BLACK LIKE US

A Century of Lesbian, Gay, and Bisexual African American Fiction

BLACK LIKE US

A Century of Lesbian, Gay, and Bisexual African American Fiction

Edited by

Devon W. Carbado, Dwight A. McBride,
and Donald Weise

Foreword by
Evelyn C. White

CLEIS
PRESS

Published in the United States by Cleis Press Inc.,
P.O. Box 14684, San Francisco, California 94114.
Printed in the United States.
Cover design: Scott Idleman
Text design: Karen Quigg
Logo art: Juana Alicia
First edition.
10 9 8 7 6 5 4 3 2 1

Permissions appear on pages 506–507.

Cover photographs clockwise from center: Langston Hughes, Wallace Thurman, Thomas Glave, E. Lynn Harris, Samuel R. Delany, Jewelle Gomez, James Baldwin, Becky Birtha, Owen Dodson, Audre Lorde, Melvin Dixon, Jacqueline Woodson, Alice Dunbar-Nelson.

LIBRARY OF CONGRESS CATALOGING-IN-PUBLICATION DATA

Black like us : a century of lesbian, gay, and bisexual African American fiction / edited by Devon W. Carbado, Dwight A. McBride, and Donald Weise. — 1st ed.
        p. cm.
    Includes bibliographical references.
    ISBN 1-57344-108-2 (trade paper)
    1. American fiction—African American authors. 2. African American lesbians—Fiction. 3. African American gays—Fiction. 4. African American—Fiction. 5. Gays' writings, American. 6. Bisexuals—Fiction. 7. Lesbians—Fiction. 8. Gay men—Fiction. I. Carbado, Devon W. II. McBride, Dwight A. III. Weise, Donald

    PS648.H57 B58 2002
    813'.5080896073—dc21

                                    2002023719

To Dale Frett

&

To Asmara Tringali

We are not the first to suffer, rebel, fight, love and die. The grace with which we embrace life, in spite of the pain, the sorrows, is always a measure of what has gone before.

—ALICE WALKER, *Revolutionary Petunias*

Contents

FOREWORD

Evelyn C. White

READ? WRITE? AFRICAN AMERICANS ARE DESCENDANTS OF people who were forbidden, on the penalty of death, to engage in such pursuits. Then, as now, the oppressor understood that knowledge leads the dispossessed to power. That power is the springboard to freedom. And most importantly, that freedom can lead to bliss. The kind of bliss that Langston Hughes describes in "Blessed Assurance," his story about the erotic love between two black men that is made plain in the stained-glass sanctity of the historic black church. As the Shakespeare of Harlem was known to have said himself: Do Jesus! Lawd Today!

As the nation marks the 100th anniversary of the birth of Langston Hughes (an Aquarian born February 1, 1902), how wonderful it is that Cleis Press has been called to release *Black Like Us: A Century of Lesbian, Gay, and Bisexual African American Fiction*. I'm happy to leave the debate about who, within our ranks, meets the standards for gay "certification" to those who revel in such sensationalism. Indeed, I'm inclined to agree with the divinely inspired Assotto Saint who once noted that black folk have more salient issues to ponder. Namely, how we might best "rise to the love that we need."

To be sure, *Black Like Us* is resplendent with the fierce jubilation of black queer literary genius—as the creators have seen fit to share their gifts. As with its precursors (most notably *Home Girls, In the Life, Brother to Brother,* and *Afrekete*), *Black Like Us* aims at inclusion. The "hot/not" battle lines and encampments that have, unfortunately, been pervasive in media-marketed gay culture and politics are refreshingly absent here. During an era when "We Are the World" has proven to be more than a warm and fuzzy cliché, the collection stands as an exemplary twenty-first century model for our movement—one that provides a foundation for all future scholars of gay and lesbian artistry. To say nothing of the multitudes of black gay youth searching for voice, visibility, and mirror reflections.

And on that note, this landmark volume makes clear that while we have often been forced to traverse "the rough side of the mountain," black queers have never journeyed alone. Within these pages, readers will discover the history, geography, hopes, and dreams of a people who have tried to love in the crucible of racism, sexism, and homophobia that is as much a part of the American fabric as the vaunted "amber waves of grain." Offered in the soaring voices of Alice, Langston, Jewelle, Darieck, Alexis, Samuel, Shay, E. Lynn, and many others, we, too, sing America. Perhaps that sweet, sweet soul brother Marvin Gaye said it best: "Come get to this."

PREFACE

I name myself "lesbian" because this culture oppresses, silences, and destroys lesbians, even lesbians who don't call themselves "lesbians." I name myself "lesbian" because I want to be visible to other black lesbians. I name myself "lesbian" because I do not subscribe to predatory/institutionalized heterosexuality. I name myself lesbian because I want to be with women (and they don't all have to call themselves "lesbians"). I name myself "lesbian" because it is part of my vision. I name myself lesbian because being woman-identified has kept me sane. I call myself "Black," too, because Black is my perspective, my aesthetic, my politics, my vision, my sanity.
— CHERYL CLARKE, *from* "New Notes on Lesbianism"

It is not enough to tell us that one was a brilliant poet, scientist, educator, or rebel. Whom did he love? It makes a difference. I can't become a whole man simply on what is fed to me: watered down versions of Black life in America. I need the ass-splitting truth to be told, so I will have something pure to emulate, a reason to remain loyal.
— ESSEX HEMPHILL, *from* "Loyalty"

MOST LITERARY INTERPRETATIONS OF BLACK LESBIAN, GAY, and bisexual literature focus either on race or on sexuality. Readers sympathetic to gay and lesbian studies typically invoke sexual orientation over race in looking at this work; those who are sympathetic to black studies typically invoke race over sexual orientation. This dichotomous approach to the literature—that it is either black or gay—helps explain the ongoing controversy within some black intellectual circles about the sexual identity of Langston Hughes and the sexual politics of his work, for example.

But as Cheryl Clarke explains, race and sexuality are connected. She identifies as both black *and* lesbian. According to Clarke, both of these aspects of her identity inform her aesthetics, her politics, and her vision. Either/or readings of writers like Clarke obscure not only that African Americans comprise a distinguished list of lesbian and gay artists whose work has helped to liberate sexuality from repressive and disciplinary conventions. Such readings also obscure the fact that gays, lesbians, and bisexuals comprise a distinguished list of African Americans whose work has helped to liberate race from its entrapment within narrow conceptions of identity and civil rights.

Thus *Black Like Us*. Stated simply, the purpose of this book is to showcase the African American lesbian, gay, and bisexual literary tradition in a way that affirms rather than negates the interconnections among race, gender, and sexuality. To do so, *Black Like Us* brings together thirty-six authors whose combined body of work covers one hundred years—from the writings of the Harlem Renaissance and the Great Migration of the Depression era to the protest literature of post-war civil rights activism and the fiction of the present day that unabashedly transcends sexual identity.

The table of contents lists equal parts men and women, some of whom are lesbian, some gay, some bisexual, some reportedly asexual, but all of whom are "queer"—and not only in terms of sexuality, but in terms of race and gender as well. The employment of the term "queer" is of course controversial, particularly when applied to African Americans; many black people across the range of sexual orientation object to its white cultural connotation, if not the word's association with sexual pathology. Consequently, large numbers of African Americans resist identifying themselves as queer, preferring instead the more acceptable labels lesbian, gay, homosexual, or even the relatively recent "same-gender-loving." Then, too, there are men and women who decline to claim a sexuality under any label whatsoever. Given this social backdrop, it is important to make clear that the term "queer" as employed in this book signifies identity and ideological nonconformity—not a particular sexual orientation. Part of what *Black Like Us* aims to show is that many of the writers in this volume were queer in terms of how they defined and embodied their racial identity, queer in terms of their conception and performance of their gender, queer in how they articulated and practiced politics, as well as queer in their intimate relationships and sense of sexual identity.

The majority of authors in this anthology have published at least one novel or short story collection. When taken together, these works represent an impressive cross section of fictional genres, including, but not limited to, romance, science fiction, fantasy, young adult, autobiography, humor, coming out, and AIDS literature. Not all of these works, however, are thought to be essentially "homosexual," though each contains some form of homosexual content and all are categorized as African American writing. Forthright depictions of queer sexuality, quite expectedly, correlate to the cultural climate of the day. Thus, lesbian and gay fiction in general grew significantly with the advent of modern sexual liberationist politics in the 1960s, with an especially active thrust after 1980. Hence, this anthology is weighted toward the last quarter century, with pre-Stonewall authors represented as fully as possible.

As this is fundamentally a book about the ways in which race, sexuality, and gender are experienced by black Americans, all of the contributors—with the exceptions of authors Rosa Guy and Michelle Cliff, who immigrated to New York as young children—were born and raised in the United States. This serves the vital function of presenting the first comprehensive collection of twentieth-century African American lesbian, gay, and bisexual writing, but also assists in establishing a more richly detailed consideration of history as it is experienced within a specific country and culture.

Additionally, the selections included in *Black Like Us* are exclusively works of fiction. Many of these authors began their careers publishing short stories, establishing their names in magazines and anthologies. The very nature of these publications called for brevity of form and, in the case of the more politically engaged periodicals, sufficient polemical opportunities that were ideally suited to the short story format. For unlike poetry, fiction enabled authors to explore character and circumstance in depth, often toward rhetorical ends. In the case of African American lesbian and gay men, however, fiction also permitted authors to incorporate controversial and overtly autobiographical same-sex content that if candidly expressed might have embarrassed or harmed one's literary reputation. As for those artists who openly affirmed their sexual identity in print, short stories and novels presented great imaginative opportunities to dramatize fully the stories of characters "in the life."

Many people would be surprised to learn that black lesbian, gay, and bisexual literature appeals to diverse audiences. While a handful of the authors featured in *Black Like Us* are read by mainstream audiences of popular fiction, others are read by lesbians and gay men (across race), or by African Americans (across sexual orientation). Still other contributors are familiar primarily to black lesbian, gay, and bisexual audiences. And a few are essentially unread outside of academia. While many readers are certain to find works by their favorite authors, very few readers of *Black Like Us* will be familiar with all of the selections, let alone will have read them. As one might expect, this literature reflects the lives of black lesbians, gays, and bisexuals, seldom involving the experiences of black queer men and women exclusively. Therefore, *Black Like Us* gives voice to mothers, fathers, grandparents, children, ex-husbands, neighbors, classmates, friends, and associates of black lesbians and gays, all of whom contribute to the diversity of what might be called the black homosexual condition. Yet, in some sense, singling out a black homosexual "condition" or "experience" proves as challenging as labeling human sexuality, and indeed may be just as shortsighted. Furthermore, one reasonably might inquire as to the propriety or necessity of showcasing an author's work in the context of his or her sexuality—or race or gender, for that matter. To put all of this more directly, would not a more effective way to honor black lesbian, gay, and bisexual authors be to free their work entirely from the constraints of identity politics? The answer may depend on whether one believes, as Essex Hemphill did, that who we are in terms of our sexuality and sexual practices "makes a difference." *Black Like Us* argues—strongly—that sexuality, like gender and race, matters.

Black Like Us is organized into three sections, corresponding with three historical periods: The Harlem Renaissance, 1900–1950; The Protest Era, 1950–1980; and Coming Out Black, Like Us, 1980–2000. Each section is introduced by a historical essay that situates black queer fiction in terms of the corresponding cultural, political, legal, and literary conditions under which each author worked. To that end, the introductions combine extended discussions of black lesbian, gay, and bisexual expression with comparably elaborate treatments of the political currents that shaped the sexual identities of these authors and the corresponding gay-identified, or non-gay-identified, content of their work. Informing this approach is the notion that the cultural and political context within which an author produces literature provides at least one interpretive framework for evaluating and making sense of the work.

The methodological approach we take in the introductions is "integrative." That is, each introduction attempts simultaneously to engage black history, women's history, and gay and lesbian history (to employ the conventional identity labels), as well as to illuminate the literary movements of each of the foregoing groups. We adopt this methodology for two principal reasons. The first is to make clear that race, gender, and sexual orientation are interconnected aspects of personhood. The second and related reason is to deliberately complicate our understanding of history, civil rights, and social and literary movements. Typically, we study black history as though it were disconnected from women's history; often we study gay and lesbian history as though it were somehow not a part of women's history; and rarely do we study black history in the context of making sense of gay and lesbian history (or vice versa). The tendency is to study literary movements in the same disaggregated way. Indeed, in conducting the research for this book, we could not find a single piece of scholarship that comprehensively delineates the connections among the literary productions of blacks, women, and gays and lesbians (again, using the conventional identity labels), let alone works that situate those connections vis-à-vis history, politics, law, and civil rights over the span of the last century. While the introductions we provide are certainly not comprehensive, they do attempt to "defractionalize" the dominant understanding of the literary productions of subordinated groups as well as the social contexts within which those productions took place.

If *Black Like Us* was conceived to encourage an intersectional approach to black queer literature, the book also was conceptualized to expand the literary canon of black queer writing. All too frequently, the canon is reduced to a few distinguished authors: James Baldwin, Audre Lorde, and Langston Hughes. Although the works of these authors are undeniably important and often groundbreaking, they are part of a larger, politicized literary tradition. Almost certainly, none of these landmark authors would have wished to see their writing set above or apart from other black queer artists. For just as writers of the pre-Stonewall era drew inspiration from their antecedents, so too have contemporary black lesbian, gay, and bisexual authors carried forward the black lesbian and gay literary tradition in ways perhaps unimaginable to their predecessors.

Still, *Black Like Us* is not a definitive study of black queer fiction. In spite of the breadth of its undertaking, the book is intended merely as a point of departure. Nor does the inclusion of any piece constitute an endorsement of its literary quality or ideological orientation. As you will see, some of the literature is better than others; some more political than others; some more sexually explicit than others; some more black gay/lesbian–affirming than others; some more conservative, even problematic, than others. Guiding the selection process was our aim of presenting a broad representation of the literature and avoiding, to the extent possible, policing the literary quality or ideology of the work.

Yet there are numerous writers whose work is not represented in this collection. Were this a multivolume project, there no doubt would have been room for a broader sampling. One could quite easily fill a book of this size with the black lesbian, gay, and bisexual fiction published during the last decade alone—and still exclude popular authors. This is one of the reasons *Black Like Us* includes an extensive bibliography: to provide readers with an opportunity to pursue the literature in greater depth for a better appreciation of the wider literary tradition that includes poetry, memoirs, histories, anthologies, plays, academic studies, and other works. All of this is to say that to some extent *Black Like Us* is just the beginning. Our sense is that this beginning is long overdue.

Devon W. Carbado
Dwight A. McBride
Donald Weise
April 2002

ACKNOWLEDGMENTS

Funding for *Black Like Us* was provided by The Institute of American Cultures Research Grant in Ethnic Studies at University of California–Los Angeles (UCLA); UCLA School of Law; the African American Studies Center at UCLA; the University of Illinois at Chicago (UIC) Humanities Institute; and the UIC Department of English. Editorial and research assistance was provided by Nancy Freeman, Courtney D. Johnson, Justin A. Joyce, and Darcy Thompson.

We would like to acknowledge the cooperation of Gary Lambrev and the staff of the Martin Luther King, Jr., branch of the Oakland Public Library; Jim Van Buskirk and the staff of the Main branch of the San Francisco Public Library; Karen Sundheim and the staff of the Harvey Milk/Eureka Valley branch of the San Francisco Public Library; the staff of the Hugh and Darling Law Library at UCLA; the African American Studies Media Center at UCLA; the Beinecke Rare Book and Manuscript Library, Yale University; and University of Delaware Library Special Collections Department.

Among the enthusiastic booksellers who cheered us onward are Holly Bemiss of A Different Light Books; Tisa Bryant of Modern Times bookstore; Suzanne Corson of Boadecia's Bookstore; Crissa Cummings of Books Inc.; Blanche Richardson of Marcus Books; and Jerry Thompson of Black Spring Books. Most of all, we wish to thank Richard Labonté, whose pioneering career as a gay bookseller not only informed the content of *Black Like Us*, but also brought many of the authors in this book to the attention of lesbian and gay readers for the first time.

For encouragement, support, and feedback on this project, special thanks goes to Robert L. Allen, Thomas Avena, Derrick Bell, Keith Boykin, Jennifer Brody, Elaine Brown, Paul Chamberlain, George Chauncey, Cheryl Clarke, Michelle Cliff, Kimberlé Crenshaw, John

D'Emilio, Brian Freeman, Barbara Gittings, Thomas Glave, Jewelle Gomez, Laura Gomez, Jim Hall, James Earl Hardy, Cheryl Harris, David Hilliard, Sharon Holland, Darnell Hunt, Ellen Lafferty, Arthur Little, Regina Marler, Lisa C. Moore, Charles I. Nero, Joan Nestle, Harold Ober Associates Inc., Bill Richter, Michael Ruggiero, Stewart Shaw, Gloria Smart, Carlton Elliott Smith, Valerie Smith, Renée Swindle, Joël B. Tan, Kendall Thomas, Giovanna Tringali, Mariah Wilkins, Patricia Williams, Jacqueline Woodson, and Richard Yarborough.

We are particularly indebted to Ann Allen Shockley, an authority on African American literature and black gay and lesbian writing whose support from the start was indispensable. She generously answered questions, questioned answers, clarified points, and affirmed our choices as only a mentor could. As if one mentor were not enough, we were fortunate to have a second in the spirited Evelyn C. White, to whom we owe thanks. She brought wisdom, wit, and candor, and her camaraderie was a driving inspiration. Additionally, we wish to recognize the ever-present influence of Joseph Beam, Essex Hemphill, bell hooks, Akasha (Gloria) Hull, Marlon Riggs, and Barbara Smith. These writers above all others influenced *Black Like Us.* Cumulatively, their scholarship, ideas, and very lives made this book possible, and the editors owe any success of the project to their formative work.

A special measure of gratitude is reserved also for Cleis Press publishers Frédérique Delacoste and Felice Newman. Their insights brought new dimensions to the book, and their support was steadfast and exemplary. *Black Like Us* is a testament to Cleis Press's active commitment to the furtherance of black lesbian and gay literature.

Thanks also to Scott Idleman and Karen Quigg for their exquisite book design, and to Mark Woodworth for his expertise in tackling a herculean copyediting assignment.

And much appreciation goes to the dedicated sales force and brilliant marketing team at Publishers Group West—especially Elise Cannon, Karen Cross, Kymberly Miller, Mark Ouimet, and Kim Wylie—for getting this book into the hands of readers everywhere.

1900–1950

THE HARLEM RENAISSANCE

"...the perfumed orchid of the New Negro Movement"

WRITING IN 1920, AS THE EPOCH THAT LATER CAME TO BE known as the Harlem Renaissance was gathering momentum, W. E. B. DuBois heralded a "New Negro" aesthetic. "A renaissance of American Negro literature is due," he proclaimed; "the material about us in the strange, heart-rending race tangle is rich beyond dream and only we can tell the tale and sing the song from the heart."[1] According to DuBois, the "New Negro" would challenge racial stereotypes that had suppressed blacks for centuries. Unlike the "old Negro" associated with the antebellum South, this new generation of early-twentieth century artists would embrace literature as a source of liberation, employing ennobled representations of the African American experience to "uplift the race" from its maligned past. For DuBois, however, this "race tangle" would not be taken up by just anyone. Race matters, perhaps even the salvation of the black race itself, were the province of an elite class of blacks, an exemplary subminority of men and women steeped in culture and education—the "Talented Tenth." DuBois firmly believed that this distinguished group—ten percent of the overall black population—would lead the coming renaissance and rescue African Americans from the racially subordinating conditions under which they lived. "The Negro race, like all races, is going to be saved by its exceptional men," he remarked in his seminal essay "The Talented Tenth," published in 1903. "The problem of education, then, among Negroes must first of all deal with the Talented Tenth; it is the problem of developing the Best of this race that they may guide the Mass away from the contamination and death of the Worst, in their own and other races."[2]

While DuBois forecast a new literary movement, the Harlem Renaissance had in fact already begun. Spanning roughly the years from the end of the First World War in 1918 to at least the mid-1930s of the Great Depression, the Harlem Renaissance represents a significant era of African American artistic productivity. In this respect, DuBois was prescient in foretelling the significance of this period in terms of art, culture, and politics. Still, his notion of the Talented Tenth, though not an unreasonable response to severe racial backlash following the war, deprived him of the foresight necessary to understand that a literary renaissance of such breadth would resist essentialist notions of racial uplift. For the ideological orientation of the Harlem Renaissance fundamentally challenged the idea that a privileged minority of intellectuals could, or should, represent African Americans en masse.

Nor would the black majority, particularly young people, abide by the marginalization and exclusion that DuBois's antiracist vision invited. Excluded from the Talented Tenth were the "low-down folks," as Langston Hughes called the remaining ninety percent of African Americans. "[A]nd they are the majority—may the Lord be praised!" Forecasting predictions of his own in "The Negro Artist and the Racial Mountain," a 1926 essay, Hughes observed that "perhaps these common people will give the world its truly great Negro artist, the one who is not afraid to be himself." Hughes's thinking was that "[w]hereas the better-class Negro would tell the artist what to do, the people at least let him alone when he does appear.... We younger Negro artists who create now intend to express our own individual dark-skinned selves without fear or shame."[3]

The African American lesbian, gay, and bisexual fiction published during the first half of the century is in many respects a study in this conflict over how postbellum blacks might best represent their "dark-skinned selves"—both to other blacks as well as to the world at large. In the case of sexual minorities, the intraracial differences among New Negro factions on issues of race and class were further complicated by considerations of sexuality and gender, though seldom were sexual topics raised as a legitimate point of debate. Beginning in 1926 with Richard Bruce Nugent's "Smoke, Lilies, and Jade," the first-known overtly homosexual work published by an African American, same-sex desire, if not thrust into the open, was at least showcased as a controversial theme for black writers to address explicitly. And while African American lesbian or bisexual authors such as Angelina Weld Grimké and Alice Dunbar-Nelson had in fact been publishing politically engaged work since the late-nineteenth and early twentieth-century, this literature was either unconcerned with homosexuality or, when same-sex subject matter was incorporated, often left unpublished, as with Grimké's love poems and Dunbar-Nelson's short stories. Although present-day black lesbian, gay, and bisexual fiction may have its origins in this body of fledgling literature, these early writings are not "gay-identified," in the contemporary sense of the term. Nor would authors such as Grimké, Dunbar-Nelson, or Nugent have identified their own sexual orientation as such. Notwithstanding the fact that the Harlem Renaissance enjoys a popular reputation as a period of extreme sexual permissiveness and gay-themed artistic expression, homosexuality retained an outlaw status that few blacks embraced at the time and, given the extreme racial subordination of the period, that still fewer would have championed alongside matters of race and class. Even queer writers of overtly gay-themed work—among them Langston Hughes, Claude McKay, and Wallace Thurman—took care to conceal their sexuality from the overwhelmingly disapproving public eye, employing a variety of socially acceptable covers (most notably marriages of convenience in the instances of Countee Cullen and Thurman).

But if modern sexual terminology fails to capture the sexual culture within which the Harlem Renaissance was played out, so too does the notion that the events in Harlem of the 1920s constituted a renaissance among African American artists fail to capture fully the artistic legacy of the New Negro Movement. To many observers, the renaissance dates more inclusively not from the close of the First World War but instead from the politically charged climate of the post–Civil War Reconstruction era. From its start in 1865, Reconstruction, sometimes called the "Second American Revolution," was a period of progressive politics in which the federal government and supportive whites assisted newly emancipated blacks in an effort to build a more democratic society. Combined with the drastic social and political changes that accompanied the abolition of slavery in 1863 was the need to rebuild the war-torn South. In effect, three constitutional amendments—the Thirteenth (abolishing slavery), ratified in 1865; the Fourteenth (conferring citizenship) in 1868; and the Fifteenth (granting black males the right to vote) in 1870—along with a series of Republican-orchestrated Reconstruction Acts that placed southern states under military control to ensure the enfranchisement of African American men, proved insufficient protections against civil rights violations. Indeed, the job of Reconstruction in the South, even in its most radical moments, was never stable. Former Confederates were bitter about losing the war, and many resentful white Southerners perceived the rapid advancements that Reconstructionist programs demanded on behalf of blacks as being too much, too fast. African Americans had in fact made significant economic and political inroads. From 1870 to 1901, for example, two black men, Blanche Bruce and Hiram Revels, joined the U.S. Senate, and twenty black congressmen entered the House of Representatives. Southern whites found these and other forms of racial progress disruptive of the racial hierarchy to which they had become accustomed economically, socially, and politically. Thus, they deployed a variety of measures, including violence and terror, to reestablish total political control of the southern states and to undo black racial gains. This politics of backlash was helped by the Compromise of 1877, pursuant to which Republican legislators withdrew federal troops from the South, essentially granting the South "home rule," while congressional Democrats conceded the deadlocked 1876 presidential election to the Republican candidate, Rutherford B. Hayes.

In the aftermath of Reconstruction's demise the segregationist era of "Jim Crow" was born. In certain respects, Jim Crow was as bad as institutionalized slavery, and in some instances worse. Subject to much of the same repression under comparably exploitive social conditions in similarly violent circumstances, blacks were for all purposes abandoned without protection by the government. By the 1890s southern states were instituting stronger segregation laws, a situation that the Supreme Court encouraged when it upheld the legality of "separate-but-equal" segregation in *Plessy v. Ferguson* (1896). Meanwhile, blacks were lynched with unprecedented frequency, as many as one hundred women and men a year. It is in the context of the violent antiblack politics of the 1880s that Ida B. Wells launched her famous antilynching crusade. A journalist and newspaper editor whose early articles "Our Women" and "Race Pride" reflected a political commitment to both race and gender, Wells was among the most ardent public critics not only of lynching but also of the federal government's complicity in offering no protection to its victims. Writing in the tradition of the abolitionists Frederick Douglass and Frances Ellen Watkins Harper, Wells authored the pamphlets *Southern Horrors: Lynch Law in All Its Phases* (1892) and *A Red Record: Tabulated Statistics and Alleged Causes of Lynching in the United States* (1895). Both documents reshaped the post-Reconstruction public discourse, in part by arguing that lynchings were driven not by black men sexually assaulting white women but by white resentment over the political advancement of African Americans. "Why," Wells asked, "is mob murder permitted by a Christian nation? What is the cause of this awful slaughter? This question is answered almost daily—always the same, shameless falsehood that 'Negroes are lynched to protect womanhood.'" According to Wells, "This is the never-varying answer of lynchers and their apologists. All know that it is untrue." She argued that "The cowardly lyncher revels in murder, then seeks to shield himself from public execration by claiming devotion to woman. But truth is mighty and the lynching record discloses the hypocrisy of the lyncher as well as his crime."[4]

Wells's confrontational politics differed substantially from the accommodationist beliefs of Booker T. Washington, the preeminent black civil rights leader of the late-nineteenth century whose teachings set the tone for post-Reconstruction racial discourse. Washington, a former slave and author of the best-selling autobiography *Up from Slavery* (1901), was the influential cofounder of the Tuskegee Institute, a vocational school created for blacks in 1881, which emphasized industrial education over academic learning. "Our greatest danger," Washington posited in his "Atlanta Address," a career-defining speech delivered at the Cotton States Exposition in 1895, "is that in the great leap from slavery to freedom we may overlook the fact that the masses of us [blacks] are to live by the productions of our hands." He urged black Americans "to keep in mind that we shall prosper in proportion as we learn to dignify and glorify common labor, and put brains and skill into the common occupations of life." Central to his thinking was the idea that "No race can prosper till it learns that there is as much dignity in tilling a field as in writing a poem. It is at the bottom of life we must begin, not at the top. Nor should we permit our grievances to overshadow our opportunities."

But Washington's comments were directed not only at African Americans. Part of the ideological project of his speech was to make clear to white Americans that the "New Negro" would be driven not by a politics of resentment but by a commitment of loyalty. "As we have proved our loyalty to you [whites] in the past, nursing your children, watching by the sick bed of your mothers and fathers, and often following them with tear-dimmed eyes to their graves, so in the future, in our humble way, we shall stand by you...."[5] For Washington, racial subordination was an unavoidable and perhaps even permanent reality of African American life. Thus his was a politics of pragmatism that encouraged blacks to strive patiently toward economic rather than racial equality. His conservatism proved popular even with progressive whites, as well as with industrialists like Andrew Carnegie and John D. Rockefeller, who supported Washington's program to the extent that he was useful in combating labor unions. Among blacks, however, Washington's reputation engendered greater controversy. Wells notably resurrected the defunct Afro-American League, a black unity organization started in 1890, as the newly established Afro-American Council in 1898, in part to counter the racial politics of white accommodation.

Among Ida B. Wells's other groundbreaking accomplishments was the creation in 1912 of the Alpha Suffrage Club of Chicago, believed to be the first organization of black women suffragists. During the political turmoil of the Reconstruction era, women's suffrage had gained greater momentum with women activists than at any time since the first clear expression of women's "right to vote" by Elizabeth Cady Stanton and Lucretia Mott at the Woman's Rights convention in 1848. By century's end, and in the spirit of Sojourner Truth, who had linked race and gender concerns in her famous "Ain't I a Woman" speech of 1851, African American women had formed a network of clubs. The National League of Colored Women (formed in 1892) and the National Federation of Afro-American Women (1896) represented more than one hundred black women's groups. The 1896 merger of these two national bodies resulted in the National Association of Colored Women (NACW), whose motto "Lifting As We Climb" signified the organization's concern with racial uplift and the betterment of black womanhood as a central platform. "[S]elf-preservation demands that [black women] go among the lowly, to whom they are bound by ties of race and sex," remarked Mary Church Terrell, cofounder and first president of the NACW.[6] Although the club movement was dominated by middle-class women such as Terrell, some of whom sought to educate the black underclass on domestic issues like housekeeping and child-care, the NACW more importantly served as a leading voice in the suffragist cause until the Nineteenth Amendment passed in 1920. Writing in "Woman Suffrage and the Fifteenth Amendment" in 1915, Terrell emphasized that her women's rights platform was rooted in racial solidarity: "Even if I believed that women should be denied the right of suffrage, wild horses could not drag such an admission from my pen or my lips, for this reason: precisely the same arguments used to prove that the ballot be withheld from women are advanced to prove that colored men should not be allowed to vote." It occurred to Terrell that "The reasons for repealing the Fifteenth Amendment differ but little from the arguments advanced by those who oppose the enfranchisement of women." Thus, she believed that it would be "inconsistent" for black people to "use their influence against granting the ballot to women, if they believed that colored men should enjoy this right which citizenship confers."[7]

The black women's club movement, and the NACW in particular, served as well to inspire the politics of the National Association for the Advancement of Colored People (NAACP). The organization was established in 1909 after white activists Mary White Ovington, Oswald Garrison Villard, and William English Walling issued a "Call" to commemorate the centennial of Abraham Lincoln's birth with a conference on race relations. "This government cannot exist half-slave and half-free any better today than it could in 1861," the Call declared. "We call upon the believers in democracy to join in a national conference for the discussion of present evils, the voicing of protests, and the renewal of the struggle for civil and political liberty."[8] Working toward the advancement of people of color, the NAACP operated originally as a white-governed organization, though it became more fully African American–oriented in 1920 under the black leadership of James Weldon Johnson and later under Walter White. Of the three original founders, however, it was Ovington, a Socialist reformer from a privileged family background, who had first conceived of the group and persuaded her male partners to join her cause. For she saw the post-Reconstruction "Negro Problem" as a continuation of the abolitionist struggle, only infused with the implicitly feminist thrust behind the suffragist movement. "I believe that women for a long time to come, whether they have suffrage or not, will need to be banded together against oppression," she remarked in "Socialism and the Feminist Movement," a 1914 critique of the Socialist Party for failing to support a woman's right to vote. "[T]hey will also recognize that as women they have an obligation to stand with all other women who are fighting for the destruction of masculine despotism and for the right of womankind."[9] Indeed, among the sixty names undersigning the Call, one-third were women's. Moreover, Ovington ensured the inclusion of African American women, particularly leaders like Ida B. Wells and Mary Church Terrell, whose NACW motivated Ovington toward a broader incorporation of gender and race relations in the NAACP. Writing of her visit to the NACW convention in 1919, Ovington commented, "I never saw anything like it before or since." Part of what surprised her was black women's political and social activism. She wrote: "[T]he white world, and white women especially, have no appreciation for the amount of social service work that colored women, without wealth or leisure, have accomplished."[10]

Joining the Call for a conference on race relations was W. E. B. DuBois, the controversial author of *The Souls of Black Folks* (1903). In that landmark collection that presaged his formation of the militant Niagara Movement in 1905, DuBois openly attacked the powerful Tuskegee Machine, a gesture that marked a radical departure from the tradition of black conservatism in favor of "persistent manly agitation [as] the way to liberty." Although poorly funded and short-lived, the Niagara Movement, with little support from whites, sought full enfranchisement of African Americans, proclaiming that "We refuse to allow the impression to remain that the Negro-American assents to inferiority, is submissive under oppression and apologetic before insults."[11] Beyond the financial strains and political pressure applied by Tuskegee loyalists, members disagreed on "nonracial" issues, notably women's role in the Movement. Cofounder Monroe Trotter objected even to their participation, which DuBois countered by creating the Massachusetts Niagara Women's Auxiliary in 1906. When the NAACP invited DuBois to join its fledgling white staff three years later, he was thus prepared to disband his work with Trotter to become founding editor of *The Crisis,* the NAACP journal that would serve as the primary vehicle for his racial uplift polemic on the "Talented Tenth."

While DuBois's and the NAACP's racial platform was not unproblematic with respect to gender—Ida B. Wells, for example, was an early detractor, charging that she had been excluded by the organizing committee—*The Crisis* nevertheless became a vocal advocate for women's rights. "The statement that woman is weaker than man is sheer rot: It is the same thing we hear about 'darker races' and 'lower classes,'" DuBois put forth in a 1915 article that urged black men to vote on behalf of women's suffrage in the forthcoming election. "Difference, either physical or spiritual, does not argue weakness or inferiority. That the average woman is spiritually different from the average man is undoubtedly just as true as the fact that the average white man differs from the average Negro." The question for DuBois was whether and how these "differences" should matter. Differences between blacks and whites, he argued, are "no reason for disenfranchising the Negro or lynching him." Nor, he reasoned, should differences between the sexes justify the subordination of women. In this sense, DuBois's political project transcended race. He even went so far as to assert that "The meaning of the twentieth century is the freeing of the individual soul."[12]

The topic of sexual orientation, however, lacked a forum in early black civil rights activism, even though one would presume that black lesbians, black gay men, and black bisexuals had been involved in American social protest struggle as long as blacks had participated in such movements. Sexual minorities had been silenced out of shame, fear of criminal retribution, and, importantly, a lack of understanding of the inherently political nature of sexual identity. Furthermore, many blacks had only recently become better acquainted with the politics of race, and the majority of African Americans, to no one's surprise, prized black enfranchisement above all else. If the "freeing of the individual soul" had at last been enlarged to include black women, it had not been extended to homosexuals and bisexuals who were black. As DuBois's "Talented Tenth" platform placed extreme emphasis on black respectability, the "outlaw" community of homosexuals early in the century, no matter their education or social status, were effectively sidelined. When the issue of homosexuality did in fact appear in the black political discourse of the time, it often surfaced in the context of "illegal" activity, from which even DuBois was not exempt. Writing in his memoirs, he remarked, "In the midst of my career there burst upon me a new and undreamed aspect of sex. A young man, long my disciple and

student, then my co-helper and successor to part of my work, was suddenly arrested for molesting men in public places."[13] The young man in
his charge was Augustus Granville Dill, whom DuBois's biographer
described delicately as "fastidious and a predestined bachelor."[14] Meeting
for the first time during Dill's undergraduate years at Atlanta University
around 1900, the two scholars coedited several influential sociological
studies, including *Efforts for Social Betterment among Negro Americans*
(1909), a study of black women's self-help organizations. So close was
their friendship that when DuBois left his teaching position at Atlanta
University to join the NAACP, Dill replaced him on faculty until he too
came on board *The Crisis* as business manager in 1913. Smooth working
relations between the two continued for almost fifteen years, until,
much to DuBois's dismay, Dill was arrested in 1928 for having gay sex in
a subway toilet. Although Dill's mentor had never "contemplated continuing my life work without you [Dill] by my side," he nonetheless
terminated his protégé.[15] Apparently troubled by this decision for the
rest of his life, DuBois wrote in 1958, "I had before that time no conception of homosexuality. I had never understood the tragedy of Oscar
Wilde. I dismissed my co-worker forthwith, and spent heavy days regret-
ting my act."[16]

Indeed, Wilde's 1898 court trial and sentencing for violation of
England's Labourche Amendment (an 1885 law that had added oral sex
to the list of homosexual offenses punishable by incarceration) was an
internationally sensational scandal, cautioning, if not further suppressing, overt expressions of homosexuality. The tragedy's impact reached
as far away as the United States, where, according to Neil Miller, some
nine hundred sermons against Wilde were preached between 1895 and
1900 alone. It was under the shadow of such dire circumstances that renderings of male homosexuality in American fiction began quietly to
emerge. The first gay-themed novels of the twentieth century, such as
Edward I. Prime-Stevenson's *Imre: A Memorandum* (1906) and his study
of gay pioneers John Addington Symonds and Edward Carpenter entitled *The Intersexes: A History of Similisexualism as a Problem in Social Life*
(1908), were self-published or printed overseas in limited editions, often
under pseudonyms. The first openly gay novel by an nationally recognized American author to appear under his own name, however, was
Henry Blake Fuller's *Bertram Cope's Year* (1919). Following the armistice
of the First World War, two notable authors addressing explicit gay

subject matter were Robert McAlmond, whose self-published collection *Distinguished Air (Grim Fairy Tales)* (1925) features what some critics believe to be the first depiction of a gay bar in American fiction, and Richard Bruce Nugent's homoerotic, bisexually themed short story "Smoke, Lilies, and Jade" (1926).

Nugent, who published this landmark story under the pen name Richard Bruce to protect the privacy of his socially established family, was a self-described flamboyantly gay bohemian—"the perfumed orchid of the New Negro Movement"—who has come to be more closely identified with the queer spirit of the Harlem Renaissance than perhaps any other author.[17] His story "Smoke, Lilies, and Jade" was widely considered the first identifiably gay work of fiction by an African American male. "Smoke, Lilies, and Jade" depicts transgressive black sexuality in a way that shook the foundations of DuBois's "Talented Tenth" philosophy. Indeed, merely calling another man "beautiful," as Nugent had done by naming the love interest Beauty, was a bold act. For as the author remarked in an interview during the 1980s, "You didn't call a man beautiful. I did."[18] Originally, the story was undertaken on a dare, when it was first proposed for the debut issue of *Fire!!* (1926), a radical but short-lived New Negro magazine started by Nugent, Langston Hughes, and Wallace Thurman. "Wally [Thurman] and I thought that the magazine would get bigger sales if it was banned in Boston. So we flipped a coin to see who wrote bannable material. The only two things we could think of that were bannable were a story about prostitution or about homosexuality." Nugent took the topic of homosexuality, while Thurman contributed a piece on prostitution in "Cordelia the Crude" (1926). Thurman, author of the gay-oriented novels *The Blacker the Berry* (1929), which also prominently considers skin color consciousness among blacks, and *Infants of the Spring* (1932), a merciless parody of the Harlem Renaissance written as the movement was winding down, similarly embraced the black counterculture, as demonstrated notably by his list of personal abhorrences, which included all African American "uplift" propaganda, black novelists, morals, religion, and "sympathetic white folks," among many others.[19] Speaking to this rather sudden "visibility" of black male homosexuality in Harlem, Nugent added years later, "You did what you wanted to. Nobody was in the closet. There wasn't any closet."[20]

Speaking in 1968, Nugent remarked of "Smoke, Lilies, and Jade" that he "didn't know *it was gay* when [he] wrote it,"[21] illustrating the caution that must be exerted in equating gay men's nonconformism in the 1920s with their willingness to self-identify as homosexual or bisexual in the modern context of gay liberation politics. For many celebrated black gay or bisexual writers of the period succumbed to societal pressures to the extent that many married in spite of ongoing attraction to men. Each writer, however, managed "heterosexual" relations in his own way. Thurman, for example, who was arrested for public sex with a man just two days after his first visit to New York in 1925, apparently hid his homosexuality from his wife during their six-month union, whereas Nugent, who claims to have loved the woman he wed in 1952 (though he does not say what forces motivated him to marry a woman whom he admits he did not love physically), continued affairs with men openly throughout their seventeen-year marriage. As if concealing his sexual orientation were not cover enough, Thurman took the additional step of announcing publicly that he was not a homosexual, adding that the rumor was an attempt by the black establishment to tarnish his reputation and undermine his career.

Perhaps most noteworthy was Countee Cullen, the young poet laureate of the Harlem Renaissance, who in 1928 wed Nina Yolande DuBois, the only daughter of W. E. B. DuBois. Cullen, who was familiar with the nineteenth-century "homophile" writings of gay men like Edward Carpenter, appears to have recognized his gayness in childhood. Moreover, Cullen's postmarital preference for his best man and intimate friend Harold Jackman, to whom he dedicated his only novel *One Way to Heaven* (1932), was borne out for everyone to see when, just three months after the wedding, the two men sailed to Paris without Yolande. Significantly, DuBois, whose recounting of the Augustus Dill incident demonstrates his near-complete ignorance of homosexual matters, perhaps optimistically (or maybe more in the interest of politely avoiding opprobrium) attributed the couple's 1930 breakup not to Cullen's obvious sexual orientation but rather to his own daughter's troublesome nature.

Cullen, who boasted, "I am going to be a poet—not a Negro poet,"[22] as he embarked on his writing career in 1924, famously employed lyrical African American themes throughout his successful if short lifetime, winning favorable comparisons even to luminaries such as Keats and Whitman before his death in 1946. Raised as a child prodigy, Cullen strove to impress his gifts on others by means of his tastefully poetic renderings of New Negro moral values. Many of his ostensibly race-based works, however, also contain pronounced homosexual overtones. Beginning with his debut collection, entitled *Color* (1925), Cullen alludes indirectly to gayness in both "The Shroud of Color" ("I strangle in this yoke drawn tighter than/The worth of bearing it, just to be man/I am not brave enough to pay the price/In full; I lack the strength to sacrifice") and "For a Poet" ("I have wrapped my dreams in a silken/cloth,/And laid them away in a box of gold").[23] Curiously, both poems are dedicated to men whose names are unknown to Cullen's editor, Gerald Early, who nevertheless concluded in his footnotes to *My Soul's High Song: The Collected Writings of Countee Cullen* (1991) that these men are merely friends or neighbors, even though it is equally plausible, absent any biographical information and in light of the homosexual currents beneath the poems, that these two men might have been Cullen's lovers. Gay traces may also be found in his next book, *Copper Sun* (1927), particularly in "More Than a Fool's Song" ("In Christian practice those who move/To symbols strange to us/May reckon clearer of His love/Than we who own His cross").[24] Alain Locke, an influential black gay Howard University professor and "Talented Tenth" champion who served as one of the guiding forces behind Cullen's literary output, proclaimed, "Ladies and gentleman! A genius! Posterity will laugh at us if we do not proclaim him now."[25]

Apart from his dedicated mentoring of young writers like Countee Cullen, Locke gained his own notoriety with *The New Negro* (1925), his groundbreaking anthology of stories, poetry, and essays by the most prominent and promising names in the field of African American literature of the 1920s. Although Zora Neale Hurston, whose story "Spunk" appears in the anthology, attributes the original discovery of many New Negro writers such as herself and Cullen to the pioneering work of Charles S. Johnson, Locke nevertheless established his reputation as one of the foremost arbiters of the Harlem Renaissance with the publication of this book. Aristocratic by birth and the first black Rhodes Scholar, Locke espoused an elitist view of race representation that favored "high art" over so-called "lower forms" such as jazz and blues music. Writing in his foreword to *The New Negro*, Locke commented, "So far as he is culturally articulate, we shall let the Negro speak for himself."[26] Locke's position on artistic expression was that blacks should rely on their African past as a source of art, illustrating how New Negro artists could take up a much maligned ancestry and elevate it to the level of high art. If he considered his part in the New Negro movement to be one of mentorship, or in his words "a philosophical mid-wife to a generation of younger Negro poets, writers, and artists," Locke's handling of gifted youth, particularly young men such as Cullen and Langston Hughes, extended as well into the realm of sexual interest.[27] A letter to Hughes (whom Locke sought to enroll at Howard University, where Hughes had been invited to share the professor's home) was sent "to tell you [Hughes] how much I love you."[28] Hughes, unlike Cullen, with whom he was often paired as literary competitor, avoided the role of acolyte to Locke, maintaining an aloof but friendly distance from the man of letters. Despite his preoccupation with promoting a movement of social respectability, Locke nonetheless seems to have understood the dilemma of a black gay man aspiring to be integrated into a society that finds black homosexuality unwelcome. In another letter to Hughes, he wrote, "My tragedy is that I cannot follow my instincts—too sophisticated to obey them, not too sophisticated not to hear them...."[29]

Langston Hughes, widely considered the most popular male writer of the Harlem Renaissance, if not among the most esteemed authors of twentieth-century America, established a popular reputation with his first book, *The Weary Blues* (1926), a poetry collection that includes the much-quoted verse "The Negro Speaks of Rivers" ("I've known rivers ancient as the world and older than the flow/of human blood in human veins")[30] and whose overall traditionalist content impressed New Negro advocates as a hopeful new addition to their fledgling literary canon. With his next volume, *Fine Clothes to the Jew* (1927), however, Hughes disappointed these admirers, incorporating instead risqué themes in poems like "Red Silk Stockings" ("Put on yo' red silk stockings,/Black gal./Go out an' let de white boys/Look at yo' legs").[31] As this latter poem indicates, Hughes's writing style was accessible to the ordinary reader, often employing black dialect, while addressing themes of social and economic concerns especially familiar to working-class blacks. If Hughes's work occasionally engendered controversy, so too did his enigmatic sexual orientation. Although he confessed to a 1926 sexual encounter with a sailor, close friends and colleagues such as Cullen, Locke, and Nugent have described the author as "asexual." Careful readings of his later poetry nevertheless suggest a homosexual voice, whether or not Hughes himself was gay. Particularly noteworthy is his

collection *Montage of a Dream Deferred* (1951), which includes "Cafe: 3 A.M."
("Detectives from the vice squad/with weary sadistic eyes/spotting fairies./
Degenerates,/some folks say./But God, Nature/or somebody/made them
that way") and "Tell Me" ("Why should it be *my* loneliness/why should it
be *my* song/why should it be *my* dream/deferred/overlong?").[32]

The publication of Hughes's *Weary Blues* was made possible
through the assistance of Carl Van Vechten, an avant-garde white gay
music critic, photographer, and best-selling novelist whose forays into
Harlem helped "open" the black community to other whites and, perhaps more importantly, brought national attention to African Americans
such as Hughes for the first time. No stranger to controversy himself,
Van Vechten published the provocatively titled *Nigger Heaven* (1926), a
sensation in both the commercial and cultural senses. The book, which
offered an "insider's" look at black Harlem, sold out immediately, while
DuBois, Locke, and Cullen took the title alone as a starting point for
their objections to the work that depicts tawdry images of black life. Yet
other noted African American writers like James Weldon Johnson,
author of *The Autobiography of an Ex-Colored Man* (1912), praised the
novel in the Urban League's *Opportunity* magazine, remarking that Van
Vechten had "achieved the most revealing, significant and powerful
novel based exclusively on Negro life yet written...."[33] If Van Vechten is
essentially a forgotten novelist to present-day readers, he is better
remembered for his close platonic friendship with Hughes. "Your letters
are so very charming, dear Langston, that I look forward to finding one
every morning under the door," Van Vechten wrote to Hughes in the
first month of their lifelong correspondence that began in May 1925.
"The poems [*Weary Blues*] came this morning and I looked them over
again. Your work has such a subtle sensitiveness that it improves with
every reading.... [Alfred] Knopf is lunching with me today and I shall
ask him to publish them."[34] Unlike black mentors such as Alain Locke,
the white Van Vechten was well-placed in New York literary circles and
could therefore see his protégé's work through to publication with no
less than the prestigious Knopf company. Still, for Hughes and other
African American artists of the era, Van Vechten served not merely as a
conduit to white social connections, as many white patrons of the
period functioned. Rather, as Emily Bernard writes in *Remember Me to
Harlem: The Letters of Langston Hughes and Carl Van Vechten* (2001),
"What they [black writers] saw in Van Vechten was more than a useful

contact; he was a fellow champion of free expression in black arts and culture."[35]

Another ardent Van Vechten supporter was Zora Neale Hurston, who remarked in his defense over the *Nigger Heaven* controversy, "If Carl Van Vechten were a people instead of a person, I could then say, these are my people."[36] For Hurston, like the aforementioned black male writers of the Harlem Renaissance, the New Negro mandate of black respectability was a force to be resisted, if not subverted with transgressive renderings of African American experience. Writing in the autobiographical *Dust Tracks on a Road* (1942), for example, she recalls the motivation in undertaking her first novel, *Jonah's Gourd Vine* (1934): "What I wanted to tell was a story about a man, and from what I had read and heard, Negroes were supposed to write about the Race Problem. I was and am thoroughly sick of the subject. My interest lies in what makes a man or woman do such-and-so, regardless of color. It seemed to me that the human beings I met reacted pretty much the same to the same stimuli."[37] Indeed, Hurston's body of work marks a point of departure in African American women's fiction up to that time. Previously, landmark novels like Jessie Fauset's *There Is Confusion* (1924) and Nella Larson's *Quicksand* (1928) and *Passing* (1929), which also offer the first candid appraisals of black women's sexuality in African American women's fiction, placed primary importance on book-length considerations of racial themes such as color and "passing" among the black middle class. Instead, Hurston's work, notably *Their Eyes Were Watching God* (1937), which Barbara Smith described as "one of a handful of books in existence that take Black women seriously,"[38] ushers in a more radical shift in black women's fiction in which, if racial themes are downplayed, they are done so only to the extent that the impact of sexual politics on poor, often rural, black women's lives may be addressed more forthrightly. "In Biblical times a woman had few choices. She could be an idle queen or independent and an outcast. The only proper role was that of wife," Smith added. "In *Their Eyes Were Watching God* Hurston questions these assumptions still in force some two thousand years later."[39]

While by the 1930s considerations of gender assumption had begun to be incorporated into black women's writings with greater prominence, poet and playwright Angelina Weld Grimké had been writing "woman-identified" literature since the early twentieth century. Born in 1880 to aristocratic biracial parents whose intellectual ancestry included the famous white abolitionists and early women's rights advocates Sarah M. Grimké and Angelina Grimké Weld (for whom the author was named), Angelina Weld Grimké produced works that infused the family tradition of racial uplift ideology with radical social protest propaganda. Her most prominent work, the antilynching play *Rachel* (1916), which was the first African American work to be performed by an all-black cast of actors for white audiences, was sponsored by the NAACP specifically to counter the racist depiction of blacks in D. W. Griffith's film *Birth of a Nation* (1915). Same-sex longings, however, were reserved by Grimké for the more private form of her love poetry, much of which remains unpublished even today. Poems such as "Rosabel" ("Rose whose heart unfolds, red petaled/Prick her slow heart's stir/Tell her white, gold, red my love is—/And for her,—for her") and "A Mona Lisa" ("I should like to creep/Through the long brown grasses/That are your lashes"), while not explicitly lesbian, nevertheless enable the author to address romantic sentiments to a female lover in a gender-neutral voice.[40] Undeniably overt homosexual sentiments, by comparison, can be found in Grimké's correspondence with friend Mamie Burrill. An 1896 letter from Burrill to Grimké asks, "Could I just come to meet thee once more, in the old sweet way, just coming at your calling, and like an angel bending o'er you breathe into your ear, 'I love you.'"[41] While one must once again exercise caution in attributing contemporary homosexual labels to people who lived long ago, a letter from Grimké to Burrill speaks clearly of lesbian love. Asking Burrill to be her "wife," Grimké writes, "Oh Mamie if you only knew how my heart overflows with love for you and how it yearns and pants for one glimpse of your lovely face…. Now may the Almighty father bless thee little one and keep thee safe from all harm, your passionate lover."[42]

If open references to lesbianism seldom appear in the poetry and short stories of black bisexual author Alice Dunbar-Nelson, she similarly chose to record them in more discreet outlets. Dunbar-Nelson, a popular elder poet of the Harlem Renaissance and an early activist in the black women's club movement, published her first book, *Violets and Other Tales* (1895), when only twenty years old and a second book, *The Goddess of St. Rocque and Other Stories*, just four years later. Shortly afterward, she met her first husband, Paul Lawrence Dunbar, the most famous black American poet of the day, retaining his name following their separation in 1902 and his death in 1906. Although Dunbar-Nelson remarried in 1916—"a good professional union," in the words of Akasha (Gloria) Hull, editor of *Give Us Each Day: The Diary of Alice Dunbar-Nelson* (1984)[43]—the author remained sexually available to women, as did any number of married black women club members, as the diary reveals. According to an August 1, 1928, entry, Dunbar-Nelson noted,

> Narka [Mrs. Narka Lee-Rayford of the National Federation of Colored Women] comes to the house for "comfort." We want to make "whoopee." So we telephone Mrs. Petis' home to see if Leitha Fleming is there. She has just come home. We go.... They are eating cream—Leitha, Mrs. Glass and another little soul or two.... Life is glorious. Good home made white grape wine. We really make whoopee. Leitha and Narka strike up a heavy flirtation. My nose sadly out of joint. Something after two Narka starts to drive home alone, just as Bobbo [Dunbar-Nelson's husband] comes up. Such a glorious moonlight night....[44]

At the same time, Dunbar-Nelson's diary also indicates that her affections for men were genuine, albeit conventional, rather than another manifestation of forced heterosexual conformity common to the period. Writing in 1931, she commented, "[L]ove and beautiful love has been mine from many men, but the great passion of four or five transcended that of other women—and what more can any woman want?"[45] Dunbar-Nelson otherwise remained private in regard to her sexuality, subject to the proprieties shared by such New Negro advocates of her generation as DuBois and Locke. In the case of black women writers, especially lesbians and bisexuals, however, an added dimension of gender-specific sexual restraint came into play, as Hull importantly observed: "They were always mindful of their need to be living refutations of the sexual slurs to which Black women were subjected and, at the same time, as much as white women, were also tyrannized by the still-prevalent Victorian cult of true womanhood."[46]

Challenging early-twentieth century gender identity from an overtly lesbian perspective in fiction were the first identifiably lesbian novels published in the United States. Arguably the most influential of these works was British author Radclyffe Hall's *The Well of Loneliness* (1928), an explicit if bleakly interpreted plea for social tolerance of homosexuals. When the book was charged with obscenity by American courts in 1929, one judge proclaimed, "The book can have no moral value since it seems to justify the right of the pervert to prey upon normal members of the community," declaring Hall's novel "offensive to public morals and decency."[47] Nevertheless, the work became a literary touchstone for women writers of all sexual orientations for generations. Prior to *The Well of Loneliness,* Sarah Orne Jewett had been publishing woman-identified fiction since 1869, most notably *The Country of the Pointed Firs* (1896). Although her novels are not lesbian-specific, historians have made a case for Jewett's homosexuality based on her unpublished poetry and a thirty-year intimate involvement (or "Boston Marriage," to borrow the phrase that describes long-terms relations between upper-class nineteenth-century women) with writer Annie Fields. The novels of Djuna Barnes furthered open representations of lesbianism, principally with the self-published *Ladies Almanack* (1928), a satire of sapphic Paris, and the landmark novel *Nightwood* (1936). In spite of the author's courage in incorporating overtly homosexual themes, Barnes did not personally identify as a lesbian, pointing out instead that she "just loved Thelma," referring to her eight-year relationship with artist Thelma Wood. Also residing in Paris among white American lesbian expatriates was Gertrude Stein, whose *Tender Buttons* (1912), "Miss Furr and Miss Skeen" (1922), and the posthumously published 1903 homoerotic novel *Q.E.D.* (1950) gave the modernist avant-garde a decidedly lesbian voice.

In Harlem of the 1920s, however, the modernist avant-garde was showcased by no one more boldly than by the heiress A'Lelia Walker, daughter of Madam C. J. Walker, a self-made millionaire whose fortune derived from the invention of hair-straightening products. Although A'Lelia Walker was neither an artist nor intellectual (she "spent the Renaissance playing bridge," David Levering Lewis observed dryly),[48] she was known principally for her lavish gay parties at her Hudson River estate and in her Manhattan apartment, dubbed "The Dark Tower." Her guest list regularly included royalty and visiting dignitaries, not to mention a veritable roll call of Harlem Renaissance celebrities like DuBois, Cullen, Hurston, Van Vechten, and Hughes, the last of whom remarked that Walker's social connections "would turn any Nordic social climber green with envy."[49] Often described for her tall, striking appearance, not to mention her riding crop and jeweled turbans, Walker was provocative by nature, as when she threw a segregated dinner party where whites were served chitterlings and bootleg liquor, while blacks were seated separately in more lavish quarters and offered caviar and champagne. For Richard Bruce Nugent, however, these functions were nothing more than "a place for A'Lelia to show off her blackness to whites."[50] And while she went through four short-lived marriages, she is remembered for having been surrounded by attractive women, all of whom "were crazy about her."[51] Furthermore, it has been argued that Walker's openness to homosexuals engendered greater tolerance of lesbian and gay men by setting a progressive example for other socially prominent African Americans to follow. Still, her "funny parties," as black lesbian Mabel Hampton called the more intimate gatherings at The Dark Tower, illustrate the extent to which the millionairess was willing to participate in Harlem's sexual bohemia. "They were kinds of orgies. Some people had clothes on, some didn't," Hampton recalled years later, speaking of one evening in particular when men and women, gay and straight, black and white partied at Walker's home. "People would hug and kiss on pillows and do anything they wanted to do. You could watch if you wanted to. Some came to watch, some came to play. You had to be cute and well-dressed to get in."[52]

Performing in all-black shows at Harlem's Garden of Joy and the Lafayette Theater as a dancer in the 1920s, Mabel Hampton was acquainted with most of the black lesbian and bisexual entertainers of the Harlem Renaissance, such as Gladys Bentley, perhaps the best-known "bulldagger" on stage during the era. Bentley, a butch woman who had left Philadelphia in 1923 to live openly in Harlem, won head-lining fame as a male impersonator at The Clam House, a speakeasy popular among black lesbians and gay men. Dressed in an elegant men's suit, top hat, and cane, the three-hundred-pound-plus star sang off-color renditions of blues standards. If Bentley's shows shocked Harlemites, the entertainer's off-stage behavior—such as marrying her white woman lover in a well-publicized civil union—was a public illustration that she was willing to employ lesbianism as the very foundation of her celebrity persona. Late in life, however, Bentley took great care to distance herself from her homosexual past. "For many years I lived in a personal hell," she began apologetically in a 1952 article of redemption entitled "I Am a Woman Again," published in *Ebony* magazine. "Like a great number of lost souls, I inhabited that half-shadow no-man's land which exists between the boundaries of the two sexes.... I earned large sums of money and thrilled to recognition, still, in my secret heart, I was weeping and wounded because I was traveling the wrong road to real love and true happiness...until the miracle happened and I became a woman again."[53] Bentley's self-described "miracle" in reality consisted of hormone therapy, faith in God, and, maybe most importantly to *Ebony*'s audience, marriage to a man, which she describes as the "awakening within me of the womanliness I tried to suppress." Photographs accompanying the article depict the author at home turning back her husband's bed and taste-testing meals she has prepared for him, while printed captions assure readers that "Miss Bentley enjoys the domestic role she has shunned for years."[54] Although her marriage was short-lived, and she confessed to remaining "haunted by the sex underworld in which I once lived," Bentley nonetheless asked that her message be embraced as a source of hope for lesbians and gay men. "I want the world to know that those of us who have taken the unusual paths to love are not hopeless; that we can find someone in the opposite sex who can teach us love as love ought to exist."[55]

In many respects, Bentley's purported transition from lesbian nonconformist to husband-happy homemaker tellingly demonstrates the extent to which even gay-identified homosexuals in the declining years of the Harlem Renaissance felt increased pressure toward "normalcy" at any cost. Writing in his study of gay New York, George Chauncey observed, "After a decade in which gay men and a smaller number of lesbians had become highly visible in clubs, streets, newspapers, novels, and films, a powerful backlash to the Prohibition-era 'pansy craze' developed. The anti-gay reaction gained force in the early to mid-thirties as it became part of a more general reaction to the cultural experimentation of the Prohibition years and to the gender rearrangements of the Depression. As the onset of the Depression dashed the confidence of the 1920s, gay men and lesbians began to seem less amusing than dangerous."[56] The federal government's prohibition against alcohol, beginning in 1917, not only had failed to end the manufacture of liquor but had driven the drinking-life underground, creating a demiworld where lines of socially acceptable behavior regarding sex, gender, and race were unregulated and therefore blurred. In the wake of Prohibition's repeal in 1933, however, government agencies enforced a new series of morality-based legal codes that sought to control the consumption of alcohol, as well as the settings in which it was served. The

state of New York, for example, set up the State Liquor Authority, which
threatened to revoke liquor licenses from anyone serving "undesir-
ables," including homosexuals, prostitutes, and gamblers. Consequently,
police closed hundreds of gay bars and gay-patronized establishments,
while homosexual men were rounded up in tourist-friendly city centers
like Times Square and dispersed to the far reaches of Greenwich Village
and Harlem. By the 1930s, Prohibition advocates such as The Women's
Christian Temperance Union (WCTU) were no longer needed to perform the function of safeguarding morals. Instead, the government had
set itself up as both cultural arbiter and watchdog, defining acceptable
parameters for sexual expression, with extreme prejudice guaranteed to
those who deviated.

Amid this heightened antihomosexual repression, gay men
nonetheless produced a number of gay-themed works challenging sexual convention with forthright depictions of homosexuality. The
publication of Foreman Brown's novel *Better Angel* (1933) and *The Young
and the Evil* (1933) by coauthors Charles Henri Ford and Parker Tyler
indicated a shift in the willingness of male authors to publish openly
homosexual fiction, which Christopher Isherwood expanded further
with *Goodbye to Berlin* (1939), an autobiographical rendering of gay life
in Weimar Germany that later was released in a single volume along
with *The Last of Mr. Norris* (1935) and *Sally Bowles* (1937) as *The Berlin
Stories* (1975). Among black writers, however, Wallace Thurman's *Infants
of the Spring* (1932), written at the onset of the Depression, became the
last openly homosexual novel by a gay African American until Owen
Dodson's *Boy at the Window* (1951) was published twenty years later.
Although Thurman was not the only black gay or bisexual author published during that period, he was in fact alone in incorporating explicitly
homosexual content into African American gay writing. The bisexual
Jamaican-born novelist Claude McKay, whose *Home to Harlem* (1929) was
the first commercially successful novel by a black author, for example,
never acknowledged his own homosexuality in print. Even his memoir,
A Long Way from Home (1937), avoids mention of sexual identity.
Langston Hughes's two autobiographies, *The Big Sea* (1940) and *I Wonder
As I Wander* (1956), are also noteworthy for their silence on the topic of
sexual orientation. Perhaps understandably, the combination of a
Depression-era economy (unemployment in Harlem had reached fifty
percent), along with daily realities of racial and sexual oppression, made

overt references to black gayness especially unattractive, if not outright dangerous, to black gay and bisexual authors of the period.

By comparison, African American heterosexuals like Richard Wright gained early fame during the post–Harlem Renaissance years with autobiographically based works that inspired the pioneering careers of Ralph Ellison, James Baldwin, and other influential writers of the following decade. Wright's landmark first novel, the politically defiant *Native Son* (1940), sold more than two hundred thousand copies in one month, showcasing African American fiction for mainstream readers who previously had limited their race-based reading to nineteenth-century slave narratives. Actor and singer Paul Robeson, who starred in the stage adaptation of Wright's third book, *Black Boy* (1945), remarked of *Native Son*, "Wright portrays the Negro as he was and is,—courageous, and forever struggling to better his condition; the Negro descended from Nat Turner, Sojourner Truth, Vesey, Frederick Douglass, and countless others who fought that Americans of African blood should also be free and (in the words of Lincoln), 'enjoy their constitutional rights.'"[57] Like Robeson, Wright was a black Communist Party member who applied Marxist teachings popular among radical-left circles to American race relations. "I owe my literary development to the Communist Party and its influence, which has shaped my thoughts and creative goals," Wright commented in 1938 at the time his short story collection, *Uncle Tom's Children,* was published. "It gave me my first full bodied vision of Negro life in America."[58] Yet unlike Wright, who renounced his party membership in 1942, Robeson deepened his political commitment until his death, incurring enmity from the same civil rights establishment that had barred homosexuals for equally disruptive racial identities. The NAACP's Walter White, for example, attacked Robeson with language that might as easily describe the prevailing attitude among African Americans of the 1940s toward lesbians and gay men, remarking in the national black press, "Robeson is a bewildered man who is more to be pitied than damned."[59] Additionally, Robeson's "highly charged erotic life," in the words of biographer Martin Duberman, became a source of exploitation for white conservatives eager to discredit this outspoken critic of American colonialism as a "moral transgressor."[60]

Following the entry of the United States into World War II, government surveillance of sexual transgressors was widespread and advanced. Whereas lesbians and gay men had been policed before, never had homosexuals been sought out from the general population as a matter of military policy. From 1941 to 1945 approximately nine thousand soldiers and sailors suspected of being gay were discharged from military service through the Armed Forces' newly instituted psychiatric screening process. Nevertheless, units such as the Women's Army Corps (WAC) attracted and retained large numbers of lesbians, with some experts placing the number of lesbians in the military at eighty percent of the overall population of women serving in the war.[61] As Lillian Faderman commented,

> For those who already identified themselves as lesbians, military service, with its opportunities to meet other women and to engage in work and adventure that were ordinarily denied them, was especially appealing. For many others who had not identified themselves as lesbians before the war, the all female environment of the women's branches of the armed forces, offering as it did the novel emotional excitement of working with competent, independent women, made lesbianism an attractive option.[62]

Even among civilians, the women's labor force grew from 12 million workers in 1941 to 19 million in 1945. Moreover, wartime labor shortages brought about by the transfer of more than 12 million men overseas necessitated in some instances that positions previously filled exclusively by white males were filled temporarily by women, including black women, whose numbers in the workforce suddenly tripled.[63] The war's end, however, not only brought a halt to the demand for "womanpower" but also instigated a cultural push for women to return to conventional gender roles familiar in prewar civilian life. Chief among these expectations was that women should embrace the traditional domestic identities of wife, mother, and homemaker. "After the war, when the surviving men returned to their jobs and homes that the women needed to make for them so that the country could return to 'normalcy,'" Faderman wrote, "love between women and female independence were suddenly nothing but manifestations of illness, and a woman who dared to proclaim herself a lesbian was considered a borderline psychotic."[64]

In the aftermath of World War II, political conservatives took advantage of the postwar gender backlash to launch an especially aggressive campaign against homosexuals. At first, this platform was manifested as an "anticommunist" agenda, whose basic function actually had less to do with dismantling American Communism than with advancing right-wing Cold War policy. Beginning with a 1950 report by the State Department that 91 people, "mostly homosexuals" (in the words of the department head), had resigned or been discharged in the process of routine security checks, and throughout the subsequent hearings in which Senator Joseph McCarthy insisted that one "flagrantly homosexual" State Department worker had been reinstated "under pressure" from an unnamed, high-ranking State Department official, gay men and lesbians were added to the list of so-called un-American conspirators.[65] Shortly thereafter, the chairman of the Republican National Committee announced that "perhaps as dangerous as the actual Communists are the sexual perverts who have infiltrated our Government in recent years…. It is the talk of Washington."[66] Indeed, one Washington, D.C., vice squad officer informed Congress that 4,500 of the 5,000 known homosexuals in Washington were government employees,[67] while a pair of Hearst newspaper reporters raised the number to 6,000, yet calling that "a fraction of the total of their kind in the city."[68] It was in the context of this antigay hysteria that a Senate subcommittee was launched to investigate gay "infiltration" in the federal government, much as "red sympathizers" had been targeted by Congress with the founding of the House Un-American Activities Committee (HUAC) in 1947. The subcommittee's research concluded, unsurprisingly, that these "clandestine relationships" and "recruiting agents" did in fact jeopardize public safety, pointing out that a homosexual has "a corrosive influence upon his fellow employees. These perverts will frequently attempt to entice normal individuals to engage in perverted practices. This is especially true in the case of young and impressionable people who might come under the influence of a pervert." As such, Republican President Dwight Eisenhower in 1953 added "sexual perversion" to the list of offenses for which one was banned by law from federal jobs.

Still, this onslaught of political hostilities also functioned as a catalyst for establishing the first postwar gay protest group, Bachelors Anonymous, in 1948. "The anti-Communist witch-hunts were very much in operation; the House Un-American Activities Committee had investigated Communist 'subversion' in Hollywood. The purge of homosexuals from the State Department took place," remarked gay rights pioneer and Bachelors Anonymous founder Harry Hay. "The country, it seemed to me, was beginning to move toward fascism and McCarthyism; the Jews wouldn't be used as a scapegoat this time.... McCarthy was setting up the pattern for a new scapegoat, and it was going to be us—Gays. We had to organize, we had to move, we had to get started."[69] Bachelors Anonymous, known alternately as the International Bachelors Fraternal Order for Peace and Social Dignity, was a service organization dedicated to the defense of the "androgynous minority."[70] Prior to this period, the only instance of overt gay activism in the United States had been Henry Gerber's short-lived Society for Human Rights in 1925. "I had always bitterly felt the injustice with which my own American society accused the homosexual of 'immoral acts,'" Gerber wrote. "One of our greatest handicaps was the knowledge that homosexuals don't organize. Being thoroughly cowed, they seldom get together. Most feel that as long as some homosexual acts are against the law, they should not let their names be on any organization's mailing list any more than notorious bandits would join a thieves' union."[71] The Society for Human Rights was disbanded when several members were charged with violating a federal law that prohibited sending obscene material through the mail. "[W]e were up against a solid wall of ignorance, hypocrisy, meanness, and corruption. The wall had won."[72] Although Bachelors Anonymous encountered similar legal prejudice, the group evolved in 1950 into the Mattachine Society, the leading homosexual political protest vehicle of the mid-twentieth century.

Appropriately enough, it was James Baldwin who invited public discussion about the intersection of race and gender—discussions that anticipated the complexities and tensions of pursuing civil rights across specific identity categories. Writing in "Preservation of Innocence," a 1949 essay that predates the birth of the modern civil rights movement, he spoke of the naturalness of homosexuality:

> We are forced to consider [the] tension between God and nature and are thus confronted with the nature of God because He is man's most intense creation and it is not in the sight of nature that the homosexual is condemned, but in the sight of God. This argues a profound and dangerous failure of concept, since an incalculable number of the world's humans are thereby condemned to something less than life; and we

> may not, of course, do this without limiting ourselves....
> Experience, nevertheless, to say nothing of history, seems
> clearly to indicate that it is not possible to banish or to falsify
> any human need without ourselves undergoing falsification
> and loss.[73]

In fact, however, notwithstanding Baldwin's efforts to normalize homo-sexuality, lesbians and gay men remained largely banished from mainstream culture of the time, which "condemned" a significant por-tion of the American population to "something less than life." What precisely this represented for black lesbian, gay, and bisexual people remained a source of contention in liberation struggles for decades to come. In the meantime, openly homosexual fiction by black lesbians and gay men, if not finding voice amid Cold War repression, found inspiration in the pioneering works of the Harlem Renaissance. The identifiably lesbian and gay African American literary movement that had begun in the 1920s was subverted by cultural watchdogs and New Negro propagandists, yet an influential literary tradition, however tenu-ous, had been established. If nothing else, the spirit of these literary forebears was manifested in the writings of a new generation of postwar lesbian and gay artists who began the project of reframing this "falsifi-cation and loss" with groundbreaking works. More than transforming the social, cultural, and political context within which they were written, these works would help radicalize cultural definitions of African American sexual identity over the next half century.

ALICE DUNBAR-NELSON

■ ■ ■

[1875–1935]

BORN IN NEW ORLEANS TO MIDDLE-CLASS PARENTS OF MIXED
racial heritage, Alice Ruth Moore possessed a gifted intellect, along with
a near-white complexion, thus distinguishing herself early in color-
conscious African American and Creole social circles. At age fifteen she
entered Straight College, graduating with a teaching degree two years
later. Following a brief period as a public school teacher, she moved
north in 1896 where later she studied English literature at Cornell,
Columbia, and the University of Pennsylvania. It was while living in New
York City that she met and married Paul Laurence Dunbar, the first
nationally recognized African American poet. Although Dunbar's infidelities and alcoholism eventually led to the couple's separation in 1902,
a less publicly acknowledged problem in the relationship was his wife's
color prejudice. Being Creole herself, she had conflicted relations with
dark African Americans such as her husband. Indeed, she did not self-
identify as *Negro*, the prevailing term for African Americans of the
time, preferring instead *mulatto*, which Dunbar-Nelson and many
other light-skinned blacks argued was a class apart and above their
darker-complexioned peers. Nevertheless, the author retained her
estranged husband's prestigious name, even after his death in 1906 and
her subsequent marriage to newspaperman Robert Nelson in 1916.

Dunbar-Nelson has the distinction of publishing the first collection
of short stories by an African American woman—though these stories,
like much of the author's early work, were devoid of black characters.
The conventionally romantic stories in *The Goddess of St. Rocque and Other
Stories* (1899) were populated with Creole and Cajun characters whom

Dunbar-Nelson did not think of as "black." Not all of her stories were conventional romances, however. She addressed gender and race explicitly in her early fiction, but these stories remained unpublished until *The Collected Works of Alice Dunbar-Nelson* was edited by the black lesbian feminist scholar Akasha (Gloria) Hull in the 1980s.

Although she won early attention for her short fiction, Dunbar-Nelson is remembered for her poetry. She published in prestigious African American periodicals such as the Urban League's *Opportunity; The Crisis,* published by the NAACP; and a number of influential anthologies, including James Weldon Johnson's *Book of American Negro Poetry* in 1931.

Dunbar-Nelson also distinguished herself as a leader in both the early women's suffrage movement and the ongoing struggle for racial equality. Her activism belied the often genteel content of her published fiction. Dunbar-Nelson made good use of the limelight that accompanied her position as an elder writer of the Harlem Renaissance and the widow of Paul Laurence Dunbar. Putting her notoriety to use, she was an ardent public speaker and a prolific journalist on behalf of "race and sex" for the rest of her life. Indeed, her outspoken opinions led to her dismissal from a teaching position in 1920, after she attended a conference in the home of Republican presidential candidate Warren G. Harding.

Dunbar-Nelson's intimate, and far less socially acceptable, affairs are recorded in the diary she kept in 1921 and again from 1926 to 1931. Among the details of the author's personal and financial struggles—as well as her ongoing devotion to Robert Nelson—are open allusions to her lesbian relationships, including relations with fellow-members in the black women's club movement, which provided an informal social network for Dunbar-Nelson and other African American lesbian and bisexual women. She was working as a newspaper columnist and lecturer when she died from heart failure in 1935.

From *The Collected Works of Alice Dunbar-Nelson* comes an unpublished early story entitled "Natalie." Characteristic of the autobiographical Creole fiction that established the author's early literary reputation, "Natalie" departs from convention by means of its suggestive lesbian content that passes as juvenile fiction. When read in the context of Dunbar-Nelson's diary, however, the work assumes a double meaning.

Natalie

[1898]

Natalie swung herself down from the breakwater to the white sands below, and walked along on the edge of the sea, her feet leaving prints that filled with water, and were quickly effaced. She swung her brown arms in the fading sunset light, and sniffed the whiffs of salt air with keenly appreciative nostril, swinging as she trotted along with long, clean-limbed step. Natalie was happy in her little sunset world down here by the water's edge.

Suddenly she paused and her big black eyes widened angrily. Someone had invaded her territory and was coming towards her.

Down here on the sands at this edge of the beach was Natalie's own kingdom, and woe unto the trespasser who dared within its boundaries. At Mandeville, you know, there are places where the fickle Lake Ponchartrain encroaches too frequently and too violently upon the homes of men, therefore, it has to be kept back by stoutly built break- waters, as its no less turbulent cousin, the Mississippi river is kept from swamping New Orleans across the way by levees. Then, too, there are spots here and there where the lake kisses the shores in regulation beach-like manner, or mingles with swamp and bayou over morass and tangled moss thicket. When the tide was low, one might walk on the sands below until the beachy places were found. Down here at the West End of the town, the natives called Natalie's kingdom because of the absolute sway she exercised over those sands and marshes and little beauty spots of scenery and waves.

Walking towards her now on the sunset lighted sands, evidently tak- ing great delight in wetting her delicate slippers, came a fair-haired, rose-tinted creature, in an ethereal film of fluffy lawn and flower-covered hat. Natalie surveyed her curiously. She knew the type well; the delicate summer boarder who came to idle time away, was afraid of everything under the sun, and generally treated Natalie either with supercilious indifference or with contemptuous patronage. She knew them and hated them accordingly. But this one must be of a different kind, else how did she get down that perilous climb, and why was she unaccompa- nied by maid or mother? The newcomer was also surveying Natalie with admiration plainly depicted in her eyes.

Contrary to her usual custom, the queen approached the trespasser and said, "Who are you and what are you doing here?" She spoke in French, and the blonde shook her head and said sadly,

"You'll have to speak English."

Natalie's self-importance rose in a corresponding degree as the girl's eyes surveyed her healthful frame with wonderment, and she repeated the question in a mixture of bad English and gestures.

Olivia replied that her family had moved into the house at the corner for the summer. The big house hidden in red roses and magnolia trees.

"The Torrés house?" asked Natalie.

Olivia nodded her head wisely, and discussing the beauties of the place, they walked along the sunset sands. They had just reached the stage when confidences were in progress, when a sharp voice above their heads caused them to look up. They were passing beneath the fishing wharf of the house, and a fretful looking, over-dressed lady with a white lace parasol was leaning over the railing.

"Olivia!" she screamed sharply, "What are you doing down there? Come up here this minute."

Olivia started nervously; it was evident that she was afraid of her mother.

"How can I get up?" she inquired.

"You'll have to climb, yes," said Natalie, "cause the nearest slope is a leetle more than a half mile down."

So boosted up by Natalie's strong, bared arms, and clinging to the scrubby bushes that grew through the cracks of the breakwater, Olivia gained the beach smiling, flushed, triumphant, only to be met with a scowl on the face of the over-dressed lady.

"What do you mean," she said sharply, "by acting like a regular tomboy, and running about with such a person already?"

Olivia hung her head, but said nothing, only walked into the house, and sat on her father's knee.

"Papa," she spoke slowly, and with tears in her eyes, "I climbed down the breakwater just now, and met such a nice girl on the sands. She's what they call a 'Cajan' here; awfully pretty, and nice, and so smart, papa! She speaks such good French, I didn't dare answer her in anything but English. Her name is Natalie Leblanc, and she lives down where the bayou meets the lake. She told me that she never liked summer boarders because they were always so stuck-up, but she liked me, because I seemed to have some sense. And she's so healthy, papa, and strong, why she almost lifted me over the breakwater. And, papa, please sir, mayn't I go with her? She says she'll show me all the beauty places, and teach me how to swim and row and fish and all that."

"Whew?" replied Mr. Spiers, "you two must have flown into each other's arms to have learned all that."

"She's a nice girl, papa, fourteen years, only you'd never think so. She's so much taller and stouter than I am."

At the supper table that night Mr. Spiers said to his wife, "Carrie, I want you to let Olivia take off those fancy clothes and get some blood in her face; she looks like a wax doll. Let her run and jump and climb and get sunburned. It'll do her good."

"Gracious me, John," exclaimed Mrs. Spiers, "you'll have the child a regular hoyden; when will she learn dignity?"

"Six years from now is time enough. I hate these little old women that are coming up now. Let her go with the natives, they'll teach her more healthy topics of conversation than that fashionable city set."

Olivia said nothing, but her pale little face lighted with pleasure, and she flashed a grateful look at her father across the table. Next morning, Mr. Spiers went back to the city, and the family settled in their beautiful, rose-embowered, rambling old home for the summer.

Natalie was swinging dreamily on her front gallery in a hammock made of barrel staves and sacking. A peaceful noonday silence hung over all save for the persistent trilling of a mockingbird in the moss-laden oak tree, and an occasional hoarse grunt from an alligator in the black waters of the bayou. The persimmon tree shook a shower of snowy fragrant blossoms at its foot, as the breezes that came from Nott's Point swept its branches. It was a quaint little, one-sided house, shingle-roofed, and moss-covered, its gray sides guiltless of paint. But the wide gallery that went all the way around the house was scrubbed white, and sprinkled after the good old fashion, with white sand, while the walk that led from the battered gate was sanded carefully, swept clean, and bordered with precise rows of poppies and larkspurs. Natalie's eyes closed as she dreamily answered the mockingbird's trills with snatches of a Creole melody.

A timid knock roused her to a standing position, and there half opening the gate, stood Olivia.

"Entrez, entrez!" cried Natalie impulsively, "Oh, mais, ma foi, you look nice, you seem sensible now," with an approving glance at Olivia's gingham dress, white sunbonnet and sand shoes. "Stay with me all the day, yes, and we shall have such fun, such a nice time, yes, we will."

So Olivia stayed, and was introduced to the grandmother Mme. Leblanc, very old and dignified and gentle. She was escorted proudly around the big yard with its duck pond and plum orchard; initiated into the mysteries of the artesian well. In Mandeville, you know slow little town as it is, everyone uses the artesian well in preference to anything else, so that every one has most clear, cold, and sparkling water at all times. This one of Natalie's fell into a big stone basin, overgrown with scarlet creepers, and waterlillies on the clear pool. Upon the stone beneath the trickling stream there was a glass, and Natalie explained how glasses could be colored by simply letting them stay under the action of the water for a day, then the sulphur and iron would turn the white into a clear amber with iridescent lights throughout. Within the old-fashioned kitchen there were many glasses which Natalie had colored, and nothing more daintily clear could be imagined.

This was only the beginning of a close intimacy between the girls. There were long rambles down the bayou shores into the piney woods of the old oak, that stood sentinel-like over the water's edge, intimacies with the quaint Indians in the St. Tammany settlement; rowings around the lake's edges and up the bayou in a dory, singing French songs that Natalie could make sound so prettily; swims in the brown lake water; a healthy brownness in Olivia's face, and a pleased sparkle about Natalie in the newfound affection that was so strange to her.

But she could not be induced to visit Olivia's home at the Torrés place. "Madame, your maman, cares not for me," she would say in response to Olivia's entreaties to come to the house, "and I think it better to stay away. You come to me, we will be happy, yes."

When Mr. Spiers came over on the steamer Saturday evening to stay until Monday morning, nothing pleased him better than to see his "little country girl" so healthy, though the stylish mother grieved to see the unfashionable tan on the girl's cheeks.

One day, however, Natalie wanted Olivia for a piney woods ramble to gather pine cones which would be made into picture frames. So with bonnet and basket, she swallowed her pride, and trudged up the beach to the Torrés place. Mrs. Spiers leaned over the picket fence with a bored expression and a frown. It was dull in this unfashionable town with nothing of interest save the daily watch for the arrival of the New

Camelia, which came puffing across the lake's bosom every evening, the engine's arms working up and down with monotonous precision. One regatta of very miniature proportions, with a very tame hop at Colomés' hotel, a daily drive to the post office, with an occasional visitor constituted the round of pleasures for the season. Mrs. Spiers wanted to go home, but Olivia wanted to stay, and Olivia generally had her way with her father. Natalie's voice aroused Mrs. Spiers from an unpleasant reverie.

"Is Oleevia home?"

She looked up crossly. "Olivia?" she said.

"Yes, madame," and Natalie gave her one of her most polite French bows, while Mrs. Spiers drew herself up haughtily.

"I think you are making a mistake," she said icily, "you probably mean *Miss* Olivia."

"Yes, madame, I mean Ma'amselle Oleevia Spiers."

At this moment, the subject of discussion tripped down the flower-lined walk of the old-fashioned garden.

"Oh, Natalie," she cried joyously, and would have kissed her friend, but the mother held her back.

"Do you mean to tell me, Olivia, that this—this—person calls you by your first name as if she were your equal? Do you permit that?"

Both girls' faces crimsoned; the one with a fair flush of mortification, the other with a darker tint of injured pride and anger.

"Mama—" began Olivia pleadingly, but Mrs. Spiers was thoroughly angry now.

"In the future, girl," she continued addressing Natalie, "I want you to call my daughter *Miss* Olivia. I require that of all inferiors."

Natalie's dark-tressed head rose proudly, "I am not an inferior, madame," she replied. "In age and in education, I am Oleevia's equal, yes, and in birth, and breeding, I am superior to madame herself," and walked away proudly, swinging her gay-colored Indian basket with erect head, while Olivia burst into shamed tears, and was promptly hustled inside.

Natalie did not go to the woods to get the pine cones, but walked swiftly home and threw herself moodily into the homemade hammock.

"They are all alike," she mused, "these city people with their airs, and I was foolish to try and be friendly. Serves me right, yes. Mais, much as I like," clenching her fists, "I'd pop before I'd call her mademoiselle, ah, non, non!"

Thus ended the pleasant intimacy between the girls, and Natalie went on in her old way, rowing her dory into the bayou, and fishing for the beautiful trout in its black waters; queening it over the children in the village, and dreaming the hot hours of the day away in the hammock or under the big oak. On Sundays, she would meet Olivia at the quaint little old church on the back road, and smile pleasantly as she knelt to tell her beads, or bowed at the tinkling of the hoarse, little host-bell.

The summer passed away, and merged into the autumn months; the poppies blazed red in the gardens, and the goldenrod gleamed in the woods and hedges. From all sides sounded the crack of the hunter's rifle, and the crackling of dropping nuts on the brown leaves in the crisp, clear air. It was pecan threshing time, and all the small town was busy in the work of threshing the pecan trees and packing the long brown nuts into barrels for shipping. Natalie's time was so taken with helping to thresh trees, gathering in the autumn-tinted persimmons and paddling in the swampy lagoons to shoot the small birds that flocked on the water's edge that Olivia was almost forgotten.

It was on a Sunday evening that a strong southeast wind came with a rush and roar over the angry waters of the lake from Nott's Point, and sent the heavy swell booming high against the breakwater. Natalie's little kingdom down on the sands was completely submerged in about eight feet of water, and the angry waves tossed up onto the shore, dashing clouds of spray into the very houses.

All the population of Mandeville was out on the beach, they dared not go on any pier, for every one of them, even to the steamer landing seemed in imminent danger of being swept away at any moment. Everyone was watching the brave little New Camelia as she battled against the wind and waves coming from Covington and the Tchefuncta River past Mandeville on the way to New Orleans. Again and again, shrilly tooting her displeasure did she skim around the landing, endeavoring to find a stopping place, but in vain, and after a final shrill squeal, she started towards New Orleans, now bounding high on the crest of a wave, now delving deep into a trough, the engine arms frantically waving up and down. Natalie, with heavy black hair, wind-blown and tangled stood in the midst of a crowd of her friends talking loudly with the rest so as to be heard above the wind and water, and at the same time furtively watching the evident distress of Mrs. Spiers and Olivia, who stood apart and wrung their hands with fright.

Everyone remembers until yet, that awful Sunday night. How in the pitchy darkness the fearful southeast wind blowing in the waters from the Gulf of Mexico through the Rigolets, upturned immense centurion oaks, and crushed solid old houses as though they were so many eggshells; how the cattle bellowed as they were swept away into the writhing, tossing waters, and how on the Monday, when the slow daylight dawned over the frightened, praying town, it revealed a complete submergment of four feet, with natives perched in every possible place, and the angry lake still tossing its heavy swells over the crushed breakwater, and dashing logs, and wood, remnants of piers and bathhouses into one's very bedroom.

Natalie's house had escaped, and the water yet lacked three inches of being in the rooms; so cheerfully making the nervous grandmother comfortable, she took her dory from its place on the back gallery, and paddled out into the desolate, frightened Louisiana Venice to give her helping smile to the distressed natives, with offers of her home to those whom falling trees or wild waves had made homeless. Picking up struggling chickens from stray bushes, where bedraggled and wild-eyed they had sought refuge, and a mewing, clawing kitten, and piling them all in the stern, too frightened to fight with each other, she rowed up the canal that had once been the main street until she came to Olivia's house. A sudden impulse caused her to slip her oars, and look up into the windows where she saw Olivia's white, frightened face.

"Natalie," called the girl, and ran out on the gallery, while the dory paddled into the ruined yard, "Oh Natalie, mama is so frightened! She is wild to go home on the Camelia, see, it is coming over now, and Mr. Colomés and Mr. Mathias have all been here, telling her she can't possibly get to the boat, and she's having hysterics, and oh, Natalie, I'm *so* frightened!" and she clung to the dory wildly.

At that moment, Mrs. Spiers came out on the gallery followed by M'sieu Colomés, the hotel man, who with shrugs and gesticulations was saying,

"Madame, is ver' unwise, ver' unwise; mais, non, madame will surely drown if she attempts to catch the bateau."

But madame was determined, so with a final shrug at the perversity of "dose Americain," M'sieu Colomés jumped into his pirogue and paddled away in disgust, determining to wash his hands of the whole affair. Madame turned to Natalie with a despairing gesture.

"You can row, Natalie," she pleaded, "take us to the landing."

"Ah," thought Natalie, 'I am not 'that person' now." But she said nothing, only turned and looked out upon the waste of waters. As far as the eye could reach the lake rolled in long, heavy, groundswells that sobbed in sullen anger under a gray sky at the mischief they had done. About a hundred feet from the gallery stood a row of slender storm-swept saplings outlining the edge of the former breakwater. Just at this line, the swells broke sharply throwing lines of foam into the inundated streets. The brave little Camelia was puffing and working in another attempt to reach the landing, but this time from New Orleans. The landing a halfmile away showed out into the angry waters a broken pile of lumber, the pier reaching to the shore had been reduced to stumps.

Natalie shaded her eyes, and took in the details of the scene at a single glance.

"Eet might be posseeble," she said musingly, "to row down the strit, yes, to the landing pier, then try the waves, but it would be dangerous, yes. Madame, the danger is over, stay in Mandeville until the water goes down."

But Madame was hysterically angry at the idea. Her husband was uneasy, she knew, and there was no possible way of letting him know that she and Olivia were safe. Then just look at those waves, and that was enough! Who knew but in the night they might rise and sweep the entire town away. Even now, the house rocked on its foundations. The servants who had gone out the night before, had not been able to return and the two were alone.

Natalie looked at her earnestly as she talked. Madame had tried all that money and persuasion could do, no one dared brave those waves to meet the boat. Moreover, all the skiffs in Mandeville, save five, had gone to pieces in the storm. Olivia was crying silently, dreading the angry waters.

"For Oleevia, I'll take you," said Natalie at length, "For your 'Mees Oleevia,'" she couldn't help growing sarcastic under the circumstances.

The few people who gazed out of windows and from galleries of the houses remaining on the beach marveled to see Natalie's brown arms pulling the now heavily laden dory up the street. Mrs. Spiers and the valise were stored in the boat among the wet chickens and the trembling kitten, while Olivia steered. It was easy enough rowing up the street in the comparatively calm water, but the superhuman effort came when it

was time to get into the lake towards the boat which had now reached
the landing, puffing and blowing, and tugging at the cable which bound
her to the broken anchor-post.

It was only a hundred yards out, but it needed a man's herculean
strength to pull against the fearful force of the heavy, incoming waves.
A foot would be gained, only to be lost and beaten back for three feet or
more. Mrs. Spiers, too frightened to speak looked desperately about her,
while Olivia prayed silently as she steered. From the deck of the steamer,
the Captain and crew watched the dory with a field glass. "If only we
could help her!" they cried, but every boat had been swept from the
steamer in that awful twenty mile battle from New Orleans.

Pull, strain, tug every nerve did Natalie, and a little headway was
made. Now her strength seemed gone, and it looked as if she must suc-
cumb and let the boat drift and be dashed into pieces on the shore. But
onward she forged, her strong hand bending as she plunged the boat
through a stubborn swell.

"Oh, Marie, mere de Dieu," prayed Natalie, "dans cette heure de
travail, pitie-moi; donnez-moi ton secours."

For a weary hour she fought with blistered hands and failing heart
against the surging swells and driving wind until near the sides of the
steamer, when a lasso-like rope came whizzing to the dory. Mrs. Spiers,
white and trembling made it fast to the seats, and in another instant,
they were all on deck, surrounded by the wondering crew, safe, but
exhausted, and sobbing, every one of them.

"And after mama being so mean to her too," cried Olivia in the first
flush of excitement.

Mrs. Spiers and Olivia went to New Orleans, while the captain sent
one of his strongest men to row Natalie home. That night, the Torrés
house crumbled to the ground, its old foundation undermined by the
water.

But was Natalie ever forgotten? Go to Mandeville to-day and you'll
find her there yet, though this happened eight years ago. But see the
comforts around Mme. Leblanc—the books and music and pleasant
little luxuries. And when Natalie goes to New Orleans for the Carnival
week, Mr. Spiers introduces her to everyone as the "plucky little girl who
rowed my wife and daughter out of a death-trap, by Jove!"

Angelina Weld Grimké

■ ■ ■

[1880–1958]

POET AND PLAYWRIGHT ANGELINA WELD GRIMKÉ WAS BORN
to a white mother and a black father, who raised their only daughter in
the progressive, upper-class society of old Boston. Her father, Archibald
Grimké, was a former slave and a nephew of the famous white abolitionist and women's rights activist Angelina Grimké Weld, for whom the
author was named. He was also a noted intellectual who served as president of the influential American Negro Academy and executive director
of the NAACP. His moderate platform (shared by many African
American leaders of the period) dissuaded his only daughter from militant politics. Instead, young Angelina was taught to aspire to the
"talented tenth" throughout her privileged upbringing.

Grimké's most famous work, *Rachel,* a play portraying the devastating
effects of lynching on a middle-class African American family, proved a
powerful plea for racial justice when it was first performed under the auspices of the NAACP in 1916. In fact, the play is believed to be the first
instance of African American "uplift" propaganda ever staged, as well as
the first successful drama by a black American writer. *Rachel*—originally
given the titles *The Pervert* and the equally curious *Blessed Are the Barren*—
is told from the perspective of a refined young black woman who, like
Grimké herself, vows that she will never marry or have children. Racism
rather than gender nonconformism, however, informs this decision—
when Rachel's father and brother are lynched, and her adopted black son
is called a "nigger," she swears she will not bring another child into the
world to be subjected to such treatment. In spite of the success of the play,
Rachel was Grimké's only book-length work published during her lifetime.

Grimké's poetry—her most prolific genre—contains explicit references to lesbianism. Her two most widely published romantic poems, "A Mona Lisa" and "As the Green Lies Over the Earth," are addressed to women. Furthermore, Grimké's correspondence with women friends displays unambiguously intimate affections. Despite the ostracism she presumably experienced as a biracial lesbian or the bisexual author of explicitly lesbian verse, she avoided openly identifying her work as "homosexual." Readers could assume that the speaker in her romantic poetry was a man writing to a woman. Consequently, Grimké's poems are featured prominently in prestigious collections of the time, including Countee Cullen's *Caroling Dusk* and Charles S. Johnson's *Ebony and Topaz*. Nevertheless, Grimké's repute as a poet, not to mention her commitment to writing, diminished suddenly in 1930 with her retirement from teaching and the death of her father, to whom she had committed much of her adult life. Depressed and living in self-imposed exile from friends, Grimké, for all purposes, ended her career long before her death in 1958.

Among Grimké's most memorable short fiction is "The Closing Door." Written specifically for Margaret Sanger's *Birth Control Review* and published in the magazine's September–October 1919 issue, the story deals with lynching and matricide. Although lesbianism is only very broadly hinted at in the opening lines, this unconventionally tragic depiction of motherhood speaks from the perspective of an especially anguished outsider.

The Closing Door

[1919]

I t was the mother heart of Agnes that had yearned over me, had pity
upon me, loved me and brought me to live in the only home I have
ever known. I have cared for people. I care for Jim; but Agnes Milton
is the only person I have ever really loved. I love her still. And before it
was too late, I used to pray that in some way I might change places with
her and go into that darkness where though, still living, one forgets sun
and moon and stars and flowers and winds—and love itself, and existence means dark, foul-smelling cages, hollow clanging doors, hollow
monotonous days. But a month ago when Jim and I went to see her, she
had changed—she had receded even from us. She seemed—how can I
express it?—blank, empty, a grey automaton, a mere shell. No soul
looked out at us through her vacant eyes.

We did not utter a word during our long journey homeward. Jim
had unlocked the door before I spoke.

"Jim," I said, "they may still have the poor husk of her cooped up
there but her soul, thank God, at least for that, is free at last!"

And Jim, I cannot tell of his face, said never a word but turned away
and went heavily down the stairs. And I, I went into Agnes Milton's
flat and closed the door. You would never have dreamed it was the same
place. For a long time I stood amid all the brightness and mockery of
her sun-drenched rooms. And I prayed. Night and day I have prayed
since, the same prayer—that God, if he knows any pity at all may soon,
soon release the poor spent body of hers.

I wish I might show you Agnes Milton of those far off happy days.
She wasn't tall and she wasn't short; she wasn't stout and she wasn't thin.
Her back was straight and her head high. She was rather graceful,
I thought. In coloring she was Spanish or Italian. Her hair was not very
long but it was soft and silky and black. Her features were not too sharp,
her eyes clear and dark, a warm leaf brown in fact. Her mouth was really
beautiful. This doesn't give her I find. It was the shining beauty and
gayety of her soul that lighted up her whole body and somehow made
her her. And she was generally smiling or chuckling. Her eyes almost
closed when she did so and there were the most delightful crinkles all
about them. Under her left eye there was a small scar, a reminder of

some childhood escapade, that became, when she smiled, the most adorable of dimples....

It was a Tuesday morning about four months, maybe, after my first experience with the closing door. The bell rang three times, the postman's signal when he had left a letter. Agnes came to her feet, her eyes sparkling:

"My letter from Bob," she said and made for the door.

She came back slowly, I noticed, and her face was a little pale and worried. She had an opened and an unopened letter in her hand.

"Well, what does Bob say?" I asked.

"This—this isn't from Bob," she said slowly. "It's only a bill."

"Well, go ahead and open his letter," I said.

"There—there wasn't any, Lucy."

"What!" I exclaimed. I was surprised.

"No. I don't know what it means."

"It will come probably in the second mail," I said. "It has sometimes."

"Yes," she said, I thought rather listlessly.

It didn't come in the second mail nor in the third.

"Agnes," I said. "There's some good explanation. It's not like Bob to fail you."

"No."

"He's busy or got a girl maybe."

She was a little jealous of him and I hoped this last would rouse her, but it didn't.

"Yes, maybe that's it," she said without any life.

"Well, I hope you're not going to let this interfere with your walk," I said.

"I had thought—" she began, but I cut her off.

"You promised Jim you'd go out every single day," I reminded her.

"All right, Agnes Milton's conscience," she said smiling a little. "I'll go then."

She hadn't been gone fifteen minutes when the electric bell began shrilling continuously throughout the flat.

Somehow I knew it meant trouble. My mind immediately flew to Agnes. It took me a second or so to get myself together and then I went to the tube.

"Well," I called. My voice sounded strange and high.

A boy's voice answered:

"Lady here named Mrs. James Milton?"

"Yes." I managed to say.

"Telegram fo' you'se."

It wasn't Agnes, after all. I drew a deep breath. Nothing else seemed to matter for a minute.

"Say!" the voice called up from below. "Wot's de mattah wid you'se up dere?"

"Bring it up," I said at last. "Third floor, front."

I opened the door and waited.

The boy was taking his time and whistling as he came. "Here!" I called out as he reached our floor.

It was inside his cap and he had to take it off to give it to me.

I saw him eyeing me rather curiously.

"You Mrs. Milton?" he asked.

"No, but this is her flat. I'll sign for it. She's out. Where do I sign? There? Have you a pencil?"

With the door shut behind me again, I began to think out what I had better do. Jim was not to be home until late that night. Within five minutes I had decided. I tore open the envelope and read the message.

It ran: "Bob died suddenly. Under no circumstances come. Father."

The rest of that day was a nightmare to me. I concealed the telegram in my waist. Agnes came home finally and was so alarmed at my appearance, I pleaded a frightful sick headache and went to bed. When Jim came home late that night Agnes was asleep. I caught him in the hall and gave him the telegram. She had to be told, we decided, because a letter from Mississippi might come at any time. He broke it to her the next morning. We were all hard hit, but Agnes from that time on was a changed woman.

Day after day dragged by and the letter of explanation did not come. It was strange, to say the least.

The Sunday afternoon following, we were all sitting, after dinner, in the little parlor. None of us had been saying much.

Suddenly Agnes said:

"Jim!"

"Yes!"

"Wasn't it strange that father never said how or when Bob died?"

"Would have made the telegram too long and expensive, perhaps," Jim replied.

We were all thinking, in the pause that followed, the same thing, I dare say. Agnes' father was not poor and it did seem he might have done that much.

"And why, do you suppose I was not to come under any circumstances? And why don't they write?"

Just then the bell rang and there was no chance for a reply.

Jim got up in his leisurely way and went to the tube.

Agnes and I both listened—a little tensely, I remember.

"Yes!" we heard Jim say, and then with spaces in between:

"Joe?—Joe who?—I think you must have made a mistake. No, I can't say that I do know anyone called Joe. What? Milton? Yes, that's my name! What? Oh! Brooks. Joe Brooks?—"

But Agnes waited for no more. She rushed by me into the hall.

"Jim! Jim! It's my brother Joe."

"Look here! Are you Agnes' brother, Joe?" Jim called quickly for him. "Great Jehoshaphat! Man! Come up! What a mess I've made of this."

For the first time I saw Jim move quickly. Within a second he was out of the flat and running down the stairs. Agnes followed to the stair-head and waited there. I went back into the little parlor, for I had followed her into the hall, and sat down and waited.

They all came in presently. Joe was older than Agnes but looked very much like her. He was thin, his face really haggard and his hair quite grey. I found out afterward that he was in his early thirties but he appeared much older. He was smiling, but the smile did not reach his eyes. They were strange aloof eyes. They rested on you and yet seemed to see something beyond. You felt as though they had looked upon something that could never be forgotten. When he was not smiling his face was grim, the chin firm and set. He was a man of very few words, I found.

Agnes and Jim were both talking at once and he answered them now and then in monosyllables. Agnes introduced us. He shook hands, I thought in rather a perfunctory way, without saying anything, and we all sat down.

We steered clear quite deliberately from the thoughts uppermost in our minds. We spoke of his journey, when he left Mississippi, the length of time it had taken him to come up and the weather. Suddenly Agnes jumped up:

"Joe, aren't you famished?"

"Well, I wouldn't mind a little something, Agnes," he answered, and then he added: "I'm not as starved as I was traveling in the South, but I have kind of a hollow feeling."

"What do you mean?" she asked.

"Jim-Crow cars," he answered laconically.

"I'd forgotten," she said. "I've been away so long."

He made no reply.

"Aren't conditions any better at all?" she asked after a little.

"No, I can't say as they are."

None of us said anything. She stood there a minute or so pulling away at the frill on her apron. She stopped suddenly, drew a long breath, and said:

"I wish you all could move away, Joe, and come North."

For one second before he lowered his eyes I saw a strange gleam in them. He seemed to be examining his shoes carefully from all angles. His jaw looked grimmer than ever and I saw a flickering of the muscles in his cheeks.

"That would be nice," he said at last and then added, "but we can't, Agnes. I like my coffee strong, please."

"Joe," she said, going to the door. "I'm sorry, I was forgetting."

I rose at that.

"Agnes, let me go. You stay here."

She hesitated, but Joe spoke up:

"No, Agnes, you go. I know your cooking."

You could have heard a pin drop for a minute. Jim looked queer and so did Agnes for a second and then she tried to laugh it off.

"Don't mind Joe. He doesn't mean anything like that."

And then she left us.

Well, I was hurt. Joe made no attempt to apologize or anything. He even seemed to have forgotten me. Jim looked at me and smiled his nice smile, but I was really hurt. I came to understand, however, later. Presently Joe said:

"About Agnes! We hadn't been told anything!"

"Didn't she write about it?"

"No."

"Wanted to surprise you, I guess."

"How long?" Joe asked after a little.

"Before?"

"Yes."

"Four months, I should say."

"That complicates matters some."

I got up to leave. I was so evidently in the way.

Joe looked up quietly and said:

"Oh! don't go! It isn't necessary."

I sat down again.

"No, Lucy, stay." Jim added. "What do you mean 'complicates?'"

Joe examined his shoes for several moments and then looked up suddenly.

"Just where is Agnes?"

"In the kitchen, I guess." Jim looked a trifle surprised.

"Where is that?"

"The other end of the flat near the door."

"She can't possibly hear anything, then?"

"No."

"Well, then, listen Jim, and you, what's your name? Lucy? Well, Lucy, then. Listen carefully, you two, to every single word I am going to say." He frowned a few moments at his shoes and then went on: "Bob went out fishing in the woods near his shack, spent the night there, slept in wet clothes, it had been raining all day, came home, contracted double pneumonia and died in two days time. Have you that?"

We both nodded. "That's the story we are to tell Agnes."

Jim had his mouth open to ask something, when Agnes came in. She had very evidently not heard anything, however, for there was a little color in her face and it was just a little happy again.

"I've been thinking about you, Joe," she said. "What on earth are you getting so grey for?"

"Grey!" he exclaimed. "Am I grey?" There was no doubt about it, his surprise was genuine.

"Didn't you know it?" She chuckled a little. It was the first time in days.

"No, I didn't."

She made him get up, at that, and drew him to the oval glass over the mantel.

"Don't you ever look at yourself, Joe?"

"Not much, that's the truth." I could see his face in the mirror from where I sat. His eyes widened a trifle, I saw, and then he turned away abruptly and sat down again. He made no comment. Agnes broke the rather little silence that followed.

"Joe!"

"Yes!"

"You haven't been sick or anything, have you?"

"No, why?"

"You seem so much thinner. When I last saw you you were almost stout."

"That's some years ago, Agnes."

"Yes, but one ought to get stouter not thinner with age."

Again I caught that strange gleam in his eyes before he lowered them. For a moment he sat perfectly still without answering.

"You can put it down to hard work, if you like, Agnes. Isn't that my coffee I smell boiling over?"

"Yes, I believe it is. I just ran in to tell you I'll be ready for you in about ten minutes."

She went out hastily but took time to pull the portiere across the door. I thought it strange at the time and looked at Jim. He didn't seem to notice it, however, but waited, I saw, until he had heard Agnes' heel taps going into the kitchen.

"Now," he said, "what do you mean when you say that is the story we are to tell Agnes?"

"Just that."

"You mean—" he paused "that it isn't true?"

"No, it isn't true."

"Bob didn't die that way?"

"No."

I felt myself stiffening in my chair and my two hands gripping the two arms of my chair tightly. I looked at Jim. I sensed the same tensioning in him. There was a long pause. Joe was examining his shoes again. The flickering in his cheeks I saw was more noticeable.

Finally Jim brought out just one word:

"How?"

"There was a little trouble," he began and then paused so long Jim said:

"You mean he was—injured in some way?"

Joe looked up suddenly at Jim, at that, and then down again. But his expression even in that fleeting glance set me to trembling all over. Jim, I saw, had been affected too. He sat stiffly bent forward. He had been in the act of raising his cigarette to his lips and his arm seemed as though frozen in mid-air.

"Yes," he said, "injured." But the way in which he said "injured" made me tremble all the more.

Again there was a pause and again Jim broke it with his one word: "How?"

"You don't read the papers, I see," Joe said.

"Yes, I read them."

"It was in all the papers."

"I missed it, then."

"Yes."

It was quiet again for a little.

"Have you ever lived in the South?" Joe asked.

"No."

"Nice civilized place, the South," Joe said.

And again I found myself trembling violently. I had to fight with might and main to keep my teeth from chattering. And yet it was not what he had said but his tone again.

"I hadn't so heard it described," Jim said after a little.

"No?—You didn't know, I suppose, that there is an unwritten law in the South that when a colored and a white person meet on the sidewalk, the colored person must get off into the street until the white one passes?"

"No, I hadn't heard of it."

"Well, it's so. That was the little trouble."

"You mean—"

"Bob refused to get off the sidewalk."

"Well?"

"The white man pushed him off. Bob knocked him down. The white man attempted to teach the 'damned nigger' a lesson." Again he paused.

"Well?"

"The lesson didn't end properly. Bob all but killed him."

It was so still in that room that although Jim was sitting across the room I could hear his watch ticking distinctly in his vest pocket. I had been holding my breath when I was forced to expel it, the sound was so loud they both turned quickly towards me, startled for a second.

"That would have been Bob." It was Jim speaking.

"Yes."

"I suppose it didn't end there?"

"No."

"Go on, Joe." Even Jim's voice sounded strained and strange.

And Joe went on. He never raised his voice, never lowered it. Throughout, his tone was entirely colorless. And yet as though it had been seared into my very soul I remember word for word, everything he said.

"An orderly mob, in an orderly manner, on a Sunday morning— I am quoting the newspapers—broke into the jail, took him out, slung him up to the limb of a tree, riddled his body with bullets, saturated it with coal oil, lighted a fire underneath him, gouged out his eyes with red hot irons, burnt him to a crisp an' then sold souvenirs of him, ears, fingers, toes. His teeth brought five dollars each." He ceased for a moment.

"He is still hanging on that tree.—We are not allowed to have even what is left."

There was a roaring in my ears. I seemed to be a long way off. I was sinking into a horrible black vortex that seemed to be sucking me down. I opened my eyes and saw Jim dimly. His nostrils seemed to be two black wide holes. His face was taut, every line set. I saw him draw a great deep breath. The blackness sucked me down still deeper. And then suddenly I found myself on my feet struggling against that hideous darkness and I heard my own voice as from a great distance calling out over and over again, "Oh, my God! Oh, my God! Oh, my God!"

They both came running to me, but I should have fainted for the first and only time in my life but that I heard suddenly above those strange noises in my ears a little choking, strangling sound. It revived me instantly. I broke from them and tried to get to the door.

"Agnes! Agnes!" I called out.

But they were before me. Jim tore the portiere aside. They caught her just as she was falling.

She lay unconscious for hours. When she did come to, she found all three of us about her bed. Her bewildered eyes went from Jim's face to mine and then to Joe's. They paused there, she frowned a little. And then we saw the whole thing slowly come back to her. She groaned and closed her eyes. Joe started to leave the room but she opened her eyes quickly and indicated that he was not to go. He came back. Again she closed her eyes.

And then she began to grow restless.

"Agnes!" I asked, "is there anything you want?"

She quieted a little under my voice.

"No," she said, "No."

Presently she opened her eyes again. They were very bright. She looked at each of us in turn a second time.

Then she said: "I've had to live all this time to find out."

"Find out what, Agnes?" It was Jim's voice.

"Why I'm here—why I'm here."

"Yes, of course." Jim spoke oh! so gently, humoring her. His hand was smoothing away the damp little curls about her forehead.

"It's no use your making believe you understand, you don't."

It was the first time I had ever heard her speak irritably to Jim. She moved her head away from his hand.

His eyes were a little hurt and he took his hand away.

"No." His voice was as gentle as ever. "I don't understand, then."

There was a pause and then she said abruptly:

"I'm an instrument." No one answered her.

"That's all—an instrument."

We merely watched her.

"One of the many."

And then Jim in his kindly blundering way made his second mistake.

"Yes, Agnes," he said, "Yes."

But at that, she took even me by surprise. She sat up in bed suddenly, her eyes wild and staring and before we could stop her, began beating her breast.

"Agnes," I said, "Don't! Don't!"

"I shall," she said in a strange high voice.

Well, we let her alone. It would have meant a struggle.

And then amid little sobbing breaths, beating her breast the while, she began to cry out: "Yes!—Yes!—I!—I!—An instrument of reproduction!—another of the many!—a colored woman doomed!—cursed!—put here!—willing or unwilling! For what?—to bring children here—men children—for the sport—the lust of possible orderly mobs—who go about things—in an orderly manner—on Sunday mornings!"

"Agnes," I cried out. "Agnes! Your child will be born in the North. He need never go South."

She had listened to me at any rate.

"Yes," she said, "in the North. In the North.—And have there been no lynchings in the North?"

I was silenced.

"The North permits it too," she cried. "The North is silent as well as the South."

And then as she sat there her eyes became less wild but more terrible. They became the eyes of a seeress. When she spoke again she spoke loudly, clearly, slowly:

"There is a time coming—and soon—when no colored man—no colored woman—no colored child, born or unborn—will be safe—in this country."

"Oh Agnes," I cried again, "Sh! sh!"

She turned her terrible eyes upon me.

"There is no more need for silence—in this house. God has found us out."

"Oh Agnes," the tears were frankly running down my cheeks. "We must believe that God is very pitiful. We must. He will find a way."

She waited a moment and said simply:

"Will He?"

"Yes, Agnes! Yes!"

"I will believe you, then. I will give Him one more chance. Then, if He is not pitiful, then if He is not pitiful,—" But she did not finish. She fell back upon her pillows. She had fainted again.

Agnes did not die, nor did her child. She had kept her body clean and healthy. She was up and around again, but an Agnes that never smiled, never chuckled any more. She was a grey pathetic shadow of herself. She who had loved joy so much, cared more, it seemed, for solitude than anything else in the world. That was why, when Jim or I went looking for her we found so often only the empty room and that imperceptibly closing, slowly closing, opposite door.

Joe went back to Mississippi and not one of us, ever again, mentioned Bob's name.

And Jim, poor Jim! I wish I could tell you of how beautiful he was those days. How he never complained, never was irritable, but was always so gentle, so full of understanding, that at times, I had to go out of the room for fear he might see my tears.

Only once I saw him when he thought himself alone. I had not known he was in his little den and entered it suddenly. I had made no sound, luckily, and he had not heard me. He was sitting leaning far forward, his head between his hands. I stood there five minutes at least, but not once did I see him stir. I silently stole out and left him.

It was a fortunate thing that Agnes had already done most of her sewing for the little expected stranger, for after Joe's visit, she never touched a thing.

"Agnes!" I said one day, not without fear and trepidation it is true. "Isn't there something I can do?"

"Do?" she repeated rather vaguely.

"Yes. Some sewing?"

"Oh! sewing," she said. "No, I think not, Lucy."

"You've—you've finished?" I persisted.

"No."

"Then—" I began.

"I hardly think we shall need any of them." And then she added, "I hope not."

"Agnes!" I cried out.

But she seemed to have forgotten me.

Well, time passed, it always does. And on a Sunday morning early Agnes' child was born. He was a beautiful, very grave baby with her great dark eyes.

As soon as they would let me, I went to her.

She was lying very still and straight, in the quiet, darkened room, her head turned on the pillow towards the wall. Her eyes were closed.

"Agnes!" I said in the barest whisper. "Are you asleep?"

"No," she said. And turned her head towards me and opened her eyes. I looked into her ravaged face. Agnes Milton had been down into Hell and back again.

Neither of us spoke for some time and then she said:

"Is he dead?"

"Your child?"

"Yes."

"I should say not, he's a perfect darling and so good."

No smile came into her face. It remained as expressionless as before. She paled a trifle more, I thought, if such a thing was possible.

"I'm sorry," she said finally.

"Agnes!" I spoke sharply. I couldn't help it.

But she closed her eyes and made no response.

I sat a long time looking at her. She must have felt my gaze for she slowly lifted her lids and looked at me.

"Well," she said, "what is it, Lucy?"

"Haven't you seen your child, Agnes?"

"No."

"Don't you wish to see it?"

"No."

Again it was wrung out of me:

"Agnes, Agnes, don't tell me you don't love it."

For the first and only time a spasm of pain went over her poor pinched face.

"Ah!" she said, "That's it." And she closed her eyes and her face was as expressionless as ever.

I felt as though my heart were breaking.

Again she opened her eyes.

"Tell me, Lucy," she began.

"What, Agnes?"

"Is he—healthy?"

"Yes."

"Quite strong?"

"Yes."

"You think he will live, then?"

"Yes, Agnes."

She closed her eyes once more. It was very still within the room. Again she opened her eyes. There was a strange expression in them now.

"Lucy!"

"Yes."

"You were wrong."

"Wrong, Agnes?"

"Yes."

"How?"

"You thought your God was pitiful."

"Agnes, but I do believe it."

After a long silence she said very slowly:

"He—is—not."

This time, when she closed her eyes, she turned her head slowly upon the pillow to the wall. I was dismissed.

And again Agnes did not die. Time passed and again she was up and about the flat. There was a strange, stony stillness upon her, now, I did not like, though. If we only could have understood, Jim and I, what it meant. Her love for solitude, now, had become a passion. And Jim and I knew more and more that empty room and that silently, slowly closing door.

She would have very little to do with her child. For some reason, I saw, she was afraid of it. I was its mother. I did for it, cared for it, loved it.

Twice only during these days I saw that stony stillness of hers broken.

The first time was one night. The baby was fast asleep, and she had stolen in to look at him, when she thought no one would know. I never wish to see such a tortured, hungry face again.

I was in the kitchen, the second time, when I heard strange sounds coming from my room. I rushed to it and there was Agnes, kneeling at the foot of the little crib, her head upon the spread. Great, terrible racking sobs were tearing her. The baby was lying there, all eyes, and beginning to whimper a little.

"Agnes! Oh, my dear! What is it?" The tears were streaming down my cheeks.

"Take him away! Take him away!" she gasped. "He's been cooing, and smiling and holding out his little arms to me. I can't stand it! I can't stand it."

I took him away. That was the only time I ever saw Agnes Milton weep.

The baby slept in my room, Agnes would not have him in hers. He was a restless little sleeper and I had to get up several times during the night to see that he was properly covered.

He was a noisy little sleeper as well. Many a night I have lain awake listening to the sound of his breathing. It is a lovely sound, a beautiful one—the breathing of a little baby in the dark.

This night, I remember, I had been up once and covered him over and had fallen off to sleep for the second time, when, for I had heard absolutely no sound, I awoke suddenly. There was upon me an overwhelming utterly paralyzing feeling not of fear but of horror. I thought, at first, I must have been having a nightmare, but strangely instead of diminishing, the longer I lay awake, the more it seemed to increase.

It was a moonlight night and the light came in through the open window in a broad, white, steady stream.

A coldness seemed to settle all about my heart. What was the matter with me? I made a tremendous effort and sat up. Everything seemed peaceful and quiet enough.

The moonlight cut the room in two. It was dark where I was and dark beyond where the baby was.

One brass knob at the foot of my bed shone brilliantly, I remember, in that bright stream and the door that led into the hall stood out fully revealed. I looked at that door and then my heart suddenly seemed to stop beating! I grew deathly cold. The door was closing slowly, imperceptibly, silently. Things were whirling around. I shut my eyes. When I opened them again the door was no longer moving; it had closed.

What had Agnes Milton wanted in my room? And the more I asked myself that question the deeper grew the horror.

And then slowly, by degrees, I began to realize there was something wrong within that room, something terribly wrong. But what was it?

I tried to get out of bed, but I seemed unable to move. I strained my eyes, but I could see nothing—only that bright knob, that stream of light, that closed white door.

I listened. It was quiet, very quiet, too quiet. But why too quiet? And then as though there had been a blinding flash of lightning I knew—the breathing wasn't there.

Agnes Milton had taken a pillow off of my bed and smothered her child.

One last word. Jim received word this morning. The door was finished closing for the last time—Agnes Milton is no more. God, I think, may be pitiful, after all.

LANGSTON HUGHES

■ ■ ■

[1902–1967]

THE BEST-REMEMBERED WRITER OF THE HARLEM RENAISSANCE
and possibly the most famous African American author of the first half
of the last century, James Langston Hughes was born in Joplin, Missouri,
to a historically prominent family. Among his maternal ancestors were
the first dean of Howard University Law School, John Mercer Langston,
who also served a term in the U.S. House of Representatives in 1888, and
an abolitionist grandfather who had fought with John Brown at Harper's
Ferry. In spite of this distinguished heritage, however, Hughes's home
life was characterized by parental neglect and the family's frequent relo-
cation. Consoling his feelings of isolation with books, he discovered an
aptitude for writing at an early age. He was just nineteen when he published both his first short story, "Mexican Games," and his first poem,
"The Negro Speaks of Rivers," which he dedicated to W. E. B. DuBois,
who printed both pieces in 1921. Hughes abruptly dropped out of
Columbia University that same year and sailed to Europe and West
Africa, where he performed a series of menial jobs until returning to
Harlem in 1924.

The author's prolific career took off in 1926 with the simultaneous
publication of his first book of poetry, *The Weary Blues,* and his landmark
essay, "The Negro Artist and the Racial Mountain," which argued on
behalf of racial pride in art. With his first novel, *Not Without Laughter*
(1931), Hughes became increasingly outspoken on behalf of leftist politics, traveling to Cuba, the Soviet Union, and Spain on the proceeds
earned from the book. He also addressed racial concerns, prominently
in *The Chicago Defender* and *New Masses,* among other periodicals of the

1940s. Jazz music was another influential component in his writings, notably in *Montage of a Dream Deferred* (1951), a book of poetry incorporating the frenetic, discordant sounds of bebop, and in *Ask Your Mama: 12 Moods for Jazz* (1961), which has been called his finest collection. By the time of the Civil Rights era, however, Hughes had fallen out of favor with black militants, many of whom perceived his once-radical work as outdated and no longer sufficiently representative of African Americans. Nevertheless, the author demonstrated a profound understanding of and devotion to the many modes of black life in America, writing poems, short stories, plays, and journalism until his death in 1967.

While the author's history as a "race man" is well documented, the nature of his sexual identity remains controversial among scholars. The debate centers on whether Hughes was heterosexual or, in light of the evidence, bisexual or homosexual. Complicating the issue further is the fact that most gay men who knew the author personally recall him as "asexual"; that is, Hughes, according to friends, desired neither men nor women, even though affairs with both sexes are known to have taken place at least once. Whatever his sexual identity may have been, Hughes incorporated explicitly gay subject matter into his writing, though much of it appears in later collections published long after the Harlem Renaissance had ended. "Blessed Assurance," a short story from his last anthology, *Something in Common and Other Stories* (1963), is a candid example that reflects a sensitive appreciation for queer identity amid the social conservatism of the African American church.

Blessed Assurance

[1963]

Unfortunately (and to John's distrust of God) it seemed his son was turning out to be a queer. He was a brilliant queer, on the Honor Roll in high school, and likely to be graduated in the spring at the head of the class. But the boy was colored. Since colored parents always like to put their best foot forward, John was more disturbed about his son's transition than if they had been white. Negroes have enough crosses to bear.

Delmar was his only son, Arletta, the younger child, being a girl. Perhaps John should not have permitted his son to be named Delmar—Delly for short—but the mother had insisted on it. Delmar was *her* father's name.

"And he is *my* son as well as yours," his wife informed John.

Did the queer strain come from *her* side? Maternal grandpa had seemed normal enough. He was known to have had several affairs with women outside his home—mostly sisters of Tried Stone Church, of which he was a pillar.

God forbid! John, Delly's father thought, could he himself have had any deviate ancestors? None who had acted even remotely effeminate could John recall as being a part of his family. Anyhow, why didn't he name the boy at birth *John, Jr.,* after himself? But his wife said, "Don't saddle him with Junior." Yet she had saddled him with Delmar.

If only Delly were not such a sweet boy—no juvenile delinquency, no stealing cars, no smoking reefers ever. He did the chores without complaint. He washed dishes too easily, with no argument, when he might have left them to Arletta. He seldom, even when at the teasing stage, pulled his sister's hair. They played together, Delly with dolls almost as long as Arletta did. Yet he was good at marbles, once fair at baseball, and a real whiz at tennis. He could have made the track team had he not preferred the French Club, the Dramatic Club, and the Glee Club. Football, his father's game in high school, Delly didn't like. He couldn't keep his eye on the ball in scrimmage. At seventeen he had to have glasses. The style of rather exaggerated rims he chose made him look like a girl rather than a boy.

"At least he didn't get rhinestone rims," thought John half-thought didn't think felt faint and aloud said nothing. That spring he asked, "Delmar, do you have to wear *white* Bermuda shorts to school? Most of the other boys wear Levi's or just plain pants, don't they? And why wash them out yourself every night, all that ironing? I want you to be clean, son, but not *that* clean."

Another time, "Delmar, those school togs of yours don't have to match so perfectly, do they? Colors *blended,* as you say, and all like that. This school you're going to's no fashion school—at least, it wasn't when I went there. The boys'll think you're sissy."

Once again desperately, "If you're going to smoke, Delmar, hold your cigarette between your *first* two fingers, not between your thumb and finger—like a woman."

Then his son cried.

John remembered how it was before the boy's mother packed up and left their house to live with another man who made more money than any Negro in their church. He kept an apartment in South Philly and another in Harlem. Owned a Cadillac. Racket connections—politely called *politics.* A shame for his children, for the church, and for him, John! His wife gone with an uncouth rascal!

But although Arletta loathed him, Delly liked his not-yet-legal step-father. Delly's mother and her burly lover had at least had the decency to leave Germantown and change their religious affiliations. They no longer attended John's family church where Delmar sang in the Junior Choir.

Delly had a sweet high tenor with overtones of Sam Cooke. The women at Tried Stone loved him. Although Tried Stone was a Baptist church, it tended toward the sedate—Northern Baptist in tone, not down-home. Yet it did have a Gospel Choir, scarlet-robed, since a certain untutored segment of the membership demanded lively music. It had a Senior Choir, too, black-robed, that specialized in anthems, sang "Jesu, Joy of Man's Desiring," the Bach cantatas, and once a year presented the *Messiah.* The white-robed Junior Choir, however, even went so far as to want to render a jazz recessional—Delly's idea—which was vetoed. This while he was trying to grow a beard like the beatniks he had seen when the Junior Choir sang in New York and the Minister of Music had taken Delly on a trip to the Village.

"God, don't let him put an earring in his ear like some," John prayed. He wondered vaguely with a sick feeling in his stomach should he think it through then then think it through right then through should he try then and think it through should without blacking through think blacking out then and there think it through?

John didn't. But one night he remembered his son had once told his mother that after he graduated from high school he would like to study at the Sorbonne. The Sorbonne in Paris! John had studied at Morgan in Baltimore. In possession of a diploma from that *fine* (in his mind) Negro institute, he took pride. Normally John would have wanted his boy to go there, yet the day after the Spring Concert he asked Delmar, "Son, do you still want to study in France? If you do, maybe—er—I guess I could next fall—Sorbonne. Say, how much is a ticket to Paris?"

In October it would be John's turn to host his fraternity brothers at his house. Maybe by then Delmar would—is the Sorbonne like Morgan? Does it have dormitories, a campus? In Paris he had heard they didn't care about such things. Care about such what things didn't care about what? At least no color lines.

Well, anyhow, what happened at the concert a good six months before October came was, well—think it through clearly now, get it right. Especially for that Spring Concert, Tried Stone's Minister of Music, Dr. Manley Jaxon, had written an original anthem, words and score his own, based on the story of Ruth:

> Entreat me not to leave thee,
> Neither to go far from thee.
> Whither thou goeth, I will go.
> Always will I be near thee...

The work was dedicated to Delmar, who received the first hand-written manuscript copy as a tribute from Dr. Jaxon. In spite of its dedication, one might have thought that in performance the solo lead—Ruth's part—would be assigned to a woman. Perversely enough, the composer allotted it to Delmar. Dr. Jaxon's explanation was, "No one else can do it justice." The Minister of Music declared, "The girls in the ensemble really have *no* projection."

So without respect for gender, on the Sunday afternoon of the program, Delmar sang the female lead. Dr. Jaxon, saffron-robed, was at the organ. Until Delmar's father attended the concert that day, he had no inkling as to the casting of the anthem. But when his son's solo began, all John could say was, "I'll be damned!"

John had hardly gotten the words out of his mouth when words became of no further value. The "Papa, what's happening?" of his daughter in the pew beside him made hot saliva rise in his throat—for what suddenly had happened was that as the organ wept and Delmar's voice soared above the choir with all the sweetness of Sam Cooke's tessitura, backwards off the organ stool in a dead faint fell Dr. Manley Jaxon. Not only did Dr. Jaxon fall from the stool, but he rolled limply down the steps from the organ loft like a bag of meal and tumbled prone onto the rostrum, robes and all.

Amens and *Hallelujahs* drowned in the throats of various elderly sisters who were on the verge of shouting. Swooning teenage maidens suddenly sat up in their pews to see the excitement. Springing from his chair on the rostrum, the pastor's mind deserted the pending collection to try to think what to say under the unusual circumstances.

"One down, one to go," was all that came to mind. After a series of pastorates in numerous sophisticated cities where Negroes did everything whites do, the Reverend Dr. Greene had seen other choir directors take the count in various ways with equal drama, though perhaps less physical immediacy.

When the organ went silent, the choir died, too—but Delmar never stopped singing. Over the limp figure of Dr. Jaxon lying on the rostrum, the "Entreat me not to leave thee" of his solo flooded the church as if it were on hi-fi.

The members of the congregation sat riveted in their pews as the deacons rushed to the rostrum to lift the Minister of Music to his feet. Several large ladies of the Altar Guild fanned him vigorously while others sprinkled him with water. But it was not until the church's nurse-in-uniform applied smelling salts to Dr. Jaxon's dark nostrils, did he lift his head. Finally, two ushers led him off to an anteroom while Delmar's voice soared to a high C such as Tried Stone Baptist Church had never heard.

"Bless God! Amen!" cried Reverend Greene. "Dr. Jaxon has only fainted, friends. We will continue our services by taking up collection directly after the anthem."

"Daddy, why did Dr. Jaxon have to faint just when brother started singing?" whispered John's daughter.

"I don't know," John said.

"Some of the girls say that when Delmar sings, they want to scream, they're so overcome," whispered Arletta. "But Dr. Jaxon didn't scream. He just fainted."

"Shut up," John said, staring straight ahead at the choir loft. "Oh, God! Delmar, *shut up!*" John's hands gripped the back of the seat in front of him. "Shut up, son! *Shut up,*" he cried. "Shut up!"

Silence...

"We will now lift the offering," announced the minister. "Ushers, get the baskets." Reverend Greene stepped forward. "Deacons, raise a hymn. Bear us up, sisters, bear us up!"

His voice boomed:

Blessed assurance!

He clapped his hands once.

Jesus is mine!

"Yes! Yes! Yes!" he cried.

Oh, what a fortress

Of glory divine!

The congregation swung gently into song:

Heir of salvation,

Purchase of God!

"Hallelujah! Amen! Halle! Halle!"

Born of the Spirit

"God damn it!" John cried. "God *damn* it!"

Washed in His blood...

WALLACE THURMAN

■ ■ ■

[1902–1934]

BY 1926, AN EMERGING GROUP OF YOUNG AFRICAN AMERICANS
had begun to openly defy the racial uplift propaganda of W. E. B.
DuBois and other "talented tenth" advocates. Chief among these transgressors was the novelist, editor, and critic Wallace Thurman. The Salt
Lake City native had arrived in Harlem the previous year. In New York,
his intellectual brilliance was immediately put to use as an editor at *The
Messenger,* a radical monthly magazine, and in the employ of black labor
leader A. Philip Randolph. Thurman is best-known for his novel, *The
Blacker the Berry* (1929), which addresses the then-taboo subjects of
intraracial color prejudice and homosexuality. These were two especially
personal issues for this dark-skinned, gay African American, who argued
that both "outsider" identities had held back his career.

Although writers like Thurman and Langston Hughes had publicly
opposed the repressive political and artistic standards of uplift propagandists, never before had anyone devoted a periodical exclusively to
this topic. The 1926 debut of Thurman's *Fire!!,* an experimental periodical whose subtitle announced that it was "Devoted to Younger Negro
Artists," rocked the moral rigidity of the Harlem Renaissance. Writers
such as Zora Neale Hurston, Countee Cullen, Richard Bruce Nugent,
Gwendolyn Bennett, and Langston Hughes himself contributed poems
and stories that were at times sexually explicit and often controversial in
their treatment of homosexuality and prostitution, among other topics.

Despite Thurman's lofty aims, however, *Fire!!* folded after only one
issue owing to financial difficulties, which plagued him the rest of his
short life. Fundamental to these difficulties was his lavish lifestyle.

Known as an extravagant partier and heavy drinker, Thurman supported himself variously as a reader for The Macauly Company—the only African American of the time employed in an editorial position by a major New York publishing house—and as a ghostwriter for *True Story* magazine, where he published pulp fiction under the pen name Ethel Belle Mandrake. His greatest commercial success was the production of his play, *Harlem* (1929). Thurman's final novel, *The Interne* (1932), offered a fictional exposé of the appalling conditions of City Hospital, where he died of tuberculosis at age thirty-two.

Although several satires of the Harlem Renaissance were published during the 1930s, Thurman's *Infants of the Spring* (1932) is the most caustic. This excerpt opens on the night of the rent-party at Niggeratti Mansion, Thurman's fictional rendering of "Niggeratti Manor," as Zora Neale Hurston had dubbed his home in Harlem. Central to the scene is Raymond, a stand-in for the author, who struggles to find his place among the odd gathering of blacks and whites, intellectuals and revelers, all the while drinking with typical Thurman abandon. Among the real-life targets who appear in this segment under disguised identities are Dr. Alain Locke (Dr. Parkes), Zora Neale Hurston (Sweetie Mae Carr), Langston Hughes (Tony Crews), Countee Cullen (DeWitt Clinton), and Richard Bruce Nugent (Paul Arbian).

from **Infants of the Spring**

[1932]

It was the night of the Donation Party. For ten days preparations had been made. For ten days Raymond's typewriter and the telephone had been overworked, bidding people to report to Niggeratti Manor on the designated night. The wolf must be driven from the door. Paul had scuttled through Greenwich Village, a jubilant Revere, sounding the tocsin. Euphoria and Eustace had canvassed their Harlem friends. Barbara had been called in for a consultation and departed ebullient, a zealous crusader. A large crowd had been assured. The audacious novelty of the occasion had piqued many a curiosity. And of course there was promise of uninhibited hijinks.

Ten o'clock. Only a few guests had arrived, laden with various bundles of staple foods. Eustace's studio and the nearby kitchen were to be the focal points for the party because in the basement there would be fewer stairs for the drunks to encounter, and more room for dancing.

Ten-thirty. The Niggeratti clique, supplemented by a few guests, had gathered around the punch bowl on the kitchen table. The concoction, fathered by Eustace, was tasty and strong.

"Ol' Mother Savoy has surpassed herself tonight," Paul murmured between drinks.

Also on the table were a half dozen bottles of gin, and Raymond noted that it was to one of these that Stephen was clinging tenaciously.

"Have some punch?"

"No," Stephen answered Raymond shortly and continued to gulp down glass after glass of straight gin.

"Go easy, Steve. The night's young."

"What of it?" He walked away from the table and leaned against the wall in a far corner of the room.

Before Raymond had time to consider his friend's unusual behavior, a host of people boisterously invaded the room, dropping packages, clamoring for drinks.

"Two cans of corn," someone shouted.

"Pound of sugar here."

"Some yaller corn meal. Hot ziggitty."

"'Taters. 'Taters. Nice ripe 'taters."

"Wet my whistle, Eustace. I lithp."

Samuel emerged from the crowd and taking hold of Raymond's arm pulled him aside. It was the first time they had met since their quarrel some weeks before. Samuel was contrite, anxious for a reconciliation. He had reasoned to himself that he had been too quick to lose his temper. People like him—people with a mission in life—must expect to be the recipients of insults and rebuffs. How could he help others when he could not control himself? Samuel felt that he had betrayed his purpose in life by reacting positively to Raymond's drunken statements.

"Ray, I owe you an apology."

"For what?"

"For what happened."

"Oh, that. Forget it." Raymond turned away and rejoined the exuberant crowd centered around the kitchen table.

"Ray." It was Paul. "Meet a friend of mine."

By his side was a grinning black boy.

"Ray, this is Bud. He's a bootblack, but he has the most beautiful body I've ever seen. I'll get him to strip for the gang soon."

The boy grinned sheepishly. But he did not seem the least bit abashed. Before Raymond could make any comment, Paul had propelled his charge toward Eustace's studio. Raymond followed. The room was crowded with people. Black people, white people, and all the in-between shades. Ladies in evening gowns. Ladies in smocks. Ladies in tailored suits. Ladies in ordinary dresses of every description, interspersed and surrounded by all types of men in all types of conventional clothes. And weaving his way among them, green dressing gown swishing, glass tray held tightly in both hands, was Eustace, serving drinks to those who had not yet found the kitchen oasis.

"Folks," Paul shouted above the din, "this is Bud. He has the most perfect body in New York. I'm gonna let you see it soon."

"Bravo."

"Go to it."

"Now?"

Paul and his protégé were surrounded by an avid mob.

Raymond sauntered back into the kitchen. Stephen was still standing in his isolated corner, a full glass progressing toward his lips. His face was flushed. His eyes half closed. Raymond started toward him.

"Hi, Ray." Someone jerked the tail of his coat. It was Bull. Beside him was Lucille.

"Hen's fruit." Bull deposited a sack full of eggs on top of the refrigerator.

"Eve's delight." A bag of apples was thrust into Raymond's hand by some unknown person.

"An' my sweet patootie has the bacon," Bull continued, jerking an oblong package from beneath Lucille's arm. Raymond put the apples beside Bull's eggs.

"Hello, 'Cile. Thanks, Bull."

"Oh, Ray." It was Barbara. She was followed and surrounded by a group of detached, anemic white men and women, all in evening dress, all carrying packages of various sizes and shapes.

"This is Ray, folks," Barbara announced to her companions. They all smiled dutifully and began relieving themselves of their bundles.

Barbara appropriated Raymond's hand and placed something in his palm.

"For Negro art," she whispered, then, slipping quickly away, corralled her friends and ushered them toward the punch bowl. Raymond opened his palm and gasped at the sight of a twenty-dollar bill.

"Good God, what a mob." Lucille was beside him. He pocketed the money Barbara had given him and regarded Lucille coolly.

"Still hep on your man?"

"Why, Ray," she began, then quickly regaining control of herself, riposted merrily, "and *how*." She then started to move away.

Raymond forestalled her by firmly clenching her wrist in his hand.

"How long you gonna play this game?" he asked sternly.

"What ol' black game?"

"You know damn well…"

"Here's a drink, baby." Bull handed Lucille a glass of punch. Raymond released her wrist, glared at the two of them, walked to the table, pushed his way through the crowd, seized a glass, and handed it to Euphoria, now guardian of the punch bowl, to fill.

After having had several drinks, he threaded his way back into Eustace's studio. It was more crowded and noisy than before. Someone was playing the piano, and in a small clearing the ex-wife of a noted American playwright was doing the Black Bottom with a famed Negro singer of spirituals.

"Ain't I good?" she demanded of her audience. "An' you ain't seen nothin' yet."

With which she insinuated her scrawny white body close to that of her stalwart black partner and began performing the torrid abdominal movements of the "mess-a-round."

"How d'y'do, Ray."

Raymond turned to see who had spoken. On the davenette against the wall was a well known sophisticated author and explorer of the esoteric. He was surrounded by four bewildered-looking, corn-fed individuals. He introduced them to Raymond as relatives and friends from his native middle west. It was their first trip to Harlem, and their first experience of a white–black gathering.

Raymond sat down beside them, talking at random, and helping himself to the bottles of liquor which the cautious author had recruited from his own private stock.

Soon there was a commotion at the door. It cleared of all standees, and in it was framed the weird Amazonian figure of Amy Douglas, whose mother had made a fortune devising and marketing hair preparations for kinky-haired blackamoors. Amy, despite her bulk and size—she was almost six feet tall and weighed over two hundred pounds—affected flimsy frocks and burdened her person with weighty brilliants. A six months stay in Europe had provided her with a series of foreign phrases with which to interlard her southern dialect. Being very black, she went in for skin whiteners which had been more effective in certain spots than in others. As a result, her face was speckled, uncertain of its shade. Amy was also generous in the use of her mother's hair preparations, and because someone had once told her she resembled a Nubian queen, she wore a diamond tiara, precariously perched on the top of her slickened naps.

Majestically she strode into the room, attended as usual by an attractive escort of high yaller ladies in waiting, and a chattering group of effeminate courtiers.

Raymond excused himself from the people with whom he had been sitting and started once more for the kitchen. While trying to pierce through the crowd, he was halted by Dr. Parkes, a professor of literature in a northern Negro college, who, also, as Paul so aptly declared, played mother hen to a brood of chicks, he having appointed himself guardian angel to the current set of younger Negro artists.

"I've been trying to find you for the past hour."

"Sorry, Dr. Parkes...but in this mob..."

"I know. Perhaps I should await a more propitious moment, but I wanted to ask you about Pelham."

"Pelham?"

"Yes."

"Oh, he's still in jail. That's all I know. His trial isn't far off. I've forgotten the exact date."

"What effect do you think this will have on you?"

"On me? I don't know what you mean."

"Don't you think this scandal when publicized will hurt all of you who lived here with Pelham?"

Raymond laughed.

"I hadn't thought of that. This might be Paul's opportunity to get his name in the paper."

"Who's taking my name in vain?" Paul appeared, still leading his dark shadow by the hand. "Oh, Dr. Parkes," he continued excitedly, "meet Bud. He's got..."

Raymond escaped and worked his way over to the piano. He stopped to chat with Aline and Janet, who had staggered in some time before with a group of conspicuously and self-consciously drunk college boys.

"Hi, Ray."

"What say, keeds?"

"Where's Steve?" they asked in unison.

"Find the gin," he replied and moved away.

Meanwhile four Negro actors from a current Broadway dramatic hit harmonized a popular love song. Conversation was temporarily hushed, laughter subsided, and only the intermittent tinkle of ice in an upturned glass could be heard as the plangent voices of the singers filled the room.

There was a burst of applause as they finished, followed by boisterous calls for an encore. After a moment's conference, the singers obligingly crooned another mellifluous tune.

Raymond retraced his steps, greeting people, whispering answers to questions buzzed into his ear. Finally he was once more in the kitchen.

It was one-thirty. The twenty dollar bill had been given to Eustace, who had sent for another dozen bottles of gin. A deposed Russian countess was perched atop the gas range talking animatedly in broken English to Paul's Spartan bootblack. The famed American playwright's ex-wife had developed a crying jag. No one could soothe her but the stalwart singer of Negro spirituals. Near them hovered his wife, jealous, bored, suspicious, irritated rather than flattered by the honeyed, Oxonian witticisms being cooed into her ear by a drunken English actor.

The noise was deafening. Empty gin bottles on the floor tripped those with unsteady legs. Bull's bag of eggs had been knocked to the floor. Its contents were broken and oozed stickily over the linoleum. Someone else had dropped a bag of sugar. The linoleum was gritty. Shuffling feet made rasping sounds.

Two-thirty. Raymond began to feel the effects of the liquor he had consumed. He decided to stop drinking for a while. There was too much to see to risk missing it by getting drunk.

In the hallway between the kitchen and Eustace's studio, Euphoria sought to set a group of Negro school teachers at ease. The crowd confused them as it did most of the Harlem intellectuals who had strayed in and who all felt decidedly out of place. Raymond noticed how they all clung together, how timid they were, and how constrained they were in conversation and manner. He sought Stephen. He wanted to share his amusement at their discomfiture and self-consciousness. It gave him pleasure that he should have such a pertinent example of their lack of social savoir, their race conscious awareness. Unable to recover from being so intimately surrounded by whites, they, the school teachers, the college boys, the lawyers, the dentists, the social service workers, despite their strident appeals for social equality when among their own kind, either communed with one another, standing apart, or else made themselves obnoxious striving to make themselves agreeable. Only the bootblack, the actors, the musicians and Raymond's own group of friends comprised the compatible Negroid elements.

This suggested a formal train of thought to Raymond's mind. Ignoring all those who called to him, he sought for Stephen. But Stephen was nowhere to be found, either in the kitchen, or in the studio where some unidentified russet brown girl was doing a cooch dance to a weird piano accompaniment.

Raymond made a tour of the house, surprised many amorous couples in the darkened rooms upstairs by turning on the light, disturbed the fanciful aggregation of Greenwich Village uranians Paul had gathered in Raymond's studio to admire his bootblack's touted body, and irritated and annoyed two snarling women who had closeted themselves in the bathroom, but still Stephen was not to be found.

Disconsolately, Raymond discontinued his search and returned to the main scene of the party. All were convivial and excited. Various persons sang and danced. Highballs were quickly disposed of. A jazz pianist starred at the piano. There was a rush to dance. Everyone seemed to be hilariously drunk. Shouts of joy merged into one persistent noisy blare. Couples staggered from the kitchen to the studio and back again. Others leaned despairingly, sillily against the walls, or else sank helplessly into chairs or window sills. Fresh crowds continued to come in. The Donation Party was successful beyond all hopes.

Raymond felt a tug on his arm. It was Samuel. His face was flushed. His eyes were angry. Raymond tried to elude him.

"I've got to talk to you, Ray." He held tightly to Raymond's arm.

"Wait till tomorrow. Who in the hell can talk with all this noise?"

"But you don't know what's happened!"

"And I don't give a good..."

"Listen, Ray, for God's sake," Samuel interrupted. "Find Steve and get him out of here. He's terribly drunk and in an awful mess."

"What the hell are you talking about?"

"He, Aline and Janet just had a scrap."

"Where is he?"

"I don't know, Ray. No one can find him. He was standing in the door there...to Eustace's place. All at once there was a great confusion. I pushed through the crowd just in time to hear Steve shout: 'You goddamn sluts.' And before I could grab him, he had hit Janet in the face, took a punch at Aline and rushed away."

"Oh, Jesus. Which way did he go?"

"Out the front door."

The two of them forged their way through the crowd and went out into the street. Without a word they raced to the end of the block, peeped into the speakeasy, then glanced down the intersecting thoroughfare. Stephen was nowhere in sight.

"See what you've done," Samuel shouted. "You've got a decent boy into a sordid mess. I told him not to live with niggers. I knew what'd happen."

But Raymond heard not one word of his tirade, for he had rushed away from Samuel, and run back to the house alone.

The party had reached new heights. The lights in the basement had been dimmed, and the reveling dancers cast grotesque shadows on the heavily tapestried walls. Color lines had been completely eradicated. Whites and blacks clung passionately together as if trying to effect a permanent merger. Liquor, jazz music, and close physical contact had achieved what decades of propaganda had advocated with little success.

Here, Raymond thought, as he continued his search for Stephen, is social equality. Tomorrow all of them will have an emotional hangover. They will fear for their sanity, for at last they have had a chance to do openly what they only dared to do clandestinely before. This, he kept repeating to himself, is the Negro renaissance, and this is about all the whole damn thing is going to amount to.

Stephen was nowhere to be found. Nor were Aline or Janet or anyone else who might tell him what had happened. Raymond felt nauseated. The music, the noise, the indiscriminate love-making, the drunken revelry began to sicken him. The insanity of the party, the insanity of its implications, threatened his own sanity. It is going to be necessary, he thought, to have another emancipation to deliver the emancipated Negro from a new kind of slavery.

He made his way to the kitchen, rejoined the crowd around the punch bowl, and, for the next hour or more, drank incontinently. He grew drunker by the moment. He had a faint idea that Euphoria was dragging him aside and telling him that the noise must be toned down, and that there must be no more brawls, or bawdy parties in the bedrooms. The next thing he remembered was snatching Lucille away from some unidentified man, and dragging her viciously into the pantry.

"Y' want a cave man, eh?" he shouted. All else was vague and jumbled. Five minutes later he passed quietly out on the pantry floor.

RICHARD BRUCE NUGENT

■ ■ ■

[1902–1987]

PERHAPS THE MOST IDENTIFIABLY GAY WRITER OF THE
Harlem Renaissance, Richard Bruce Nugent is remembered more for his
Bohemian flamboyance than his slim body of work. His literary notoriety
comes primarily from *Fire!!* (1926), the controversial but short-lived periodical he coedited with the gay African American novelist Wallace Thurman.
Along with Langston Hughes's 1926 essay "The Negro Artist and the Racial
Mountain," *Fire!!* was the generational landmark that signaled the end of
the Harlem Renaissance as a movement concerned with "talented
tenth" propaganda. After *Fire!!,* young African American writers began
to acknowledge themes of racial and sexual transgression more openly
in their work, though hardly as frequent topics for discussion.

Nugent was born to what he called a "bohemian" middle-class family in Washington, D.C. His mother played piano and his father sang,
encouraging their son toward the arts. Nugent was a teenager when his
father died and the family moved to New York City. During a return visit
to his hometown the author met Langston Hughes, W. E. B. DuBois, and
Alain Locke at the salon of the poet Georgia Douglas Johnson. In 1925,
Nugent returned to Harlem. Locke, a closeted black gay mentor of
young, predominantly male, Harlem Renaissance talent, continued a
lifelong correspondence with Nugent, despite any risks involved in asso-
ciating with Nugent's unconcealed homosexual persona.

Along with writings by Langston Hughes and Zora Neale Hurston,
Fire!! included Nugent's most famous work, "Smoke, Lilies, and Jade."
Believed to be the first explicitly gay story published by an African
American writer, the dreamy, heavily elliptical plot concerns the

intoxicated musings of a young, bisexual artist whose late-night wanderings in Harlem lead him to a sexual encounter with a handsome male
stranger known only as Beauty. That this mysterious lover was known to
be a composite sketch—of Rudolph Valentino, Langston Hughes, Harold
Jackman, and the author himself—adds still another layer of controversy
to a story that was already scandalous by virtue of its openly transgressive
themes of homosexuality and drug usage.

Smoke, Lilies, and Jade

[1925]

He wanted to do something...to write or draw...or something...but it was so comfortable just to lay there on the bed...his shoes off...and think...think of everything...short disconnected thoughts—to wonder...to remember...to think and smoke...why wasn't he worried that he had no money...he *had* had five cents...but he had been hungry...he *was* hungry and still...all he wanted to do was...lay there comfortably smoking...think...wishing he were writing...or drawing...or something...something about the things he felt and thought...but what did he think...he remembered how his mother had awakened him one night...ages ago...six years ago...Alex...he had always wondered at the strangeness of it...she had seemed so...so...so just the same...Alex... I think your father is dead...and it hadn't seemed so strange...yet...one's mother didn't say that...didn't wake one at midnight every night to say...feel him...put your hand on his head...then whisper with a catch in her voice...I'm afraid...sh don't wake Lam...yet it hadn't seemed as it should have seemed...even when he had felt his father's cool wet forehead...it hadn't been tragic...the light had been turned very low...and flickered...yet it hadn't been tragic...or weird...not at all as one should feel when one's father died...even his reply of...yes he is dead...had been commonplace...hadn't been dramatic...there had been no tears... no sobs...not even a sorrow...and yet he must have realized that one's father couldn't smile...or sing any more...after he had died...every one remembered his father's voice...it had been a lush voice...a promise... then that dressing together...his mother and himself...in the bathroom...why was the bathroom always the warmest room in the winter...as they had put on their clothes...his mother had been telling him what he must do...and cried softly...and that had made him cry too but you mustn't cry Alex...remember you have to be a little man now...and that was all...didn't other wives and sons cry more for their dead than that...anyway people never cried for beautiful sunsets...or music...and those were the things that hurt...the things to sympathize with...then out into the snow and dark of the morning...first to the undertaker's...no first to Uncle Frank's...why did Aunt Lula have to act like that...to ask again and again...but when did he die...when did he

die...I just can't believe it...poor Minerva...then out into the snow and
dark again...how had his mother expected him to know where to find
the night bell at the undertaker's...he was the most sensible of them all
tho...all he had said was...what...Harry Francis...too bad...tell mamma
I'll be there first thing in the morning...then down the deserted streets
again...to grandmother's...it was growing light now...it must be terrible
to die in daylight...grandpa had been sweeping the snow off the
yard...he had been glad of that because...well he could tell him better
than grandma...grandpa...father's dead...and he hadn't acted strange
either...books lied...he had just looked at Alex a moment then continued sweeping...all he said was...what time did he die...she'll want to
know...then passing thru the lonesome street toward home...Mrs.
Mamie Grant was closing a window and spied him...hallow Alex...an'
how's your father this mornin'...dead...get out...tch tch tch an' I was
just around there with a cup a' custard yesterday...Alex puffed content-
edly on his cigarette...he was hungry and comfortable...and he had an
ivory holder inlaid with red jade and green...funny how the smoke
seemed to climb up that ray of sunlight...went up the slant like just
imagination...was imagination blue...or was it because he had spent his
last five cents and couldn't worry...anyway it was nice to lay there and
wonder...and remember...why was he so different from other people...
the only things he remembered of his father's funeral were the crowded
church and the ride in the hack...so many people there in the church...
and ladies with tears in their eyes...and on their cheeks...and some men
too...why did people cry...vanity that was all...yet they weren't exactly
hypocrites...but why...it had made him furious...all these people crying...it wasn't *their* father...and he wasn't crying...couldn't cry for
sorrow altho he had loved his father more than...than...it had made
him so angry that tears had come to his eyes...and he had been ashamed
of his mother...crying into a handkerchief...so ashamed that tears had
run down his cheeks and he had frowned...and some one...a woman...
had said...look at that poor little dear...Alex is just like his father...and
the tears had run fast...because he *wasn't* like his father...
he couldn't sing...he didn't want to sing...he didn't want to sing...Alex
blew a cloud of smoke...blue smoke...when they had taken his father
from the vault three weeks later...he had grown beautiful...his nose had
become perfect and clear...his hair had turned jet black and glossy and
silky...and his skin was a transparent green...like the sea only not so

deep...and where it was drawn over the cheek bones a pale beautiful red appeared...like a blush...why hadn't his father looked like that always... but no...to have sung would have broken the wondrous repose of his lips and maybe that was his beauty...maybe it was wrong to think thoughts like these...but they were nice and pleasant and comfortable...when one was smoking a cigarette thru an ivory holder...inlaid with red jade and green...........

he wondered why he couldn't find work...a job...when he had first come to New York he had...and he had only been fourteen then was it because he was nineteen now that he felt so idle...and contented... or because he was an artist...but was he an artist...was one an artist until one became known...of course he was an artist...and strangely enough so were all his friends...he should be ashamed that he didn't work...but...was it five years in New York...or the fact that he was an artist...when his mother said she couldn't understand him...why did he vaguely pity her instead of being ashamed...he should be...his mother and all his relatives said so...his brother was three years younger than he and yet he had already been away from home a year...on the stage...making thirty-five dollars a week...had three suits and many clothes and was going to help mother...while he...Alex...was content to lay and smoke and meet friends at night...to argue and read Wilde... Freud...Boccaccio and Schnitzler...to attend Gurdjieff meetings and know things...Why did they scoff at him for knowing such people as Carl...Mencken...Toomer...Hughes...Cullen...Wood...Cabell...oh the whole lot of them...was it because it seemed incongruous that he...who was so little known...should call by first names people they would like to know...were they jealous...no mothers aren't jealous of their sons...they are proud of them...why then...when these friends accepted and liked him...no matter how he dressed...why did mother ask...and you went looking like that...Langston was a fine fellow...he knew there was some-thing in Alex...and so did Rene and Borgia.... and Zora and Clement and Miguel...and...and...and all of them...if he went to see mother she would ask...how do you feel Alex with nothing in your pockets...I don't see how you can be satisfied...Really you're a mystery to me...and who you take after...I'm sure I don't know...none of my brothers were lazy and shiftless...I can never remember the time when they weren't send-ing money home and when your father was your age he was supporting a family...where you get your nerve I don't know...just because you've

tried to write one or two little poems and stories that no one understands...you seem to think the world owes you a living...you should see
by now how much is thought of them...you can't sell anything...and you
won't do anything to make money...wake up Alex...I don't know what
will become of you........

it was hard to believe in one's self after that...did Wilde's parents
or Shelley's or Goya's talk to them like that...but it was depressing to
think in that vein...Alex stretched and yawned...Max had died...
Margaret had died...so had Sonia...Cynthia...Juan-Jose and Harry...all
people he had loved...loved one by one and together...and all had
died...he never loved a person long before they died...in truth he was
tragic...that was a lovely appellation...The Tragic Genius...think...to go
thru life known as The Tragic Genius...romantic...but it was more or
less true...Alex turned over and blew another cloud of smoke...was all
life like that...smoke...blue smoke from an ivory holder...he wished he
were in New Bedford...New Bedford was a nice place...snug little
houses set complacently behind protecting lawns...half open windows
showing prim interiors from behind waving cool curtains...inviting...like
precise courtesans winking from behind lace fans...and trees...many
trees...casting lacy patterns of shade on the sun dipped sidewalks...small
stores...naively proud of their pseudo grandeur...banks...called institutions for saving...all naive...that was it...New Bedford was naive...after
the sophistication of New York it would fan one like a refreshing
breeze...and yet he had returned to New York...and sophistication...was
he sophisticated...no because he was seldom bored...seldom bored by
anything...and weren't the sophisticated continually suffering from
ennui...on the contrary...he was amused...amused by the artificiality of
naivety and sophistication alike...but may be that in itself was the
essence of sophistication or...was it cynicism...or were the two identical...blew a cloud of smoke...it was growing dark now...and the smoke
no longer had a ladder to climb...but soon the moon would rise and
then he would clothe the silver moon in blue smoke garments...truly
smoke was like imagination.........

Alex sat up...pulled on his shoes and went out...it was a beautiful
night...and so large...the dusky blue hung like a curtain in an immense
arched doorway...fastened with silver tacks...to wander in the night
was wonderful...myriads of inquisitive lights...curiously prying into
the dark...and fading unsatisfied...he passed a woman...she was not

beautiful...and he was sad because she did not weep that she would never be beautiful...was it Wilde who had said...a cigarette is the most perfect pleasure because it leaves one unsatisfied...the breeze gave to him a perfume stolen from some wandering lady of the evening...it pleased him...why was it that men wouldn't use perfumes...they should...each and every one of them liked perfumes...the man who denied that was a liar...or a coward...but if ever he were to voice that thought...express it...he would be misunderstood...a fine feeling that...to be misunderstood...it made him feel tragic and great...but may be it would be nicer to be understood...but no...no great artist is...then again neither were fools...they were strangely akin these two...Alex thought of a sketch he would make...a personality sketch of Fania... straight classic features tinted proud purple...sensuous fine lips...gilded for truth...eyes...half opened and lids colored mysterious green...hair black and straight...drawn sternly mocking back from the false puritanical forehead...maybe he would make Edith too...skin a blue...infinite like night...and eyes...slant and grey...very complacent like a cat's... Mona Lisa lips...red and seductive as...as pomegranate juice...in truth it was fine to be young and hungry and an artist...to blow blue smoke from an ivory holder............

here was the cafeteria...it was almost as tho it had journeyed to meet him...the night was so blue...how does blue feel...or red or gold or any other color...if colors could be heard he could paint most wondrous tunes...symphonious...think...the dulcet clear tone of a blue like night...of a red like pomegranate juice...like Edith's lips...of the fairy tones to be heard in a sunset...like rubies shaken in a crystal cup...of the symphony of Fania...and silver...and gold...he had heard the sound of gold...but they weren't the sounds he wanted to catch...no...they must be liquid...not so staccato but flowing variations of the same caliber... there was no one in the cafe as yet...he sat and waited...that was a clever idea he had had about color music...but after all he was a monstrous clever fellow...Jurgen had said that...funny how characters in books said the things one wanted to say...he would like to know Jurgen...how does one go about getting an introduction to a fiction character...go up to the brown cover of the book and knock gently...and say hello...then timidly...is Duke Jurgen there...or...no because if one entered the book in the beginning Jurgen would only be a pawn broker...and one didn't enter a book in the center...but what foolishness...

Alex lit a cigarette...but Cabell was a master to have written Jurgen...and an artist...and a poet...Alex blew a cloud of smoke...a few lines of one of Langston's poems came to describe Jurgen.....

Somewhat like Ariel.
Somewhat like Puck
Somewhat like a gutter boy
Who loves to play in muck.
Somewhat like Bacchus
Somewhat like Pan
And a way with women
Like a sailor man......

Langston must have known Jurgen...suppose Jurgen had met Tonio Kroeger...what a vagrant thought...Kroeger...Kroeger... Kroeger...why here was Rene...Alex had almost gone to sleep...Alex blew a cone of smoke as he took Rene's hand...it was nice to have friends like Rene...so comfortable...Rene was speaking...Borgia joined them...and de Diego Padro...their talk veered to...James Branch Cabell...beautiful...marvelous...Rene had an enchanting accent...said sank for thank and souse for south...but they couldn't know Cabell's greatness...Alex searched the smoke for expression...he...he...well he has created a phantasy mire...that's it...from clear rich imagery...life and silver sands...that's nice...and silver sands...imagine lilies growing in such a mire...when they close at night their gilded underside would protect...but that's not it at all...his thoughts just carried and mingled like...like odors...suggested but never definite...Rene was leaving...they all were leaving...Alex sauntered slowly back...the houses all looked sleepy...funny...made him feel like writing poetry...and about death too...an elevated crashed by overhead scattering all his thoughts with its noise...making them spread...in circles...then larger circles...just like a splash in a calm pool...what had he been thinking...of...a poem about death...but he no longer felt that urge...just walk and think and won- der...think and remember and smoke...blow smoke that mixed with his thoughts and the night...he would like to live in a large white palace...to wear a long black cape...very full and lined with vermilion...to have many cushions and to lie there among them...talking to his friends...lie there in a yellow silk shirt and black velvet trousers...like music-review artists talking and pouring strange liquors from curiously beautiful bottles...bottles with long slender necks...he climbed the noisy stair of the odorous tenement...smelled of fish...of stale fried fish and dirty milk bottles...he rather liked it...he liked the acrid smell of horse manure too...strong...thoughts...yes to lie back among strangely fashioned cushions and sip eastern wines and talk...Alex threw himself on the bed...removed his shoes...stretched and relaxed...yes and have music waft softly into the darkened and incensed room...he blew a cloud of smoke...oh the joy of being an artist and of blowing blue smoke thru an ivory holder inlaid with red jade and green...

the street was so long and narrow...so long and narrow...and blue... in the distance it reached the stars...and if he walked long enough...far enough...he could reach the stars too...the narrow blue was so empty... quiet...Alex walked music...it was nice to walk in the blue after a party...Zora had shone again...her stories...she always shone...and Monty was glad...every one was glad when Zora shone...he was glad he had gone to Monty's party...Monty had a nice place in the village...nice lights... and friends and wine...mother would be scandalized that he could think of going to a party...without a copper to his name...but then mother had never been to Monty's...and mother had never seen the street seem long and narrow and blue...Alex walked music...the click of his heels kept time with a tune in his mind...he glanced into a lighted cafe window...inside were people sipping coffee...men...why did they sit there in the loud light...didn't they know that outside the street...the narrow blue street met the stars...that if they walked long enough...far enough...Alex walked and the click of his heels sounded...and had an echo...sound being tossed back and forth...back and forth... some one was approaching...and their echoes mingled...and gave the sound of castanets...Alex liked the sound of the approaching man's footsteps...he walked music also...he knew the beauty of the narrow blue...Alex knew that by the way their echoes mingled...he wished he would speak...but strangers don't speak at four o'clock in the morning...at least if they did he couldn't imagine what would be said... maybe...pardon me but are you walking toward the stars...yes, sir, and if you walk long enough...then may I walk with you I want to reach the stars too...perdone me senor tiene vd. fosforo...Alex was glad he had been addressed in Spanish...to have been asked for a match in English...

or to have been addressed in English at all...would have been blasphemy just then...Alex handed him a match...he glanced at his companion apprehensively in the match glow...he was afraid that his appearance would shatter the blue thoughts...and stars...ah...his face was a perfect compliment to his voice...and the echo of their steps mingled...they walked in silence...the castanets of their heels clicking accompaniment...the stranger inhaled deeply and with a nod of content and a smile...blew a cloud of smoke...Alex felt like singing...the stranger knew the magic of blue smoke also...they continued in silence...the castanets of their heels clicking rhythmically...Alex turned in his doorway...up the stairs and the stranger waited for him to light the room...no need for words...they had always known each other.........as they undressed by the blue dawn...Alex knew he had never seen a more perfect being...his body was all symmetry and music...and Alex called him Beauty...long they lay...blowing smoke and exchanging thoughts... and Alex swallowed with difficulty...he felt a glow of tremor...and they talked and...slept...

Alex wondered more and more why he liked Adrian so...he liked many people...Wallie...Zora...Clement...Gloria...Langston...John... Gwenny...oh many people...and they were friends...but Beauty...it was different...once Alex had admired Beauty's strength...and Beauty's eyes had grown soft and he had said...I like you more than any one Dulce...Adrian always called him Dulce...and Alex had become confused...was it that he was so susceptible to beauty that Alex liked Adrian so much...but no...he knew other people who were beautiful...Fania and Gloria...Monty and Bunny...but he was never confused before them...while Beauty...Beauty could make him believe in Buddha...or imps...and no one else could do that...that is no one but Melva...but then he was in love with Melva...and that explained that...he would like Beauty to know Melva...they were both so perfect...such compliments...yes he would like Beauty to know Melva because he loved them both...there...he had thought it...actually dared to think it...but Beauty must never know...Beauty couldn't understand...indeed Alex couldn't understand...and it pained him...almost physically...and tired his mind...Beauty...Beauty was in the air...the smoke...Beauty...Melva... Beauty...Melva...Alex slept...and dreamed........

he was in a field...a field of blue smoke and black poppies and red calla lilies...he was searching...on his hands and knees...searching...

among black poppies and red calla lilies...he was searching and pushed aside poppy stems...and saw two strong white legs...dancer's legs...the contours pleased him...his eyes wandered...on past the muscular hocks to the firm white thighs...the rounded buttocks...then the lithe narrow waist...strong torso and broad deep chest...the heavy shoulders...the graceful muscled neck...squared chin and quizzical lips...grecian nose with its temperamental nostrils...the brown eyes looking at him...like... Monty looked at Zora...his hair curly and black and all tousled...and it was Beauty...and Beauty smiled and looked at him and smiled...said... I'll wait Alex...and Alex became confused and continued his search...on his hands and knees...pushing aside poppy stems and lily stems...a poppy...a black poppy...a lily...a red lily...and when he looked back he could no longer see Beauty...Alex continued his search...thru poppies...lilies...poppies and red calla lilies...and suddenly he saw...two small feet olive-ivory...two well turned legs curving gracefully from slender ankles...and the contours soothed him...he followed them...past the narrow rounded hips to the tiny waist...the fragile firm breasts...the graceful slender throat...the soft rounded chin...slightly parting lips and straight little nose with its slightly flaring nostrils...the black eyes with lights in them...looking at him...the forehead and straight cut black hair and it was Melva...and she looked at him and smiled and said...I'll wait Alex...and Alex became confused and kissed her...became confused and continued his search...on his hands and knees...pushed aside a poppy stem...a black-poppy stem...pushed aside a lily stem... a red-lily stem...a poppy...a poppy...a lily...and suddenly he stood erect...exultant...and in his hand he held...an ivory holder... inlaid with red jade...and green............

and Alex awoke...Beauty's hair tickled his nose...Beauty was smiling in his sleep...half his face stained flush color by the sun...the other half in shadow...blue shadow...his eye lashes casting cobwebby blue shadows on his cheek...his lips were so beautiful...quizzical...Alex wondered why he always thought of that passage from Wilde's Salome... when he looked at Beauty's lips...I would kiss your lips...he *would* like to kiss Beauty's lips...Alex flushed warm...with shame...or was it shame...he reached across Beauty for a cigarette...Beauty's cheek felt cool to his arm...his hair felt soft...Alex lay smoking...such a dream...red calla lilies...red calla lilies...and...what could it all mean...did dreams have meanings...Fania said...and black poppies...thousands...millions...

Beauty stirred...Alex put out his cigarette...closed his eyes...he mustn't see Beauty yet...speak to him...his lips were too hot...dry...the palms of his hands too cool and moist...thru his half closed eyes he could see Beauty...propped...cheek in hand...on one elbow...looking at him...lips smiling quizzically...he wished Beauty wouldn't look so hard...Alex was finding it difficult to breathe...breathe normally...why *must* Beauty look so long...and smile *that* way...his face seemed nearer...it was...Alex could feel Beauty's hair on his forehead...breathe normally...breathe normally...could feel Beauty's breath on his nostrils and lips...and it was clean and faintly colored with tobacco...breathe normally Alex...Beauty's lips were nearer...Alex closed his eyes...how did one act...his pulse was hammering...from wrists to finger tip...wrist to finger tip...Beauty's lips touched his...his temples throbbed...throbbed...his pulse hammered from wrist to finger tip...Beauty's breath came short now...softly staccato...breathe normally Alex...you are asleep...Beauty's lips touched his...breathe normally...and pressed...pressed hard...cool...his body trembled...breathe normally Alex...Beauty's lips pressed cool...cool and hard...how much pressure does it take to waken one...Alex sighed... moved softly...how does one act...Beauty's hair barely touched him now...his breath was faint on...Alex's nostrils...and lips...Alex stretched and opened his eyes...Beauty was looking at him...propped on one elbow...cheek in his palm...Beauty spoke...scratch my head please Dulce...Alex was breathing normally now...propped against the bed head...Beauty's head in his lap...Beauty spoke...I wonder why I like to look at some things Dulce...things like smoke and cats...and you...Alex's pulse no longer hammered from...wrist to finger tip...wrist to finger tip...the rose dusk had become blue night...and soon...soon they would go out into the blue...........

the little church was crowded...warm...the rows of benches were brown and sticky...Harold was there...and Constance and Langston and Bruce and John...there was Mr. Robeson...how are you Paul...a young man was singing...Caver...Caver was a very self assured young man... such a dream...poppies...black poppies...they were applauding... Constance and John were exchanging notes...the benches were sticky...a young lady was playing the piano...fair...and red calla lilies...who had ever heard of red calla lilies...they were applauding...a young man was playing the viola...what could it all mean...so many poppies...and

Beauty looking at him like...like Monty looked at Zora...another young
man was playing a violin...he was the first real artist to perform...he had
a touch of soul...or was it only feeling...they were hard to differentiate
on the violin...and Melva standing in the poppies and lilies...
Mr. Phillips was singing...Mr. Phillips was billed as a basso...and he had
kissed her...they were applauding...the first young man was singing
again...Langston's spiritual...Fy-ah-fy-ah-Lawd...fy-ah's gonna burn ma
soul...Beauty's hair was so black and curly...they were applauding...
encore...Fy-ah Lawd had been a success...Langston bowed...Langston
had written the words...Hall bowed...Hall had written the music...the
young man was singing it again...Beauty's lips had pressed
hard...cool...cool...fy-ah Lawd...his breath had trembled...fy-ah's
gonna burn ma soul...they were all leaving...first to the roof dance...
fy-ah Lawd...there was Catherine...she was beautiful tonight...she
always was at night...Beauty's lips...fy-ah Lawd...hello Dot...why don't
you take a boat that sails...when are you leaving again...and there's
Estelle...every one was there...fy-ah Lawd...Beauty's body had pressed
close...close...fy-ah's gonna burn my soul...let's leave...have to meet
some people at the New World...then to Augusta's party...Harold...
John...Bruce...Connie...Langston...ready...down one hundred thirty-
fifth street...fy-ah...meet these people and leave...fy-ah Lawd...now to
Augusta's party...fy-ah's gonna burn ma soul...they were at Augusta's...
Alex half lay...half sat on the floor...sipping a cocktail...such a
dream...red calla lilies...Alex left...down the narrow streets...fy-ah...up
the long noisy stairs...fy-ahs gonna bu'n ma soul...his head felt swollen...
expanding...contracting...expanding...contracting...he had never
been like this before...expanding...contracting...it was that...fy-ah...
fy-ah Lawd...and the cocktails...and Beauty...he felt two cool strong
hands on his shoulders...it was Beauty...lie down Dulce...Alex lay
down...Beauty...Alex stopped...no no...don't say it...Beauty mustn't
know...Beauty couldn't understand...are you going to lie down too
Beauty...the light went out expanding...contracting...he felt the bed
sink as Beauty lay beside him...his lips were dry...hot...the palms of his
hands so moist and cool...Alex partly closed his eyes...from beneath
his lashes he could see Beauty's face overhis...nearer...nearer...Beauty's
hair touched his forehead now...he could feel his breath on his
nostrils and lips...Beauty's breath came short...breathe normally
Beauty...breathe normally...Beauty's lips touched his...pressed

hard...cool...opened slightly...Alex opened his eyes...into Beauty's...
parted his lips...Dulce...Beauty's breath was hot and short...Alex ran
his hand through Beauty's hair...Beauty's lips pressed hard against his
teeth...Alex trembled...could feel Beauty's body...close against his...hot...
tense...white...and soft...soft...soft.........

they were at Forno's...every one came to Forno's once maybe only
once...but they came...see that big fat woman Beauty...Alex pointed to
an overly stout and bejeweled lady making her way thru the maze of
chairs...that's Maria Guerrero...Beauty looked to see a lady guiding
almost the whole opera company to an immense table...really
Dulce...for one who appreciates beauty you do use the most abominable
English...Alex lit a cigarette...and that florid man with white
hair...that's Carl...Beauty smiled...The Blind bow boy...he asked...Alex
wondered...everything seemed so...so just the same...here they were
laughing and joking about people...there's Rene...Rene this is my
friend Adrian...after that night...and he felt so unembarrassed...Rene
and Adrian were talking...there was Lucricia Bori...she was bowing at
their table...oh her cousin was with them...and Peggy Joyce...every one
came to Forno's...Alex looked toward the door...there was Melva...Alex
beckoned...Melva this is Adrian...Beauty held her hand...they
talked...smoked...Alex loved Melva...in Forno's...every one came there
sooner or later...maybe once...but.........

up...up...slow...jerk up...up...not fast...not glorious...but slow...up...up
into the sun...slow...sure like fate...poise on the brim...the brim of
life...two shining rails straight down...Melva's head was on his shoulder...his arm was around her...poise...the down...gasping...straight
down...straight like sin...down...the curving shiny rail rushed up to
meet them...hit the bottom then...shoot up...fast...glorious...up into
the sun...Melva gasped...Alex's arm tightened...all goes up...then
down...straight like hell...all breath squeezed out of them...Melva's
head on his shoulder...up...up...Alex kissed her...down...they stepped
out of the car...walking music...now over to the Ferris Wheel...out and
up...Melva's hand was soft in his...out and up...over mortals...mortals
drinking nectar...five cents a glass...her cheek was soft on his...up...
up...till the world seemed small...tiny...the ocean seemed tiny and
blue...up...up and out...over the sun...the tiny red sun...Alex kissed

her...up...up...their tongues touched...up...seventh heaven...the sea had swallowed the sun...up and out...her breath was perfumed...Alex kissed her...drift down...soft...soft...the sun had left the sky flushed...drift down...soft down...back to earth...visit the mortals sipping nectar at five cents a glass...Melva's lips brushed his...then out among the mortals...and the sun had left a flush on Melva's cheeks...they walked hand in hand...and the moon came out...they walked in silence on the silver strip...and the sea sang for them...they walked toward the moon...we'll hang our hats on the crook of the moon Melva...softly on the silver strip...his hands molded her features and her cheeks were soft and warm to his touch...where is Adrian...Alex...Melva trod silver...Alex trod sand...Alex trod sand...the sea *sang* for her...Beauty...her hand felt cold in his...Beauty...the sea *dinned*...Beauty...he led the way to the train...and the train dinned...Beauty...dinned...dinned...her cheek *had* been soft...Beauty...Beauty...her breath *had* been perfumed...Beauty...Beauty...the sands *had* been silver...Beauty...Beauty...they left the train...Melva walked music...Melva said...don't make me blush again...and kissed him...Alex stood on the steps after she left him and the night was black...down long streets to...Alex lit a cigarette...and his heels clicked...Beauty...Melva...Beauty...Melva...and the smoke made the night blue...

Melva had said...don't make me blush again...and kissed him...and the street had been blue...one *can* love two at the same time...Melva had kissed him...one *can*...and the street had been blue...one *can*...and the room was clouded with blue smoke...drifting vapors of smoke and thoughts...Beauty's hair was so black...and soft...blue smoke from an ivory holder...was that why he loved Beauty...one *can*...or because his body was beautiful...and white and warm...or because his eyes...one *can* love........

....*To Be Continued...*

COUNTEE CULLEN

■ ■ ■

[1903–1946]

WIDELY CONSIDERED THE PREMIER POET OF THE HARLEM
Renaissance, Countee Cullen was the most famous African American
literary figure of the late 1920s. Indeed, among black poets up to that
point, only Phillis Wheatley in the eighteenth century and Paul
Laurence Dunbar, a popular poet at the time of Cullen's birth, compare
in stature.

Although the details surrounding the author's origins are uncertain, Cullen was adopted by one of Harlem's leading fundamentalist
ministers and his wife sometime before 1918. The puritanism of his
adopted father, Frederick (reported to have been an effeminate, latent
homosexual himself), may have influenced his son's lifelong effort to
shroud his private life, notably his homosexuality. Even Cullen's high-
profile marriage in 1928 to W. E. B. DuBois's only daughter, Yolande, did
not dispel rumors of the author's well-known preference for his handsome friend and lover Harold Jackman; nor for that matter did the
couple's hushed divorce just four years later hamper further speculation
as to Cullen's true sexual orientation.

Cullen's literary success was launched at an early age with the back-
to-back publication of three highly popular books of verse: *Color* (1925),
Ballad of the Brown Girl (1927), and *Copper Sun* (1927). Most of the poems
in those collections had been modeled on the English romantic poets
and composed while Cullen was a student at New York University and
Harvard, where he, unlike most African Americans, had been formally
educated in poetry. White and black critics alike proclaimed his brilliance, and there was even talk that Cullen's appeal might cross over

color lines. When the national economy soured in the 1930s, however, the author's renown began to wane. The mixed reception of his most ambitious work to date, *The Black Christ and Other Poems* (1929), was an unexpected blow. Switching genres, he followed up with the publication of his first and only novel, *One Way to Heaven* (1932), as well as *The Medea and Some Poems* (1935), a drama set to music by gay composer Virgil Thompson and believed to be the first major translation of a classical work by a black writer. Cullen supplemented his income as a public school instructor, teaching French to young James Baldwin, among other pupils. The author was working on a stage musical at the time of his death from high blood pressure and uremic poisoning at age forty-three.

In spite of his lofty reputation as a poet, Cullen's *One Way to Heaven* is a "low-down" satire of the Harlem Renaissance in the manner of Wallace Thurman's *Infants of the Spring*. Indeed, both novels were published in 1932 and each pokes fun at the most celebrated personalities of the era, including Langston Hughes and Carl Van Vechten. Unlike Thurman, however, Cullen's career once held special promise for New Negro advocates, who had looked to his early fame as a hopeful source of racial uplift. With *One Way to Heaven,* however, black critics charged that he had degraded African Americans. Perhaps tellingly, the novel is dedicated to Harold Jackman.

W hen Constancia had hit upon the kind and generous impulse of marrying Mattie from her home, she had had no ulterior motive in view, had envisaged no future date when Sam would add to her popularity and prestige by contributing to the success of one of her evenings, even though at the expense of the Duchess of Uganda. But Constancia had been born under a lucky star and belonged to that fortunate group to whom, having much, the heavens with inexplicable and illogical generosity promise more.

That a wedding may be a matter of great momentary importance, yet not magical enough to change the ingrained thoughts and actions of a lifetime in the twinkling of an eye, Mattie was to learn slowly and sorrowfully in her fitful experience with Sam. When he asked her to marry him, he had done so only after what to him was due deliberation, and with the wavering intention that surely he would find work to do the next day or the next week after his marriage. It was, however, fully two months after, and then only due to Constancia's intervention, that he drew in his long legs from in front of the parlor stove and set out to earn his share of his and Mattie's living.

Mattie had been too deep in love and too lost in religion to scold, or to show by word or look that she was hurt or disappointed. With her religion had come a fatalism, and she was leaving all to the Lord. Daily Aunt Mandy nagged her for keeping a good-for-nothing man lying around the house and in her way, although daily the old lady took out her cards, read Sam's fortune, and then became his partner in one of the many card games he had taught her. Daily Mattie was forced to answer in the negative when Constancia asked if Sam had started to work. Finally, Constancia had taken the matter in hand herself, and with Mattie at her side had routed Sam away from the fire one March morning, and had taken him to a job. It was a job with a uniform, much to Aunt Mandy's joy, and with great prestige and privilege attached, although the nature of it was not entirely to Mattie's liking. It savored too much of the world, the flesh, and the devil. Constancia had been able to do nothing better than to secure Sam the role of ticket-chopper in one of the small variety and movie houses of the neighborhood. It was work which could be manipulated with one hand, and which at the same time, with the attendant uniform, afforded Sam a real opportunity to show off his fine height and slim, swaggering figure.

It was a gorgeous uniform of smooth bright green material, with square padded shoulders, gold epaulettes, and with black braid fronting the sleeves and surrounding the buttonholes through which large brass buttons shot their fire. Sam felt like a general or drum-major, and thought that working might not be so distasteful as long as he could be attired in such a manner.

The evening on which he first donned his glory happened to be one on which Mattie had been retained at Constancia's, where a party was being given for Herbert Newell, a young Negro who had just published a novel. As the doors of the theater swung open to liberate its audience from the land of fancy and at the same time to liberate Sam from his toil, he thought it might be a pleasant idea if he passed by Constancia's in order to wait for Mattie and to walk home with her, and incidentally to let her feast her eyes upon his new-spun raiment. Unfortunately, he liked himself so well in his new finery that he thought it worthy of a stimulant, with the result that by the time he reached Constancia's home it was only by the bright lights which illumined the house from roof to cellar, and by that second sense which some drunken men seem to acquire, that he was able to locate his destination.

The party was for Herbert Newell, but the evening became that of the duchess and of Sam. Not many people had read Herbert's novel, although it had been out for several months and had been commented upon in the Negro and white press (denounced by the former as an outrage against Negro sensibilities, and lauded by the latter as being typically Negro), yet almost everyone present came up to the author, shook his hand, and congratulated him. Poor outspoken Lottie Smith naïvely made herself an enemy for life by admitting that she was waiting to borrow Constancia's copy of the new book. Herbert, a very dark, belligerent young Negro, was brutally frank, and shocked several of the more sentimentally minded guests by informing them that art as such didn't mean anything to him, and that he had not written his book for the sake of anything so nebulous, but merely to make some money.

"Not," he added, "that I expect to make it from Negroes."

"I suppose I shall buy it," sighed Mrs. Vanderbilt-Jones in a tone of deep resignation. "I'll buy it out of pride of race, although from what

I hear, I shall hardly like it, I fear. I don't see why our writers don't write about *nice* people sometimes." She gazed grandiloquently around the room to show Herbert the fine material at hand.

"Yes, Herbert," interposed Constancia, who had just come up at this point. "I understand that the heroine of your book is a prostitute, and that the hero is a stevedore. How can anything good come out of Nazareth, or anything to which we as a race can point to with pride come out of a combination like that? I quite agree with Mrs. Vanderbilt-Jones. You should have written about people like Counselor Spivens, who has just been incarcerated for a year for converting to his own use money awarded one of his clients in an equal-rights case; or like Dr. Strong, whose new limousine is the reward of Heavens knows how many abortions; or you might have woven a highly colorful tale around Mrs. Vanderbilt-Jones's own niece, Betty, who just..."

"Constancia," interrupted the old lady as she flounced off, "if I didn't love you so much I should positively hate you."

Constancia smiled and laid her hand on Herbert's arm. "Write whatever you want, Herbert, and don't give a continental about them. It will take them centuries, anyway, to distinguish between good and bad, and what is nice and what is really smeared over with a coating which they call nice. I just heard poor Mrs. De Peyster Johnson, to whose credit it can at least be said that she has read your book, declare, simply because you are a New Negro and therefore dear to her heart, that your novel was as good as anything that Wells or Bennett had written. And when I added that it was much better than anything written by any of the Russians, she agreed heartily. That's race pride with a vengeance for you, and self-criticism that isn't worth a penny."

"I wish they were all like you, Constancia," Herbert assured her. "I'd know then that they had some intelligence, and that when they condemned my book they had something to back up their dislike, and that when they said they liked it they were really doing something more sincere than making conversation with me. Half a dozen of them tonight have already asked me what the white people will think about the race when they read my book. Good God! I wasn't writing a history about the Negro. I was trying to write a novel."

"Yes," agreed Constancia as she waved to the duchess and to Lady Hyacinth Brown, who had just come in, "I suppose there are any number of us who pass perfectly wretched nights sleeping on our backs instead of on our stomachs, which we would find more comfortable, because we fear what the white world might say about the Negro race."

"Sometimes it makes me feel like I should like to chuck it and pass for something else," said Herbert, seriously, although a nearby glass which gave back his countenance showed one which was far too sable to pass as anything Caucasian, not even excepting the Italian and the Spanish.

"I never feel like that," said Constancia. "God knows there is nothing chauvinistic about me. I often think the Negro is God Almighty's one mistake, but as I look about me at white people, I am forced to say so are we all. It isn't being colored that annoys me. I could go white if I wanted to, but I am too much of a hedonist; I enjoy life too much, and enjoyment isn't across the line. Money is there, and privilege, and the sort of power which comes with numbers; but as for enjoyment, they don't know what it is. When I go to so-called white parties sometimes and look around me, I have a feeling that the host has been very wise in breaking down color conventions, and that in most cases his reason is selfish instead of being due to an interracial complex. I have seen two Negroes turn more than one dull party, where I was longing for home and Harlem, into a revel which Puck himself would find it hard to duplicate. As for variety, I think I should die if I were obliged to look into the mirror daily and to see nothing but my own parchment-colored skin, or to turn and behold nothing but George's brown visage shining back at me all day long, no matter how much adoration it reflected. When I get tired of George and myself I have simply to phone for Stanley Bickford—and Greenland's icy mountains couldn't send me anything more Nordic, with a nose more aquiline, with more cerulean eyes, or with hair one bit more prickly and blond. Let me dial another number and I have the Duchess of Uganda, black as the ace of spaces and more beautiful than Lucifer, or Lottie Smith, brown as a berry and with more real vivacity than a twirling dervish. No, thanks, I wouldn't change. So long as I have my happiness to consider, I'll not go to the mountain. If the mountain wants me, let it come to me. It knows where I am."

"I am going to write a book about you some day, Constancia," threatened Herbert.

"If you call it *Nice People,* it will be a terrible misnomer," said Constancia, turning to greet the duchess and Lady Hyacinth Brown, who were rushing over to their hostess in concerted excitement, if the floating undulation of Lady Hyacinth, a mode of ambulance which she never abandoned even in her most tense moments, and the waddling propulsion of the duchess may be termed rushing. Behind them like a lost shadow stalked Donald Hewitt.

Some day Lady Hyacinth and the duchess, the latter more deservedly, will find a chronicler worthy of recounting their adventures and of properly fixing their status in Harlem society. They were an excellent foil to one another; yet each was so much the other's complement that since the inception of the Back-to-Africa movement, and since the laying of the accolade upon them, they had been inseparable companions, both working for the same cause, each respecting the power of the other, and neither in the least jealous of her sister's attainments.

By way of explaining the duchess and Lady Hyacinth, it may be noted that the Back-to-Africa movement was the heart and entrails of a society whose aim it was to oppose to the American slogan of "The United States for the White Man" the equally non-inclusive shibboleth of "Africa for the Black Man," in this case, the favored descendant of Ham being the American branch. The society held its meetings in a large barn-like building which had once been a church, and certainly one not dedicated to the gods of Africa. Credit must be given the society for realizing the importance of something which most organizations for civic or racial betterment are inclined to ignore, namely an appeal to the pleasurable instincts of man. With the Back-to-Africa movement went costumes that rivaled those of the private guard of the king of England; parades up and down the broad avenues of Harlem every Sunday and once or twice during the week; thunderous orations at the seat of the cabal; and wild, heady music blared forth by a specially trained, constantly practicing brass band. Added to this was the beautifully naïve and romantic way in which the society marched forward to meet the future. Its members were not doomed, like the Israelites, to sweat and toil and perish many in the wilderness before tasting any of the joys of their Canaan. The Back-to-Africa movement realized that it was simply a matter of constantly lessening time before Africa should be back in the hands of its rightful sons and daughters; therefore, in order to speed the zeal of the members, the officers began to parcel out what they already considered as properly, even if only remotely, theirs. Out of deference to the existing powers they did not proclaim an Emperor of Africa, but they did elect a President for the Nonce. With his election their deference to lesser dignitaries ceased, and the far-off, unsuspecting African territories were parceled out left and right, as dukes, counts, and marquises of Africa were created without stint and without thought of the complications which might arise should the Negroes, once returned to their ancestral home, decide upon a republican form of government.

It had been a bright day indeed for her who had been born simple Mary Johnson (as she was often reminded by Constancia when the spirit of the malicious was upon her) when the President for the Nonce of the African Empire, in recognition of fifteen thousand dollars which her argumentative talents had garnered for the general coffers of the society, had bidden her kneel, had laid his accolade upon her, and then had bidden her rise, Mary Johnson no longer, but Mary, Duchess of Uganda, first of her line, and spiritual and temporal head of the house of Uganda.

It had been a day no less luminous and no less marked of Heaven when she whose husband was a mere government employee, too stubbornly entrenched in the monthly assurance of a government check to see rising into the future the glorious edifices of the New Africa, had also knelt to rise, in recognition of ten thousand dollars raised for the general coffers, Mrs. Hyacinth Brown no longer but Lady Hyacinth Brown, undisturbed by the social complications of a mulish husband who must continue to be introduced as plain Mr. Brown.

With their advent into the nobility, there came a rise in social importance if not in actual social status. Few Harlem hostesses could forbear the pleasurable thrill of including on their guest lists the names of the duchess and of Lady Hyacinth. To be sure, as the wife of a railway mail clerk, Lady Hyacinth had already possessed a not unenviable niche in Harlem society; whereas the duchess, as a once-talented, if now slightly declining elocutionist, had also been greatly in demand; but the glories of governmental patronage and of elocution were shabby indeed in comparison with those of nobility. Lady Hyacinth, being the less complicated personage, is the more quickly disposed of. She was a special type from which a well-known and disturbing generality has been drawn for almost every play or novel written to combat miscegenation. Any young Englishman, colonial expatriate, or Southern aristocrat left unprotected with her for five minutes was certain to develop an incurable case of *mammy palaver*. Her elongated languorous body, deep-sunken eyes shaded with heavy velvet lashes, the perfect blending of colors in her skin, and her evident consciousness of her seductive powers, would have arrested any author in search of the perfect half-caste siren. The only drawback was that one soon tired of Lady Hyacinth; she was neither witty, amusing, nor intelligent; she was merely disturbingly beautiful. She was clever enough, however, to ally herself with the duchess and, when the moment presented itself, to shine by silent comparison.

But the duchess was a character, a creation, a personage in whose presence one felt the stir of wings and heavenly vibrations. Constancia declared the duchess was as beautiful as Satan; but she erred; there was nothing Satanic or diabolic about the duchess, not even when she was descanting upon the beauties of that Africa which she had never seen. Indeed, looking at her, one was apt to feel, if he could forget the body to which it was attached, that some divine sculptor had taken a block of the purest black marble and from it had chiseled that classic head. She reminded one of beautiful Queen Nefertiti. In her youth, when her figure, trim and lissom, was a perfect adjunct to the beauty of her face, the duchess had been the toast of half of Negrodom, including many who until they gazed upon her had never felt that beauty could reside in blackness unadulterated. Now in her fortieth year, only in the shapelessness of that bulk with which the years had weighted her down, did she give evidence of the cruelty of time; her face still retained the imperishable beauty of black marble.

The duchess had come along in a day and time when the searing flare for the dramatic which gnawed at her entrails had had no dignified outlet. There was little which a black girl, however beautiful, might do on the stage; and because Mary Johnson, even as a girl, had been the soul of dignity, she had put the stage out of her mind as something unattainable, and had decided to be an elocutionist. Even so, the way had been hard and thorny. The duchess was not one to truckle; she certainly had not forsworn the stage in order to lend herself as a diseuse to anything less than dignified, and to little less than might be labeled classic. Therefore to Negro audiences which might have rallied to her support, had she regaled them with the warm dialect of "When Malindy Sings" and "The Party," she chose to interpret scenes from "Macbeth," "Hamlet," and "The Merchant of Venice." To audiences and intelligences to whom it was utterly unimportant whether the quality of mercy was strained or not, she portrayed in a beautiful and haunting voice the aspirations of a dark Lady Macbeth, the rich subtleties of a sable Portia, and the piteous fate of a black Desdemona.

And success had not been hers.

Finally, as many another artist has turned from the dream of his youth to something baser but more remunerative, the duchess, in the face of want, had turned from elocution to dressmaking. Her nimble fingers and inventive mind had done for her what her voice had failed to accomplish; money had rolled in until she had finally been able to open two shops, and to do nothing herself save supervise.

But the worm of an unfulfilled ambition lay tightly curled at the root of material success; and at the dropping of a handkerchief the duchess would willingly recite for any club, charity benefit, or simple social gathering.

With the passing of the years she had developed a decided predilection for martial pieces and had added to her standard Shakespearian repertoire such hardly perennials as "I am dying, Egypt, dying," "The Charge of the Light Brigade," and "The Black Regiment." The recital of the gallant doings at Balaclava had once thrown her into a state of embarrassment from which only Constancia's quick wit had saved her. The members of the United Daughters of African Descent still chuckle at the memory of it.

It happened at the annual meeting of the Daughters, a conclave at which Constancia, in the guise of mistress of ceremonies, had finally heeded the duchess' importunings, and had called upon her for a recitation. The duchess was charmed, and she looked to Tennyson's poem to help her to eclipse totally all other participants on the program. She began beautifully, her "Half a league, half a league, half a league onward" soaring over the benches into the gallery of the auditorium and completely terminating every whisper. Never before had the Daughters given such gracious attention. But midway of the glorious account, at what would seem the crucial moment, something went blank in the duchess' mind, or, to be more exact, her memory failed her absolutely. Her right arm was raised, her right foot extended and pointed, as she proclaimed "Cannon to right of them." Twice she repeated the designation of that particular section of cannon. Her memory still in abeyance, she was so discountenanced and flustered at the fourth repetition that even her usual beautiful diction suffered, with the result that she uttered unmistakably, "*Cannern* to right of them." It was then that Constancia, who was seated behind her, pulled the duchess' sleeve, at the same time importuning her in a whisper which escaped no one, "For God's sake, Duchess, genuflex and sit down."

A singular comradeship had sprung up between the duchess and Donald Hewitt, and Harlem soon became accustomed to the sight of the tall, fair-haired, imbibing Englishman, more often tottering than maintaining that dignity which is held synonymous with his nationality, accompanied by the short, hard-breathing, elocutionist. They complemented one another's educations admirably. Into dens and retreats of which she had never dreamed the duchess followed Donald, squeezed her gargantuan form into diminutive chairs, and bravely sipped at strange, fiery beverages while Donald gulped down others by the score. Impervious to the imprecations hurled at them by those with whom they collided, they would often dance everyone else from the floor until they alone were left, free to dip and glide and pirouette from one end of the dance space to the other. Then back at their seats, just as his head began to sag and his eyes to glaze, Donald would lean across the table, plant the blond refractory head firmly on his crossed elbows, and beseech the duchess to recite. It is to be doubted that the melancholy soliloquy of Denmark's prince or the gentle pleadings of Portia have ever been uttered under stranger auspices. Over the savage blare of brass and the shrill screeching of strings, cutting into the thick, sickening closeness of cabaret smoke, drowning the obscene hilarity of amorous women, reprimanding the superimposed braggadoccio of inebriated males, the beautiful voice of the duchess would rise, clear and harmonious, winging across the table to Donald. *"To be or not to be..."* The pure sweet voice of African nobility would go on soothing one of England's disillusioned children with the divine musings of England's best. *"Nymph, in the orisons, Be all my sins remembered."* Often as not when the last soft syllable fell from the duchess' lips, England's son would be peacefully sleeping; for always when the duchess began a Shakespearian recitation, Donald was forced to veil his eyes. With the most charming frankness he had explained his reason for this seeming discourtesy to Constancia, one evening when she came upon him with covered eyes while the duchess, as Ophelia, was declaiming, *"O heat, dry up my brains! tears seven times salt, Burn out the sense and virtue of mine eye!"*

"I adore the duchess," Donald had apologized, "but I simply cannot look at her when she does Shakespeare. Her voice is as divine as any I have ever heard, but her color and form collide with all my remembered Ophelias and Portias. I cannot get those tall, flaxen-haired women of my race out of my mind; they linger there so obstinately that the duchess, so physically dissimilar, for all the ebony loveliness of her face, looms like a moving blasphemy on the horizon of my memory. But you won't tell her, Constancia, will you?"

Constancia had promised to keep his secret; so Donald continued, whenever it was a question of the duchess' Shakespearian repertoire, for which he himself often asked, to shade his eyes, thereby gaining for himself the reputation of being her most sincere and enamored admirer.

It was never a question of anything more between them than open and candid comradeship; they amused one another, and life seemed more pleasant to them because of the acquaintance. Such a mild state of affairs irked Lady Hyacinth, who looked upon Donald with a favorably prejudiced eye which, alas! found no answering gleam in those blue orbs so childishly centered upon the duchess.

It was give and take between Donald and the duchess. If he dragged her off nightly to mushroom-growth cabarets, or insisted upon taking her to Park Avenue teas where she was lorgnetted and avoided by all except her constant companion and a few daring males, she also had her hour. Docilely Donald followed her to Back-to-Africa meetings, where he sat, hot and uncomfortable, beneath the hostile gaze of thousands for whom he was but another inquisitive and unde- sired representative of all that was bleached and base; and it was only the duchess' extended scepter that secured him grace and safety. The duchess piloted him in and out of dark, mysterious hallways, made him climb innumerable flights of creaking stairs as she went her rounds soliciting funds for the movement. Never did he balk, for always he envisioned the evening's close—music, dancing, the slow fumes from forbidden beverages insinuating their wily passage into his brain, and across the table from him a beautiful black, middle-aged sybil ready to lull him to sleep with the opium of the world's dramatic wisdom.

Constancia, although ordinarily charity itself, had no sympathy with the duchess' nostalgia for Africa, and had never opened her purse to the duchess' insistent and plaintive pleadings for a donation to the cause. "I am in favor of back-to-nature movements," she excused herself, "for everybody except George and myself. George knows nothing about African diseases, and I can't abide tsetse flies, tarantulas, and dresses made out of grass. No, thank you, I wouldn't change Seventh Avenue for the broadest boulevard along the Congo."

"You are totally devoid of race pride, Constancia," the duchess had complained, bitterly, an indictment against which Constancia knew it was useless to defend herself.

Donald, equally unsympathetic to the Back-to-Africa movement, and marveling how any inhabitant of Harlem could look forward with relish to life in Africa, had been less impervious to his comrade's entreaties. He had capitulated by giving the duchess a princely check, accompanied by the ungentlemanly and unphilanthropic wish that it might do the movement no good whatever, and that, should it ever be used toward the purchase of a ship, that unholy conveyance might get no further than New York Harbor.

The reason for the duchess' and Lady Hyacinth's excitement the night of the party for Herbert Newell was soon made apparent. Both the noble ladies were panting with an unsimulated eagerness to be the first to break the important news, but Donald, who was ironically calm, if a bit unsteady, stole their thunder.

"The duchess has just discovered a marvelous record concerning the aviatic exploits of one Lieutenant Julian," he explained. "A marvelous poem, set to entrancing, barbaric music. The noble sentiments expressed in the verses make the duchess and Lady Hyacinth certain that the record can be a mighty weapon in awakening the American Negro to a sense of his duty. In order to aid the duchess in a work with which I have not the slightest sympathy, I have just donated one hundred of these records to the cause. The duchess contemplates sending them to all the centers where there are branches of the Back-to-Africa movement. I've brought along one for you to listen to."

They had to crowd close to the victrola in order to hear; for near by Mrs. Vanderbilt-Jones and Agatha Winston, a sleek, *café-au-lait* soubrette, who had just returned from eighteen months of European triumphs, were having a shouting bout. Agatha had gone to London over three years past with a sepia-colored musical comedy which had not caused a conflagration on the Thames. The sponsor of the engagement had paid the actors a tithe of the wages promised them, and then had left them to scuttle for themselves. And they had scuttled in dreary, dejected bands of three and four, some back to America, others across Europe as far as Russia, improvising as they went. An egotistic streak had caused Agatha to shun all offers of partnership, and to shift for herself. She had worked her way to Paris, where a slight ability to sing and dance, the knack of crossing her eyes, and of twisting her limbs out of joint, while attired in the minimum amount of clothes permitted by the French penal code, had soon made her the darling of France. She was now back in America for a brief visit to Harlem, intent on dazzling a world too immersed in having a good time to be more than faintly amused by a French maid, the display of divers gifts from infatuated European royalty, and the consciousness that it all emanated from a talent which could be duplicated and eclipsed in any Harlem pleasure cave.

"An Earl with a coat of mail and everything, and I turned him down." Agatha's voice soared in strident self-approval over the soft preparatory grating of the needle.

"And to think you could have been an earless, the first colored earless in the world, a stepping-stone for the race," Mrs. Vanderbilt-Jones shouted back her disapproval, and clucked her tongue.

Clustered around the victrola, Constancia, the duchess, Lady Hyacinth, and Donald formed a trembling and excited group which was soon augmented by Lottie Smith, who, never having been to Europe, couldn't abide Agatha's airs. As the first bars of the rich mongrel music, in which notes of Africa, Harlem, and the Orient could be traced, flooded the room, Lottie rolled her eyes upward in an ecstatic convulsion and snapped her fingers rhythmically, while the duchess stood with bowed and pensive head, as if the strains of a Negro "Marseillaise" were causing her ample bosom to seethe and stir with patriotism. In gusty Jamaican pride the voice of the singer heralded the exploits of Lieutenant Julian:

> At last, at last, it has come to pass,
> *Hélas, hélas!* Lieutenant Julian will fly at last,
> Lindbergh flew over the sea,
> Chamberlin flew to Germany,
> Julian said Paris or eternity.

The chorus with which this melodic eulogy opened set the keynote of racial pride and hope which was to run through the amazing verses:

> Negroes everywhere,
> Negroes in this hemisphere,
> Come, come in a crowd,
> Come let us all be proud,

When he conquers the wave and air,
In his glory we are going to share.
He said Paris or eternity.

White men have no fear,
White men have conquered the air,
Julian with him will compare,
About his life he has no fear,
Why should we not do what we can
To help this brave colored man.
He said Paris or eternity.

"They simply *cannot* love like *colored* men," Agatha's indecent and compromising avowal shocked in midair with the termination of the panegyric on Lieutenant Julian.

The duchess heaved a mammoth sigh, and wiped away a pearly tear as the last heroic strains died off.

"What do you think of it?" she asked Constancia, who had not yet recovered.

"Very soulful, Duchess," Constancia assured her.

"And its possibilities?" persisted the duchess.

"Limitless," conceded Constancia.

"I love the change from alas to *hélas* in the chorus," said Lady Hyacinth, dreamily. "I don't know why, but it gives me a catch in my throat, probably because it's so foreign and unexpected."

"I don't think it's so hot as sense," confessed Lottie, bluntly, "but the music would make a grand stomp; it's so aboriginal."

"I am going to use it on the lecture platform," said the duchess, "as I go from city to city addressing our branches. It will inspire thousands to a sense of the possibilities inherent in the simplest black man. I do wish, however, that he had said *Africa* or eternity instead of *Paris*. That would be so much more effective for my purpose."

"Lottie," urged Constancia, anxious to sidetrack the duchess from her favorite topic of African redemption, "won't you sing something for us, the 'St. Louis Blues,' perhaps?"

"There's nobody to play for me," demurred Lottie, "or I would. Stanley's not here yet."

"You might sing *a capella*," suggested Constancia.

"I'm sorry, Constancia," said Lottie. "You know you never have to beg me, but I don't know 'A Capella' and there's nobody to play it, if I did. Maybe the duchess will recite. I love to hear her do that piece where she goes mad and talks so crazy."

"I suppose she means Ophelia," said the duchess, haughtily, ignoring Lottie and addressing herself to Constancia.

"Yes," confessed Lottie, unabashed, "that's the one. I think it's *simply* a scream."

"I assure you that it wasn't written as a scream, Miss Smith"—the duchess' dark eyes were charged with enough indignation and disgust to annihilate a less imperturbable soul than Lottie.

"Have it your own way, Duchess," Lottie retorted, "but it's a scream to me."

The duchess did not stoop to further argument, fearful lest an extended discussion rob her of this opportunity to shine.

"I don't feel very Shakespearian tonight," she confided to Constancia. "I feel martial. I feel the urge to recount the heroic doings of my people. I could do either 'Black Samson of Brandywine' or 'The Black Regiment.' Which shall it be?"

"Why not do both, Duchess?" asked Donald, gallantly.

"You dear greedy boy, I will," the duchess conceded as she tousled his hair and inwardly thanked him from the bottom of her heart for affording her an excuse to render both recitations. "I shall start with 'The Black Regiment.' But I must have silence."

She stepped to the center of the floor, where, after bowing profoundly, she stood in meditative and dignified reproval until all the diminutive whispers, sudden coughs, and epileptic squirmings had ceased.

O black heroic regiment whose bravery has been recounted so nobly by the poet Boker, your immortality is assured so long as there remains a Negro elocutionist to chant your glory! From your dust may flowers rise as garlands for the head of the duchess and all her kind! Well might Ethiopia's estranged children, captives in a hostile land, let roll down their gay painted cheeks, a few furtive tears, as the duchess, trembling with pride and devotion, unleashed that divine voice:

> Dark as the clouds of even,
> Banked in the western heaven,
> Waiting the breath that lifts
> All the dread mass, and drifts

Tempest and falling brand,
Over a ruined land—
So still and orderly
Arm to arm, and knee to knee
Waiting the great event,
Stands the Black Regiment.

Down the long dusky line
Teeth gleam and eyeballs shine;
And the bright bayonet,
Bristling and firmly set,
Flashed with a purpose grand
Long ere the sharp command
Of the fierce rolling drum
Told them their time had come
Told them what work was sent
For the Black Regiment.

There was no need for Donald to veil his eyes now. The duchess was in her element. As if the ghostly regiment stood behind her listening in serried ranks of impalpability to the recital of their bravery, her voice now soft and tender, now rich with frenzy, now high and courageous as if in the midst of battle, swept everything before her. Listening to her, her auditors felt that there was nothing in heaven and hell which their race might not surmount, and even Constancia felt a hard unfamiliar tightening of the throat. And then that opulent petition to which the lords of the land would never open their ears brought the poem to its close:

Hundreds on hundreds fell;
But they are resting well;
Scourges and shackles strong
Never shall do them wrong.
Oh! to the living few,
Soldiers, be just and true!
Hail them as comrades tried;
Fight with them side by side;
Never in field or tent
Scorn the Black Regiment!

By all that is fine and touching there should have been no applause, there should have been nothing but dark bowed heads, their obeisance hiding proud, glistening eyes. And for a full minute the duchess should have stood there, Ethiopia eloquent, stretching forth her hands for justice and equity in exchange for courage and proven fidelity.

And then while the rumor of great and mighty actions was still with them, while the ghosts of the Black Regiment were yet there, suffused with the memory of their mortal greatness, the duchess should have evoked the towering majesty of "Black Samson of Brandywine," that fierce black scythe of destruction whom a black poet has sung and whom black declaimers kept alive.

But, alas for the serene and somber Spirit which hopes to reign supreme and tranquil at a Negro gathering. Shut laughter and raillery out; with cotton in every crevice and keyhole bid them begone, yet will they filter their way back through the shaft of light that steals in under the lowered window-shade!

Even as the duchess, sensing the dramatic opportunities of the moment, made the transition from regiment to lone soldier, cleared her throat, and introduced, "Black Samson of Brandywine"—at that moment even, he who in a bright green uniform with gold epaulettes had made his dizzy way from glass to glass through a maze of streets to Constancia's home, stood beautifully balancing himself in the doorway. The gold buttons flashed their radiance into the room, and mingled their fire with the amber, unclouded enchantment in Constancia's eyes. Like a lioness defending her young, the duchess turned with open mouth and outraged countenance to confront the intruder, while Lottie Smith rose from her chair, shrieking, "It must be Black Samson himself!"

"No," disagreed the enchanted Constancia, as with one hand she supported the tottering duchess, while with the other she beckoned Sam to abandon his perilous perch on the threshold, for a place among the company, "it's only the Emperor Jones!"

Later, as they walked home through the fine Harlem twilight, Mattie rebuked Sam for having endangered her position by his precipitate and unsolicited entrance into her mistress' home; but in her purse was a crisp new bill of generous denomination and in her ears still echoed the laughter with which Constancia had said: "The duchess and Sam made my *soirée*. As I refuse to donate to the Back-to-Africa movement, I am giving this to Sam. And don't scold him."

1950–1980

THE PROTEST ERA

"I dream of your freedom/as my victory..."

Late in the life of James Baldwin, a television journalist queried the author about his early decision to write as an openly gay African American novelist. "You were black, impoverished, and homosexual," the interviewer began. "You must have said to yourself, 'Gee, how disadvantaged can I get?'" Baldwin answered, "No, I thought I hit the jackpot. It was so outrageous you could not go any further. You had to find a way to use it." [1]

THE POSTWAR YEARS MARKED THE BEGINNINGS OF AN ERA OF activism that would irrevocably shape black lesbian and gay writing and thought. Nowhere was this movement for civil rights more readily visible to the world than among African Americans. One of the first events to shake the foundation of American race relations was the *Brown v. Board of Education* decision. "Separate but equal" treatment, the Supreme Court declared in that historic 1954 ruling, "generates a feeling of inferiority...[and] has no place [in American society]." [2] Although the *Brown* decision went largely unenforced for many years—and some would say it has remained unenforced up to this day—the decision nevertheless presented civil rights activists with the legal grounds to gain recourse against racial discrimination in other public arenas, including accommodations and transportation. Moreover, the *Brown* decision sent a message to the world that American democracy was not, with respect to race, a complete failure. This message was important given that America was attempting to "contain" communism and promote democracy in Asia, Africa, and Latin America. Indeed, the media throughout the United States and around the world celebrated *Brown* as a "blow to communism."[3]

But only one year later, when Rosa Parks was arrested on a city bus for protesting segregation ordinances in 1955, it became clear that *Brown*'s "blow" to racism was going to be limited. At the time, Dr. Martin Luther King, Jr., was just twenty-five years old and newly installed as minister of Dexter Avenue Baptist Church in Montgomery, Alabama. Under King's leadership more than 42,000 African Americans boycotted Montgomery's buses for thirteen months, until the Supreme Court in December 1956 outlawed restricted seating not only in Montgomery but throughout the United States. The victory, however, was hardly King's alone. "Much credit has been given publicly to the Rev. Martin Luther King, the Negro leader, and he deserves credit indeed," remarked one of King's advisors. "But success was achieved by a revolt of the people. In particular, the women of Montgomery have made this possible."[4] Jo Ann Robinson, president of the local Women's Political Council (WPC), had written to the mayor in 1954, threatening a citywide boycott of buses by more than two dozen local organizations if segregation in the public transit system was not reformed at least to the extent that blacks would be allowed to take unoccupied seats in the front of buses. Furthermore, the WPC, nine months prior to the arrest of Parks, had chosen its own test litigant, fifteen-year-old Claudette Colvin, who had been taken into custody by police for refusing to give up her bus seat in March 1955. "We had planned the protest long before Mrs. Parks was arrested," Robinson recalled. "There had been so many things that happened, that the black women had been embarrassed over, and they were ready to explode."[5] Support for Colvin vanished, however, when organizers learned that the unmarried high school student was pregnant and therefore lacking what Robinson described as "the caliber of character" needed to galvanize the city around a boycott.[6]

The question of who would represent African Americans in protest was hotly contested from the beginning of the postwar movement. Ella Baker, a veteran activist of social reform and executive director of the Southern Christian Leadership Conference (SCLC), struggled with King over leadership of the movement. Founded in 1957 as an assembly of ministers, the SCLC sought to build on the momentum in Montgomery with a wider, southern-based plan of action. With King as its president the organization strove to "redeem the soul of America" through nonviolent resistance. But King often disregarded Baker's input on important matters, and strained relations are evident in Baker's remark "Martin did not make the movement; the movement made Martin."[7] Despite her executive position and notwithstanding the role she played as a founding member of SCLC, Baker's gender for all practical purposes disqualified her as a civil rights leader. "[T]hose men didn't have any faith in women, none whatsoever," wrote SCLC director of education Septima Clark.[8] As a woman, Baker could never be what Hazel Carby referred to as a "race man."[9]

Disenchanted by the politics of SCLC, Baker resigned from SCLC and helped form the Student Nonviolent Coordinating Committee (SNCC) in 1960. Composed of organizers from the lunch counter sit-ins that had begun in Greensboro, North Carolina, that same year, SNCC combined nonviolent opposition to racial discrimination with a class analysis that had been historically absent from most establishment protest groups. Originally, King had hoped that SNCC would serve as the youth division of SCLC, but Baker vociferously opposed a formal political relationship between the two groups, whereupon King abandoned the idea. For Baker had envisioned a "group-centered" leadership that would challenge not only white racism but also the gender politics of conventional protest organizations. "I don't think you could go through the Freedom Movement without finding that the backbone of the support of the Movement were women," she observed in 1969. "When demonstrations took place and when the community acted, usually it was some woman who came to the fore."[10]

Homosexuality proved fully as controversial as gender politics in the postwar movement. In 1942, some fifteen years before SCLC was formed, Bayard Rustin helped found the Congress of Racial Equality (CORE), a pacifist organization that pioneered Gandhian tactics of nonviolence in U.S. race relations. Although Rustin's homosexuality was widely known among activists, his 1953 arrest on "morals charges," stemming from sex with two men in a parked car, effectively "outed" him to the larger American public. News reports linked Rustin to CORE's parent organization, the Fellowship of Reconciliation (FOR), a religious-based group that more or less dismissed him within a week after the incident. Rustin's sexual orientation had been discussed openly in the national press before—*Jet* magazine, for example, captioned a photograph of his 1948 meeting with Indian Prime Minister Nehru with the question, "Is Homosexuality Becoming Respectable?"[11]—but never before had the issue been put so forcefully to FOR.

Two years after his controversial departure from FOR, however, Rustin was back at the center of the movement as special advisor to Montgomery's bus protest organizers. Until the boycott, King, according to Rustin, knew little about Mahatma Gandhi and did not self-identify as a pacifist. "He was still working out of the framework of Christian love. I believe he soon came to see what I had recognized while working with Gandhi's movement in India—that you ought not to separate the secular from the religious."[12] Rustin at the time was among the leading American authorities on nonviolent direct action, and soon it became the centerpiece of King's ideology.

Nevertheless, Rustin's sexual orientation remained a source of friction in spite of his influence on civil rights activism, or perhaps because of it. In 1960, for example, the black Democratic Congressman Adam Clayton Powell of New York threatened to report to the press a fabricated homosexual coupling of Rustin and King unless the minister canceled his plans for a demonstration at the Democratic national convention. Rather than stand firm against this groundless charge, King acquiesced, advising Rustin to sever all relations with SCLC. Among the activists most shocked by King's capitulation was novelist James Baldwin, who wrote that King had "lost much moral credit...in the eyes of the young, when he allowed Adam Clayton Powell to force the resignation of his extremely able organizer and lieutenant...."[13]

Rustin's appointment to lead the 1963 March on Washington was equally contentious. Roy Wilkins, the NAACP's leader and one of the key march strategists, argued that civil rights opponents might seize on Rustin's homosexuality and his brief affiliation with the Communist Party in the 1930s to discredit both the march and its supporters. Despite Wilkins's protestations and the upheaval they engendered,

King, along with a majority of the leaders of the march, supported
Rustin. "[King] looked on every human being as a child of God," Rustin
later explained. "He had absolute respect for individuals and individual
differences. He felt they should all be treated equally." King's ecumeni-
cal approach to human diversity, Rustin pointed out, "never diminished
his considerable affection for the Gay people on his staff, and certainly
not myself."[14]

Accordingly, King—now backed by labor leader A. Philip
Randolph, the pioneering elder statesman of the movement, and
SNCC's John Lewis—supported Rustin's appointment, with Wilkins
agreeing to allow Rustin to lead the march under the diminished title of
deputy director. Still, the announcement that Rustin would assume this
leadership position did not go unnoticed. Strom Thurmond, the segregationist senator from South Carolina who would later oppose the
nomination of Thurgood Marshall, the first black Supreme Court justice, jeopardized Rustin's already vulnerable authority by denouncing
him as a sexual degenerate from the Senate floor just days prior to the
event. This, of course, was precisely the sort of controversy Wilkins had
feared. But, in a political about-face, the NAACP director championed
Rustin. "We have found in the past six weeks that he is a man of exceptional ability, who has delivered an extraordinary project that should
have required a full three months but is being completed in two,"
Wilkins answered in Rustin's defense.[15] In the end the march proved to
be the largest public demonstration for civil rights in U.S. history, contributing to the passage of both the landmark Civil Rights Act of 1964
and the Voter's Rights Act in the following year.

Not all African Americans, however, applauded the march.
Malcolm X, the firebrand Black Muslim minister who publicly ridiculed
"the farce on Washington," signaled the impending tactical shift among
black activists by the mid-1960s. "Revolutions are never based upon love-
your-enemy-and-pray-for-those-who-despitefully-use-you. And revolutions
are never waged singing 'We shall overcome.' Revolutions are based on
bloodshed."[16] White liberals and the civil rights establishment had
repeatedly betrayed the trust of time-worn nonviolent demonstrators
like SNCC chairman Stokely Carmichael, who drew on Malcolm X's
teachings to espouse "Black Power" beginning in 1966. At this juncture,
when African Americans began to separate themselves from whites,
women activists began speaking out on sexism in the civil rights struggle.

Mary King and Casey Hayden, two white SNCC staff members, wrote a 1964 position paper, "Women in the Movement," which was distributed anonymously among organizers. They argued, among other things, the following:

> The average SNCC worker finds it difficult to discuss the woman problem because of the assumptions of male superiority...[which] are as widespread and deep-rooted and [every bit as]...crippling to the woman as the assumptions of white supremacy are to the Negro.... [SNCC] should force the rest of the movement to stop the discrimination and start the slow process of changing values and ideas so that all of us gradually come to understand that this is no more a man's world than it is a white world.[17]

Although SNCC executive secretary James Forman recognized that "subtle and blatant forms of discrimination against women" existed both inside and outside the organization, Carmichael dismissed the authors' complaint as a diversion by white women who believed Black Power would politically displace them.[18] Carmichael's response might help to explain why, according to Paula Giddings, African American women did not rise en masse with white women against sexism. While Giddings did not deny the existence of black male chauvinism, she argued that African American women did not perceive sexual discrimination—at least within the black civil rights movement generally and SNCC in particular—to be nearly as damaging as white women claimed. Presumably, part of what informed that perspective was the fact that black women members such as Donna Richards Moses, Diane Nash, and Ruby Doris Smith were involved in SNCC's decision-making processes. And more generally, "The influence of *Black* women was actually increasing at the time; it was *White* women who were being relegated to minor responsibilities..."[19] (emphasis added). Because this political relegation was race-specific, many black women simply did not perceive it to be about gender per se.

As white women activists joined predominantly white organizations like Students for a Democratic Society (SDS) and the burgeoning women's movement, the Black Panther Party offered African American women a revolutionary alternative to the reform-oriented protest tradition.

The Party welcomed progressive whites as political allies, thereby appealing to both black women and black men who were interested in racially inclusive forms of black liberation. Founded in 1966 by Huey P. Newton and Bobby Seale, the Black Panther Party initially was an armed self-defense force whose ten-point platform called for full employment, housing, education, and an end to police brutality, among other demands. Almost from the Party's inception, women members, including Elaine Brown, Kathleen Cleaver, and Ericka Huggins, held leadership roles, with Brown chairing the Party during the mid-1970s. Lesbians and gay men also served the organization, sometimes openly and occasionally in positions of national authority. "There were gay operatives in the Black Panther Party working at the highest levels of leadership," remarked Black Panther Party founding member and former chief of staff David Hilliard. "Lesbian relationships were more acceptable in the Party than homosexual relations between men. But the uneasiness over gay men was expressed primarily by men, most of whom were insecure with their own sexuality. Still, no one ever asked you to define your sexual orientation. We didn't divide ourselves like that. First and foremost you were a Black Panther."[20]

An enduring point of controversy remains the inflammatory rhetoric of Eldridge Cleaver, Black Panther Party minister of information, whose best-selling *Soul on Ice* (1968) likens homosexuality to "a sickness" and chronicles the author's past exploits "practicing" rape on African American women until he became "smooth enough" to assault "white prey."[21] Cleaver's politics of gender and sexual orientation was extreme, yet his chauvinism did not go unchecked. Writing in a 1970 essay "The Women's Liberation and Gay Liberation Movements," Black Panther leader Huey P. Newton laid out the Party's political platform with regard to sex and gender in unequivocally inclusive terms. "We must understand [homosexuality] in its purest form…. That is, a person should have the freedom to use his body in whatever way he wants. Whatever your personal opinions and your insecurities about homosexuality and the various liberation movements among homosexuals and women (and I speak of the homosexuals and women as oppressed groups), we should try to unite with them in a revolutionary fashion."[22] Never before had a black civil rights group recognized lesbians and gay men as an oppressed population (perhaps "the most oppressed people in the society," according to Newton) facing a struggle for acceptance and equality comparable to that of African Americans. For the first time in the movement's history, blacks sought political coalitions with gay activists based on their similar oppression.

Issues of sexual identity complicated relations within the emerging women's movement as well, just as gender and sexual orientation had proved controversial in the civil rights and black liberation movements. Consider, for example, the National Organization for Women (NOW), whose initial response to lesbianism was at best cautious and at worst unabashedly hostile. NOW was founded in 1966 by twenty-nine women, including feminist pioneer Betty Friedan, as the first postwar feminist organization to advocate women's rights on a national scale. Its corner-stone "Bill of Rights for Women" demanded passage of the Equal Rights Amendment to the U.S. Constitution, enforcement of Title VII (pro-hibiting both sexual and racial discrimination), and equal education and employment opportunities for women. NOW's focus on women's rights, as opposed to women's liberation, however, signaled its primary difference from radical feminist groups emerging at that time. As Susan Brownmiller put it, "At its inception the women's movement appeared to have two distinct wings—the reformers of NOW and the radicals of Women's Liberation."[23] These two wings differed not only in ideological orientation but also in the nature of their political action. While the reformers of NOW preferred traditional forms of protest (litigation and political lobbying, for instance), radical feminists were far more confrontational. Women's Liberation brought to the attention of the American public antiviolence issues such as rape and sexual harassment, while insisting that lesbian issues be incorporated into the broader goals of the feminist movement.

Friedan and like-minded feminists felt concern that a radical femi-nist agenda would discredit the women's movement. (This, of course, parallels the respectability concerns of black leaders at the turn of the twentieth century.) Friedan called lesbians "the lavender menace" of feminism, a remarkable statement given that relatively few lesbians in the movement openly identified as such. In the words of Karla Jay,

> It was one thing to hang out in a bar where everyone simply assumed similar sexual proclivities.... It was quite another to announce one's lesbianism and then demand it take center

stage in a room full of straight feminists who were likely to be heterosexists...and who had just issued an ultimatum to keep on sleeping with men as part of a program to mend the oppressors' ways.[24]

Nevertheless, antilesbianism in the women's movement was confronted head-on in May 1970 after NOW omitted the Daughters of Bilitis from its list of sponsors of the Second Congress to Unite Women. On the first evening of the congress, several hundred women sat waiting for a panel to begin when the lights suddenly went out. When they were switched back on, seventeen women dressed in T-shirts emblazoned with the words "Lavender Menace" lined the auditorium aisles to address homosexuality in the women's movement. By the end of the demonstration, more than thirty women from the audience had joined protesters on stage as the first post-Stonewall group to focus on lesbian issues.

From this gathering the Lavender Menace—or Radicalesbians, as the group was renamed—presented a statement to the closing session of the congress, which read:

1. Be it resolved that the Women's Liberation Movement is a Lesbian plot.
2. Resolved that whenever the label "Lesbian" is used against the movement collectively, or against women individually, it is to be affirmed, not denied.
3. In all discussions of birth control, homosexuality must be included as a legitimate form of contraception.
4. All sex education curricula must include Lesbianism as a valid, legitimate form of sexual expression and love.[25]

The Lavender Menace produced a manifesto, "The Woman-Identified Woman," which defined lesbianism as "the rage of all women condensed to the point of explosion."[26] The more fundamental purpose of the manifesto was to convey the idea that "Homosexuality is a by-product of a particular way of setting up roles (or approved patterns of behavior) on the basis of sex; as such it is an inauthentic (not consistant with 'reality') category. In a society in which men do not oppress women, and sexual expression is allowed to follow feelings, the categories of homosexuality and heterosexuality would disappear."[27] After continuous pressure,

NOW passed a resolution in 1971 acknowledging "the oppression of lesbians as a legitimate concern of feminism."[28]

If Betty Friedan's work defined early feminist discourse, Kate Millet's groundbreaking *Sexual Politics* (1970) advanced the movement toward a more fundamental understanding of the inherently political nature of sexual relations between men and women. Since all societies are patriarchies, Millet asserted, so-called "masculine" and "feminine" traits cannot be attributed to human nature. According to her, "the enormous area of our lives, both in early 'socialization' and in adult experience, labeled 'sexual behavior,' is almost entirely the product of learning." For Millet, "even the act of coitus itself is the product of a long series of learned responses...to the patterns and attitudes, even as to the object of sexual choice, which are set up for us by our social environment."[29] Adrienne Rich's essay "Compulsory Heterosexuality and Lesbian Existence" (1978), which demonstrated how heterosexuality oppresses all women, furthered Millet's insights by dissecting the politics of sexual orientation. Rich conceived of heterosexuality, like other disciplinary aspects of identity (such as motherhood), as a "political institution." She put the point this way:

> When we look hard and clearly at the extent and elaboration of measures designed to keep women within a male sexual purlieu, it becomes an inescapable question whether the issue feminists have to address is not simple "gender inequality" nor the domination of culture by males nor mere "taboos against homosexuality," but the enforcement of heterosexuality for women as a means of assuring male right of physical, economic, and emotional access.[30]

For Rich, women, regardless of their sexual orientation, could benefit from the liberating potential of understanding what she called "lesbian existence" ("the fact of the historical presence of lesbians and our continuing creation of the meaning of that existence") and the "lesbian continuum" ("a range—through each woman's life and throughout history—of woman-identified experience, not simply the fact that a woman has had genital sexual experience with another woman").[31]

Race matters were just as divisive among feminists. Toni Morrison, writing in the *New York Times* in 1971, spoke of the overwhelming distrust black women felt toward the women's movement. "It is white, therefore suspect," she observed in "What the Black Woman Thinks." According to Morrison, "In spite of the fact that liberating movements in the black world have been catalysts for white feminism, too many movements and organizations have made deliberate overtures to enroll blacks and have ended up by rolling over them."[32] The establishment of the National Black Feminist Organization (NBFO) thus marked a turning point in the history of feminism. The organization emerged out of a meeting of some thirty African American feminists in 1973. In its Statement of Purpose, NBFO announced:

> Black women have suffered cruelly in this society from living the phenomenon of being both black and female, in a country that is both racist and sexist.... We must, together, as a people, work to eliminate racism, from without the black community, which is trying to destroy us as an entire people; but we must remember that sexism is destroying and crippling us from within.[33]

When, in 1974, several members of the Boston chapter of NBFO felt that the larger organization was not adequately concerned with issues relevant to disenfranchised populations of African American women, they established The Combahee River Collective (CRC). "The most general statement of our politics at the present time," wrote Barbara Smith, Demita Frazier, and Beverly Smith in the Collective's "Black Feminist Statement," "would be that we are actively committed to struggling against racial, sexual, heterosexual, and class oppression." This struggle required that black feminists develop an "integrated analysis and practice based upon the fact that the major systems are interlocking.... As black women we see black feminism as the logical political movement to combat the manifold and simultaneous oppressions that all women of color face."[34]

Black feminism was truly a departure not only from traditional white feminism but also from a lesbian feminism that advocated "dyke separatism" from the women's and gay male movements. The CRC, for example, built coalitions with women of all races and sexual orientations, as well as with African American men. Its mission statement made it clear that "Although we are feminists and lesbians, we feel solidarity with progressive black men and do not advocate the fractionalization that white women who are separatists demand.... We struggle with black men against racism, while we struggle with black men about sexism."[35]

With the advent of modern black feminism, African American women had begun to draw correlations between the black civil rights struggle and women's liberation. As with the women's movement, black feminists looked to black women writers for political leadership. Toni Cade Bambara, writing in *The Black Woman* (1970), likened the atmosphere of the period to an embrace: "a hardheaded attempt to get basic with each other."[36] Although she made no mention of lesbianism in her book, *The Black Woman* broke new ground by becoming the first collection of African American feminist thought. Among the anthology's important contributions was Bambara's own inquiry into the authenticity of feminist protest literature. Citing the works of Anaïs Nin, Simone de Beauvoir, Doris Lessing, and Betty Friedan, she remarks, "The question for us arises: how relevant are the truths, the experiences, the findings of white women to Black women? Are women after all simply women?"[37] Friedan's best-selling work *The Feminine Mystique* (1963), which has been described as the genesis for the new women's movement, argued that traditional gender expectations limited women to "careers" as housewives and mothers. The book was soundly criticized for its shortcomings, including its white middle-class orientation. As bell hooks explained,

> Specific problems and dilemmas of leisure-class housewives were real concerns that merited consideration and change but they were not the pressing concerns of masses of women. Masses of women were concerned about economic survival, ethnic and racial discrimination. Although many women longed to be housewives, only women with leisure time and money could actually shape their identities on the model of the feminine mystique.[38]

Hook's suggestion, with which many black feminists agree, was that *The Feminine Mystique* was written for white, middle- and upper-class heterosexual women.

In her influential essay "Toward a Black Feminist Criticism" (1977), Barbara Smith called for a truly inclusive black feminist movement, citing the "near nonexistence" of black lesbian writing and the struggles of African American women authors in general. For Smith, then, there existed a nexus between the literary production of black lesbian work and the political goals of black feminism: "A viable, autonomous Black feminist movement in this country would open up the space needed for the exploration of Black women's lives and the creation of consciously Black woman-identified art."[39] This, Smith reasoned, is precisely what white feminism managed to achieve for white women's literature. Thus, while white women's experiences—including, to some extent, the experiences of white lesbians—were appearing in literature with increasing visibility during the 1970s, the experiences of black women, and especially black lesbians, were largely invisible and untold. "I finally want to express how much easier both my waking and sleeping hours would be if there were one book in existence that would tell me something specific about my life," Smith concluded. "One book based in Black feminist and Black lesbian experience, fiction or nonfiction. Just one work to reflect the reality that I and the Black women whom I love are trying to create."[40]

The modern lesbian, gay, and bisexual liberation movement began with a street rebellion against police harassment at the Stonewall Inn bar in New York City in 1969. Street chaos quickly turned to organizing, as gay people attempted to build a movement from the outburst. Leading the postriot talks was the Mattachine Society, an important political player in the so-called "homophile movement." Formed in 1950 as a predominantly white male, middle-class organization, Mattachine challenged the popular interpretation of homosexuality as a mental illness, insisting instead that lesbians and gay men are a legitimate minority group:

> The Mattachine Society holds it possible and desirable that a highly ethical homosexual culture emerge, as a result of its work, paralleling the emerging cultures of our fellow minorities... the Negro, Mexican, and Jewish Peoples. The Society believes homosexuals can lead well-adjusted lives once ignorance, and prejudice, against them is successfully combated, and once homosexuals themselves feel they have a dignified and useful role to play in society.[41]

Under the leadership of Harry Hay, the club drew on aspects of radical left politics to battle police entrapment and other forms of persecution directed at gay men.

Daughters of Bilitis (DOB) was founded in 1955 as the first lesbian organization in the United States. Although DOB shared the Mattachine's purpose of "improving the image" of homosexuals—and in fact attempted to work cooperatively with the Society—some male Mattachine members viewed DOB as a separatist and politically divisive organization. Many members of DOB, by contrast, believed that Mattachine had made no meaningful effort to understand the nexus between gender and sexual orientation for women. As DOB cofounder Del Martin demanded to know from an assembly of Mattachine members, "What do you men know about Lesbians?"[42]

Few African Americans were visible within the early homophile movement; fewer still held positions of leadership. Ernestine Eckstein, who served as a DOB chapter vice president, was one of the few African Americans lesbians in DOB. Speaking in "Interview with Ernestine," an article published in the June 1966 issue of *The Ladder*, a DOB publication, she commented, "I feel the homophile movement is more open to Negroes than, say, a lot of churches…. Unfortunately, I find there are very few Negroes in the homophile movement. I keep looking for them, but they're not there. Why not?" Eckstein herself provided a partial answer: "Negroes are not now at the stage where they can begin to explore."[43]

Prior to entering both Mattachine and DOB in 1963, Eckstein, a former activist with the NAACP and CORE, had never heard the word *homosexual*, much less identified her sexual attraction to women as *lesbianism*. She was the only African American to participate in the historic 1965 Washington, D.C., protest in which lesbian and gay demonstrators carried placards outside the White House calling for an end to federal employment discrimination. Asked whether she had found correlations between the homophile movement and the black civil rights struggle, Eckstein replied,

> There's only a very rough parallel. Generally, NAACP is the most conservative of all civil rights groups. And some homophile groups are the same, with the same sort of predisposition to take things easy, not to push too fast, not stick their

necks out too far…. I think in the homophile movement, some segments will have to be so vocal and so progressive, until they eventually push the ultra-conservative segments into a more progressive line of thinking and action.[44]

Sharing Eckstein's isolation from other African American lesbians was Audre Lorde, whose *Zami: A New Spelling of My Name* (1982) chronicled her experiences in New York's lesbian enclaves during the 1950s. Writing in retrospect, Lorde offered a complicated analysis of intraracial tensions among black lesbians of the period that spoke to the dangers of being both black and openly homosexual in the Cold War years. "Sometimes we'd pass Black women on Eighth Street—*the invisible but visible sisters*…and our glances might cross, but we never looked into each other's eyes," Lorde recalls. "We acknowledged our kinship by passing in silence, looking the other way. Still, we were always on the lookout…for the telltale flick of the eye, that certain otherwise prohibited openness of expression, that definiteness of voice which would suggest, I think she's gay."[45] The few identifiably homosexual black women whom Lorde encountered in Greenwich Village shared little by way of community, seeming instead to understand that their rarity enhanced their value in lesbian circles. If the 1950s was an especially lonely time for black lesbians, the isolation toughened those strong enough to withstand the intense cultural repression. "In a paradoxical sense, once I accepted my position as different from the larger society as well as from any single sub-society—Black or gay—I felt I didn't have to try so hard. To be accepted. To look femme. To be straight. To look straight. To be proper. To look 'nice.' To be liked. To be loved. To be approved," Lorde wrote. "What I didn't realize was how much harder I had to try merely to stay alive, or rather, to stay human. How much stronger a person I became in that trying."[46]

Although the early homophile organizations provided a much-needed social space for gay men and lesbians, the moderate political platforms of the Mattachine Society and DOB soon fell out of step with the counterculture politics of the Stonewall generation. Stonewall politics, after all, had not emerged out of a political vacuum. The new gay liberation movement reflected the broader social movements of the time—black civil rights groups, the New Left, the antiwar movement, and feminism. Among the most vocal groups to emerge in 1969 was the

Gay Liberation Front (GLF). This radical organization embraced multi-issue politics that broke with the gay civil rights agenda of pursuing equality on narrow, identity-based terms. "We are a revolutionary group of men and women, formed with the realization that complete sexual liberation for all people cannot come about unless existing social institutions are abolished," the group proclaimed. "We reject society's attempt to impose sexual roles and definitions of our nature."[47] From the outset, GLF made it clear that while it was interested in contesting sex roles, it would also work in coalitions with groups fighting oppression based on class and race.

Whether gays and lesbians would unite with nongay groups was a point of contention in the fledgling lesbian and gay movement. No sooner had GLF established its voice in the community than a number of disgruntled members, favoring a return to gay-centered politics, departed to start the Gay Activists Alliance (GAA), a militant, direct-action organization solely dedicated to gay concerns, in December 1969. While the single-issue focus helped force politicians to address homosexual rights for the first time, this narrow approach had alienating consequences as well. Lesbians and gay men of color often felt particularly marginalized within these largely white organizations, as did lesbians in general whose complaints of sexism went unaddressed. "Black women didn't have the time for Gay Activists Alliance. We didn't have time to sit on the fence while our people were dying," remarked Candice Boyce. "To be a white male in America and realize your gayness and find out that you're oppressed is a very different thing than being oppressed all your life as a woman of color."[48]

Lesbians began splitting away from gay groups to form their own organizations. Lesbian separatism thus became popular among "women-identified-women," who believed that only by severing relations with all men, and in some instances with heterosexual women too, could lesbians transcend patriarchal oppression. Radical groups like the Furies argued that lesbianism was "the greatest threat that exists to male supremacy." In her essay "The Shape of Things to Come," Furies cofounder Rita Mae Brown wrote in 1972, "If women still give primary commitment and energy to the oppressors how can we build a strong movement to free ourselves?... Are Blacks supposed to disperse their communities and each live in a white home?... Only if women give their time to women, to a woman's movement, will they be free. You do not free yourself by polishing your chains, yet that is what heterosexual women do...."[49] Jill Johnston even foresaw an independent Lesbian Nation. Just as black nationalists failed to include homosexuality in their political vision, however, white lesbian separatists overlooked racial concerns. As Margaret Sloan observed, "I can't call you my sister until you stop participating in my oppression."[50]

By the middle-1970s African American lesbians and gay men had taken political matters into their own hands. Many fled predominantly white gay liberation and lesbian groups to address their own concerns as queer people of color. Marsha P. Johnson and Sylvia (Ray) Rivera, two street queens who had been involved in the Stonewall uprising, formed Street Transvestite Action Revolutionaries (STAR) in 1970 to address homelessness among young queers of color like themselves. Salsa Soul Sisters was founded in 1974 by the Rev. Dolores Jackson, Harriet Austin, Sonia Bailey, and Luvenia Pinson, among others. This pioneering group provided an alternative to the bar-oriented lesbian community, because "...there was no other organization that we knew of in the New York area, existing for or dealing with the serious needs of third world gay women." Its newsletter, *Third World Women's Gay-zette,* launched in 1976, was the first periodical specifically for lesbians of color. Salsa Soul Sisters later became African Ancestral Lesbians United for Societal Change, the oldest black lesbian organization in America.[51] In 1978, the National Coalition of Black Gays (NCBG) brought African American lesbian and gay issues to a national level. The NCBG (renamed the National Coalition of Black Lesbians and Gays in 1985 to recognize lesbianism explicitly) emerged as a prominent political player during the first March on Washington for Lesbian and Gay Rights, in 1979, where the organization hosted the first National Third World Lesbian and Gay Conference.

Politically moderate African American activists, on the other hand, began to establish leadership positions within traditional white gay protest vehicles. Melvin Boozer, a young, up-and-coming African American politico active in Washington, D.C., circles, came out publicly after attending the March on Washington for Lesbian and Gay Rights. Soon he was working as a lobbyist for the National Gay Task Force, a lesbian and gay civil rights advocacy group established in 1973, and he was elected the first black president of GAA. Boozer achieved historical acclaim in 1980 as a delegate to the Democratic National Convention.

There, seventy-five openly lesbian and gay delegates nominated him for vice president of the United States, the first gay person ever to receive a major party nomination. Speaking to the convention, Boozer observed, "Would you ask me how I dare to compare the civil rights struggle with the struggle for lesbian and gay rights? I know what it means to be called a nigger and I know what it means to be called a faggot, and I understand the difference, in the marrow of my bones. And I can sum up that difference in one word: nothing. Bigotry is bigotry."[52] Although he predictably stepped down in deference to the Democratic Party's nominee, Walter Mondale, Boozer's symbolic point had been made. Race and sexual orientation issues were no longer necessarily an "either/or" question for black lesbians and gay men.

While African American lesbians and gay men made political strides, the larger gay movement of the 1970s lost political momentum. True, the community had achieved an unprecedented degree of visibility after Stonewall, and for the first time ever, large numbers of lesbians and gay men came out to publicly proclaim their identities. Even among veteran activists, however, social protest seemed to have lost its urgency. Many lesbians had withdrawn from gay civil rights organizations that they saw as male dominated, while gay men lived a separatist existence of their own, frequenting all-male bars, discos, and bathhouses.

The movement was jolted from complacency, however, in 1977, when Anita Bryant, a born-again Christian entertainer, helped overturn a gay rights ordinance in Dade County, Florida. Bryant's "Save Our Children" crusade, a forerunner to the right-wing "family values" campaigns of the 1980s, operated under the slogan "Homosexuals cannot reproduce, so they must recruit."[53] Then in 1978, California State Senator John Briggs doubled the attack on gay civil liberties with Proposition 6, known as the Briggs Initiative, which sought to outlaw homosexuals from teaching positions in the state's public schools. Suddenly, lesbians and gay men nationwide were united against this renewed backlash of repression. As Candice Boyce of Salsa Soul Sisters remarked, "The homophobia of Anita Bryant was the homophobia of the country."[54] Proposition 6 was defeated with the help of San Francisco Supervisor Harvey Milk, whose 1977 election marked a major milestone when he became the first openly gay elected official in a metropolitan American city. The Dade County gay rights ordinance, by contrast, represented a belated victory many years later when it was narrowly reinstated in 1998.

Nonetheless, lesbians and gay men had at last established a formidable political front against homophobia by 1980, advancing the cause for gay rights on unequivocally queer-identified terms.

Lesbian and gay writing matured during this period as well. Beginning with the advent of pulp fiction in the 1950s, stories featuring overt lesbianism were found in mainstream outlets such as drugstores and newsstands. Although these often-lurid paperback books were frequently written by men as a voyeuristic source of arousal for other heterosexual males, pulp novels nevertheless provided lesbian readers with at least distorted visibility in midcentury fiction. "Lesbians bought these books with relish because they learned to read between the lines and get whatever nurturance they needed from them," wrote Lillian Faderman. "Where else could one find public images of women loving women?"[55] With the publication of Patricia Highsmith's *The Price of Salt* (1952), though, lesbian authors began to transform the pulp genre. Highsmith's romance novel, published under the pen name Claire Morgan, challenged conventional attitudes about sexual orientation, becoming perhaps the first lesbian book to end not with the homosexual protagonist's shame-induced suicide but instead with a hopeful future. Ann Bannon's *Odd Girl Out* (1957), the first of the author's five influential novels in the pre-Stonewall years, similarly broke through sexual stereotypes of the genre with thoughtful accounts of lesbian life. The emergence of gay liberation in the 1960s politicized the lesbian literary tradition more fully with the publication of Jane Rule's *Desert of the Heart* (1964), Isabel Miller's *A Place for Us* (1967), and Rita Mae Brown's *Rubyfruit Jungle* (1974). As Naiad Press publisher Barbara Grier remarked, "The politicizing nature of the literature, albeit exclusively fiction, can be convincingly cited as one of the catalytic agents for the women's movement."[56]

Yet African American lesbianism was conspicuously absent from the pre-Stonewall outpouring of white lesbian fiction. Ann Allen Shockley's novel *Loving Her* (1974) thus broke new ground as the first novel to feature a black lesbian protagonist. Although Shockley did not label her own sexual orientation, her writing nevertheless demonstrated a complex understanding of race, gender, and sexual orientation seldom found in African American literature or lesbian fiction up to the 1970s. Indeed, the only other novel published by a black woman writer with relatively explicit lesbian themes is Rosa Guy's young adult novel *Ruby* (1976). Presumably, Shockley recognized that her own work was both genre transcending and creating. She observed in 1979 in her provocative essay "The Black Lesbian in American Literature" that "Until recently, there has been almost nothing written by or about the Black Lesbian in American literature—a deficiency suggesting that the Black Lesbian was a nonentity in imagination as well as reality."[57] Shockley rightly links the historic absence of lesbian content in black women's literature to the widespread acceptance within the black community that race is the "strongest oppression" among African Americans. Moreover, she attributes the dearth of homosexual content in the work of black women writers to the fear of being labeled homosexual. To be sure, white women were also concerned with being labeled lesbian. Yet African Americans ran the additional risk of alienating themselves from their racial community— the very community in which they sought social and political refuge from racism. Few authors would willingly take that risk. "Black women writers live in the Black community and need the closeness of family, friends, neighbors, and co-workers who share the commonality of ethnicity in order to survive in a blatantly racist society," Shockley observed. "This need is foremost, and often supersedes the dire need for negating misconceptions and fallacies with voices of truth."[58]

Whether playwright Lorraine Hansberry left lesbian characters out of her work from fear of ostracism or simply in the interest of appealing to the same audience that had embraced her award-winning debut play, *A Raisin in the Sun* (1959), she nevertheless remained silent on the topic of lesbianism in her best-known dramas. She depicted female homosexuality in her unfinished play, *Toussaint* (1961), and she wrote about male homosexuality in *The Sign in Sidney Brustein's Window* (1964). She came out privately following her separation from her husband in 1957. Shortly after her marriage ended, she wrote two letters supporting gay liberation. "I'm glad as heck that you exist," she told the staff of *The Ladder* who printed her letters anonymously. "I feel that women, without fostering any strict separatist notions, homo or hetero, indeed have a need for their own publications and organizations." Hansberry reasoned that such outlets could create a new consciousness about discrimination against gays and lesbians: namely, "that homosexual persecution and condemnation has its roots not only in social ignorance, but a philosophically active anti-feminist dogma."[59]

Hansberry elaborated on the topic of women's liberation in her 1957 essay "Simone de Beauvoir and *The Second Sex*." Praising Beauvoir's book as possibly "the most important work of this century," she wrote, "The problem...is not that woman has strayed too far from 'her place' but that she has not yet attained it; that her emergence into liberty is, thus far, incomplete, even primitive."[60] For Hansberry, part of the goal of women's liberation was to imagine what, outside of the context of patriarchy, womanhood would mean. Precisely where and how lesbianism would figure in this reimagining is unclear. There is some suggestion, however, that Hansberry considered sexual orientation, particularly vis-à-vis a person's public celebrity, or professional identity, to be a private matter: "With regard to the writer...there are two aspects of his being: his work, which is important, and his personal life, which is really none of our business."[61]

And yet black lesbian and bisexual women of the Stonewall era made their complex identities "our business." Specifically, these writers explored their most personal experiences in groundbreaking works that explicitly addressed the intersection of homosexual persecution and feminism—and both, significantly, from an African American perspective. Audre Lorde, for one, openly challenged conventional literary representations of lesbianism and blackness with an "outsider's" perspective in her poetry collections *The First Cities* (1968), *Cabels to Rage* (1970), *From a Land Where Other People Live* (1973), *The New York Head Shop and Museum* (1974), *Coal* (1976), and *The Black Unicorn* (1978), which is often considered her masterpiece. Included in the latter work, for example, is "Woman," a candid expression of lesbian sensuality:

> I dream of a place between your breasts
> to build my house like a haven
> where I plant crops
> in your body
> an endless harvest
> where the commonest rock
> is moonstone and ebony opal
> giving milk to all my hungers
> and your night comes down upon me
> like nurturing rain.[62]

Whether she is considering overtly political themes, as with the 1977 poem "Assata," written for the imprisoned Black Panther Assata Shakur ("I dream of your freedom/as my victory/and the victory of all dark women"),[63] or the erotic rendering of lesbian love, all of Lorde's poetry is fundamentally protest writing. As she explained it, "[T]he question of social protest and art is inseparable for me.... I loved poetry and I loved words. But what was beautiful had to serve the purpose of changing my life, or I would have died. If I cannot air this pain and alter it, I will surely die of it. That's the beginning of social protest."[64]

Anita Cornwell, a pioneering black lesbian journalist whose writings were first published in periodicals such as *The Ladder* and *Negro Digest*, offered a slight departure from Lorde's observations. Writing in her foreword to Cornwell's *Black Lesbian in White America* (1983), a collection of articles and autobiographic portraits from the 1960s and '70s, author Becky Birtha explained, "Incorporated into all of her work was an acute political analysis of both racial and sexual oppressions, an analysis both radical and feminist, though the work was written long before those words were in common use together."[65] A publisher's note even claimed that Cornwell's voice was in fact the first raised among black lesbian feminists. Featured in this collection is "The Black Lesbian in a Malevolent Society" (1977), a noteworthy essay in which the author stated, "I find it difficult to imagine anyone more oppressed than the Black Lesbian in America. Perhaps that is why so many still cling so desperately to their niche in the closet even during these times of so-called sexual revolution."[66] Unlike Lorde, however, Cornwell expressed a degree of willingness to align herself politically with the predominantly white feminist movement over the black civil rights establishment, which she critiques as sexist. Indeed, notwithstanding the tensions she experienced as a black lesbian within a white, heterosexual feminist movement, Cornwell remained ideologically oriented toward feminism: "For anyone born poor Black and female in this white, middle-class, male-oriented society had damn sure better quickly learn the concepts of Feminism if she wants to survive."[67]

Joining the earliest "out" black women writers, if not one of the first openly lesbian poets, was Pat Parker. Speaking to the "inseparable struggles" of black lesbian feminism, Parker commented,

If I could take all my parts with me when I go somewhere, and
not have to say to one of them, "No, you stay home tonight,
you won't be welcome," because I'm going to an all-white
party where I can be gay, but not Black. Or I'm going to a
Black poetry reading, and half the poets are antihomosexual,
or thousands of situations where something of what I am cannot come with me. The day all the different parts of me can
come along, we would have what I would call a revolution.[68]

Beginning with the publication of *Child of Myself* (1971), followed by *Pit
Stop* (1974), *Womanslaughter* (1978), and *Jonestown and Other Madness*
(1985), Parker explored controversial elements of the African American
lesbian experience, including internalized homophobia, racist feminists, and black male chauvinism, among other politically charged
subject matter. In *Movement in Black* (1978), a volume of poems she
wrote between 1961 and 1978, for example, she mingled race and gender with humor in "For the White Person Who Wants to Know How to
Be My Friend" ("The first thing you do is to forget that i'm Black./
Second, you must never forget that i'm Black...And even if you really
believe Blacks are better/lovers than whites—don't tell me. I start think-
ing/of charging stud fees"), while a more complicated convergent
point is found in "Brother" ("Brother/i don't want to hear/about/how
my real enemy/is the system./i'm no genius,/but I do know/that sys-
tem/you hit me with/is called/your fist").[69] Commenting on the racial
salience of blackness in Parker's work, Cheryl Clarke remarked, "Pat
Parker projected her blackness to its raw vernacular core—part of the
freight for being a dyke. One's blackness must never be in question
when so much else is under attack and suspicion."[70]

In many respects, gay and lesbian life in midcentury America might perhaps be best characterized as a series of ongoing attacks and suspicions,
which quite literally equated homosexuality with criminality and psychological disorders. During the 1950s, however, a number of influential
nonfiction books had begun to help liberate gay thinking from the
closet. Among the formative works that would later impact, and to some
degree make possible, openly homosexual writings by black lesbian and
gay men was poet Robert Duncan's essay "The Homosexual in Society"
(1944), the first instance of an American writer's "outing" himself in

explicit terms. Also helping to normalize homosexuality was the publication of Dr. Alfred C. Kinsey's *Sexual Behavior in the Human Male* (1948), which reported that thirty-seven percent of the men surveyed admitted to at least one postadolescent encounter with another male that led to orgasm. Debunking conventional arguments on the matter, Kinsey claimed that "persons with homosexual histories are to be found in every age group, in every social level, in every conceivable occupation, in cities and on farms, and in the most remote areas of the country."[71] Following Kinsey's breakthrough was Donald Webster Cory's *The Homosexual in America* (1951), the first book-length study of American homosexual politics. Although critics have remarked on the work's self-hating tone, some of Cory's arguments anticipate by more than twenty years the sexual liberation politics of the 1970s:

> The homosexual often feels the source of his difficulty lies in the fact that he is born into a hostile world, and this hostility is inherent, he believes, in that he lives in a heterosexual society. He is in my opinion, entirely wrong in this concept. The root of the homosexual difficulty is that he lives, not in a heterosexual world but in an anti-sexual world.[72]

These and other seminal writings brought a new political consciousness to gay male fiction, and perhaps to a lesser extent to lesbian fiction as well. While male homosexuality remained a well-observed literary taboo, and African American male homosexuality even more so, the topic was no longer feared by those writers willing to risk the attendant penalties for incorporating gay concerns into their work.

Concurrent with the release of the Kinsey findings was the publication of the first gay-themed novels of the postwar era. John Horne Burns's *The Gallery* (1947), Gore Vidal's *The City and the Pillar* (1948), and Truman Capote's *Other Voices, Other Rooms* (1948) each received widespread acclaim, even though Burns and Vidal were attacked by the press for their sexual candor. In Vidal's case, his next five novels were "blacked out" by reviewers who refused to cover his books, until his novel *Julian* (1963) hit best-seller lists over a decade later. James Baldwin's *Giovanni's Room* (1956) joined the era's list of critically praised gay works, though the author had already addressed homosexuality in "The Preservation of Innocence" (1949), a magazine article that significantly was not reprinted in *Notes of a Native Son* (1955). "Let me suggest that his [the homosexual's] present debasement and our obsession with him corresponds to the debasement of the relationship between the sexes," Baldwin commented in the article that was published several years ahead of his first novel, *Go Tell It on the Mountain* (1953). "His ambiguous and terrible position in our society reflects the ambiguities and terrors which time has deposited on that relationship.... If we are going to be natural then this [homosexuality] is part of nature; if we refuse to accept this, then we have rejected nature."[73] Another early treatment of homosexuality appeared in his short story "Outing" (1951), though he employed representations of gayness more forthrightly in later fiction such as *Another Country* (1962), *Tell Me How Long the Train's Been Gone* (1968), and *Just Above My Head* (1979). While Baldwin, like a number of other gay authors of the period, resisted labeling human sexuality with social definitions (as Baldwin explained it, "I love men but I'm not a homosexual"),[74] and in spite of the fact that he also refused to call himself a black writer, Baldwin's ground-breaking career nevertheless set a literary precedent for openly gay African American fiction.

Yet Baldwin was not alone among African American male authors depicting gay content in fiction of this period. Ralph Ellison's *Invisible Man* (1952) and Chester Himes's *Cast the First Stone* (1952) both feature openly homosexual characters. The latter work is even set in the context of a prison "love story." Owen Dodson's *Boy at the Window* (1951), however, was the first gay-themed novel published by an African American homosexual in the 1950s. The autobiographical plot concerns a nine-year-old boy's coming to terms with his sexuality after his mother's death. Although its gay subject matter is largely confined to cautious renderings of sexual exploration, the novel subtly depicts what Dodson's biographer called "a stunted and guilty homosexuality."[75] It is worth noting here that in spite of the political strides of gay literature and progressive medical research of the time, much of the writing by homosexual and bisexual men could also be described aptly as "stunted" or "guilty." Indeed, the intensely repressive social climate of the period that penalized gay sex as criminal virtually mandated guilt on the part of homosexuals. Recall that in 1950, Senator Joseph McCarthy announced that 205 State Department employees were Communist Party members, thereby launching the government-orchestrated "witch-hunts" that quickly added gays to the list of political dissidents already under attack by the authority of the government. Moreover, the controversy engendered by a public accusation of homosexuality could devastate one's career and social standing, regardless whether one was in fact gay. For African Americans, particularly black gay men such as Dodson who were employed at leading cultural institutions like Howard University, forthright literary expressions of homosexuality were perhaps understandably "stunted." Significantly, *Boy at the Window* was also the first gay-oriented novel published by a black homosexual since Wallace Thurman's *Infants of the Spring* in 1932.

Although the 1940s were an especially dour time for African American queer writers, that period witnessed the early radicalization of white gay men's literature with the coalescence of the "Beat" movement after the war. At the center of the predominantly gay group were Allen Ginsberg, Jack Kerouac, and William Burroughs, with Neal Cassady, Herbert Huncke, Peter Orlovsky, and others forming the larger circle. Beginning with Ginsberg's *Howl and Other Poems* (1956), an unabashed poetic tribute to gay sex, the Beats became the center of public controversy. When *Howl* was seized by police on grounds of "indecency" in 1957, the book's highly publicized obscenity trial placed the Beats on the literary map. Kerouac's *On the Road* (1957) enhanced the group's visibility. However, *The Subterraneans* (1958) was an openly queer novel that, like many other literary representations of homosexuality at the time, consciously avoided revealing the autobiographical origins of the book's gay content. The works of Burroughs, by contrast, not only publicly acknowledged the writer's own homosexuality but went so far as to depict S/M and group sex in novels like *Naked Lunch* (1959). If the Beats failed to transform the culture of male chauvinism often associated with them and their output, these authors nevertheless elevated the "outsider" status of gay men to unprecedented political levels of nonconformity. "In their rejection of the nuclear family, their willingness to experiment sexually, and, most importantly, their definition of these choices as social protest, the beats offered a model that allowed homosexuals to view their own lives from a different angle," wrote John D'Emilio. Through the Beats, gay men could conceive of themselves as norm-breakers rather than degenerates, "nonconformists rather than deviates."[76]

With the political and literary breakthroughs of the 1950s and early 1960s, nonconformity assumed greater diversity in the writings of gay men of color. The black queer writer Samuel R. Delany turned to the science fiction and fantasy genre with innovative depictions of outcast protagonists who transcend conventional gender expectations. His first published novel, *The Jewels of Aptor* (1962), foreshadowed more complicated renderings of sexuality both in the short story "Aye, and Gomorrah..." (1967) and in the novel *The Einstein Intersection* (1967), which explores the ways in which "difference" is confronted by and assimilated within a dominant alien culture. Homoeroticism, however, appears explicitly in *Dhalgren* (1975) and continues in *Tales of Nevèryon* (1979). "The constant and insistent experience I have had as a black man, as a gay man, as a science fiction writer in racist, sexist, homophobic America," Delany commented, "...colors and contours every sentence I write."[77] Socially marginalized settings also serve as the basis for the work of the gay Latino author John Rechy, whose experience as a male prostitute inspired his best-known works. *City of Night* (1963) concerns the sexual underworld of male prostitution, while later works such as *Numbers* (1967) and the nonfiction *Sexual Outlaw* (1977) treat promiscuity and homosexual identity even more forthrightly. Although critics have charged Rechy with an unduly harsh rendering of gay life, the author insisted that his work reflects "a realistic appraisal of the [gay] world...a very despairing, lonely world in many respects."[78]

By the late 1970s three critically acclaimed, commercially successful novels by white homosexual authors—Edmund White's *Nocturne for the King of Naples* (1978), Andrew Holleran's *Dancer from the Dance* (1978), and Larry Kramer's *Faggots* (1978)—set post-Stonewall gay literature on an unprecedented course of openness. Particular to these liberated gay novels was a new-style protagonist for whom societal marginalization was not necessarily disadvantageous but to some degree preferred. As David Bergman wrote, these stories are populated by "gay men who live in an exclusively gay neighborhood, have exclusively gay associates, spend their afternoons at the gym and their nights either at the bathhouse or dance bars, and manage somehow through marginal jobs, trust funds, or the kindness of strangers to live lives of drugs, dancing, physical beauty, and sex."[79]

Although Bergman's observation that these and other breakthrough novels by gay white authors, including Felice Picano's *The Lure* (1978), meant that booksellers and publishers could no longer deny the commercial demand for popular gay fiction, the reception of black gay novelists in the publishing world remained for all purposes unaffected for nearly a decade. While one can only speculate that the reasons might be simply the realities of racism and homophobia, it seems probable, if not more instructive, to point out that white publishers also may not have imagined a viable audience for black gay books—notwithstanding that there had been an audience for black gay fiction as long as there had been one for gay books. Indeed, the publishing market for African American fiction did not more fully emerge until the 1990s, when blockbuster successes like Terry McMillan's *Waiting to Exhale* (1992) demonstrated to publishers and the larger literary world the existence of an enthusiastic but underserved African American reading public.

Still, an unanswerable question remains: How did Black gays and lesbians experience the almost exclusively white gay literary terrain of the day? Joseph Beam, writing in his introduction to the black gay anthology *In the Life* (1986), expressed a view that was perhaps shared by many African American lesbians and gay men of the period:

> I had grown weary of reading literature by white gay men who fell, quite easily, into three camps: the incestuous literati of Manhattan and Fire Island, the San Francisco cropped-mustache-clones, and the Boston-to-Cambridge politically correct radical faggot. None of them spoke to me as a Black gay man.... I called a personal moratorium on the writings by white gay men, and read, exclusively, works by lesbians and Black women. At the very least, their Black characters were credible and I caught glimpses of my reality in their words.[80]

Although the literature of white gay men continued to incorporate many of the stereotypes that Beam decried, by the late 1980s writings by African American lesbians, gay men, and bisexuals were entering the mainstream more frequently. Cumulatively, these works provided alternative perspectives of lesbian and gay life unimaginable only a decade earlier. The postwar protest movements for racial and sexual equality helped to infuse black queer literature with unprecedented sexual candor and political intent. While these movements fully liberated neither the writing nor the authors from extant social prejudices, they helped to expand the black lesbian, gay, and bisexual literary tradition begun in the Harlem Renaissance. This expansion provided new possibilities and hope for generations to come.

By the late 1970s, the topic of homosexuality in the greater African American community together with issues of race within the broader lesbian and gay population remained largely sidelined. Despite a quarter century of liberation movements, the voices of black lesbians, black gay men, and black bisexuals were often marginalized, even silenced, during this period of intense public protest. To be certain, the entire civil rights struggle empowered African Americans regardless of gender or sexual orientation, just as the gay movement empowered homosexuals and bisexuals regardless of gender or race, quite as the feminist movement empowered women irrespective of race or sexual orientation. In spite of internal differences that sometimes splintered and occasionally destroyed social protest groups, all these organizations nonetheless contributed to the larger struggle for equality that benefited African American lesbians and gay men. Furthermore, and perhaps more central to the focus of this book, the social protest model served the essential function of radicalizing notions of identity politics, which empowered black lesbian, gay, and bisexual writers to incorporate comparably radical themes of race, gender, and sexuality into their works. Unambiguous depictions of same-sex relations in a decidedly African American context were only one among many hallmarks particular to the emerging literature.

Owen Dodson

■ ■ ■

[1914–1983]

THE WORKS OF SUCH CIVIL RIGHTS PIONEERS AS W. E. B. DuBois and Booker T. Washington introduced Owen Dodson early to the classic African American writings. Although Dodson's family had little money—his mother died when he was twelve and his father, a freelance journalist, served as director of the National Negro Press Association—he was able to attend Bates College and Yale University, even after the family's situation worsened with the onset of the Depression. Dodson earned an MFA degree in playwrighting in 1939 and went on to teach drama at Howard University for twenty-three years. He produced a voluminous body of work, including two novels, two books of poetry, and thirty-seven plays and operas.

Dodson's debut play, the prize-winning *Divine Comedy* (1938), set the course for his career as one of the most prolific African American dramatists ever. By the 1950s, he had also taken up fiction. His first novel, *Boy at the Window* (1951), a semiautobiographical story about a sensitive boy who loses his mother, alludes to the author's homosexuality, but only suggestively and always innocently from a child's perspective. Based on the success of *Boy at the Window*, Dodson was awarded a Guggenheim Fellowship in 1952 to complete the sequel, *Come Home Early, Child,* which deals with the protagonist's sexual coming of age. Significantly, the follow-up novel went unpublished until 1977, seven years after Dodson had retired from his position as chair of the drama department at Howard. He continued to write, direct, and produce stage work until his death from a heart attack in 1983.

In this excerpt from *Boy at the Window,* Coin, the novel's nine-year-old protagonist, meets Ferris, an older boy visiting his aunt in Washington, D.C. While coming to an awareness of his budding sexual identity, Coin finds himself struggling with the memory of his mother.

from **Boy at the Window**

[1951]

When he first entered the Gem Movie Playhouse, on Seventh Street, the darkness reminded him of underwater and deep periods of sleep and down in the damp cellar on Berriman Street. He thought of the woods, near Atkins Avenue, with trees at the top spreading, long branches shaking hands and all the birds you could hardly ever see. The kids called them the up-in-the-tree birds. Now it was brighter and he felt alone, more alone than ever, with kids everywhere. In his remembered woods he saw a squirrel leap from branch to branch in the nanny goat lady's oak tree. He wished the animal would hop to him. Come to him like on the day his mother died, the sparrow came and he knew the chirping was asking for crumbs. He bit his left thumbnail off and placed it between his two front teeth and worked it in and out there. He slid down into his seat and looked at the silver screen. Tom Mix raced along low slopes toward a sign that read EL PASO. He caught up a girl riding on the behind of the bad guy's horse. A whole flock of men waited in the distance with guns. Then all of a sudden a shot banged out of the piano in the front of the theatre and the bad guy's horse's front legs hit up in the air kicking. The pretty girl slid down the slick behind of the horse like on a slide in the playground and she was on a cactus plant crying to beat the band. Coin let out a long ahhhhh geeeeeeeee. That was when he noticed the boy beside him.

"That's all right," said the boy, "it's only a picture; it ain't real."

"Yeah," said Coin. But it was realer than that and he wanted to help the girl up and bring some iodine. Iodine all over her arms and behind. It wasn't real, that's right, he thought. And Rudolph Valentino wasn't real. "Valentino was dead living on the silver screen," Mrs. Jeffers had said last summer between her crying. So now he knew. And he knew the boy realized the same thing, so he answered, "Yeah, yeah, I know that."

When the lights went on he smelled the perfume like toilet smell and baby talcum powder mixed. He wanted to rush into fresh air. A big bag of peanuts was thrust under his nose and he took a handful as the seat snapped up and the kids began to rush out in scrambled talk, piano pounding and giggling. The boy at his side asked, "You goin' out or stayin' for the next show?"

"I'm goin'. I gotta wait for my uncle."

In the light outside the movie he sneaked a look at the boy. He was older than him. His hair grew forward and his eyes were real black and white, like the color black had been separated from the white by a jacknife. The boy's face shone. Not greasy but the leaping shiny of autos. His fingers looked strong and hard as he asked Coin to have some more peanuts.

"Fillin'. Almost a meal, that's what peanuts is. Peanuts is the best thing in Washington, District of Columbia." And he cocked his head from side to side and began a smile that showed laughing teeth. "This Washington ain't the other, Washington, the state. Teacher said so."

"Yeah," said Coin twisting his face on a sour peanut. Probably one of Mrs. Carth's. He smiled too. They were both smiling at each other and Coin couldn't stop.

"Can't you say nothin' but yeah?" the boy asked Coin.

"Yeah. What's your name?"

"That's more like it. Whoever ain't got the grit to talk ain't from nothin' or nowhere. My name's Ferris."

"I ain't heard of no name like that."

"Well, that's my name. Ferris. I was named after the wheel, Ferris wheel. Sometimes I feel like a wheel too, feel like I'm goin' round and round up and down. I can turn a cartwheel, too."

"Ferris sounds made up."

"A Ferris wheel got lights on it. Lights in a ball of glass. Seen 'em in a carnival in Kentucky. A big ring lighted in the sky. Music, too. When my Mama was carryin' me she was ridin' the wheel. That's how come my name."

"Your Mama took a baby up in them swingin' seats?"

"That was before I was born."

"She couldn't have been carryin' you then."

"Yes, she was. My Mama was."

"Not before you were born."

"You don't know from nothin'. How you suppose babies is made?"

"Well, you know," Coin answered vaguely. He bit a peanut loud. "Say, Ferris, look at that big airplane flying up there. It looks like a grasshopper with double wings."

"Hey, hey all over. Look at that big airplane," Ferris repeated. "Don't you know babies is carried?"

"Sure I do."

"You do! Then tell me if you're so knowing." Coin just shuffled along and looked like he was interested in the sky and the airplane that was out of sight. But Ferris kept at it like rubbing in sandpaper. All Coin could think of was that he was delivered when he was born. He looked slantways at Ferris and thought, old country boy. He don't know from doodley-squat.

Ferris began to laugh sharp and gooey like an egg-beater going.

"Don't you know all carry their young. Except some birds. They lay 'em in eggs."

"Uh huh," Coin managed to say.

"Furthermore, do you know how babies is conceived?"

"Conceived?"

"Began and started, boy you is the dumbest boy this side Kentucky."

They had reached a small park surrounded by stores and houses, where hardly anybody was.

Ferris sat down on the first bench and kept on talking. "Babies is made from a man and a woman. I seen it. Man goes in and after the woman is fat for nine months, baby comes crying. That's the gist of it."

Coin had heard of that but he didn't believe babies came from it. He didn't come from nothing dirty like that. "My mother and father never did anything like that."

Ferris laughed. "How do you think you're here eatin' peanuts and talkin' to me?"

"My mother never did nothin' dirty like that and you better shut up. You better shut right up, if you don't want a punch in your friggin' nose." Coin felt hot all over like a blazing was inside him. He stood up over Ferris with fists clenched and tears in his eyes, muttering to the boy lying on the bench rolling with laughing. "You're a bastard, you're a bas-tard. Bastard, bastard. Double bastard. Get up and fight."

Ferris sat up quickly.

"Maybe your mother did that thing but mine never did. My mother's the salt of the earth. She was the salt…"

"Hey boy. Hey, hey." Ferris put his arms friendly around Coin and Coin thrust him off. Ferris landed on the bench.

"I don't allow nobody to call me that. If you wanta fight, put 'em up. Put 'em up." Ferris' eyes were turning red as Coin talked.

Coin was shaking and sweat was on his forehead as a small group of boys began crowding, egging them on.

"Better knock him in the head before he gets up offa that bench."

"He's afraid: ha ha ha."

"They both sissies, that's what."

"Nobody better not call me no bastard." Ferris, growling like a dog, got to his feet and faced Coin. Coin hitched his knickers up and hitched them up again. Ferris narrowed his eyes. Then they stood dead still staring into each other's eyes.

One sideline kid shouted, "Shucks, ain't no use waitin', ain't no use waitin'. They both sissies."

Just then a fly began to tickle on Coin's nose and he raised a hand to brush it off. He felt a slam in his right eye and saw firecracker stars of all colors. Raising his fists to hit at Ferris, he tripped. His knickers had fallen down. Ferris was on top of him and he heard all the yelling children, felt blow after blow on his cheeks and chest. He knew he was a mess. When one sock of Ferris' went into his right eye, he saw a shooting star land and his mother's face came out of it. A blue face laughing and stars splintering in her hair. That was when he made force in his left arm and flinging it up gripped Ferris' head in a half-nelson. He heard his voice sputtering, "Do you give up, do you give up, do you give up?"

With every repeat of the phrase he locked Ferris' head tighter till he thought Ferris must be dead. They were both sweating and dirt scratched everywhere on Coin's body. His mother was sitting in the window and the little man of sunshine bowed and bowed over her white hair; he saw her face in the coffin with red stuff on the cheeks and the lips bugged close. Mama over the washtub and Mama inspecting him saying: get up get up get up before you get so dirty Popa will be mad. Mama and johnnycake. Ferris was still as nothing and the sideline boys were still but he asked the question, "How is babies born, how, how, how...no dirty, no dirty...?"

Ferris' voice came at last as Coin released him, "Babies...?"

"Take it all back!"

"Babies...is delivered," Ferris voice was panting. Through his sweat Coin looked at him close. Ferris' eyes began to get big.

"All right, all right," Coin said. "You give up?"

"I gives up."

With the excitement over the kids drifted away. Coin didn't know what to say. Ferris was over by the bench. He picked up the bag that had had peanuts in it, gathered it together at the top and blew hard. The bag puffed out. Taking it out of his mouth he twisted the ragged edges and popped the paper ball with his fist. Coin turned around to a smiling Ferris.

"There ain't, there ain't not even one peanut left."

They smoothed their clothes in silence and drank at a fountain. Ferris broke the silence first.

"I ain't asked you your name."

"Coin."

"Like a penny?"

"Yeah."

Ferris laughed until be bent over. "Whoooooo wheeeee whooooo ummmmmmmm. That's the funniest yet. Why boy, you as bad as me in name."

"Yeah," grinned Coin.

Ferris whooped harder. He turned a cartwheel and yelled, "I'm gonna spend you, boy." He ran along a path quick as hot cakes, quick as sixty and Coin was at his heels laughing with his nose running and the sunlight sharp in his hurting eyes but he didn't care.

At the edge of the park a man was ringing a Santa Claus bell, standing by a dirty white cart looking like who-struck-john. The boys stopped short. Ferris went over to the cart with bottles of all flavors in them and a big hunk of ice and a scooping cup.

"Coin, you like scraped ice and flavorin'?"

"Thanks."

"Don't ever say thanks till you get somethin' to thank for," said Ferris handing him a snowball of shaved ice with mint green flavoring.

"Ferris, you know, you're one of the nicest friends I ever had. You're the nicest."

"You know why? I was raised on a sugar tit."

"You ought to come by my room and meet my uncle. He's blind but he can really get around with that stick."

"Wish I could, Coin, but I gotta get to the station. Lord, that reminds me, what time do you reckon it is? Mister, what time is it?"

The man at the cart took an alarm clock from under his apron.

"Twenty minutes to six."

"What are you in such a big hurry for, Ferris?"

"I'm going home tonight, goin' to Kentucky. And I ain't gonna miss the seven o'clock train. I'm gonna scoot out of this Washington, District of Columbia, so fast the wind gonna wonder how I flew."

"I'm sorry you're leavin' just when I found someb…" Coin couldn't swallow his last scraps of ice and he liked mint flavoring too. "Can I go to the station with you?"

"You better come. We can walk from here."

"How about your bag and things?"

"My Aunt Louise sent everything along ahead, before she went to work, and left a lunch box in the bag room. I got the ticket here."

"Lord," sighed Ferris as they walked along kicking stones and cans ahead, "Lord, I sure will be glad to get back. Wake up in the morning and it's so quiet and no noise to make you sick. Just before the sun come out, the birds commence to sing and by midday you can hardly bear it. Their music everywhere; catbirds, finches, little finches, redbirds, chickadees. Sure will be glad to get back. An' fishin', too, in the crick. Stand sometime in quicksand…"

Coin's face was almost stuck under Ferris' mouth.

"…of course I hold onto a branch. Sometimes gold minnows fairly blazin'. And sometimes I just lie down in the high grass and look up in the sky…look like a big old blue tent. Brush snake doctors away."

"What are snake doctors?"

"Boy, you don't know nothing. They flies that tend sick snakes. Got wings like glass when they fly in the sun. They pretty but they mean. I ain't scared of them though. Just lay down in the high grass and watch the clay hills, 'long about sunset, roll away like molasses puddin's."

"I can just see them."

"Lord, I hope that train fairly races. This city makes me nervous. All the autos jar me so. Feel like a bell ringin' in me."

Coin saw it all and wished he could just leave everybody and thing and get on that train with Ferris. And he could send for Esther maybe. Esther could teach both of them after regular school.

Ferris was singing:

> Honey in the bee ball,
> I can't see ya'll.
> A bushel of ree,
> A bushel of rye,
> All that ain't hid
> On judgement day,
> Better holler I.

"What's that, Ferris?"

"Hide-and-seek song."

"We play that all the time. Hide and go seek."

"Boy, don't cut out the monkey with me. I made that game up myself."

"After you got there you wouldn't have to worry about a thing. My Aunt Hallie and me do right well…"

"Don't you live with your mother?"

"My Mama…oh, my Mama's up in Chicago. She do right well too. She went away a long time ago, took the brass bed and a big yellow leghorne hat and dressed in yellow, but she send big boxes for Christmas and love and kisses."

Coin looked swiftly at his friend and heard the crying underneath the cocksure voice.

"My Mama's name is in the Bible, too, Anna Matilda Robinson. Teacher say Anna mean full of grace. Is your Mama's name in the Bible?"

"I never looked. I don't know."

They walked along in silence. Coin began to try to think of all the time he had looked in the Bible and whether he remembered the name Naomi on any page or under a picture. He remembered fifty names at once but not Naomi anywhere. Anna mean full of grace. Naomi mean…? What does Naomi mean?

"I was sayin' Coin, if you got there…my Aunt Hallie and me do right well. We got a oriental rug on the floor. You can tell it's genuine, too, because it got ORIENTAL stamped right on the back of it. Chinese people wove it all by hand. We got a gold chair, too, come out of the Jewish people's church. My aunt paid fifty dollars for it. Come all the way from Louisville. Come out to our house in a car. Course the gold's worn off a little. But we gonna fix that. I seen some gold paint in the Five an' Ten Cent Store. Only thing we people down in Kentucky don't have that city people got is electric and gaslights and house toilets that people sit on."

"What kind of toilets have you?" Coin was thinking of all that number one and number two in the fields and everywhere.

"Wood ones out in the back yard. Ours close to the water well. Make it convenient, too."

"Who else is in your family that lives with you besides your Aunt Hallie?"

"Nobody. Sometimes my Mama send somebody down from Chicago. But they don't do nothing much but laugh with Aunt Hallie and sit on the back porch eating Concord grapes in September. Don't stay but a few weeks and then Aunt Hallie and me settle down to winter talking. Mostly about my Uncle Wayne Anthony. He's dead now. He was something, now let me tell you. He was a moonshiner of reputation. Use to go about with Reverend Talifer. Reverend Talifer was a preacher with gravy and moans. Could preach up a storm. Sometimes he'd preach a funeral and have the whole family fallin' out and nobody left to walk with the coffin but pallbearers and they'd be cryin' so hard almost drop the casket. Ever go to a funeral, Coin?"

Coin nodded his head. He didn't want to think about funerals. There would be no more funerals with him. But he couldn't help listening to Ferris. He wondered if all it was true. But it didn't matter much. He felt happy like when he was in the movies and everything happened you never saw happen in daylight and probably never could. Ferris talked on like piano music.

"In this one funeral Mrs. Messiah from Bucket Crick. They was carryin' her to the grave singing *Now We Take This Feeble Body*. She were no more feeble. Weighed almost a ton of stones. The day was rainin' and windy. Pallbearers' white gloves filled with red mud and all. They started lowerin' the body down and got it down when one of the men's gloves slipped off and got caught in the wind. Got full of wind and puffed out and flew away like a dove. Folks got down on their knees and prayed…they hustled up collections and in a month hired the gravestone cutter from Louisville to carve a dove of peace to place on the grave. Folks keep it decorated with flowers. Afraid not to. And Reverend Talifer died of the shakes two weeks after. Fell into a coma callin' for Uncle Wayne Anthony's moonshine. Before he took sick he baptized me in the river. The water was cold. I trembled, boy. *He* wore a furlined robe. Think probally that's why he died. He had the crossed eyes. You ever drink moonshine, Coin?"

"No."

"I only did once, tasted pretty good. Like molasses with somethin' sharp in it. Sassafras taste. Made me feel like I was risin' and fallin' and everythin' I wanted seem to come true. Felt like I was walkin' the waters and standin' on quicksand an' never sink one inch. Didn't drink it but the one time. Reverend Talifer sent me out to Uncle Wayne Anthony's. You leave fifty cents on a stump in the woods and go away to drink from a cool stream an' when you come back your gallon jug is full. Asked

Uncle Wayne Anthony how he made it. You put your molasses barrel in
the cellar and sprinkle kerosene on the inside and then light it."

"Didn't the barrel burn?"

"You sure can cut the monkey in your mind, Coin; no, it didn't burn,
that made the agin' charcoal. Then you pour in your corn whiskey and let
it get strong for a year. Sometimes they take it out sooner. Tasted better,
they tell me. Lord, never forget Reverend Talifer moanin' before he died,
moanin' that he didn't want to die and go to hell before he got to go to
Chicago. Uncle Wayne Anthony went once. When he come back they said
he was crazy. But I just listened to his stories. Say they got enough lights
there to fairly blaze up the sky. What time you reckon it is, Coin?"

There was no time on any of the buildings they passed. Coin could
see the arches of the station and the statues standing around the top.
The capitol dome in the distance looked like a wedding cake. An auto
honked as they raced across the clearing leading to the station and they
stood stock-still while the driver laughed. Ferris poked out his tongue
and muttered something.

Afterwards Coin could never quite figure how Ferris got his lunch
box before the train pulled out. It all happened so fast. The conductor
was yelling out "all aboard" when he remembered the melted chocolate
bar he bought to give Ferris. Steam was rising from the wheels and people were running and hopping up the steep steps. Ferris was behind a
dusty window with his nose pressed looking at him and waving. Suddenly
Coin ran up the steps and into the hot coach. Thrusting the wet Hershey
bar into Ferris' free hand he ran out to the platform again. A whistle
blew and he heard the first chunk-chunks before the train started. His
heart was in his mouth. Ferris was going. Coin cupped his hands suddenly and called, "What's your address?"

Ferris pointed to his ears and shook his head. Coin made out like
he was writing as he called the question another time. Ferris began to
write in the dust of the windowpane as the train started moving. Coin
trotted by the side and as the chunk-chunks got louder, the wheels
whirled faster. Coin could hardly keep up. He couldn't read a thing
Ferris was writing. Something like a W but it was all backwards. No. It was
an M—M-A-D—if he was cross-eyed he could read it in no time. The
train was going lickety-split and he could hardly keep up with the tears
running down his eyes and he couldn't see even if he could read
backwards. M-A-D...what's the next letter? He couldn't make out if it

was a C or an X or what. The last thing he remembered was Ferris' face behind letters and dust; the big eyes looking at him. The questions about Concord grapes and how far was Kentucky, where his mother's name was in the Bible, the answers were running away.

"Ferris, Ferris, Ferris, write me, write me a letter, write me..." He bunked into a post. When he sprang up the train was turning around the bend and he couldn't tell which coach Ferris was on.

JAMES BALDWIN

■ ■ ■

[1924–1987]

BORN THE ELDEST OF EIGHT CHILDREN, JAMES BALDWIN grew up in an emotionally and physically abusive home where he was ridiculed as ugly and unintelligent by his mother's second husband, a fundamentalist Baptist preacher. Baldwin coped with these difficult circumstances in part by turning to books, becoming a voracious reader throughout adolescence. In the process he distinguished himself as a gifted pupil. By the age of fourteen, the poverty and sordid environs of Depression-era Harlem drove Baldwin to the safety of the Pentecostal Church. There he served as a child minister for three years, before resigning over his distaste of the hypocrisy of organized religion. This brief tenure in the pulpit shaped the author's literary style, which reflected biblical imagery, cadences, and rhetoric.

After his stepfather's death in 1943, Baldwin moved from Harlem to Greenwich Village, where he hoped that the bohemian climate would encourage his writing. During this period, he began a tentative first novel that later evolved into his debut book, *Go Tell It on the Mountain* (1953), and made the acquaintance of author Richard Wright. As a black gay writer, however, Baldwin found the racial prejudice of the Village to be as fundamentally limiting to his career as the homophobia he had fled in Harlem. Thus, he bought a one-way ticket to France in 1948, leaving the United States for what he hoped would be a more socially tolerant culture. It was while living as an expatriate that Baldwin published his first wave of landmark works, including his essay collection *Notes of a Native Son* (1955). He also wrote his first public defense of homosexuality, "The Preservation of Innocence," his boldest declaration of gay identity politics until he published the gay love story *Giovanni's Room* in 1956.

Baldwin's agent suggested that he burn the manuscript of *Giovanni's Room,* rather than risk the critical fall-out that traditionally accompanied the publication of an openly homosexual work by an American author. Never before had an explicitly gay novel been published by an African American author. Baldwin softened the critical blow by denying that *Giovanni's Room* was a homosexual book, insisting instead that it was really about the fear to love. He also did not identify himself as homosexual, nor for that matter did a number of gay authors of the period. Indeed, Baldwin, like so many other homosexuals, had even been engaged to be married. Still, his most intimate relationships were with men, notably his partner Lucien Happersberger.

Baldwin resided in France until his death from cancer in 1987, only returning to America briefly in 1957 and again in 1960 to participate in the burgeoning African American civil rights movement. In fact, his controversial third novel, *Another Country* (1962), tells the story of a racially and sexually diverse cast of young Americans, who struggle to understand each other despite their differences. This pre–Stonewall era novel is remarkable not only for its absence of shame around explicitly gay subject matter but also for its graphic depiction of African American homosexuality—a significant departure for the author, who cautiously had chosen white protagonists in *Giovanni's Room.*

In these two excerpts from *Another Country,* Rufus, a penniless, black bisexual musician, has momentarily turned to hustling to survive. Vivaldo, his white writer friend, recalls the tensions that have marked their often troubled friendship.

Now, bowed down with the memory of all that had happened since that day, he wandered helplessly back to Forty-second Street and stopped before the large bar and grill on the corner. Near him, just beyond the plate glass, stood the sandwich man behind his counter, the meat arrayed on the steam table beneath him. Bread and rolls, mustard, relish, salt and pepper, stood at the level of his chest. He was a big man, wearing white, with a blank, red, brutal face. From time to time he expertly knifed off a sandwich for one of the derelicts within. The old seemed reconciled to being there, to having no teeth, no hair, having no life. Some laughed together, the young, with dead eyes set in yellow faces, the slackness of their bodies making vivid the history of their degradation. They were the prey that was no longer hunted, though they were scarcely aware of this new condition and could not bear to leave the place where they had first been spoiled. And the hunters were there, far more assured and patient than the prey. In any of the world's cities, on a winter night, a boy can be bought for the price of a beer and the promise of warm blankets.

Rufus shivered, his hands in his pockets, looking through the window and wondering what to do. He thought of walking to Harlem but he was afraid of the police he would encounter in his passage through the city; and he did not see how he could face his parents or his sister. When he had last seen Ida, he had told her that he and Leona were about to make it to Mexico, where, he said, people would leave them alone. But no one had heard from him since then.

Now a big, rough-looking man, well dressed, white, with black-and-gray hair, came out of the bar. He paused next to Rufus, looking up and down the street. Rufus did not move, though he wanted to; his mind began to race, painfully, and his empty stomach turned over. Once again, sweat broke out on his forehead. Something in him knew what was about to happen; something in him died in the freezing second before the man walked over to him and said:

"It's cold out here. Wouldn't you like to come in and have a drink with me?"

"I'd rather have a sandwich," Rufus muttered, and thought *You've really hit the bottom now.*

"Well, you can have a sandwich, too. There's no law that says you can't."

Rufus looked up and down the street, then looked into the man's ice-cold, ice-white face. He reminded himself that he knew the score, he'd been around; neither was this the first time during his wanderings that he had consented to the bleakly physical exchange; and yet he felt that he would never be able to endure the touch of this man. They entered the bar and grill.

"What kind of sandwich would you like?"

"Corned beef," Rufus whispered, "on rye."

They watched while the meat was hacked off, slammed on bread, and placed on the counter. The man paid and Rufus took his sandwich over to the bar. He felt that everyone in the place knew what was going on, knew that Rufus was peddling his ass. But nobody seemed to care. Nobody looked at them. The noise at the bar continued, the radio continued to blare. The bartender served up a beer for Rufus and a whiskey for the man and rang up the money on the cash register. Rufus tried to turn his mind away from what was happening to him. He wolfed down his sandwich. But the heavy bread, the tepid meat, made him begin to feel nauseous; everything wavered before his eyes for a moment; he sipped his beer, trying to hold the sandwich down.

"You were hungry."

Rufus, he thought, you can't make this scene. There's no way in the world you can make it. Don't come on with the man. Just get out of here.

"Would you like another sandwich?"

The first sandwich was still threatening to come up. The bar stank of stale beer and piss and stale meat and unwashed bodies.

Suddenly he felt that he was going to cry.

"No, thank you," he said, "I'm all right now."

The man watched him for a moment.

"Then have another beer."

"No, thank you." But he leaned his head on the bar, trembling.

"*Hey!*"

Lights roared around his head, the whole bar lurched, righted itself, faces weaved around him, the music from the radio pounded in his skull. The man's face was very close to his: hard eyes and a cruel nose and flabby, brutal lips. He smelled the man's odor. He pulled away.

"I'm all right."

"You almost blacked out there for a minute."

The bartender watched them.

"You better have a drink. Hey, Mac, give the kid a drink."

"You sure he's all right?"

"Yeah, he's all right, I know him. Give him a drink."

The bartender filled a shot glass and placed it in front of Rufus. And Rufus stared into the gleaming cup, praying, Lord, don't let it happen. Don't let me go home with this man.

I've got so little left, Lord, don't let me lose it all.

"Drink. It'll do you good. Then you can come on over to my place and get some sleep."

He drank the whiskey, which first made him feel even sicker, then warmed him. He straightened up.

"You live around here?" he asked the man. If you touch me, he thought, still with these strange tears threatening to boil over at any moment, I'll beat the living shit out of you. I don't want no more hands on me, no more, no more, no more.

"Not very far. Forty-sixth Street."

They walked out of the bar, into the streets again.

"It's a lonely city," the man said as they walked. "I'm lonely. Aren't you lonely, too?"

Rufus said nothing.

"Maybe we can comfort each other for a night."

Rufus watched the traffic lights, the black, nearly deserted streets, the silent black buildings, the deep shadows of doorways.

"Do you know what I mean?"

"I'm not the boy you want, mister," he said at last, and suddenly remembered having said exactly these words to Eric—long ago.

"How do you mean, you're not the boy I want?" And the man tried to laugh. "Shouldn't I be the best judge of that?"

Rufus said, "I don't have a thing to give you. I don't have nothing to give nobody. Don't make me go through with this. Please."

They stopped on the silent Avenue, facing each other. The man's eyes hardened and narrowed.

"Didn't you know what was going on—back there?"

Rufus said, "I was hungry."

"What are you, anyway—just a cock teaser?"

"I was hungry," Rufus repeated; "I was hungry."

"Don't you have any family—any friends?"

Rufus looked down. He did not answer right away. Then, "I don't want to die, mister. I don't want to kill you. Let me go—to my friends."

"Do you know where to find them?"

"I know where to find—one of them."

There was a silence. Rufus stared at the sidewalk and, very slowly, the tears filled his eyes and began trickling down his nose.

The man took his arm. "Come on—come on to my place."

But now the moment, the possibility, had passed; both of them felt it. The man dropped his arm.

"You're a good-looking boy," he said.

Rufus moved away. "So long, mister. Thanks."

The man said nothing. Rufus watched him walk away.

Then he, too, turned and began walking downtown. He thought of Eric for the first time in years, and wondered if he were prowling foreign streets tonight. He glimpsed, for the first time, the extent, the nature, of Eric's loneliness, and the danger in which this placed him; and wished that he had been nicer to him. Eric had always been very nice to Rufus. He had had a pair of cufflinks made for Rufus, for Rufus' birthday, with the money which was to have bought his wedding rings: and this gift, this confession, delivered him into Rufus' hands. Rufus had despised him because he came from Alabama; perhaps he had allowed Eric to make love to him in order to despise him more completely. Eric had finally understood this, and had fled from Rufus, all the way to Paris. But his stormy blue eyes, his bright red hair, his halting drawl, all returned very painfully to Rufus now.

Go ahead and tell me. You ain't got to be afraid.

And, as Eric hesitated, Rufus added—slyly, grinning, watching him: "You act like a little girl—or something."

And even now there was something heady and almost sweet in the memory of the ease with which he had handled Eric, and elicited his confession. When Eric had finished speaking, he said, slowly;

"I'm not the boy for you. I don't go that way."

Eric had placed their hands together, and he stared down at them, the red and the brown.

"I know," he said.

He moved to the center of his room.

"But I can't help wishing you did. I wish you'd try."

Then, with a terrible effort, Rufus heard it in his voice, his breath:

"I'd do anything. I'd try anything. To please you." Then, with a smile, "I'm almost as young as you are. I don't know—much—about it."

Rufus had watched him, smiling. He felt a flood of affection for Eric. And he felt his own power.

He walked over to Eric and put his hands on Eric's shoulders. He did not know what he was going to say or do. But with his hands on Eric's shoulders, affection, power, and curiosity all knotted together in him—with a hidden, unforeseen violence which frightened him a little; the hands that were meant to hold Eric at arm's length seemed to draw Eric to him; the current that had begun flowing he did not know how to stop.

At last, he said in a low voice, smiling, "I'll try anything once, old buddy."

Those cufflinks were now in Harlem, in Ida's bureau drawer. And when Eric was gone, Rufus forgot their battles and the unspeakable physical awkwardness, and the ways in which he had made Eric pay for such pleasure as Eric gave, or got. He remembered only that Eric had loved him; as he now remembered that Leona had loved him. He had despised Eric's manhood by treating him as a woman, by telling him how inferior he was to a woman, by treating him as nothing more than a hideous sexual deformity. But Leona had not been a deformity. And he had used against her the very epithets he had used against Eric, and in the very same way, with the same roaring in his head and the same intolerable pressure in his chest.

Vivaldo lived alone in a first-floor apartment on Bank Street. He was home, Rufus saw the light in the window. He slowed down a little but the cold air refused to let him hesitate; he hurried through the open street door, thinking, Well, I might as well get it over with. And he knocked quickly on Vivaldo's door.

There had been the sound of a typewriter; now it stopped. Rufus knocked again.

"Who is it?" called Vivaldo, sounding extremely annoyed.

"It's me. It's me. Rufus."

The sudden light, when Vivaldo opened the door, was a great shock, as was Vivaldo's face.

"My God," said Vivaldo.

He grabbed Rufus around the neck, pulling him inside and holding him. They both leaned for a moment against Vivaldo's door.

"My God," Vivaldo said again, "where've you been? Don't you know you shouldn't do things like that? You've had all of us scared to death, baby. We've been looking for you everywhere."

It was a great shock and it weakened Rufus, exactly as though he had been struck in the belly. He clung to Vivaldo as though he were on the ropes. Then he pulled away.

Vivaldo looked at him, looked hard at him, up and down. And Vivaldo's face told him how he looked. He moved away from the door, away from Vivaldo's scrutiny.

"Ida's been here; she's half crazy. Do you realize you dropped out of sight almost a month ago?"

"Yes," he said, and sat down heavily in Vivaldo's easy chair—which sagged beneath him almost to the floor. He looked around the room, which had once been so familiar, which now seemed so strange.

He leaned back, his hands over his eyes.

"Take off your jacket," Vivaldo said. "I'll see if I can scare up something for you to eat—are you hungry?"

"No, not now. Tell me, how is Ida?"

"Well, she's *worried,* you know, but there's nothing wrong with her. Rufus, you want me to fix you a drink?"

"When was she here?"

"Yesterday. And she called me tonight. And she's been to the police. Everybody's been worried, Cass, Richard, everybody—"

He sat up. "The police are looking for me?"

On a Saturday in early March, Vivaldo stood at his window and watched the morning rise. The wind blew through the empty streets with a kind of dispirited moan; had been blowing all night long, while Vivaldo sat at his worktable, struggling with a chapter which was not going well. He was terribly weary—he had worked in the bookstore all day and then come downtown to do a moving job—but this was not the reason for his paralysis. He did not seem to know enough about the people in his novel. They did not seem to trust him. They were all named, more or less, all more or less destined, the pattern he wished them to describe was clear to him. But it did not seem clear to them. He could move them about but they themselves did not move. He put words in their mouths which they uttered sullenly, unconvinced. With the same agony, or greater, with which he attempted to seduce a woman, he was trying to seduce his people: he begged them to surrender up to him their privacy. And they refused—without, for all their ugly intransigence, showing the faintest desire to leave him. They were waiting for him to find the key, press the nerve, tell the truth. *Then,* they seemed to be complaining, they would give him all he wished for and much more than he was now willing to imagine. All night long, in an increasing rage and helplessness, he had walked from his worktable to his window and back again. He made himself coffee, he smoked cigarettes, he looked at the clock— and the night wore on, but his chapter didn't and he kept feeling that he ought to get some sleep because today, for the first time in several weeks, he was seeing Ida. This was her Saturday off, but she was having a cup of coffee with one of her girl friends in the restaurant where she worked. He was to meet her there, and then they were to visit Richard and Cass.

Richard's novel was about to be published, and it promised to be very successful. Vivaldo, to his confusion and relief, had not found it very remarkable. But he had not had the courage to say this to Richard or to admit to himself that he would never have read the novel if Richard had not written it.

All the street sounds eventually ceased—motors, and the silky sound of tires, footfalls, curses, pieces of songs, and loud and prolonged good nights; the last door in his building slammed, the last murmurs, rustling, and creaking ended. The night grew still around him and his apartment grew cold. He lit the oven. They swarmed, then, in the bottom of his mind, his cloud of witnesses, in an air as heavy as the oven heat, clustering, really, around the desired and unknown Ida. Perhaps it was she who caused them to be so silent.

He stared into the streets and thought—bitterly, but also with a chilling, stunned sobriety—that, though he had been seeing them so long, perhaps he had never known them at all. The occurrence of an event is not the same thing as knowing what it is that one has lived through. Most people had not lived—nor could it, for that matter, be said that they had died—through any of their terrible events. They had simply been stunned by the hammer. They passed their lives thereafter in a kind of limbo of denied and unexamined pain. The great question that faced him this morning was whether or not he had ever, really, been present at his life. For if he had ever been present then he was present still, and his world would open up before him.

Now the girl who lived across the street, whose name, he knew, was Nancy, but who reminded him of Jane—which was certainly why he never spoke to her—came in from her round of the bars and the coffee houses with yet another boneless young man. They were everywhere, which explained how she met them, but why she brought them home with her was a somewhat more sinister question. Those who wore their hair long wore beards; those who wore theirs short felt free to dispense with this useful but somewhat uneasy emphasis. They read poetry or they wrote it, furiously, as though to prove that they had been cut out for more masculine pursuits. This morning's specimen wore white trousers and a yachting cap, and a paranoiac little beard jutted out from the bottom half of his face. This beard was his most aggressive feature, his only suggestion of hardness or tension. The girl, on the other hand, was all angles, bone, muscle, jaw; even her breasts seemed stony. They walked down the street, hand in hand, but not together. They paused before her stoop and the girl staggered. She leaned against him in an agony of loathing, belching alcohol; his rigidity suggested that her weight was onerous; and they climbed the short steps to the door. Here she paused and smiled at him, coquettishly raising those stony breasts as she pulled back her hair with her hands. The boy seemed to find this delay intolerable. He muttered something about the cold, pushing the girl in before him.

Well, now, they would make it—make what? Not love, certainly— and should he be standing at this window twenty-four hours hence, he would see the same scene repeated with another boy.

How could they endure it? Well, he had been there. How had he endured it? Whiskey and marijuana had helped. He was a pretty good liar and that had helped; and most women inspired great contempt in him and that had helped. But there was more to it than that. After all, the country, the world—this city—was full of people who got up in the morning and went to bed at night and, mainly, throughout their lives, to the same bed. They did whatever it was they were supposed to do, and they raised their children. And perhaps he didn't like these people very much, but, then, he didn't, on the other hand, know them. He supposed that they existed because he had been told that they did; presumably, the faces he saw on subways and in the streets belonged to these people, who were admirable because they were numerous. His mother and father and his married sister and her husband and their friends were part of this multitude, and his younger brother would belong to them soon. And what did he know about them, really, except that they were ashamed of him? They didn't know that he was real. It seemed that they didn't, for that matter, know that *they* were real, but he was insufficiently simple to find this notion comforting.

He watched a lone man come up the street, his tight black overcoat buttoned to the neck, looking back from time to time as though he hoped he were being followed. Then the garbage truck came up the street, like a gray brainless insect. He watched the garbage being loaded. Then there was nothing, no one. The light was growing stronger. Soon, alarm clocks would begin to ring and the houses would expel the morning people. Then he thought of the scene which would now be occurring between the boy and the girl in the room.

The yellow electric light, self-consciously indirect, would by now have been discovered to be useless and would have been turned off. The girl would have taken off her shoes and turned on her radio or her hi-fi set and would be lying on the bed. The gray light, coming in through the monk's-cloth blinds, would, with the malice of the noncommittal, be examining every surface, corner, angle, of the unloved room. The music would not be loud. They would have poured drinks by now and the girl's drink would be on the table. The boy's would be between his hands. He would be sitting on the bed, turned a little away from the girl, staring at the floor. His cap would have been pushed further back. And the silence, beneath the music, would be tremendous with their fear. Presently, one of them would make a move to conquer this. If it were the girl, the movement would be sighing and halting—sighing because of need, halting because of hostility. If it were the boy, the movement would be harshly or softly brutal: he would lunge over the girl as though rape were in his mind, or he would try to arouse her lust by means of feathery kisses, meant to be burning, which he had seen in the movies. Friction and fantasy could not fail to produce a physiological heat and hardness; and this sheathed pressure between her thighs would be the girl's signal to moan. She would toss her head a little and hold the boy more tightly and they would begin their descent into confusion. Off would come the cap—as the bed sighed and the gray light stared. Then his jacket would come off. His hands would push up the sweater and unlock the brassiere. Perhaps both might wish to pause here and begin a discovery of each other, but neither would dare. She moaned and clung to darkness, he removed the sweater. He struggled unlovingly with her breasts;

the sound of her gasps foreshadowed his failure. Then the record on the hi-fi came to an end, or, on the radio, a commercial replaced the love song. He pulled up her skirt. Then the half-naked girl, with a small, apologetic murmur, rose from the bed, switched off the machine. Standing in the center of the room, she might mock her nakedness with a small, cruel joke. Then she would vanish into the john. The boy would finish his drink and take off everything except his undershorts. When the girl reappeared, both would be ready.

Yes, he had been there: chafing and pushing and pounding, trying to awaken a frozen girl. The battle was awful because the girl wished to be awakened but was terrified of the unknown. Every movement that seemed to bring her closer to him, to bring them closer together, had its violent recoil, driving them farther apart. Both clung to a fantasy rather than to each other, tried to suck pleasure from the crannies of the mind, rather than surrender the secrets of the body. The tendrils of shame clutched at them, however they turned, all the dirty words they knew commented on all they did. These words sometimes brought on the climax joylessly, with loathing, and too soon. The best that he had ever managed in bed, so far, had been the maximum of relief with the minimum of hostility.

In Harlem, however, he had merely dropped his load and marked the spot with silver. It had seemed much simpler for a time. But even simple pleasure, bought and paid for, did not take long to fail—pleasure, as it turned out, was not simple. When, wandering about Harlem, he came across a girl he liked, he could not fail to wish that he had met her somewhere else, under different circumstances. He could not fail to disapprove of her situation and to demand of her more than any girl in such a situation could give. If he did not like her, then he despised her and it was very painful for him to despise a colored girl, it increased his self-contempt. So that, by and by, however pressing may have been the load he carried uptown, he returned home with a greater one, not to be so easily discharged.

For several years it had been his fancy that he belonged in those dark streets uptown precisely because the history written in the color of his skin contested his right to be there. He enjoyed this, his right to *be* being everywhere contested; uptown, his alienation had been made visible and, therefore, almost bearable. It had been his fancy that danger, there, was more real, more open, than danger was downtown and that he, having chosen to run these dangers, was snatching his manhood from the lukewarm waters of mediocrity and testing it in the fire. He had felt more alive in Harlem, for he had moved in a blaze of rage and self-congratulation and sexual excitement, with danger, like a promise, waiting for him everywhere. And, nevertheless, in spite of all this daring, this running of risks, the misadventures which had actually befallen him had been banal indeed and might have befallen him anywhere. His dangerous, overwhelming lust for life had failed to involve him in anything deeper than perhaps half a dozen extremely casual acquaintanceships in about as many bars. For memories, he had one or two marijuana parties, one or two community debauches, one or two girls whose names he had forgotten, one or two addresses which he had lost. He knew that Harlem was a battlefield and that a war was being waged there day and night—but of the war aims he knew nothing.

And this was due not only to the silence of the warriors—their silence being, anyway, spectacular in that it rang so loud: it was due to the fact that one knew of battles only what one had accepted of one's own. He was forced, little by little, against his will, to realize that in running the dangers of Harlem he had not been testing his manhood or heightening his sense of life. He had merely been taking refuge in the outward adventure in order to avoid the clash and tension of the adventure proceeding inexorably within. Perhaps this was why he sometimes seemed to surprise in the dark faces which watched him a hint of amused and not entirely unkind contempt. He must be poor indeed, they seemed to say, to have been driven here. They knew that he was driven, in flight: the liberal, even revolutionary sentiments of which he was so proud meant nothing to them whatever. He was just a poor white boy in trouble and it was not in the least original of him to come running to the niggers.

This sentiment had sometimes seemed to stare out at him from the eyes of Rufus. He had refused to see it, for he had insisted that he and Rufus were equals. They were friends, far beyond the reach of anything so banal and corny as color. They had slept together, got drunk together, balled chicks together, cursed each other out, and loaned each other money. And yet how much, as it turned out, had each kept hidden in his heart from the other! It had all been a game, a game in which Rufus had lost his life. All of the pressures that each had denied had gathered together and killed him. Why had it been necessary to deny anything? What had been the point of the game? He turned into the room again and lit a cigarette and walked up and down. Well, perhaps they had been afraid that if they looked too closely into one another each would have found—he looked out of the window, feeling damp and frightened. Each would have found the abyss. Somewhere in his heart the black boy hated the white boy because he was white. Somewhere in his heart Vivaldo had feared and hated Rufus because he was black. They had balled chicks together, once or twice the same chick—why? And what had it done to them? And then they never saw the girl again. And they never really talked about it.

Once, while he was in the service, he and a colored buddy had been drunk, and on leave, in Munich. They were in a cellar someplace, it was very late at night, there were candles on the tables. There was one girl sitting near them. Who had dared whom? Laughing, they had opened their trousers and shown themselves to the girl. To the girl, but also to each other. The girl had calmly moved away, saying that she did not understand Americans. But perhaps she had understood them well enough. She had understood that their by-play had had very little to do with her. But neither could it be said that they had been trying to attract each other—they would never, certainly, have dreamed of doing it that way. Perhaps they had merely been trying to set their minds at ease; at ease as to which of them was the better man. And what had the black boy thought then? But the question was, What had *he* thought? He had thought, Hell, I'm doing all right. There might have been the faintest pang caused by the awareness that his colored buddy was doing possibly a little better than that, but, indeed, in the main, he had been relieved. It was out in the open, practically on the goddamn table, and it was just like his, there was nothing frightening about it.

He smiled—*I bet mine's bigger than yours is*—but remembered occasional nightmares in which this same vanished buddy pursued him through impenetrable forests, came at him with a knife on the edge of precipices, threatened to hurl him down steep stairs to the sea. In each of the nightmares he wanted revenge. Revenge for what?

He sat down again at his worktable. The page on the typewriter stared up at him, full of hieroglyphics. He read it over. It meant nothing whatever. Nothing was happening on that page. He walked back to the window. It was daylight now, and there were people on the streets, the expected, daytime people. The tall girl, with the bobbed hair and spectacles, wearing a long, loose coat, walked swiftly down the street. The grocery store was open. The old Rumanian who ran it carried in the case of milk which had been deposited on the sidewalk. He thought again that he had better get some sleep. He was seeing Ida today, they were having lunch with Richard and Cass. It was eight o'clock.

He stretched out on the bed and stared up at the cracks in the ceiling. He thought of Ida. He had seen her for the first time about seven years ago. She had been about fourteen. It was a holiday of some kind and Rufus had promised to take her out. And perhaps the reason he had asked Vivaldo to come with him was because Vivaldo had had to loan him the money. *Because I can't disappoint my sister, man.*

It had been a day rather like today, bright, cold, and hard. Rufus had been unusually silent and he, too, had been uncomfortable. He felt that he was forcing himself in where he did not belong. But Rufus had made the invitation and he had accepted; neither of them could get out of it now.

They had reached the house around one o'clock in the afternoon. Mrs. Scott had opened the door. She was dressed as though she, too, were going out, in a dark gray dress a little too short for her. Her hair was short but had lately been treated with the curling iron. She kissed Rufus lightly on the cheek.

"Hey, there," she said, "how's my bad boy?"

"Hey, yourself," said Rufus, grinning. There was an expression on his face which Vivaldo had never seen before. It was a kind of teasing flush of amusement and pleasure; as though his mother, standing there in her high heels, her gray dress, and with her hair all curled, had just done something extraordinarily winning. And this flush was repeated in his mother's darker face as she smiled—gravely—back at him. She seemed to take him in from top to toe and to know exactly how he had been getting along with the world.

"This here's a friend of mine," Rufus said, "Vivaldo."

"How do you do?" She gave him her hand, briefly. The brevity was not due to discourtesy or coldness, simply to lack of habit. Insofar as she saw him at all, she saw him as Rufus' friend, one of the inhabitants of the world in which her son had chosen to live. "Sit down, do. Ida'll be right out."

"She ready?"

"Lord, she been getting ready for days. Done drove me nearly wild." They sat down. Vivaldo sat near the window which looked out on a dirty back yard and the back fire escape of other buildings. Across the way, a dark man sat in front of his half-open window, staring out. In spite of the cold, he wore nothing but an undershirt. There was nothing in the yard except cans, bottles, papers, filth, and a single tree. "If anything had happened and you hadn't showed up, I hate to think of the weeping and wailing that would have gone on in this house." She paused and looked toward the door which led to the rest of the apartment. "Maybe you boys like a little beer while you waiting?"

"That all you got to offer us?" Rufus asked, with a smile. "Where's Bert?"

"Bert's down to the store and he ain't back yet. You know how your father is. He going to be sorry he missed you." She turned to Vivaldo. "Would you like a glass of beer, son? I'm sorry we ain't got nothing else—"

"Oh, beer's fine," said Vivaldo, looking at Rufus, "I'd love a glass of beer."

She rose and walked into the kitchen. "What your friend do? He a musician?"

"Naw," said Rufus, "he ain't got no talent."

Vivaldo blushed. Mrs. Scott returned with a quart bottle of beer and three glasses. She had a remarkably authoritative and graceful walk. "Don't you mind my boy," she said, "he's just full of the devil, he can't help it. I been trying to knock it out of him, but I ain't had much luck." She smiled at Vivaldo as she poured his beer. "You look kind of shy. Don't you be shy. You just feel as welcome here as if you was in your own house, you hear?" And she handed him his glass.

"Thank you," said Vivaldo. He took a swallow of the beer, thinking she'd probably be surprised to know how unwelcome he felt in his own house. And then, again, perhaps she wouldn't be surprised at all.

"You look as though you dressed up to go out someplace, too, old lady."

"Oh," she said, deprecatingly, "I'm just going down the block to see Mrs. Braithwaite. You remember her girl, Vickie? Well, she done had her baby. We going to the hospital to visit her."

"Vickie got a baby? *Already?*"

"Well, the young folks don't wait these days, you know that." She laughed and sipped her beer.

Rufus looked over at Vivaldo with a frown. "Damn," he said. "How's she doing?"

"Pretty well—under the *circumstances.*" Her pause suggested that the circumstances were grim. "She had a right fine boy, weighed seven pounds." She was about to say more; but Ida entered.

Rosa Guy

■ ■ ■

[1925–]

AS A CHILD, ROSA CUTHBERT IMMIGRATED FROM TRINIDAD TO Harlem in 1932. Two years later when her mother became ill and died, Cuthbert and her sister were sent to Brooklyn to live with a cousin, a disciple of black nationalist leader Marcus Garvey, whose politics influenced her later activism. In 1937, her father also died, leaving the two girls in the care of foster homes. At age fourteen, Cuthbert quit school for a job in a lingerie factory, where she became involved in the labor movement. In 1941, she married Warner Guy, had a child the next year, and divorced eight years later.

Guy became active in the American Negro theater during World War II. Central to her work as an actor and playwright was the goal of creating authentic African American drama devoid of traditional racial stereotypes. To this end, she cofounded the Harlem Writers Guild in 1951, a groundbreaking workshop for black writers that included Maya Angelou and Paule Marshall, among other emerging artists.

Guy's first novel, *Bird at My Window* (1966), portraying the social adversities of black men, was dedicated to the recently slain Malcolm X. The assassination of Martin Luther King, Jr., in 1968 led the author to tour the South, where she interviewed young people for her essay collection, *Children of Longing* (1970).

Guy is internationally renowned as a writer of young adult fiction, having established her literary reputation with publication of *The Friends* (1973) and *Ruby* (1976), the first of her many young adult novels. *Ruby* is set in a West Indian household in Harlem. As with Guy's most popular stories for young adults, her protagonist is a young black woman facing overwhelming odds. Unlike the author's other works, however, *Ruby* deals directly with lesbianism, making the book the first young adult novel to depict a lesbian affair. Ruby is a desperately lonely eighteen-year-old, whose mother has died, leaving her and sister Phyllisia under the watchful eye of their tyrannical father. When Ruby meets Daphne, a beautiful, strong-willed classmate of exceptional intelligence, her love for the outgoing young woman becomes a hopeful source of liberation. In this excerpt, Ruby, who is frightened of Daphne, gathers the courage to speak to her.

The moment the door slammed behind Calvin the next morning Ruby was up and dressing. Phyllisia opened one eye, and began complaining. "But Ruby, it's Saturday. What do you have to do this early?"

"I have to see someone."

"On a Saturday morning?"

Ruby rushed out without answering, and only when she actually found herself in the streets did she begin to doubt her intentions. Saturday was a morning that people stayed in bed. What if she was intruding where she was not wanted? Yet she quickened her steps, afraid of changing her mind. Turning the corner, Ruby bumped into someone. They side-stepped in the same direction at least three times before looking at each other.

"Ruby!"

"Orlando!" The meeting made them speechless. Then, to break the awkward silence, Orlando waved the container of milk he held in his hand.

"I just came from the store."

"I—I am taking a walk."

"Can—can I walk with you?"

"No—I'm afraid not. I—I want to be alone."

"Oh." He touched her hand. She drew away. "Well, anyway it's nice seeing you."

"But you can always see me, Orlando. All you have to do is turn your head when I pass."

"I—I mean to talk to…"

"Then—you can say hello."

"And get another bloody nose? But I'd even take that chance if I had a little encouragement."

"Encouragement? I always look at you. And anyway why blame me if you're afraid of my father?"

His pleasant manner changed. "Afraid? Look, once a guy gets mauled by a lion, he gets mighty careful about touching the cub."

"Not if he's a real man."

"Even if he is a brave man. It's you who don't have courage, Ruby. You're old enough to tell your old man—"

"I have to go now." She cut him off abruptly.

"But you're still so beautiful," he said. "I think you're the most beauti—" She ran, trying to push his words out of her ears; him out of her mind. But as she rode downtown she could not help reflecting that he had grown even better-looking than she remembered. He seemed taller, thicker, and he had begun to grow a beard.

Ruby hurried off the bus and to the building she had gone into the day before, only to find that it was not easy to enter this morning—not easy at all.

Why did I come? What will I say? What do I want from her? I don't know...I don't know...

She walked to the next corner, stood uncertainly. Then she walked back, stood again in front of the house, looking in. She walked to the opposite corner and wondered if she should wait for a bus. She walked back to the building, moving aside to allow a drunken-looking couple to enter. Panicking at the thought of following them in, she started again toward the bus stop, and might have gone home this time if she had not noticed a man leering at her from a parked car.

Lifting her head proudly, she went into the building, walked through the dark, dark hallway to the elevator, and pushed the button. She waited with impatience as the car creaked painfully downward and the elevator door reluctantly opened. She entered, praying apprehensively as the tired car labored back up, and thanked God when it stopped on the fourth floor.

She followed the letters on the doors to apartment 4E. But when she reached the door, she was unable to ring the bell. "I am not bold," she muttered. "I am not bold at all." Back at the elevator she was reluctant to get in it again and suffer its age, aches, tiredness. She decided to take the stairs, but only went down two steps before she turned, ran back up and rang the apartment bell.

Waiting was agony. Seconds, minutes eased away while her heart pounded in her chest, her ears, her temples. She heard no sound and thought that perhaps it was because of the pounding in her body. She leaned against the door, and the stillness she heard within the apartment was a waiting stillness. She stared hard at the peep-hole, wondering if someone was standing there staring back at her, refusing to open simply because it was her standing there. She flattened herself against the wall.

What am I doing here? What am I doing here? I must be mad...mad to be here...at the door of a stranger...a stranger who obviously despises me...I must be mad...

Suspense, fright, her lack of purpose forced her away from the door. She walked quickly toward the stairs.

"The name is Ruby Cathy, isn't it?"

Ruby whirled around. The door had cracked open and the words were spoken through the unlit, chain-latched opening in the doorway.

"Ye—es." Her unsteady answer did not appear to satisfy the listener, and, after a pause, she stumbled on. "Your—your friend gave me your address." Her voice trailed off. She did not want to lie. She had not come to lie. But how tell that hostile, unseen presence that she had followed her home from school one day? What was her reason? "I—I wanted to talk to you."

"Well fathers!" A soft exclamation. "Whatever friend can you mean? I have so few—and even my worst enemy knows better than to wake me up early on a Saturday morning." The tone—intellectual, carefully rounded, and pointed to embarrass—killed all hopes for understanding. And wasn't that the reason she had come?

"I—I—want—I—need..."

"These are not my office hours." The hostility deepened. Tears sprang into Ruby's eyes.

"Please, please," she sobbed softly. "I'm unhappy. I'm so unhappy."

"Stop that!" The voice was sharp; almost brutal. But the chain was lifted, the door opened. "Did you come to cry at my door and disturb my neighbors? Come in." And, as Ruby hesitated, "Don't stand there wetting my welcome mat. Come in, come in."

Daphne led her down a long, darkened hallway from where she could see the sun lighting the drawn shades of the living room. But Daphne's room struck her first. It was before the living room, at a corner where the hall turned sharply. Upon entering, Ruby noticed a second door in her room, closed off by heavy, wine-colored drapes, matching the drawn draperies at the window, which obviously led back into the L-shaped hall.

Daphne's room was bright, however, from overhead lights. It was a large room, furnished with a big mahogany desk and chair, a mahogany bureau, a ceiling-to-floor lamp, and a convertible couch-bed. The walls were lined with crammed bookcases.

Daphne sat down at the desk and motioned Ruby to the unmade bed. Ruby sat down primly on the edge, trying not to stare. Daphne was lovely. She wore shortie, see-through pajamas which revealed nothing more than that there was little softness about her. Her legs were well shaped, muscular; her shoulders broad, yet femininely rounded; her stomach flat and hard. Muscles accentuated her slim arms. Yet her hair, crispy-curly, tied with a string, hung to her shoulders, in a disarray Ruby found charming, softening the effect of her thick neck, her square jaw. Her feet were as well manicured as her long tapering fingers. Ruby had never seen such lovely feet. Struggling against showing her admiration, she settled for staring at Daphne's feet, and stared so intensely that Daphne's toes began to wiggle. This forced Ruby to raise her eyes, slowly; slowly noticing, even as she did—self-consciously—the smooth-ness of Daphne's taut, tan skin.

Then she was looking into the eyes, the gray eyes in which the mer-est glint of humor surfaced—mocking, waiting. The silence stretched out and Daphne's controlled face made clear her invention not to break it. Ruby reached in her mind for words.

"I—I…" She swallowed. Finally she blurted: "You don't like me, do you?"

Daphne's face relaxed in surprise. "As I live and breathe!" she exclaimed softly. "Did you wake me up on a Saturday morning to ask me that?" Reaching behind her on the desk she took a ten-inch toothpick from an inkwell and began digging around her large white teeth. Ruby gazed fascinated. They were so large, so lovely.

"But you don't—do you?" What did it matter that her words made little sense? At least it was a starting point.

"I don't believe it." Daphne blinked, deliberately. "But since you ask, let's put it this way. I neither like nor dislike you. That's the way I feel about most people. There are some, however, that I don't dig. You— happen to be one of them." Slipping slang into conversation was her way of showing that it was not her natural speech pattern, that she did it from choice. It seemed to matter to her that this was understood.

"Why? Tell me why? What have I ever done?"

"Everything to make me dislike you. But, as I said, I am not the disliking…"

"We have never even talked."

"I never talked to Hitler. I never talked to Wallace. I never talked to Tshombe, and I certainly never talked to Uncle Tom…."

"So you think I'm an Uncle Tom too?"

"I guess you want me to be frank. So let me say I think that you are worse than an Uncle Tom. At least Uncle Toms tom to survive. But you bow and scrape with such open-eyed sincerity. You are the most sincere person about kissing..."

"I only help Miss Gottlieb because she is old and crippled."

"Most of those teachers are old and they are all damn cripples," Daphne said scornfully. "Their society made them that way and they don't need our help to stay that way."

"Miss Gottlieb is so helpless."

"And she needs *you* to help her? She made it clear that she doesn't. She treats you like dirt. She treats us *all* like dirt. That's part of her disease. She actually believes we *are* dirt."

"I don't think that you..."

"She needs us, yes. But not in the way you think. And we help her. We help her by just sitting in her classroom so that she can vent her hatred on us or else she'd go mad. Who else can she vent her hatred on?"

"You don't understand," Ruby insisted patiently. "I can't look at anyone and see them..."

"What would she have done if you had never left your island? Have you ever asked yourself that? Don't you think she would have found someone else? Don't you think that she has always found someone through the years whom she makes the target of all her lovely invectives?"

"Miss Gottlieb doesn't mean half the things she says. She says them be—"

"Because they are in her to say." It was obvious that Daphne, as in school, believed only in her own ideas. "And because they're in her she will be saying them until the other half of her dies, and she will be thinking them until the last pinpoint of light goes out in her brain.

"She and those like her hate us for being black, and they hate us because they need us. Who else can crippled outcasts like them teach? Decent schools will not have them. They sit there being paid to tell us all kinds of things against ourselves; then they hate us if we don't accept it as gospel.

"They build themselves like gods on our backs, destroy us so that we are little imitations of themselves. Only most of us can't hide our distortions with higher education. Their educational system only makes us fit for the ghettoes, where we end up destroying each other.

"You see? That's what being God is all about. So, if they are such gods, why do they need *your* help?"

Anger flushed Daphne's face, the hate she denied quivered there, blazed out of her eyes. "But you, you have to prove you are bigger, better. Virgin Mary. Pontius Pilate, Ju—"

"Stop it! Don't. Please don't. Can't you see, I am not an American! I cannot hate like you!"

Daphne's head snapped to attention. Her smoldering eyes cooled slowly, grew thoughtful, reflective. Perhaps in the labyrinth of her mind the thought was raised that she had ruled out options, jumped to conclusions for which there might be more than one answer. She leaned forward, pointing her finger.

But at that moment someone brushed the curtain. Ruby turned, caught a fleeting impression of a man: tall, white. The curtain, however, was only slightly drawn and it remained only an impression. She turned back, but the chance for communication had slipped by in that second. Daphne sat back in her chair, toothpick between her teeth, a sardonic expression on her face.

Silence settled between them, heavy, undefinable, and Ruby, searching through Daphne's eyes, found in them an agelessness, a network of complexities far beyond her abilities to cope with.

Is it possible to be in the same city...the same class...certainly the same age group...and be so far apart? If so, then why am I here? What strange force directed me here...when it was so hard...so terribly hard?

She stood up, defeat weighing heavy on her thighs. She remained by the bed, needing words, words that eluded her. She looked at Daphne, begging for help. But Daphne refused her, and Ruby stood in that heavy silence, looking into the face with the mocking eyes, the mocking smile that was forcing the meeting, the moment, into history. Then suddenly the silence was broken, the weight lifted.

"Damn, Daphne, you got to start preaching so early in the morning?"

Ruby knew it was Daphne's mother because of her eyes. The woman stepped into the room past the heavy curtains, her manner brisk and breezy. "Damn, can hear you clear to the Bronx."

Apart from the eyes; the difference between them was startling. Where Daphne was at least six feet tall, Mrs. Duprey was possibly two or three inches over five. She was tiny, from her well-formed features down to her feet encased in spiked heels. She was fair, much fairer than

Daphne, and her hair was red, touched-up, although she had a red-head's complexion. Where Daphne's skin was smooth, poreless, Mrs. Duprey's was coarse with enlarged pores, giving her the look of hard living rather than of aging. But nowhere was the contrast so startling as in their speech patterns.

"Hey kitten." Mrs. Duprey flashed Ruby a professional smile. "You see what happens when you get up so damn early? A goddamn early worm is always snatched by a waiting bird. And the bird that sticks *its* beak out too early has had it at the claws of some vulture."

"Mumsy, this is Ruby." Daphne smiled affectionately, ignoring her mother's jibes. "She's in my class. We were here discuss—"

"Yeah, I heard," Mrs. Duprey said sarcastically. Then to Ruby: "I got to give it to you, baby. You sure know where to come to get the bull."

Mrs. Duprey's need to tear through her daughter's arrogance gave Ruby a feeling of comfort. It rounded the edge off her ignorance, redressed the balance in the room, handed her an ease with which she could speak to Daphne again.

"It *is* rather early," Daphne said, undaunted. "But we will forgive her this time, won't we Mumsy?" She went to her mother, hugged her roughly, kissed her, and teasingly ruffled the well-groomed hair.

Mrs. Duprey pushed Daphne away angrily, glared at her, and patted her hair into place. "Anyhow," she said, "I got to get my heels clicking. We underdevelopeds got to serve our time."

"Mumsy works as a barmaid in a restaurant..."

"In the heart of Harlem," Mrs. Duprey supplied, her voice edged in sarcasm. "The last stand of us high-yellers. Once upon a time we were all the craze, from one part of New York City to the other. But now, Black Is Beautiful. Those places that pay gets either blacks or whites. Either the afros or the straights. We in-betweeners are being eased out into the greasy spoons." She swayed out of the room, her high heels clicking.

"Mumsy used to be in show business, aiming for the big time," Daphne explained, a smile flitting across her face. Then, as though by common consent as the high heels clicked down the hall, they remained silent, listening. When the door slammed, Daphne yawned, continued. "She wanted to be a woman-libber but has to settle for being a liberated black. She's bitter." Stretching, she added, "And so you have met my family. They are fine people."

Nothing to answer. Nothing to add. Ruby walked to the door, stood, reluctant to open it, waiting. Waiting for Daphne to stop her. She touched the doorknob. "Daphne, do you think that Miss O'Brien is a cripple like the rest of the teachers in the system?"

She felt, rather than saw, the head jerk to attention. Daphne's tone was cool, cautious. "There are always rules that are proven by the exception—and these exceptions we should take advantage of." Ruby waited. Nothing more? "She is also a strong woman who can bend to pick up her own pointers."

Ruby opened the door, sifting Daphne's words for hidden meanings. It was too difficult. "I—I'm sorry I disturbed you. I—I just thought it would be nice to have a friend. I—am lonely."

"You-don't-know-what-the-word-lonely-means."

Daphne spoke slowly, holding Ruby at the door with her emphasis. "I happen to be the loneliest person in the world—with reason, to be sure. Do you see all those books? I have read them all—or almost. I am self-educated. That hardly attracts many friends. My father used to say that if you don't educate yourself, you won't get educated. And he was right. He started me reading when I was five, sent me to private school when I was twelve, and then he died.

"Can you imagine what it is, sitting in classrooms with pink-faced teachers who cannot teach, knowing more than they can ever know? That-is-the-loneliest-trip-in-the-world."

"You taught yourself everything? Even math?"

"What came hard I was tutored for. My mother paid. She did it under duress, but she did it."

"You are hard on her."

"We are hard on each other," Daphne said brusquely. "I just happen to be bigger. But she can put down those size threes of hers and a hurricane can't budge her."

Ruby looked around the room. Phyllisia would be in heaven here. "You really read all of these books?"

"My father was a black nationalist. Books were his bible."

"And he died."

"Yes."

"My mother is dead."

"What did she die of?"

"Cancer."

"One can almost call that a noble disease."

"What did your father die of?"

Sudden agitation came over Daphne. She hammered her fist on her palm angrily. "Well," she said finally, "it wasn't noble, that's for sure." Then, pulling herself together, she added, "Let us just say he went out of here on a hummer."

Feeling the intensity of Daphne's anger, Ruby did not ask what she meant. Instead she announced, "I guess I'd better be going."

"Before you tell me why you came?" The sardonic smile back on her face, Daphne stretched out on the bed.

"I—I told you."

"I didn't hear."

"I—I wanted to be your friend."

"And so now you are leaving. You get me out of bed early on a Saturday morning to tell me what you can say any day in school? You are satisfied?" Ruby looked at the floor. "Do you think you have achieved what you came for—or have you changed your mind?"

"No—no, I haven't changed…"

"Then why are you leaving?"

"Because I…Because I…"

"Dear me, sirs. What trouble she goes through to make friends and how easily discouraged she becomes." Getting up from bed, Daphne went to stand over Ruby, looking down as though from a great height. She held Ruby's chin, tilted her head back, kissed her full on the lips. Ruby gasped indignantly, her brown eyes wide, insulted.

Laughing, Daphne walked away, lay across the bed. "Good-bye, Bronzie. That is another trait I detected in you. Did anyone ever tell you what a great hypocrite you are?"

"Bronzie?" Ruby did not move. "Bronzie?"

"Yes. That's my private name for you. Bronzie. Brown, brown eyes, brown skin, brown hair—a perfect, natural bronze—and a hypocrite."

"Why would you say that? It's not true! I never lie!"

"I bet you don't. I just bet you don't. That's your great tragedy. You never think. You just say a lot of garbage that comes to mind and you call that truth. Good-bye. Go on—go out of that door. But don't forget—above all to thine own self be true, and it follows—etcetera, etcetera. Go on home."

But now it was Daphne who was lying Ruby realized. Daphne who was telling her to go yet not allowing her to go. Her tone was angry, a demanding anger. She was challenging her, daring her to walk out of that door, daring her to say good-bye. And Ruby could not walk away, could not say those parting, never-to-be-spoken-again words.

Ruby walked over to the bed, sat next to Daphne, touched the broad shoulder. "Daphne?" Then she was in the strong arms, feeling the full strength of those arms. Her mouth was being kissed, and she responded eagerly to those full, blessedly full lips. At last she found herself, a likeness to herself, a response to her needs, her age, an answer to her loneliness.

"If you don't know what you are doing"—Daphne pushed her away, searched her eyes—"you had better stop and ask somebody."

"Daphne. Daphne. I have never had a nickname before. I love that name—Bronzie."

AUDRE LORDE

■ ■ ■

[1934–1992]

THE MOST REVERED AFRICAN AMERICAN LESBIAN WRITER OF
her time, Audre Lorde stood as the political conscience of a generation
of lesbian feminists. She admonished white, middle-class feminist aca-
demics for what she saw as their complacency in the face of classism and
racism. "The master's tools will never dismantle the master's house," she
wrote, a reference to what she saw as the hypocrisy of white lesbian
feminism. She called on antiracist white feminists and lesbians to "reach
down into that deep place of knowledge inside herself and touch that
terror and loathing of any difference that lives there."

Born to working-class West Indian immigrants, Lorde was raised in
New York City. On graduating from Columbia University in 1961, she
married Edwin Ashley Rollins, with whom she had two children, before
divorcing in 1970. Lorde worked as a public librarian in Manhattan until
1968, when a grant from the National Endowment for the Arts enabled
her to take a position as poet in residence at Tougaloo College in
Mississippi.

That same year saw the publication of her debut book of poetry,
The First Cities (1968), followed by the more politically charged *Cabels to
Rage* (1970), the National Book Award nominee *From a Land Where Other
People Live* (1973), and later her most critically acclaimed collection, *The
Black Unicorn* (1978). Among the distinguishing features of Lorde's
poetry are her openness around her lesbianism and her outspoken
stance on matters of racial and sexual liberation. Indeed, her artistic
concerns suited the political climate and cultural transitions of the
1960s. For Lorde, however, her writing was more than merely protest

literature; it was, as she described it, the very sustenance for her well-being, if not survival, as an African American lesbian living with homophobia, racism, and sexism. Her work has also been cited as an especially fundamental source of inspiration for subsequent black lesbian poets, including Pat Parker and Cheryl Clarke, among others.

Lorde also wrote several landmark works of nonfiction, including two autobiographical texts, *The Cancer Journals* (1980), a chronicle of her struggle with breast cancer, and *Zami: A New Spelling of My Name* (1982), Lorde's classic account of her coming of age in the pre-Stonewall era. In titling her fictive memoir *Zami*, a West Indian name for women who work together as friends and lovers, Lorde was suggesting that white American demarcations of lesbianism fail to appreciate the complexities of black women's culture that fall beyond conventional parameters of sexual labels. This complication of sexual and racial identity politics is also a hallmark of her essay collections, *Sister Outsider: Essays and Speeches* (1984) and *A Burst of Light* (1988). Before her death from cancer in 1992, Lorde was the recipient of a number of prestigious awards, including being named the first woman Poet Laureate of New York State in 1991.

This excerpt from the final chapter of *Zami* introduces Afrekete, or "Kitty," a young African American lesbian whom Audre meets in 1957. The book is subtitled a "biomythology," indicating that traditions of autobiography and memoir have been overturned with the use of "mythology" or fiction. Thus, while the work recalls the author's life from her early years, it does not function as a conventional memoir. *Zami* is remarkable for its rare and authentic rendering of 1950s lesbian culture from the point of view of a black lesbian feminist.

from Zami: A New Spelling of My Name

[1982]

Gerri was young and Black and lived in Queens and had a powder-blue Ford that she nicknamed Bluefish. With her carefully waved hair and button-down shirts and gray-flannel slacks, she looked just this side of square, without being square at all, once you got to know her.

By Gerri's invitation and frequently by her wheels, Muriel and I had gone to parties on weekends in Brooklyn and Queens at different women's houses.

One of the women I had met at one of these parties was Kitty.

When I saw Kitty again one night years later in the Swing Rendezvous or the Pony Stable or the Page Three—that tour of second-string gay-girl bars that I had taken to making alone that sad lonely spring of 1957—it was easy to recall the St. Alban's smell of green Queens summer-night and plastic couch-covers and liquor and hair oil and women's bodies at the party where we had first met.

In that brick-faced frame house in Queens, the downstairs pine-paneled recreation room was alive and pulsing with loud music, good food, and beautiful Black women in all different combinations of dress.

There were whip-cord summer suits with starch-shiny shirt collars open at the neck as a concession to the high summer heat, and white gabardine slacks with pleated fronts or slim ivy-league styling for the very slender. There were wheat-colored Cowden jeans, the fashion favorite that summer, with knife-edge creases, and even then, one or two back-buckled grey pants over well-chalked buckskin shoes. There were garrison belts galore, broad black leather belts with shiny thin buckles that originated in army-navy surplus stores, and oxford-styled shirts of the new, iron-free dacron, with its stiff, see-through crispness. These shirts, short-sleeved and man-tailored, were tucked neatly into belted pants or tight, skinny straight skirts. Only the one or two jersey knit shirts were allowed to fall freely outside.

Bermuda shorts, and their shorter cousins, Jamaicas, were already making their appearance on the dyke-chic scene, the rules of which were every bit as cutthroat as the tyrannies of Seventh Avenue or Paris. These shorts were worn by butch and femme alike, and for this reason were slow to be incorporated into many fashionable gay-girl wardrobes, to keep the signals clear. Clothes were often the most important way of broadcasting one's chosen sexual role.

Here and there throughout the room the flash of brightly colored below-the-knee full skirts over low-necked tight bodices could be seen, along with tight sheath dresses and the shine of high thin heels next to bucks and sneakers and loafers.

Femmes wore their hair in tightly curled pageboy bobs, or piled high on their heads in sculptured bunches of curls, or in feather cuts framing their faces. That sweetly clean fragrance of beauty-parlor that hung over all Black women's gatherings in the fifties was present here also, adding its identifiable smell of hot comb and hair pomade to the other aromas in the room.

Butches wore their hair cut shorter, in a D.A. shaped to a point in the back, or a short pageboy, or sometimes in a tightly curled poodle that predated the natural afro. But this was a rarity, and I can only remember one other Black woman at that party besides me whose hair was not straightened, and she was an acquaintance of ours from the Lower East Side named Ida.

On a table behind the built-in bar stood opened bottles of gin, bourbon, scotch, soda and other various mixers. The bar itself was covered with little delicacies of all descriptions; chips and dips and little crackers and squares of bread laced with the usual dabs of egg-salad and sardine paste. There was also a platter of delicious fried chicken wings, and a pan of potato-and-egg salad dressed with vinegar. Bowls of olives and pickles surrounded the main dishes, with trays of red crab apples and little sweet onions on toothpicks.

But the centerpiece of the whole table was a huge platter of succulent and thinly sliced roast beef, set into an underpan of cracked ice. Upon the beige platter, each slice of rare meat had been lovingly laid out and individually folded up into a vulval pattern, with a tiny dab of mayonnaise at the crucial apex. The pink-brown folded meat around the pale cream-yellow dot formed suggestive sculptures that made a great hit with all the women present, and Pet, at whose house the party was being given and whose idea the meat sculptures were, smilingly acknowledged the many compliments on her platter with a long-necked graceful nod of her elegant dancer's head.

The room's particular mix of heat-smells and music gives way in my mind to the high-cheeked, dark young woman with the silky voice and appraising eyes (something about her mouth reminded me of Ann, the nurse I'd worked with when I'd first left home).

Perching on the edge of the low bench where I was sitting, Kitty absently wiped specks of lipstick from each corner of her mouth with the downward flick of a delicate forefinger.

"Audre...that's a nice name. What's it short for?"

My damp arm hairs bristled in the Ruth Brown music, and the heat. I could not stand anybody messing around with my name, not even with nicknames.

"Nothing. It's just Audre. What's Kitty short for?"

"Afrekete," she said, snapping her fingers in time to the rhythm of it and giving a long laugh. "That's me. The Black pussycat." She laughed again. "I like your hairdo. Are you a singer?"

"No." She continued to stare at me with her large direct eyes.

I was suddenly too embarrassed at not knowing what else to say to meet her calmly erotic gaze, so I stood up abruptly and said, in my best Laurel's-terse tone, "Let's dance."

Her face was broad and smooth under too-light make-up, but as we danced a foxtrot she started to sweat, and her skin took on a deep shiny richness. Kitty closed her eyes part way when she danced, and her one gold-rimmed front tooth flashed as she smiled and occasionally caught her lower lip in time to the music.

Her yellow poplin shirt, cut in the style of an Eisenhower jacket, had a zipper that was half open in the summer heat, showing collar-bones that stood out like brown wings from her long neck. Garments with zippers were highly prized among the more liberal set of gay-girls, because these could be worn by butch or femme alike on certain occasions, without causing any adverse or troublesome comments. Kitty's narrow, well-pressed khaki skirt was topped by a black belt that matched my own except in its newness, and her natty trimness made me feel almost shabby in my well-worn riding pants.

I thought she was very pretty, and I wished I could dance with as much ease as she did, and as effortlessly. Her hair had been straightened into short feathery curls, and in that room of well-set marcels and D.A.'s and pageboys, it was the closest cut to my own.

Kitty smelled of soap and Jean Naté, and I kept thinking she was bigger than she actually was, because there was a comfortable smell about her that I always associated with large women. I caught another spicy herb-like odor, that I later identified as a combination of coconut oil and Yardley's lavender hair pomade. Her mouth was full, and her lipstick was dark and shiny, a new Max Factor shade called "WARPAINT."

The next dance was a slow fish that suited me fine. I never knew whether to lead or to follow in most other dances, and even the effort to decide which was which was as difficult for me as having to decide all the time the difference between left and right. Somehow that simple distinction had never become automatic for me, and all that deciding usually left me very little energy with which to enjoy the movement and the music.

But "fishing" was different. A forerunner of the later one-step, it was, in reality, your basic slow bump and grind. The low red lamp and the crowded St. Alban's parlor floor left us just enough room to hold each other frankly, arms around neck and waist, and the slow intimate music moved our bodies much more than our feet.

That had been in St. Alban's, Queens, nearly two years before, when Muriel had seemed to be the certainty in my life. Now in the spring of this new year I had my own apartment all to myself again, but I was mourning. I avoided visiting pairs of friends, or inviting even numbers of people over to my house, because the happiness of couples, or their mere togetherness, hurt me too much in its absence from my own life, whose blankest hole was named Muriel. I had not been back to Queens, nor to any party, since Muriel and I had broken up, and the only people I saw outside of work and school were those friends who lived in the Village and who sought me out or whom I ran into at the bars. Most of them were white.

"Hey, girl, long time no see." Kitty spotted me first. We shook hands. The bar was not crowded, which means it probably was the Page Three, which didn't fill up until after midnight. "Where's your girlfriend?"

I told her that Muriel and I weren't together any more. "Yeah? That's too bad. You-all were kinda cute together. But that's the way it goes. How long you been in the 'life'?"

I stared at Kitty without answering, trying to think of how to explain to her, that for me there was only one life—my own—however I chose to live it. But she seemed to take the words right out of my mouth.

"Not that it matters," she said speculatively, finishing the beer she had carried over to the end of the bar where I was sitting. "We don't have but one, anyway. At least this time around." She took my arm. "Come on, let's dance."

Kitty was still trim and fast-lined, but with an easier looseness about her smile and a lot less make-up. Without its camouflage, her chocolate skin and deep, sculptured mouth reminded me of a Benin bronze. Her hair was still straightened, but shorter, and her black Bermuda shorts and knee socks matched her astonishingly shiny black loafers. A black turtleneck pullover completed her sleek costume. Somehow, this time, my jeans did not feel shabby beside hers, only a variation upon some similar dress. Maybe it was because our belts still matched—broad, black, and brass-buckled.

We moved to the back room and danced to Frankie Lymon's "Goody, Goody," and then to a Belafonte calypso. Dancing with her this time, I felt who I was and where my body was going, and that feeling was more important to me than any lead or follow.

The room felt very warm even though it was only just spring, and Kitty and I smiled at each other as the number ended. We stood waiting for the next record to drop and the next dance to begin. It was a slow Sinatra. Our belt buckles kept getting in the way as we moved in close to the oiled music, and we slid them around to the side of our waists when no one was looking.

For the last few months since Muriel had moved out, my skin had felt cold and hard and essential, like thin frozen leather that was keeping the shape expected. That night on the dance floor of the Page Three as Kitty and I touched our bodies together in dancing, I could feel my carapace soften slowly and then finally melt, until I felt myself covered in a warm, almost forgotten, slip of anticipation, that ebbed and flowed at each contact of our moving bodies.

I could feel something slowly shift in her also, as if a taut string was becoming undone, and finally we didn't start back to the bar at all between dances, but just stood on the floor waiting for the next record, dancing only with each other. A little after midnight, in a silent and mutual decision, we split the Page together, walking blocks through the West Village to Hudson Street where her car was parked. She had invited me up to her house for a drink.

The sweat beneath my breasts from our dancing was turning cold in the sharpness of the night air as we crossed Sheridan Square. I paused to wave to the steadies through the plate glass windows of Jim Atkins's on the corner of Christopher Street.

In her car, I tried not to think about what I was doing as we rode uptown almost in silence. There was an ache in the well beneath my stomach, spreading out and down between my legs like mercury. The smell of her warm body, mixed with the smell of feathery cologne and lavender pomade, anointed the car. My eyes rested on the sight of her coconut-spicy hands on the steering wheel, and the curve of her lashes as she attended the roadway. They made it easy for me to coast beneath her sporadic bursts of conversation with only an occasional friendly grunt.

"I haven't been downtown to the bars in a while, you know? It's funny. I don't know why I don't go downtown more often. But every once in a while, something tells me go and I go. I guess it must be different when you live around there all the time." She turned her gold-flecked smile upon me.

Crossing 59th Street, I had an acute moment of panic. Who was this woman? Suppose she really intended only to give me the drink which she had offered me as we left the Page? Suppose I had totally misunderstood the impact of her invitation, and would soon find myself stranded uptown at 3:00 A.M. on a Sunday morning, and did I even have enough change left in my jeans for carfare home? Had I put out enough food for the kittens? Was Flee coming over with her camera tomorrow morning, and would she feed the cats if I wasn't there? If I wasn't there.

If I wasn't there. The implication of that thought was so shaking it almost threw me out of the car.

I had had only enough money for one beer that night, so I knew I wasn't high, and reefer was only for special occasions. Part of me felt like a raging lioness, inflamed in desire. Even the words in my head seemed borrowed from a dime-store novel. But that part of me was drunk on the thighed nearness of this exciting unknown dark woman, who calmly moved us through upper Manhattan, with her patent-leather loafers and her camel's-hair swing coat and her easy talk, from time to time her gloved hand touching my denimed leg for emphasis.

Another piece of me felt bumbling, inept, and about four years old. I was the idiot playing at being a lover, who was going to be found out shortly and laughed at for my pretensions, as well as rejected out of hand.

Would it be possible—was it ever possible—for two women to share the fire we felt that night without entrapping or smothering each other? I longed for that as I longed for her body, doubting both, eager for both.

And how was it possible, that I should be dreaming the roll of this woman's sea into and around mine, when only a few short hours ago, and for so many months before, I had been mourning the loss of Muriel, so sure that I would continue being broken-hearted forever? And what then if I had been mistaken?

If the knot in my groin would have gone away, I'd have jumped out of the car door at the very next traffic light. Or so I thought to myself.

We came out of the Park Drive at Seventh Avenue and 110th Street, and as quickly as the light changed on the now deserted avenue, Afrekete turned her broad-lipped beautiful face to me, with no smile at all. Her great lidded luminescent eyes looked directly and startlingly into mine. It was as if she had suddenly become another person, as if the wall of glass formed by my spectacles, and behind which I had become so used to hiding, had suddenly dissolved.

In an uninflected, almost formal voice that perfectly matched and thereby obliterated all my question marks, she asked,

"Can you spend the night?"

And then it occurred to me that perhaps she might have been having the same questions about me that I had been having about her. I was left almost without breath by the combination of her delicacy and her directness—a combination which is still rare and precious.

For beyond the assurance that her question offered me—a declaration that this singing of my flesh, this attraction, was not all within my own head—beyond that assurance was a batch of delicate assumptions built into that simple phrase that reverberated in my poet's brain. It offered us both an out if necessary. If the answer to the question might, by any chance, have been no, then its very syntax allowed for a reason of impossibility, rather than of choice—"I can't," rather than "I won't." The demands of another commitment, an early job, a sick cat, etc., could be lived with more easily than an out-and-out rejection.

Even the phrase "spending the night" was less a euphemism for making love than it was an allowable space provided, in which one could move back or forth. If, perhaps, I were to change my mind before the traffic light and decide that no, I wasn't gay, after all, then a simpler companionship was still available.

I steadied myself enough to say, in my very best Lower East Side Casual voice, "I'd really like to," cursing myself for the banal words, and wondering if she could smell my nervousness and my desperate desire to be suave and debonair, drowning in sheer desire.

We parked half-in and half-out of a bus stop on Manhattan Avenue and 113th Street, in Gennie's old neighborhood.

Something about Kitty made me feel like a roller coaster, rocketing from idiot to goddess. By the time we had collected her mail from the broken mailbox and then climbed six flights of stairs up to her front door, I felt that there had never been anything else my body had intended to do more, than to reach inside of her coat and take Afrekete into my arms, fitting her body into the curves of mine tightly, her beige camel's-hair billowing around us both, and her gloved hand still holding the door key.

In the faint light of the hallway, her lips moved like surf upon the water's edge.

It was a 1½ room kitchenette apartment with tall narrow windows in the narrow, high-ceilinged front room. Across each window, there were built-in shelves at different levels. From these shelves tossed and frothed, hung and leaned and stood, pot after clay pot of green and tousled large and small-leaved plants of all shapes and conditions.

Later, I came to love the way in which the plants filtered the southern exposure sun through the room. Light hit the opposite wall at a point about six inches above the thirty-gallon fish tank that murmured softly, like a quiet jewel, standing on its wrought-iron legs, glowing and mysterious.

Leisurely and swiftly, translucent rainbowed fish darted back and forth through the lit water, perusing the glass sides of the tank for morsels of food, and swimming in and out of the marvelous world created by colored gravels and stone tunnels and bridges that lined the floor of the tank. Astride one of the bridges, her bent head observing the little fish that swam in and out between her legs, stood a little jointed brown doll, her smooth naked body washed by the bubbles rising up from the air unit located behind her.

Between the green plants and the glowing magical tank of exotic fish, lay a room the contents of which I can no longer separate in my mind. Except for a plaid-covered couch that opened up into the double bed which we set rocking as we loved that night into a bright Sunday morning, dappled with green sunlight from the plants in Afrekete's high windows.

I woke to her house suffused in that light, the sky half-seen through the windows of the top-floor kitchenette apartment, and Afrekete, known, asleep against my side.

Little hairs under her navel lay down before my advancing tongue like the beckoned pages of a well-touched book.

How many times into summer had I turned into that block from Eighth Avenue, the saloon on the corner spilling a smell of sawdust and liquor onto the street, a shifting indeterminate number of young and old Black men taking turns sitting on two upturned milk-crates, playing checkers? I would turn the corner into 113th Street towards the park, my steps quickening and my fingertips tingling to play in her earth.

And I remember Afrekete, who came out of a dream to me always being hard and real as the fine hairs along the under-edge of my navel. She brought me live things from the bush and from her farm set out in cocoyams and cassava—those magical fruits which Kitty bought in the West Indian markets along Lenox Avenue in the 140s or in the Puerto Rican *bodegas* within the bustling market over on Park Avenue and 116th Street under the Central Railroad structures.

"I got this under the bridge" was a saying from time immemorial, giving an adequate explanation that whatever it was had come from as far back and as close to home—that is to say was as authentic—as was possible.

We bought red delicious pippins, the size of french cashew apples. There were green plantains, which we half-peeled and then planted, fruit-deep, in each other's bodies until the petals of skin lay like tendrils of broad green fire upon the curly darkness between our upspread thighs. *There were ripe red finger bananas, stubby and sweet, with which I parted your lips gently, to insert the peeled fruit into your grape-purple flower.*

I held you, lay between your brown legs, slowly playing my tongue through your familiar forests, slowly licking and swallowing as the deep undulations and tidal motions of your strong body slowly mashed ripe banana into a beige cream that mixed with the juices of your electric flesh. Our bodies met again, each sur-face touched with each other's flame, from the tips of our curled toes to our tongues, and locked into our own wild rhythms, we rode each other across the thundering space, dripped like light from the peak of each other's tongue.

We were each of us both together. Then we were apart, and sweat sheened our bodies like sweet oil.

Sometimes Afrekete sang in a small club further uptown on Sugar Hill. Sometimes she clerked in the Gristede's Market on 97th Street and Amsterdam, and sometimes with no warning at all she appeared at the Pony Stable or Page Three on Saturday night. Once, I came home to Seventh Street late one night to find her sitting on my stoop at 3:00 A.M., with a bottle of beer in her hand and a piece of bright African cloth wrapped around her head, and we sped uptown through the dawn-empty city with a summer thunder squall crackling above us, and the wet city streets singing beneath the wheels of her little Nash Rambler.

There are certain verities which are always with us, which we come to depend upon. That the sun moves north in summer, that melted ice contracts, that the curved banana is sweeter. Afrekete taught me roots, new definitions of our women's bodies—definitions for which I had only been in training to learn before.

By the beginning of summer the walls of Afrekete's apartment were always warm to the touch from the heat beating down on the roof, and chance breezes through her windows rustled her plants in the window and brushed over our sweat-smooth bodies, at rest after loving.

We talked sometimes about what it meant to love women, and what a relief it was in the eye of the storm, no matter how often we had to bite our tongues and stay silent. Afrekete had a seven-year-old daughter whom she had left with her mama down in Georgia, and we shared a lot of our dreams.

"She's going to be able to love anybody she wants to love," Afrekete said, fiercely, lighting a Lucky Strike. "Same way she's going to be able to work any place she damn well pleases. Her mama's going to see to that."

Once we talked about how Black women had been committed without choice to waging our campaigns in the enemies' strongholds, too much and too often, and how our psychic landscapes had been plundered and wearied by those repeated battles and campaigns.

"And don't I have the scars to prove it," she sighed. "Makes you tough though, babe, if you don't go under. And that's what I like about you; you're like me. We're both going to make it because we're both too tough and crazy not to!" And we held each other and laughed and cried about what we had paid for that toughness, and how hard it was to explain to anyone who didn't already know it that soft and tough had to be one and the same for either to work at all, like our joy and the tears mingling on the one pillow beneath our heads.

And the sun filtered down upon us through the dusty windows, through the mass of green plants that Afrekete tended religiously.

I took a ripe avocado and rolled it between my hands until the skin became a green case for the soft mashed fruit inside, hard pit at the core. *I rose from a kiss in your mouth to nibble a hole in the fruit skin near the*

*navel stalk, squeezed the pale yellow-green fruit juice in thin ritual lines back and
forth over and around your coconut-brown belly.*

*The oil and sweat from our bodies kept the fruit liquid, and I massaged it
over your thighs and between your breasts until your brownness shone like a light
through a veil of the palest green avocado, a mantle of goddess pear that I slowly
licked from your skin.*

Then we would have to get up to gather the pits and fruit skins and
bag them to put out later for the garbagemen, because if we left them
near the bed for any length of time, they would call out the hordes of
cockroaches that always waited on the sidelines within the walls of Harlem
tenements, particularly in the smaller older ones under the hill of
Morningside Heights.

Afrekete lived not far from Genevieve's grandmother's house.

Sometimes she reminded me of Ella, Gennie's stepmother, who
shuffled about with an apron on and a broom outside the room where
Gennie and I lay on the studio couch. She would be singing her non-
stop tuneless little song over and over and over:

> Momma kilt me
> Poppa et me
> Po' lil' brudder
> suck ma bones.

And one day Gennie turned her head on my lap to say uneasily, "You
know, sometimes I don't know whether Ella's crazy, or stupid, or divine."

And now I think the goddess was speaking through Ella also, but
Ella was too beaten down and anesthetized by Phillip's brutality for her
to believe in her own mouth, and we, Gennie and I, were too arrogant
and childish—not without right or reason, for we were scarcely more
than children—to see that our survival might very well lay in listening to
the sweeping woman's tuneless song.

I lost my sister, Gennie, to my silence and her pain and despair, to
both our angers and to a world's cruelty that destroys its own young in
passing—not even as a rebel gesture or sacrifice or hope for another living of the spirit, but out of not noticing or caring about the destruction.
I have never been able to blind myself to that cruelty, which according to
one popular definition of mental health, makes me mentally unhealthy.

Afrekete's house was the tallest one near the corner, before the high rocks of Morningside Park began on the other side of the avenue, and one night on the Midsummer Eve's Moon we took a blanket up to the roof. She lived on the top floor, and in an unspoken agreement, the roof belonged mostly to those who had to live under its heat. The roof was the chief resort territory of tenement-dwellers, and was known as Tar Beach.

We jammed the roof door shut with our sneakers, and spread our blanket in the lee of the chimney, between its warm brick wall and the high parapet of the building's face. This was before the blaze of sulphur lamps had stripped the streets of New York of trees and shadow, and the incandescence from the lights below faded this far up. From behind the parapet wall we could see the dark shapes of the basalt and granite outcroppings looming over us from the park across the street, outlined, curiously close and suggestive.

We slipped off the cotton shifts we had worn and moved against each other's damp breasts in the shadow of the roof's chimney, making moon, honor, love, while the ghostly vague light drifting upward from the street competed with the silver hard sweetness of the full moon, reflected in the shiny mirrors of our sweat-slippery dark bodies, sacred as the ocean at high tide.

I remember the moon rising against the tilted planes of her upthrust thighs, and my tongue caught the streak of silver reflected in the curly bush of her dappled-dark maiden hair. *I remember the full moon like white pupils in the center of your wide irises.*

The moons went out, and your eyes grew dark as you rolled over me, and I felt the moon's silver light mix with the wet of your tongue on my eyelids.

Afrekete Afrekete ride me to the crossroads where we shall sleep, coated in the woman's power. The sound of our bodies meeting is the prayer of all strangers and sisters, that the discarded evils, abandoned at all crossroads, will not follow us, upon our journeys.

When we came down from the roof later, it was into the sweltering midnight of a west Harlem summer, with canned music in the streets and the disagreeable whines of overtired and overheated children. Nearby, mothers and fathers sat on stoops or milk crates and striped camp chairs, fanning themselves absently and talking or thinking about work as usual tomorrow and not enough sleep.

It was not onto the pale sands of Whydah, nor the beaches of Winneba or Annamabu, with cocopalms softly applauding and crickets keeping time with the pounding of a tar-laden, treacherous, beautiful sea. It was onto 113th Street that we descended after our meeting under the Midsummer Eve's Moon, but the mothers and fathers smiled at us in greeting as we strolled down to Eighth Avenue, hand in hand.

I had not seen Afrekete for a few weeks in July, so I went uptown to her house one evening since she didn't have a phone. The door was locked, and there was no one on the roof when I called up the stairwell.

Another week later, Midge, the bartender at the Pony Stable, gave me a note from Afrekete, saying that she had gotten a gig in Atlanta for September, and was splitting to visit her mama and daughter for a while.

We had come together like elements erupting into an electric storm, exchanging energy, sharing charge, brief and drenching. Then we parted, passed, reformed, reshaping ourselves the better for the exchange.

I never saw Afrekete again, but her print remains upon my life with the resonance and power of an emotional tattoo.

Samuel R. Delany

■ ■ ■

[1942–]

BORN TO A MIDDLE-CLASS FAMILY OF NEW YORKERS, SAMUEL R. Delany was a child prodigy whose literary gifts were fostered at an early age by a solid grounding in the arts. His prolific career began with the publication of his first science fiction novel, *The Jewels of Aptor* (1962), when he was only nineteen years old. A string of Nebula Award–winning works followed, among them the queer-oriented novels *Babel-17* (1966) and *The Einstein Intersection* (1967), as well as his gender-bending short story "Aye, and Gomorrah…" (1967), establishing Delany as the first African American science fiction writer to incorporate sexually transgressive themes. In spite of this success, he nearly abandoned literature for music in 1967, going so far as to move into an East Village commune with his band. Here he lived openly as a bisexual, an experience that influenced his appreciation for unconventional sexual identities. Indeed, the issue of marginalization, whether sexually or racially based, is a recurring topic in much of Delany's work.

The author returned to writing in 1970, publishing distinctly gay material in *Dhalgren* (1975), an epic-length novel whose intellectual, esoteric thrust appealed to readers beyond the traditional science fiction audience, making the book one of the best-selling science fiction novels of all time. Delany's homoerotic Nevèryon series followed in 1979 with the publication of *Tales of Nevèryon*, the first of four books that concluded with *The Bridge of Lost Desire* (1987) almost a decade later. The winner of the Hugo Award for science fiction as well as the Bill Whitehead Memorial Award for Lifetime Excellence in Gay and Lesbian Literature, Delany has also published several works of nonfiction,

including critical studies of literature, a number of hardcore gay porno-
graphic novels, a volume of memoirs entitled *Motion of Light in Water: Sex
and Science Fiction Writing in the East Village, 1957–1965* (1988), and the
well-received *Times Square Red, Times Square Blue* (1999).

In Delany's most openly queer work from the pre-Stonewall era,
"Aye, and Gomorrah...," gender-neutered astronauts known as "Spacers"
travel through space in search of *frelk*, a perverted race of outcasts with
a fetish for Spacers.

Aye, and Gomorrah....

[1967]

And came down in Paris:

Where we raced along the Rue de Medicis with Bo and Lou and Muse inside the fence, Kelly and me outside, making faces through the bars, making noise, making the Luxembourg Gardens roar at two in the morning. Then climbed out and down to the square in front of St. Sulpice where Bo tried to knock me into the fountain.

At which point Kelly noticed what was going on around us, got an ashcan cover, and ran into the pissoir, banging the walls. Five guys scooted out; even a big pissoir only holds four.

A very blond young man put his hand on my arm and smiled. "Don't you think, Spacer, that you...people should leave?"

I looked at his hand on my blue uniform. *"Est-ce que tu est un frelk?"*

His eyebrows rose, then he shook his head. "Une *frelk*," he corrected. "No, I am not. Sadly for me. You look as though you may once have been a man. But now..." He smiled. "You have nothing for me now. The police." He nodded across the street where I noticed the gendarmerie for the first time. "They don't bother us. You are strangers, though..."

But Muse was already yelling. "Hey come on! Let's get out of here, huh?" And left. And went up again.

And came down in Houston:

"God damn!" Muse said. "Gemini Flight Control—you mean this is where it all started? Let's get *out* of here, *please!*"

So took a bus out through Pasadena, then the monoline to Galveston, and were going to take it down the Gulf, but Lou found a couple with a pickup truck—

"Glad to give you a ride, Spacers. You people up there on them planets and things, doing all that good work for the government."

—who were going south, them and the baby, so we rode in the back for two hundred and fifty miles of sun and wind.

"You think they're frelks?" Lou asked, elbowing me. "I bet they're frelks. They're just waiting for us to give 'em the come-on."

"Cut it out. They're a nice, stupid pair of country kids." "That don't mean they ain't frelks!" "You don't trust anybody, do you?"

"No."

And finally a bus again that rattled us through Brownsville and across the border into Matamoros where we staggered down the steps into the dust and the scorched evening with a lot of Mexicans and chickens and Texas Gulf shrimp fishermen—who smelled worst—and we shouted the loudest. Forty-three whores—I counted—had turned out for the shrimp fishermen, and by the time we had broken two of the windows in the bus station, they were all laughing. The shrimp fishermen said they wouldn't buy us no food but would get us drunk if we wanted, 'cause that was the custom with shrimp fishermen. But we yelled, broke another window; then, while I was lying on my back on the telegraph office steps, singing, a woman with dark lips bent over and put her hands on my cheeks. "You are very sweet." Her rough hair fell forward. "But the men, they are standing around watching *you*. And that is taking up *time*. Sadly, their time is our money. Spacer, do you not think you…people should leave?"

I grabbed her wrist. *"Usted!"* I whispered. *"Usted es una frelka?"*

"Frelko in español." She smiled and patted the sunburst that hung from my belt buckle. "Sorry. But you have nothing that…would be useful to me. It is too bad, for you look like you were once a woman, no? And I like women, too…."

I rolled off the porch.

"Is this a drag, or is this a drag!" Muse was shouting. "Come *on!* Let's *go!"*

We managed to get back to Houston before dawn, somehow.

And went up.

And came down in Istanbul:

That morning it rained in Istanbul.

At the commissary we drank our tea from pear-shaped glasses, looking out across the Bosphorus. The Princes Islands lay like trash heaps before the prickly city.

"Who knows their way in this town?" Kelly asked.

"Aren't we going around together?" Muse demanded. "I thought we were going around together."

"They held up my check at the purser's office," Kelly explained. "I'm flat broke. I think the purser's got it in for me," and shrugged. "Don't want to, but I'm going to have to hunt up a rich frelk and come on friendly," went back to the tea; *then* noticed how heavy the silence had become. "Aw, come *on,* now! You gape at me like that and I'll bust every bone in that carefully-conditioned-from-puberty body of yours. Hey you!" meaning me. "Don't give me that holier-than-thou gawk like you never went with no frelk!"

It was starting.

"I'm not gawking," I said and got quietly mad.

The longing, the old longing.

Bo laughed to break tensions. "Say, last time I was in Istanbul— about a year before I joined up with this platoon—I remember we were coming out of Taksim Square down Istiqlal. Just past all the cheap movies we found a little passage lined with flowers. Ahead of us were two other spacers. It's a market in there, and farther down they got fish, and then a courtyard with oranges and candy and sea urchins and cabbage. But flowers in front. Anyway, we noticed something funny about the spacers. It wasn't their uniforms: they were perfect. The haircuts: fine. It wasn't till we heard them talking— They were a man and woman dressed up like spacers, trying to *pick up frelks!* Imagine, queer for frelks!"

"Yeah," Lou said. "I seen that before. There were a lot of them in Rio."

"We beat hell out of them two," Bo concluded. "We got them in a side street and went to *town!*"

Muse's tea glass clicked on the counter. "From Taksim down Istiqlal till you get to the flowers? Now why didn't you say that's where the frelks were, huh?" A smile on Kelly's face would have made that okay. There was no smile.

"Hell," Lou said. "Nobody ever had to tell me where to look. I go out in the street and frelks smell me coming. I can spot 'em halfway along Piccadilly. Don't they have nothing but tea in this place? Where can you get a drink?"

Bo grinned. "Moslem country, remember? But down at the end of the Flower Passage there're a lot of little bars with green doors and marble counters where you can get a liter of beer for about fifteen cents in lira. And there're all these stands selling deep-fat-fried bugs and pig's gut sandwiches—"

"You ever notice how frelks can put it away? I mean liquor, not… pig's guts."

And launched off into a lot of appeasing stories. We ended with the one about the frelk some spacer tried to roll who announced: "There're two things I go for. One is spacers; the other is a good fight…."

But they only allay. They cure nothing. Even Muse knew we would spend the day apart, now.

The rain had stopped, so we took the ferry up the Golden Horn. Kelly straight off asked for Taksim Square and Istiqlal and was directed to a dolmush, which we discovered was a taxicab, only it just goes one place and picks up lots and lots of people on the way. And it's cheap.

Lou headed off over Ataturk Bridge to see the sights of New City. Bo decided to find out what the Bolma Boche really was; and when Muse discovered you could go to Asia for fifteen cents—one lira and fifty krush—well, Muse decided to go to Asia.

I turned through the confusion of traffic at the head of the bridge and up past the gray, dripping walls of Old City, beneath the trolley wires. There are times when yelling and helling won't fill the lack. There are times when you must walk by yourself because it hurts so much to be alone.

I walked up a lot of little streets with wet donkeys and wet camels and women in veils; and down a lot of big streets with buses and trash baskets and men in business suits.

Some people stare at spacers; some people don't. Some people stare or don't stare in a way a spacer gets to recognize within a week after coming out of training school at sixteen. I was walking in the park when I caught her watching. She saw me and looked away.

I ambled down the wet asphalt. She was standing under the arch of a small, empty mosque shell. As I passed, she walked out into the court-yard among the cannons.

"Excuse me."

I stopped.

"Do you know whether or not this is the shrine of St. Irene?" Her English was charmingly accented. "I've left my guidebook home."

"Sorry. I'm a tourist too."

"Oh." She smiled. "I am Greek. I thought you might be Turkish because you are so dark."

"American red Indian." I nodded. Her turn to curtsy.

"I see. I have just started at the university here in Istanbul. Your uniform, it tells me that you are"—and the pause, all speculations resolved—"a spacer."

I was uncomfortable. "Yeah." I put my hands in my pockets, moved my feet around on the soles of my boots, licked my third from the rear left molar—did all the things you do when you're uncomfortable. You're so exciting when you look like that, a frelk told me once. "Yeah, I am." I said it too sharply, too loudly, and she jumped a little.

So now she knew I knew she knew I knew, and I wondered how we would play out the Proust bit.

"I'm Turkish," she said. "I'm not Greek. I'm not just starting. I'm a graduate in art history here at the university. These little lies one makes up for strangers to protect one's ego…why? Sometimes I think my ego is very small."

That's one strategy.

"How far away do you live?" I asked. "And what's the going rate in Turkish lira?" That's another.

"I can't pay you." She pulled her raincoat around her hips. She was very pretty. "I would like to." She shrugged and smiled. "But I am…a poor student. Not a rich one. If you want to turn around and walk away, there will be no hard feelings. I shall be sad though."

I stayed on the path. I thought she'd suggest a price after a little while. She didn't.

And *that's* another.

I was asking myself, *What do you want the damn money for anyway?* when a breeze upset water from one of the park's great cypresses.

"I think the whole business is sad." She wiped drops from her face. There had been a break in her voice, and for a moment I looked too closely at the water streaks. "I think it's sad that they have to alter you to make you a spacer. If they hadn't, then *we.*… If spacers had never been, then we could not be…the way we are. Did you start out male or female?"

Another shower. I was looking at the ground and droplets went down my collar.

"Male," I said. "It doesn't matter."

"How old are you? Twenty-three, twenty-four?"

"Twenty-three," I lied. It's reflex. I'm twenty-five, but the younger they think you are, the more they pay you. But I didn't want her *damn* money—

"I guessed right then." She nodded. "Most of us are experts on spacers. Do you find that? I suppose we have to be." She looked at me with wide black eyes. At the end of the stare, she blinked rapidly. "You would have been a fine man. But now you are a spacer, building water-conservation units on Mars, programming mining computers on

Ganymede, servicing communication relay towers on the moon. The alteration…" Frelks are the only people I've ever heard say "the alteration" with so much fascination and regret. "You'd think they'd have found some other solution. They could have found another way of neutering you, turning you into creatures not even androgynous; things that are—"

I put my hand on her shoulder, and she stopped like I'd hit her. She looked to see if anyone was near. Lightly, so lightly then, she raised her hand to mine.

I pulled my hand away. "That are what?"

"They could have found another way." Both hands in her pockets now.

"They could have. Yes. Up beyond the ionosphere, baby, there's too much radiation for those precious gonads to work right anywhere you might want to do something that would keep you there over twenty-four hours, like the moon, or Mars, or the satellites of Jupiter—"

"They could have made protective shields. They could have done more research into biological adjustment—"

"Population Explosion time," I said. "No, they were hunting for an excuse to cut down kids back then—especially deformed ones."

"Ah, yes." She nodded. "We're still fighting our way up from the neopuritan reaction to the sex freedom of the twentieth century."

"It was a fine solution." I grinned and absently rubbed my crotch. "I'm happy with it." I've never known why that's so much more obscene when a spacer does it.

"Stop it," she snapped, moving away.

"What's the matter?"

"Stop it," she repeated. "Don't do that! You're a child."

"But they choose us from children whose sexual responses are hopelessly retarded at puberty."

"And your childish, violent substitutes for love? I suppose that's one of the things that's attractive. You really don't regret you have no sex?"

"We've got you," I said.

"Yes." She looked down. I glanced to see the expression she was hiding. It was a smile. "You have your glorious, soaring life—*and* you have us." Her face came up. She glowed. "You spin in the sky, the world spins under you, and you step from land to land, while we…" She turned her head right, left, and her black hair curled and uncurled on the shoulder of her coat. "We have our dull, circled lives, bound in gravity, *worshiping* you!" She looked back at me. "Perverted, yes? In love with a bunch of corpses in free fall!" Suddenly she hunched her shoulders. "I don't like having a free-fall-sexual-displacement complex."

"That always sounded like too much to say."

She looked away. "I don't like being a frelk. Better?"

"I wouldn't like it either. Be something else."

"You don't choose your perversions. *You* have no perversions at all. *You're* free of the whole business. I love you for that, spacer. My love starts with the fear of love. Isn't that beautiful? A pervert substitutes something unattainable for 'normal' love: the homosexual, a minor, the fetishist, a shoe or a watch or a girdle. Those with free-fall-sexual-dis—"

"Frelks."

"Frelks substitute"—she looked at me sharply again—"loose, swinging meat."

"That doesn't offend me."

"I wanted it to."

"You don't have desires. You wouldn't understand."

"Go on."

"I want you because you can't want me. That's the pleasure. If someone really had a sexual reaction to…us, we'd be scared away. I wonder how many people there were before there were you, waiting for your creation. We're necrophiles. I'm sure grave robbing has fallen off since you started going up. But you don't understand." She paused. "If you did, then I wouldn't be scuffing leaves now and trying to think from whom I could borrow sixty lira." She stepped over the knuckles of a root that had cracked the pavement. "And that, incidentally, is the going rate in Istanbul."

I calculated. "Things still get cheaper as you go east."

"You know," and she let her raincoat fall open, "you're different from the others. You at least *want* to know—"

I said, "If I spat on you for every time you'd said that to a spacer, you'd drown."

"Go back to the moon, loose meat." She closed her eyes. "Swing on up to Mars. There are satellites around Jupiter where you might do some good. Go up and come down in some other city."

"Where do you live?"

"You want to come with me?"

"Give me something," I said. "Give me something—it doesn't have to be worth sixty lira. Give me something that you like, anything of yours that means something to you."

"No!"

"Why not?"

"Because I—"

"—don't want to give up part of that ego. None of you frelks do!"

"You really don't understand I just don't want to buy you?"

"You have nothing to buy me with."

"You are a child," she said. "I love you."

We reached the gate of the park. She stopped, and we stood time enough for a breeze to rise and die in the grass. "I…" she offered tentatively, pointing without taking her hand from her coat pocket. "I live right down there."

"All right," I said. "Let's go."

A gas main had once exploded along this street, she explained to me, a gushing road of fire as far as the docks. Overhot and overquick, it had been put out within minutes. No building had fallen, but the charred facias glittered. "This is sort of an artist and student quarter." We crossed the cobbles. "Yuri Pasha, number fourteen. In case you're ever in Istanbul again." Her door was covered with black scales; the gutter was thick with garbage.

"A lot of artists and professional people are frelks," I said, trying to be inane.

"So are lots of other people." She walked inside and held the door. "We're just more flamboyant about it."

On the landing there was a portrait of Ataturk. Her room was on the second floor. "Just a moment while I get my key—"

Moonscapes! Marsscapes! On her easel was a six-foot canvas showing the sunrise flaring on a crater's rim! There were copies of the original Observer pictures of the moon pinned to the wall, and pictures of every smooth-faced general in the International Space Corps.

On one corner of her desk was a pile of those photo magazines about spacers that you can find in most kiosks all over the world: I've seriously heard people say they were printed for adventurous-minded high school children. They've never seen the Danish ones. She had a few of those too. There was a shelf of art books, art history texts. Above them were six feet of cheap paper-covered space operas: *Sin of Space Station #12, Rocket Rake, Savage Orbit...*

"Arrack?" she asked. "Ouzo, or pernod? You've got your choice. But I may pour them all from the same bottle." She set out glasses on the desk, then opened a waist-high cabinet that turned out to be an icebox. She stood up with a tray of lovelies: fruit puddings, Turkish delight, braised meats.

"What's this?"

"Dolmades. Grape leaves filled with rice and pignolias."

"Say it again?"

"Dolmades. Comes from the same Turkish word as 'dolmush.' They both mean 'stuffed.'" She put the tray beside the glasses. "Sit down."

I sat on the studio-couch-that-becomes-bed. Under the brocade I felt the deep, fluid resilience of a glycogel mattress. They've got the idea that it approximates the feeling of free fall. "Comfortable? Would you excuse me for a moment? I have some friends down the hall. I want to see them for a moment." She winked. "They like spacers."

"Are you going to take up a collection for me?" I asked. "Or do you want them to line up outside the door and wait their turn?"

She sucked a breath. "Actually, I was going to suggest both." Suddenly she shook her head. "Oh, what do you want!"

"What will you give me? I want something," I said. "That's why I came. I'm lonely. Maybe I want to find out how far it goes. I don't know yet."

"It goes as far as you will. Me? I study, I read, paint, talk with my friends"—she came over to the bed, sat down on the floor—"go to the theater, look at spacers who pass me on the street, till one looks back; I am lonely too." She put her head on my knee. "I want something. But," and after a minute neither of us had moved, "you are not the one who will give it to me."

"You're not going to pay me for it," I countered. "You're not, are you?"

On my knee her head shook. After a while she said, all breath and no voice, "Don't you think you...should leave?"

"Okay," I said, and stood up.

She sat back on the hem of her coat. She hadn't taken it off yet. I went to the door.

"Incidentally." She folded her hands in her lap. "There is a place in New City you might find what you're looking for, called the Flower Passage—"

I turned toward her, angry. "The frelk hangout? Look, I don't need money! I said anything would do! I don't want—"

She had begun to shake her head, laughing quietly. Now she lay her cheek on the wrinkled place where I had sat. "Do you persist in mis-understanding? It is a spacer hangout. When you leave, I am going to visit my friends and talk about...ah, yes, the beautiful one that got away. I thought you might find...perhaps someone you know."

With anger, it ended.

"Oh," I said. "Oh, it's a spacer hangout. Yeah. Well, thanks."

And went out. And found the Flower Passage, and Kelly and Lou and Bo and Muse. Kelly was buying beer so we all got drunk, and ate fried fish and fried clams and fried sausage, and Kelly was waving the money around, saying, "You should have seen him! The changes I put that frelk through, you should have seen him! Eighty lira is the going rate here, and he gave me a hundred and fifty!" and drank more beer. And went up.

RED JORDAN AROBATEAU

■ ■ ■

[1943–]

AN AFRICAN AMERICAN FEMALE-TO-MALE TRANSSEXUAL WRITER, Red Jordan Arobateau is known for his series of popular S/M novels. Born to a working-class Honduran father and light-skinned African American mother, Arobateau was raised on Chicago's South Side. His mixed racial heritage allowed him to pass for white, but he embraced his blackness, even taking on his mother's maiden name of Jordan. Arobateau identified himself as homosexual for the first time while reading a lesbian pulp novel in 1960. This discovery led him to San Francisco, where he found his voice as a writer during the 1970s. After his father died in 1973, Arobateau felt free to write about the taboo subject matter that established his reputation as a prolific writer of S/M erotica.

His first novel, the self-published *Bars Across Heaven* (1977), was an autobiographical story about a black lesbian street hustler named "Flip" Jordan. As with much of Arobateau's fiction, the novel is set in black urban settings, where prostitution, pawnshops, and drugs are part of black lesbian life. *Bars Across Heaven* was followed by forty self-published books of fiction, including collections of short stories with such provocative titles as "Golden Showers," "Gang Rape," "Reflections of a Lesbian Trick," and "Pleasure in the Glitter Gutter." Some critics have responded to his work by arguing that his sexually explicit work could not have been written by a woman—even though Arobateau identified as a lesbian until his gender transition in 1998. But as scholar Ann Allen Shockley said, in the title of her 1982 profile, Red Jordan Arobateau is "A Different Kind of Black Lesbian Writer." Indeed, his work had been rejected by all the feminist and gay presses until Judy Grahn published his short story "Suzie Q" in the anthology *True to Life Adventure Stories* (1978).

In this story, Arobateau gives voice to Suzie Q, a spirited black lesbian prostitute. Written in the vernacular of black street language, the story is a significant departure in black lesbian fiction. Indeed, "Suzie Q" is a rarity among African American women's fiction in general. As this excerpt demonstrates, working-class issues complicate oversimplified discussions of race and sexual orientation among black lesbians.

She breezed into the club with a strong rap. Television was into women's lib and it was a new day. Women was tired of giving up their money to a nigger. A ho was no longer a bitch.

The bar was filled with white hippies. Wall painted black, and red lamps along the sides. A horse-shoe shaped bar that someone had thrown together up front, dance floor behind it. Tables and chairs along the wall. Suzie thought how much it looked like Pappy's which had hos lined up gabbing or nodding out, leaning up against the counter where fried chicken and soft drinks was for sale, when they should be out on the curb working. Nothing but women on the barstools; black and red shadows cast on their faces that were boyish smooth and hairless. But there was a difference. These women here were lesbians.

She was a character with the appearance of mini mouse. Skinny legs. Her shoes too big for her feet. —She'd bought 'em, now she'd have to wear 'em. Bronze complexion, her hair cornrowed—at ten cents a braid down at the Kings and Queens Beauty Salon—but hiding under a wig that sat on her like a hat. Full lips, big round eyes with a hardened look that she could turn on or off. Of medium height— 5'5"—and weight, 130 pounds well proportioned on her frame. Not an extra ounce of fat from all that walking and standing. Her spirits are exuberant tonight. A party mood. Body full of energy—that came from her mind, for physically she was worn out. Suzie had on a tiny little outfit pink, showing a big expanse of bare copper colored skin on arms and legs that bore plenty of bruises. Scars darker then others, some fresh bluish marks.

She had got to the club—half way 'cross town—by showing the bus driver an old transfer she'd found in the street. The first bus she'd got on, the driver had read it and told her: "THIS IS NO GOOD LADY." Suzie yelled back: "DID IT COME OUT YO' POCKET?" Dismounted, walked 5 blocks, tried another bus, and as she'd sashayed down the aisle weary, in a world-wise manner, the driver didn't have enough nerve to call her back and demand she feed the fare box those precious coins.

A bedraggled pheasant, she walked in the door, her plumage dragging. "The only reason why I come back here wuz we *pahteed* last time we wuz here. Folks get down, girl, with whistles and bells and tambourines, and they *dannnce!*"

Of course that was the only reason for being here that she'd admit.

On the bus ride, she'd seen out the window black youths do Kung Fu like alley cats leaping into thin air, backs arched. And she made a mental note to herself, "that's the next thang, soon as I get my place, get my kids, I'm gonna learn Karate, and I'll chop a niggers head off if he mess with me one more time."

Red and black lights revolved, her brain spun. Sleepless too many nights. The wig sat listlessly on her head. The bar curved away from her into the distance, as if embracing the cash register. Not but a few women, holding conversations in low tones. Monday, it was an off night. A high ceiling, and the bar echoed with notes from a jukebox. "Last time I wuz here they had a live band. Guess 'cause it's Monday…but that's cool."

Suzie's not too smart, but very verbose. A meager intelligence had been allotted to her, plus no education going for her. In addition, she's young and hasn't gained wisdom. But it don't stop her, not one bit! Talkative. One white woman, the sophisticated kind has come up; despite that $40 like the skins of frogs—green, slippery against her thigh, tucked in the top of her stockings, Suzie tells the woman, "Buy me a drank, I'm broke." And her eyes, a moment ago wide, staring into space as she jiggled her legs and tapped her nails on the bar, her look immediately hardens. "Ain't got a cent, it's the end of the month," she adds. "Oh really?" Says the woman looking directly in her eyes. She's overweight, older, in her 40's and has a pantsuit over her pear-shaped body, and a friendly smile on her face. Gives the young woman a knowing look. Suzie's strong hustling rap won't get over too swell here. It wasn't necessary, and most women can see thru it.

The lady buys her a drink. Soon the two are rapping. Words spill out Suzie's mouth one after another. A little wad of white stuff is in the corner of her mouth, not wiped away and her eyes glazed—from not eating or sleeping. The woman asks her if she'd like to dance. "No. My body hurts. I'm fucccccked up."

She gives up on trying to view the women as a trick. Tho she may never abandon the hustle that she's developed over the last 5 years—thru necessity—Suzie is not as cold hearted as she might seem at first.

She talks about her life, her kids, her man, and why she's here. The woman nods solemnly. After a couple of drinks in the all-women bar, which is still empty, it's early, just 10pm, when the red lights are revolving over the barflies like goldfish in a bowl— "Your body is beautiful." The woman says with a knowing twinkle. And touches her arm briefly. Suzie nods, "Right on." She says nodding like she's a million miles away, "but no touching please." "I'm sorry." The woman says, modestly. "That's allright— I know you don't know any better." Suzie says, chin in the air. —She can't stand for people to touch her—unless she's getting paid for it.

Down the bar at one end of its magnet-ends, two women are throwing the dice cups. "A HORSE ON YOU." One yells.

Finally the woman leaves. She has to be at work at the office 9 the next morning. "TAKE CARE OF YOUR BODY!" She calls out in a friendly tone, and waves goodbye.

"I will, I'm number one." Suzie says, but no one hears her, and the woman is gone out the door.

Red and black shadows play up the walls for her to watch—nothing else much is happening. Relaxing in a stretch of bar all to herself—empty stools on both sides, full lips touch the rim of her glass, the beverage is almost gone, soon she'll have to worry about getting the next drink, but those green bucks in her stocking she will preserve to the bitter end.

One arm stretches to her purse a few inches away on the wet-stained bar. Bruises on the warm brown flesh; she retrieves a cigarette, snaps her lighter: "No more, I'm gonna learn Karate, Kung Fu, K-nife and K-razor…and K-gun. Sheit."

All thoughts of women's liberation are out. —There were still many obstacles so many miles high and wide. She's just trying to survive number one. Get her a little money together and get her own place and get her kids back from her mother's. This was her struggle. She wished it was less real and mo' fantasy, like a Mickey Mouse cartoon where the villain gets WHOOPED over the head with a board. But this female liberation like drops of water one by one was beginning to touch her life with information; beginning with the pussy between her own legs, it's as real as life and death. Stark as a heart attack.

Flash. —It was always him first, never her. And she was sick of being in the life, already. Tired of a backstreet reputation and a sordid existence.

The Good News of liberation had begun to attack this sistah's brain with doubts as to her present profession.

The stop watch in her life. The second glimpse at herself. She was about to move into a new dimension.

In 1977, women were divided.

"My kids are first. They come first. My kids. I got two, a girl, 6, the boy, 4. They're number one. I'm getting my apartment and get my kids back." She tells the bartender vehemently. The bartender agrees and she moves on down the line filling glasses. Suzie's thick lips close together—lipstick is wearing off, and her brown eyes stare into the pit of sleeplessness inside her brain.

"When I left Flash Gordon he was sitting there in nothing but his fur-lined hat with his hair in rollers underneath. Pectoral muscles in his big brown chest, curly hair disappearing down his stomach in an arrow pointing right at the only thing he's got that's worth anything—his dick. Big brown feets on the shag rug, and a mean expression on his face.

Now don't get me wrong, Flash Gordon is not the kids' father. I just chose Flash last month.

I'm in the life."

The clock moved swiftly towards 12 midnight.

No cars were out in front of the club. Gaps of parking places. Next door to a shoddy hotel. Bottles once filled with wine along the gutters can be seen in the empty spaces. But by 12:30, inside was a little party happening. Bright colors of pantsuits and evening gowns. Folks blowing whistles. You see, welfare folks own no cars. And this Monday was the 30th, Mothers Day, so quite a little crowd had arrived.

A butch came to the bar. Brown hair in a short natural, spiffily attired in jacket and pants to match plus vest. Platform shoes on her small feet that elevated her to 5'5" tall. Her brown face held no outward sign of the emotions within her, coolly she strode to the bar.

When she bought her first beverage of the evening—a Coca Cola dyed pink in a tall glass, with it came a napkin and a note that read:

FOR YOUR OWN PROTECTION PLEASE END YOUR CONVERSATIONS INSIDE THE BAR AND NOT OUT IN FRONT OF THE BAR AFTER 2:00 OR YOU WILL BE ARRESTED. SO BE FOREWARNED, IT'S FOR YOUR OWN PROTECTION.

The police had been cracking down on the club—they considered it a dive—but, anybody could see, as the black and red lights danced their rays over the revelers who leapt into the air like gazelles, it was not nothing bad going on here, it just bes a party!

The stud sat down at the bar—after debating whether or not to occupy a booth. But you can't meet anybody that way. Slid onto the barstool with the weariness in her bones of a nigger. —That perpetual weariness of bearing up under stress. Lots of extra problems of homosexuals; she looked around to see what they bes into, these others like her. "If I had a daughter I would name her Gamine. It means plucky. Ability to stick it out. To endure hardships or humiliation without complaint."

The butch sat, elbows on the bar and a hat sat on her head, her feminine features; a corsage on her lapel, and the rest of her in the masculine-woman suit, vest, doubled breasted jacket and two-toned platform shoes.

Red lamps shone from the bar, streaked her face with colors. Let us share the butch's secret thoughts: Hungry for a woman, to press her heart against. Chest to chest as if pressing the love from her heart into the woman's heart. The woman's naked body under her own—spreading her legs. The butch goes down, licking her; the tip of her tongue flicking, probing, gently pushing the folds of the labia back with her fingers. Smooth, grainy, that female smell in her nostrils, mouth sucking, tongue alternately seeking out that hood shaped spot, and the pearl emerges. — The femme's clitoris becomes hard. The butch's tongue moving faster, harder in that most loving of physical acts. The femme moans as she lays back on the bed, her body goes taut, fingers alternately grasping the butch's hair, and the sheet of the bed at either side. The butch alternately sucks and licks the woman's vagina, concentrating on the clitoris, then the woman puts her whole mouth against her woman's sex, sucking, while reaching up and fondles her breasts at the same time. The smell of their own strong sexuality. Then her mouth pulls away while her hand reaches down to manipulate the pearl tongue between the woman's legs, while mouth sucking the nipple of one breast and wrapping her arms around her body to play with the woman's other nipple. Gently she push her fingers into her mate's pussy, thrusting a little ways, one finger in and out, then, as the vagina got bigger, two, then three fingers; at the same time alternately kissing the femme's mouth or sucking her nipple. The love partner moans, arms wrapped around her lover's body, arching her back, the butch slides down the femme's raptured body, and goes down, again sucking her clitoris, while her fingers move in and out of her vagina at the same time. The femme climaxes moaning, her body hot, shuddering in short jerks, a sob deep in her throat.

Now the butch stands over her mate at the side of the bed. The femme caresses the masculine woman's thighs. Carefully she moves back the skin of her labia with her fingers and tentatively flicks the tip of her tongue, exploring, tasting, seeking the clitoris. She cups her hands around the butch's buttocks, pulling the butch to her, till her fuzzy head is buried in pubic hair and gets the woman's sex in her whole mouth, sucking, and the butch's hips thrusting so that her sex goes up and down on the woman's lips in short jerks. But she doesn't come that way, instead, gently pushes her mate back on the bed, the femme spreads her legs for her, slowly sliding up around her body, as she gets between them, the butch's pussy against the femme's and pumps fast 'till the heat building up inside to a climax, pounding to a finish, a huge explosion like her whole body sobbing, or breathing. Hearts still beating, totally relaxed they lie beside each other. Then, they repeat this procedure for at least one more go round, but probably two. Three orgasms each, in other ways, maybe 69. The two of them sharing. They are both starved for a woman, it's been such a long time. The beginning of a good thing...

Now, we exit the butch's skull, as she sits, twirling ice in the glass, eyes staring into space, not a trace of what she's thinking betrayed on her cool face.

So, she was in Soulville, and there she met a woman.

Suzie Q was being a hooker. But not for long. Fast talking, gum smacking, red nail polish. She bes faaasssst!

"I told her I was a player from New York, tho actually I'm from the Sunset district 30 blocks away. And that my name was Gamine, and she couldn't pronounce it and called me Gama, like in Gamma ray. All night long and informed me *her* name was Suzie Q. But occasionally she'd slip up and say she was Mildred Johnson. For instance, 'My mother told me, Mildred, you...' And etc. With all these lies we told from the get go, we were destined to go far. Even if for no better reason then to see what it bes like.

"Now I only told her I was a player because I know a ho when I sees one. Actually I'm a draftsperson. I draw blueprints for an architect firm. I'm a square. I just told her I was a player, I thought it would make her feel more at home. I didn't want to brag up my good fortune or tell her what I have because her life wasn't going well, I could see that. Black and blue marks over her pretty skin. Her life was on the rocks, and so she was being snotty.

"Her name was 'Suzie Q. 21 years old.' But probably younger. She had a man—Flash Gordon named after the cartoon hero—his street name, and she was contemplating leaving him. Tired of his manhandling her. I thinks to myself, 'Oh no, trouble.' And also, 'Why can't the black sistah keep her shit together? Why they always have to complicate thangs by having a no good nigger—of either sex—in the background?'

"However, against my better judgement, I gave her my phone number—the real one, at the apartment I was staying at. I guess she made me curious."

Later in the week, one night as the New York player was squeezing into sleep over the threshold, RANG RANG! goes the phone.

It was Suzie Q.

Her soft voice greeted the butch from the other end of the line, as that brown body uncurled amidst a sea of powder blue sheets. "May I speak to Gamma Ray please?" "GAMMA RAY? WHAT? WHO? HUH?" The butch says. For a minute this went on. She practically had to fight with the mysterious caller, telling her there was no Gamma Ray there, until she recognized the voice. Suddenly the remembrance of that alias she'd given flooded back into mind, and the whole evening came back. The vision of a pretty woman in a pink outfit. "OH. OHH! DIS IS ME!" The butch said at last, wiping some sleep out of her brain. "Uh, sorry…I thought you was someone else."

"WHO?" "Your old lady?" She queried.

"Naw. I ain't got an old lady." The stud says sleepily—and that was mistake number two.

At the other end of the line in a ramshackle motel room, Suzie Q sat on the edge of the sofa. Thick lips had just a faint hue of lipstick—the rest worn off. Her eyes wide, glazed. A combination of no sleep alcohol and pills. The young woman spoke into the phone: "It's Flash Gordon he's driving me crazy. He just gave me an ass whuppen. My haid hurts. And he told me 'BITCH BLIP DE BLOP DE BLOOP DE BLAM!' So I tried to kill myself. I took 20 black beauties and I been up since Monday." (It was Friday.) "So I thought I'd call you." And, without even a "let me tell you what happened can you spare a few minutes?" she launches into a detail blow by blow description of the unconscious workings of her life.

In a monotone voice, yet gabbing a mile a minute, Suzie went on. It seems she had been down on the strip—those few blocks of motels and dilapidated buildings known as the red light district, in Pappy's, one of the drinking and feeding joints where the hustlers hang out, and, as usual, she was acting crazy. Pappy's needs a paint job, has an uneven flo', 10 stools with ripped vinyl covers. They sell chicken, soda pop and the ladies of the evening go in there to get out of the cold and off their feet. Also, much dope exchanges hands.

"This old man shuffles up to me, gurl, he's got a face like a bulldog, and snaggle toothed 'n he's so black yuh could paint a white line up his back and use him for a street 'n he growls, 'how about some pussy on credit? I'll pay you Friday, I gets my social security.' 'NOT IN LIFE!' I says. And turns on my heel to end the conversation.

"But the old farmer taps me on the shoulder. 'Well then,' he says, 'What about $10. It's all Ah got.' I replied, 'I ain't fucken' fo' free, it's $20.' He says, 'I'll give you $10 and some weed.' 'Cash only.' I replied coolly.

"'I'll get the $20.' He says. 'Will you be here in half an hour? I got a buddy who owns the gas station down the way, I can get it from him, sugar.' Now I knows about this old man, he likes to slobber all over you 'n there's no way I'm gonna date him, not with all those other tricks riding around. He's nasty. It's not worth the trouble.

"'Naw, not today.' I says. 'I ain't doin no fucken' tonight, I'm tired. —My feet hurt.' 'But,' he says, 'Ah just want to…' And I walk away. See I just don't want to be bothered with no tricks. Period. And I'm determined to have a party with no tricks. Period. Nobody slobbering on me, grabbing on me, trying to run their sorry game down on me or nothing. Period. And I'm determined to have a party time and treat *me* right tonight. I'm feeling independent, and gonna do what I wants to do.

"So I walk over to the jukebox, but the old man shuffles after me and says, 'Well honey, all I want to do is eat you out.' By this time I'm sick of him, gurl, he's so *ugly*, so I says, 'NOT UNLESS YOU CAN FIND A RUBBER TO FIT YOUR FACE.' And EVERYBODY all up and down Pappy's howls with laughter.

"So that took care of that. I looks at the rows of bad soul hits on the jukebox lit by blue and orange lights and wishes I had a dime to play. If I dated the old man I'd still have that time to account for to my man and so I couldn't spend the money anyway, so what's the difference? Now I was drunk and highsiding. It ain't nothing but a party.

"The heat's outside checking ID's, so rows of hookers are lounging around, they can't work. No pimps nowhere. Just chit-chatting, shooting that bullshit—talking about their mens, bragging up their men's dicks, they men's clothes, they men's rides, they men's this and thats, how good they mens treats them, while underneath everybody in the place knows they niggers ain't worth shit.

"So the walls of Pappy's are ringing with cusswords and loud talk and all the hos getting bold with no mens around to keep them in line. Frankly it looks just like the gay bar. All womens. I'm thinking on this in secret. I'd never admit this to none of them bitches down at Pappy's, they's never let me hear the end of it."

The clock on the wrist of a hooker flashes red numerals an instant then goes out. She tosses her hand impatiently. Time ticks. Suzie Q is down the bar gambling just as loud as the next gal.

Meanwhile, RANG RANG! Goes the phone inside a tiny motel room. A hefty man lies on the couch watching TV in fur lined hat, bare chest, fur trimmed trousers with suspenders and bare feet. Toenails polished— clear. Pimp style. He rolls off the couch, grunts, runs his hand over his thick jaw, there is stubble on it. He has thick black eyebrows. Walks across the floor, and grabs the ringing phone in his huge meat-chopping hand.

Down at Pappy's, Suzie gabs on into the night with any ho who will listen. The heat is gone, the girls are back outside at work—but she's feeling independent, and not in the mood. She don't know it, but the grapevine is simmering. A nosey bitch has snitched to her man, and her man calls Suzie's man and runs down the story:

"What's wrong there at the crib Flaaasssh my man? Is you getten weak, you can't manage yo' ladies no mo'?" Came an ignorant drawl, snake-like thru the phone, hostilly. "Word has it yo' bitch Suzie Q turned down a $20 date with a regular trick 'n all she had to do was lay up there with her legs cocked and let the freak suck her off, man. One of my bitches dated him last week."

3 am on the ho stroll. Black night streaked by silver from the lampposts. WHIZZZ of cars passing by outside. Tired hos is gabbing indoors. The heat is gone, but so is the tricks. And that's when a bitch challenges Suzie Q, coldly dropping the fact that Flash had paid that white woman

to go out with him, and at least her man nevah *nevah* did nothing that chicken shit; dropped this like a penny into an empty collection plate so it rattled in silence—rubbing salt in the wounds.

Suzie Q gave some smart answer, parrying the knife thrust, as cold bovine eyes of the older hos studied her, however they didn't have long to judge her expression—to see the effect of their words—time was precious and there was too much other stuff to gab about. Secretly all the whores were eager to say their piece—their piece about something, even if they had to dream up a piece to say, being they didn't have nothing exciting to talk about—except millions of bragged up dollars that they would never see again (that they never had in the first place, but if they had had, they still wouldn't have, because they greedy mens choked their purses wringing every last cent out and made them turn it loose).

Ms. Q kept up her front—a nonchalant smile, eyes behind sunglasses wouldn't reveal much anyhow. But her brain was smoking. Now that had been on her mind for weeks. A white bitch Flash had met in a club waitressing. She worked the San Francisco stroll and dealt dope on the side. She meant plenty money, and Flash was trying to get her to choose, but he had blown his cool by buying her more than one drink. The dice shook up in the fickle fist of fate, rolled out—no dice.

He's blown $100 taking her out—she'd out-hustled him. A bill— flushed down the toilet for all the good it had done them. Now, this had been working in the back of Suzie Q's mind for weeks. How she'd worked tooth and nail for that hundred, hustling her ass up and down Grove street. At least Flash could have got him an outfit, or put the down payment on a ruby ring to show for it. —But what did they have? Hard feelings.

"The more I thought about it, the madder I got.

"4 am rolled around and I didn't have the first penny to break luck of that evening. —And I'd been out since 9 p.m. Well, I was mad as a muthafucker. Mad about not having my kids. Mad about not having no money. Mad about that $100 Flash had blown. Mad that I haven't got nowhere since I been in the fast life—but empty praise from my man, and yes he takes care of my clothes and the room rent, but I'm not getting nowhere, and I'm mad, but I'm scairt too. Eight hours at work and nothing to show for myself. —In Flash's book that's enough warrants for a whupping. And I didn't have change for a dime girl. Not even to call one of my regulars. A trick who's always good for $30.

"I was mad, so I went in the toilet of Pappy's and wrote with my lip-stick on the walls:

"'FLASH GORDEN AIN'T SHIT, THE NIGGER SPENDS HIS LADIES $ ON SQUARE BITCHES. ASK ANYONE. ONE OF THE BEST NIGGERS TODAY IS BILLY THE KID.'

"Then I pulled down my panty hose hiked up my skirt and pissed into the toilet.

"Now I knew Billy the Kid my man couldn't *stand*. The nigger was lame. Wore a pee-yellow hat, piss pants and a yellow suit jacket the color of dried pee, and it was the ultimate insult to use my man's name and this lame tin-head nigger's name in the same breath. But I was smoking. And then I lipsticked a big red X thru the notice that said: 'FLASH GOR-DEN GIVES COCK AND COKE TO HIS BITCHES.'

"That I'd wrote the week before—to brag him up to the other ladies down on Grove street, tho we all knows ain't none of them niggers no good 'cept Charlie Brown, and he an old nigger and can't take care of but one bitch. And also X'd out:

'FLASH GORDON IS A BITCHES DELIGHT, GIVES PLENTY COCK AND COKE AND TREATS HIS WOMENS RIGHT.'

"I smoked a joint, and adjusted my wig in the mirror, and reapplied my makeup—using a purple tube, being I'd squashed the color I was wear-ing making signs. When I got out it was 5 am, and the streets was empty. But it was still dark, and it looked like tricking time to me! But no action. —The hos ain't heard of daylights saving time I guess."

Suzie Q walked wide-legged down the street in her too-big shoes grumbling to herself and trying to think up an excuse to tell Flash when she got home and didn't have no money to show. Down past the stoplight in the middle of the Boulevard some fucked-up whore was challenging the world with sex. A sorry creature in a maxi coat, red, with a red hood, down to her ankles, short skirt, hard painted face. She had reached the border line between her profession and psychosis. And this was appar-ent. Slowly she sauntered in front of a lane of traffic. The car slowed to a stop and the whore strutted across its path terribly slowly, staring at the occupants of the car in a manner, suggestive.

"DO YOU WANT A DATE?" Sex power welled up in her body. It was sad. The totality of her being focused into this one act—screwing for money. The complex human organism reduced to one function. Her face was stone. Painted many colors, and many fools had worshiped her.

Now she was getting ugly, her heart was a hideous mess. She might spend 16 hours on the street and only come back with $5. —Which she sparechanged. Her manner was frightening. She was insane.

The little trooper in the pink dress strode along, pointed toe shoes first, thick mouthed with a wad of gum. Her eyes in the gutter contemplating. Where oily water was green with streaks of silver.

"And I think about Janice. She's not pan' the police and the reason her not pan' the police 'cause she's got something on the judge. Because he the one bought some pussy. She know the whore-detective too, for the simple reason he's getten' some leg. I think about Janice and I gets mad. See, Janice a call girl, and she don't give up no money. She's her own selfs private call girl. I know this broad don't have no pimps or *nothing*. And I don't care *what* my man tell me about how all self-respecting call girls *he* know has a nigger they gives their money too, I knows for a fact all call girls don't give up their $."

Suzie walked on, grumbling. The motel lights were on, and a few cars drove down the boulevard. Her shadow was 15 feet high diagonally on the pavement cast from an angle of the neon lights.

She ambled past the "YO' MAMMY IS A HO" sign spray painted in huge red letters. Where as in Berkeley the hippies spray paint buildings with things like "DOWN WITH THE FACIST PUPPET GOVERNMENT IN VIETNAM!" But on Grove street, 'bout the best they can do is: "YO' MAMMY IS A HO AND SO IS YO' PAPPY." And somebody chalked, "YO' PAPPY IS A PUNK," under *that*.

She walks up from Grove street to the main intersection and sashayes into a fancy restaurant. Air-conditioned, rows of booths, roomy, tastefully covered in gold imitation leather, with a view out of plate glass windows. Decor of wrought metal and wood. Several waitresses bustle about, check pads in their hands, in spiffy uniforms. Her heavy lidded eyes appraise the scene—nobody's in there she knows. She sits down at the counter and orders a coffee and stirs 4 teaspoons of sugar in it; takes the metal container in her brown hand with chipped nails, and pours in as much cream as will fit in the cup. And vows to sit there 'till somebody she know comes in—because she don't have a quarter to pay for the coffee.

"I has my 2 twenties, even, hid in my stocking, but I ain't gonna break that, that's to give to my momma for the kids. And so I sit there waiting, and stirring. And waiting, and stirring. And waiting, and stirring. And I think back to how life bes like when I was a square bitch."

JULIE BLACKWOMON

■ ■ ■

[1943–]

BORN JULIA CARTER IN SALUDA, VIRGINIA, THE AUTHOR renamed herself Julie Blackwomon to affirm her newly realized identity after she came out as a lesbian in 1973.

Blackwomon's first major poem, "Revolutionary Blues" (1977), brought her to prominence as a lesbian writer of color. Soon she began to write fiction as well. Among the major themes in her writing are intraracial tensions between African American lesbians and homosexuality in the black community. Although she has published only one collection of stories, *Voyages Out 2: Short Lesbian Fiction* (1990) (a two-author story anthology that also features the writing of white lesbian author Nona Caspers), and a chapbook entitled *Revolutionary Blues and Other Fevers* (1984), Blackwomon's work has appeared in numerous anthologies, including *Lesbian Poetry: An Anthology, Home Girls: A Black Feminist Anthology,* and *She Who Was Lost Is Remembered: Healing from Incest Through Creativity.*

From *Voyages Out 2* comes "Symbols," a humorous though insightful story concerning Barry, whose wife Dee has recently ended their marriage with the sudden announcement of her lesbianism—a plot mirroring Blackwomon's own life. With her focus on Barry, Blackwomon speaks to the ways in which coming out of the closet is more than just a "gay thing."

Symbols

[1990]

I

"Do you have to wear that?" He was walking down Walnut Street without looking at her. His hands were in his pockets and he was staring down at his spitshined brown shoes.

"Do I have to wear what?"

He looked over at her now. She wore a short Afro and large hoop earrings that brushed her neck when she turned to look at him.

"Do you have to wear that thing around your neck?" he said. They were on their way to a play he'd already seen months before. The tickets were a Father's Day gift from his brother, Arthur. They had come inside a white envelope and were hand-delivered by a thin woman with ultra long, flame red fingernails. She was supposed to have been his blind date. This had also been arranged by his brother. On the way home from seeing the play the first time the woman had casually dropped her hand into his lap. He wasn't interested though. He was afraid he'd catch some disease that he would take back to Dee, the woman walking beside him now.

It was late afternoon and sweltering. As Barry and Dee walked toward the theater, Barry carried his beige jacket draped across his arm because he expected the theater to be air-conditioned and also because this was a special occasion: the first time they'd had dinner together after a six month separation. He was disappointed that she had shown up in jeans and a short-sleeved Danskin but he refused to accept this as a negative omen. He had picked her up a couple hours earlier and they had dined in the quiet restaurant with the hanging chandeliers. It was the same place he had taken her to celebrate their eighth year together. The other celebration had represented their third year of marriage. They had lived together five years before his divorce from his first wife became final. His ex-wife got the house, the second car and a third of his salary until Joshua, then six, and Elizabeth, then seven, turned eighteen. He got the right to marry Dee and introduce her to his kids.

He'd seen her a total of six times since he reluctantly moved out of their apartment, four times when he'd returned on the pretext of picking up some clothes. Once she'd called him about two A.M. because she'd lost the keys to her motorcycle in Fairmount Park. He'd gotten out of bed at half past two, driven around in the semidarkness until he'd found her, then he'd driven her home to pick up her extra set of keys. He had waited there with his motor running until she'd kick-started the bike and then he sat watching the red and amber taillight and the reflection of her helmet moving down Kelly Drive. Then he'd put his Chrysler into gear and headed for home. He noticed that she had appeared depressed and anxious but she had allowed him to hold her hand in the car. He had driven back to his parents' house wondering whether or not that was significant.

At the restaurant earlier today, he had not become upset when Dee insisted on splitting the bill. He found the idea amusing, as if this were their first date and she had to make sure she didn't owe him anything, wouldn't have to go to bed with him afterwards. Still, he knew better than to laugh. He could be liberal if he had to, but mostly he was just satisfied to be spending time with her again.

When he picked her up for their date he had already angered her by inadvertently extending the boundaries of their agreement for seeing each other. As he stepped inside the apartment she embraced him, and when their pelvises touched it ignited a spontaneous bolt of electricity that coursed through his groin and he had been unable to suppress a groan. She had pulled away embarrassed and he'd had to listen to the ground rules of their relationship again. Friendship. They got past that once he explained to her quite truthfully that he was just happy spending time with her again. He had not added that friendship was acceptable only if that was all that was offered.

Everything was fine until he noticed the thing around her neck. Even after he'd first seen it he walked several blocks distracted in his conversation, trying not to say anything. But then she looked over at him with his hands in his pockets and asked, "What's the matter?"

He said, "Nothing."

And she said, "You know I can always tell when something's bothering you." It was then that he'd asked if she had to wear that thing.

She reached up and grabbed her double women's symbol as if it was so much a part of herself she could find it at night in a room totally devoid of light, as she might find her arm. "This?" she asked.

"Yeah," he nodded his head and looked away at passengers erupting out of a bus at the corner of 16th and Locust Streets. "That's a lesbian symbol, isn't it?"

"Why, yes," she said, a trace of irritation (or was it defiance?) in her voice. They stared at each other in separate pools of silence.

"Does it bother you?" she asked finally.

"Well, yeah..." This was no time to lie. He started to say something else but stopped himself.

"Why?"

"Huh?"

"Why does it bother you?" She stopped walking and stared him in the face, trying to hold his gaze, but he looked away—down at his shoes, at the bus about to pull away from the curb.

It bothers me because I love you. Because I need you to want me the way I still want you. Because the symbol suggests you never will.

"I don't know, it just does," he said aloud.

"And you want me to take it off?"

"I don't want to fight about it, Dee." He touched her elbow and nudged her forward.

She allowed herself to be led a few steps, then balked. If there was one thing he could not stand, it was a public scene.

"Look, this is what I am, Barry. I wear it with a degree of pride, alright? Asking me to take it off would be like asking me to take down my freedom flag." He pictured the red, green and black freedom flags that were sewn on the pockets of her work suits. The ones she wore as a gym teacher.

"Dee, I know you're a lesbian," he said softly. From the comer of his eye he peeped at the passing dyads and, leaning closer, said "lesbian" without moving his lips, as if he didn't want anyone to hear the word "lesbian" coming from his mouth. "I know you're a lesbian," he repeated with the same strained effort, "but you're with me now."

"I'm lesbian wherever I go, and this goes wherever I go." She held it out in front of her as if it were an amulet warding off evil spirits.

He sighed deeply and moved his jacket to his other arm. Telling her to be quiet now, he decided, would be the worst thing he could do. Changing the subject wouldn't work either. When Dee was being self-righteous there was no hushing her up. Once during an argument he'd made the mistake of asking her to be quiet so the neighbors would not hear and Dee started yelling at the top of her voice while he ran around the apartment furiously pulling down the windows. The memory brought a frown to his face.

A tall, blond man in horn-rimmed glasses bumped into Barry and Barry stepped back and apologized. He moved to the side of Anthony's Pizza Parlor where Dee was leaning against the wall, one foot propped up behind her. She was still holding the women's symbol, cradling it protectively, her hand resting against her orange Danskin. She wore a button pinned to her shoulder bag with "Hera" stamped on it. Hera was the name of the women's bookstore where Dee did volunteer work. Actually it was a lesbian bookstore but he didn't like to think about that. He didn't like to think of Dee referring to herself as lesbian at all. Thoughts like that confounded and depressed him, creating questions about their relationship he hadn't the courage to face.

He looked across Walnut Street at a block-long line of people waiting to see *Star Wars*. A patrol car was passing slowly, the officer inside watching Dee, an "Is he bothering you miss?" expression on his face.

"Why don't we just forget about the play." She sounded as tired as he felt.

"And waste forty dollars!" He took her elbow and nudged her forward then felt the weight of her resistance and stopped again. Depression engulfed him like a wet cloud. When he turned to face her again she had both hands on her hips and she was frowning. He sucked his teeth and leaned back against the wall, his hands in his pockets. This was not supposed to be happening. He was ready to just give up, give Dee the tickets and go on home alone. Only Dee wouldn't accept the tickets.

"Why do you always manage to make me feel guilty?" she asked.

"I'm not trying to make you feel guilty," he said, "I just don't want to see the play anymore."

"Maybe it's too early for us to try to spend time together," Dee said.

"Or maybe it's too late," Barry mumbled. He held no hope of salvaging the evening.

"Huh?"

"Never mind," he said, "I'll take you home."

II

Later in his apartment, with his feet on the coffee table and a beer in his hand, Barry wondered how Dee could suddenly decide at twenty-nine that she liked women better than men. Shouldn't there have been some clues? In her adolescence? Eighteen months ago she'd told him she "thought" she might have "homosexual tendencies." She borrowed books from the library. They both borrowed books from the library. And since he had no doubt that she did love him once and perhaps loved him still, deep down, why now, in the tenth year of what she'd referred to as the best relationship she'd ever had, was she wanting to be with women?

The only other lesbian he'd known was Myrtle McHenry, a tall thick-shouldered woman who, even in junior high school, more closely resembled a man than a woman. Once, three of the boys from Bainbridge Street had grabbed Myrtle and tried to yank her clothes off to see what she wore underneath. They succeeded but Barry wondered if the razor slash that still puckers Junebug's left eyebrow had been worth finding out that Myrtle wore her breasts tied down with an ace bandage and that she donned white cotton panties under her men's pants. At any rate, Barry saw no connection between Myrtle and Dee except that Dee maintained that North Philadelphia stroll she developed as a kid growing up in the Raymond Rosen projects.

Thinking about her now he could still see a trace of the adolescent Dee. Six months in charm and modeling school had not erased her tendency to bounce like a Philly corner boy. When she wore her hair straightened and curled, and when she wore those cute little skirts and pumps she did not appear as, well, androgynous as she did now. There was a boyishness about her that her voluptuous ass could not deny. That was what first attracted him to her, her ass.

They met in Washington, D.C. during Ralph Abernathy's first mass civil rights demonstration after Dr. King's death. Barry had been separated from the bus he rode down on and it had taken off without him. He jumped on the bus chartered by the union from Dee's job and asked it if was going back to Philly.

"Somebody got left. Somebody got left," the voice in sing-song fashion came from a seat just behind the driver. Barry looked over at an attractive young woman in a powder-blue shell wearing a curly brown wig. He smiled but he did not think it amusing. He was embarrassed and concerned about getting back home. He turned to the woman with the teasing voice. She had full lips and a mole on the side of her face.

"Is this bus going back to Philly?"

"Yep," she replied with an impish grin.

"Can I ride with you?"

"I guess so but you'd better check with the shop steward. "

Barry sat down in the seat in front of her and rode with his head craned backwards, talking with her for about forty-five minutes. Some boozed-up coworkers were singing golden oldies in the back of the bus and he was beginning to get nauseous from riding backwards. Finally, she asked him if he wouldn't be more comfortable if he sat beside her.

At a rest stop he got his first glance at her ass and, although there were other things he liked about her, it was the sight of her exiting the bus in front of him in those tight jeans that made him ask her out.

She stood him up the first time they were supposed to go out. Left him standing in front of a laundromat in South Philadelphia while a group of white teenagers on roller skates played hockey in the middle of the street. He waited an hour in his charcoal gray suit and black tie and then he went home. When he called her later from a pay phone she told him she had forgotten. Later she told the truth: she had gotten cold feet. Never before had she dated a married man.

The second time they went out he took her to a race track, partly because he liked horse racing but mostly because the race track was in New Jersey. He didn't want to have to concern himself with being seen.

Afterwards he dropped her off at an address in North Philadelphia and Dee would later tease him about going home horny while she made love with her ex-boyfriend. She said he shouldn't have been jealous because he went home each night to his wife. He had tried repeatedly to explain that he hadn't slept with his wife in a very long time. Sometimes Dee believed this and sometimes she didn't, but it was more or less true. For the year before he met Dee he had rarely slept with his wife. Sometimes he just went into the bedroom with a "you're my wife..." attitude. But it was rarely worth the effort to make love with a woman who just laid there and waited until it was over. Even at that he was afraid of getting her pregnant. They already had two children and a marriage that was obviously finished.

In contrast, he and Dee had had an almost idyllic relationship. He didn't believe it when she said she was attracted to women. It had surprised him when she started going to the lesbian community center. Next had come the volunteer work at Hera, then the consciousness-raising group followed promptly by a slew of "dates." He had withstood the casual flings much better than he had endured the first weekend she spent out of town.

That Sunday he read the sports page, did the *New York Times* crossword puzzle and she still hadn't come home. She called from the train station but there was time only for "hello" and "got here safely" and reassurances that she would be back in time to go to dinner with him Sunday evening. Then the phone went dead and he imagined she was walking towards a cab, her lover carrying her bags. It was already half past two and he wanted to get out of the house, walk over to Hank's, or maybe drive over to his parents' house to see if the kids were visiting. Mostly he just wanted to get out of the house to make the waiting easier. Since ten that morning he had been preparing for her arrival, straightening up the living room, fielding questions from family and friends. "She didn't tell me she had a friend in New York," her Aunt Bertha had said. It was the absurdity of it all that prompted him to call her at her lover's apartment. Why was he sitting home acting like her secretary while she carried out her long distance affair?

He was sitting on the couch, the T. V. tuned to a talk show featuring some politicians all dressed in suits of varying shades of gray. They were debating something Barry could not hear because the volume was turned all the way down. The radio was on, tuned to "Amazon Country," the local women's radio station. Dee had discovered it from a newspaper she picked up at the lesbian center. On Sunday afternoon he and Dee usually listened to that station and, although he now thought of changing the station to some music, he sat leaning over the coffee table staring, eyes unfocused, at a book on the aerospace industry. He was supposed to be studying for a test for a promotion at his job in the accounting department in city hall. He thought about Dee's journal/telephone book on the nightstand next to her side of the bed.

He stood up then and, as he leaned over to switch the dial, his jealousy aroused, he thought suppose she didn't go to New York to see a woman. Suppose she went to see a man? The thought of Dee impaled beneath a naked, sweating man filled him with such despair he immediately sank back down under the weight of it. It had brought back memories of his ex-wife, Jeannie, and her "cousin from Georgia." One hot August night when he'd come home early from his Friday night poker game, he had seen what he thought was his wife getting into a car with Georgia license plates. It had been dark, the street poorly lit and he'd been almost half a block away. He called out her name, then chased behind the car running hard the way they taught him in track. He'd been gaining on the red taillights too until the car suddenly sped up and he stopped, exhausted. It had looked like his wife, in the car, the height was the same, she wore the same curly bush. But later, in their bedroom, he in his jockey shorts and she in her yellow nightie, the door closed so the kids couldn't hear them, she'd denied it all.

The more he obsessed about it, the more he convinced himself that the only reasonable course of action was to call Dee at her lover's apartment.

"Hello," the husky voice on the other end sounded almost like Dee when just awakened. Why was she asleep at two in the afternoon?

"Hello," he said tentatively, then more confidently, "May I speak to Dee Spicer please?"

"Who is this?" the voice asked suspiciously.

"Barry—Barry Spicer," he said struggling to keep his voice calm and free of hostility. Had they been making love? "May I speak to my wife please?"

There was a loud clatter that hurt his ears, the phone being dropped.

"Why did you give that man my number? I don't play that shit!" The voice coming through the dropped receiver, crisp, angry.

"I didn't give him your number." Dee now, annoyed and defensive.

He could deal with Dee's anger, but a more horrid fear took away his breath. What if Dee refused to come to the phone? What if they hung up on him? He realized now that the question of male or female was trivial. It would be no less painful if she were with a man.

"Hello," Dee was on the phone now, her voice guarded.

He breathed a sigh of relief and then his mind went blank... "Uh, Dee?"

"Why did you call me here, Barry?" She sounded unconcerned. Suppose he was sick? Suppose he needed her to sign him in or out of a hospital? He was angry then as if he were actually in a hospital and his wife responded as if she were more concerned about appeasing her girlfriend.

"Where did you get this number, Barry?"

"I got it out of your telephone book."

A voice in the background, the girlfriend, "Hang up the phone."

"Barry, you shouldn't have called me here."

He heard the intrusive voice again, "Hang up the phone. You can't talk to your man on my damn phone."

"Tell that bitch to shut up," Barry said.

Both voices through the receiver, muffled conversation he could not decipher.

Dee back on the line again. "Is everything alright there?" she asked.

"Yeah, you coming home soon?"

"I'll be catching the five forty-five."

"I'll meet you at the station, okay?"

"Sure…you really shouldn't have called me here."

"I miss you," he said.

"We'll talk about it," she said and hung up.

They talked about it three months later on the tennis court. It was like old times; an impromptu picnic on a lazy Sunday morning, a six-pack of beer, potato salad, fried chicken and barbecue from a rib joint on South Street.

The difference in their relationship was reflected in Dee's tennis game. She had always been a fierce competitor. She hated to lose almost as much as Barry did and would play any ball at which she had the remotest chance. He liked that about her. But that day she hit the ball tentatively. Even the suggestion that she was letting him win was not sufficient to prevent her lackluster taps across the net or her flailing helplessly at balls that the old Dee would have chased down at top speed. When Barry won the last set, Dee broke down and cried right there on the tennis court. He was embarrassed. Not knowing what else to do he put his arms around her and walked her off the court.

"Why are you crying?" he asked her.

"I don't know, I'm just so unhappy." She dabbed at her eyes with a napkin but the tears kept flowing. She was sitting on a picnic table, her tennis racket lying across her lap.

Dee had broken up with the woman from New York. He didn't fool himself into thinking that it had anything to do with him. The bottom line was that even though she went to Gay Activists Alliance meetings on Monday nights, the Lesbian Center on Saturdays, Club Olympia, a Black Gay/Lesbian club once a week, Dee came home to sleep every night. He thought things were returning to normal. It shocked him to hear of her acute unhappiness.

"I'm sorry I'm making you unhappy," she said.

"I can take care of myself," he said. He had been afraid she would bring up the subject of breaking up again. The last time they discussed his unhappiness was that Sunday evening three months ago after she had returned from New York. Afterwards they had split all the bills and divided up all the housework. At least in theory they were roommates.

Barry looked with envy at a couple in identical white short sets who were kissing at the net. He grabbed another napkin and helped Dee dab at her eyes too.

"Maybe you ought to talk to somebody..." he said. He was afraid of offending her and said the words softly so she could not hear him if she didn't want to, "...like a therapist or something? I mean," he rambled on, "I mean it wouldn't imply there's anything wrong with you or any-thing." He shrugged his shoulders. "I saw one myself right after I got out of the Marines." She squirmed in his arms as if he was holding her too tightly and he released her. For the first time he allowed himself to con-sider the possibility that she might feel smothered.

"Maybe I should just move out for a while," he said. "Give you a chance to decide what you really want to do?"

As a last effort to salvage his marriage he moved out of the apartment and returned to his parents' house. It was intended as a temporary move.

He had been out of the house a month when Dee agreed to see the shrink. Twice they both went to see a young white woman with long hair and sandals who told Dee she wasn't really a lesbian, but that she just wasn't dealing with some resentment she had against her father.

They both went back to the library for more books. He became drawn to the ones on bisexuality and began to think of her in those terms. He lowered his expectations. It occurred to him that they could go on like this forever: Dee going to gay bars and gay activist meetings a couple days per week, and being Mrs. Barry Spicer the rest of the week. It worked with other couples, why not with them? He had called her up, invited her to dinner and a play to talk about it.

III

The next weekend Barry sat with Arthur in the living room of their par-ents' house with the still-unused theater tickets in his pocket. He had inadvertently pulled them out when he reached into his jacket pocket at the Garden State Race Track.

"Do you notice how Dee walks sometimes, man, the way she bounces when she walks?" Barry asked.

"Yeah, man," Arthur said casually chewing on his pipe stem. They were waiting until their father returned from the circus with the two sets of kids. Arthur's wife, Helene, was visiting her relatives in South Jersey.

"I don't think Dee and I are getting back together, man. "

"You like Donna's cousin, Terry?" Arthur's eyes brightened, which irritated Barry. Arthur never liked Dee. Terry was the thin one with the red fingernails, the woman Arthur once fixed Barry up with. She didn't know who George Jackson was and saw no reason Ray Charles should not perform in South Africa. And her nails were too long. She was not Dee. "It doesn't have anything to do with Terry, it's just about Dee and me," Barry said.

"No problem," Arthur said. He sat watching while Barry drummed his fingers on the end table.

"What's the longest time you've ever been separated from a woman and still got back together with her?"

"About a year and a half. I used to go with this bisexual who came to me to get tuned up between affairs with women. She was a neat lady," he said with some regret. They were both silent for a moment, then Arthur said, "But, you know if a woman likes chocolate ice cream she ain't gonna settle for vanilla for too long." He relit his pipe and studied Barry's face.

"But wouldn't they rather have both if they could?" Barry said.

"Maybe. But you can't have both, man. Not for long."

He met Dee's new girlfriend when he went to get the rest of his clothes. When he saw her in the hall he knew immediately who she was. Partly it was his sixth sense, but mostly it was because she wore a lavender T-shirt that had "Killer Dyke" silk-screened on the front in large silver letters. She had passed him on the second landing. He found her standing in the kitchen when he let himself in with his key. Dee was standing at the stove frying steak. Dee, too, had on one of those absurd lavender T-shirts, only hers read "Sappho" on the front.

"I think I passed you in the hall," the girlfriend said, holding out her hand and smiling the smile of a current lover who could afford to be gracious.

"Pleased to meet you." He could play the polite game too. Well, at least the girlfriend wasn't offering tea as if she had already moved in. He shook her hand. It was soft. Much softer than Dee's. Dee's lover had no ass but she had firm breasts that sat up under her shirt. She wore no bra. There would be no mistaking her for a boy. She was soft, petite and feminine and he could have forgiven her everything except the "Killer Dyke" T-shirt. If they walked down the street like that—advertising— everybody would know. Suppose his parents saw them? Or his kids? Except for Dee's earrings and her breasts, which were smaller than her girlfriend's, she might easily have been mistaken for a teenaged boy. The idea revolted him and he frowned involuntarily. He disliked lesbians now. All of them.

He walked into the bedroom closet and pulled out two suitcases Dee had already packed. On the way out he stopped in the kitchen again, curious. Dee was chopping cucumbers for a salad. The girlfriend sat at the table reading to Dee from what appeared to be a poetry book. He put the suitcases back into the closet. He would get them another time when he would not have to walk past Dee's lover to get them out.

He motioned to Dee from the kitchen doorway. "Can I speak to you, Dee?" Dee looked up at him then over at her lover. She rinsed her hands at the sink and followed him out into the hallway.

"You're in love with her, huh?"

Dee nodded her head.

"I guess this is it." He handed her the key and stood there as if he couldn't decide what he should do next.

"Maybe in a few months we can talk some more?" Dee said.

"I wouldn't bet the mortgage on that," he said. But he smiled when he said it. Almost as an afterthought, he threw her an air kiss. And then he walked out closing the door softly behind him.

Outside it had begun to rain, but he didn't want to go back inside the apartment to get his umbrella. He walked past his car parked across the street, then stopped and looked up at the apartment window. Dee was at the sink washing dishes. He rolled his collar up and continued walking towards Center City. He decided to call Terry. Maybe he could get her to cut those damn fingernails.

ALICE WALKER

■ ■ ■

[1944–]

NOVELIST AND WRITER ALICE WALKER REDEFINED BLACK women's fiction with explicit depictions of women's sexuality, including taboo subject matter such as lesbianism and incest among African Americans. With groundbreaking works such as *The Color Purple* (1982), she not only affirmed lesbianism as a source of liberation for black women but also established her voice as an internationally renowned author and activist. Indeed, *The Color Purple* won both the Pulitzer Prize for Fiction and the National Book Award in 1983, as well as becoming a major motion picture in 1985.

Born the youngest of eight children to a sharecropping family in Eatonton, Georgia, Walker as a girl was blinded in her right eye by a BB gun accident, leading to a self-imposed isolation in which she discovered books and fed her early love for reading. After finishing high school and being named valedictorian in 1961, Walker began her college career at Spelman College, graduating from Sarah Lawrence College in 1965. She then married Mel Leventhal, a white activist attorney, whom she met while working in the civil rights movement of the late 1960s, and with whom she had a daughter, author Rebecca Walker. It was during her marriage to Leventhal that Walker published both her first novel, *The Third Life of Grange Copeland* (1970), and her first volume of poetry, *Once* (1968).

A prolific period followed, during which she produced, among other works, the novel *Meridian* (1976) and edited a groundbreaking collection of Zora Neale Hurston's writing, *I Love Myself When I Am Laughing...And Then Again When I'm Looking Mean and Impressive* (1979).

She picked up characters from *The Color Purple* in the novels *Temple of My Familiar* (1989) and *Possessing the Secret of Joy* (1992), the latter an outspoken indictment against the African practice of female genital mutilation. Walker also effectively employed nonfiction prose to further her politics, most notably in her essay collections *In Search of Our Mother's Gardens: Womanist Prose* (1983) and *Living by the Word: Selected Writings, 1973–1987* (1988). Walker's first declaration of her bisexuality to appear in print was published in *Essence* magazine in 1996, just as her first book of autobiographical writings, *The Same River Twice: Honoring the Difficult* (1996), was brought out.

In addition to her extensive career as a novelist and essayist, Walker is a respected writer of short stories, with several collections, including *In Love and Trouble: Stories of Black Women* (1973), *You Can't Keep a Good Woman Down* (1981), and *The Way Forward Is with a Broken Heart* (2000), which features the following story, "This Is How It Happened."

This Is How It Happened

[2000]

This is how it happened. After many years of being happier than anyone we knew, which worried me, my partner of a dozen years and I broke up. I still loved him, in a deeply familial way, but the moments of palpable deadness occurring with ever greater frequency in our relationship warned me we'd reached the end of our mutual growth. How to end it? How to get away?

My old friend Marissa, with whom I'd been infatuated years ago in Brooklyn, came to San Francisco for a visit. She was a dyke, pure and strange, and I could never see her without a certain amount of awe. She was the most beautiful of women, shapely and brown, but she could also wire houses and fix cars. All the while speaking in the softest of voices and never showing any of her innate wildness until left alone on the dance floor. She immediately caused the other dancers to disappear and the dance floor itself to retreat until it seemed to be in a forest somewhere and the five thousand or so years of a lackluster patriarchy fairly forgotten.

We had met while I was in a marriage with a decent, honorable man who had not danced in six or seven years, and she was living with a woman who told her what to eat, think and wear. I didn't know this when we met, of course. Because she was an electrician and earned her own living I found her strong, independent, free. In retrospect we decided, once we'd been separated for some years from our earlier partners, we'd been infatuated with the image of each other that we needed to help us flee.

"I thought you always knew exactly what you were doing," she said. "To have married someone nice to support you while you perfected your craft as an artist. To have had children with someone who supported you and them. Oh," she continued, "the list was long."

I was amazed. "It was all instinct," I said. "I had seen so many women married to men who squashed their development. Any hint of such a personality turned me off. And of course," I said, "I never seriously considered women." Nor had I understood I could.

"Well," she said, "you wouldn't have done any better with the one I found. Libby is just the man her father was. Domineering, bossy, a real pain in the neck." She sighed. "And after the first couple of years, no sex."

"No sex?" How could sexy Marissa not be having sex?

Marissa shrugged. "It's a curious thing to encounter the father of your woman leering out at you. Which is what happened when Libby drank. She'd forget we'd argued and that I'd been humiliated over some outrageous behavior of hers. She'd get sentimental in her drunkenness and want to make love. By force if necessary. I was repelled."

I too had enjoyed making love with Tripper for many years. Then it seemed to me my sexual rhythm was broken. I no longer experienced any periods of horniness, as I had earlier in my life. Eventually I realized it was because over time Tripper's sexual needs set the times of love's occasions. I was never able to say no, but my body did. It withheld its pleasure, since its own desire was not permitted to set the pattern of celebration and release.

Why didn't either of us speak up? Marissa and I often asked each other. We agreed that we'd tried, but habits, once formed, had proved hard to break, and retreat and silence had offered a spuriously virtuous comfort. Our mothers' behavior, probably, copied while we were very young, too early to recognize it for the depression it was.

The week I left Tripper he was still interested in making love to me, and suggested a "good-bye fuck" even though my body had not for many months expressed the slightest desire. In fact, it had expressed just the opposite, with its pancake-flat nipples and a vulva so dry I'd thought I'd prematurely entered "the change."

When Marissa came to pick me up Chung was in the kitchen attempting to repair the toaster. His straight black hair, with the dapper streak of gray on the left side, hung in his eyes, and his somewhat paunchy torso, sans shirt, glistened with sweat. When we'd met I'd practically drooled over his body. I still admired it, but in a more critical way. I loved the fact that he was short, and that when we kissed, we could look squarely into each other's eyes. Also that my arms reached easily around him—Tripper had been both large and tall—and I could grab a nice handful of his butt. Marissa took a beer from the fridge and sat gap-legged at the table sipping it and watching him struggle with the toaster as long as she could stand it. By the time I was ready to go she'd ripped it from his fingers and declared it dead and therefore inefficient. Chung, who has a sense of humor if not much vitality at this stage in his life, grabbed a beer for himself and was still laughing as we went out of the house.

I backed my battered pea-green Karman Ghia out of the driveway
and then stopped to put down the top. Marissa and I flew down the
streets giddy as teenagers, serene as the old friends we were.

At the dance, as I suspected, Marissa was queen. The best dancers
sought her out and she outdanced all of them. It was the kind of dykey
joint that still intimidated me. The kind with lots of women in all manner of dress and an obligatory three or four men. I was always wondering
about the men. Who were they? Why were they there? Were they bounc-
ers? Were they brothers of some of the women? Lovers of some of the
women? Straight? Bisexual? Gay?

What men? was always Marissa's response when I asked her about them.

Tonight as always I sat quietly in a corner hoping not to be
approached. Unless it was by a particular woman across the room who
attracted me by the sexiness of her dress—I'd discovered I liked
femme-looking women, with their low-cut dresses and light, pinky-plum
colors. But butches too—like Marissa, who wore tight jeans, a leather
jacket and a scarf around her neck—could be almost unbelievably alluring. Marissa would dance with me until my lack of wildness bored her.
Then she'd whirl out on the dance floor dancing only with partners
who, in their abandon, reminded her of herself. Or, she'd dance alone,
a voluptuous brown-skinned woman with dreadlocks to her ass, and
everyone watching her imagined her dancing just for them, in silvery
moonlight beneath a canopy of ancient trees, naked.

After sleeping together once or twice why hadn't we become
lovers? I often asked myself. Perhaps because you can't recall whether it
was once or twice, said Marissa, when I queried her. I certainly loved and
admired her. Yet she seemed somehow beyond me, freer. I felt I'd never
catch up. Her "way" seemed natural to her. I would have to learn it. This
frightened, irritated and depressed me. I tried to imagine Marissa in a
heterosexual relationship and it made me laugh. I tried to imagine the
two of us as a couple and it made me uneasy.

Sitting in my corner drinking a margarita I was for a moment
unaware I'd been watching a woman standing by the door holding a
baby in her arms. This was so incongruous—the loud music, the ener-
getic dancing, the drinking and smoking—that I immediately rose and
walked over to her, offering her the seat next to mine. She could not
come over just yet, she explained, because she was selling some articles
of apparel from Guatemala which I now noticed she carried in a large

denim bag at her feet. I was shocked by this, I don't know why. But within minutes I was holding the baby, a fitfully dozing black-eyed boy, who was not an infant but a two-year-old, and she was squatting beside her merchandise where much to my surprise she seemed to make sales by simply rummaging for a particular item in her bag and then briefly flinging it over a cleared spot on the floor. Money changed hands rapidly and soon she'd sold enough colorfully striped cotton trousers, headbands and vests to satisfy her for the evening. Dragging what was left in her bag she hurried over to us. The baby strained against my arms as she approached, and resolutely wriggled off my lap and toddled up to her. When they met, on the fringe of the whirling dancers, who any minute I expected to stomp on him, she smiled down at him and stopped to swing him up in her arms. At that moment the Drifters or some other old group was singing the golden oldie "With Every Beat of My Heart," and the two of them danced a moment cheek to cheek. Her hair was in short, thick, warrior erect dreadlocks. She was wearing pants that looked like a skirt, and a light blue denim shirt with an open collar. Beneath the shirt was a peach-colored tank. She wore earrings. Bracelets. And on her feet, sturdy brown boots.

It happened in the moment they were dancing, the child closing his eyes in a swoon of delight. The woman a being I'd never seen before.

MICHELLE CLIFF

■ ■ ■

[1946–]

JAMAICA-BORN LESBIAN AUTHOR MICHELLE CLIFF BRINGS AN immigrant's perspective to outsider sexual identity. A light-skinned girl, Cliff often passed as white during her childhood in New York City's Jamaican community. Her alienation and feelings of difference shaped her search for self-expression, which is a consistent theme in her fiction, essays, and poetry.

Cliff's family eventually moved back to Jamaica; she returned to New York in the 1960s to attend college. She worked at W. W. Norton as an editor in the 1970s and served as coeditor and publisher of the lesbian feminist journal *Sinister Wisdom* with partner Adrienne Rich in the 1980s.

Cliff's first book, *Claiming an Identity They Taught Me to Despise* (1980), is a collection of essays about the impact of racism and colonization on the women in her family. Her first novel, *Abeng* (1984), introduces Clare Savage, a young, light-skinned Jamaican woman. Savage's strained relations with her family, homeland, and dark-skinned friends serve as the foundation for the book's sequel, *No Telephone to Heaven* (1987), which also features a cross-dressing gay man who befriends Clare. While lesbian identity informs Cliff's writing, racial and gender concerns are her primary topics.

In the short story "Ecce Homo," however, homosexuality runs as a major a theme alongside race. Set in fascist Rome, the piece is about a black gay American linguist whose outlaw sexuality—coupled with his blackness—lands him in a concentration camp.

Ecce Homo

[2000]

*Dream...on black wings...you come whenever sleep...sweet god, truly...
sorrow powerfully...to keep separate...I have hope that I shall not share...
nothing of the blessed...for I would not be so.* —SAPPHO #63

The story as I was told it begins in Rome.

There is a man who is a linguist. He is accomplished in several languages. Western and nonwestern. He gets a job as a translator in the U.S. Embassy. He translates for Italians who clamor for visas. Jews among others.

His is a low-level position for a man of his qualifications.

He is black which is of concern to his country.

He is homosexual but they seem unaware.

He counts his blessings beside the Trevi Fountain.

All in all he has been comfortable in Rome.

His is an adopted country.

He was brought to America when he was fourteen. His are a nomadic people. Strivers, always in search of a better place. His mother and father—he was blessed with both—settled in Philadelphia. He did well in school, near the top of his graduating class.

He availed himself of Lincoln, the Black Princeton.

One evening in the Pizza Navona he is sitting at an outdoor restaurant. He has ordered a glass of Pinot Grigio—Campanile '36—and is lighting a Muratti cigarette. The restaurant—the storyteller cannot recall the name—is located at the south end of piazza, and from his table the linguist can see Bernini's *Il Moro* and takes heart.

That very evening he meets a man, an Italian.

A simple meeting: the Italian stops by the linguist's table, asks for a cigarette, a light.

They stroll the Roman streets, light at the Italian's apartment.

They become lovers.

On the weekends they spend time in a hilltown beyond the hills of the city the Italian knows from childhood.

They speak freely. The storyteller says that was when they fell in love.

But too soon Americans have to leave. The linguist—like it or not—is a naturalized American. As such he must go.

But the linguist does not want to abandon his beloved. The linguist—the Negro who speaks in tongues—of rivers—unlike the tongues of the women back home (home the place that is unAmerica) in the pocomania shacks—twirling their spirituous tongues—was once tongue tied—

"What's the matter, boy?"   "Wha' do you, bwai?"

"Is Cat got you tongue?"

"Don' mek me give you one tongue-lashing."

Now his tongue is the most skilled part of him.
He works with his tongue. He makes love with his tongue.
He knows when to hold his tongue.

The linguist tries to arrange a visa but the beloved is a known quantity and the application is denied.
He will not leave.
And that—the storyteller says—is the beginning of the end.

One night the fascists descend on the rooms the two men share in the Piazza della Repubblica. They are removed suddenly, without incident, but for the incident of their removal.

When he was a boy, before the family left for America, he read in a newspaper about two men apprehended because they were found together. A laborer, a casual laborer, the paper had reported, and a bank clerk. They were discovered in "an obscene condition"—a child, he did not know what this meant. When the two men were arraigned on a charge of public indecency (they'd been discovered under a pier near the Myrtle Bank Hotel) hundreds packed the court-room—including mothers and their children. Later the two men were given twelve strokes of the Cat and five years hard labor.

The police take the two men to the nearby train station where they are loaded on a car bound for a camp.

Do you remember the end of *The Garden of the Finzi-Contini?* The film, this does not happen in the book. The schoolroom where the deportees are taken to be sorted and shipped. The train station in this story has a similar feel right now. There are still the stalls selling bottles of Acqua Mia and

San Benedetto, bunches of grapes in white paper, newspapers, magazines, paperbound libretti—the air smells of cigarette smoke and oranges and damp—the ordinariness of it all—strikes them—commerce, train travel— the schoolroom smelling of chalkdust—and people who have been tagged.

The two men arrive at the camp together. Thank God they have not been separated. But they will do well to ignore one another. To ignore one another while looking out for the other—that is their task.

They mask their longing.

They are assigned forced labor. Breaking rocks. Drawing the rocks, wagonload by wagonload, up the side of the quarry, stacking them in pyramids. The guards, wielding sledgehammers, smash the pyramids; the prisoners return to the pit of the quarry and break more stones, draw them to the lip of the quarry, stack them.

The two men are mocked, called names only the linguist understands.

Outside the windows of the storyteller's flat the sun is going down over the Pacific, beyond the Golden Gate.

The storyteller does not know how the two managed to escape. We will have to bring our imaginations to bear.

It must be night. Under cover of night they drift to the edge of the camp. In the darkness they burrow out under the barbed wire. Something like that. An opportunity has presented itself and they take it.

They find their way into some woods.

They live in the heart of the woods in the heat of a war as lovers. They live on mushrooms and lamb's quarters and wild birds the Italian traps. And the storyteller knows this is romantic, but let's let them have it. They make a place to sleep in a tree trunk heavy with moss and shelved with lichen.

A decayed, decadent nest.

The gunfire which seems to encircle them is coming closer to them. They whisper about which course to take. They sleep with their legs wrapped together. One man's penis nestles against the other's flank. When it rains, the rain draws a curtain around them.

They decide they will try to find Switzerland. They laugh. At least they have a plan. The linguist will pretend to be the Ethiopian servant of the Italian: "A spoil of war," the linguist whispers.

Now they're getting somewhere.

Suddenly luck finds them. They stumble upon a company of American troops—Negro soldiers encamped nearby. The linguist explains—omitting the triangle—now but a ghost on his chest.

Time passes. Switzerland is forgotten.

The Negro soldiers get orders to move north and drop the men at a way station where displaced people wait.

The two are processed.

The linguist is returned to his adopted country.

The Italian is made a prisoner of war.

The linguist says, "When this is all over I will send for you."

This is a slender thread.

In the end it is no use.

The beloved hangs himself shortly after he is taken prisoner.

The linguist, this being postwar New York City, gets a job in the kitchens of the Waldorf-Astoria. He translates for the Hungarian chef.

When he hears of the Italian's death he breaks down.

He is committed to the Metropolitan State Hospital where he will die.

A man is seated under a silk cotton tree in the Blue uniform of the mad. There are no silk cotton trees anywhere near this place.

Epiphytes—plants that live on air—disport themselves above his head. Bromeliads whose sharp pink blooms last months.

The rainforest just beyond the man in mad dress reminds him of the forest where they hid, two men trying to be safe. But his mind's eye moving closer he notes the difference.

In a contest—in a fancy dress parade of Green—the rainforest would win: a dead heat between the iguana and the breadfruit.

Home.

He places the beloved on the bench beside him. They face the Green impenetrable, listen to its suddenness of sound: shrieks, howls, echoes from within brick walls.

The constrictors would tie with the man in mad dress for silence.

He holds his tongue.

CHERYL CLARKE

■ ■ ■

[1947–]

ONE OF THE MOST WIDELY PUBLISHED LESBIAN POETS WRITING today, Cheryl Clarke was born in Washington, D.C., to parents who respected and affirmed the experiences of black women and instilled a sense of self-determination in their daughter. As a literature student at Howard University in the 1960s, she discovered the works of James Baldwin and the male Black Arts poets of the period—an influence that politicized her. At Rutgers University, in the late 1960s, she read Gwendolyn Brooks, Audre Lorde, and Ntozake Shange, women whose voices profoundly shaped her craft. Clarke's work draws on historical imagery to comment on contemporary concerns, especially from the perspective of an African American feminist.

Since coming out as a lesbian in 1973, Clarke has published four books of poetry: *Narratives: Poems in the Tradition of Black Women* (1982), *Living as a Lesbian* (1986), *Humid Pitch: Narrative Poetry* (1989), and *Experimental Love* (1993). She is also noted for her provocative essays "Lesbianism: An Act of Resistance" and "The Failure to Transform Homophobia in the Black Community," which appeared in *This Bridge Called My Back: Writings by Radical Women of Color* and *Home Girls: A Black Feminist Anthology* respectively.

Clarke's work concentrates on the experiences of black lesbians and black women in general, often speaking to the converging points of racism and sexism in American culture. "Women of Summer" (1977) offers a fictional account of African American lesbians in the black liberation movement during the waning civil rights era of the latter 1970s.

Women of Summer

[1977]

I f we can just get through this state, N. thought, as she rode the bus next to her comrade, J., who slept nervously next to her.

Forty-five minutes. The friend would be waiting for them at the station outside the town where they would spend twenty-four hours before going south to her grandmother's house in a small sharecropping town. She and J. would hold up there until they decided on their next point of action.

As she fitfully checked the cars that passed the bus—none of them resembling the charcoal Oldsmobile driven by the state troopers—N. was reminded of the limousine that Poochie had kidnapped the smug deputy police commissioner in.

"Took the mother-fucker in his own ride," Poochie had laughed sullenly as he pushed the wiry, belligerent white man, blindfolded and at gunpoint, into the basement of L. F.'s brownstone.

"Look at the Long Ranger peein in his boots," J. had crooned while she frisked the pockets of their hostage and Poochie disposed of the stolen blue uniform he had worn in disguise to pose as the deputy commissioner's driver.

By the time N. had met Poochie at the docks in a navy blue Rambler, he had sufficiently schooled their hostage that any move of resistance would be treated as an attack on the people. The high-level cop had been cowed enough to submit docilely to the blindfolding, handcuffing, and gagging. N. stripped him of his badge and they both forced him into the back seat of the vehicle. N. took the wheel, while Poochie went back to the limousine to leave a brown envelope containing a typewritten communique:

DEPUTY POLICE COMMISSIONER PATRICK HALLORAN IS A PRIS-
ONER OF THE PEOPLE. IF PIG JEFFERSON MADIGAN IS NOT
TERMINATED FROM YOUR VIGILANTE SQUAD IN 48 HOURS HAL-
LORAN WILL SUFFER THE SAME DEATH AT THE HANDS OF THE
PEOPLE AS YOUNG SISTER AVA CROCKER SUFFERED AT THE
HANDS OF YOUR VIGILANTE, JEFFERSON MADIGAN.   —SHAKA

J. was dreaming of L. F., her old madame, handing her a folded newspaper void of print. Blood seeped from its folds. She saw collage images of herself reaching into her stocking leg and taking hold of her blade while the malicious "john" dismissed the threat and lunged himself forward until his chest absorbed the blade to its hilt. She jerked herself awake, in a sweat. The latter was a five-year-old rerun, the former was a variation of a new suspense film her mind had been conjuring of late.

N. put her arms around J. and gave her a reassuring hug: "Be easy, sister."

N. remembered the day after Halloran's body was found. H. had come to L. F.'s house. She and J. thought he would blame them for Poochie's death. She heard H.'s soft voice again and vaguely smiled, reassured:

"Poochie was a street warrior. He made the commitment to die long before they murdered him in that parking lot. His executioners will not go unpunished. But not now. You must fly, while the pigs are disconcerted over Halloran's funeral and increasing security around Madigan. They know Poochie did not work alone. They are searching for other warriors and calling in their informers. Here are bus tickets. Friends will meet you in the next state and get you further south. Sleep with your shoes and clothes on. Keep your pieces nearby. Be silent and unseen. Peace be with you, now, my sisters. Allah will protect you. The struggle continues."

N. nudged J. awake as the bus pulled into the station. An empty blue and white patrol car was parked in the lot adjacent to the bus station. J. ignored its presence, but not its threat. They disembarked, scanning the area for the car H. had said would be waiting for them. They saw it and proceeded to get in. The friend smiled, checked her rearview mirror, and drove off. The patrol car remained parked.

"Welcome sisters," the friend greeted. "You'll stay with us for twenty-four hours."

In about five minutes, the friend drove onto a short, curbless street lined with matchbox duplexes, Cadillacs, 225s, Grand Prixs, and VWs. Folks were sitting out on their steps. Young folk were holding conferences over fences, and little children were trading secrets by the street. Two young ones were shooed away by the imposition of the friend's vintage Dodge on their spot.

"You chaps stay outta the street. Good evenin Miz Johnson. Kinda chilly this evenin. These are my friends from New England. They on they way south. Outta school and travelin," said the big woman.

N. and J. smiled quickly and coldly, nodding their heads.

"When you leavin?" Mrs. Johnson queried out of politeness.
"Tomorrow," N. asserted coolly. "Soon's we rest up and eat. Been travelin
by bus for six hours."

Into the house. The friend turned on the radio in the front room.
"Let's go into the kitchen. It's my turn to fix dinner. I better start getting
it together."

"Who you fixin dinner for?" J. cross-examined her.

"You all, me, and my housemate. She doesn't get home for a couple
of hours," the friend answered casually as she sprinted for the icebox door.

Green pepper, a half-used onion, an egg, bread crumbs, and
chopped meat were pitched backwards on the drain board. The friend
began chopping the ingredients for a meat loaf.

"Hand me that garlic powder in the cupboard, somebody. While
you in there, get the Worcestershire sauce. We gon do it up right."

"You from round here, sister?" N. asked.

"No. Further west."

The sound of the radio intruded upon the domestic quiet.

Bad Black News. Straight from the street to your soul!
The funerals of deputy police commissioner Patrick Halloran
and his alleged kidnapper and assassin, Carl "Poochie"
Williams, were held today. Williams was slain by police and
FBI in the parking lot behind his wife's building five days ago.

An estimated five hundred people attended Halloran's
funeral. The mayor and police commissioner and four other
police and city officials were his pallbearers.

Shortly after the funeral, WBAD reporter Samad Zayd got
these statements from Mayor Albright and Police Commissioner
Riley:

"The murder of Deputy Police Commissioner Halloran
was a cruel and vicious act. No stone will be left unturned in
our investigation and destruction of the black terrorist organization, SHAKA.

"Pat Halloran was my friend and colleague. He was a husband, father, and grandfather. He will be mourned by his
family as well as by his fellow police officers. With the assistance of the FBI we are calling in suspected sympathizers of

SHAKA for questioning. We have detained Erlene Williams, the murderer's wife, in custody. We are investigating all evidence that might lead to the capture of Williams' accomplices. We ask for the cooperation of the black community so that we might destroy this band of police murderers."

Almost simultaneously, WBAD Bad Black News reporter Tamu Malik recorded Imam Hassan Shahid's eulogy for the deceased Poochie Williams. Williams was mourned by his wife, who attended under the guard of federal investigators, his five-year-old daughter, his mother and father, and 200 friends. Shahid cried throughout his speech, which attacked police killings of black people:

"...How many deaths have black people suffered at the hands of gun-crazy police? Halloran was an enemy of our people though he might never have raised a gun to shoot a black person. He harbored a known murderer of our people— Jefferson Madigan, a devil who gunned down fourteen-year-old Ava Crocker. Our brother warrior, Poochie, always struggled to turn the fascists' murderous force back on them. But he rests now with Allah who will grant that Poochie's spirit fertilize our revolution. A-Salaam A-laikum, brothers and sisters. The struggle continues."

WBAD reports that officer Madigan is still under heavy guard, for fear that SHAKA might carry out its sentence of execution against him. Madigan was not indicted for the murder of Ava Crocker, the fourteen-year-old black girl whom he killed during the process of arrest. Madigan claimed that the youngster was a known drug dealer and that she resisted arrest when Madigan stopped her at twelve midnight on June 15 while on routine patrol.

Police sources reported to WBAD that Williams was also wanted for questioning in the partial bombing of the police station in the precinct where young sister Ava was killed. A witness, who saw two figures fleeing from the direction of the station house immediately preceding the explosion, identified Williams from police mug shot files. The witness could not determine the race or sex of a person whom he described as light-skinned and running beside the person alleged to have been Williams. Police say a woman might have been his accomplice.

Now back to music straight from the street to your soul on WBAD!

For the first time, the friend noticed N.'s light skin and straight, short hair. She took the elbows of N. and J. and escorted them out to the back yard.

"Where were you all when Poochie was murdered?"

"I was barricaded in an old whorehouse when my old madame brought me the paper. All I read was the headlines," answered J.

"I was reporting to my parole officer," N. answered with a smile in her voice. "When I heard the news over her desk radio, she asked me did I know him."

"Well, if we're lucky, you'll be in violation of your parole next week. Mine got a warrant on me by now. I ain't reported in three months," said J.

"How did the pigs get Poochie?"

"Informer," J. asserted.

"It was just a matter of time before they got him if he stayed in the city," N. corrected J. "After that tugboat captain saw Halloran's limousine at the docks, he called the pigs. When they read the communique from SHAKA, the FBI came in on the case. They opened their file on what they call 'Black Militants' and did a massive shakedown of all of us in the area. Poochie had been one of the eight brothers and sisters who was tried and imprisoned for a bombing conspiracy that was instigated by an agent provocateur. Naturally, he would be among the first ones the pigs would come looking for."

"Poochie wanted Madigan, though," J. commented impatiently.

"I followed the Madigan affair pretty close. And I must admit that I wasn't surprised when the grand jury didn't indict him," stated the friend.

"In a way Madigan not being indicted by the grand jury was a victory for black people," mused J.

"Why so?" asked the friend.

"Cuz niggers need to be constantly reminded that there ain't no hope."

"And that wasn't no witness that 'identified' Poochie and some 'light-skinned figure' running away from the police station the night it was bombed. It was an informer. They gonna pin every unsolved crime in the city on Poochie to make people think revolutionary justice is the act of one of a few anti-social niggers who have a 'burning' hatred of white people," N. agreed with J.

The friend escorted them back inside. She sprinted again over to the oven door and looked in at her meatloaf.

"Let's set the table and eat. My housemate can eat when she gets home. We won't have to wait."

N. and J. searched frantically for eating utensils in the unfamiliar kitchen, one of many they had found themselves in during the last six months. N. volunteered to make a salad and, hot as it was, J. perked some coffee.

"Will your grandmother be happy to see you all?" the friend directed at both of the strange women who seemed to be getting more comfortable in the work of preparing some grits.

"I know we can stay there. That's all I know," N. said curtly.

At that point a short, dark-skinned woman entered the door with an English racer and a knapsack strapped to her back. She parked the bike in a corner and came to the kitchen at the sound of voices and movement. She smiled a greeting at the two strangers and walked over to the big friend, reaching up and massaging her shoulder while the big friend bent over and kissed her lightly.

"This is my housemate, earlier than I expected. Dinner's ready. Let's chomp."

"In a minute," answered the small woman and slipped her knapsack off her shoulder as she headed toward a closet in the dining area. She pushed a black leather hassock over to the closet and climbed up on it. She rummaged noisily through packages of various junk on the closet shelf. She jumped off the hassock and stuck two rectangular objects into her knapsack.

"Those car tags?" J. queried.

"Yeah, better put them in my bag fore I forget them for tomorrow," the small friend responded, as if put off by the question.

"Oh, you the one that's drivin us to W.," J. nodded.

The tag-woman was about 4 feet 11 inches, N. guessed. She didn't appear to be a short person. She shuffled into the kitchen and returned with a fully-heaped plate. Saying nothing, she started right into scarfing with the three of them.

"Tastes good, roomie. I was hungry as forty," the small woman said.

"Yeah, was good. First time in days I been able to relax long enough to eat food," N. chimed in.

"Um," belched J.

"How about some cards?" the tag-woman suggested.

"Right on. They used to call me Six Low Sue in the House of D," J. bragged as she curled her lips and spread her nostrils.

"I was hopin you all would play some Pinochle," the big friend countered.

"Oh, let's play Bid Whist. Too many cards in Pinochle," J. pleaded.

The big friend got out a straight deck, riffled it, laid it to the right for J. to cut. She dealt, and N. bid: "Three Low."

"This ain't Pinochle, sister. The bid only goes around once. Four-No," challenged the tag-woman.

J. looked askance at the dealer and her partner, N., and bid: "Six Low."

"Six-No...Uptown," said the big friend and picked up her kitty. J. threw two jokers out of her hand and exchanged them for two useless cards from the discard pile.

"Shit," J. muttered.

"Don't worry partner. We'll set them," N. asserted.

After the big friend played seven spades from Ace to seven, she looked at N. and smiled, "Looks like you all might be goin to Boston tonight before you go to W."

"I got one book," J. defended.

"You ain't have shit in your hand cept those two jokers. I know why they called you Six Low Sue if all you can do is bid a Six Low," said N. disgustedly.

"Don't get down on your partner, you gon need her for that one book," the tag-woman advised.

The big friend played a Queen of Hearts in the last trick of the game and J. bested her with the King hold card.

"Well, I guess you can all rest here for the night. You won't be going to Boston, after all," the big friend teased.

"I am going to bed though. That Six-No took me out," N. confessed.

J. shook her head, yawning, in agreement.

The big friend showed them upstairs to a large room with a king-size bed and laid towels at its foot.

As she was getting ready to rest her bag on a chair in the room, N. stopped in mid-motion and said to the big woman, "We can sleep downstairs on the couch and floor. We don't have to sleep in your bed, sister."

J. curled her lips in response to N.'s willingness to sacrifice their comfort for a floor and a couch.

"No, I'll sleep downstairs and my housemate can sleep in the guest room. The bed in there is only large enough for one. Y'all can have our room. Goodnight. Sleep well," the big woman urged.

The two comrades began undressing, dismissing H.'s advice to sleep with their clothes on. J. noticed a newspaper and sat on the bed to scan its contents.

"I'm tired of mourning men. I told Poochie to let me slice that prick's throat. Then we wouldn'a had to deal with no gun. He coulda been outa the state by the time they found Halloran's body and then we coulda been on our way."

"And why'd he have to go back to Erlene's? He ain't seen her in months. He wasn't no fool, now. He musta known they'd be camped out there waitin for him. Bad time for him to get sentimental," N. replied.

"Sentimental, shit. The nigger had a death wish."

"Oh, you know they'd been on his ass since the bombing."

"But how come they keep saying *he* 'murdered' that motherfucker. They can't find no gun. I got rid of that myself and of that Rambler. The only thing they coulda pinned on him was the bombing," J. reflected.

"I wish some other black folk would be askin themselves *that* question out loud."

"All that rhetoric about warriors dyin in the struggle and all that maudlin bullshit coming from the PBA about Halloran's wife and family, and everybody's forgotten that Ava Crocker's murderer is still breathin air and collectin a salary."

"Poochie knew he was gonna die, but why'd he have to go back to Erlene's? Why'd he have to put her life in danger? She woulda got to him. Now, she's charged with harborin a fugitive. Ain't nobody talking about that. Is SHAKA gonna take care of her child?" N. asked.

"Shit. The warriors still ain't into that even if they women is carrying bayonets as well as babies on they backs."

"Same ole same ole. We just 'accomplices' like the news says. Even if we do make the bombs that blow up those police stations and whatever else. You know, Simba wasted that bomb puttin it in the wrong place. So, of course it didn't blow up the area it was supposed to blow up! And had the nerve to get salty with Z., saying she ain't make it 'right'." N. laughed, remembering the incident.

"The next man I work with that don't treat me like a comrade just might get cut," J. asserted with a yawn.

"Let's not bad-mouth the dead. Poochie did what he thought he had to do, I guess. He *was* a warrior."

"We warriors, too. This ain't the spook who sat by the door," J. hissed.

Realizing she had gotten her comrade's back up, N. whispered soothingly, "Let's get some sleep, baby."

They lay in bed afraid of sleep, for the nakedness of unconsciousness rendered them vulnerable. They also feared the thoughts that gather about wakefulness. They turned around to face one another simultaneously. They clutched hands and smiled.

"Did you ever know you would be in this deep?" N. asked.

"Yes, and so did you."

N. rubbed J.'s face with the back of her hand as J.'s eyes fluttered closed.

N. wondered when the police and feds would release their names and when their pictures would be posted in post offices. If L. F. could hold those boxes and that ditto machine she had ripped off from the student center until H. gave her word of new quarters, other warriors would be protected.

J. began to sleep fitfully. The image of the deputy police commissioner recurred all night long. He lay on some floor, spurting a red spray like a deflating white toy whale. Poochie was also in the dream, leaping into the air with a red stream trickling from his crotch. CMPN, J. saw herself giggling. The conked head and gold-toothed sardonic smile was playing across his reddish-brown skinned face, changing into a frown of surprised pain as the middle-aged "john" backed off of her knife.

"Wake up, baby, wake up!" N. rubbed her comrade's shoulder.

"Whew!" J. wiped her sweaty brow in relief. "Glad to see you and the morning again!"

"Havin that dream again, girl?" N. asked consolingly.

"That one and some new ones. But you'd think that the two years L. did for runnin her house and the four years I did for doin my knife trick on that m.f. woulda been enough repentance."

"Hell, I still dream about courtrooms and 'Heah Come Da Judge' and my suckered brother."

"Think we can stick together?" J. asked, forlorn.

"For awhile. Till we find out where the action's happenin or until the pigs know we're travelin together. Might find some interestin work pickin tobacco. Might be able to get some folks angry enough there to start a little underground railroad."

"We might hafta split up. It won't take them long to find an informer who'll give your name. If they ain't already found one." J. yawned and closed her eyes again in sleep.

N. drifted into an early morning sleep, too. She awoke to the sound of conversation outside the bedroom window. It came from the front porch. Mrs. Johnson was telling the two friends that the police had been checking an abandoned car parked on their street for two days. N. jumped out of bed and peered out the window. She was just in time to see the patrol car pulling slowly away from their street. N. expelled a hiss and switched on a small table radio.

Bad Black News straight from the street to your soul! City police have reported that the fifteen-year-old son of police officer Jefferson Madigan, recently acquitted of murder charges, did not return to his classroom after lunch yesterday afternoon. His parents reported that he did not return home after school. Police have put out an all-points bulletin with the description of the youngster. Madigan and his family have been under police guard for six months.

Erlene Williams, wife of slain SHAKA warrior, Poochie Williams, has been retained in custody for harboring her husband, a known fugitive, and is under $50,000 bail.

Babylon Defense Committee for Political Prisoners has stated that police have produced no conclusive evidence that Williams executed Deputy Police Commissioner Patrick Halloran or that he bombed a police station and are holding Mrs. Williams illegally.

That's it for news. Now, back to music straight from the street to your soul.

J. jack-knifed to a sitting position and N. stood frozen by the window. They looked at one another with did-you-hear-what-I-heard expressions.

"Right on, SHAKA and Bad Black News straight from the street to my soul," J. exulted, scratching her knitted-knotted head with both hands.

"M. sent him outta the classroom and K. and W. got him in the little boys' room. Right on. Bloods are definitely crazy out here. Even with his police guard, SHAKA still snapped him. I just feel a little guilty that the kid is such an innocent bystander, who probably hates his father too," N. confessed.

"M. is a better teacher since she let us rap to her about 'revolutionary education.' And anyway, we can't take the chance that the little m.f. will grow up just like his daddy. Maybe this little episode will teach him not to be a nigger hater."

"Maybe it will, maybe it won't, that is if he lives through the experience."

"Oh, you know they ain't gonna kill the little m.f.," J. responded, making N. feel almost foolish.

"Yeah, well I'm not so convinced that the warriors don't take the eye-for-an-eye outlook—no pun intended—more seriously than you," said N., wanting to conclude their bickering.

In preparation for their showers J. took her .32 from out of her duffle bag. "I never was one for getting caught in the shower…"

"Go ahead, woman," N. commanded gruffly.

"You sure is evil this morning, comadre."

They showered, dried themselves, and oiled their bodies distractedly, each in turn having offered to scrub, dry, and oil the back of the other.

They joined the friends at breakfast.

"The city's poppin," said the tag-woman, as she greeted the two women with squeezes and hugs.

The big friend sipped her coffee, lit a cigarette, frowned, and motioned all three women to the back. They settled on the porch again. The tag-woman carried the coffee-tray as J. carried the cups. N. brought the black leather hassock out and placed it close, almost underneath the wicker chair of the big friend.

"Your stuff is together," said the big friend in solemn, clipped tones. "You have two driver's licenses and two student i-dees. All four up to date but bearing four different names. Our contacts were only able to secure one passport, with legally validated photos. I am certain neither of you will have any trouble making up to look like the women in the photos, since all niggers look alike. You all can decide between you who uses it, if that becomes necessary." She paused to drag off her cigarette and shrug her shoulders. J. became impatient with her seeming smugness. And N. nearly laughed at the flat, pat rap the big woman must have given countless times.

After a dramatic exhale of the smoke, the woman continued, "You have some money here, which should sustain you until you reach your first destination. If you run into some bread, we would be grateful for a return of any portion of it so we can continue to do our work. I assume you have equipment to protect yourselves."

N. and J. looked at her blankly.

"Okay, when you get to your grandmother's be open and friendly, because if it's small and rural, by dawn everybody's going to know you are there anyway. So, don't raise any questions by being secret. N., you're your grandmother's grandchild home from college and J., you're a fellow student visiting the South for the first time."

Appearing to have absorbed her limit, N. said, "I know how to deal with that scene, sister. My grandmother will take care of us."

"Okay, but will she be hip to calling you by a different name? Can she deal with who you are, if it comes down to having to square with her?" the friend tested N. Turning and looking directly at J., almost throwing down the glove, the friend asked, "Can you take low to white folk?..."

N. interrupted the friend's interrogation, "Sister, my mother told me that for thirty years both my grandparents fed and sheltered and aided blacks escaping from prison farms down there. My grandmother took low to white people for thirty years so she and my grandfather could do *their* work. She sharecropped, took in wash, cleaned white people's houses and buildings until she saved enough money to build her own house. So, she don't owe white people nuthin, cept a bullet through the head. And it wouldn't be the first time she shot a white man. She keeps a .28 in her night table and a shotgun at her door—for rabbits, she says—but it's in her hand everytime she opens the door."

"I ain't never known a rabbit to knock," said the big friend smiling, retreating from her verbal foray. She continued with the instructions: "You'll get to W. around nine tonight. Roomie here will take you to our friend's club. It's a cool place. She's running it for her sister for the summer. You'll stay there for five hours. Three for her to close the joint and two for her to blow some z's. The nearest city to your destination is five hours from W. You'll be dropped just outside a city by the name of T.

T. has a sometime bus service to a town ten miles from your grand-mother's. Hitch or hike to your grandmother's. It'll be nice weather for bare feet and rolled-up jeans with shirttails tied above the waistline." The friend paused again to dump her ashes and crush her cigarette.

"If you must contact us at any time, call information. We're listed as Scott. And you can call collect," added the tag-woman encouragingly.

"Think you'll dig the country?" the big friend taunted J.

J. and N. took turns braiding their hair and reacting silently to the cloak-and-dagger instructions of the big woman. J. had been wanted at least ninety times—seventy of those being bogus—before this recent knowing and not-knowing hocus-pocus. But this time she also knew that this flight was not a "flight to avoid prosecution" as much as it was to take her skill and fervor elsewhere. "Next time I go to jail, I'll be a corpse first," J. had decided. N. appreciated the thoroughness and drama of the friends, their warm impersonalness, their caring. In all her years of radi-cal campus politics, taking over buildings, burning files, receiving stolen goods, bombings, N. had never heeded the get-out-before-they-get-you advice of friends, enemies, or well-wishers. "Let them come and get me. They better have a warrant or a subpoena. I can go to court. I been to jail before…" But not like that last time. Not like that last isolation. She couldn't be an activist in the joint. She had always justified her guilty silence while in prison by saying things like, "I'll do better next time I'm in the joint." But she knew she would do everything in her power not to go back, just as she did everything in her power to get paroled.

"Let's raise, sisters. We got a four- to five-hour drive with traffic," said the tag-woman.

J. and N. went obediently upstairs to change their clothes. J. put on a khaki shirt and coveralls. N. wore cut-offs, sweat socks and sneakers, and pulled a white tee shirt over her head that sported the letters U. of M.

"Let's hat up. This state is hangin heavy on our heels," J. advised.

The tag-woman was at the door waiting and ready. The big friend came over to the door and kissed her roommate heavily on the lips and embraced the two women. "Go well," she said softly to all three.

"We gonna need the juju dust of Marie LeVeaux to get us where we goin, it's so far into the sticks," laughed J., finally seeming to relax.

The tag-woman opened the door and J. and N. followed. Mrs. Johnson sat on the steps of her porch between two of her children. "Have a nice trip, all of you."

"Thanks and it was nice meeting you. Maybe next time we visit we can spend more time together," N. proffered warmly.

"Alright now. I'm gonna hold you to your word."

The tag-woman hopped into an old Ford and adjusted the seat and switched on the radio. J. and N. piled in after her.

Bad Black News straight from the street to your soul:

City police have received a communique from SHAKA. Eliot Madigan, Jefferson Madigan's fifteen-year-old son, was apparently kidnapped by SHAKA members in the lavatory of his high school—much to the dismay of his police guards, who were posted outside the lavatory when the kidnapping is said to have taken place.

"See! " exclaimed J. "I told you those niggers was bad! "

...This new SHAKA communique was received by WBAD producer Chembe Rogers, as well as by city police. It is addressed, "To Our People." We will read an excerpt:

"In the name of black children, we have taken Eliot Madigan a prisoner of war. He will remain unharmed if the city police and FBI release Erlene Williams into the custody of her own community and if the prosecutor signs an affidavit in the presence of Mrs. Williams' Imam, Hassan Shahid, and her mother, Mrs. Essie Davis, dismissing all charges of harboring a fugitive. Eliot Madigan will be returned to safety if his father, Jefferson Madigan, resigns from the police force. If he does not, Eliot Madigan will be given the same chance as his father gave Ava Crocker. The struggle continues."

Police Commissioner Riley had no comment...

Now, back to soul on the beat radio from WBAD— straight from the street to your soul.

"That's what the niggers shoulda done at first. But no, they had to be bad black warriors and capture a chief pig," growled N.

"I need some tampons, right now," J. commanded.

It was a sunny day and folk were shopping, congregating, and shooting the breeze as the tag-woman drove through the town in search of tampons. The early summer air was still oozing the moisture of spring under their skins, making N. and J. almost regret their flight. J. spotted a black cop mounted atop a brown nag.

As he nodded to J., whose stare had conjured his eyes around, she murmured, "Does that nigger think he's in Marlboro Country?"

N. and the tag-woman laughed at the analogy.

The tag-woman parked and asked J. her preference of tampons. "Regular," J. responded.

The tag-woman sighed and jumped out of the car with, "Back in a minute."

Both J. and N. were alternately drawn into their separate thoughts and distracted by the clusters of activity on the street.

The tag-woman returned with a box of "Super."

"I said 'Regular,' sister."

"I forgot. Want me to take them back?"

"Drive on, baby. Let's make it," N. asserted.

The ride to W. was a silent ride with the radio blaring music, news, and static.

"The business in the city with Madigan's son is probably gonna keep the FBI busy for a week," the tag-woman offered, to break the ice-like smoothness of the silence among the three of them.

"I doubt it. The feds is all over," J. responded dispassionately.

"Think they know who the woman is who bombed the station with Poochie?" the tag-woman asked, but the women were again silent.

N. wondered how long she could remain in her limbo of above-underground, if it might be better to try to get to the frozen tundra of Canada. She fantasized about organizing and teaching young brothers and sisters who sharecropped in her grandmother's town. No time to be having Bethune aspirations, she thought. She hoped J. could tolerate the inactivity of the Southern scene. She wondered, casually, if her grandmother would become an aider. Would she understand the necessity for fighting the white man openly and aggressively—no more rabbits? Then her thoughts fell upon the reality of her covert position— the result of open aggression.

J. felt sullen about having to leave the tense pace of her city for what she imagined to be the sultry, lazy stroll of the country. She hoped she could double her consciousness enough to be an ingratiating darkie and a subversive field nigger. From the first time the pigs came to her house to arrest her for a B 'n' E, she had vocalized her contempt of white men and their presumed authority. Five years ago when an Italian judge sentenced her to ten years for manslaughter, she blaringly questioned his lineage before the court. His pride offended, he sentenced her to six months extra for contempt. After having been mercilessly beaten with an electric cord by a prison matron and restrained in her bed for three weeks in a psychiatric cell block, she especially couldn't take but too low to white folk. She wondered if she and N. could hook up with any of those bad niggers who always lurk in the woods of small Southern towns, that don't no crackers mess with cuz they know the niggers is crazy and ain't afraid to shoot them. Or were they mythical like many things in Disneyland, U.S.A.

"After seeing Miss Jane Pittman on t.v., the whole world must think niggers in the South always resisted peacefully and only talked the rhetoric of freedom and got killed by the honky," N. sliced through their preoccupied silence.

"And all the women did was live one hundred years and cry over their men being killed," the tag-woman said, seizing upon N.'s invitation to converse.

"Don't forget," said J., "that the high point in any nigger's life is to drink out of the honky's water fountain in front of other niggers with picket signs and pigs with riot gear on and cattle prods dangling alongside they pricks."

The tag-woman pulled off the road onto a shoulder shrouded by pines. "Be with you in five minutes." She grabbed her bag and was out of the car and seemed to be removing her front car tag. She proceeded to the rear and seemed to be doing the same thing. She returned to her car and her riders, adjusted her mirror, and swerved back onto the road. The tag-woman asked J. to open the glove compartment and pass her the registration. As J. did so, the tag-woman fished in her jacket pocket and pulled out a similar looking document which she gestured toward J. to replace in the glove compartment. "We'll be in W. in ninety minutes," she said.

This is WNAZ news at 3:30 P.M. President Nixon maintains that he will stand firm against impeachment.

Israeli air forces are bombing Lebanese borders.

Governor George Wallace today accused the Republican Administration of making the middle class bear the brunt of the economic recession.

One hundred medical experts reported to the Senate Committee on Health and Nutrition that the rate of starvation is higher than it has ever been.

_____ City police officer, Jefferson Madigan, resigned from the city police force this afternoon to secure the release of his fifteen-year-old son, Eliot, who was kidnapped by black terrorists, who have also claimed responsibility for the bombing of a police station and the kidnap and murder of that city's deputy police commissioner, Patrick Halloran.

Now, we return you to our program of music to suit your every mood.

"Shit, what about Erlene?" N. implored.

"What about us?" J. answered.

"The woman you'll hook up with in W. runs a tiny bar called 'The Sanctuary'—oddly enough. At one time she was involved in prison work, until a stoolie told one of the matrons that she was spreading communism." The tag-woman tried to change the subject, wanting to keep the two women focused on the here-and-now—never mind about what the radio ain't said.

"Oh yeah?" N. responded more out of politeness than interest.

"She's a real sister in the struggle," the tag-woman assured N. and J., who appeared bored with her story.

A state police car glided past them. The two policemen, wearing black wrap-around sunglasses, looked askance at the tag-woman's car as she pulled abreast of them.

This is Soul Starship coming to you from the Black Metropolis. We'll continue with our program of rock, blues, and jazz after the evening news.

_____ City police found Eliot Madigan unharmed in the phone booth of a filling station on the east side of the city. Eliot is the fifteen-year-old son of Jefferson Madigan, the policeman who was recently acquitted of murder charges. His son was held prisoner by SHAKA, a black revolutionary group, until the release of Erlene Williams, who had been in police custody, and the resignation of Officer Madigan from the city police force.

Mrs. Williams, widow of slain black revolutionary Carl "Poochie" Williams, was released shortly before young Madigan was found.

Police are now looking for two women, believed to have been accomplices of Poochie Williams in the kidnap and killing of deputy police commissioner Patrick Halloran and in the partial bombing of a police station on the east side of the city. Police have not revealed the names of the women, but believe they are fleeing north and have put out an all points bulletin on the two suspects.

Now back to Soul Starship in the Black Metropolis.

"Uh-oh, that means they know we're moving south," J. emitted in a disgusted tone.

"Then it may not be wise to wait five hours before you travel on. But then again it may not be wise to travel on," the tag-woman suggested as she gassed her car up to seventy-five.

"Humph, you better slow down or we won't have to make any decisions," said N., eyeing the speedometer.

"No, I don't want to hold up in no W. I want to keep going," said J.

"I guess I'm with my partner," N. said.

"Right on," said the tag-woman.

In another thirty minutes, the tag-woman was pulling off the highway into W. and driving through the city, which was lit only by traffic lights and headlights. They got out of the car in an alley which led them through a wooden door of a red brick building. A woman with long, straight brown hair, glasses, and a small, wiry frame admitted them to an office with a cot, water cooler, a small refrigerator, and a cluttered desk.

"Welcome to the Sanctuary," she greeted the three women, smiling.

"What's happenin?" the tag-woman answered distantly.

J. looked suspiciously at the white woman. N. placed a reassuring hand on J.'s shoulder.

"I leave you in good hands," said the tag-woman.

"Hey, hey, no you don't. We ain't buying insurance here," called J., grabbing the tag-woman by the shoulder and pushing her into the hall. "What's the idea of leaving us with that whitey?!"

"Hold on, sister. You ain't in a position to be a separatist now. You might find yourself being aided by anybody. We have credibility. Would we put you in the hands of anybody who hadn't proven herself a friend? We ain't lost or had anybody informed on yet. That woman knows the roads. She'll be a good cover for you, too. If you don't trust her, tell her so. She'll get you a black driver, but I bet you'll be stopped before you get out of R."

J. jerked her hands away sullenly and returned to the white woman's office, where she and N. were chatting softly over a road map as the white woman cleaned her shotgun with castor oil.

"It might be a good idea to leave sooner than planned," suggested the tag-woman, who had followed J. back into the room.

"Yes, I think so. I'll tell my bartender to close up. Then, we can leave in an hour."

"I'm bookin," said the tag-woman and stood on tiptoe to embrace N. and J. She shook the white friend's hand shyly. "Stay well."

The new friend put the parts of her shotgun together, loaded it, and pulled the safety catch forward.

"Stay back here and I'll go out and tell my bartender to close for me. Then we can leave."

As the white woman left, J. grabbed N. and pulled her ear to her lips. "I don't trust no white person to take me to the corner store…"

"Just be cool. She's been around. She useta be with the Brigade. She's spent two and a half years in the joint. I remember her case. She's too well known to go back underground. So, now she's an aider. She was with S.N.C.C. in Durham till the nationalists took it over. She really does know the roads. If we travel her route, we'll be there in five hours. So, relax," N. pleaded.

The woman came back into her office a half hour later to find J. and N. curled around one another in a troubled sleep on her cot. She woke J. easily, who started and then wheezed a sigh of relief in recognition of the new friend.

"Sorry, took longer than I expected. There was a pig out front and I had to go through a routine with him about the rooms back here. They harass us as a matter of course."

"What'd you tell him?" J. asked nasty-like.

"That he couldn't search anything unless he had a signed warrant," the new friend answered in a reasoning tone.

Soon, the woman led them to a light blue wood-paneled Ford station wagon with M. tags. They loaded their bags in the rear, hopped in the wagon, and waited for the aider to adjust her seat and begin to drive.

The three women said nothing. The aider kept her eyes peeled to the front. Not even the radio was on. The handle of the white woman's shotgun rested intimately against N.'s heel. The roads drew them and enchanted them with crisp, dry summer greenness. N. and J. were surprised by the aloofness of the white woman. When would they have the chance to come down on whatever liberal, communist, feminist we-can-be-together rap they hadn't had to hear because of their isolation for so many heavy months?

N. recalled the nightmarish spectacle of M., her brother, and herself in the courtroom, fighting for their lives. M. had been so drugged, because of the bullet pain in his shoulder. She had been so traumatized emotionally the day M.'s lawyer had asked that their cases be severed. She remembered how naked she'd felt when she jumped up and screamed curses at the lawyer—a charlatan whom all the movement people said was radical political because he'd got so many brothers and sisters off with light sentences. He'd claimed their charges were different, that M.'s health was poor and he could not withstand the rigors of the trial, and that N.'s contemptuous behavior was jeopardizing the success of her brother's case.

She remembered that betrayal. She remembered that she'd had to settle for a public defender, when her own lawyer dropped her case because she could no longer afford his fees and her parents had refused to help her because they were sinking all their resources into M.'s defense. The public defender told her to plead guilty and get a lighter sentence. She knew better. She pleaded not guilty, acted as her own witness, and told the court that whatever her brother did he was still her brother and she would protect him. The public defender asked to be relieved of the case. She defended herself. She was sentenced to ten years. Her brother got ninety years. She was out in four. He was still in the joint. She never recovered from hating M. for his stupidity in allowing their cases to be severed. She never tossed from her mind his passivity before the white male authority of his lawyers and all the others. She also couldn't help but feel, despite her love of women, that the white man's authority was easily transferred to his woman, for it had been a white woman judge who sentenced both her brother and herself to their respective prison terms.

J. was quite resentful at the silent aplomb of this white woman. The bitch really is cold, thought J. She's wheeling this tank like a truck driver and this road is dark as a mother-fucking cave. "Put on your high beams," J. ordered her.

"They're on," said the woman casually. The woman resembled all those nuns who'd flogged her in the Catholic girls' home the state had sent her to for "incorrigibility," J. thought.

"What're you in this for? Excitement? You get your liberal jollies off helpin some bad niggers out?"

"I haven't asked you any questions, have I?"

"That's not the point. I wanna know what your stake is in this."

"You might have to do the same for me one day—some people already have. I'd hate to have to question your loyalty on the basis of your skin color," the aider snarled, not even turning her head to look at her interrogator.

"Bullshit," J. spewed back.

"How much further, I have to pee," N. interrupted this promising argument.

"About two hour's drive. I'll pull over here," said the woman in a relieved tone. N. got out of the car with a farcical, panicky gesture. J. and the aider exchanged hostile glances.

"How'd you get inside the prisons? What group do you work for?" J. started up again.

"I don't belong to any group. I used to get in on a clergy pass. I provided 'spiritual' guidance."

J. did not appreciate her humor. "You a nun?"

"No."

N. knocked at the window and halted J.'s next comment. "Let's go. Turn on the radio," N. directed the aider.

This is WPEC, your country station bringing you the best in country music. Dutton County Board of Education has refused to allow neighboring Marlow County nigra chil'ren to attend its schools to create racial balance.

Three nigra convicks have escaped from P. Farms prison. State troopers, sheriff's men, and deputized community residents are combing the area.

Jennifer Christmas, a known felon and arsonist, is wanted for questioning by _____ City police in connection with the kidnap and murder of deputy police commissioner Patrick Halloran, whose body was found a week ago in an abandoned car. Christmas is believed to be fleeing north in the company of another nigra woman. Christmas is also a nigra.

CLICK! "I'm sick of listening to this corn-pone mouth," J. snapped.

The friend burned the roads. N. felt the gravelly road boil in offense. A gray and yellow patrol car followed and drew abreast; the pink-faced driver, whose stomach pillowed the steering wheel, waved for them to pull over.

"He's by himself. It's dawn and the shotgun's right under my foot," N. whispered to both the aider and J.

"That mother-fucker's awfully sure of himself. He would want to be careful travelin alone with all those bad niggers on the loose," J. hissed.

"Ee-een kwot a her-ree, aincha may-um?" the brute smiled, showing two solid gold crowned canine teeth among his tobacco stained dentures.

"Oh, aw-fi-suh, Ah promised Cal-line, our girl, Ah'd git her grits to a bus station in D. by seven a-clock. I kinda los mah way and track a-time. They gotta ketch that bus or they'll lose they jobs in R.," the aider feigned a syrupy plea.

"Lah-cense and reg'stration, may-um."

"Heah, awf-fi-suh. Pleeze, her-ree," the aider panted.

The pink and paunchy ugly cop perused the items given him by the aider. J. and N. were constipated with anxiety.

"You ole Apple Orchard Bayard's daughter? How's yo daddy? He's a fine Southern maa-en. Stands up fuh Dixie. Go head, may-um. Hope Ah ain't cost you no inconvenience."

VROOM! "He can be so sure of women. So fucking patronizing and cute. He didn't even have sense enough to feel threatened by that shotgun I know he saw under my foot," the aider fumed.

"If he'd tarried any longer that barrel woulda been up his nose," N. assured her.

"Is that Apple Orchard dude really your old man?" J. asked in unself-conscious curiosity.

"No, his daughter was my roommate in college. I borrowed her license at a class reunion two months ago and nature took care of the rest."

Both N. and J. laughed hysterically as the redness of the friend's anger gradually withdrew like the mercury of a thermometer.

After ninety-odd minutes of silence, N. and J. were delivered to a dusty bus station. They got their makeshift back packs and stood at the passenger side window of the aider's car.

"A bus should be here in forty minutes. It'll take you to within twenty-five miles of your destination. Stay well," the aider said to both of them, but made eye contact only with N. N.'s eyes followed the car's trail of dust.

"There she goes-off in a mighty cloud of dust and a hearty 'Hi-Ho, Silver,'" J. taunted.

The bus was hot, old, and segregated. J. and N. caused a near stir when they sat toward the front of the bus. No one said anything, but the stares and glares spoke for them. The black folk on the bus either looked out the dirty bus windows or bowed their heads in exasperation or shame. N. and J. just stood their ground, and pretended not to notice. The road gave them an uncomfortable ride as the pre-noon sun created a glare on the windows. They felt dusty, clammy, and strangely hungry.

"We shoulda brought some fried chicken in a greasy brown paper bag and been right in style," J. quipped. The bus stopped at numberless little towns, corners, roads—some with markers, some anonymous, except to the particular inhabitants who disembarked with each snappy halt the driver made.

"The next one's ours. Feel like hitchin?" N. asked J.

J. rolled her eyes. "What choice do we have?"

"We could walk."

"I'm really sick of this trip, girl."

They descended from the raggedy bus and started footing it east on the dirt road. Few cars passed them and those that did weren't going to stop.

"Maybe I oughtta go barefoot then somebody would surely pity this homeless darkie."

"You have such a stereotyped mind, you know. You haven't even been here ten minutes and already you know how the whole thing works. Can't you just be cool?" N. shouted at J. for the first time, defensive about her Southern roots.

"Sorry, sister. But every stereotype has borne itself out in the last five hours," J. said, apologetic but unable to resist this last dig.

N. laughed uproariously. "Well, one thing I know—I ain't no stereotype."

The sound of a vehicle pulling over behind them made them reach for their equipment, but a loud, friendly voice calling to them halted that action. "You ladies want a ride?" a young, brown-skinned man yelled from a dusty black pick-up truck.

"We're going ten miles east," N. answered, smiling.

"Come on, get in."

"Thanks," N. and J. said simultaneously, happy to get out of the sun.

"I live over thataway. On my way back from a brick-layin job. I work for my father. He's a bricklayer," the youngster, who appeared to be no more than fifteen, bragged.

"We're visiting my grandmother, Hattie Moses. We came down from school. This is my roommate, Connie. My name's Paulene," N. said hospitably.

"Pleased to meet you. My name's Logan."

The women settled back, lit cigarettes, and breathed easily for the first time in several days. The young man, respecting their rest, was quiet and reassuring.

"Here's y'all's stop. I gotta turn off here, now. My father's expecting me home. Say hello to Miss Hattie for me."

The two women waved at the boy. After a moment's hesitation, they both moved tentatively toward a small clapboard house held up on cinderblocks. "This is it, Connie," N. said to J., clasping her hand.

"Right on, Paulene," J. responded, sealing the pact.

N. knocked hard.

"Who's there?" a voice from within called with an assertive tremor.

"Your granddaughter, Nannie."

The door opened slowly to a forty-five degree angle.

"The leaves told me my people was comin," a tall, cordovan colored-woman of about eighty smiled as she slid a shotgun back into its place beside the door.

1980–2000
COMING OUT BLACK, LIKE US
"Now I speak and my burden is lightened…"

WRITING IN 1983, AUDRE LORDE, LIKE MANY AFRICAN AMERICAN lesbian, gay, and bisexual people who had come of age during the civil rights era, understood the limitations of liberation movements fraught with divisiveness. "[I]f there is one thing we can learn from the 60s it is how infinitely complex any move for liberation must be. For we must move against not only those forces which dehumanize us from outside, but also against those oppressive values which we have been forced to take into ourselves."[1] In spite of the political strides of the African American civil rights struggle of the 1960s and the gay rights movement of the 1970s, black lesbians and gay men faced an unfinished agenda in the 1980s—an agenda that challenged the ways in which Americans viewed black homosexuality as much as it revealed the ways in which black homosexuals viewed themselves and each other.

African Americans had employment and educational opportunities that were unencumbered by institutionalized segregation. While racial disparities persisted, and while the struggle for equality was far from over, blacks no longer were mandated to the lowest social caste. Race pride had trumped old stereotypes with empowering slogans such as the 1960s' "Black is beautiful." These strides had a cost, however. The

African American community was increasingly divided by income, leading to a renewed criminalization of the black underclass—sometimes with the complicity of other African Americans. With the rise of middle-income blacks also came calls for dismantling affirmative action programs, which, critics argued, were now unnecessary. Complicating matters further was the opinion held by some African Americans that advances among black women, as well as black gay men and lesbians, in the areas of jobs and social status threatened the stability of the black family.

A similar dynamic occurred among lesbians and gay men, with no less troubling consequences. Homosexuals were "coming out" in unprecedented numbers, discovering their political clout as an identifiably gay community. Openly homosexual candidates were being elected to political office, while lesbians and gay men—including black lesbians and gays—stepped forward in journalism, professional sports, music and the arts, and the armed forces to challenge debilitating sexual stereotypes. For the first time ever, the burgeoning gay rights movement had become a formidable force against antigay prejudice as well as a source of inspiration for lesbians and gay men everywhere. But as with African Americans, social progress had its drawbacks. Whereas pre-Stonewall homosexuals were persecuted by virtue of their "invisibility," out gays of the post-Stonewall era were met by a relentless homophobic backlash. Cultural watchdogs on the right moved forward with antigay initiatives intended to curtail lesbian and gay civil rights, if not drive homosexuals back into the closet.

The enlarged presence of gay people in everyday life also brought the unavoidable issue of sex to the forefront of political and cultural debates. Gay men's sexuality was thrust into news headlines with the first reports of AIDS in 1981. Surfacing as a mysterious illness among gay men, AIDS was first dubbed "gay cancer" but was soon renamed Acquired Immune Deficiency Syndrome (AIDS), when medical professionals realized that heterosexuals were vulnerable, too. Consequently, gay activists were the first to attempt to get the public, the government, and the gay community itself to take the sudden crisis seriously. Larry Kramer voiced alarm in "1,112 and Counting," an essay published in the gay press in 1983. "If this article does not scare the shit out of you, we're in real trouble," he wrote. "If this article does not arouse anger, fury, rage, and action, gay men have no future on this Earth. Our continued existence depends on how angry you can get."[2] When Kramer wrote the piece, 1,112 AIDS cases had been reported, up alarmingly from only 41 cases cited in the *New York Times* the previous year. By the end of 1985, however, the number had exploded to 11,980, while reported AIDS-related deaths rose from 641 in 1982 to 6,973 in 1984. These numbers impressed on Kramer the conviction that "In all the history of homosexuality we have never before been so close to death and extinction."

Because early warnings from gay pundits like Kramer were directed at the predominantly white gay male population that was perceived to be most at risk, at first activists failed to consider, let alone address, race concerns in AIDS organizing. By 1987, African Americans and Latinos represented more than forty percent of AIDS cases, even though they accounted for only about twenty percent of the U.S. population. Among women, the racial numbers were even more stark. In 1988, black women and Latinas made up more than seventy percent of all women with AIDS, with black women alone accounting for forty-nine percent of the total. Meanwhile, of children with AIDS, fifty-seven percent were black, twenty-three percent Hispanic. Despite the highly disproportionate impact of AIDS on minority communities, AIDS education and prevention funding nevertheless flowed to groups serving gay white males.

Within the African American community, civil rights leaders contributed to the shortfall of services by maintaining that AIDS was not a black civil rights issue. As Cathy Cohen explained in *The Boundaries of Blackness: AIDS and the Breakdown of Black Politics* (1999), a number of factors contributed to this misimpression. African Americans feared that engaging in AIDS activism, for example through programs of needle exchange and sex education, would confirm the historical (mis)association of black people with drug use and sexual deviance (specifically, homosexuality and sexually transmitted diseases). According to Cohen, the initial response to AIDS by national black political organizations such as the NAACP, the Urban League, and the SCLC was one of denial. In fact, NAACP literature failed to mention AIDS until 1989, by which point more than 17,000 African Americans had died from the disease.[3] Complicating matters was the problem of black establishment organizations' singling out women and children as "innocent victims." The exclusion of gay men, drug users, and sex workers from the debate led such groups as the Minority AIDS Project, Gay Men of African Descent (GMAD), AMASSI, and the National Task Force on AIDS Prevention

(NTFAP), the first federally funded AIDS service organization focusing on black men who have sex with men, to challenge the legitimacy of black leadership as the AIDS crisis worsened throughout the 1980s and 1990s. As a result, today most black civil rights organizations have learned to respond to AIDS as a civil rights issue. Indeed, NAACP President and CEO Kweisi Mfume was named the 2002 spokesperson for National Black HIV/AIDS Awareness Day. Inaugurated a year earlier, the day constitutes a nationwide, black community effort to draw attention to and educate people about the impact of AIDS on African Americans.

The black community's troubling response to AIDS has been strained further by some African Americans' reducing homosexuality to a white cultural phenomenon. This misconception has shaped the conservative sexual politics behind much black antiracist discourse. Molefi Asante's *Afrocentricity: The Theory of Social Change* (1980), for instance, asserted that homosexuality is not an "Afrocentric relationship." Nathan Hare and Julia Hare's *The Endangered Black Family: Coping with Unisexualization and the Coming Extinction of the Black Race* (1984) elaborated on this idea, claiming that there is "no need to engage in endless debates about the pros and cons of homosexuality.... [It] does not promote black family stability and...it historically has been a product largely of Europeanized society."[4] Dr. Frances Cress Wesling, writing in *The Isis Papers: Keys to the Colors* (1990), weighed in with an observation worthy of Anita Bryant: "Black psychiatrists must understand that whites may condone homosexuality for themselves, but we as Blacks must see it as a strategy for destroying Black people that must be countered."[5] As black gay filmmaker Marlon Riggs rightly pointed out, this self-serving rehistorization advocates a mythologized past, wherein "African men were strong, noble protectors, providers, and warriors for their families and tribes." Central to this myth is the idea that "In pre-colonial Africa, men were truly men. And women were women. Nobody was lesbian. Nobody was feminist. Nobody was gay."[6]

In spite of its divisiveness, black sexual conservatism served as the cornerstone for "community-building" in the Million Man March on Washington, D.C. Organized by the Nation of Islam in 1993, the purpose of the gathering was to "build and sustain a free and empowered [black] community, a just society and a better world."[7] While the mission statement for the march did not openly condemn homosexuality, it encouraged male/female relationships, promoted patriarchal values, and was buttressed by a fundamentalist religious platform. Moreover, Nation of Islam leader Minister Louis Farrakhan had publicly denounced homosexuality on numerous occasions, positing that lesbianism is a disease produced by what he perceived to be a particular black familial dysfunction: single female-headed households. Nevertheless, some black gay men, like Dennis Holmes, president of the National Black Lesbian and Gay Leadership Forum, joined the march "to demonstrate that we are members of the black family."[8] Keith Boykin, former executive director of the Forum, participated for similar reasons. Other black gay men, however, together with many black feminists, refused to be involved, reasoning that marching would be tantamount to supporting the homophobic and sexist ideology around which the march was organized.

The black left has also had its share of problems with homophobia. When organizers of a ceremonial demonstration to commemorate the twentieth anniversary of Martin Luther King, Jr.'s "I Have a Dream" speech announced that homosexuals would not be permitted to address the audience, the National Coalition of Black Lesbians and Gays (NCBLG) stepped in to protest the exclusion. The NCBLG (renamed the National Black Lesbian and Gay Leadership Forum in 1988) lobbied the march coordinator, Congressman Walter Fauntleroy, until Audre Lorde was added to the program. The NCBLG also met with Coretta Scott King, who subsequently called for lesbian and gay civil rights legislation. By the time of the 1987 Gay and Lesbian March on Washington, D.C., the situation had hardly improved: With the notable exception of Jesse Jackson's Rainbow Coalition, no African American establishment civil rights group participated. By 1993, however, the relationship between African Americans and gay people was reconciled to the extent that the NAACP unanimously endorsed that year's Gay and Lesbian March on the nation's capital.

In matters of race representation within the white lesbian and gay rights movement, the situation was no better. The debate on gays in the military is one instructive example. In 1993, President Bill Clinton outlawed homosexuals from military service with the "Don't Ask, Don't Tell" policy. When gay personnel began to be discharged under the new policy, gay rights groups fought the ban by selecting test litigants, individuals whose distinguished record of service flew in the face of arguments that lesbians and gays threatened the purported goal of "military cohesion." Remarkably, all the high-profile plaintiffs—Margarethe Cammemeyer, Keith Meinhold, and Joseph Steffan among them—were white. This racial specificity belies the fact that an African American gay man first beat the military's prohibition on homosexuals. Perry Watkins, an Army sergeant known as "the Rosa Parks of gay soldiers," was drafted into the Vietnam War at age nineteen. From his induction in 1967, Watkins repeatedly acknowledged his sexual orientation to commanding officers. He even performed lavish, military drag shows replete with a signature seven-foot feather boa. When fellow soldiers attempted to gang rape him in a gay-bashing incident, the army began an investigation that led to Watkin's dismissal. After a ten-year legal battle, the Court of Appeals for the Ninth Circuit concluded that the army not only knew Watkins was gay but had allowed him to reenlist three times. Rather than return to the military at the court's behest, however, he opted to take an honorable discharge, $135,000 in back pay, and full retirement benefits.

For the most part, Watkins' story was ignored by gay organizers as the campaign for gays in the military took off. According to Tom Stoddard, a white gay lawyer who directed the Campaign for Military Service, "[T]here was a public relations problem with Perry."[9] Ostensibly, the problem was not simply that Watkins was black, but also that he wore a nose-ring. Speaking to the movement's decision to champion the newly "out" Cammemeyer over himself, Watkins nevertheless indicated that race was the determinant. "[W]e'll go with a [white] woman who lied for twenty years before we go with a black man who had to live the struggle nearly every day of his life."[10] Furthermore, while African American women were discharged from the military for homosexuality at twice the rate of white men, neither the mainstream press nor gay rights proponents have presented black women as victims of discrimination, let alone as icons. Indeed, the dismissal of navy personnel Wendi Williams and Alicia Harris in 1980 received even less attention than Watkins's case.

As the gay movement battled the military ban, a right-wing group called Colorado for Family Values put on the ballot a proposed amendment to the state constitution. Amendment 2 sought to repeal existing gay civil rights laws and prevent Colorado from enacting any such laws in the future. This ballot initiative was part of a larger New Rights Initiative, which redefined gay rights as "special rights" (paralleling the claim that race-based civil rights measures such as affirmative action were a form of special rights for blacks and other nonwhites). Gay civil rights groups filed suit, taking their case all the way to the Supreme Court. Its 1986 decision in *Bowers v. Hardwick,* a landmark case involving Michael Hardwick, who was arrested for having sex with another man in his own bedroom, had upheld the constitutional legality of a Georgia sodomy statute, and, by extension, the right of any state to outlaw sex between consenting adults. In the instance of Amendment 2—and much to the surprise of many activists who anticipated a return to *Bowers*—the Court invalidated the amendment. Writing for the majority of the Court in *Romer v. Evans,* Justice Kennedy maintained that "We must conclude that Amendment 2 classifies homosexuals not to further a proper legislative end but to make them unequal to everyone else.... This Colorado cannot do. A State cannot so deem a class of persons a stranger to its law."[11]

In an effort to combat right-wing offenses against sexual minorities, lesbian and gay activists had throughout the 1980s begun to reorganize old political organizations and to establish new ones, the better to answer political repression against an increasingly visible lesbian and gay population. The National Gay and Lesbian Task Force (NGLTF) marked a historic transition in the movement by becoming the first professional lesbian and gay political organization with a national agenda. By the 1990s, however, it enlarged its platform under the leadership of Urvashi Vaid to include so-called nongay matters like abortion rights and opposition to the Persian Gulf War. The broadening of NGLTF's agenda caused controversy within the organization, leading critics to insist that a fundamentally gay-oriented organization ought to remain devoted to gay-centered politics. Along with NGLTF, the Human Rights Campaign (HRC), a Washington, D.C.–based congressional lobbying organization formed in 1980, signaled the movement's new influence in shaping legislation at the national level.

While the Human Rights Campaign began a lobbying campaign in the halls of Congress, in New York City the AIDS Coalition to Unleash Power (ACT UP) took to the streets to protest a lack of effective public policy in the AIDS crisis. Organized in 1987 by Larry Kramer and some three hundred New York activists, ACT UP adopted the motto "United in anger and committed to direct action to end the AIDS crisis." The group raised public awareness about AIDS/HIV more dramatically than any other organization, expanding access to clinical trials of drugs' efficacy, pushing the U.S. Food and Drug Administration to expedite its drug approval process, and lowering the cost of medication. The confrontational street tactics of ACT UP inspired the formation in 1990 of Queer Nation, a militant "in-your-face" organization that embraced anti-assimilationism with the slogan "We're here, we're Queer, get used to it," as well as the Lesbian Avengers, a radical direct action group that gave voice to "lesbian survival and visibility."

Given the leadership role of gay men in responding to the AIDS crisis, AIDS activism is traditionally discussed in the context of the gay rights struggle. However, the women's health movement also had a defining, if seldom acknowledged, impact on AIDS activism. Throughout the 1970s, feminists challenged the oppressive health care system by taking matters into their own hands. Women's centers, support groups, and clinics advocated for a feminist approach to women's health issues. The Boston Women's Health Collective revolutionized women's health in 1976 with the publication of *Our Bodies, Ourselves,* a groundbreaking book that not only provided basic medical information from a woman's point of view but also affirmed lesbianism and discussed taboo topics like rape, incest, and abortion. The reproductive rights movement similarly established a formidable activist model. Although women had for years campaigned for the right to legal abortion, national pro-choice groups were formed in the 1960s, with both the Planned Parenthood Federation of America and the National Association for the Repeal of Abortion Laws joining the cause in 1969. When the Supreme Court invalidated anti-abortion laws throughout the United States in 1973 with the *Roe v. Wade* decision, pro-choice activists began providing abortion and contraception services, advocating federal funding of family planning, and fighting the political backlash from right-wing legislators who sought to overturn the ruling.

Despite its success, the reproductive rights movement did not consider the impact of race and class on reproductive freedom. Black feminists challenged this failing by insisting that the feminist reproductive rights campaign address issues like welfare and sterilization abuse. Black feminists argued that a connection could be drawn between media images of black women as welfare queens and the "common sense" notion that black women could be—quite literally—"fixed." A new medical device called Norplant allowed for up to five years of birth control in one dose, providing lawmakers with the means to impose short-term sterility on black women who were perceived to be unfit mothers. Although women-of-color organizations, such as the National Black Women's Health Project, challenged the regulatory efforts involving Norplant, the idea of black population control had taken hold.

Concurrently, a broad black feminist effort was under way to make all liberation movements more responsive to the experiences and needs of black women, including black lesbians. Their arguments for inclusiveness were directed not only at black antiracism; they targeted feminism as well, pushing feminists to articulate a conception of women's equality that was more all-encompassing in terms of race, sexual orientation, and class. The purpose was to make feminism more responsive to all women—not only middle- and upper-class white heterosexuals. To this end, Alice Walker coined the term "womanism," introducing it in the preface to *In Search of Our Mothers' Gardens: Womanist Prose* (1983). Her aim was to racialize not only feminism but the very notion of womanhood itself:

> I don't choose womanism because it's "better" than feminism.... Since womanism means black feminism, this would be a non-sensical distinction. I choose it because I prefer the sound, the feel, the fit of it; because I cherish the spirit of the women (like Sojourner) the word calls to mind, and because I share the old ethnic habit of offering society a new word when the old word it is using fails to describe behavior and change that only a new word can help it more fully see.[12]

Walker later applied the womanist concept more broadly to include feminists of color, as well as women who love women, in both sexual and nonsexual senses. Indeed, her Pulitzer Prize–winning novel *The Color Purple* (1982) as well as *The Temple of My Familiar* (1989) and *Possessing the Secret of Joy* (1992) have become womanist classics for their politicized representations of female sexuality, and for the inclusion of bisexuality and lesbianism.

Conflicts about class, race, and sexual orientation had also become evident in the emerging women's publishing movement of the 1970s. Historically, mainstream publishing outlets had not, for the most part, been interested in—or perhaps even aware of—works by feminists, and more particularly lesbian feminists. In response to this, women began founding their own book publishing companies, including Diana Press (1972), Daughters Inc. (1972), Naiad Press (1973), New Victoria (1976), Persephone (1976), Seal Press (1976), and Spinster's Ink (1978). The nascent feminist publishing industry became the site for some of the debates that were taking place within feminism more broadly. Women of color, for example, argued that the work published by feminist presses oversimplified gender in ways that denied, discounted, or ignored important differences of race, class, and culture. They pointed to the fact that many of the women's presses had a mediocre record with respect to bringing out books by and about women of color.

Of course, exceptions were to be found. This newly emerging publishing world—which subsequently would include Cleis Press (1980), Kitchen Table: Women of Color Press (1981), Aunt Lute (1982), Sister Vision (1985), and Firebrand Books (1986)—brought out ground-breaking works by women of color, especially lesbians of color. Spinster's Ink, for example, published Audre Lorde's *Cancer Journals* (1980), her first major work of prose. Two years later The Feminist Press published *All the Women Are White, All the Blacks Are Men but Some of Us Are Brave* (1982), in which editors Akasha (Gloria) Hull, Patricia Bell Scott, and Barbara Smith asserted that antiracist efforts on behalf of African Americans focus on black men while feminist efforts on behalf of women focus on white women. Naiad Press published a number of influential works, including Ann Allen Shockley's short story collection *The Black and White of It* (1980), J. R. Roberts's indispensable *Black Lesbians: An Annotated Bibliography* (1981), and Anita Cornwell's *Black Lesbian in White America* (1983). Still, little work was being published by women's presses reflecting the concerns and experiences of lesbians of color. This helps to explain why a significant amount of black lesbian literature during this time appeared in such theme-specific publications as *Azalea, Dyke, GPN News, Black/out: The Magazine of the National Coalition of Black Lesbians and Gays, Outweek, Conditions, Gay Black Female, off our backs,* and *Ache: The Bay Area's Journal for Black Lesbians.*

In a similar situation, African American–owned presses published few works by and about black women. An established black book-publishing industry had been promoting the writings of African American men since the early 1970s. These presses were responsible for black classics such as Robert B. Hill's *The Strengths of Black Families*

(1972), Dr. Alvin Poussaint's *Why Blacks Kill Blacks* (1972), Chanceller Williams's *The Destruction of Black Civilization* (1974), and Haki R. Madhubati's *Enemies: The Clash of Races* (1978). Yet African American publishers seldom brought out books that spoke from a black feminist-perspective. Like their white feminist and mainstream counterparts, the black presses marginalized black feminism specifically and black women generally. This began to change in the late 1980s and 1990s.

The exclusion of black women's literature from within and without the African American and feminist publishing movements provided the impetus for the founding of Kitchen Table: Women of Color Press. Created in 1981 by Barbara Smith, Audre Lorde, Cherrie Moraga, and others, the press aimed to give voice to women of color. This publishing criterion, according to Smith, was explicitly and unapologetically ideological. Works were chosen not because the author was a woman of color, but more crucially because her book "consciously examines from a positive and original perspective the specific situations and issues that women of color face."[13] This led to Kitchen Table's *This Bridge Called My Back: Writings by Radical Women of Color* (1983), first published by Persephone Press in 1981, and *Home Girls: A Black Feminist Anthology* (1983). These books enlarged the terms on which liberation movements were being carried out, leading to Kitchen Table's "Grassroots Freedom Organizing Series," which went on to publish Lorde's *I Am Your Sister: Black Women Organizing Across Sexualities* (1985) and Angela Davis's *Violence Against Women and the Ongoing Challenge to Racism* (1987).

Nor did black women's challenges to feminism and antiracism overlook the academy. Beginning in the 1970s, black women scholars began to study black women's writing within the context of African American studies and women's studies. The work of Hortense Spillers, Trudier Harris, Patricia Bell Scott, Akasha (Gloria) Hull, Paula Giddings, Mary Helen Washington, Barbara Christian, bell hooks, Hazel V. Carby, Beverly Guy-Sheftall, Patricia Hill Collins, and Michelle Wallace, among many others, helped to introduce a generation of readers to black women writers, as well as to create a literary canon of contemporary fiction for the writers themselves. The work of Akasha (Gloria) Hull, for example, reclaimed and repositioned Angelina Weld Grimké and Alice Dunbar-Nelson as pioneers of black lesbian literature. This type of scholarship not only exposed students to literary materials outside the canon, it also encouraged them to pursue similar projects of literary excavation. Indeed, this black woman–centered writing helped establish research facilities like the Schomberg Library of Nineteenth Century Black Women Writers and journals such as *Sage: A Scholarly Journal on Black Women.*

A popular lesbian feminist political expression of the 1970s was that "feminism is the theory, lesbianism is the practice." By the 1980s, lesbian feminists began to ask a more fundamental question about lesbian identity: What is lesbianism? A special issue of *Signs,* a feminist journal of women, culture, and society, framed the issue this way: "Is there somehow a transcendent lesbian identity, or only particularized identity?" Adrienne Rich's "Compulsory Heterosexuality and Lesbian Existence" (1980) answered the question by arguing for a spectrum of woman-to-woman identification that provided feminists with a basis to claim a lesbian identity that was not necessarily related to their sexual practices and preferences. Meanwhile, academic studies such as Eve Sedgwick's *The Epistemology of the Closet* (1990) and Judith Butler's *Gender Trouble: Feminism and the Subversion of Identity* (1990) conceptualized sexual orientation (like gender) as a social construction. These books among others suggested that, to borrow from Simone de Beauvoir, one is born neither homosexual nor heterosexual but rather becomes one.

Black women authors like June Jordan took that concept of constructed identity one step further. In "On Bisexuality and Cultural Pluralism," a 1995 lecture published in *Affirmative Acts: Political Essays* (1998), she remarked, "I am a cultural pluralist. And, as sexuality is a biological, psychological, and interpersonal factor of cultural experience, I am a sexual pluralist. What else could I be?"[14]

Jordan's sexual pluralism belongs to a broader black queer sexual politics that was evidenced by the literature of the time. African American lesbian and bisexual fiction of the 1990s often avoided conventional representations of lesbian sexualities. Instead, the authors of these books frequently incorporated lesbian concerns into larger considerations of African American life. Novels such as Helen Elaine Lee's *The Serpent's Gift* (1994), April Sinclair's *Coffee Will Make You Black* (1994), Jacqueline Woodson's *Autobiography of a Family Photo* (1994), Sapphire's *Push* (1996), and Shay Youngblood's *Soul Kiss* (1997) do not always speak explicitly from a homosexual perspective. Rather, these works expand the traditional terrain of lesbian fiction by addressing issues such as adolescent sexuality and domestic abuse. As these and other unconventional themes began to appear more frequently in black lesbian and bisexual writing of the 1990s, authors no longer felt required to feature same-sex desire for their work to be read as a "lesbian novel."

This redefinition of black lesbian fiction was part of a broader redefinition of lesbian writing, as Blanche McCrary Boyd's *Revolution of Little Girls* (1991) and Dorothy Allison's *Bastard Out of Carolina* (1993) attest. Their literature reflected a trend in lesbian and gay communities, with women reclaiming bisexuality and other "nonlesbian" queer identities, such as transgenderism. "I found that the lesbian community castigates bisexual women for being different from them," Sapphire remarked, "which is fine because I no longer call myself a lesbian."[15] Indeed, recent black lesbian fiction has sometimes been charged with being insufficiently lesbian-focused. Not only has this criticism been directed at black lesbian writing, it belongs to a wider critique of lesbian literature that is increasingly becoming more mainstream. To others, however, the fluidity of queer identity in black lesbian writing signaled an unprecedented freedom for black lesbians, in both their creative and personal lives.

Editors Catherine E. McKinley and L. Joyce DeLaney captured this new trend toward sexual self-definition with the 1995 publication of *Afrekete: An Anthology of Black Lesbian Writing,* the first-ever collection of African American lesbian literature. As McKinley commented in the introduction:

> *Afrekete* joins the dialogue of other creative and political move-ments...which risk essentializing both what Black female and lesbian and gay identity should be. Black lesbian writing can-not easily cling to simple notions of racial, gender, and sexual identity and the politics that overreach them. We cannot afford this any more than we can single representations of Black lesbians or a handful of generally recognized texts that portray Black lesbian lives.[16]

Two years after *Afrekete* was published, Lisa C. Moore brought out her Lambda Award–winning *Does Your Mama Know?: An Anthology of Black Lesbian Coming Out Stories,* thus launching her RedBone Press.

While black lesbian and bisexual women might not have always directly depicted sex and sexuality in their writings, their works have always reflected a concern about sexual politics, including the erotic. Lorde's "The Uses of the Erotic: The Erotic as Power" (1978) viewed sex as a source of knowledge and self-definition. Jewelle Gomez praised sex for its relationship between pleasure, power, and politics. Kathleen E. Morris' *Speaking in Whispers: African American Lesbian Erotica* (1996) and Alycee Lane's *Black Lace,* a black lesbian erotica quarterly, explicitly challenged traditional representations of African American lesbian sexuality with erotic short fiction written by and for black lesbians. As Morris observed, "We found that adherence to strict roles and fear of rejection/ ridicule in confessing fantasies left us frustrated, angry, and repressed. The erotic literature [that black lesbians] read was generally vague and 'pretty,' the characters predominantly white, and the stories didn't really move us." According to Morris, black lesbian alienation from white lesbian erotica created a sense within the black lesbian community that "someone" should write "a book of erotica…that featured us as wimmin who loved being wimmin and loving wimmin…."[17]

If sex was an empowering source of self-awareness for lesbians, it was also a tremendous source of controversy. Throughout the 1980s, debates—or "sex wars"—around the regulation of pornography, butch/femme role-playing, and S/M divided the movement along ideological battle lines. Antiporn feminists organized in 1976 under Women Against Violence Against Women (WAVAW), a protest organization targeting images in the film and recording industries. In 1979, Women Against Pornography joined the movement, and by 1980 the political influence of antiporn feminists led NOW to denounce pornography and S/M as violence. In turn, "pro-sex" feminists founded the Feminist Anti-Censorship Task Force (FACT) in 1984 to combat these and other assaults on censorship and sexual freedom. The group sought to expand public discourse about sexuality, especially as it pertained to antiporn legislation. As FACT founding member Lisa Dugan wrote, "Rather than ask, 'Is pornography good or bad for women?' we would question whether any meaningful generalizations can be made about all 'women' and pornography, and ask how and why materials defined as 'pornography' are produced and used, and in what settings, and for what purposes."[18]

In spite of these attempts to contextualize pornography, S/M literature remained controversial among lesbian feminists. However, pioneering works such as Pat Califia's *Sapphistry: The Book of Lesbian*

Sexuality (1980) and *Coming to Power: Writings and Graphics on Lesbian S/M* (1981), edited by members of SAMOIS, a lesbian/feminist S/M organization, sought to clarify distinctions between the practice of sado-masochism and the misogynistic violence it was often mistaken for. These works challenged the cultural feminist idea that S/M and other aspects of a libertarian, lesbian sex culture reflected an internalization of patriarchal norms about sexuality, an idea that subsequently would be rearticulated in the form of "dominance theory" in Andrea Dworkin's *Pornography: Men Possessing Women* (1981) and Catherine MacKinon's *Feminism Unmodified: Discourses on Life and Law* (1987).

An explicit racial dimension to S/M literature was added by black authors Red Jordan Arobateau and Marci Blackman. Jordan, a female-to-male transsexual, is the prolific author of a lesbian biker series that includes *The Black Biker* (1994), which focuses on the club's African American members and a rival gang of white lesbians called The Aryan Avengers. His series combines, in the author's own words, "street fights, interracial struggles, S/M, raunch."[19] Blackman's *Po Man's Child* (1999) similarly depicts transgressive lesbian sex seldom found in African American women's fiction. Winner of the American Library Association's award for Lesbian Fiction, the novel opens with Po, the black lesbian protagonist, suffering a serious S/M related injury when a scene with her white lover goes awry. "It's an act, a game we play. Mary picks a spot on my body, any spot; tests how hard she can pinch or bite it, how deep she can cut it, or how long she can burn it."[20] Although writers like Jordan and Blackman are in the minority of black queer writers, the barrier-breaking nature of their fiction nevertheless affirms the reality of alternative lesbian sex.

Among gay male writers of the 1980s, the debates over sex practices were clouded by the devastation of the AIDS epidemic. Working with the ter-minology of the time, gay novelists first addressed AIDS obliquely as "gay cancer" in books like Robert Granit's *Another Runner in the Night* (1981) and Andrew Holleran's *Nights in Aruba* (1983). The first published AIDS-centered novel, however, was Paul Reed's *Facing It* (1984). Books like *The Darker Proof: Stories from a Crisis* (1987) by Edmund White and Adam Mars Jones, Robert Ferro's *Second Son* (1988), and David B. Feinberg's *Eighty-Sixed* (1989) followed. Additionally, some of the most successful early works were plays, beginning with Jeff Hagedorn's *One* (1983),

William A. Hoffman's *As Is* (1985), and Larry Kramer's *The Normal Heart* (1985). As with Tony Kushner's *Angels in America* (1993), these plays offer clear indications of how AIDS impacts the lives of people living with the disease, as well as the lives of those who care for them. Still, this burgeoning body of AIDS writing not only raised public awareness of the epidemic but also brought unprecedented visibility to gay male life. As Edmund White observed, "The paradox is that AIDS, which destroyed so many...has also, as a phenomenon, made homosexuality a much more familiar part of the American landscape."[21]

With the exception of Samuel R. Delany, who addresses AIDS in *Flight from Nevèryon* (1985), the "American landscape" had yet to come to terms with AIDS and homosexuality among gay men of color, particularly African Americans. Joseph Beam's groundbreaking *In the Life: A Black Gay Anthology* (1986) consequently launched the first post-Stonewall movement of openly gay work by black men. The book brought the writings of Melvin Dixon, Essex Hemphill, and Donald Woods to the attention of mainstream gay and lesbian readers for the first time. Among its selections is Craig G. Harris's short story "Cut Off from Among Their People," a piece that offers both an early representation of AIDS from a black gay perspective and a candid view on homophobia in the African American community. The publication of a companion volume, *Brother to Brother: Collected Writings by Black Gay Men* (1991), which Hemphill completed after Beam died of AIDS in 1988, furthered the movement with writing by David Frechette, Isaac Julien, Kobena Mercer, and Marlon Riggs, among others.

Brother to Brother joined a short list of lesser-known collections that had begun to highlight the newly emergent black gay literary movement. Other Countries, a collective of African American gay writers founded in 1986, published two anthologies, *Other Countries: Black Gay Voices* (1988) and the Lambda Award–winning *Sojourner: Black Gay Voices in the Age of AIDS* (1993). One of the contributors to these books was Assotto Saint, who also edited the award-winning anthology *The Road Before Us: 100 Gay Black Poets* (1991) and *Here to Dare: 10 Black Gay Poets* (1992), which includes G. Winston James, Marvin K. White, and others. White's own book of poetry, *Last Rights* (1999), brought the tradition of black gay AIDS-inspired poetry up to date. His poem "and your names," for example, is a role call of black gay artists who have died, such as Marlon Riggs, Essex Hemphill, Assotto Saint, and Wayne Corbitt: "i still call your names/because you have all left me/moved on and/moved me/to poetry."[22] Indeed, the work of these authors have been a visionary source of inspiration to young black gay men, much as James Baldwin's writing had been for a generation of authors coming of age during the Stonewall period.

Rounding out the collections of the period is Michael J. Smith's *Black Men/White Men: A Gay Anthology* (1983), which, as the title suggests, explores the interracial component of the black gay experience. Smith, the white founder of Black and White Men Together (BWMT), a social network of gay "interracialists," included poems, stories, essays, and interviews that purport to speak from "the Black and interracial gay experience," even though much of the book's content eroticizes black men from a white gay viewpoint. In spite of this shortcoming, however, Smith featured his historic profile of the first openly gay professional baseball player, Glenn Burke. The African American outfielder had came out publicly when an article, "The Double Life of a Gay Dodger," was published in *Inside Sports* magazine in 1982. "I'd finally gotten to the point where it was more important to be myself than a baseball player."[23] Burke's career began with the Los Angeles Dodgers in 1972, peaking in 1977 with his participation in the World Series. His future suddenly soured in 1978, when he was traded to the Oakland A's amid rumors that homosexuality and his close friendship with Dodger manager Tommy Lasorda's gay son had jeopardized his position on the team. Certainly this was Burke's impression: "Deep inside I know the Dodgers traded me because I was gay."[24] When he was dismissed from the A's in 1980, and with no new offers to play, Burke retired from baseball. Commenting on the decision to disclose his sexual orientation, he remarked, "If I can make friends honestly, it may be a step towards gays and straight people understanding each other. Maybe they'll say, 'He's all right, there's got to be a few more all right.'"[25]

Themes of black/white love also began to appear in black gay novels. Larry Duplechan's *Eight Days a Week* (1985) suggests that even to the extent that black men and white men desire each other, the very fact of that desire—that it is constituted in a black/white racial context—can overwhelm a relationship. Melvin Dixon's *Vanishing Rooms* (1991) illustrates how racial insensitivity, or at least a lack of racial understanding, can manifest itself even in the context of a loving relationship between a black man and a white man. The author presents this dilemma in the

following exchange between Jesse, a black gay dancer, and his white
lover, Metro, who asks:

> "But why do you always act like black people are the only ones
> oppressed? There are other oppressed people."
>   "Like who?"
>   "Gays, Jews. Even poor boys from the South. Don't you
> think we have some weight to bear? Don't you think we hurt
> sometimes?"
>   "You're white, Metro. At a distance you blend in with the
> crowd. Shit, they can see me coming, and in a riot they don't
> stop me to ask if I've been to college or live in the suburbs.
> They start beating any black head they find."[26]

Canaan Parker's *The Color of Trees* (1992) and Darieck Scott's *Traitor
to the Race* (1995) explore racial tensions and homophobia as well. While
Parker's book suggests that gay male relationships can be constituted by
a kind of race transcendence or, at least, need not be complicated by race,
Scott's novel raises a fundamental question about the politics of racial
desire: whether black men's sexual relations with white men constitute
self-loathing.

Not all the debates on race and sexuality depicted in black gay
fiction of this era, however, occur within the confines of an interracial
gay male couple, or even in the context of the gay community. Many
novels reflect a black-centered or "Afrocentric" consciousness that
transcends the "gay ghetto." In some instances, sexual identity is
depicted in predominantly, and sometimes exclusively, heterosexual
African American settings. Don Belton's *Almost Midnight* (1986), Randall
Kenan's *A Visitation of Spirits* (1989), and Bil Wright's *Sunday You Learn
How to Box* (2000) center gayness within the larger black population.
White homosexuality, and to some degree whiteness and homosexuality
across the board, is peripheral. More specifically, these gay works,
though not dogmatically "Afrocentric," call into question the notion
that homosexuality is something experienced only within the white
lesbian and gay community.

Black-centered fiction assumes a more self-consciously Afrocentric
vision in the novels of James Earl Hardy. While his *B-Boy Blues* (1994),
subtitled *A Seriously Sexy, Fiercely Funny, Black-on-Black Love Story*, embraces

gay Afrocentrism, the book also critiques misconceptions of its superiority. Mitchell, its central character, has the following to say about interracial dating:

> We...are often depicted in some passionate embrace with a white man, particularly in safer-sex ads. The message is insidious, insulting, and very clear; we don't fuck each other, we don't love each other, and, hence, we're better off fucking and loving a white man. No wonder so many of us believe Black men loving Black men is a revolutionary thing when it isn't.[27]

B-boys, or "banjee-boys," are given an added dimension in *The Brothers of New Essex: Afro-Erotic Adventures* (2000), an illustrated collection of black gay homoerotic stories by the African American graphic artist known as Belasco. The racial specificity of his work, which includes highly sexualized, all-black male settings, aims, in the artist's own words, "to fill a void of what I felt was a lack of strong, black male images in the realm of illustrated homoerotica." Unlike the homoerotica of white gay artists like Tom of Finland and Robert Mapplethorpe who fetishize black men, Belasco's nudes are rendered from a black gay perspective.

The transformative aspect of black-on-black gay love is also framed memorably in Marlon Riggs's *Tongues Untied* (1989). The documentary film's closing title even reads, "Black men loving Black men is *the* revolutionary act." Featuring performance, poetry, and autobiographical vignettes played against the backdrop of social prejudice, *Tongues Untied* affirms the diversity of black gay identity in celebratory, often sexually explicit terms: "I was blind to my brother's beauty, and now I see my own. Deaf to the voice that believed we were worth wanting, loving each other. Now I hear. I was mute, tongue-tied, burdened by shadows and silence. Now I speak and my burden is lightened. Lifted. Free." The candor of *Tongues Untied* inspired Brian Freeman, Djola Branner, and Eric Gupton to form Pomo Afro Homos (Postmodern African American Homosexuals), a performance art ensemble, which was the first gay group to be funded by the National Endowment for the Arts' Expansion Arts Program. Their performance piece *Fierce Love: Stories from Black Gay Life* (1991) explored the contradictions, humor, and naturalness of African American gay male life.

If *Tongues Untied* inspired black gay art, it also generated conservative backlash. The film's graphic content came under fire by right-wing
observers like Patrick Buchanan, who denounced the work as "porno-
graphic" when the film aired on Public Television in 1991. Cheryl
Dunye's *Watermelon Woman* (1996), which focuses on black lesbian identity, would be subject to similar debate about the funding practices of
the NEA. In the meantime, Riggs continued his unabashed exploration
of gay themes in film until his death from AIDS complications in 1994.
His final project, *Black Is, Black Ain't* (1995), is a broad examination of
contemporary African American culture that calls into question strict
notions of racial authenticity. As Riggs remarked, "My struggle as a
black, gay man with HIV is to constantly negotiate the attempts within
myself, as well as within the larger society, to deny some part of who I am.
For me to have to constantly say, 'No, I am who I am, and I am proud of
that. And that includes all of the above.'"[28]

The dramatic challenges faced by black gay and bisexual men struggling with self-acceptance lies at the core of the novels of E. Lynn Harris,
whose characters often lead double lives, concealing their sexuality from
others, if not from themselves. With top-selling titles like *Invisible Life*
(1991), *Just As I Am* (1994), *And This Too Shall Pass* (1996), and *Abide with
Me* (1999), Harris has become the most commercially successful African
American gay author since James Baldwin, opening opportunities for new
queer black writers to follow. His reputation among gays, however, has not
always been congratulatory. Lines such as "I sometimes prayed for a pill I
could take to destroy my homosexual feelings" complicate his relationship
with gay men and lesbians.[29] Still, it is surprising that the enormous popularity of his ground-breaking novels went unrecognized by the national
gay press until *The Advocate* printed an interview with the author in 1997.
Explaining the indifference of the white gay mainstream toward his work,
Harris suggested that perhaps it was "because I'm not interested in the
politics of 'being gay'.... To say the white gay community is racist is...well,
they just wouldn't get it. They live in their own world."[30]

By the end of the 1990s, an unprecedented breadth of writing from
African American gay men had established a literary tradition that main-
streamed the experiences of at least some black gays. This included
memoirs like Gordon Heath's *Deep Are the Roots: Memoirs of a Black
Expatriate* (1992), Bill T. Jones's *Last Night on Earth* (1995), Alvin Ailey's
Revelations (1995), and tell-all books by drag/transgendered entertainers

like RuPaul's *Lettin' It All Hang Out* (1995) and Lady Chablis's *Hiding My Candy* (1996). Cultural studies such as Keith Boykin's *One More River to Cross: Black and Gay in America* (1996) and Robert F. Reid-Pharr's *Black Gay Man: Essays* (2001) sought to bridge divides with an analysis of both homophobia in the black community and racism in the gay community. A number of biographies on long-marginalized black gay figures such as James V. Hatch's *Sorrow Is the Only Faithful One: The Life of Owen Dodson* (1995), David Hadju's *Lush Life: A Biography of Billy Strayhorn* (1996), Jervis Anderson's *Bayard Rustin: Troubles I've Seen* (1997), and David Adams Leeming's *Amazing Grace: A Life of Beauford Delaney* (1998) restored the truth of these men's sex lives to the historical record.

Finally, a new wave of anthologies that feature black gay and lesbian writing in the same volume has created a wider body of queer literary work. These books present the work of new young writers, and even include white authors, heterosexual black authors, or authors whose sexual identities do not conform to the labels "lesbian" and "gay." Among these anthologies are *Go the Way Your Blood Beats: An Anthology of Lesbian and Gay Fiction by African American Writers* (1996), *Shade: An Anthology of Fiction by Gay Men of African Descent* (1996), *Má-ka: Diasporic Juks: Contemporary Writing by Queers of African Descent* (1997), *Dangerous Liaisons: Blacks, Gays, and the Struggle for Equality* (1999), *Fighting Words: Personal Essays by Black Gay Men* (1999), and *The Greatest Taboo: Homosexuality in Black Communities* (2000). *Black Like Us* takes its place in this new inclusive literary tradition.

Cumulatively, this body of work satisfies Essex Hemphill's insistence that lesbian, gay, and bisexual men reclaim their voices and affirm their lives on their own terms. As Hemphill wrote: "I believe the task for the politically active, courageous black homosexual who has not chosen to be isolated is to begin to sensitize our families, friends, and communities to our concerns and to create images of ourselves in true proportions to who we are. The black community cannot afford to indulge in excluding black homosexuals or in condemning us. Nor can black homosexuals afford the exclusive, powerless indulgence of being a subculture, fearful and unwilling to defend our right to legitimate human rights and dignity."[31] Far from constituting a "powerless indulgence," the work of the past twenty years has established a literary tradition that will render it impossible for future generations to refer to black lesbian, gay, and bisexual experience as an "invisible life."

BECKY BIRTHA

■ ■ ■

[1948–]

BORN IN HAMPTON, VIRGINIA, TO A DIVERSE EXTENDED FAMILY
that included African American, Irish, Cherokee, and Catawaba people,
Becky Birtha was culturally aware at an early age. Her mother, a children's librarian, introduced her young daughter to African American
literature, while teachers encouraged her experiments as a writer. In
1968, she moved to Berkeley, where she participated in the student
uprisings in People's Park before returning to the East to continue her
education at SUNY Buffalo and Vermont College, where she completed
her MFA in Creative Writing in 1984.

After Birtha came out as a lesbian in 1976, her writing assumed new
emotional and political dimensions. She wrote about women's relationships, sexuality, passion, and self-acceptance in her short story
collections *For Nights Like This One: Stories of Loving Women* (1983) and
Lovers' Choice (1987), and in her book of poems, *The Forbidden Poems*
(1991). The author's work has been published in more than fifty journals and twenty anthologies, notably *Women on Women, Breaking Ice,* and
Does Your Mama Know?: An Anthology of Black Lesbian Coming Out Stories.
Awarded the Pennsylvania Council for the Arts Individual Fellowship in
Literature, a National Endowment for the Arts Creative Writing
Fellowship, and a Pushcart Prize in 1988, Birtha has established her
name as a respected African American lesbian figure.

"In the Life," the closing story in *Lovers' Choice,* perhaps the
author's most popular book, speaks to the lives of elderly black lesbians
in unabashedly sexual, if not supernatural, terms that seem almost to
transcend death.

In the Life

[1987]

G race come to me in my sleep last night. I feel somebody presence, in the room with me, then I catch the scent of Posner's Bergamot Pressing Oil, and that cocoa butter grease she use on her skin. I know she standing at the bedside, right over me, and then she call my name.

"Pearl."

My Christian name Pearl Irene Jenkins, but don't nobody ever call me that no more. I been Jinx to the world for longer than I care to specify. Since my mother passed away, Grace the only one ever use my given name.

"Pearl," she say again. "I'm just gone down to the garden awhile. I be back."

I'm so deep asleep I have to fight my way awake, and when I do be fully woke, Grace is gone. I ease my tired bones up and drag em down the stairs, cross the kitchen in the dark, and out the back screen door onto the porch. I guess I'm half expecting Gracie to be there waiting for me, but there ain't another soul stirring tonight. Not a sound but singing crickets, and nothing staring back at me but that old weather-beaten fence I ought to painted this summer, and still ain't made time for. I lower myself down into the porch swing, where Grace and I have sat so many still summer nights and watched the moon rising up over Old Mister Thompson's field.

I never had time to paint that fence back then, neither. But it did-n't matter none, cause Gracie had it all covered up with her flowers. She used to sit right here on this swing at night, when a little breeze be blow-ing, and say she could tell all the different flowers apart, just by they smell. The wind pick up a scent, and Gracie say, "Smell that jasmine, Pearl?" Then a breeze come up from another direction, and she turn her head like somebody calling her and say, "Now that's my honey-suckle, now."

It used to tickle me, cause she knowed I couldn't tell all them flow-ers of hers apart when I was looking square at em in broad daylight. So how I'm gonna do it by smell in the middle of the night? I just laugh and rock the swing a little, and watch her enjoying herself in the soft moonlight.

I could never get enough of watching her. I always did think that
Grace Simmons was the prettiest woman north of the Mason-Dixon line.
Now I've lived enough years to know it's true. There's been other
women in my life besides Grace, and I guess I loved them all, one way or
another, but she was something special—Gracie was something else
again.

She was a dark brownskin woman—the color of fresh gingerbread
hot out the oven. In fact, I used to call her that—my gingerbread girl.
She had plenty enough of that pretty brownskin flesh to fill your arms
up with something substantial when you hugging her, and to make a
nice background for them dimples in her cheeks and other places I
won't go into detail about.

Gracie could be one elegant good looker when she set her mind to
it. I'll never forget the picture she made, that time the New Year's Eve
party was down at the Star Harbor Ballroom. That was the first year we
was in The Club, and we was going to every event they had. Dressed to kill.
Grace had on that white silk dress that set off her complexion so perfect,
with her hair done up in all them little curls. A single strand of pearls
that could have fooled anybody. Long gloves. And a little fur stole. We was
serious about our partying back then! I didn't look too bad myself, with
that black velvet jacket I used to have, and the pleats in my slacks pressed
so sharp you could cut yourself on em. I weighed quite a bit less than I
do now, too. Right when you come in the door of the ballroom, they
have a great big floor to ceiling gold frame mirror, and if I remember
rightly, we didn't get past that for quite some time.

Everybody want to dance with Gracie that night. And that's fine
with me. Along about the middle of the evening, the band is playing a
real hot number, and here come Louie and Max over to me, all long-
face serious, wanting to know how I can let my woman be out there
shaking her behind with any stranger that wander in the door. Now they
know good and well ain't no strangers here. The Cinnamon & Spice
Club is a private club, and all events is by invitation only.

Of course, there's some thinks friends is more dangerous than
strangers. But I never could be the jealous, overprotective type. And the
fact is, I just love to watch the woman. I don't care if she out there shaking it with the Virgin Mary, long as she having a good time. And that's
just what I told Max and Lou. I could lean up against that bar and watch
her for hours.

You wouldn't know, to look at her, she done it all herself. Made all her own dresses and hats, and even took apart a old ratty fur coat that used to belong to my great aunt Melinda to make that cute little stole. She always did her own hair—every week or two. She used to do mine, too. Always be teasing me about let her make me some curls this time. I'd get right aggravated. Cause you can't have a proper argument with somebody when they standing over your head with a hot comb in they hand. You kinda at they mercy. I'm sitting fuming and cursing under them towels and stuff, with the sweat dripping all in my eyes in the steamy kitchen and she just laughing. "Girl," I'm telling her, "you know won't no curls fit under my uniform cap. Less you want me to stay home this week and you gonna go work my job and your job too."

Both of us had to work, always, and we still ain't had much. Everybody always think Jinx and Grace doing all right, but we was scrimping and saving all along. Making stuff over and making do. Half of what we had to eat grew right here in this garden. Still and all, I guess we was doing all right. We had each other.

Now I finally got the damn house paid off, and she ain't even here to appreciate it with me. And Gracie's poor bedraggled garden is just struggling along on its last legs—kinda like me. I ain't the kind to complain about my lot, but truth to tell, I can't be down crawling around on my hands and knees no more—this body I got put up such a fuss and holler. Can't enjoy the garden at night proper nowadays, nohow. Since Mister Thompson's land was took over by the city and they built them housing projects where the field used to be, you can't even see the moon from here, till it get up past the fourteenth floor. Don't no moonlight come in my yard no more. And I guess I might as well pick my old self up and go on back to bed.

Sometimes I still ain't used to the fact that Grace is passed on. Not even after these thirteen years without her. She the only woman I ever lived with—and I lived with her more than half my life. This house her house, too, and she oughta be here in it with me.

I rise up by six o'clock most every day, same as I done all them years I worked driving for the C.T.C. If the weather ain't too bad, I take me a walk—and if I ain't careful, I'm liable to end up down at the Twelfth Street Depot, waiting to see what trolley they gonna give me this morning. There ain't a soul working in that office still remember me. And they don't even run a trolley on the Broadway line no more. They been running a bus for the past five years.

I forgets a lot of things these days. Last week, I had just took in the clean laundry off the line, and I'm up in the spare room fixing to iron my shirts, when I hear somebody pass through that squeaky side gate and go on around to the back yard. I ain't paid it no mind at all, cause that's the way Gracie most often do when she come home. Go see about her garden fore she even come in the house. I always be teasing her she care more about them collards and string beans than she do about me. I hear her moving around out there while I'm sprinkling the last shirt and plugging in the iron—hear leaves rustling, and a crate scraping along the walk.

While I'm waiting for the iron to heat up, I take a look out the window, and come to see it ain't Gracie at all, but two a them sassy little scoundrels from over the projects—one of em standing on a apple crate and holding up the other one, who is picking my ripe peaches off my tree, just as brazen as you please. Don't even blink a eyelash when I holler out the window. I have to go running down all them stairs and out on the back porch, waving the cord I done jerked out the iron—when Doctor Matthews has told me a hundred times I ain't supposed to be running or getting excited about nothing, with my pressure like it is. And I ain't even supposed to be *walking* up and down no stairs.

When they seen the ironing cord in my hand, them two little sneaks had a reaction all right. The one on the bottom drop the other one right on his padded quarters and lit out for the gate, hollering, "Look out, Timmy! Here come Old Lady Jenkins!"

When I think about it now, it was right funny, but at the time I was so mad it musta took me a whole half hour to cool off. I sat there on that apple crate just boiling.

Eventually, I begun to see how it wasn't even them two kids I was so mad at. I was mad at time. For playing tricks on me the way it done. So I don't even remember that Grace Simmons has been dead now for the past thirteen years. And mad at time just for passing—so fast. If I had my life to live over, I wouldn't trade in none of them years for nothing. I'd just slow em down.

The church sisters around here is always trying to get me to be thinking about dying, myself. They must figure, when you my age, that's the only excitement you got left to look forward to. Gladys Hawkins stopped out front this morning, while I was mending a patch in the top screen of the front door. She was grinning from ear to ear like she just spent the night with Jesus himself.

"Morning, Sister Jenkins. Right pretty day the good Lord seen fit to send us, ain't it?"

I ain't never known how to answer nobody who manages to bring the good Lord into every conversation. If I nod and say yes, she'll think I finally got religion. But if I disagree, she'll think I'm crazy, cause it truly is one pretty August morning. Fortunately, it don't matter to her whether I agree or not, cause she gone right on talking according to her own agenda anyway.

"You know, this Sunday is Women's Day over at Blessed Endurance. Reverend Solomon Moody is gonna be visiting, speaking on 'A Woman's Place in the Church.' Why don't you come and join us for worship? You'd be most welcome."

I'm tempted to tell her exactly what come to my mind—that I ain't never heard of no woman name Solomon. However, I'm polite enough to hold my tongue, which is more than I can say for Gladys.

She ain't waiting for no answer from me, just going right on. "I don't spose you need me to point it out to you, Sister Jenkins, but you know you ain't as young as you used to be." As if both of our ages wasn't common knowledge to each other, seeing as we been knowing one another since we was girls. "You reaching that time of life when you might wanna be giving a little more attention to the spiritual side of things than you been doing…"

She referring, politely as she capable of, to the fact that I ain't been seen inside a church for thirty-five years.

"…And you know what the good Lord say. 'Watch therefore, for ye know neither the day nor the hour…' But, 'He that believeth on the Son hath everlasting life…'"

It ain't no use to argue with her kind. The Lord is on they side in every little disagreement, and he don't never give up. So when she finally wind down and ask me again will she see me in church this Sunday, I just say I'll think about it.

Funny thing, I been thinking about it all day. But not the kinda thoughts she want me to think, I'm sure. Last time I went to church was on a Easter Sunday. We decided to go on accounta Gracie's old meddling cousin, who was always nagging us about how we unnatural and

sinful and a disgrace to her family. Seem like she seen it as her one mission in life to get us two sinners inside a church. I guess she figure, once
she get us in there, God gonna take over the job. So Grace and me
finally conspires that the way to get her off our backs is to give her what
she think she want.

Course, I ain't had on a skirt since before the war, and I ain't aiming to change my lifelong habits just to please Cousin Hattie. But I did
take a lotta pains over my appearance that day. I'd had my best tailor-
made suit pressed fresh, and slept in my stocking cap the night before
so I'd have every hair in place. Even had one a Gracie's flowers stuck in
my buttonhole. And a brand new narrow-brim dove gray Stetson hat.
Gracie take one look at me when I'm ready and shake her head. "The good
sisters is gonna have a hard time concentrating on the preacher today!"

We arrive at her cousin's church nice and early, but of course it's a
big crowd inside already on accounta it being Easter Sunday. The organ
music is wailing away, and the congregation is dazzling—decked out in
nothing but the finest and doused with enough perfume to outsmell
even the flowers up on the altar.

But as soon as we get in the door, this kinda sedate commotion
break out—all them good Christian folks whispering and nudging each
other and trying to turn around and get a good look. Well, Grace and
me, we used to that. We just find us a nice seat in one of the empty pews
near the back. But this busy buzzing keep up, even after we seated and
more blended in with the crowd. And finally it come out that the point
of contention ain't even the bottom half of my suit, but my new dove
gray Stetson.

This old gentleman with a grizzled head, wearing glasses about a
inch thick, is turning around and leaning way over the back of the seat,
whispering to Grace in a voice plenty loud enough for me to hear, "You
better tell your beau to remove that hat, entering in Jesus' Holy Chapel."

Soon as I get my hat off, some old lady behind me is grumbling.
"I declare, some of these children haven't got no respect at all. Oughta
know you sposed to keep your head covered, setting in the house of
the Lord."

Seem like the congregation just can't make up its mind whether
I'm supposed to wear my hat or I ain't.

I couldn't hardly keep a straight face all through the service. Every
time I catch Gracie eye, or one or the other of us catch a sight of my hat,

we off again. I couldn't wait to get outa that place. But it was worth it. Gracie and me was entertaining the gang with that story for weeks to come. And we ain't had no more problems with Cousin Hattie.

Far as life everlasting is concerned, I imagine I'll cross that bridge when I reach it. I don't see no reason to rush into things. Sure, I know Old Man Death is gonna be coming after me one of these days, same as he come for my mother and dad, and Gracie and, just last year, my old buddy Louie. But I ain't about to start nothing that might make him feel welcome. It might be different for Gladys Hawkins and the rest of them church sisters, but I got a whole lot left to live for. Including a mind fulla good time memories. When you in the life, one thing your days don't never be, and that's dull. Your nights neither. All these years I been in the life, I loved it. And you know Jinx ain't about to go off with no Old *Man* without no struggle, nohow.

To tell the truth, though, sometime I do get a funny feeling bout Old Death. Sometime I feel like he here already—been here. Waiting on me and watching me and biding his time. Paying attention when I have to stop on the landing of the stairs to catch my breath. Paying attention if I don't wake up till half past seven some morning, and my back is hurting me so bad it take me another half hour to pull myself together and get out the bed.

The same night after I been talking to Gladys in the morning, it take me a long time to fall asleep. I'm lying up in bed waiting for the aching in my back and my joints to ease off some, and I can swear I hear somebody else in the house. Seem like I hear em downstairs, maybe opening and shutting the icebox door, or switching off a light. Just when I finally manage to doze off, I hear somebody footsteps right here in the bedroom with me. Somebody tippy-toeing real quiet, creaking the floor boards between the bed and the dresser...over to the closet...back to the dresser again.

I'm almost scared to open my eyes. But it's only Gracie—in her old raggedy bathrobe and a silk handkerchief wrapped up around all them little braids in her head—putting her finger up to her lips to try and shush me so I won't wake up.

I can't help chuckling. "Hey Gingerbread Girl. Where you think you going in your house coat and bandana and it ain't even light out yet. Come on get back in this bed."

"You go on to sleep," she say. "I'm just going out back a spell."

It ain't no use me trying to make my voice sound angry, cause she
so contrary when it come to that little piece of ground down there I
can't help laughing. "What you think you gonna complish down there
in the middle of the night? It ain't even no moon to watch tonight. The
sky been filling up with clouds all evening, and the weather forecast say
rain tomorrow."

"Just don't pay me no mind and go on back to sleep. It ain't the
middle of the night. It's almost daybreak." She grinning like she up to
something, and sure enough, she say, "This the best time to pick off
them black and yellow beetles been making mildew outa my cucumber
vines. So I'm just fixing to turn the tables around a little bit. You gonna
read in the papers tomorrow morning bout how the entire black and yellow beetle population of number Twenty-seven Bank Street been wiped
off the face of the earth—while you was up here sleeping."

Both of us is laughing like we partners in a crime, and then she off
down the hall, calling out, "I be back before you even know I'm gone."

But the full light of day is coming in the window, and she ain't
back yet.

I'm over to the window with a mind to holler down to Grace to get
her behind back in this house, when the sight of them housing projects
hits me right in the face: stacks of dirt-colored bricks and little caged-in
porches, heaped up into the sky blocking out what poor skimpy light
this cloudy morning brung.

It's a awful funny feeling start to come over me. I mean to get my
housecoat, and go down there anyway, just see what's what. But in the
closet I can see it ain't but my own clothes hanging on the pole. All the
shoes on the floor is mine. And I know I better go ahead and get washed,
cause it's a whole lot I want to get done fore it rain, and that storm is
coming in for sure. Better pick the rest of them ripe peaches and tomatoes. Maybe put in some peas for fall picking, if my knees'll allow me to
get that close to the ground.

The rain finally catch up around noon time and slow me down a
bit. I never could stand to be cooped up in no house in the rain. Always
make me itchy. That's one reason I used to like driving a trolley for the
C.T.C. Cause you get to be out every day, no matter what kinda weather
coming down—get to see people and watch the world go by. And it ain't
as if you exactly out in the weather, neither. You get to watch it all from
behind that big picture window.

Not that I woulda minded being out in it. I used to want to get me a job with the post office, delivering mail. Black folks could make good money with the post office, even way back then. But they wouldn't out you on no mail route. Always stick em off in a back room someplace, where nobody can't see em and get upset cause some little colored girl making as much money as the white boy working next to her. So I stuck with the C.T.C. all them years, and got my pension to prove it.

The rain still coming down steady along about three o'clock, when Max call me up say do I want to come over to her and Yvonne's for dinner. Say they fried more chicken that they can eat, and anyway Yvonne all involved in some new project she want to talk to me about. And I'm glad for the chance to get out the house. Max and Yvonne got the place all picked up for company. I can smell that fried chicken soon as I get in the door.

Yvonne don't never miss a opportunity to dress up a bit. She got the front of her hair braided up, with beads hanging all in her eyes, and a kinda loose robe-like thing, in colors look like the fruit salad at a Independence Day picnic. Max her same old self in her slacks and loafers. She ain't changed in all the years I known her—cept we both got more wrinkles and gray hairs. Yvonne a whole lot younger than us two, but she hanging in there. Her and Max been together going on three years now.

Right away, Yvonne start to explain about this project she doing with her women's club. When I first heard about this club she in, I was kinda interested. But I come to find out it ain't no social club, like the Cinnamon & Spice Club used to be. It's more like a organization. Yvonne call it a collective. They never has no outings or parties or picnics or nothing—just meetings. And projects.

The project they working on right now, they all got tape recorders. And they going around tape-recording people story. Talking to people who been in the life for years, and asking em what it was like, back in the old days. I been in the life since before Yvonne born. But the second she stick that microphone in my face, I can't think of a blessed thing to say.

"Come on, Jinx, you always telling us all them funny old time stories."

Them little wheels is rolling round and round, and all that smooth, shiny brown tape is slipping off one reel and sliding onto the other, and I can't think of not one thing I remember.

"Tell how the Cinnamon & Spice Club got started," she say.

"I already told you about that before."

"Well tell how it ended, then. You never told me that."

"Ain't nothing to tell. Skip and Peaches broke up." Yvonne waiting, and the reels is rolling, but for the life of me I can't think of another word to say about it. And Max is sitting there grinning, like I'm the only one over thirty in the room and she don't remember a thing.

Yvonne finally give up and turn the thing off, and we go on and stuff ourselves on the chicken they fried and the greens I brung over from the garden. By the time we start in on the sweet potato pie, I have finally got to remembering. Telling Yvonne about when Skip and Peaches had they last big falling out, and they was both determine they was gonna stay in The Club—and couldn't be in the same room with one another for fifteen minutes. Both of em keep waiting on the other one to drop out, and both of em keep showing up, every time the gang get together. And none of the rest of us couldn't be in the same room with the two a them for even as long as they could stand each other. We'd be sneaking around, trying to hold a meeting without them finding out. But Peaches was the president and Skip was the treasurer, so you might say our hands was tied. Wouldn't neither one of em resign. They was both convince The Club couldn't go on without em, and by the time they was finished carrying on, they had done made sure it wouldn't.

Max is chiming in correcting all the details, every other breath come outa my mouth. And then when we all get up to go sit in the parlor again, it come out that Yvonne has sneaked that tape recording machine in here under that African poncho she got on, and has got down every word I said.

When time come to say good night, I'm thankful, for once, that Yvonne insist on driving me home—though it ain't even a whole mile. The rain ain't let up all evening, and is coming down in bucketfuls while we in the car. I'm half soaked just running from the car to the front door.

Yvonne is drove off down the street, and I'm halfway through the front door, when it hit me all of a sudden that the door ain't been locked. Now my mind may be getting a little threadbare in spots, but it ain't wore out yet. I know it's easy for me to slip back into doing things the way I done em twenty or thirty years ago, but I could swear I distinctly remember locking this door and hooking the key ring back on my belt loop, just fore Yvonne drove up in front. And now here's the door been open all this time.

Not a sign a nobody been here. Everything in its place, just like I left it. The slipcovers on the couch is smooth and neat. The candy dishes and ash trays and photographs is sitting just where they belong, on the end tables. Not even so much as a throw rug been moved a inch. I can feel my heart start to thumping like a blowout tire.

Must be, whoever come in here ain't left yet.

The idea of somebody got a nerve like that make me more mad than scared, and I know I'm gonna find out who it is broke in my house, even if it don't turn out to be nobody but them little peach-thieving rascals from round the block. Which I wouldn't be surprised if it ain't. I'm scooting from room to room, snatching open closet doors and whipping back curtains—tiptoeing down the hall and then flicking on the lights real sudden.

When I been in every room, I go back through everywhere I been, real slow, looking in all the drawers, and under the old glass doorstop in the hall, and in the back of the recipe box in the kitchen—and other places where I keep things. But it ain't nothing missing. No money—nothing.

In the end, ain't nothing left for me to do but go to bed. But I'm still feeling real uneasy. I know somebody or something done got in here while I was gone. And ain't left yet. I lay wake in the bed a long time, cause I ain't too particular about falling asleep tonight. Anyway, all this rain just make my joints swell up worse, and the pains in my knees just don't let up.

The next thing I know Gracie waking me up. She lying next to me and kissing me all over my face. I wake up laughing, and she say, "I never could see no use in shaking somebody I rather be kissing." I can feel the laughing running all through her body and mine, holding her up against my chest in the dark—knowing there must be a reason why she woke me up in the middle of the night, and pretty sure I can guess what it is. She kissing under my chin now, and starting to undo my buttons.

It seem like so long since we done this. My whole body is all a shimmer with this sweet, sweet craving. My blood is racing, singing, and her fingers is sliding inside my nightshirt. "Take it easy," I say in her ear. Cause I want this to take us a long, long time.

Outside, the sky is still wide open—the storm is throbbing and beating down on the roof over our heads, and pressing its wet self up against the window. I catch ahold of her fingers and bring em to my lips. Then I roll us both over so I can see her face. She smiling up at me through the dark, and her eyes is wide and shiny. And I run my fingers down along her breast, underneath her own nightgown....

I wake up in the bed alone. It's still night. Like a flash I'm across the room, knowing I'm going after her, this time. The carpet treads is nubby and rough, flying past underneath my bare feet, and the kitchen linoleum cold and smooth. The back door standing wide open, and I push through the screen.

The storm is moved on. That fresh air feel good on my skin through the cotton nightshirt. Smell good, too, rising up outa the wet earth, and I can see the water sparkling on the leaves of the collards and kale, twinkling in the vines on the bean poles. The moon is riding high up over Thompson's field, spilling moonlight all over the yard, and setting all them blossoms on the fence, to shining pure white.

There ain't a leaf twitching and there ain't a sound. I ain't moving either. I'm just gonna stay right here on this back porch. And hold still. And listen close. Cause I know Gracie somewhere in this garden. And she waiting for me.

ALEXIS DEVEAUX

■ ■ ■

[1948–]

POET AND PLAYWRIGHT ALEXIS DEVEAUX WAS BORN IN HARLEM
and raised by her extended family, who assisted the author's mother and
eight siblings. She began a lifelong affiliation with community activism
in 1969, taking jobs with the New York Urban League, The Frederick
Douglass Community Arts Center, and the Bronx Office of Probations.
In 1977, DeVeaux created the Flamboyant Ladies Theater Company, a
Brooklyn-based black women's performance salon, and three years later
she formed the Gap Toothed Girlfriends Writing Workshop, which published two books of poetry and fiction. Receiving her undergraduate
degree from Empire State College in 1976, the author went on to earn
an MA degree in American Studies from SUNY Buffalo in 1989.

DeVeaux is the author of seven plays, perhaps most notably her two
works produced for national public television, *Circles* (1972) and *The
Tapestry* (1976). Her protest play *No* (1981), a woman-identified work
that has been compared favorably to *For Colored Girls Who Have Considered
Suicide/When the Rainbow Is Enuf,* brought unexpected notoriety when its
Harlem performance instigated a series of angry letters and reviews, one
written by a disgruntled male critic who went so far as to argue the
nonexistence of lesbianism in Africa. Among DeVeaux's most popular
nontheatrical works are a young adult novel, *An Enchanted Hair Tale*
(1987); a fictional biography of Billie Holiday, *Don't Explain: A Song of
Billie Holiday* (1980); and a poetry collection, *Blue Heat: Poems and
Drawings* (1985). The recipient of a Creative Artists in Public Service
grant from the New York State Council on the Arts and a National

Endowment for the Arts Fellowship in 1981, DeVeaux served as editor-at-large for *Essence* magazine throughout the 1980s.

In "Bird of Paradise" (1992), DeVeaux's use of lyrical, poetic language and laconic sentence fragments evoke a powerful emotional landscape as Camille, a young archaeology student, tells her mother for the first time about her girlfriend.

Bird of Paradise

Dig One:

Up here on the fourth floor is cold with a hint of spring to come Camille's first month back in Harlem. Snow falls a thin cantata against their windows in the light of night light. Under her pink pastel night-gown the mother Phelia stretches. Her hand fine as gold dust powder runs along her stomach over her navel. This umbilical cord of feelings the body never forgets the rip of tissue that was childbirth. After she said her piece Camille waited for Phelia to speak.

Where you meet her?

She's from Kingston.

She dig up stuff too?

No. She's a singer. You'll like her.

Don't tell me who to like.

She turns her back to the daughter. In the only bed their matchbox apartment ever had so they shared it all these years. Shared the habits of sleeping that were a comfort without question to each of them from the first day Phelia brought Camille home from the hospital. Phelia's still opened eyes blaze a blackness with the grip of quicksand. She did not have to like what she didn't understand. Like how the child spoke French fluently. The big words Camille used that made her feel stupid. The names of rocks and stones that fell easily from Camille's young lips. And this. Laying beside her. A woman. With a woman for a lover. Was she going to be happy? Have children of her own one day? Know when it was time to let them go?

When Camille awakes abruptly it is 5am. Her mother is not in bed.

Phelia?
Is not in the bathroom. Or the kitchen down the hall.
Phelia?

Is barely lit with the light of morning the small livingroom holds against
a somber blue wall. Phelia is a shadow on the edge of the sofa. She flicks
her cigarette in an ashtray atop the coffee table.

You coming back to bed?
All that education you got girl
you ain't learned to sleep by yourself yet?

Camille stands in the livingroom doorway. Everything in this room she
thinks everything the television sofa and matching armchair the shelves
of knick-knacks and Atlantic City mementos the white lamps and
mahogany endtables the pictures of herself and Phelia the one picture
of her father everything including the window and this arched doorway
has gotten doll house small the two years she's been away digging up evidence of escaped slaves and maroon societies deep in the hills of
Jamaica. Some bones don't want to be dug up Camille thinks but does
not say. Some animals eat their young.

Dig Two:

It was the first room she stopped in every day after school. She'd
sprawl on the bed. Stare at the chiseled face of her great grandmother
framed in the faded black and white Civil War photograph staring
back at her from the wall. It was Phelia's face in there. In the history
of those coal black cheeks. In her needle sharp gaze carved by the
meanness of slavery. In this alcove of a room in the afternoon quiet
when Phelia had the day shift at the bar the redskinned moon faced
girl entertained herself making up stories. About the dark glass bottles of Shalimar Perfume and lavender waters her mother kept atop
the maple vanity chest. And the love letters from Camille's father
Phelia kept in the bottom drawer. Stories about who he was half
Cherokee. How Phelia said he was built like a boxer. Walked low to
the ground. Like that night at the bar when Phelia met him. He said

he was from N'Awlins and preferred the name Talking Brook to Curtis. And then one day he said baby I got to go.

Dig Three:

How come you don't have no lover Phelia?
Had your father.
What about now?
All I want now is for you to finish college. Become a famous archaeologist like you want to.
That's all you want?
Whatchu want Camille?
To know how you feel.
I feel tired when I get off work.

Dig Four:

When Phelia came home from work she went straight to the bathroom. To wash off the smell of bar stories and tips. In the steam of the shower she'd rinse clean of the night's back and forth on her feet. Juggling glasses and broken conversations. From one side of the bar to the other. Pouring drinks. Mixing one part liquor to three parts I'm a damn good barmaid proud of what I do. Which kept them fed and clothed. With a roof over their heads. Whenever Camille needed extra money for books Phelia laid on the table what the girl's scholarship did not cover. The longed for getting it done done now.

Dig Five:

At the kitchen window the evening quarter moon watches Camille watch Phelia scrape what is left of her dinner into the garbage can. Watches as the daughter turns the mother turns in the orbit of motherhood.

Bring your friend by the bar Phelia says time for me to meet her.

Who knows when the front door closes behind Phelia gone to work what the moon sees in the afterbirth of mother–daughter love. What stars feel in the quiver of its throat. What a shard of moon sees on the breast of night.

Dig Six:

When Phelia opened the door she saw it right away. On the kitchen table. Was a note from Camille. And the one bird of paradise its royal plumage orange and electric purple in a glass vase next to the note was a flower she had never seen before. Phelia sat down at the table staring at it. Secretly tickled. It was just like Camille. Something new to see whether she understood it or not. She'd done a good job raising the girl alone. There was nothing to regret. In her heart she knew that. And let go.

JEWELLE GOMEZ

■ ■ ■

[1948–]

BOSTON-BORN WRITER JEWELLE GOMEZ WAS RAISED BY HER working-class extended family, including a great-grandmother who instilled in the young author a strong appreciation of history and social activism. Coming of age during the civil rights era, she developed a political awareness that led her to the antiwar and black liberation movements of the 1960s and the lesbian feminist movement of the 1970s. A Columbia University School of Journalism graduate, she was among the original board members of the Gay and Lesbian Alliance against Defamation (GLAAD), a gay media watchdog organization founded in 1985, as well as a member of the Feminist Anti-Censorship Task Force, a sex-positive group that countered the women's movement to ban pornography.

Gomez is the author of two poetry collections, *The Lipstick Papers* (1980) and *Flamingoes and Bears* (1987); a book of essays, *Forty-three Septembers* (1993); and a short fiction collection, *Don't Explain* (1998). Her best-known work, however, is the award-winning vampire novel *The Gilda Stories* (1991).

Told from the perspective of a black lesbian feminist, *The Gilda Stories* subverts the literary tradition of white male protagonists who dominate science fiction/horror stories. As with all of Gomez's writing, issues of racial, sexual, and gender identity politics are integrated into a uniform analysis of societal oppression. Spanning two centuries, the novel opens in 1850 with a runaway slave known only as The Girl taking sanctuary in the home of Gilda, whose secret identity as a lesbian vampire is known only by her lesbian-vampire-lover and helpmate, Bird.

from **The Gilda Stories**

[1991]

In her lifetime, Gilda had killed reluctantly and infrequently. When she took the blood there was no need to take life. But she knew that there were those like her who gained power as much from the terror of their prey as from the life substance itself. She had learned many lessons in her time. The most important had been from Sorel and were summed up in a very few words: the source of power will tell in how long-lived that power is. He had pointed her and all of his children toward an enduring power that did not feed on death. Gilda was sustained by sharing the blood and by maintaining the vital connections to life. Her love for her family of friends had fed her for three hundred years. When Bird chose to join her in this life, Gilda was filled with both joy and dread. The weight of the years she had known subsided temporarily; at last there would be someone beside her to experience the passage of time. Bird's first years at Woodard's were remote now—Bird moving silently through their lives, subtly taking control of management, finding her place closer and closer to Gilda without having to speak of it.

Before she had even considered bringing Bird into her life she had wanted to feel her sleeping beside her. She had not been willing to risk their friendship, though, until she was certain. And Bird had opened to her, deliberately, to let her know her desires were the same as Gilda's. When they first lay together, Gilda sensed that Bird already knew what world it was Gilda would ask her to enter. She had teased Gilda later with sly smiles, about time and rushing through life, until Gilda had finally been certain Bird was asking to join her.

Despite the years of joy they had known together, tonight, walking along the dark road, Gilda felt she had lived much too long. Only now was it clear to her why. The talk of war, the anger and brutality that was revealed daily in the townspeople, was a bitter taste in her mouth. She had seen enough war and hatred in her lifetime. And although her abolitionist sentiments had never been hidden, she didn't know if she had the heart to withstand the rending effects of another war.

And as always, when Gilda reflected on these things she came back to Bird: Bird, who had chosen to be a part of this life, a choice she seemed to have made effortlessly. Gilda had never said the word *vampire*.

She had only asked if Bird would join her as partner in the business and in life. In the years since she'd come to the house she always knew as much as was needed and challenged Gilda any time she tried to hide information from her. Bird listened inside of Gilda's words, hearing the years of isolation and discovery. There was in Gilda an unfathomable hunger—a dark, dry chasm that Bird thought she could help fill.

But now it was the touch of the sun and the ocean Gilda hungered for, and little else. She ached to rest, free from the intemperate demands of time. Often she'd tried to explain this burden to Bird, the need to let go. And Bird saw it only as an escape from *her*—rather than a final embrace of freedom.

Thoughts jostled inside her as she moved—so quickly she was invisible—through the night. She slowed a few miles west of the Louisiana state line, then turned back toward her township. When she came to a road leading to a familiar horse ranch within miles of her farmhouse, she slackened her pace and walked to the rear of the woodframe building.

All of the windows were black as she slipped around to the small bunkhouse at the back where hands slept. She stood in the shadows listening. Once inside she approached the nearest man, the larger of the two she could see in the darkness. She began to probe his dreams, then sensed an uncleanness in his blood and recoiled. His sleeping face did not bear the mark of the disease that coursed through his body, but it was there. She was certain. Gilda was saddened as she moved to the smaller man who slept at the other end of the room.

He had fallen asleep in his clothes on top of the blankets and smelled of whiskey and horses. She slipped inside his thoughts as he dreamed of a chestnut-colored bay. Under his excitement lay anxiety, his fear of the challenge of this horse. Gilda held him in sleep while she sliced through the flesh of his neck, the line of her nail leaving a red trail. She extended his dream, making him king of the riders as she took her share of the blood. He smiled with triumph at his horsemanship, the warmth of the whiskey in him thundering through her. She caught her breath, and the other ranch hand tossed restlessly in his sleep. Although she no longer feared death she backed away, her instincts readying her hands to quiet the restless worker if he awoke. Her touch on the other sleeper sealed his wound cleanly. Soon his pulse was steady and he continued to explore the dreams she had left with him. As their breathing settled into a calm rhythm, Gilda ran from the bunkhouse, flushed with the fullness of blood and whiskey.

The road back felt particularly dark to Gilda as she moved eastward. The clouds left little moonlight visible, but she was swift. Blood pounded in her head, and she imagined that was what she would feel once she finally lay down in the sea and gave up her life. Her heart beat with excitement, full of the need to match its rhythm with that of an ocean. There, Gilda would find her tears again and be free of the sounds of battles and the burden of days and nights piled upon each other endlessly. The dust from the road flew up around her as she made her way toward home. She remembered the dusty trek that was the one clear image of her childhood. They had been going toward water, perhaps the sea. The future had lain near that sea, somehow. It was survival for her mother, father, and the others who had moved relentlessly toward it. Now it was that again for Gilda—now and more. The sea would be the place to rest her spirit.

Once back in her room she changed her dusty jacket and breeches and sat quietly alone in the dark. As dawn appeared on the horizon behind the house, Gilda let down her dark hair and was peaceful in her earthen bed. She was relieved to finally see the end of the road.

In the soft light of a fall afternoon the Girl worked in the garden as she had done for so many years. By now she knew the small plot well, picking the legumes and uprooting the weeds without much thought, enjoying the sun and air. When she looked up at the house Bird waved to her, then pulled the curtain tight across the window of Gilda's room. The Girl's reverie was lazy and undirected. She started at Minta's shadow when it crept over her.

They both sat quietly for some time before the Girl asked Minta, "How long you been here at Woodard's?"

"I was younger than you was when you come," she answered proudly, "but I think I'm gonna move on soon, though. Been savin' my money and thinkin' about goin' west where Rachel is. Look around for a while."

"How long Bird...has Bird been here?" the Girl asked, picking her way through the rules of grammar.

"I don't know. Long as any of us can remember. She left once, that's what I heard Bernice say, but she come back quick. Them Indian folks she come from didn't want her back."

Both girls were quiet for a moment, each feeling younger than either had since going out into the world on her own. Minta spoke with hard resolve as if to cover her vulnerability. "When I leave, I'm gone. Gonna make me a fortune in California, get away from this war talk."

"You think Rachel let you stay with her?"

"Well, she sent me a letter with her address and everything. She went to that man Miss Gilda said would give her a hand if she need it. And he put her up in a place 'til she got her own and said he'd help her find a little shop." Minta could feel the Girl's unspoken doubt. She pushed ahead with assurance as much for herself as for the Girl. "She right there on the water and got lotsa business. And she say there not enough women for anybody." A smirk opened her mouth then, but she tried to continue in a businesslike way. "She want to move if she save the money. Get in a quiet district with the swells." Simply talking about Rachel and her new life seemed to make Minta breathless. "She said the women and men there wear the prettiest clothes she ever seen. She want to get a place nearer to the rich people and leave them sailors behind."

The Girl looked aghast, trying to picture Rachel alone in a western city, owning a shop, mixing with rich people who weren't trying to get in her bed. But the image was too distant to get it into focus.

"Say, you think you want to come too? I bet we could get us a little business goin' out there the way you can sew and all."

Leave Gilda and Bird? The thought was a shock to the Girl who had never considered such a possibility; it seemed ludicrous as she knelt under the warm sun feeling the softness of the earth's comfort beneath her. And even with the war coming and talk of emancipation and hardship, the Girl had little in mind she would run away to. "Naw, this is my home now, I guess."

"Well, you just be careful."

"What do you mean?"

"Watch yourself, is all." Minta said it softly and would speak no more. The Girl was puzzled and made anxious by the edge in Minta's voice as well as the silence that followed. Her look of frustration tugged at Minta. "There's lots of folks down this way believe in ha'nts and such like. Spirits. Creoles, like Miss Gilda, and Indians, they follow all that stuff." Minta spoke low, bending at the waist as if to make the words come out softer. "I like her fine, even though some folks don't. Just watch, is all." She skittered through the garden to the kitchen door.

The Girl finished her weeding, then went to the kitchen steps to rinse her hands at the pump and dust her clothes. Bernice watched from the back porch.

"What you say to Minta, she run upstairs?"

"I ain't certain. She's so nervous I can't get hold to what she sayin' half a while. I know she wants me to go out there with her to stay with Rachel."

"What else?"

"She afraid of something here. Sometimes I think maybe it's Miss Gilda. What you think?"

Bernice's face closed as if a door had been locked. "You ain't goin', is you?"

"I'm here for the war no matter what, if there's gonna be one."

"Listen gal, you been lucky so far. You got a life, so don't toss it in the air just to stay 'round here." Behind Bernice's voice the Girl could sense her conflict, her words both pushing the Girl away and needing her to stay.

"My life's here with you and Miss Gilda and Bird. What would I do in California—wear a hat and play lady?" she said, laughing loudly, nervously. She saw the same wary look on Bernice's face that had filtered through Minta's voice.

"What is it? Why you questioning me with that look?" the Girl asked with a tinge of anger in her voice.

"Nothin'. They just different. Not like regular people. Maybe that's good. Who gonna know 'til they know?"

"You sayin' they bad or somethin'?" The challenge wavered in the Girl's throat as her own questions about Gilda and Bird slipped into her mind.

"No." The solid response reminded the Girl of how long Bernice had been at Woodard's. "I'm just saying I don't know who they are. After all the time I been here I still don't know who Miss Gilda is. Inside I don't really know what she thinkin' like you do with most white folks. I don't know who her people is. White folks is dyin' to tell each other that. Not her. Now Bird, I got more an idea what she's up to. She watch over Miss Gilda like...like..." Bernice's voice trailed off as she struggled for words that spoke to this child who was now almost a woman.

"That ain't hurt you none, now has it?" The Girl's response was hard with loyalty to the women who'd drawn her into their family.

"Not me. I'm just waitin' for the river to rise." Bernice didn't really worry about who Gilda and Bird were. Her concern was what would become of this Girl on her own.

On a day soon after Gilda took the Girl and Bird with her to the farmhouse, Minta stood by the empty horse stall nearest the road. Her face was placid, yet she was again bent at the waist as if still whispering. The Girl caught a glimpse of her when the buggy rounded the bend in the road, and she leaned over looking back. She was excited about this journey away from the house, but Minta's warnings itched her like the crinoline one of the girls had given her last Christmas.

The evening sky was rolling with clouds as they drove the buggy south to the farm, yet the Girl could feel Gilda's confidence that there would be no storm. They talked of many things but not the weather. Still, from simply looking into Gilda's eyes and touching Bird's hand she knew there was a storm somewhere. She felt a struggle brewing and longed to speak out, to warn them of how much everyone in town would need them when the war came. She knew that would not be the thing to say—Gilda liked to circle her point until she came to a place she thought would be right for speaking. It didn't come on the road to the farmhouse.

When the three arrived at the farmhouse, the Girl stored her small traveling box under the eaves in the tiny room she slept in whenever they visited here. She wondered if Minta knew Gilda spoke without speaking. That might be the reason she had cautioned her. But the Girl had no fear. Gilda, more often aloof than familiar, touched the Girl somehow. Words were only one of many ways of stepping inside of someone. The Girl smiled, recollecting her childish notion that Gilda was a man. Perhaps, she thought, living among the whites had given her a secret passage, but knowledge of Gilda came from a deeper place. It was a place kept hidden except from Bird.

The fields to the north and west of the farmhouse lay fallow, trimmed but unworked. It was land much like the rest in the Delta sphere, warm and moist, almost blue in its richness—blood soil, some said. The not-tall house over the shallow root cellar seemed odd with its distinct aura of life set in the emptiness of the field. Gilda stood at the window looking out to the evening dark as Bird moved around her placing clothes in chests. Gilda tried to pull the strands together, to make a pattern of her life that was recognizable, therefore reinforceable. The farmhouse offered her peace but no answers. It was simply privacy away from the dissembling of the city and relief from the tides, which each noon and night pulled her energy, sucking her breath and leaving her lighter than air. The quietness of the house and its eagerness to hold her safe were like a firm hand on her shoulder. Here Gilda could relax enough to think. She had hardly come through the door before she let go of the world of Woodard's. Still her thoughts always turned back toward the open sea and the burning sun.

The final tie was Bird. Bird, the gentle, stern one who rarely flinched yet held on to her as if she were drowning in life. Too few of their own kind had passed through Woodard's, and none had stayed very long. On their one trip west to visit Sorel, neither could tolerate the dust and noise of his town for more than several weeks. And until the Girl's arrival, Gilda had met no one she sensed was the right one. To leave Bird alone in this world without others like herself would be more cruel than Gilda could ever be. The Girl must stay. She pushed back all doubts: Was the Girl too young? Would she grow to hate the life she'd be given? Would she abandon Bird? The answer was there in the child's eyes. The decision loosened the tight muscles of Gilda's back as if the deed were already done.

The Girl did not know why they had included her in the trip to the farmhouse this time. They rarely brought her along at midseason. The thought that they might want her to leave them made her more anxious than Minta's soft voice. Yet each day Bird and she sat down for their lessons, and in the evening, when Gilda and Bird talked quietly together, they sought her out to join them. She would curl up in the corner, not speaking, only listening to the words that poured from them as they talked of the women back at the house, the politics in town, the war, and told adventurous stories. The Girl thought, at first, that they were made up, but she soon heard in the passion of their voices the truth of the stories Gilda and Bird had lived.

Sometimes one of them would say, "Listen here, this is something you should know." But there was no need for that. The Girl, now tall and lean with adulthood, clung to their words. She enjoyed the contrasting rhythms of their voices and the worlds of mystery they revealed.

She sensed an urgency in Gilda—the stories had to be told, let free from her. And Bird, who also felt the urgency, did not become preoccupied with it but was happy that she and Gilda were spending time together again as it had been before. She unfolded her own history like soft deerskin. Bird gazed at the Girl, wrapped in a cotton shirt, her legs tucked under her on the floor, and felt that her presence gave them an unspoken completeness.

She spoke before she thought. "This is like many times before the fire in my village."

"Ah, and who's to play the part of your toothless elders, me or the Girl?" Gilda asked, smiling widely.

The Girl laughed softly as Bird replied, "Both."

Gilda rose from the dark velvet couch. Her face disappeared out of the low lamplight into the shadow. She stooped, lifted the Girl in her arms, and lay her on the couch. She sat down again and rested the Girl's head in her lap. She stroked the Girl's thick braids as Bird and she continued talking.

In the next silence she asked the Girl, "What do you remember of your mother and sisters?" The Girl did not think of them except at night, just before sleeping, their memory her nightly prayers. She'd never spoken of them to Gilda, only to Bird when they exchanged stories during their reading lessons. Now the litany of names served as memory: Minerva, small, full of energy and questions; Florine, two years older than the Girl, unable to ever meet anyone's eyes; and Martha, the oldest, broad-shouldered like their mother but more solemn. She described the feel of the pallet where she slept with her mother, rising early for breakfast duties—stirring porridge and setting out the rolls. She described the smell of bread, shiny with butter, and the snow-white raw cotton tinged with blood from her fingers.

Of the home their mother spoke about, the Girl was less certain. It was always a dream place—distant, unreal. Except the talk of dancing. The Girl could close her eyes and almost hear the rhythmic shuffling of feet, the bells and gourds. All kept beat inside her body, and the feel of heat from an open fire made the dream place real. Talking of it now, her body rocked slightly as if she had been rewoven into that old circle of dancers. She poured out the images and names, proud of her own ability to weave a story. Bird smiled at her pupil who claimed her past, reassuring her silently.

Each of the days at the farmhouse was much like the others. The Girl rose a bit later than when they were in the city, for there was little work to be done here. She dusted or read, walked in the field watching birds and rabbits. In the late afternoon she would hear Bird and Gilda stirring. They came out to speak to her from the shadows of the porch, but then they returned to their room, where the Girl heard the steady sound of their voices or the quiet scratching of pen on paper.

The special quality of their life did not escape the Girl; it seemed more pronounced at the farmhouse, away from the activity of Woodard's. She had found the large feed bags filled with dirt in the root cellar where she hid so long ago. She had felt the thin depth of soil beneath the carpets and weighted in their cloaks. Although they kept the dinner hour as a gathering time, they had never eaten in front of her. The Girl cooked her own meals, often eating alone, except when Bird prepared a corn pudding or a rabbit she had killed. Then they sat together as the Girl ate and Bird sipped tea. She had seen Gilda and Bird go out late in the night, both wearing breeches and woolen shirts. Sometimes they went together, other times separately. And both spoke to her without voices.

The warning from Minta and the whispers of the secret religion, vodun, still did not frighten her. She had known deep fear and knew she could protect herself when she must. But there was no cause for fear of these two who slept so soundly in each other's arms and treated her with such tenderness.

On the afternoon of the eighth day at the farmhouse the Girl returned from a walk through the fields to get a drink of water from the back pump. She was surprised to hear, through the kitchen window, Gilda's voice drawn tight in argument with Bird. There was silence from the rest of the room, then a burst of laughter from Gilda.

"Do you see that we're fighting only because we love each other? I insist we stop right this minute. I won't have it on such a glorious evening."

The Girl could hear her moving around the small wooden table, pulling back a chair. Gilda did not sit in the chair, instead lowering herself onto Bird's lap. Bird's expression of surprise turned into a laugh, but the tension beneath it was not totally dispelled.

"I'm sick of this talk. You go on about this leaving as if there is somewhere in the world you could go without me."

Her next words were cut short by Gilda's hand on her mouth. And then Gilda's soft, thin lips pressed her back in the chair.

"Please, my love, let's go to our room so I can feel the weight of your body on mine. Let's compare the tones of our skin as we did when we were young."

Bird laughed just as she was expected to do. The little joking references to time and age were their private game. Even knowing there was more to the kisses and games right now, she longed to feel Gilda's skin pressed tightly to her own. She stood up, still clasping Gilda to her breasts, and walked up the stairs with her as if she were a child.

The Girl remained on the porch looking out into the field as the sun dropped quickly behind the trees. She loved the sound of Gilda and Bird laughing, but it seemed they did so only when they thought no others were listening. When it was fully dark she went into the kitchen to make supper for herself. She put on the kettle for tea, certain that Bird and Gilda would want some when they came down. She rooted through the day jars until she had pulled together a collection of sweet-smelling herbs she thought worthy. She was eager to hear their laughter again.

MELVIN DIXON

■ ■ ■

[1950–1992]

THE AFRICAN AMERICAN VERNACULAR TRADITION OF THE migrant black community in which Melvin Dixon was raised in Stamford, Connecticut, largely shaped the style and subject matter of much of his writing. He grew up listening to folkloric stories brought from the South by people like his parents, who hailed from the Carolinas. By the age of seventeen, Dixon published his first poem, and his first plays were produced at Wesleyan University before his graduation in 1971. He wanted to be a novelist, however, and it was during his graduate years at Brown University that he wrote his first novel. This unpublished work foreshadows themes that appear later in his debut novel, *Trouble the Water* (1989), an award-winning southern gothic story about a black Harvard professor's return to his past.

Dixon's second novel, the critically praised *Vanishing Rooms* (1991), also examines themes of African Americans attempting to reconcile history, with the notable exception that the book's plot centers on an interracial gay male couple in New York City. Arguably the author's most important work, *Vanishing Rooms* boldly pushes boundaries with forthright considerations of gay racism and explicit homophobic violence. Dixon was also a well-respected scholar, publishing a critical study, *Ride Out the Wilderness: Geography and Identity in Afro-American Literature* (1987), and in 1991 a translation of Léopold Sédar Senghor's collected poetry. Dixon contributed to a number of groundbreaking black gay anthologies, notably Essex Hemphill's *Brother to Brother: Collected Writings by Black Gay Men* and *Sojourner: Black Gay Voices in the Age of AIDS*. The author was teaching at City University of New York at the time of his death from AIDS in 1992.

Fundamental to the plot of *Vanishing Rooms* is the story of Lonny, a young gay-basher who has killed Metro, the white lover of Jesse, the novel's African American protagonist. Although much of the book concerns Jesse's attempt to surmount his grief around Metro's murder, this confessional excerpt is revealing for the ways in which Dixon objectively allows the white attacker to share his troubling perspective of the killing.

from **Vanishing Rooms**

[1991]

L ike I keep telling you. October is a bitch, a mean, red bitch. And you still don't believe me. Shit, you got the red leaves, you got early nightfall and twisted chilly mornings freezing you back into bed. You got people in scarves and caps tilted to the side like Hollywood detectives. You got October. What more do you want? You want red leaves clogging the sewers? You want legs and arms splayed out like tree limbs after a storm? You really don't believe in fall, huh, or how people can change too, just as fast? You want all this? Then you're no better than that faggot who wanted me.

He said his name was Metro. Just like that, he said it, out of the blue. So I said, "Yeah." Nothing more. The way he looked at me I could tell he was thinking he'd seen me around and knew I'd seen him around, too, and after saying hello just once he could come up to me a week later and tell me his funny name.

I was on my way to meet Cuddles who had the smoke this time. I had my mind on herb and didn't really see him until he was close enough to speak. "Metro," he said. I thought he was asking for directions. But he stuck out his hand, 'cause it wasn't a place he was telling me, it was his name. I felt a load on me from the moment he spoke. All I said was "yeah." He didn't take the hint. He waited for more. Maybe he was thinking the cat got my tongue and he wanted it. I looked closer. He was about my height and build. Had wavy hair, not stringy like mine. He looked like any guy, except he spoke in a drawl straight out of *Gone with the Wind,* then changed back to a normal voice, like my voice changes sometimes, but not that bad. He said again his name was Metro. What could I do? He waited for me to tell him my name, but I never did. I finally said, "You know what you are?"

"Metro."

"Shit, man, you better get out of my face." And I left him standing there, looking like he just lost some money or came home to find his apartment broken into and his stereo and favorite record gone. With the wind. How do I know he even had a stereo? I don't know. He never invited me in to smoke dope or listen to records. Which is the only reason anyone would go with him. With a name like Metro, what would you expect?

I didn't expect nothing at all. The third time I seen him walking into the corner building, I knew he lived there. I wasn't meeting Cuddles that time. I didn't know why I was even in the neighborhood. You get used to meeting friends in the late afternoon and it gets to be routine. Metro was dressed in a suit, no jeans, no flannel plaid, no white undershirt poking from inside the open collar. He looked like one of those Wall Street businessmen, he looked so square, so regular. He might have been somebody's husband or somebody's father even though he wasn't that old. You should know about fathers. They're the most important people to a kid trying to be a man, when everyone is out to get you or fix you into a can or a crate going six feet down.

My father built things. He was a carpenter mainly. He'd build things, take things apart, and build them again. But he was also an electrician, a house painter, a wallpaper hanger, a welder, a car mechanic, a plumber. All for money and for fixing up other people's houses. He could fix anything. A regular Jack-of-all-trades. I remember he used to make toys for us at Christmas because he couldn't buy any. We was living in the Bronx then, and my father would load up his beat-up station wagon every morning and go off on the jobs people called him for. He owned his business. He was his own business. That's what Moms said to write in the blank beside "father's occupation" on school registration forms every September: "self-employed." I didn't even know what it meant, because my father never talked to us. He didn't tell us about who we were. I mean, as a family. And since I didn't know who I was aside from nothing or no one, I thought I could be anybody I damn well pleased.

"You ain't never had a chance, have you?" Moms said once.

"What are you talking about? I'm anybody I'm strong enough to be."

"And mean enough," she said, shaking her head like she did when my father died. He worked all the time and kept his feelings locked inside him until his heart burst open. The fucking load he must have been carrying. Shit, I coulda carried some of that load.

"You ain't never had a chance," Moms said again.

"I make my own chances. I'm self-employed."

Naw, Metro couldn't have been anybody's husband or father. You could tell by the way he walked and, if you listened close enough, by the way he talked. He had what you call opportunities. Maybe if you don't ever have kids you can build things for yourself. Do things. He just made the mistake of wanting to do me.

"You can come up to visit sometime, you know. Now that you know where I live."

"You mean me?"

"Sure. What's your name?"

"Lonny."

"I'm Metro."

"You told me before. Remember?"

"Yes. I thought you didn't remember. You didn't say anything."

"I didn't know what to say. Besides, where'd you get a name like that?"

"You'll see."

"Listen man, you trying to get wise or something?"

"Let's be friends, Lonny."

"I got to go now."

"Some other time, then?"

"Sure, man, sure."

"Call me Metro. I like that."

"Sure.

I got away and ran all the way to Cuddles' place. He wasn't even expecting me. But I was there just the same, leaning against the corner beam of the loading platform. It was about five feet off the ground so that the packing trucks could be loaded from the level of the storage and work areas. I could have been holding up the very corner of the building myself, or at least the sign saying Holsworth Meat and Poultry Packing, where you could actually see the sides of beef, the blood and fat making the loading-platform floor slippery and the whole place smell like rotten armpits.

Maybe it was the heat. Or just me, hot with my tangled nerves sizzling electric. All from talking with that guy Metro and running at breakneck speed to Cuddles' job like it was the only safe place. I was hot standing there thinking about Metro and hating myself for letting him talk like that to me. Shit, he talked like he knew who I was or who I could be. Like he could actually see into my corduroy jacket, his eyes like fingers in my clothes—touching me. You ever get that feeling talking to someone? Shit. I hated him for thinking he knew who I was and could come on to me like I was some bitch. He didn't know who he was messing with. Sure, I told him my name. We was just talking. Wouldn't you talk before you realized his eyes were fingers crawling all over you? I know you would, mostly because you'd think a guy wouldn't do that to another guy.

Later, you'd swear he hadn't touched you. Wouldn't you? You'd think that talking was all right. It was only some words between you, not hands. You'd think that as long as he didn't touch you it would be all right to speak. Long as neither of you was touching. It don't mean that you're one of them, just 'cause you say "Lonny," like I did. We was only talking, man. But when you realized his eyes were fingers taking hold, you'd hate him even more for pulling it off, undressing you right there with his eyes and laughing at your naked ass or shriveled-up cock. You'd be mad enough to kill him.

"You lying," Cuddles says when I tell him. "You lying, man."

"Naw, I ain't."

"Shit, man. Wait till I see Maxie and Lou."

"What for?"

"We oughta kick his ass."

"Look, Cuddles. Maybe we can just forget it, huh?"

"Naw, man. You one of us. What happens to you, happens to us. You forgetting the pledge."

"What pledge?" I ask after him, and he's dancing on the same short circuit I'm on.

When we catch up with Maxie and Lou, it's Cuddles doing the talking. "Man, we should celebrate," he yells, looking me over.

"Celebrate what?" I ask.

"Losing your cherry to a faggot, what else?" he says.

My face burns. "He didn't touch me, man."

"Aw, Lonny, we know you got a little bit," says Maxie grinning.

"Don't start no shit," says Lou.

"Maybe that's what I'm smelling," says Cuddles, moving up then back from me and flailing his arms like he's brushing me off.

"You mean the shit on *your* breath," I say, stepping up to him.

And Maxie jumps up and goes "Whoa," and Lou goes "Whoa," and I go "Whoa."

Cuddles backs off. "I'll fix your ass," he says. "Fix it real good."

"Aw, man, we been low too long now, let's ride high," says Maxie.

"Beer and smoke?" I ask.

"Yeah."

"Let's ride and fuck the night," adds Lou. He revs up the cycle with Cuddles holding tighter to him than I ever held. At the first red light Cuddles turns to me, saying he'll fix me real good. I tell him where to put that shit.

Around midnight, after five trips to Burger King for fries and hot apple pies to ease the munchies, we get back to the garage in Chelsea. I'm high, yeah, I admit it. Feeling good. We stop cutting up with each other and just enjoy being so bloated we can barely move. We keep talking shit, though, like it's all we can say. But I still feel funny about meeting Metro earlier in the afternoon. A numbing tingle comes through my face like I'm getting high all over again or just burning slowly inside. Then I feel light again as if something is about to happen to ease the beer and marijuana out of me on a cool streak, and I'd lift off the garage floor, lift up from the street and glide out to 12th Street and Bleecker and on to West 4th, where I'd be sure to see him and we'd talk. Just talk. Maybe this time I would get to hear his stereo. Maybe he likes the same music I do. Maybe he really is like me or Maxie or Cuddles or Lou, just a little haywire.

But we leave the garage again and move in a group through the meat-packing section of West 12th and down toward Bleecker where men walk alone or in twos, passing us. Lou scowls. Cuddles sets his shoulders broad. We're a solid block, and tough. Them faggots is just maggots on rotting meat. They move away from us and off the sidewalk quick. Lou and Cuddles laugh, and I hardly know their voices. When I laugh too, just to be laughing, the chuckle comes out of some pit inside me, and the voice ain't mine, honest. Like the shit you don't know you carry around until it starts to stink.

Some guy up ahead is selling loose joints for a dollar. "All our joints loose," says Maxie, laughing and trying to unzip his pants. When we come up to him Maxie asks, "Got fifteen?"

"We'll get blasted to hell," I say. But no one answers. They all look like they know something I don't know.

Maxie asks for change of a twenty. I see Cuddles and Lou sneak in close, so I move in close. The guy fumbles around in his pockets and gives me the joints to hold. As soon as he brings out a wad of bills it's a flurry of green and fists. Cuddles first, then Maxie, Lou, and me pounding hard on the upbeat.

"That's all the money I got," the guy whines. Cuddles pushes him away from us. The flash of metal makes the kid back right into Lou who feels his ass. Cuddles gets a feel, too. The guy's face goes red and his voice trembles, "Leave me alone. You got what you wanted."

"You oughta be glad we don't make you suck us off," Lou says, pushing him away. "Now get the fuck outta here."

The kid disappears down a side street. We count the new joints and money and move in close ranks like an army of our own, the baddest white boys out that night. Everyone else moves off the sidewalk as we approach, some we even push into the street, just close enough to a car to scare them clean out of their designer jeans and alligator shirts. The funniest shit is that some of them have on leather bomber jackets, and here we are doing the combat. We blow some of the cash at the liquor store off Sheridan Square.

On a vacant stoop near West 4th Street, we finish off the beer and the joints and divide up the rest of the money. Everything is sweet now. Sure we have our fights and fun and great highs. So what if they don't last long? Sure as shit and just as loud as the beer and smoke would let him, Cuddles goes, "Lonny, man, how's Beatrice these days?"

"Don't be bringing my Moms into your shit," I say.

"Keep it clean, guys," says Maxie.

"I was trying to keep it clean," Cuddles starts. "But the bitch had her period right when I was fucking her."

In a second I'm on him with fists and feet. He deserves no better. "We dancing this one, asshole."

"Yo, man, cool it," says Lou. He and Maxie pull me off Cuddles, but not until I land some good ones. Cuddles is too high to fight good. I could be faster myself, but what the hell.

"Aw man," Cuddles says, rolling to his side, sliding down the concrete stairs away from me. "I just wondered if she knew about your boyfriend. You know, the one you said lived around here."

"Whoa," says Maxie. "Lonny getting faggot pussy again? Keeping it all to himself?"

"It ain't true, man," I say.

"What ain't true?"

"This guy just told me his name, that's all. I didn't say nothing else. Nothing."

"Why he tell you his name then?"

"'Cause he wanted to, that's why. You jealous, Cuddles?"

"Shit, man."

"He wanted to do something, I guess," I say.

"Of course he wanted to," says Maxie.

"He was trying to rap to me," I say, but I'm talking too much and can't stop. "Like I was some bitch."

"He touch you, man? He touch you?" Maxie asks.

"Shit," says Cuddles. "Faggots everywhere."

"I ain't no faggot," I say.

"He touch you, man?" asks Maxie.

"Like you touched that reefer kid back there?"

"That's different, Lonny. We was on top."

"Shit," says Cuddles. "Pass me another joint."

"Me too."

"Pass Lonny another joint. He cool."

"Thanks."

Hours pass. Or minutes that seem like hours. The streets are suddenly quiet and so are we. But that kind of quiet—sneaking up and banging like a fist on your face—makes you think something's about to happen and no laughing or getting high can stop it. What you do won't be all that strange, either, more like something you always thought about doing but never did. I hate that feeling. It makes me think that something's burning in me that I don't know about. And I've got to let it out or choke on the fumes.

Cuddles is the first to see him strolling down the street. He nudges me and Maxie. Maxie nudges Lou, who's half-asleep and stroking himself hard again.

"Aw, shit." My voice gives it away.

"That's him, ain't it?" asks Cuddles. "That's Lonny's faggot, ain't it?"

"I didn't say that," I say, but it's too late.

"He the one touch you?" asks Maxie.

"That's the one," says Cuddles.

"How do you know?"

"*You* told me," Cuddles says, but his voice also tells me something I can't get ahold of. They ease into the street and wait. I join just to be joining them. Metro approaches dizzily, either drunk or high or plain out of it, but not as bad as the rest of us. Cuddles speaks up like he has it all worked out in his head.

"Hey, baby," he goes, in a slippery, chilly voice.

"Huh?" says Metro.

"Hey, subway, baby," Cuddles goes again.

"The A train, right? I just took the A train," says Metro.

"We got another train for you, baby. A nice, easy ride."

I can't believe what Cuddles is saying. I try to hide my surprise by not looking at Metro, but they both scare me like I've never been scared before. It's something I can't get hold of or stop.

"Metro. Why do they call me Metro?" he goes, talking to himself all out of his head now. Does he even see these guys, hear them?

"Hey, baby," says Lou, getting close to him.

I stay where I am near the concrete steps.

"Oh, baby," says Maxie, joining in.

"They call me the underground man," says Metro, his words slurring. "You wanna know why? I'll tell you why." His eyes dart to all of us, locking us in a space he carries inside for someone to fill. Then he sees me for the first time. He stops, jaws open, eyes wide. "Is that you, Lonny?"

I say nothing. The guys are quiet, too.

"You wanna know why, Lonny? 'Cause I get down under. Underground. Metro. Get it?" Then he laughs a high, faggoty laugh. And I don't know him anymore. He stops suddenly. No one else is laughing. He feels something's wrong. He looks straight at me, then at the others now tight around him.

"Lonny, what's going on? Who are these guys?"

Cuddles touches him, his hand gliding down Metro's open shirt. Metro's eyes get round.

"Lonny, I don't know these guys."

"That's all right," says Maxie. "We're Lonny's friends. Ain't that right, Lonny?"

I say nothing. Lou kicks me square in the shins. "Yeah," I say. "Yeah." But nothing more.

"And when Lonny tells us you go under, man, you give it up nice and easy, don't you?" says Cuddles.

Metro reaches into his pockets and pulls out a raggedy leather wallet. "I don't have much money." He shows the wallet around so we see the single ten-spot inside. "That's all there is. You want it? It's all I have."

"No, baby," says Cuddles. "Keep your money. Right, fellahs?"

"Right."

Metro looks worried. "My watch? I don't have anything else. Nothing, honest. You can check if you want."

"We don't want your watch," says Lou. His hand falls to Metro's ass, feeling it. Then to the front, gathering Metro's balls into a hump and slowly releasing them.

"Lonny says you been after him."

"After him? I don't understand. What are they saying, Lonny?"

I don't say nothing, but I want to say something. When I step closer, I feel metal pointing in my side, a blade tearing my shirt. Cold on my skin.

"Yeah," I say. "You been after me."

Cuddles steps up. "You wanted to suck his cock? Take it up the ass?"

"Hold it, Cuddles," I say.

"Naw, you hold it," says Maxie. "You could be like that too, for all we know. Ain't that right, fellahs?"

"Shit, man. You tell him, Cuddles. Tell him he's crazy to think that. You seen me with that girl."

"Naw, man. You show us," Cuddles says.

They hustle me and Metro to an alley near the abandoned building and stoop. Maxie and Lou hold Metro by the armpits. Cuddles twists my arm behind my back, and from his open breath I know he's grinning ear to ear. "Aw, man," he whispers to me. "We just having fun. Gonna shake him up a little."

"What about me?"

Cuddles says nothing more. He looks at the others.

Maxie pushes Metro to the ground. The alley carries his voice. "You wanted to suck him, huh? Well, suck him."

Cuddles unzips my pants.

"I didn't touch you, Lonny. I never touched you."

"You lying, subway man," says Cuddles.

"Ask him," says Metro. "Did I touch you, Lonny? Ever? You can tell them. Please, Lonny. I never touched you."

All eyes are on me now, and even in the dark I can see the glimmer of Metro's eyes looking up from the ground. From the sound of his voice I can tell he's about to cry. Suddenly, the click of knives: Lou's and Maxie's. Metro faces away from them and can't see. I see them, but I say nothing. Cuddles twists my arm further. The pain grabs my voice. His blade against my skin. "I told you I'd get back at you, shithead."

Pain all in me. Metro jerks forward. "Ouch," he says feeling a blade, too. Then Metro's mouth in my pants. Lips cold on my cock. Then warmer. Smoother. Teeth, saliva, gums. I can't say nothing, even if I want to.

It don't take me long. I open my eyes. Metro's head is still pumping at my limp cock, but his pants are down in the back, and Lou is fucking him in the ass. Lou gets up quickly, zips up his pants. Maxie moves to take his place. I move out of Metro's mouth, open in a frown this time or a cry. Maxie wets his cock and sticks it in. Cuddles pumps Metro's face where I was. Metro gags. Cuddles slaps his head back to his cock, and I hear another slap. This one against Metro's ass, and Lou and Maxie slap his ass while Maxie fucks him. Lou has the knife at Metro's back and hips. He traces the shape of his body with the blade. Metro winces. "Keep still, you bastard. Keep still," Lou says.

I try to make it to the street, but Cuddles yanks me back. He hands me a knife and I hold it, looking meaner than I am. You ain't never had a chance, I'm thinking and realizing it's for Metro, not for me. Cuddles finishes and pulls out of Metro's dripping mouth. His fist lands against Metro's jaw, slamming it shut. I hear the crack of bone and a weak cry. The next thing I know, Maxie, still pumping Metro's ass and slapping the cheeks with the blade broadside, draws blood, and once he finishes he shoots the blade in, then gets up quick, pulling the knife after him. Lou's hand follows. Then a flash of metal and fists.

"Shit, man. Hold it," I yell. "I thought we was only gonna fuck him. What the hell you guys doing?"

"Fucking him good," says Lou.

"Stop. For God's sake, stop."

But they don't stop.

"Oh my God. Oh my fucking God." It's all I can say, damn it. And I hear my name.

"Lonny?"

"Oh my God."

"Lonny?" Metro's voice is weak, his words slurring on wet red leaves. "Help me."

Lou and Maxie jump together. "Let's get the fuck outta here."

"Yeah," says Cuddles. He kicks Metro back to the ground where his arms and legs spread like the gray limbs of a tree.

"Oh my fucking God." I keep saying it, crying it. But it's too late. The guys scatter into the street like roaches surprised by light. Running.

They're running. I look back at Metro and he rolls toward me. His still eyes cut me like a blade. "Never touched you," the eyes say. "Never touched you."

I hold my breath until my ears start to pound. I hold my head. I run, stop, run again. The knife drops somewhere. I run again. Don't know where the fuck I'm going, just getting the hell out of there. Don't see anybody on the street and not for the rest of the night. Not Lou, not Cuddles. Not anybody else at all.

October is red, man. Mean and red. Nobody came back there but me, see. And Metro was gone, by then. Somebody had raked the leaves into a clean pile. I ran through it and scattered the leaves again. Once you get leaves and shit sticking all on you, you can never get them off. And when you start hearing the scratchy, hurt voices coming from them, the leaves I mean, not patches of skin or a body cut with knives, or a palm of broken fingers, you'll start talking back, like I do. You stop hanging out at the meat-packing warehouses on West 12th or walking the loading platform mushy with animal fat and slime where your sneaks slip—not Adidas, but cheaper ones just as good.

When I found Cuddles and told him about the talking red leaves, he said to get the fuck away from him, stop coming around if I was gonna talk crazy and dance out of fear like a punk. But I wasn't dancing. My feet was trying to hold steady on the loading platform, but my sneaks wouldn't let me. You ever hear the scratchy voices of leaves? You ever try to hold steady on slippery ground?

They had the body marked out in chalk on the ground behind some blue sawhorses that said "Police Line—Do Not Cross." It was right where we left him. I saw it glowing. "Here's Metro," I told myself. Here's anybody, even me. A chalk outline and nothing inside. A fat white line of head, arms, body, and legs. A body curled into a heap to hold itself. Like a leaf or a dead bird, something dropped out of the sky or from a guy's stretched-out hand. It was amazing. But it was also the figure of somebody. A man. Any man. So I walked around the outline, seeing it from different angles. How funny to see something that fixed, protected from people or from falling leaves or from the slimy drippings from sides of beef. The outline wasn't Metro. It was somebody like me.

Once I saw the chalk figure I couldn't get enough of it. I kept coming back and walking slower and slower around it, measuring how far it was from the police barricade and from where I stood looking down at it, sprawled where we left him. But I figured out a way to keep looking at it and not step in the garbage scattered nearby. You know, leaves, rags, torn newspapers, bits of dog hair, blood maybe, and lots more leaves. I went three steps this way and three steps that way, keeping the chalk outline in sight and missing the garbage and dogshit. One-two-three, one-two-three. Up-two-three, down-two-three. When I saw one of the neighbors watching from a window, I cut out of there. By then I knew what I had to do.

I came back that night. The chalk shape was glowing like crushed jewels under the streetlights. I took off my shirt and pants and didn't even feel cold. I crossed the barricade and sat inside the chalk. The glow was on me now. It was me. I lay down in the shape of the dead man, fitting my head, arms, and legs in place. I was warm all over.

The police came and got me up. Their voices were soft and mine was soft. They pulled a white jacket over me like some old lady's shawl. I shrugged a little to get it off, but my arms wouldn't move. When I looked for my hands, I couldn't find them. The police didn't ask many questions, and I didn't say nothing the whole time. At the precinct, a doctor talked to me real quiet-like and said the leaves would go away forever if I told him everything that happened to the dead man and to me. But they didn't call him Metro, they called him some other name with an accent in it. A name I didn't even know. I asked the doctor again about the red leaves. He promised they would go away. "What about the blood?" I asked. "Will I step in the blood?"

"Not if you come clean," he said.

"What about my sneaks?" I asked him. "Will they get dirty?

Donna Allegra

■ ■ ■

[1953–]

POET, SHORT STORY WRITER, AND DANCER DONNA ALLEGRA was born in Brooklyn in 1953. She studied dramatic literature, theater, and history at both Bennington College and New York University. Allegra is the author of a collection of short fiction, *Witness to the League of Blond Hip Hop Dancers* (2000), which was nominated for the 2001 Violet Quill Award by Inside/Out Books. Her poems and stories have been published in numerous journals and magazines, such as *Essence, Sinister Wisdom,* and *Common Lives/Lesbian Lives,* as well as in several anthologies, among them *Home Girls: A Black Feminist Anthology* and *Best Lesbian Erotica.* She has won the Pat Parker Memorial Poetry Prize and was runner-up for the Audre Lorde Poetry Prize in 1994. The author's dance, music, theater, book, and film reviews have appeared in *Colorlife!, The Lesbian Review of Books, Sojourner,* and several other publications. Allegra credits Jemima, one of the first African American lesbian writing groups, as an especially vital influence on her literary career.

As with much of her work, Allegra's short story "Dance of the Cranes" focuses on women coming together culturally—in this instance, in African dance—to confront and overcome a myriad of social oppressions, including the sexism associated with all-male environments and the homophobia sometimes encountered in communities of color.

Dance of the Cranes

[1997]

"It's my mother's favorite dance," had become Lenjen's automatic answer. She didn't fidget while the security guard eyed her, his arms stitched across his chest. She was an old hand at facing the scowls that accompanied, "What kind of name is that? What's it mean?"

The guard continued to block the entrance, frowning over the new names kids had these days, baptisms he could barely pronounce, much less spell. Without waiting for further interrogation, Lenjen explained, "It comes from a West African dance."

Finally he hmphed, dismissing her while giving her body another squint from the corners of his eyes, then sat back to his copy of *The Watchtower*. She took that as permission to enter the court yard and join her mother in the dance class beyond the gate. It was only then that she saw Cayenne, waving her to hurry.

"You didn't have to start a war with him, honey."

"I didn't start it, Mama. I'm always patient when I tell people my name, but he was acting stupid," Lamban protested, then cringed. She hated sounding like a kid.

"The brother was probably just showing an interest in you," her mother said, as if explaining simple addition, but for Lenjen, edgy from the delay, the math didn't add up.

She'd spent a large part of her childhood traveling to West African classes where Cayenne's passion for Senegambian dance from the Old Mali Empire could be satisfied. As a baby, Lenjen would lay quietly in her bunting, absorbed by the hypnotic drum rhythms. The growing girl ran and played with other small children whose mothers had also brought them to the studio. Lenjen would watch with a smoldering interest when the adults danced their way across the studio floor, their bodies elastic with extravagant motions. She stared as if snake-charmed into the circle these women formed at the end of class when everyone had a chance to do a solo within the volcanic ring of dancers.

Eventually she joined the children's line, and the fire for West African dance caught her in its grip, first as a playful tickling at her toes, then consuming her in its wake.

At 13, Lenjen stood tall, awkward, elegant in her long limbs fitted for the dance of the cranes—a bird known more for wading in the water than paddling its wings through the sky. She never understood the full extent of her name until the Wednesday evening Senegalese dance class when Sulaiman, fiddling with one of the cowrie shells braided into a crown across his forehead, explained that the movements for lenjen mimicked a crane in a marsh. This made sense. She'd already concluded that African people liked animals, particularly birds, to shape their dances.

Lenjen had turned 14 six months after she and Cayenne moved from Newark to Harlem, primarily because it'd then be easier for the two of them to revel in African dance. Mother and child duly went everywhere in Harlem, Brooklyn, and Greenwich Village where Cayenne could find a class.

Lenjen was by then a solid folkloric dancer, though not always obedient to styles that American Blacks took up as the traditional African way. "Some of those supposed-to-be-traditions are dead for a reason, Ma," Lenjen said. More often than not, she would refuse to wear a lapa in dance class, aggravating Cayenne.

Cayenne had specially bought fabric made in Senegal from one of the merchants who sold jewelry wares, lapa outfits, and American-style dresses sewn in African fabrics. The woman had even shown Lenjen how to wrap the fabric around her waist for a lapa, a staple in any African woman's wardrobe. "Like this," the market woman demonstrated with the two edges of cloth she pulled first across her backside, then around the front of her waist to tie a knot, "so the extra cloth won't get in your way when you kick up those long legs."

Cayenne noted the sweatpants and T-shirt Lenjen placed into a Capezio dance bag and fumed over how, once again, Lenjen completely disregarded yet another womanly way.

But Lenjen knew she didn't want to end up as some man's woman. Somehow she couldn't convince her mother that she wasn't like the sisters so eager to have babies. Even so, it pained her to go against the grain of right and proper African womanhood—that is, in the ways that the grown-ups she was most familiar with would have right and proper African womanhood be.

To soothe her mother's irritation, Lenjen tried telling Cayenne, "Ma, I hate it when the drummers hoot and holler like their brains fell out when I dance."

Cayenne rolled her eyes toward the ceiling. "They're paying you a compliment, honey. You should be glad the men like you." Lenjen sucked her teeth with ingratitude.

"I know I can shake a tail feather, and I'm fast on my feet, but I'm showing off for the other dancers, and the fellas just make it into something stupid." Lenjen stopped short of saying how eagerly she looked to the grown women for approval. She longed for their encouraging attention as the dancing circle at the end of class settled down from a boiling caldron to a simmering stew.

"You won't feel that way much longer, missy. I'll bet my bottom dollar on that." Cayenne spoke with finality, certain she knew the last word to this story.

"I'm not like that, Mommy." She hated the pleading tone trailing her words, but Cayenne had already left the room.

Lenjen wanted her mother to understand how she drank from the current of energy that flowed from the dancing women, that they were the ones who enriched her blood. She wasn't putting her passion on the floor for some mating game. But Cayenne's mind was set, and Lenjen didn't want to whine after her to explain. When Cayenne returned with her own dance outfit in hand, mother and daughter let the matter rest so they wouldn't be late to class. They kept the peace on the common ground they held around the dance and music from the 14th-century Mali empire and other regions of the Senegambia in West Africa.

"You have your bus money?" Cayenne prompted.

Lenjen sent her mother a scolding look.

"Don't give me those eyes. We don't want to be late," Cayenne exaggerated her defensiveness.

"Hurry up, Ma. I'm waiting, and you're the one who's not ready."

"All right, old lady. Fourteen going on 40," Cayenne grumbled as the bus lumbered into their stop.

They always arrived before the rest of the Sunday flock who regularly gathered at the armory in Brooklyn or at the Sounds in Motion studio on Tuesdays on 125th Street. On Saturdays the community of dancers converged on a recreation center in Newark, and this evening they'd join the dance congregation at the Cathedral of St. John the Divine.

As the bus rumbled down Amsterdam Avenue, its buildings maintaining a ruined majesty, Lenjen relaxed into a reverie. She missed

people when they didn't come to class; even women she didn't particularly like pained her with their absence. When a woman with the slightly
sad and dreamy face had started showing up to Wednesday night classes,
Lenjen pegged her as a newcomer. This woman too had a name taken
from a West African dance. She'd heard a woman with three gold teeth
call out in surprise, "Lamban!"

Lenjen had always favored lamban, the social celebration dance for
rites of passage—birth, puberty, marriage—but now that dance took on
new meaning for her. She felt pulled toward the woman, allured by the
way Lamban carried herself and would be a part of the group but somehow kept to the sidelines.

Initially Lenjen imagined her feeling of kinship arose on account
of the genesis of their names—both from West African dances—and the
similar sounds of Lenjen and Lamban. That made them two of a kind.
But she also thrilled that Lamban wore African pants and didn't hold
back from trying the men's steps.

As the bus hulked toward their stop, Lenjen hoped Lamban would
start coming to Tanya's class on Fridays and prayed the woman would be
in Sulaiman's class this evening. Her thoughts stirred with rising excitement: maybe Lamban would be in the sabar class next Tuesday. She'd
have to start coming to the Armory on Saturdays. That was the class of
the week where all the African queens showed up in force.

But maybe, Lenjen reasoned against her quickening thoughts,
the woman went to Newark on Sundays. Clearly an accomplished
dancer, with movements articulate and strong, she always put her own
vibe into the steps. She had to be taking class somewhere regularly,
Lenjen argued with herself. It took a long time to learn West African
dance. Good Haitian and Brazilian dancers came across awkward and
stupid-looking when they entered the West African tradition. Even
though some of the Haitian and Brazilian dance steps were similar, a
whole different energy would spin the West African movements in
motion. You had to learn the entire alphabet of each particular people's dance language before your body could say its words and form
sentences.

Lenjen felt strange and giddy as she pondered where this unusual
woman had been taking class. *I could ask her,* she hesitantly proposed to
herself. *Grown-ups think teenagers are children anyway, so I could ask as if I
really were younger. I can make like I do to get people in class to show me steps so*

that I can catch their phrasing. Then I can ask where she takes class, and I can ask her to show me what she knows about lamban!

I like that she's so strong and handsome, not pretty and silly about it. That stupid drummer, Ralph—always with something to say about a woman's body after she passed out of earshot—has a point: She is juicy delicious, and I think she's dreamy.

The bus jolted and then sunk to a halt. "Lenjen, wake up, little sister. Here's our stop!"

During the warm-up calisthenics that Sulaiman directed, Lamban, twice Lenjen's age, sensed someone watching her. She turned her head and saw Lenjen look down, the girl's face an Etch-A-Sketch from expression to blankness. It was more than a sixth sense that told her she had drawn Lenjen's eye.

She moved with caution when it came to revealing her interest for anyone in class, but she liked this teenager who was all limbs and as quick to frown someone off as grin them in. Something familiar about the girl tickled Lamban. In class the previous week Lamban had asked her line partner, a Bajan woman called Merle, "Whose daughter is that beanpole?"

"Lenjen? She's Cayenne's girl. She's gotten big all of a sudden," and Merle frowned at her recognition that the girl was now a teen.

Lamban tried to cover her curiosity by hastily adding, "That baby-face on stilts is so open and alive when she dances. She has a sweet feeling to her." Merle had nodded, and Lamban marveled how Lenjen could remain quietly self-contained among so many boisterous people. *Maybe she's given up on being taken seriously around all these adults,* Lamban thought, turning away from the dancers to hitch her lapa for a more comfortable fit. Lenjen was the rare bird who didn't wrangle for attention and demand to be noticed. The girl had a quality to her that Lamban found dear.

It pained Lamban to imagine that Lenjen probably kept herself quiet because otherwise the men in class would never leave her alone. She sipped from her water bottle and in her peripheral vision, Lenjen looked like some imagined African royalty—delectable as she blossomed into a young woman's beauty.

She coughed and spilled some water. A patch of envy spread across her chest for how Lenjen had grown up with African dance and didn't have to start in Senegambian folklore as an adult. Not all people took to the demands of West African dance, but those who did held tight to this ground and made it a home.

As Sulaiman guided the 30 dancers through a series of hip rolls, Lamban savored the curiosity she felt emanating from Lenjen. *Probably doesn't know the half of her beauty,* Lamban thought. Young women could look so unearthly at times.

She once again praised the powers that had brought her back to the African dance scene. She'd taken herself away, needing a break from the clutch of frustration, an involuntary muscle that kicked in against her will. It held her at breath when she cared so strongly for women in a community that valued only male–female couplings as important. She couldn't understand how women who had the pride enough not to straighten their hair still left themselves by the wayside. Why did those sisters pump up boys' already-overblown on a sense of themselves? These were the very men who didn't allow room for the women rooting for them to have space on stage.

Lamban wondered if she could see this pattern of the heterosexual social dance because she entered the world as a lesbian. But she was also a dancer and West African folklore gave her heart its rhythm. She'd stayed away from these dance classes for months, and a few people let her know they'd noticed and were glad to see her return.

That first evening back, the woman who became her line partner for the night said, "Hello, stranger. Haven't see you in a dog's age. You been busy, huh?"

Lamban heartened that she'd not been forgotten, surprised she'd even been missed. As much as she chafed against the ultra-heterosexuality of the African dance community, she did love the people. They'd all been taking classes and sharing high energy for years now. She knew individual spirits, had watched their children grow, and her soul had mingled in the communion of rhythms for dance.

Still, the boys could be real pains in the ass when they paraded their notions of manhood. "Hold back, girl. You're making me look bad. I'm supposed to be the strong one. You chill out."

Lamban felt she couldn't be as freely loving to the sisters as she wanted—she didn't want anyone calling her "queer" in that tone of contempt she knew so well. She cringed at the disdain straight women could put forth for lesbians only. She never heard them voice anger for the men who deserted families. Or condemn pimps, rapists, molesters, and murderers.

She'd felt confounded yet again by attitudes she'd overheard that evening in the dressing room. "That sister should know better; men can't help themselves." Is that how they felt about men who wouldn't step up to the plate for the children they helped create?

But the African dancer in her could be fed only within this sphere. And not all the women were "Black-maled" into keeping themselves back so that some men could hold on to an illusion of superiority. Sisters weren't stupid. It was just those misguided and loud-about-it few who let themselves be quelled and then energetically tried to send other women astray.

"Jumping jacks," Sulaiman ordered. He simply smiled at the groans that issued from around the room.

Lamban knew as well as Sulaiman did that these women welcomed the good feeling that came with pushing their muscles. She felt so good to be back in this class, she wondered why she'd ever left. No, she knew the reasons; they just weren't tormenting her like a headache fevered by the devil's hammer.

She'd been through the fire, sorted through her ashes and determined she wouldn't hurt herself again by denying her lesbian self. She'd tried hiding this truth from anyone who got friendly with her. When she couldn't pretend anymore, instead of going to class, she stayed home and cried night after night for a week.

She switched to Haitian and Brazilian classes downtown. Those rhythms fed another part of her soul, but her spirit longed for the dances of Senegal, Mali, and Guinea. She ached to do djola, mandgiani, wolof-sodon, goumbe, lenjen, sabar, and her beloved lamban. A cramped tendon in her spirit throbbed for release, just as her muscles would want more stretch when she didn't extend her body to the full range of its ability.

Lamban still grieved that being a lesbian could make her an outlaw to a group of people who did the most spiritually sustaining thing she knew in life. She'd needed all those months away to love herself again. The time in seclusion let her grow a perspective, like new skin. That's how lobsters did it—when the old shell became too small for the mature body, they'd go to a protected place where they could shed the old covering safely. In that haven, they could curl naked and vulnerable until a new covering grew in.

"Are you getting warm?" Sulaiman asked the group who responded with "Yeah!" and "Give us a break."

It had taken time for Lamban to understand what had bent her so far out of shape. She'd ignored the many off-notes she felt as she smiled eagerly to people who gave her suspicious looks. She'd remained fervent in pursuit of dance and felt she couldn't afford to challenge a woman who, when Lamban had come into the bathroom, had self-righteously declared to another, "There's no funny women in Africa you know."

Were they talking about her? Lamban's underarms grew moist. She wasn't sure and had been afraid to eye the speaker with a frown intended to challenge the woman. Wasn't this the one who'd once bragged, "I changed that AC/DC into a real man, and he's my husband now." That man had left her not so long ago, Lamban remembered as she'd hurriedly gotten dressed. Still, she hadn't opened her mouth to wrestle with the woman's viewpoint.

Lamban couldn't admit then, that as much as she loved her lesbian self—a favorite part which she would swear before anyone that the African powers had made her—she sought her image in mirrors that didn't reflect her. How many times had she heard, "Friends are OK and all that, but every woman needs a man"? The distortion occurred as if by osmosis, and she had no tools to correct the vision. Not seeing other lesbians and gay men stand in her corner made it all too easy for her truth to be clipped of wings.

For a long time it had been all right with Lamban not to ask for anything, to give the listening ear to the sisters when they talked about their men and babies. But after a while, she too needed to be heard, needed simple recognition that she, a lesbian woman, was one on a scale of dissonant notes that Black Americans could always harmonize. She needed these individuals to ask about her girlfriend or give a touch of sympathy if she mentioned having trouble on the home front.

But fear kept her opinions unspoken. It didn't take long for that poverty of speech to make Lamban feel closed out from the people among whom she mingled. When her well ran dry, that's when she'd cried all those nights, aching because it hurt to be left-out and maligned.

The time in exile gave her to realize how strongly she loved West African folklore and that this culture gathered the people with whom she wanted to dance. Maybe most wouldn't welcome her as a lesbian, and she'd have to resign herself to getting a family embrace elsewhere.

But, by the same token, she didn't have to till the land for their hetero-sexuality either.

When a woman in a Brazilian dance class had complimented Lamban on her samba step—"Work them hips girl. That's the action that brings the brothers around"—Lamban shook her head and said, "It's not about that for me." Her cheeks filled with heat, but she didn't rush to assure the woman that men mattered. Lamban decided right then and there that she needed her own encouragement more than she wanted to give it away to women who pledged themselves first to men and abandoned sisters to sink at sea. Let the ones who'd shrink from her do so, but she wouldn't stay away from her rightful place in this world, and resolved to get back to West African dance. She was one of the multitude of rhythms that African people the world over could work through their bodies all at the same time.

Having a stronghold on hard-won knowledge, Lamban had earlier this evening packed her dance gear: leotards, leg warmers, tights cut off above her knees, and a piece of fabric to fasten around her hips in a wrap she liked. She'd taken care to drape the fabric almost like a baby's diaper, giving herself room to move freely and feel all her strength.

"Let's do some last stretches. You're almost done," Sulaiman coaxed.

"You're killing us before we even started, Sulai," a voice in the back of the room warned.

"This is it, I promise," and he put a hand on his hip in a classic Black woman's body posture, queening it up, making everyone grin.

Lamban returned to her old stomping grounds with a mind set to make herself at home. Shackles fell away when she no longer cared to follow in the manner of an American-style traditional African woman. No one would give her any medals for pretending to be something she wasn't. She stopped wearing lapa or dress outfits; instead she wore the dabbas, the shokotos, the African pants the men and a few women wore.

In her new ease, she marveled that she'd kept her affection for the community in class. She still recoiled from the just plain jive of some—and they weren't the majority—but she could exult in the dance, the beauty of her classmates, the drummers, and the unseen forces that brought them all together.

"OK, you're done," Sulaiman told the group who grumbled at him good-naturedly for making them break a sweat during the warm-up.

As women adjusted lapas and the drums blasted ceremonial calls, Lamban felt a trespass of eyes against her skin. She paused to examine the ravelled edge of her African fabric, looked up abruptly, and saw Lenjen quickly fold her face toward her neck, then become engrossed in re-tying her own lapa. A surge of triumph curved Lamban's lips. Lenjen was drawn to her, and she knew the reason why. She vowed to the sprit of a young girl she carried inside herself that she would lead by example if this teenager was walking the same road.

Lamban shook her head in wonder at the paradox that her period of exile granted her freedom to take root with herself. She could now say, *This is who I am, and I am a branch on this family tree.*

The bellowing drums grew thunderous in the Cathedral of the Church of St. John the Divine. Her eyes landed with affection on Sulaiman who had been teaching this Wednesday class for the past few months. *He's gay,* she thought with defensiveness to a disapproving audience. *Lots of us are queer and you know it, so don't try to act like we don't exist or that we're too weird to even conceive of,* she wanted to shout to everyone.

Scanning the room to see who else was here tonight, Lamban felt at ease. She knew the routine of changing clothes, warming up, learning the steps to the dances. The familiarity gave her confidence as she skipped downstairs to the bathroom. Before the evening ended, she'd rise to the tide of rhythm the drums called forth as dancers unfurled in a wave of prayer.

When she returned, African fabric wrapped around her hips, Lamban heard Sulaiman saying, "Pat Rollins is our guest teacher tonight, so I'll let her speak on what she's teaching us. Pat."

A woman who'd been kneeling over a djimbe drum, her back to the group, straightened and stepped forth. Lamban looked at a face planed in bronze: it might have been sculpted in Benin. She'd taken class with that Brooklyn-born, spirit-of-Guinea girl. Pat Rollins embodied a Guinea folkloric dancer to her core: strong, with faster movement than the neighboring Senegalese style, and so much more exciting.

Pat's father was a master drummer in New York. Papa Rollins had trailbazed African folkloric arts for American Blacks years before the current generation of percussionists. But Pat owned a reputation in her own right as a dancer, independent of her father's Nigerian focus. The woman could move from liquid lightning to fiery steel, Lamban thought. If she weren't beautiful, she'd be ugly. The French had a word for her: *belle laide.*

Lamban admired the hearty and outspoken woman, but some drummers wished Pat would disappear. "She's the kind who puts fear into Black men's hearts—always speaking her mind," a songbe player said to the drum circle only half-joking. Lamban surprised herself by turning to a woman standing nearby, "Well, Pat knows what she's talking about when she calls drummers on not playing the rhythms she wants."

The woman, her stance as sturdy as a market vendor's, had nodded and whispered to her nervous-looking companion, "Sometimes these drummers don't understand what the dance teacher is asking for. You get a lot of brothers acting like women don't know anything about the drum. They think they can get away with playing any old beat they want—probably because they don't know how to do what the teacher asks." The woman was almost getting into a huff.

Lamban continued the whispered conversation as the group waited for Pat to finish instructing the lead drummer. "Pat's father taught a lot of these whelps when they couldn't keep a beat," she informed the women nearby, whose eyes regarded Pat approvingly.

Lamban liked how Pat didn't hesitate to pick up a djimbe and replace a drummer without apology to show up anyone who wasn't playing what she asked. Pat even made the men keep quiet when she explained a cultural note to her dancers. Lamban noticed she wasn't the only dancer appreciating Pat for that.

The woman Lamban spoke to, dressed in a lapa and matching-top outfit, said to her friend, who was timid about being a tenderfoot in class, "There's another thing about Pat—she's really into her dancers and refuses to treat the drummers as if they were the high and holy be-all and end-all. She wants the music exact and will make those men play their butts off until they get it right."

Lamban knew that some men resented this leadership, but they'd play harder and afterward be glad they had to work their best energy to meet Pat's demands.

"Ms. Mister," Ralph, a djimbe player, called behind her back as Pat moved like a lioness from the drummers to ask Sulaiman a question. Lamban figured Ralph had heard the thrilling rumor that Pat was creating her own company to perform traditional dance. Even he couldn't deny that this group would be no less than a thundering herd, despite the drama that would follow a woman artistic director.

Sulaiman was rounding up dancers. "Pat is so knowledgeable about the folklore and such a blazing rock of a dancer that..." He didn't finish. Pat took his arm and walked him past the circle of drummers for her question.

Ralph's cramped eyebrows and skimpy whiskers gave him the look of a jackal who could barely cover his fangs as he skulked out of the way for Sulaiman and Pat. Even so, he was drooling to play in her company. Lamban wondered if he'd also heard that Pat was looking to have women compose her drum orchestra.

"Hi, everyone," Pat addressed the gathered community of dancers and drummers. "Today we're going to work on saa."

Lamban wanted to hoot for joy as she thought, *I am in heaven. The very idea of saa sends my heart soaring. Thank God, I came back to class.*

"Saa is from the bush of Guinea," Pat explained. "It used to be a women's secret society dance. The women played drums in the bush. Saa was the strength dance for the females to keep themselves together. The sisters marched saa from Guinea to Mali and back again, protesting what we nowadays can talk about as macho madness." The room quieted with attention, some faces incredulous, some as if remembering forgotten knowledge.

"The women danced saa to show they were just as strong—if not stronger—than the men. And like I said, the women played the rhythms," Pat said with a chastising look at those drummers who made faces of disbelief.

Lamban nodded her head almost imperceptibly. She noticed how, several feet away, Lenjen's face brightened with interest in Pat's preface. Lenjen took on the look of someone who'd been adrift and now steered with a new rudder toward purpose. Lamban could understand how a teenager like Lenjen might yearn to hear the greater truth behind what Pat was saying: that there is a wider realm for African women than the small plots where men wanted to kennel and keep them.

"Some brothers say it's taboo for women to play the drum, but you have to ignore them. Have you ever heard of Makeda?" People nodded, some women smiling as if anticipating praise for themselves. "She's one of the best drummers—man or woman. A lot of brothers don't like her 'cause she's so good, but that's just their jealousy."

"And that little ego thing," Cayenne called out. Several women raised a chorus of "Um hm"s that broke into tolerant laughter. Lamban's enthusiasm kept her chin nodding. She ached to connect with the smile widening Lenjen's face, the skin smooth as an apple.

Pat changed direction slightly. "Saa steps are strenuous, ladies. It's a military dance—I'm talking serious war. Don't cheat on the steps. You have to smile when you march it." She flashed a challenging brightness of teeth, as if opening her mouth set free a flock of white birds to burst into the room of respectful listeners. The teacher adjusted her lapa around her hips for a looser fit and Lenjen could tell Pat was readying to show the steps.

"Like I said, saa was a women's secret society dance, but like a lot of things, the brothers peeped it and now it's everybody's dance." Then, as if this were a discovery, she added, "Women's secret societies prove that it's important for us to get together as females to share what we are strong with. I'm ready. I hope you are."

The dancers lined up in rows of three to practice each step as they went across the floor. Lamban let two women move ahead of her and quickly stepped in place to stand in Lenjen's line. She smiled at the girl openly. "Come on, puppy. This is the women's dance of strength." Before Lamban could continue or Lenjen could answer with anything more than her own smile of delight, Pat was demonstrating the steps to saa and both dancers set to work.

At first Lenjen was annoyed that she wasn't picking up the movements with her usual ease. Distress changed to horror as the rows of dancers sailed across the floor stitching the step securely to the music, but she just wasn't grasping the needle of movements Pat had shown. Lenjen had to work hard just to do it all wrong. And when she did get a slight grip on the footwork, she had a difficult time holding on to its thread.

Her mind kept repeating the enthusiastic words, *"Come on, puppy. Saa is the women's dance of strength."* Lenjen felt near panic; she had to get this. The sisters had marched saa from Guinea to Mali then back again to make a point to brothers whose egos had taken them unnaturally out of line.

Halfway through the class, Lamban took Lenjen's hand and drew her to the side of the room. Lamban exaggerated and carved her anatomy like an ancestor figure to show Lenjen the transition which made the saa step so troublesome.

"It's a rhythm thing," Lamban said. "Count it: one and uh-two. Hold three." Lenjen felt grateful for this instruction, even as she felt shamed that this reserved woman touched Lenjen's leg, elbow, hand, like a puppet master guiding movement to her limbs.

Lenjen badly wanted to look good, was flustered by her mistakes, and hated each and every false move. She kept a thin grip on her belief that she was learning something important. She paid heed to what Lamban pointed out and let herself be a child who had something to inherit from a woman she favored.

Still, she rallied herself like a warrior readying for battle. *Every class humbles me,* she thought. *Every class brings out my weakness, shows me my power, tells me my name. It's the same for anyone else here. I'm not going through anything different than the rest of the folks trying to learn this stuff. But damn, I wish I didn't have to sweat for it today.*

Pat rode herd on the dancers to guard them from slacking off. "Keep the steps clean. Tighter," she urged. Finally she motioned the drummers to go into a new rhythm for the next dance. The drum call tickled Lenjen just short of recognition. Her body could practically taste which dance would come next, but her mouth couldn't call it by name.

Pat motioned like a choir director to the alert faces that seemed eager for her every word. "Let's slow it down some. We'll do a lamban next. What I teach is from Guinea. This lamban is for the rite of passage from girlhood into womanhood."

Pat narrowed her eyes into the group of dancers, and when her funnel of vision caught Lamban, she signaled the woman to come to the front line.

Lamban felt her blood course both humble and proud. She put more than her body into the steps that Pat laid out, aware that people watched her so they could learn. She danced full-out and amplified each part of the movement. People needed clear demonstrations, especially in African dance where every movement would not be counted and broken down. She consciously offered herself as the strong pattern for anyone who looked to pick up the impression of her footfalls.

The music of the drums drove line after line of dancers, and Pat nipped at their heels to keep the movement strong. After what seemed a flicker of time, the hurricane of dance let up from a storm to a shower of raining arms and legs. Lamban looked forward to the ending circle where they'd probably do the social dance, mandgiani, but instead Pat signaled the drummers to play yet another rhythm. After a false start with the music and a moment of confusion, Pat sang out a rhythm that the lead drummer tried to catch, while Ralph scowled bewilderment. Finally, Pat called out, "I want you to play lenjen." The lead djimbe player smiled in quick recognition and apology.

Pat skipped through the semicircle she had directed the dancers to form around the drummers, then paired people off. Lamban caught the moment when Pat's face startled in a look of uncertainty, then sureness, recognizing a resemblance in two people. She'd just put together the two dance-named women, and her smile flared with bright teeth at how she'd paired Lamban with Lenjen.

Pat then went center-circle to say, "Here's what I want: Come out with your partner in an opening step. Each of you will do a solo. Then leave together doing the same step. Take a minute to work it out, OK?"

Lamban, her flesh heated, body confident, and sense of herself strengthened from dancing, felt giddy as a lottery winner to partner with this teenager. She said yes to all of Lenjen's suggestions for the steps they would do. Lamban went gladly into a listening stance, knowing that she could channel greater good from that position. She would take in more and connect with greater ease as she deferred to someone's greater skill.

The woman and teenager worked out and rehearsed their duet and solo steps. When Pat called the dance circle to order and it came their turn to ride out on the lenjen rhythm, Lamban felt herself barely more than a shadow. Lenjen danced as if she had no bones in her body to hamper its fluidity and, indeed, sported wings instead of arms. Her steps took her high into the air, as close to flight as humanly possible.

Lamban sensed everyone else in class look with wonder at Lenjen's solo, which soared the group to a climax. On Lenjen's last go-around at jumping into the circle of paired dancers, she pulled Lamban in with her and danced elaborate patterns around her partner. In finale, she angled her body into a sequence of steps in which everyone could join, then broke off with a gambol like a kaleidoscope discovering it could also be a rainbow.

At the end of class faces glistened with the sweaty joy fashioned from something cleansed and set free. Lenjen and Lamban smiled at, looked away from and back to one another. Lamban pulled the girl to her and held her in a long, strong hug. She felt people smiling their way. And why not smile upon them? The community had just witnessed a mighty rite of passage. Two queer birds had stretched their wings, each finding a new level of flight in the dance of the cranes.

STEVEN CORBIN

■ ■ ■

[1953–1994]

NEW JERSEY–BORN NOVELIST STEVEN CORBIN WAS CONTRO-
versial for his depiction of homophobia in black families, interracial
tension in gay relationships, and the gritty realities of AIDS.

His best-known works are *Fragments That Remain* (1993), a novel
concerning a black gay actor and his troubled family, and *A Hundred
Days from Now* (1994), a bleakly interpreted love story about an HIV-
positive African American writer whose Latino lover is unexpectedly
diagnosed with AIDS. His short fiction appears in Terry McMillan's
Breaking Ice: An Anthology of Contemporary African American Fiction. He was
teaching creative writing at UCLA at the time of his death from AIDS
in 1994.

In *A Hundred Days from Now,* Dexter, an African American screen-
writer, has just met and fallen in love with Sergio, a closeted Mexican
American businessman whose self-denial about his homosexuality is further complicated by the news that he has AIDS. In spite of the interracial
differences and difficulties in caring for a partner who will not speak the
truth of his own sexual identity, Dexter lovingly assumes the role of primary caregiver. However, when Sergio comes down with AIDS-induced
Kaposi's sarcoma, and an experimental bone-marrow transplant seems
the only hope for survival, the relationship takes on deeper issues of
mortality that cut to the core of their lives. In the end, Corbin, a former
ACT UP member, presents one of the most heartrending depictions of
AIDS/HIV in black gay fiction ever published.

"I have bad news," Sergio announced to Dexter over the telephone, a week after they'd returned from Hawaii.

Dexter swallowed, held his breath, sat down on the kitchen stool, his pulse racing.

"What is it?" he managed to say without stuttering.

"Remember that spot on my back?"

Oh, my God! Dexter thought. No. It can't be. No, God, don't let it be...

"Well," Sergio continued, sighing, defeated. "It's KS all right."

Dexter tried, with everything he had, to subdue the wave of grief rising from his stomach, weaving throughout his rib cage, sliding up his throat, gagging him with tears he didn't want Sergio to hear. He was trying to be strong for Sergio. But how could he? This second symptom declared it official that Sergio had AIDS.

"I'm so sorry," Dexter said, his voice cracking.

Seven weeks. That's all it had been. Forty-nine days. He'd barely known Sergio seven weeks and he couldn't—simply refused to imagine his life without him.

After they hung up, Dexter took a long, aimless walk through the neighborhood, barely aware of which streets he turned into, or of the automobiles that were stopping for him to cross the street. No, God, he thought. I'm sorry, you can't have this one. You've taken too many from me already. Go pick on somebody else. Dexter had fallen in love, virtually against his will. He'd never met anyone like Sergio, who encompassed nearly all the qualities Dexter sought in a man—and then some.

Of all the men Dexter had dated, Sergio was the near-perfect find, the divine one. He'd already resolved to spend the remainder of his life with Sergio. But he'd never considered how much life Sergio had left. So preoccupied with every other facet of Sergio—his good looks, his Harvard education, his intellect, his charm, his extraordinary achievements—Dexter never once—*not once!*—considered Sergio's health, his longevity. Talk about priorities being out of whack.

What would Dexter do? How would he handle this? He wasn't going to abandon Sergio, that much he knew. He meant what he'd said in Honolulu. The growing proportions of the pandemic being what they were, Dexter felt his contribution to the fight, as care-giver, would make him feel more involved, no longer simply watching from the sidelines. But how does one go about day-to-day existence when it entails living with a loved one's terminal illness?

And yet, AIDS, not unlike diabetes and cancer, wasn't necessarily terminal anymore. It was evolving into a survivable disease. He knew several men—not many, an incredibly small percentage actually—who, despite the disease, were living relatively healthy, productive lives. Of course, Sergio would be one of them, one of the more fortunate statistics. But of course! Just the thought of it gave Dexter a second wind. He and Sergio would fight the virus and beat it. Dexter likened Sergio to the allegorical protagonist in Ingmar Bergman's *The Seventh Seal* who plays chess with Death. Sergio would take on this faceless, hooded opponent and checkmate him. There wasn't a doubt in his mind.

Returning home, Dexter made a few phone calls to friends for support, hoping they would tell him what he wanted—what he needed—so desperately to hear. An hour later, he jumped in his car and drove to Sergio's, unannounced.

Sergio was surprised but ecstatic to see him. Dexter grabbed him and embraced him longer and tighter than he ever had, caressing his back, reassuring Sergio that everything would be all right. When Dexter released him, neither of them knew what to say, each of them trying to be brave for the other.

Sergio explained to Dexter that his treating physician, Dr. Marc Lieberman, had prescribed a medication for the KS. Alpha interferon. Sergio had been instructed by the doctor to inject himself with this cancer-battling fluid each night to suppress the one lesion on his back and to prevent the appearance of others. Sergio had been given an instructional videocassette to learn how to properly administer it. He and Dexter stripped down to their undies and lay in bed together watching the tape, which encouraged the user to teach the method to at least one other person. Dexter was eager to learn. When the tape finished, they lay in each other's arms, Dexter's ear pressed against Sergio's chest, listening to his heart beat, his tainted blood pump and circulate, imagining the virus ticking inside his body on a search-and-destroy mission to conquer Sergio's T-cells.

"Dex?"

"What, *Serge?*" Dexter said, emphatically abridging Sergio's name in an effort to humor him.

"This is so weird, you know. I never thought I'd ever be stricken with a terminal illness. I guess it's the 'it-happens-to-the-other-guy' syndrome. And yet, I think I know when I got the virus."

"You do?"

"Yeah."

"How?"

"It's kind of like, when a woman knows the moment she's been impregnated, the precise moment of conception. It was kind of like that. It happened on Fire Island, I'm sure of it."

"I was absolutely shocked to learn I was HIV-positive," Dexter said. "I'd never been terribly promiscuous. Well, maybe sometimes. But I almost never had intercourse that wasn't 'safe sex,' even though there wasn't a term for it at the time. I just think full intercourse is such an intimate act, I couldn't do it with just anybody. I never went to the baths and stuff like that. So when the volunteer at the health center told me, I was shocked. I thought they'd given me the wrong results."

"I'm the first person I know to get AIDS," Sergio admitted, following a long, piercing silence, as he stared blankly, fixedly at the ceiling.

"You're kidding?"

"No, I'm not."

"Aren't any of your friends even HIV-positive?"

"I don't have any...any gay friends."

"You don't? Not even one?"

"Only you and Dante, my ex-lover."

"Why's that?" Dexter said, shocked, not knowing what to make of this.

"It's a long story," Sergio sighed. "I'll tell you all about it someday."

Dexter tried to imagine what it would be like to be gay and not have any gay friends outside former and present lovers. And he attempted to fathom what it was like not to know anyone who'd contracted the plague and died from it. Younger gay men, twenty-something, he could understand. But Sergio was forty-three. An anomaly. He couldn't wait to hear Sergio's "long story." Dexter was thirty-five and he'd known plenty who'd perished. In some twisted way, he envied Sergio.

"You know what, Dex?"

"What, Serge?"

"You're the best thing that's ever happened to me."

"Am I?"

"Yes, you are. You don't know what it means to me to have you here at this moment."

Dexter mentally prepped himself for the days, weeks, months ahead. He thrived on challenge; ate it for breakfast. And Sergio was nothing if he wasn't a challenge. Dexter watched as Sergio eased out of bed, grabbed his Sony Walkman, and popped an audio-cassette into it. Untangling the earphones, he plugged one into his ear, one into Dexter's, pushed the PLAY button, scooped Dexter up in his arms, and closed his eyes. Dexter's ears filled with the backdrop of ocean waves breaking and crashing on the shore, punctuated by a soothing, hypnotic voice-over.

"For the next sixty minutes," the voice-over said, "we're going to learn how to love ourselves. The most important thing in your life beginning now and forever is to love yourself, to embrace your alternative lifestyle, to love and embrace your homosexuality…"

Dexter's thoughts drifted from the tape to the disturbing advice he'd received from the Greek chorus of friends over the telephone a few hours before.

Are you crazy?! And you're gonna stay with him?

It's best to bail out now. Save yourself the grief, honey. And there will be grief. Nobody would blame you if you left him. And fuck 'em if they did!

Oh, yeah, I just remembered I'm talking to a writer. To achieve art, I guess you're supposed to suffer…

Dexter would show them, the faithless. He couldn't put his finger on it, but something, he didn't know what exactly, but something, a panacea, a cure, a fucking miracle, whatever, whatever it took, something was going to save Sergio. Dexter hoped Sergio had enough time left so that it, whatever it was, would reveal itself, show itself to them. He and Sergio just had to be patient. They just had to learn how to hurry up and wait.

Sunday night, Dexter and Sergio were driving to a dinner party at the home of Dexter's friend, a costume designer. The guests were a film producer, a former *Saturday Night Live* actress-comedienne, and a casting director. Dexter and Sergio had stopped by the bank's automatic teller and were headed for the supermarket to purchase flowers and wine.

"As a writer, what do you want to say through your art?" Sergio asked, ever the challenging inquisitor.

"That's a loaded question," Dexter replied with a chuckle. "There's a lot I want to say in my work. Aside from exploring the human condition in general, there are things I want to say about the African-American and gay experience in this country."

"I really envy you that," Sergio said. "I admire *and* envy you."

"What? Why?"

"Because you can be so...so open...so honest in your work...as a gay man, I mean."

"You think so?"

"I know so. I'm your biggest fan. And I don't think I could ever be that open and honest."

"You couldn't?"

"I'm working on it. Really, I am. That's part of why I love you, Dex, and respect you so much. I'm trying to learn from you, trying to learn to love and accept myself wholeheartedly, unconditionally, the way you love and accept yourself."

"I'm touched," Dexter replied, and blushed. "I don't know what to say."

"Dex, you're like a burst of light invading the twenty years of darkness I've been living in. How's that for metaphor?"

"Maybe you should write."

"Is your art fueled by anger?"

"Of course. That's true of most artists, period; especially those of color. There're still hundreds of stories in Hollywood that haven't been told."

"Such as?"

"Well, like what it means to grow up a black, gay male in America—"

"Didn't you deal with that in your first film?"

"Only somewhat, because it had to be made digestible for a mainstream audience. Besides, it's only one story."

"Just on a daily basis," Sergio said, sliding into his familiar role of devil's advocate, "what angers you?"

"Lots of things. Subtle things. And nothing much is subtle anymore. Like whenever we eat out, have you noticed that the waiter always talks directly to you to present the wine list and the day's special, never to me, as if I weren't even there? Or that he invariably gives the check to you and never to me? Or when I'm walking down the street behind a white woman and she clutches her bag or crosses the street, or if I happen to—"

"But wait, Dex. You can't take that personally. I mean, these women are responding from an unfounded but ingrained fear of black men that is perpetuated by the media and society—"

"What do you mean, 'Don't take it personally'?" Dexter's head instantly grew hot, repressing the words that were stuck in his throat. Here it comes, Dexter thought.

"Because their fear has nothing to do with you personally, Dex—"

"I don't care. I'm a hypersensitive man and when women or children react that way to me it hurts and angers me. There've been times when I was conservatively dressed in a suit and tie, carrying two giant bags of groceries, and they're still scared. That's just pure American racism—"

"But I think you've got to—"

"I don't care what you think, Serge. What do you know about it? Has it ever happened to you?"

Now it was out. Dexter had not meant to turn surly on Sergio, but he'd grown impatient with nonblack people instructing him as to how he should feel—or how he shouldn't feel—about racism. Sergio, moving through the United States of America with an olive complexion, sandy hair, and blue eyes, could not possibly have walked the same pot-holed roads of bigotry as had Dexter. Dexter had noticed that although Sergio identified himself as Latino and proudly and vehemently related to that side of his racial heritage, and considered himself a Mexican first and foremost, perhaps because he had been born and raised in Mexico, Dexter also observed that Sergio utilized his Anglo heritage when it was convenient, when it most benefited him—namely out in public, where people never thought he was Mexican, but always considered him to be white. And though Sergio was as culturally Latino-identified as Dexter was black-identified, just who the hell was Sergio to tell him how to feel, when Dexter had grown up smelling, tasting, breathing, swallowing, and gagging on racism since he had fallen out of the womb.

Dexter, who was driving, pulled the cherry red BMW convertible into Lucky's parking lot. He opened the door and noticed Sergio wasn't getting out.

"You coming?"

"No," Sergio said gruffly, suppressing a cough, refusing to face Dexter.

"Why not?"

"I'm really pissed at you."

"For what?"

"You know what."

Dexter slammed the door shut and entered the supermarket alone. Storming up and down the aisles, he searched for the wine section, though he knew where it was. Distracted by Sergio's stinging words, which echoed in his head, Dexter realized and accepted that they were having their first fight. But the last thing Dexter wanted was to attend this dinner party engaged in a cold war with Sergio. He had been looking forward to showing off Sergio to friends of his Sergio had never met. Only around Dexter's friends, gay or straight, could they be open and honest about their relationship. Among Sergio's friends, all of whom were hetero, it was simply out of the question.

As Dexter drove out of the parking lot, thinking of ways to reconcile without compromising himself, Sergio beat him to it.

"Let's have this out and settle it before we get to the party, okay?" Sergio suggested.

"Absolutely."

"Dex, don't you ever tell me I don't know about racism. You don't have to be black to experience it, you know—"

"I didn't say you had to—"

"You said I didn't know anything about it—"

"You don't!"

"For your information, I caught a lot of shit about being Mexican, especially in the lily white neighborhood where I grew up in Seattle. And I've had my ass kicked by black guys because I'm white. So, don't tell me—"

"I'm not denying you that, Serge. I'm only saying that to be black and male in this country is the lowest level on the totem pole. And you know it's true. Your racist experiences are not comparable to mine. I have to deal with racism every day of my life—"

"I think you're a little too angry—"

"People like you, who enjoy every racial and societal privilege there is, always think people like me are too angry—"

"All right, already!"

"Okay, then!"

Then silence befell them, filled with animated breathing, Dexter barely able to concentrate on the traffic. Dexter switched on the radio to drown out the silence and Sergio switched it off. Ten minutes later,

Sergio reached out and groped for Dexter's fingers wrapped around the stick shift.

"Friends?" Sergio said.

"Sure."

"Now," Sergio said, coughing, "we can go to the dinner party and have a great time."

What a fresh approach to fighting, Dexter thought. During Dexter's six-year live-in relationship with his ex-lover Pietro, they had never settled an argument as quickly and neatly. Chronically uncommunicative, Pietro thrived on silence and holding grudges whether they were in public, around friends, or not. And here was another kind of man, who was in touch with his feelings, and who wanted to settle a disagreement and get on with the business of communication. Gosh, Dexter thought, this man is even great at fighting and resolving issues. What a guy.

When the door opened, the first things Dexter and Sergio noticed were two cats, one Persian, the other calico, standing on top of the dining-room table, sniffing around the plates, glasses, and eating utensils. As Dexter introduced Harlan the host to Sergio, and handed Harlan the flowers and the bottle of wine, he saw that Sergio's face had turned white. Sergio acted graciously until Harlan walked away.

"Dex, I have to speak to you privately," Sergio said with urgency. They walked into a bedroom, as Dexter waved and bade distant hellos to the guests. He had no idea why Sergio was acting so strangely. In the forty-five seconds it took them to get to Harlan's bedroom in the back of the house, Dexter assumed that one of Sergio's ex-lovers, or a past trick, was among the dinner guests, which could have made for an uncomfortable, awkward evening.

"What's wrong, honey?"

"Dex, I'm sorry, but I can't eat here."

"You can't? Why not?"

"Because Harlan has cats."

"Cats? Yeah?"

"You know: toxoplasmosis?"

"Oh, my God!" Dexter said. "I never thought of that."

"What're we going to tell your friend?"

"I don't know. Let's think. Quick."

"I know what. I'll tell him I'm not feeling well."

"That doesn't sound too believable. And this guy's real sensitive about people liking his food. He's Jewish, so he can be a real Yiddisha mama about how he's been slaving over the kitchen pots for the last two days without sleep."

They walked back into the living room, where Dexter introduced Sergio to the guests. Dexter could barely remember everyone's name, though he knew them well. For the longest time, Dexter was preoccupied with what alibi they could offer Harlan. After the introductions, Dexter asked to speak privately with Sergio.

"How about if we tell him the truth?" Dexter said.

"I don't care. I still can't eat here."

"Well, maybe Harlan will have some ideas."

"I just can't eat here when it's endangering my health. I hope you understand."

"Totally. Let me call him."

Dexter called Harlan into the bedroom and shut the door.

"Harlan, we have a problem."

"What is it?" Harlan said, his eyebrows arched, a serving fork in one hand, wiping the other on his chef's apron. "Is everything all right?"

"Well," Dexter began, "Sergio can't eat here tonight."

"Why not?"

"Because you have cats...and—"

"I have a compromised immune system," Sergio interrupted.

"Compromised immune system?" Harlan said. "Okay, I've got a great idea. How about we all speak English?" Harlan suggested, always the joker.

"Sergio has AIDS," Dexter said.

"And?" Harlan said.

"Cats have toxoplasmosis," Sergio said.

"Which is?" Harlan snapped his fingers repeatedly. "English, honey, English."

"Which is a parasite that lives in their feces," Sergio said. "It's in their litter box and on their feet and paws and ultimately, it could make me very sick, even kill me."

"Especially since the cats are hanging around the place settings," Dexter said, wondering what the hell behooved people to allow their animals around places where they ate.

"I got an idea," Harlan offered. "How about if I sterilize your plate and eating utensils. Would that be better?"

"Sterilize them how?" Sergio asked.

"I'll pour boiling water over everything you use. How's that?"

Dexter didn't think Sergio would go for it. He looked at Sergio, waiting for a response. Sergio shrugged his shoulders hesitantly.

"Yeah, that'll be okay, I guess."

"Great! I'm so glad we solved that problem," Harlan said. "I mean, after all, my darlings, I've been slaving over the kitchen pots for the last two days without so much as a nap." He turned to leave the room. "Dinner in five minutes, boys!"

"See," Dexter said. "See what can happen when you're just honest?"

Sergio took Dexter's hand in his, kissed his knuckles, and led him back into the living room to mingle with the guests.

Canaan Parker

■ ■ ■

[1954–]

NEW YORK–BORN NOVELIST CANAAN PARKER GREW UP IN EAST Harlem. Following graduation from Williams College and Harvard University, he worked for the Legal Aid Society and the National Conference of Black Lawyers, where he helped draft a series of motions leading to the release of Black Panther Assata Shakur from solitary confinement. Parker also served on the Steering Committee of the Publishing Triangle, a lesbian and gay advocacy group, and was advertising director and webmaster for Outmusic. As an activist with Queer Nation, in 1992 he successfully lobbied then New York City Commissioner Mark Green to resolve a rash of gay-bashings in Chelsea. Most recently, the author served on the Advisory Committee on Gay Affairs to Manhattan Borough President C. Virginia Fields.

Parker began writing fiction in 1990 while convalescing from an illness, and by 1992 his first novel, *The Color of Trees,* was published. He followed with *Skydaddy* in 1997. His writing also appears in *Flesh and the Word 4, We Must Love Each Other or Die: The Live and Loves of Larry Kramer,* and *Lambda Book Report.*

Set in the 1960s, an era of racial integration during which the author himself came of age, *The Color of Trees* opens with Peter, an African American teenager from Harlem, having received a scholarship to attend a prestigious upstate boarding school. He attempts to navigate the racial exclusivity of the predominately white student body population—as well as deal with his growing awareness of his sexual attraction to T. J., a rambunctious white classmate.

It was obvious Ashley Downer didn't like me. Perhaps he needed someone on the corridor to have a lower status than he did. Or maybe he thought making me a target would take the pressure off him for being the class nerd.

He was too shrewd to make race the issue, at least not explicitly. My hallmates wouldn't have gone along with that. Ashley made it a question of money.

"When are you going to pay me the money you owe me, Givens?"

"I beg your pardon, Ashley?" I said.

"I'm subsidizing your scholarship. Everyone on this corridor is. What are you going to do for us in return?"

Being fourteen years old, I'd rarely been confronted with such direct hostility. I'd endured enough physical threats, of course—from the boy in fourth grade who tried to steal my coat, or the three girls in junior high who tried to take my bus pass every month. But Ashley's tactics caught me off guard.

"I think you should be working in the kitchen. Or mopping the floors. You should make up our beds every morning. It's only fair. My father is paying your tuition. All of our fathers are."

We were sitting in the Common Room on Saturday. It had been a pleasant winter afternoon, quiet and cozy, until Ashley started his tirade. Barrett Granger was there, and Kent Mason and Captain Zero. T. J. was sitting in the corner reading, one of the few times I'd ever seen him quiet.

"Say something, Givens! If you had any decency, you'd see I was right. You come all the way out here from Harlem to go to our school, and you refuse to pay your share."

"Calm down, Frogger," said Captain Zero.

"Ribbit," said Kent Mason behind Ashley's back.

"I'm serious. Don't you know what the school could do with all that scholarship money? They could hire maids. They could build a new hockey rink." Ashley turned towards Kent Mason. "I don't know about your family, Mason, but I have a maid at home. Why should I have to clean up here when there are scholarship students?"

I couldn't think of what to say. I looked around the room for support.

"I think working in the kitchen is fair for scholarship students," said Barrett.

"You guys could probably cook better," laughed Captain Zero.

"That's right. And if the Headmaster won't impose it, you should volunteer to clean our rooms. We should make it corridor policy," said Ashley.

"Frog, why don't you go lay some eggs under a rock somewhere?" T. J. interrupted. Ashley ignored him and turned his back. "Just because your father is on the board of trustees—"

"That's right. He is. And I'm going to propose it to him." Ashley turned towards me and spoke impersonally. "It's for your own good. So that you don't become confused. I've noticed lately that you've been acting confused about your background. As though you were one of us. You aren't, you know. I'm just being truthful. Your confusion could cause you problems in life."

Ashley sent a memo to the Headmaster threatening to complain to his father. The mood of the campus changed in the following days. I didn't speak to any white student. The eleven black students and the one Native American student on scholarship showed the pressure. We sat together in the cafeteria, in chapel, and in the library. Keith Hanson said we should all withdraw if the Headmaster implemented Downer's proposal. I felt awful at the thought of being forced to return home. Everywhere I went I felt like an outsider. Ashley, through his pure viciousness, received more respect from the Third Form than before. On the corridor, he glared at me with a sullen malice.

Mr. Chase called a meeting in his study with the scholarship students that Friday. He told us Briarwood was an egalitarian society, and could well afford its scholarship program, but could not afford to distract any of its students from their academic duties. Therefore no one would be required to work in the kitchen. He delivered his brief address in his usual quivering tones, beaming with beneficence as though he, at that moment, embodied the school's traditions of charity and grace. "Any questions?" he asked, smiling and quavering in his chair. Keith asked if Mr. Chase had discussed the issue with the trustees. "It's not a decision for the trustees," answered Mr. Chase.

"What about Downer's father?" asked Keith.

"I've spoken with Mr. Downer. As I said, this is my decision. Any other questions?"

When no one answered, Mr. Chase thanked us and then left the room. The twelve of us filed out of the study slowly.

"It's a good thing. I would have never stood for that," said Keith.

"It wouldn't have been that big a deal. A few nights in the kitchen," I said.

"It would have set us all apart. Waiting on them hand and foot. How could you face them in class as their servants?"

"It's over, Keith. We won."

"We'll never win from this side, brother. It's like my brother told me. 'They may let you *in,* but they will never let you *win.*'"

That night in chapel, Keith and I sat together in the choir pews at the front of the hall. There were two sets of pews that faced each other, reserved for the Second and Third Forms. After each service, the lower classes filed out of the choir pews in pairs and walked down the center aisle, leading out the congregation. Of all the people for me to walk out with tonight, there was Ashley Downer. I grimaced and hesitated. Keith gave me a shove, and I turned around to see him smirking. Ashley's face was afire. We walked stiffly down the aisle together. Behind me, barely audibly, I could hear Keith laughing in his exaggerated baritone, "Heh, heh, heh. Heh, heh, heh."

The next Saturday we were all back in the Common Room again. Ashley was stewing in a moody funk. He wouldn't just accept Mr. Chase's decision. He told me that his father would bring up the matter at the next trustees' meeting, along with a general review of the scholarship program. His eyes were beady and he looked pale, almost ill, as he spoke, shivering with hostility. "If I have my way, the whole scholarship program will be dumped."

"Fuck you, Downer," I said, having had enough.

"Fuck you, Givens."

"No, fuck you, Frog," T. J. jumped in.

"Fuck you, T. J. I'm sick of you butting into my business. Leave me alone, dammit!"

Just then Mr. Bennett came into the Common Room. "Cut out the swearing! My wife is right across the hall." T. J. apologized, and Ashley rushed out of the room.

One day the following week, T. J. caught up to me while I was crossing the quad going to class.

"I know how to nail Downer," he said.

"How?"

"That nasty little fuck. We should waste his ass."

"He's just doing it 'cause you turned him into the school clown."

"I'm no worse to him than anybody else."

"How are you going to nail him?"

"His roommate is going away this weekend."

"Acheson?"

"Make sure Acheson's going away, and let me know if he changes his plans."

Gary Acheson flew to Vail for the weekend, which meant that Ashley Downer would be alone in his room on Friday night. I made sure of this, and reported back to T. J. as he'd asked. "Fine," he said. I wondered what he had planned.

T. J.'s room was strategically located right next door to Ashley's. Perhaps he was planting some kind of booby trap.

Or blackmail? I would have gone along with anything to get Ashley off my back.

On Saturday afternoon, T. J. came into my room carrying a micro-cassette recorder.

"Listen to this."

"Oooh, Daddy. Oooh, Daddy, I'm sorry."

"What the hell is that?"

"Just listen, Givens."

"Ooooh, Daddy. I'm sorry. I'm sorry, Daddy."

"Are those bedsprings in the background?"

"Yep."

"Is that Downer?"

"No, it's Mae West, genius," T. J. said. "Of course, it's Downer."

"Adams, I swear you are psychotic."

"I told you I'd nail that amphibian fuckface."

"What do we do now?"

"If you can't figure that out, you really are retarded." T. J. removed the cassette from the recorder and handed it to me. "Happy anniversary, darling," he said, and went out the room.

A day later Ashley Downer received a note in his mailbox. The note read, "I'm sorry, Daddy. (Ribbit) I'm sorry for sending you that letter. I'm sorry you found out my little secret. I'm sorry, Daddy (Ribbit)." We didn't hear any more of Ashley's vaunted influence with his father the school trustee.

Part of me felt sorry for Ashley, even though he was a snob and a bigot. I mentioned this to Keith, and he looked at me in amazement. "People like Downer are our enemy," he exclaimed. I knew he was right, but I just couldn't find an emotion of anger or hatred inside of me.

I ran into Ashley one afternoon in downtown Green River. He was walking alone along the road, headed back towards school. I was headed in the opposite direction. He was staring at the ground, absorbed in his thoughts. I don't think he even saw me. His glasses were sitting lopsided on his face. He had on a jacket and tie, and one of his shirttails was hanging out. As he walked by me, across the road, I felt oddly connected with him, as though somehow in our souls we were alike, except that I was the more fortunate.

I think that was the reason I couldn't passionately hate Ashley. We really were alike. We were both kind of weird, quiet, bookish kids. The only difference between us was race. It would have been hard for a black kid to be labelled a nerd in a mostly white school. But if I had been white, I was sure T. J. would have tortured me just as he had the Frog; or if I'd gone to an all-black school, I would have been the unpopular outcast—especially since I didn't date girls. At Briarwood I was free to hide behind the indifference of my white schoolmates. No one was looking very hard at me. And so I didn't have to look very hard at myself.

Ashley must have suspected T. J. or me of sending the note, but he never showed any interest in revenge. He started behaving out of sorts—bewildered and lost. He didn't speak much to anyone. Gary Acheson told us Ashley had become depressed. Even T. J. stopped teasing him and calling him Frog.

Later I asked T. J. how he had bugged Ashley.

"Walkie-talkies," he said. He pulled out his set of army surplus hand radios from under his bed. "I set one to send and planted it under Gary's pillow. Then I just recorded from my radio."

"But how did you know?"

His eyes flickered suspiciously. "Safe guess," he said in a near whisper.

T. J. and I became friends after he helped me nail Ashley Downer. I couldn't very well stay rude to him after that. And I was starting to feel like a hypocrite for shunning him but playing Peeping Tom every chance I got. After all, T. J. wasn't wrong. He was just too obvious. And not just to me. His roommate Kent Mason was spreading rumors that T. J. was queer.

Of course, I had my doubts about Kent Mason, too. When Billy Green was sitting naked on the training table in the gymnasium, taping his ankles for hockey practice, Kent walked by the doorway and looked in. I swore his eyes almost popped out of his head.

One night T. J. came running out of the bathroom into my room, completely naked and dripping wet. He'd been having a water fight with Gary Acheson. My roommate Barrett laughed nervously and asked T. J. what he and Acheson were doing in the bathroom.

"Having sex!" T. J. exclaimed. Barrett just shook his head and muttered, "Jesus, Adams." I started laughing, and T. J. smiled at me, his manic black-brown eye dots twinkling under his mop of soaked hair. "What are you laughing at, Givens?" he said. He ran his fingers through his hair and spattered drops of water in my face. Then he turned and ran back into the bathroom.

"What a nut," I said to Barrett, and for the only time in the year we roomed together, we smiled.

I don't think T. J. realized what he was doing, any more than I realized how conspicuous I was when I stared at his dick by the urinals. He was just a very horny kid, his sex exploding out of him. T. J. didn't believe in self-control and he didn't believe in inhibitions. Being his friend meant I had to deal with his strange personal view of life and of the world.

Privacy meant nothing to T. J. The idea of personal barriers was as useless to him as clothing. Just by talking to him, I opened myself to a barrage of intrusions across my personal space. My appearance was now within his jurisdiction: he repeatedly suggested I grow my hair like his favorite rock star, Jimi Hendrix. "I thought you were going to grow a big afro?" he kept asking me, and I winced at the thought of myself in Jimi's frazzled, byzantine hairstyle. He could be stunningly blunt about my personal habits: "Givens, quit beating off in the shower," he hollered at me one morning. "You're wasting all the hot water."

I never saw T. J. ignore anyone, or leave anyone alone when they asked. His own nerves were radically exposed, and he couldn't abide docility in anyone else; we all had to join him in his hyperactive universe. Being quiet, egg-headed, and black, I especially piqued his curiosity, rivalling the Frog as a target of his exploratory attentions. T. J. was Dr. Frankenstein, and I and my responses were the subject of his experiments. All he wanted was to prod and test me, to piss me off or to make me laugh; to hear my jokes (few, far between, and usually not worth the wait), my problems (multitudinous), my sexual exploits (imaginary). To T. J. I was just another soul stranded on the earth, a kindred human, and therefore an opportunity for something interesting to happen.

We started to walk together to class almost every day. Since T. J. and I were both on honors, we could take morning study hall in our rooms instead of the library. Most mornings we were alone in the dormitory.

"Who's your favorite master?" he asked me one morning.

"I guess Mr. Craig," I said.

"I think Mr. Press is cool." Sanford Press was the varsity football coach, as well as our ancient history teacher and school dean. He was a big man, two hundred pounds and six feet tall, with a broad, heavy jaw and a grayish brown crew cut. It was rumored that Mr. Press had once gone through tryouts in a real pro football training camp.

"Mr. Press?" I said doubtfully. "You would pick Press."

"What's wrong with Press?"

"The Dean of Students? What if he has to kick you out?"

T. J. paused and thought. "Press would never kick me out."

"Why not?"

"He just wouldn't."

I thought of the time I'd seen Dean Press walking behind the chapel with T. J., his arm around T. J.'s shoulder. I frowned and sat up on my bed.

"You suck up to him in ancient history class," I said with a bitterness that surprised me.

"I'd like to suck up to his daughter," T. J. said. Lisa Press was a student at Trinity and spent her weekends at home with her parents. She was thin and hipless, with crystalline features and eyes that shone like blue frost in contrast to her short, black hair. More than once I had mistaken her, at a distance, for a boy.

"Let's head back to class," I said.

"Wait a minute. I have to take a piss."

"I'll come with you."

In the bathroom I sat on the sink while T. J. urinated. I looked, and his penis swelled. He turned and smiled at me casually, as if nothing were strange. "You could come home with me sometime," he said. "We could spend a weekend at my house." In the late spring of our Third Form year T. J. meant business, while I was still just a silly voyeur.

April Sinclair

■ ■ ■

[1954–]

HAVING GROWN UP ON CHICAGO'S SOUTH SIDE DURING THE
height of the civil rights era may account for novelist April Sinclair's
activist origins, if not also the period settings that characterize her
fiction. Sinclair first became involved in community issues while
studying at West Illinois University. Following graduation, the author
moved to California, where she served as director of a San Francisco
Bay Area food bank and worked with youth programs. It was while living amid the cultural diversity of Oakland that Sinclair began giving
readings of her first novel, *Coffee Will Make You Black,* which consisted
then of only twenty pages. Her storytelling talents, combined with an
outstanding gift for humor, won rave receptions from audiences who
encouraged her toward completion of the book. In fact, news of
these reportedly hilarious readings finally reached a literary agent,
who contacted the author and sold the unfinished manuscript to a
publisher.

The best-selling *Coffee Will Make You Black* (1994) is a comic
coming-of-age story about Jean "Stevie" Stevenson, a young African
American woman discovering political and sexual self-awareness during the cultural tumult of the 1960s. The major success of *Coffee Will
Make You Black* inspired its sequel, *Ain't Gonna Be the Same Fool Twice*
(1996), in which Stevie becomes sexually active in the 1970s. With lesbian themes also appearing in Sinclair's third novel, *I Left My Back Door
Open* (1999), the self-identified bisexual author is one of the most
popular African American authors publishing queer-oriented fiction
today.

In this selection from *Coffee Will Make You Black,* Stevie has reached a sexual crossroads, where erotic fantasies involving Miss Horn, the white high school nurse, surpass her cooling affections for boyfriend Sean. As with much of Sinclair's writing, racial identity complicates issues of sexual understanding, to comic ends.

from Coffee Will Make You Black

[1994]

Me and Carla were walking to school. We had just decided she should tell her new boyfriend, Ivory, to buy her the Temptations' and Smokey Robinson and the Miracles' new albums for her birthday. Carla's mother had given her a choice between a new stereo and a birthday party after Carla told her about my new box. She'd chosen the stereo. Carla finally had her room to herself. Marla and Sharla had both moved in with their boyfriends. They each had a girl and a boy now, but neither was married.

"There's Nurse Horn's car, the blue one," I said, pointing as we passed the faculty parking lot. "Carla, don't you think Mustangs are hot?"

"I already done told you that I want me a red Firebird. And you done showed me Nurse Horn's stupid car before."

"Well, have you checked out Nurse Horn's new pants uniform? And have you seen her new white earth shoes?"

"Stevie, I don't give a flying fuck about Nurse Horn or her car or her uniform! Do you hear me?"

"Dog, Carla, why you got to curse?"

"Cause you should be trippin' on the prom, steada her white ass, that's why."

"I *am* trippin' on the prom."

"So, when you gon get your dress? Don't wait till the last minute now."

"Carla, the prom is still almost two months away."

"I thought you said your auntie was taking you shopping?"

"She is, we're going Clean-Up Week to Carson's. My Aunt Sheila's got a charge there."

"Carson Pirie Scott, go 'head, girl!" Carla gave me five. "Who woulda thought you would pull a senior? Stevie, I'm jealous, girl; you should be so excited!"

"I am excited, okay?"

"Okay. So now, what the fuck are earth shoes?"

"I like the way you dribble," Sean teased me as I headed down the alley behind his house later that day. I jumped up, dripping with sweat, and made my basket. Sean grabbed the ball, slam dunking it and swinging on the rim of the hoop outside his garage door.

"It's getting late," I said, glancing up at the purple sky. The wind was kicking, but it felt good after working up a sweat. I breathed in the cool night air mixed with sweet-smelling funk. Yeah, we were sweaty, but neither of us stunk, I told myself.

Sean held me close as we snuggled, lying down in the back seat of his brother's '63 Buick in front of his house.

"Stevie, I like that you can shoot some hoops."

"Most girls wouldn't be into it, huh?"

"No, but I'm glad you're different."

"You are?"

"Yeah, I wasn't looking for the average bear."

"Me either, Sean."

"Stevie, I feel like this English writer Miss Porter told us about in class. I can't remember the dude's name, but anyway, he was at a dinner party and he heard this woman say she didn't care for any gravy. The writer dude said, 'Madam, I've been searching my whole life for someone who dislikes gravy. Let's swear eternal friendship.'"

"So I take it you don't like gravy?" I asked, smiling.

"Not really. What about you?"

"I'm not crazy about it either. But I can sho go for some pan drippings."

"I heard that!" Sean laughed.

"So, Stevie, how come you never went out for the girls' basketball team?"

"I don't know, I guess I got into the Drama Club and then I got on the newspaper this year, you know." I looked into Sean's dark brown eyes. "It really wouldn't bother you to have a girlfriend on the basketball team?"

"No, not so long as she was all woman off the court." Sean leaned over and covered my mouth with his luscious lips. I liked the taste of his tongue. I wondered what Sean would think if he knew that I day-dreamed about Nurse Horn more than him—that my favorite daydream was of Nurse Horn rescuing me from drowning and giving me mouth-to-mouth resuscitation. And sometimes I just remembered Nurse Horn hugging me against her terry-cloth bathrobe, telling me that I had potential.

I kissed Sean back, trying my best to prove to him that I was definitely all woman. Sean's wet tongue teased my ear, sending shivers through my body.

"Sean," I whispered, "I like the way you dribble too, on and off the court."

Sean pressed against me and ran his fingers through my natural. I could feel his thing through my jeans. I knew that I couldn't allow myself to get too excited. Mama said that most boys won't go any farther than you let them. "It's up to you not to let them," she'd warned. I didn't stop Sean from reaching under my T-shirt and squeezing my breasts through my bra. I didn't want him to turn off completely. My job was to keep Sean interested without going all the way.

Sean ran his hand up and down my thighs. I couldn't help but feel excited. I held my breath while he tugged at my zipper.

"No, Sean, not here," I said, as he stroked my panties. "Anybody could come by and see us."

I sat up and Sean pulled his hand away and glanced around the deserted street.

"Stevie, I couldn't help it," Sean said hoarsely. "I just got really turned on. You said, Not here, well where? We've been going together six months."

"I don't know, Sean. Maybe I'm afraid that once I do it you won't respect me anymore."

"Stevie, I respect the hell outta you now and giving yourself to me could never change that."

"I don't want to end up like Patrice, having to go to a school for unwed mothers. Did you know that by the time she found out she was pregnant Yusef was already going with Gail?"

"Stevie, Yusef Brown always was a dog."

"Well, I tried to tell her that, but Patrice wouldn't listen."

"All Yusef does is hang out on the corner and sell weed." Sean sighed. "But, Stevie, not all brothers are about nothing. If I messed a girl up, I'd stand by her."

"But, Sean, there's just no way I could get pregnant. It would kill my parents. They're counting on me. And Mrs. Stuart says, with my grades, even if my SAT scores come back average, I can still get a college scholarship. She says our time has come. I couldn't face her if I messed up."

Sean held my hand. "I heard that, hey, I'm proud of you, baby. I don't want to be a daddy right now, either. I'm going to Chicago State in the fall, remember? I've got dreams, too."

"Thanks," I whispered in Sean's ear.

"For what?"

"For understanding."

"Oh."

The next morning me and Carla sat on the school's stone steps and faced a row of fudge-colored buildings. Carla held her big sweater together with one hand as she took a drag off her cigarette. I glanced up at the cloudy morning sky.

"So finish telling me about you and Seanny last night."

"Like I told you, Carla, I felt his thing up against me. And he touched me through my panties."

"And then what happened?"

"I told him to stop."

"You told him to stop! Why?"

"You know why, because I'm scared. I can't come up pregnant." I tightened the belt on my rain-shine coat. "I finally ended up giving Sean a hand job last night."

"Again!" Carla groaned, "I don't see why you don't just get on the pill like somebody with some sense."

I shrugged. We'd had this conversation before.

"Stevie, I know Sean is patient, but a man has needs, if you know what I mean."

"Yeah, I know what you mean."

"A man is only willing to be frustrated for so long, before he starts looking for a new prom date. Get my drift?"

"Carla, you don't understand. Sean is different."

Carla blew out smoke. "He ain't that damn different. He still a man. After a while them milkshakes begin to add up. Then it's payback time," Carla added.

"Carla, I wish it didn't have to hurt. It's hard to get excited over something painful."

"It don't be hurtin' no worser than bad cramps. You done felt them before."

"I don't look forward to cramps, Carla."

"Stevie, I got a idea. You smoke you a joint and do it when you high." Carla exhaled. "You will be feeling no pain then."

I couldn't help but raise my eyebrows. "Carla, you get high now?"

"Damn, Stevie, you lookin' at me like I said I shot heroin or some shit like that. It's just a little weed."

"You've smoked marijuana before! I can't believe you never told me."

"Look, I've only done it a few times, once with my sisters and twice with Ivory."

Ivory was Carla's fine yellow nigga, as she put it. He was tall, with a big 'fro, and his rap had been so powerful that he'd stolen her away from Tyrone. Me and Mama had run into Carla and Ivory in Kmart. Mama had taken one look at his lime-colored clothes and big hat and decided Ivory was about nothing. I had finally managed to convince Mama that Ivory's pants were avocado, but she still insisted that the "negro" was no good.

"Well, how was it?"

"It was cool, you get the munchies, you wanna eat a bunch of shit. And shit be funnier than hell."

"Wow, did you do it with Ivory when you were high?"

"Yeah," Carla exhaled.

"How was it?"

"Hot! Ain't nothing better than being high as a kite and getting it at the same time."

I didn't know what to say. I'd never been high and I'd never gotten it. I tried to picture it in my mind as the bell rang.

We were in gym class, jumping over a statue of a horse. Miss Bryant had a girl standing on either side of the horse, just in case. I stood in the line waiting to take my turn. I was still tripping on what Carla had said earlier. I wondered how it felt to be high. I had never even been tipsy. I had drunk a few sips of beer when they'd passed around a can on the bus after the homecoming game last year. That had been it. Maybe I should go ahead and do it with Sean. Carla said it wouldn't hurt if I was high. Maybe a glass of wine would be enough. Who knows? I might even like it.

I balled my fists and ran toward the horse. I grabbed each side of the saddle and lifted both of my feet to clear it.

"Jean, are you all right?"

When I stopped seeing stars, I recognized Miss Bryant's thin, worried walnut-colored face.

"Girl, your feet got caught, you hit your head up underneath on that metal part." I heard Tanya's voice. The group of brown faces and blue gym suits were all one blur. My head was swimming.

"Jean, can you walk to the nurse's office, or do you need for me to send for Miss Horn?"

I looked up from the thick cotton mat, unsure where my legs were.

"She looks monked up."

"Maybe her brain is damaged, huh, Miss Bryant?"

"She should sue the school."

"You mean the Board of Education, girl."

"Quiet, girls."

"Miss Bryant, you want me to go get Nurse Horn?"

"Yes, Rosita, ask her to come right away."

I heard footsteps and looked up.

I thought I had died and gone to heaven. Nurse Horn looked like one of the angels on the stained-glass window at my church. She felt the bump on my forehead and frowned. She explained, that, no, I hadn't lost my memory like the dude on TV. There were some sighs of disappointment and this one fool kept asking me what I'd eaten for breakfast. "Raisin Bran," I answered, as Nurse Horn put her arm around my shoulder and walked me out of the gym.

The cot had never felt more comfortable. Nurse Horn had propped two flat pillows under my head. She sat in a chair next to me, talking softly.

"Jean, I think you're going to be all right, but you should go to your doctor and have your head examined."

"Have my head examined." I smiled.

"Yes, just to be safe. Jean, all kidding aside, do get checked. You're starting to get two black eyes."

I sat up. "Two black eyes!"

"Don't get excited. Here, take a look." Nurse Horn walked over to her desk and returned with a large face mirror.

I stared at my reflection. My forehead looked like a cone and I had a wide black circle under each eye. It was like I'd been worked over by the mob.

"I can't believe I look this bad!"

"Just goes to show you, looks can go just like that." Nurse Horn popped her fingers and smiled. "Well, how do you feel?"

I tried to look as pitiful as possible, I wanted every ounce of sympathy I could get out of Nurse Horn. "My head hurts and I'm still a little dizzy."

"Well, the aspirin I gave you should help. I'll keep you down here for the rest of the afternoon. I want you to see a doctor tomorrow and maybe you'll be well enough to return to school on Monday."

"I don't really have a doctor. I'll have to go to the clinic."

"That should be fine." Nurse Horn looked out the window. "It's starting to rain."

"April showers bring May flowers," I mumbled.

"Jean, you haven't been down here since the first snowfall, remember?"

"I know. Who woulda thought it would wind up being a blizzard, remember?"

"Yes, I remember."

"My cramps haven't been bad lately. I took your advice."

"You've been staying out of that ocean?" Nurse Horn asked.

"So far, and I've been eating less junk food and exercising more."

"That's good, I'm glad. I'm sorry that you're hurt, but it *is* nice seeing you. I guess I've missed lecturing you."

"I've missed you too, Nurse Horn." Seeing her in the hallways every now and then hadn't been enough.

"Well, you can always stick your head in and say, 'hi,' you know."

"You mean you want to see me in sickness and in health?"

"Sure. I certainly don't want you to develop into a hypochondriac, Jean."

I smiled. I was glad she wanted to see me.

"Do you prefer to be called Stevie or Jean?"

"My friends call me Stevie."

"Well, I'd like to be your friend. So I'll call you Stevie, if that's all right?"

"Please do."

"Is there anyone who can come get you so you don't have to walk home today?"

"No. My father has the car and he's at work. Sean might be able to get his brother to give me a ride."

"If not, I can drive you home. It might be pouring by three-thirty."

I swallowed. Had Nurse Horn said she would drive me home? I could ride in her '67 Mustang with her! I forgot my pain for a minute.

"On second thought, I believe Sean told me Brian's car is in the shop. It's getting tuned up or something," I lied.

"Well, that settles it, then. I'll give you a lift."

I had no intention of arguing with her.

The doctor shone a flashlight in my eyes and told me to take some aspirin for pain. That had been it. Daddy said the school should pay my clinic bill, but Mama said it wasn't worth the red tape to try to collect ten dollars. They'd argued back and forth at the dinner table. It was settled when Mama sent me to get her checkbook. Of course, my brothers teased me no end about my shiners. And they were forever begging me to take off my sunglasses.

A week later Carla and I were at my locker.

"You think I still need my sunglasses?"

Carla shook her head. "Not unlessen you just want to look cool."

Sean walked toward us. "Hey, Stevie, let's say we check out White Castle ninth period? They gotta special going, ten burgers for a buck."

"I wish I could, Sean, but I'm booked."

"Booked? You gotta new nigger or something?" Carla cut in. Sean smiled but he looked worried.

"No, I've got to help Nurse Horn."

Carla shook her head at me before rushing away to catch up with Ivory.

"Help Nurse Horn? Help her do what?"

"Different stuff, Sean, file, type, clean up, whatever. I'm her student helper now."

"How did you get stuck with that?"

"I had to tell Nurse Horn what the doctor said. And while I was in her office, Barbara Taylor was in there."

"So."

"Anyway, Barbara was telling Nurse Horn that she couldn't be her helper anymore, accounta she's the new captain of the girls' basketball team, and they're in the finals and all."

"So, what's that got to do with you?"

"So I asked Nurse Horn if I could be her new helper. And she said, 'Great idea.'"

Sean frowned, "Why do you have to help her ninth period? Why would you want to be tied up at the end of the day?"

"Because that's when she needs me. Earlier she's more likely to have somebody sick in there."

"What if I need you?"

"Sean, you're being silly. You go to swim-team practice three times a week. You play basketball during most of lunch period."

"That's different."

"Well, I need service points for the Junior Honor Society. Helping Nurse Horn two measly periods a week will cover it."

"I forgot about your needing service points."

"Sean, we can go to White Castle tomorrow."

"Stevie, tomorrow it will be too late. This is a one-day sale," Sean grumbled.

That's just too bad, I thought to myself.

LARRY DUPLECHAN

■ ■ ■

[1956–]

MUSIC RATHER THAN WRITING WAS LARRY DUPLECHAN'S FIRST love. Following graduation from UCLA where he majored in literature, Duplechan spent six years singing professionally in nightclubs. When he reached a crossroads in his career, he chose to take up writing fiction, a talent that had first distinguished him in high school in his native Los Angeles.

Duplechan's debut novel, *Eight Days a Week* (1985), introduces the author's alter-ego protagonist, Johnnie Ray Rousseau, a black gay vocalist with a preference for white men. Although Duplechan once referred to himself as an "assimilationist," arguing that his sexual identity was more important to him than his racial self, his sexual politics are often characterized by wry, unapologetic humor and insight into the complexities of interracial love. Duplechan's second novel, *Blackbird* (1987), looks at Johnny Ray's isolated coming of age as a gay youth. His more ambitious *Tangled Up in Blue* (1989), an AIDS novel with an all-white cast of characters.

In this excerpt from *Captain Swing* (1993), the author's most recent novel, Johnny Ray returns, this time venturing from Los Angeles to visit his estranged father, Lance, on his deathbed in St. Charles, Louisiana.

"I'm here to see my father," I said to the same braided-haired nurse I'd seen the previous day. "Lance Rousseau." The nurse glanced at her wristwatch and then briefly down at the desk and said, "They givin' him his breakfast now. You can go on in if you want to."

Nigel said, "I'll wait over there," indicating the small waiting area.

Several long, deep yoga breaths failed to calm my racing heartbeat as I approached the door to my father's room. I should have hopped the first plane home when I had the chance, I thought. Well, maybe the first train.

"Please, Mr. Rousseau," came a plaintive female voice from within the room. "How can I feed you if you won't open your mouth?" From the doorway, I could see my father, propped up in bed with several pillows, his face set, jaw clenched, a food tray set before him. Bedside, perched on a high stool, spoon in hand, was a heavyset, caramel-colored young nurse's assistant.

"I said get away from me, girl," Lance growled through clenched teeth.

"Come on now, Mr. Rousseau," the woman repeated in a voice like honey-butter laced with arsenic, "just one bite."

"No!" Lance said, teeth together as if wired shut. "You eat it."

I smiled at the little drama, at my father's childish petulance, the woman's exasperation. Suddenly I was considerably less nervous. The brawny-armed disciplinarian who had left so many stripes on my thighs, the paragon of masculinity who had made me feel so inferior for so very long, the father who had turned me from his home—that man, or what was left of him—lay all but helpless in a hospital bed, refusing to eat his porridge. Fate had had to nearly flatten Lance Rousseau before I could feel I had anything resembling the upper hand, but this was definitely it.

"Let me give it a try," I said, stepping into the small, machine-dense room. The nurse's aide turned. Lance looked across the bed, across the room. Though Lance's eyes gave me nothing, I could have sworn I saw the threat of a smile pass, if briefly, across my father's tightly shut face. "I'm his son," I added for the woman's benefit. She looked at Lance, then back at me. Perhaps finding a family resemblance in my features, almost certainly happy to be relieved of duty, she shook the spoon clean, walked over, and handed it to me. "Good luck," she said, deadpan, and left the room.

Wiggling the spoon between my fingers, I strolled toward the bed. "Hello, Dad," I said, climbing onto the stool vacated by the nurse's aide. No visible or audible acknowledgment from the man in bed. So I said, "Hello, son, how nice of you to drop everything and schlep halfway across the United States to be treated like so much dog shit by your hateful homophobic asshole father. What a good, good son you are."

Lance blinked. I considered emptying the breakfast tray onto my father's head and fingerpainting obscenities across his hospital gown in strained squash, but thought better of it. I took a couple of yoga breaths and tried again.

"How are you feeling today, Dad?" I said. Lance continued to stare straight ahead. But after a moment, he said, "I'm dying. How the hell are you?"

I suppressed a smile. It wasn't much, but it was an answer. "Well," I said, "Garbo talks. How the hell am I, you ask. Well, let's see, now... my lover was killed by a hit-and-run over a year ago and I'm still in mourning. I'm given to screaming nightmares, I've been taking an extremely habit-forming prescription drug just to keep my mind from flying apart like a New Year's party favor, and I don't know if I'll ever love again. I'm in therapy with a shrink who looks like Opie, and who tells me there's no formal timetable for grief. And right at the moment, I'm sitting in a hospital room in the middle of Nowhere City, Louisiana, staring at my dying father, who doesn't want to see me. I'm fine." It crossed my mind to mention that I'd recently made something very like whoopie with Lance's nearly nineteen-year-old nephew, but chose not to just yet.

Finding no discernible reaction from Lance, I waved the spoon I still held, made a pop-eyed, twisted-lipped Baby Jane Hudson face, and barked à la Bette Davis, "Time ta eat-cha BREAK-fast!" I scooped up a spoonful of orangish-brownish mush from one of the larger compartments of the food tray and held it toward my father's tightly closed lips. Lance continued to stare straight ahead, across the room and seemingly through the open doorway and into the hall. I raised the spoon high, then brought it slowly down in a long, wavy line. "Open up the hangar," I singsonged, "here comes the airplane." No reaction. "Come on, Dad,"

I said softly. "I know it doesn't look so good, but I'm sure it's good for you. You need to rally your strength, you know."

"What for?" Lance said, opening his lips just enough to allow the words to escape. "I'm gonna die anyhow."

"So die, already!" I shouted, slamming the spoon down onto the tray, causing the food to splatter, leaving a little sprinkling of orangish-brownish spots on my father's hospital gown. "Don't just lie there, staring out into space, talking through your teeth, throwing people out, and pointedly not eating anything. Die if you're going to die. I'm sure they could use the room, and besides—I personally can't wait to do the hokey-pokey on your grave and get on with what is laughingly called my life. So just die, okay?"

I was trembling by the time I'd finished that little tirade. I crossed my arms tightly over my ribs and waited for it to pass. When, to my surprise, Lance opened his mouth wide, eyes closed like a man about to have his gums poked by a particularly clumsy dental hygienist, I scraped up another spoonful of food and carefully introduced it into my father's gaping mouth. Lance closed his lips around the spoon, frowning at the taste of it. When I had withdrawn the empty spoon, Lance said, "You talk just like your mother. You always did."

I lifted another spoonful from the tray and said, "I'll take that as a compliment, thanks. Open." Lance took another spoonful of the indeterminate mush, then said through barely parted lips, "How is your mother?"

"She's fine," I said. I seriously considered adding something about my mother finally finding a man who treated her as she deserved, but let it go for the moment. Among the grab bag of ill feelings I was harboring for my father, I held a special grudge for the sexual infidelities—some surreptitious, others carelessly exposed, some spitefully flaunted—which had driven Clara Rousseau away from her husband after twenty-one years of marriage. Now, nearly fifteen years later, I enjoyed the idea that my father, no longer the handsome bronze charmer, without wife and decidedly without paramour, might finally have lived to regret his past actions.

"She still living with that Jew?" Lance said.

"Yes," I said with some satisfaction. "She and Daniel are in Paris at the moment. Paris, France," I added, hoping the thought of the wife he'd so stupidly allowed himself to lose, summering in the city of *toujours l'amour* with a red-haired gynecologist seventeen years her junior, might cause my father some small pain. Nothing excruciating; a nice little sting would do. I smiled and said, "She's very, very happy." I watched my father's jaw muscles tighten and knew the sting had stung. I've seldom been one for kicking a man when he's down, but I have to admit I was really enjoying this.

The better part of a minute passed before Lance said, so softly I could just hear it, "I loved that woman."

I failed to stifle a quick, high, Chihuahua-bark of a laugh. "Well, you always did have the oddest little ways of showing your affection." I scooped up another spoonful of food, held it toward my father's face, and said, "More?"

"No," Lance said through his teeth, his eyes shut tight, as if the food ceased to exist as soon as he couldn't see it.

A long minute went by. Then two. Lance lay there thinking thoughts I could only have guessed at: the loss of a good wife? the impending loss of life? the blandness of his hospital breakfast? For my own part, I spent the silence thinking about a question, one I'd waited years to ask. Just considering it brought on a case of the trembles so strong I had to lay down the spoon. I took a good, long breath and went ahead. "On the general subject of people you allegedly loved," I said, crossing my arms again tightly across my front in a self-hug, "do—did you love me?"

"What?" Lance said, his expression unchanged.

"Nothing," I said quickly, feeling a fool for asking, feeling frustrated for having to ask. "Never mind."

Lance's sudden attack of deafness, whether genuine or feigned, gave me the opportunity to backpedal, to approach the love question a bit more slowly and quietly, like a rabbit in your dahlia garden. "You always favored David so much," I began. "Not that I blame you. What father wouldn't have? He was everything a father could want in a son. Unlike some of us." My heart beat like a West Hollywood dance club on a Saturday night, but I forced myself to continue. "And I know I never brought home any basketball trophies, but I did excel in some things— my grades, my clarinet. My singing. But I—" I felt my throat tighten; I swallowed hard. "God, I must sound like Tommy Smothers, here. 'Dad always liked you best.' But, see, I never quite felt like you valued the things I did as much as you valued what David did. I so wanted to feel like you were proud of me, too. For the things I accomplished. And that you loved me, too." I paused a moment, waiting for some reaction from my father: if not some small morsel of belated reassurance, at least some knee-jerk denial of ever having withheld his approval or his love.

There I sat. Open. Vulnerable. Utterly unacknowledged.

Finally, I heard my father take in a breath through slightly parted lips.

"Proud of you," he said, neither opening his eyes nor turning his face in my direction, his voice a harsh rasp, like steel wool against your skin. The phrase emerged without inflection, not quite a question, not exactly a statement. It occurred to me that my father might be attempting to tell me that he was, in fact, proud of me, and I felt a slight adrenaline kick at the thought.

"You made me sick," he said, slowly, deliberately, his meaning quite unequivocal, each word hitting me like a roundhouse right to the stomach. "Come sashaying into my house," he continued, his lips scarcely moving, "talking about 'I'm gay,' like you so damn happy you was a faggot. Like I'm supposed to be happy about it. Bringing some little sissified white boyfriend right *in* my house. Like it wasn't enough, my son was taking some white man up the butt—I had to *meet* him, too." He made a little snorting sound around the plastic nose piece. "Proud of you," he repeated, then added, "shit."

I gripped the sides of the stool I sat on, fighting the shakes, blinking rapidly against the tears. I was *not* going to cry. I refused to give him the satisfaction of making me cry. A minute, maybe ninety seconds, and several long, deep breaths later, the trembling subsided and I decided to trust my voice not to betray my pain. I decided to pass on the opportunity to mention that I was, in fact, quite happy to be gay; to remind him that the young man I so foolishly chose to bring home to meet the folks, was a strapping six-footer and anything but "sissified"; or to volunteer that, notwithstanding my father's remark about my taking it up the butt, I'm basically a top.

I spoke softly, slowly, as evenly as I could manage.

"Why, you ugly old half-dead *piece* of an evil muthafucka. I have never in my life asked you to be proud of my gayness. I am neither proud nor ashamed of being gay. Being gay is not in and of itself an accomplishment. However," and I swallowed around a lump of soreness, "let us forget the subject of pride for just a moment"—I sniffed a wet one—"and get back to this love thing. After all, whatever else I may be, I am your firstborn son. Your only living son. And I think it's a perfectly reasonable question to ask, so I'll ask it again, in case you missed it the first time around. Do you love me"—and I paused for a bit of dramatic effect before adding, "Father?"

Lance made no sound, save for the soft hiss of his slow, even breathing. I waited.

Then I waited a little longer.

"Dad?" I leaned in toward my father's ear. "Dad?" Lance's only reply was his familiar, flutteringly glottal snore—a sound not unlike an old Volkswagen Beetle with serious muffler problems, taking a steep incline—the snore both David and I myself had inherited. While no longer the roar it had been in Lance's robust youth (when it resembled a Mack truck with no muffler at all), it was still a formidable sound, more than capable of filling a small hospital room.

"Perfect," I said aloud, taking my leave of Lance, the room, the snore.

Nigel looked up from a magazine as I approached. "How'd it go?" he asked.

"Oh, fine," I said. "I force-fed him three mouthfuls of baby food, then sang him to sleep."

Nigel's thick, black eyebrows rose and Nigel followed them up to a standing position. "You sang?"

"No," I said. "Could we go get some breakfast? I'd absolutely kill for a cheese omelette."

"How 'bout Anna Lee's?" Nigel said. I shot him a look—I was in no mood. "For breakfast, Captain," Nigel said, raising a shielding hand, "for breakfast. Anna Lee can bum her some grits and eggs and she'll sling it our way free-for-nothin'. Okay?" He smiled that smile.

E. LYNN HARRIS

■ ■ ■

[1957–]

AMONG THE MOST COMMERCIALLY SUCCESSFUL BLACK GAY novelists ever, E. Lynn Harris grew up in Little Rock, Arkansas, in the integrationist period of the 1960s. In the midst of social unrest, his mother provided a loving and stable home for Harris and his four sisters.

In 1977, Harris graduated from the University of Arkansas at Fayetteville with honors, earning the distinction of being the college's first black male cheerleader. He sold computers for thirteen years before quitting his job to write his first novel, *Invisible Life*. Failing to find a publisher for this overtly gay-themed work, Harris published the book himself in 1991. Anchor Books eventually "discovered" his novel, which had been sold through African American bookstores and beauty salons. The publication of Anchor's first trade paperback edition of *Invisible Life* in 1994 formally launched Harris's career.

Following the groundbreaking success of his debut novel, Harris continued to explore middle-class, black male homosexuality and bisexuality in the best-selling sequels *Just As I Am* (1994), *And This Too Shall Pass* (1996), *If This World Were Mine* (1997), and *Abide with Me* (1999). His next novel, *Not a Day Goes By* (2000), debuted at #2 on the *New York Times* best-seller list and was the #1 best-selling title in *Publishers Weekly* for two consecutive weeks. The author's most recent work, *Any Way the Wind Blows* (2001), was released to similar acclaim. Harris's writing also appears in *Brotherman: The Odyssey of Black Men in America, Go the Way Your Blood Beats*, and his gay novella "Money Can't Buy Me Love" was published in *Got to Be Real: Four Original Love Stories*. His novels have been nominated for several NAACP Image Awards, with *If This World*

Were Mine winning the James Baldwin Award for Literary Excellence in 1998. Appropriately, Baldwin's work has been the predominant literary model for Harris, whose career has been largely motivated by his desire to advance the African American gay male canon begun by writers such as Baldwin.

Harris gives voice to closeted and "questioning" African American gay and bisexual men who strive for self-acceptance, despite the social pressures that inhibit their growth. *Invisible Life* tells the story of Raymond, who, while in a loving relationship with his girlfriend Nicole, has been secretly involved in an affair with Quinn, a closeted husband with two children. Raymond, however, feels the need to settle down—to commit himself to a "twenty-four seven" relationship—and he even considers "giving up" homosexuality for his girlfriend.

from Invisible Life

[1991]

It's interesting what roses do to women. I sent Nicole one hundred red roses the following day with a card saying a rose for each day she had made me smile inside. My being a jerk for the last couple of days was quickly forgiven. I debated all morning on what to say to Quinn about us cooling our relationship. As I came closer to making a decision about giving up the life for good, I wondered if it was at all possible. Maybe being gay was like being an alcoholic. That with willpower and a little counseling you could just stop, that you would still be gay but just choose not to practice. Nicole and her strong religious beliefs came to mind. Did prayer change things? Whenever I was worried about something, she would simply say, "Let go, let God."

I sometimes prayed for a pill I could take to destroy my homosexual feelings. I would have taken it in a heartbeat. When I went to church with Nicole, I listened intently for answers to my questions. I wondered what you had to feel in order to be saved. Were you saved from everything?

I joined church and was baptized when I was twelve years old. It was not because I felt anything different, but because it was time. Like going to junior high when you finished the sixth grade. I accepted Christ during Vacation Bible School, partly because all my friends did. I remembered how proud my mom and pops had been the day I was baptized. I wondered why Christians just couldn't understand that Christ sent about ten percent of us down the chute just to confuse things. Maybe He had a plan yet to be revealed. That maybe we were the chosen ones. With Nicole I learned how to let go with my faith, no longer being intellectual about religion. I believed that Christ loved me no matter what. That there were no degrees of sin and I would be judged according to my heart.

The things that I would miss about the gay lifestyle were few. If I were going to give it up, the thing that I treasured the most about being gay was still intact, my friendship with Kyle. My sensibilities as a man who respected women and my ability to feel and be sensitive were characteristics I attributed to my gayness. I wouldn't miss the bars or the viciousness of the kids.

I understood that being vicious was just another defense. It was no accident that the most obviously gay men were the ones most vicious and with the quickest wit. Many times I felt sorry for those who couldn't pass. The majority didn't seemed to mind a bit. Many lived with the additional stigma the bulk of their life. They would read you before you got a chance to comment on their appearance. It didn't matter if you were gay or straight. Nothing and no one were spared their tart tongues.

Grady buzzed to tell me that Quinn and two little ones were waiting for me in the lobby. *Little ones,* I thought, what can Grady be talking about? When I arrived in the lobby, there stood Quinn with his two children, Baldwin and Maya. Quinn was holding Maya in his arms and Baldwin was standing and holding Quinn's legs. This was the first time that I had come in contact with any other part of Quinn's life.

"I'm sorry. I have to drop them off at my sister-in-law's up in Harlem," Quinn explained.

"No problem. This must be Baldwin," I said, reaching for Quinn's son. "And Maya. What a beautiful little lady."

They were both beautiful. It looked as though Quinn had spit them out. There was no denying that these were his children.

"Say hello to Uncle Ray," Quinn chided the two little ones.

As the two gave me shy greetings, I looked at Quinn with a double look... *Uncle Ray.* What was that about? As we rode uptown, I felt like an interloper in Quinn's world. He was quite the doting father, talking with Maya and Baldwin as though I weren't there. A part of me respected that and another side of me begrudged him. After dropping Baldwin and Maya off, we drove to the Tower Video store, where we picked up a couple of videos, and stopped to grab a bite to eat at the Saloon. When we had finished eating, I stood at the cashier's stand while Quinn paid the check. On the way out I heard someone call out my name. When I turned, I saw it was Basil. He was on his way into the restaurant with an attractive blue-eyed blonde who looked like a *Playboy* centerfold. We exchanged hellos and I introduced the two of them to Quinn. Quinn was polite but reserved. After a few minutes of nervous conversation, I told Basil it was good seeing him and nice meeting his lady friend, Elesa. As we were leaving, Basil said, "I'm still waiting on that call, Mr. Tyler."

"Yeah, real soon, Basil," I replied.

As we walked toward the car, Quinn asked in an annoyed tone, "What was that about?"

"What are you talking about?"

"Come on, Ray. I didn't know you knew Basil Henderson."

"Well, I really don't. I told you he was Kyle's friend."

"Well, he seemed to know you pretty well."

"We did have drinks once."

"Is that all…and why didn't you mention it to me?"

"Quinn, come on now. It was just drinks. Besides, I do have a life the rest of the week."

"Point well taken, Mr. Tyler," Quinn said in a huff.

Quinn didn't utter a word as we drove up Columbus Avenue and back to my apartment. I had never seen him behave like this. Was he jealous? The thought made me smile. When we reached my apartment, Quinn went directly into my bedroom. I grabbed a couple of beers and walked into the bedroom, where Quinn undressed in silence.

"Quinn, we need to talk," I said.

"About what?"

"About this relationship," I responded.

"What, Raymond, are you seeing someone?" Quinn asked.

"You know I've been going out with Nicole. It's getting serious."

"And?"

"Well, I'm thinking about telling her the truth. I'm trying to go back to the other side exclusively."

"Are you crazy?"

"What do you mean by that?"

"Why bring that grief on yourself? Are you trying to give me an ultimatum?"

"An ultimatum?"

"Well, I know you haven't been happy with our situation lately. But you know how I feel about you, Ray."

"No, I don't know, Quinn. Just look at you. We don't talk at all and you come in here and undress. It's like saying, 'Okay, let's fuck, so I can get home to my wife and kids.' How do you think that makes me feel?"

"Raymond, it's not like that. It's just that I thought this was what you wanted."

"No, Quinn. I want somebody in my life twenty-four seven."

Quinn rubbed his face and looked out the window. The silence of the next few minutes seemed like days. Had we finally come to the end of the road? He sat motionless on the bed in yellow silk briefs, pressing his knee into his chest. His eyes appeared bottomless. I walked over to the bed and sat next to Quinn. He took my hand and pulled it to his chest. "What are you saying, Raymond? What do you want me to say? That I love you? Well, I do."

"That's not it, Quinn. I think I'm in love with Nicole and I want to be fair to the both of you."

"And how long do you think that's going to last?"

"At least as long as your marriage," I snapped defensively.

"Oh, fuck this shit," Quinn said as he raised his voice in anger and leaped from the bed.

"Is that how you want to handle this, Quinn? Just fuck it?"

Quinn turned toward me with a look of rage in his eyes. I had not seen this side of him. His body appeared to be trembling and tears were welling up in his eyes.

"Why do we have to stop seeing each other? Do you want me to leave my wife and kids? Do you want me to move here and be with you twenty-four hours a day? I don't think this is about Nicole. I think this is about Basil or some other nigger!" Quinn shouted.

"Quinn, if I keep making room for you in my life, then I'm bound to fall in love with you. I can't do that to myself. I can't do it to those two beautiful kids."

Quinn broke into a nervous laughter. "So you're doing this for my kids. What about me and what we mean to each other? There are times when I want you, Raymond, as badly as I want my next breath."

There was a certain power in Quinn's voice and in his face. As Quinn suddenly started to get dressed, with his jeans halfway up, he sat back on the bed and began to sob softly. I stopped my search for my T-shirt and pulled him against my chest and massaged the nape of his neck as his tears fell onto my naked shoulders. I had a sudden impulse to retract my previous words and tell him that everything was going to be all right, but in my heart I knew better.

"Quinn, let's just take some time and rethink this situation. I don't want to hurt you, but I can't risk getting hurt myself," I pleaded. "This is wrong for the both of us."

"What? Being gay?"

"Not that. Quinn, you're married. Maybe it could be different if the facts were different."

Quinn looked straight ahead in silence. His body felt rigid and hard. He gently removed himself from my embrace and finished dressing and walked into the living room. My body became sick with fear that I had made the biggest mistake of my life. I joined Quinn in the living room, where he was standing, just looking around the room in a daze. He walked toward me with a blank look on his face. He gently touched my face and kissed my lips with such power that the force staggered me. His eyes were now dry but slightly pink.

Quinn looked me straight in the eyes and said, "You want the facts. The facts are that you may be throwing away the best thing that ever happened to you. Your desire for me and other men isn't going away because you think you're in love with some woman. I know because I live that lie every day. With the exception of the Saturdays I'm with you. What we have is the closest thing to real love that either one of us can ever dream of. I won't let you throw it away, Raymond," Quinn said in hurried sentences.

Quinn gave me a last kiss and embrace and headed out my door without another word or allowing me to say more. I walked to the doorway and Quinn stared at me, then turned away and headed down the long hallway, home. I felt the tears falling from my eyes when I let myself acknowledge my real feelings for Quinn. Perhaps I was going to lose his love because I had not, in the end, believed in it enough. But what kind of life would a weekends-only relationship offer me? Why double the sin? I must admit that Quinn's and my tidal wave of emotions surprised me. I guess I knew that he did in fact love me, but was that love enough?

Maybe I *was* giving him an ultimatum. What if Quinn hadn't been married with two children? What if we were just two single gay men? Would our relationship have stood a better chance of surviving? I knew one thing: with Quinn I felt safe. I could talk about work, sports and things that even Kyle didn't understand. It was a friendship similar to those with my fraternity brothers, but with sex. Torrid sex. Plus an undying devotion to each other and the ability to share a tenderness rare in both men and women. I was pushing Quinn away because I was afraid to love another man that deeply. I think when two men like Quinn and myself meet, there is a fear of losing one's self. Although we didn't play roles, it was apparent that we both were used to being in charge. In previous relationships with men, I had always held back, never giving myself totally. AIDS had a lot to do with that, but in many ways it became a *man thing* with me. I used to listen to Kyle talk about the total rapture he felt when he gave himself to another man. He would describe it like a woman talking about multiple orgasms. It sounded like a dangerous addiction that I could live without. I remember meeting a supermacho guy who supposedly had been turned out in prison. The next time Kyle and I saw him, Kyle remarked that he looked like "a queen without a country."

Maybe Quinn touched buttons within me that I didn't want to acknowledge or believe existed. I had to get out now!

SHAY YOUNGBLOOD

■ ■ ■

[1959–]

BORN IN COLUMBUS, GEORGIA, PLAYWRIGHT AND NOVELIST
Shay Youngblood graduated from the MFA in Creative Writing program
at Brown University. She is the recipient of numerous prizes and awards,
including the Lorraine Hansberry Playwrighting award, several NAACP
Theater Awards, and the Pushcart Prize for her short stories. Among her
works are the lesbian-themed short fiction collection *The Big Mama
Stories* (1989); the plays *Shakin' the Mess Outta Misery* (1994) and *Talking
Bones* (1994); and novels *Soul Kiss* (1997) and *Black Girl in Paris* (2000).
She lives in New York, where she teaches creative writing at the New York
School for Social Research.

   This excerpt from *Soul Kiss* opens in 1968 with seven-year-old
Mariah and her emotionally unstable mother shortly before their
abrupt departure for the South. There, Mariah is unexpectedly left in
the care of her mother's aunts, who become responsible for the girl
after her mother goes off with a boyfriend. Notable for the vivid descriptions and the lyrical tone of Youngblood's prose, the book also deals
subtly with sexuality, especially as it is presented through the eyes and
thoughts of a child.

When me and Mama lived together the world was a perfect place to be a little girl. I adored Mama and she adored me in return. No one else mattered. One of my first memories was watching her dress for work. Next to her reddish-brown skin, softened each night with a thin layer of Vaseline and cold cream, she wore a pink satin slip. Pink was romantic, she said, the color of love and laughing. Mama's slanted eyes, a gift, she said, from her Cherokee grandfather, were dreamy remembering how my father told her she looked like a princess when she wore pink. On the outside she wore white. Her nurse's uniform was starched, white-white, a petite size eight, with a tiny white cap perched on her short, tight, nappy curls, dyed blonde not quite down to her dark roots. White silk stockings veiled her long thin legs. Silent crepe-soled white shoes she'd let me lace up held her perfect, size six feet. Every weekday morning, on her way to the military hospital, she would walk me to school past the gray army barracks to the steel, bread-shaped huts, where we lined up for the pledge of allegiance to the flag.

Armed with a sandwich, a piece of fruit, and a word written on a small square of pink paper folded twice, I was ready for anything. The word was written in blue ink in my mother's fancy script...*pretty...sweet...blue...music...dream...* Sometimes she gave me words in Spanish...*bonita...dulce...sueños...agua...azul...* The word I kept in my mouth, repeated like a prayer when I missed her. Mama told me that she would be thinking of the same word all day. That thought made our time apart bearable. Before she left me at the door of the school she would whisper the word into my ear. I'd close my eyes and she would kiss me quickly on my neck, then let go of my hand. She always watched me through the window as I walked to my seat near the back of the room. We would mouth our word to each other once more before she disappeared. When Mama came for me in the afternoon I would take her hand and swing our arms as if we were both little girls on a walk.

"Blue. B-L-U-E. Blue is the color of sad music. Blue." I would pronounce, spell, and give the meaning of our word. Sometimes on our walks we invented words and spoke to each other in new languages. As praise, Mama would tickle me under my chin, then cup my face in her warm delicate hands and close her eyes. She would press her lips full on mine and give me what she called a soul kiss. My whole body would fever from my mother's embrace.

"I love you, Mama," I would say, looking into her eyes.

"I love you more," she answered every time, looking deep inside me.

I could read books before I could walk, Mama said. By the time I was three years old I was sitting on her lap reading to her from the newspaper. I don't remember all this, but Mama said it's so. I was so smart I got special treatment in school. "Teachers' pet" they called me, and other names I grew to hate. I didn't make friends, but I didn't need them, I had Mama. All my days at school were spent passing the time, waiting for Mama to free me from the steel breadbox. She taught me all the important things there were to know.

We lived on a military base near Manhattan, Kansas. Flat squares of grass occupied by long flat gray squares of apartments one after the other for miles and miles. There was a swing in our backyard where Mama spent hours pushing me into the sky. Sometimes I sang songs into the wind, catching pieces of cloud in my throat and swallowing them for safekeeping.

We lived in a tiny apartment. The bare walls were an unpleasant weak shade of green transformed at night by Mama's colored light bulbs into a pink velvet womb. In the living room an overstuffed red crushed velvet sofa sat in the middle of the room on gray-flecked linoleum tiles. There was a table at one end of the room and a lamp with a red-fringed shade and a big black radio on top of it. The radio's antenna was wrapped with aluminum foil so we could get better reception for the blues and jazz music that came on in the evening from someplace so far away that pulsing static accompanied each song. Mama kept the plain white shades pulled down past the window sills "to keep our business to ourselves," she said. The living room opened onto the kitchen where a bright yellow and pink flowered plastic tablecloth was spread over a wobbly card table surrounded by three silver folding chairs. A bare white bulb hung from the center of the white ceiling. White metal cabinets lined one wall and underneath them, an old-fashioned double sink with one side deeper than the other. Mama said she used to wash me in the deep part of the sink when I was small enough to hold in one hand. It always made me laugh when she said that because I couldn't imagine being that tiny. Sometimes I wished I were small enough to crawl back

inside her stomach where she said I was once small enough to fit.
I could imagine no greater comfort. The bedroom was just big enough
to fit the queen-sized bed and chest of drawers which held all our neatly
folded clothes among fragrant cedar balls. A clean white tiled bathroom
had a toilet that ran all night and a sink that dripped but also a deep,
creamy white enamel tub that was big enough to fit me and Mama
together just right.

At night we would eat directly from tin cans heated on a one-eyed
hot plate while we listened to music on the radio. In summer she said it
was too hot to light the oven, in winter she said she was too tired to cook.
On special days we had picnics, selecting cans of potted meat, stewed
tomatoes, fruit cocktail, applesauce, and pork and beans to spread on
saltine crackers or spear with sturdy toothpicks and wash down with
sweet lemon iced tea. Mama just didn't have any use for cooking and I
never missed it because this was all I knew. After supper we would take a
bath together, soaping each other with a soft pink sponge. Sometimes
she let me touch her breasts. In my tiny hands they felt like holding
clouds must. Like delicate overripe fruit. Her nipples were dark circles
that grew into thick buttons when I pressed them gently as if I were an
elevator operator. I kneeled in the warm soapy water between her legs
letting water pour over her breasts from between my small fingers and
watched her as she leaned back in the tub, her narrow eyes closed, hair
damp and matted, mouth slightly open as if she were holding her breath.
I felt so close to her, as if my skin were hers and we were one brown body.
She didn't seem to mind my curious fingers touching and soaping every
curve and mystery of her body. There were no boundaries, no place I
could not explore. After our bath we lay on the sofa in our clean white
pajamas, listening to the radio until we fell asleep. I loved sleeping with
her warm belly pressed into my back, one arm across my waist.
Sometimes she would hold my hand as we slept.

On weekends me and Mama played Ocean. Around bedtime she
would get dressed in beautiful clothes and go out dancing. She left me
alone with instructions to stay on the sofa, warning me that if I got off,
even to go to the bathroom, I might drown in the ocean. She gave me
toast left over from breakfast which I tossed bit by bit to the sharks in
the dangerous waters all around my island so they wouldn't nibble on
my toes when I slept. I remember a pink lamp with a pink bulb burning and the radio turned down low. A few drops of scotch and lots

of pink punch swirled in a chipped blue china cup burned sweetly in my throat. I drifted further out to sea than I imagined I could swim. The sharks began to circle as my eyelids dropped and the horizon across the ocean grew hazy. The sound of small waves rocked me like arms into the deepest part of sleep. Usually I began dreaming right after Mama left.

> *I look like my mother. My hair is dyed blonde, my eyes are narrow, shaped like almonds and lined in black ink. My lips are rich with soft, pink kisses. Her hair. Her eyes. Her lips. I even have my mother's breasts. Her thick, delicious nipples. In my favorite, secret dream I dress in her clothes, tight-waisted, sparkly, pink dresses, and dance in a circle of light. I dance until my feet become so light that I float across the dance floor up toward the ceiling of moving stars, then fly out of my window into other oceans.*

Mama was always there when I woke up. One time she woke me in the middle of the night crying. She told me that a special friend of hers, a hospital doctor, was being sent overseas and because Mama wasn't his wife—he had one already—she couldn't go. Because Mama was sad, I was sad. Her tears were mine. When Mama was crying, it seemed as if the whole world were crying.

Before long, right out of the blue, Mama began to change. I was scared and confused. After school I wanted to tell her about my new classmates in second grade: the Korean girl who put her hands to her face and cried quietly all day; the red-haired, blue-eyed boy from Arkansas who talked like he had rocks in his mouth; the dark-skinned, wide-eyed girl named Meera with clouds of jet-black hair she let me touch at recess and whose mother was an Indian from India. I had a new friend, new books, and a new teacher, but Mama wasn't interested in any of it. She seemed to be sleepwalking through our lives. More and more I was in charge. She let me do everything. In the afternoons I led us home. Her movements became slower, she walked as if strong hands gripped her ankles. Her eyes were dull and her voice weak. Sometimes she wouldn't speak to me, but would mouth our word for the day while I untied her shoes and kneaded feeling back into her toes. I unhooked the stockings from their garters, rolling the silk carefully down her exhausted legs. She would fall asleep, and I would fill a small blue pan

with warm water and soak her feet, massaging them gently. I would
unbutton her white uniform and hang it in the closet. The wig she had
started wearing was curly and dark. I would slide it off her head and
place it on its stand. I would take a comb and scratch the dandruff from
her scalp, oiling it with bergamot while she dozed, wondering why her
hair had begun to fall out. It was dry and coarse and no longer blonde.
I would watch her, slumped into the sofa in her pink satin slip, watching
the rise and fall of her breasts. Curling up in her lap, I would smooth the
satin over the rise of her breasts with both my hands pressing the shape
of her body from shoulders to waist, over and over again. Her eyes stayed
closed, her breathing raw and hollow. Sometimes Mama would sleep for
whole days when she wasn't working. When she woke up she wanted
water. Cool water.

Mama had an answer for everything even when she didn't know.

"Where is my father?" I would ask her in the lazy pink light before
we fell asleep at night.

"In Mexico, painting the sky blue." She drew pictures with her answers.

"Is he handsome?" I asked, secretly hoping for more.

"Very handsome. You have your father's hands," she'd say, kissing
my fingers, each one.

Her voice was twilight, and the stories she told me about him
sounded like fairy tales that found their way into my dreams. Did I
remember them or did I dream them? She never spoke of him outside
of these times between waking and dreaming.

I would close my eyes to listen, seeing every detail, my imagination
filling in all the blank spaces.

"How did you meet him? Tell me everything about him,"
I demanded. Mama closed her eyes and drifted beyond my reach. She
tossed me bits of stories to nibble on. I devoured the nights, the days of
her memories, growing fat from their richness. The details of her stories
changed over time. The season, the city, the natural disaster that took
place the day they met, the color of his eyes.

"I was happy then," she would begin each time. "I was so happy then."

One legend began: "It was springtime, in California. A light breeze
was blowing off the ocean. I had just come on duty when he walked into
the emergency room. A cut from his head was bleeding. He had fallen
off a ladder. There was pale blue paint all over his face and arms.
I thought he had fallen from the sky, he was so beautiful, like an angel.

His eyes were so black, I was afraid I would be hypnotized by them. I was taking his blood pressure when the room started to slip sideways. The earth shook me like a nervous child, and I fell into his wide, blue arms. My mind was racing so fast I could see through him. I could see you. Me being earth and him being sky, I knew we would have an angel child. And we did. I wanted to name you Angelita, Walks with Angels, but he said no, so we called you Mariah after his mother."

Other times the story went: "It was winter in New York. It was so cold the day I met your father, my eyelashes froze, and he melted them, with his breath."

Sometimes in her memory, they discovered each other on a windswept Caribbean beach: "Your father was at the top of a tall ladder the first time I saw him. A strong wind blew him right into my arms. When we first met, he painted pictures of me every day. Orange bodies with yellow faces, purple arms and red hair. He drank raspberry beer and rubbed my feet with mint leaves. When I met your father there was a strong wind in my hair twisting my mind like a hurricane."

In my mother's stories my father was always handsome and always, always there was pale blue paint all over his face and arms. I grew to love him too.

At school, me and my friends Meera and David, the blue-eyed boy from Arkansas, played Army during recess. We invented wars and fought against invisible armies of dragons and sea creatures. We always won by the time recess was over and what I liked most was that we were always on the same side.

Mama's beautiful blue script was replaced by shaky, uncertain block letters written in pencil or with a broken red crayon. The words on the slips of paper began to change. *Vieja...lluvia...ve, ve...lagrimas... mohosas...x's and o's.* Once she filled a small square of paper with z's and q's. Sometimes the paper was wet with her tears. Her writing became hard to read, the lines no longer separated or curved, going nowhere. She seemed hurt and nervous, as if she were afraid of every thing. One morning she forgot to give me a word altogether. When I reminded her she pulled a torn scrap of paper from the pocket of her uniform. Her fingers were trembling and couldn't hold the pencil I gave her, so she pressed the paper to her lips twice, then crushed it into my hand. At lunchtime, after eating the slice of dry bread and bruised banana in my lunch bag, I unfolded the paper Mama gave me and pressed it to my lips. I closed my eyes and tried to feel the warmth of her paper kisses.

One time Mama took me to the hospital where she worked. I waited out in the emergency room. One of the nurses gave me a lollipop and asked me if I could do any of the new dances. I said, "No, but I can sing." I stood up on a chair and opened my mouth. I don't know why Billie Holiday came out. "God Bless the Child" haunted the air. Sometimes Mama sang it when she was sad. The nurses and some of the sick people clapped when I was done. Mama's doctor friend was there; he said it sounded like there was an angel in my throat. I explained to him that I put clouds there for safekeeping. He said I was just like my mother. I liked him even though he was the one my mama always seemed to be crying about. I let him kiss me because Mama said it was all right. Up close he smelled sweet, like a woman not my mother.

Helen Elaine Lee

■ ■ ■

[1961–]

NOVELIST HELEN ELAINE LEE WAS AN ATTORNEY BEFORE turning to writing, attending Harvard Law School with the encouragement of her father, also a lawyer. In time, however, she realized that she did not share her father's passion for legal practice, preferring instead to write fiction. Among the short stories Lee had written during her nine years as an attorney was a dramatic, lesbian-themed story about abortion entitled "Water Call." Eventually, the piece was expanded into her debut novel, *The Serpent's Gift* (1994), which won a First Novel Award from the Black Caucus of the American Library Association. Lee has also published a second novel, *Water Marked* (1999), while her short fiction has appeared in *Callaloo*, *Afrekete: An Anthology of Black Lesbian Writing*, and *Children of the Night: The Best Short Stories by Black Writers, 1967 to the Present*. She teaches in the Program in Writing and Humanistic Studies at Massachusetts Institute of Technology.

This excerpt from *The Serpent's Gift* depicts the sexual life of Ouida, a beautiful young black manicurist employed at a barbershop in the 1920s. After succumbing to the persistent advances of a white traveling salesman, as well as furious, wordless sex with one of the barbers, Ouida finds herself sexually unsatisfied. She then becomes irresistibly drawn to Zella, a woman who "ain't normal," according to one coworker, with this attraction blossoming into a passionate coupling.

from The Serpent's Gift

[1994]

Just as LaRue was getting to know Olive, Ouida was having her own summer of discovery. She was finding out about choosing, and about a woman she had never expected to know.

Her kisses were like nighttime secrets, and Ouida swore that her laugh, like the rain, made things grow. Zella Bridgeforth touched her somewhere timeless, held her, compelled her with her rhythms, and Ouida answered her call. She chose her, after all, but the path that led to Zella took her, first, through other choices.

The summer of 1926, the summer they had met, Ouida would later think of as her "swan song." She had swung her corset-cinched body along the streets of the city with long steady strides, smiling but never meeting the eyes of those who paused from whatever they were doing to partake of her radiance. Just divorced from Junior, she was finished, finally, with trying to will their union into rightness.

As soon as she had landed her manicurist job and rented her flat, she had surveyed the range of the possible from the vantage point of her manicurist's table, feeling, for the first time in her life, that she owned the choice. From the spin of options, she made assessments. And she did some choosing.

She chose Johnston Franklin, the middle-aged white man who stopped in the shop on his business trips from Louisville. He came in and stared at her while waiting for a chair, and she met his glance, her chin in the air, and kept working. While he sat for his haircut and shave, he asked Alton, one of the barbers, who she was. When Alton didn't answer, Johnston Franklin turned in the chair, his face halfcovered with lather, and addressed Alton with a demanding look. Alton turned away and stirred his soap, assessing the cost of defiance. Finally, he said, "I think she's married, sir. Least that's what I've heard."

Johnston Franklin laughed and said, "Well I'm not interested in her husband. What is her name?"

Alton stirred his soap some more and then answered, "Ouida Staples. Miss Ouida Staples."

Ouida had noticed the exchange and could see Johnston Franklin coming her way out of the corner of her eye, but she refused to look up.

She sat at her table humming while she polished and arranged her instruments, the edge of his gold fob, a crisply creased pant leg, and the tip of an expensive shoe just within view. Finally, when he realized that she wasn't going to look up at him, he sat down and ordered a manicure. She took his hands and began her task.

"I understand your name is Ouida," he said, "and that's an unusual name." She lifted her eyes slowly, as if it was an effort, assessed his face in an instant, and returned to his hands. The barbers watched to see what she would do.

"And how *are* you today, Ouida?" Johnston Franklin tried again.

"Oh, I'm just fine," she answered with a hint of insolence as she lifted her eyes, "sir."

"Well...I don't recall seeing your lovely face in this establishment before..." Ouida kept filing, silently.

"I come in here every month or so...here on business, quite regularly, and I will certainly make it a habit to visit this establishment more often." She filed his nails silently, thinking how soft and pale his hands were.

"Well...," he ventured, "this town sure is different from my home... it's the city, all right, and I do like, now and again, seeing something besides trees...of course, this town doesn't compare to New York...now that's a different story, that's the real city. Have you ever been to New York, Ouida...Miss Ouida?"

She shook her head, and kept working on his nails. And receiving neither information nor interest, he jerked his hand away as she was finishing up, paid his bill, and left. He returned the next week, and the next, watching her from the barber chair, and when he was finished being shaved, he came up to her and leaned over her table until she met his eyes. Matter-of-factly, he said, "It would be my pleasure if we could spend some time together...tonight, perhaps."

She looked at him, her head tilted, and measured the choice. She saw a square pink face, not so different from many she had seen, well fed and well tended, and even though it wasn't a face that moved her much, she thought she could look into his restless moss green eyes for a little while. It was a face that held the promise of things she couldn't afford, and their delivery with a kind of homage.

She glanced over at the barbers, Alton and Regis, who watched the whole thing unfold and waited for her to resist sweetly, and their expectations bred defiance. The other barber, Flood, never looked her way.

"Not tonight," she answered as she stood up and went to tend to some other job, making him wait until she returned to tell him when.

It was a timeless play, the choreographed conquest of strange exotic prey, and Ouida was willing to play it for a time. It was a variation on a role she knew, and even though she was familiar with the script, she liked to think that it was she, in fact, who controlled the hunt, fooling the hunter into thinking things moved along by his design. She figured she could learn something about the rest of the world from Johnston Franklin, about the places he visited that she had never been. She liked the challenge. She liked the gifts he brought. And she liked his liking, too.

Their first night of sex, Johnston Franklin had undressed completely and was waiting for her in the bed when she came in from the bathroom, and she had stood, fully dressed, and looked at him. "Well, you certainly are direct, Johnston Franklin. You get right to the point."

She found herself calling him by his full name, even in bed. And after they had sex he talked to her of his business trips, of meetings and sales and the shops and restaurants he had visited. It was as if just being around Ouida made something in him loosen and spill out, the things he held separate from the rest of his life. Eventually, he started discharging the details of his day, his aspirations and his self-doubts, as soon as he saw her, and he talked all the way through undressing, right up to their first embrace.

He was captivated by her beauty, and her knowledge of its power, and he had seen it in the way she made him wait that first day he saw her, and had wanted it for his own, sensing there was something, some kind of magic, that she knew. He wanted to know it, too.

He wanted to know about the way she lived life up close. While he heard things and looked at colors and shapes from somewhere outside of himself, he could tell that when Ouida did something, she was right in the middle of it. He asked her to reveal to him her eye for things, and he asked her to give him the rich details she saw. "Tell me a texture," he would say, as they lay in the rich linen of his hotel, and she would begin to describe some fabric she had seen.

"Silky, like a river in sunlight, and purple, with flaws that aren't flaws, but just the way of the cloth. And it feels purple, Johnston Franklin. You know how purple feels? Rich, with a grain that's both kind to and hard on the fingertips. Now it is your turn," she said, lying back on the pillows. "Tell me about the trees you have at home."

"Okay...well...let's see," he said and then stopped. "I can't," he protested, but she continued to prod him. "Okay, okay. The trees in my front yard are oak trees. They are live oak trees."

"Live oaks," she said.

"Yes. Live oak."

"Well, that doesn't mean a whole lot to me, Johnston Franklin. Are they shaped like fat stodgy men, or lithe like young girls? Are they dark, and do other colors show through in spots? Are they sheltering, or does the rain get past the leaves? And what does the bark feel like to the touch...does it stand away or cling to the wood?"

He leaned back against the pillow and tried to imagine them.

"They're shaped...like oak trees are shaped, I guess. I never noticed. And they're green...and brown, like I suppose most trees are."

"Well, how does the trunk feel?" Ouida asked.

"They are like...they're live oak, that's all. I don't know what else to say," he stammered, as she shook her head and argued. "I know what you call them, Johnston Franklin, but what are they like to you?"

"We had them put in a long time ago...they're what everyone has...and they're old...and big...and they have leaves, like all trees. I don't know what else to say. I don't know, that's all I see."

Ouida looked at him, propped on her elbow, and then slid down under the covers and went to sleep.

Johnston Franklin visited weekly for several months, but Ouida began to withdraw from him as she felt him trying to hold her closer and closer, like a butterfly in a Ball canning jar. Waxed paper stretched across the top. Breathing holes punched through.

The last time they met, on one of his regular forays from his wife and family, he held onto her as she got up to leave, and demanded to know where she was going. Ouida pulled her arm free and gave him a decimating look as she got her things to leave. When she glanced back to look at him for the last time, she saw a child whose fingers held traces of the black and orange dust of captured butterflies.

When it was just about finished with Johnston Franklin, Ouida chose the barber, Flood, who drew her with the economy of his attention, and looked at her from underneath his eyes. The other barbers flirted with her all the time, and played at asking her out. "You shore is one fine-lookin' woman," Alton would say, leaning on the arm of his chair as he waited for his first customer, shaking his head. "When, just when, are you gon' marry me?"

"After she marry me and I leave her," Regis answered, " 'cause you know a woman fine as she is don't mean nothin' but trouble. I prefer the ugly ones, truth be told, 'cause that way you're glad when they leave you."

She laughed at them playfully, and said, "You two are just no good. What about that devoted little lady of yours at home, Alton?"

"She would understand. She know I just married her 'cause I was waitin' on you."

Flood never joined in the joking, and he barely even smiled. Ouida didn't even know if he was married, and as she wasn't looking for a husband, she didn't care. He never looked her way when Johnston Franklin came to the shop, and he never shaved him or cut his hair. He prepared all of his own lotions and tools, neither accepting nor offering help. He traveled solo, with a hardness about him that she wanted to work soft.

When Ouida had passed between barber chairs one afternoon in search of towels, and brushed against his arm, he hadn't started, or looked at her, but she had seen the muscles in his forearm tense as he gripped his comb. After that she found reasons to go by his chair. Knowing that she would have to go after him, and thrilled by the pursuit, she brought him a cup of tea one morning and left it on the counter behind his chair. He let it sit all day, never thanking her and never drinking it. She did the same thing the next day, and the next, until, holding the cup with both hands, warming his palms, he lifted it to his mouth and drank. And as he lowered the cup, he looked at her with desire, and a trace of contempt.

The next evening, she waited until Alton and McGraw were gone, and she and Flood were left to lock up. Fiddling with his scissors and combs, he slowly cleaned up his chair and the floor around it, while she arranged and rearranged her manicurist tools, unable to speak. He went for his coat and hat and headed for the door. As he reached for the doorknob, she spoke.

"Flood?"

He stood with his hand on the knob and his back to her and then he turned, and she said nothing as he stood at the door waiting for her. They walked to her flat, and as soon as they got inside the door, they tore at each other's clothes, and took each other on the bare floor, as if it couldn't be helped, as if it had to be that way, the hard urgency a hurting they both wanted to feel. As soon as it was over, he dressed and left without saying good-bye, and Ouida didn't think of the risk she had taken until it was too late.

At the barbershop, things didn't change on the surface, and Ouida knew little more about Flood than before. What she did know was that the heat, the tension between them would make him return, and she waited for him to come to her again. At times she wondered if she had dreamed it, until a week later, she had stood watching him after Alton and McGraw had left, and he looked at her and grasped the back of his chair tight, until the leather squeaked. She knew he wanted her again; and again, he waited at the door.

In their fevered loving, Ouida saw Flood surrender, silently, to something in her. She wanted to be the one who reached him, against his will, the one whom he couldn't help but come back to, the one who excavated his pain, his need, and for a time, she was willing to exchange peace for the intensity of the fight. Again and again, she tugged on the one string that joined them and she reeled him in.

When this was no longer enough, Ouida had tried to push it further, to find out who he was, but the two of them were stuck in a moment in time, repeating again and again the same act, moving nowhere. By the time she heard Zella's call, she was letting go of what she had, and didn't have, with Flood, and she chose Zella, rain-voiced, in whom she met herself.

The first time she saw her, Zella was standing on the corner waiting for a streetcar as it began to shower, and Ouida watched her digging in her bag from the barbershop window for something to shield herself, cursing as her hair got wet. As soon as she had pulled out a newspaper to cover her head, she had tossed it down and stood there laughing as her head got soaked. Ouida glanced up and saw her as she was putting her instruments away, and moved to the window to watch as Zella lifted her arms and face to the rain and shook her head, opening her generous mouth to taste the falling water.

The next time she saw her, Zella had come into the shop for a haircut on the weekday allotted for colored customers, and Ouida had watched her enter and approach Alton's chair, struck by the way she moved with authority over space. She was tall and slender, and a few years older than Ouida, almost thirty. Her skin was copper-colored and her hair was a mass of dark ringlets, but it was her large flashing black eyes that were remarkable, one smaller than the other. When she walked over to Alton's chair and sat down, he came around to face her and declared, "Now you don't need a shave, and I know you not even thinkin' 'bout cuttin' off all that pretty hair, so just what are you doin' in my chair?"

Zella frowned and gave him a look that was a challenge. "You cut hair, don't you," she stated, rather than asked, and Alton nodded. 'Well," she said, "I suspect you cut it like your customers ask you to, is that right?" and Alton nodded again. "Then I suggest you get busy with your scissors and crop mine just above my cheek. Right about here," she said, gesturing with her hand.

Alton argued with her for a while, but he gave in when Zella said, "Why is it that colored folks feel every bit of our hair ought to be on our heads! If we were as concerned with what's in our heads as we are with what's on them, we'd be a lot further along."

At that, Alton had to laugh, and he took up his scissors. He shook his head as her hair fell to the floor, and exclaimed what a shame it was the entire time, and after Zella looked at the finished product in the mirror, she got up, paid him, and left, nodding to Ouida on the way out.

"Well," Alton said, as she was leaving, "Girl, bet' not mess with that one. I know her peoples, and she ain't quite right. What I mean to say is...she ain't normal."

When Ouida stared at him, wanting to know more but afraid to ask, he continued, "I know she'd like a sweet young thing like you all for her own. Her kind, they like that."

"Now that's a lovely woman," Zella said to herself once she was outside. She turned back and caught Ouida's eye through the window, and there was between them a moment of recognition, whose power made them turn away.

Ouida went to the family house that evening and stayed the night, and Vesta sat on the edge of her bed working lotion into her face while Ouida was brushing and plaiting her hair. "Vesta, I met someone who's different," she ventured, unsure of herself.

"Different..." Vesta replied. "What does that mean?" And Ouida paused. "I don't know. Different, somehow. I don't know how to explain it."

"You gotta do better than that, Ouida," Vesta said. "It's late and I'm not up to reading minds tonight."

"Well...she gets her hair cut short, and at the shop," she began, to which Vesta raised her eyebrows. "I don't know, she's kind of not feminine, but she is feminine after all." Vesta just looked at her.

Ouida told Vesta what Alton had said and then she stopped brushing and asked, "What do you think, Vesta? You know anything about
these things?"

Vesta didn't and so she shook her head. "I've heard of people like
that, but no, I don't know at all about that sort of thing. I can say, for
sure, though, that it sounds like trouble to me," and then she finished
up with her face, turned her bed down, and curled up facing the wall.
But she lay there in the darkness considering what Ouida had said, and
it was a long time before she fell asleep.

The next time Ouida saw Zella, two weeks later, she had thought
about what Alton and Vesta had said and she was ready for Zella's greeting, but not for the way she made her feel, like a dry part of her was
being watered. "Rain," she whispered to herself, "Rain."

After her haircut, Zella sat down at Ouida's table and said, "I think
I'm due for a manicure." In fact, she had never had a manicure, but
something in Ouida's response to her glance had pulled her there, and
she had to see what her voice sounded like.

"My name is Zella," she opened, and Ouida responded, "Ouida...
Ouida is my name."

They smiled and Zella asked her what kind of name it was and
where she got it. She said, quietly, "It was passed down. Or so my mother
said." As Ouida worked on Zella's hands, she noticed how strong and
worn with experience they looked and felt, and she wanted to know
where those hands had been.

Zella began to feel the need for a weekly haircut or a manicure,
and she and Ouida found themselves sitting for hours talking while she
surrendered her fingers to Ouida's, and felt something in her tear loose.
Each time she left she told herself on the way home that she was risking
her heart foolishly, that in the end, she would be destroyed. She knew,
somehow, that Ouida had known only men, and she told herself that she
could never have her and that she had to stop going. But she always
found a reason to return.

She stayed one time until the barbershop closed, and the two of
them kept on walking down the street toward Ouida's flat. They stopped
to buy fruit and when they got to the flat, Ouida made tea and offered
Zella one of her chipped cups, and then they sat in the nook she had
made next to the kitchen with her cerulean blue chairs, telling about
themselves until their hands, both reaching for the teapot, touched.

"Say yes," Zella whispered.

"Yes," Ouida answered. "Yes."

They sat in the last light of the day as it thickened and became gold, entering through the window, coming down to them, meeting them. Lowering itself into their laps, the golden light thick with all that the day had held. Light not merely for seeing, but for touch. For love.

It was almost dawn again. Almost light, but not yet, not yet. Zella rose from the bed and went to the icebox to get a pear. She sliced it into wedges and removed the seeds, and little beads of juice stood out on the cool inner surface of the fruit. She knelt beside the bed and said, quietly, "Close your eyes."

And she turned a wedge of the iced fruit, turned it to Ouida, and the open cool innerness of the wedge met her lips. Ouida sank her mouth into it, giving in to it, and Zella fed her, after she was spent, but not really, not quite, not yet, as the fire rose in her again, mingling with the ice-hot wetness of the fruit, into an ache that had to be quenched even though it was getting light, pale light, pale and thin and tinged with blue, thin, but not yet, not yet, and it had to be now, even though there would be time for it all again and again and again across the years, it must be now and now and now.

Randall Kenan

■ ■ ■

[1963–]

RANDALL KENAN'S SCHOOL YEARS COINCIDED WITH THE FIRST
integration of public schools in Duplin County, North Carolina, an
experience the Brooklyn-born author later put to use in his fiction.
At the University of North Carolina at Chapel Hill, he initially studied physics. But literature soon won his attention, especially the works
of Toni Morrison and other African American writers, and he graduated with a degree in English literature in 1985. In fact, through the
connections of Morrison he landed his first publishing job at
Random House.

Working as a book editor, Kenan became familiar with the writing
of James Baldwin, whose autobiographically based references to race,
homosexuality, and his relationship with the black church inspired the
content of Kenan's first book, the novel entitled *A Visitation of Spirits*
(1989). Following its publication, the author left Random House for a
teaching position at Sarah Lawrence College, where he continued to
write. Among Kenan's other titles are a young adult biography, *James
Baldwin* (1994), and an ethnographic travel book, *Walking on Water:
Black American Lives at the Turn of the Century* (2000). He is the recipient
of a National Book Critics Award nomination, a Guggenheim
Fellowship, a Sherwood Anderson Award, and an American Academy of
Arts and Letters' Prix de Rome.

In "The Foundations of the Earth," a short story drawn from
Kenan's collection *Let the Dead Bury Their Dead* (1992), Maggie
MacGowan Williams, an elderly black woman living in rural North
Carolina, struggles to come to terms with the homosexuality of her

estranged (and now deceased) grandson Edward. Six months after his funeral, where Mrs. Williams had first discovered that Edward had been gay, she invites Gabriel, her grandson's white lover, to visit her in the hopes of learning more about Edward's private life.

The Foundations of the Earth

[1992]

I

Of course they didn't pay it any mind at first: just a tractor—one of the most natural things in the world to see in a field—kicking dust up into the afternoon sky and slowly toddling off the road into a soybean field. And fields surrounded Mrs. Maggie MacGowan Williams's house, giving the impression that her lawn stretched on and on until it dropped off into the woods far by the way. Sometimes she was certain she could actually see the earth's curve—not merely the bend of the small hill on which her house sat but the great slope of the sphere, the way scientists explained it in books, a monstrous globe floating in a cold nothingness. She would sometimes sit by herself on the patio late of an evening, in the same chair she was sitting in now, sip from her Coca-Cola, and think about how big the earth must be to seem flat to the eye.

She wished she were alone now. It was Sunday.

"Now I wonder what that man is doing with a tractor out there today?"

They sat on Maggie's patio, reclined in that after Sunday-dinner way—Maggie; the Right Reverend Hezekiah Barden, round and pompous as ever; Henrietta Fuchee, the prim and priggish music teacher and president of the First Baptist Church Auxiliary Council; Emma Lewis, Maggie's sometimes housekeeper; and Gabriel, Mrs. Maggie Williams's young, white, special guest—all looking out lazily into the early summer, watching the sun begin its slow downward arc, feeling the baked ham and the candied sweet potatoes and the fried chicken with the collard greens and green beans and beets settle in their bellies, talking shallow and pleasant talk, and sipping their Coca-Colas and bitter lemonade.

"Don't they realize it's Sunday?" Reverend Barden leaned back in his chair and tugged at his suspenders thoughtfully, eyeing the tractor as it turned into another row. He reached for a sweating glass of lemonade, his red bow tie afire in the penultimate beams of the day.

"I...I don't understand. What's wrong?" Maggie could see her other guests watching Gabriel intently, trying to discern why on earth he was present at Maggie MacGowan Williams's table.

"What you mean, what's wrong?" The Reverend Barden leaned forward and narrowed his eyes at the young man. "What's wrong is: it's Sunday."

"So? I don't..." Gabriel himself now looked embarrassed, glancing to Maggie, who wanted to save him but could not.

"'So?' 'So?'" Leaning toward Gabriel and narrowing his eyes, Barden asked: "You're not from a church-going family, are you?"

"Well, no. Today was my first time in... Oh, probably ten years."

"Uh-huh." Barden corrected his posture, as if to say he pitied Gabriel's being an infidel but had the patience to instruct him. "Now you see, the Lord has declared Sunday as His day. It's holy. 'Six days shalt thou labor and do all thy work: but the seventh day is the sabbath of the Lord thy God: in it thou shalt not do any work, thou, nor thy son, nor thy daughter, thy manservant, nor thy maidservant, nor thy cattle, nor thy stranger that is within thy gates: for in six days the Lord made heaven and earth, the sea, and all that in them is, and rested the seventh day: wherefore, the Lord blessed the sabbath day, and hallowed it.' Exodus. Chapter twenty, verses nine and ten."

"Amen." Henrietta closed her eyes and rocked.

"Hez." Maggie inclined her head a bit to entreat the good Reverend to desist. He gave her an understanding smile, which made her cringe slightly, fearing her gesture might have been mistaken for a sign of intimacy.

"But, Miss Henrietta—" Emma Lewis tapped the tabletop, like a judge in court, changing the subject. "Like I was saying, I believe that Rick on *The Winds of Hope* is going to marry that gal before she gets too big with child, don't you?" Though Emma kept house for Maggie Williams, to Maggie she seemed more like a sister who came three days a week, more to visit than to clean.

"Now go on away from here, Emma." Henrietta did not look up from her empty cake plate, her glasses hanging on top of her sagging breasts from a silver chain. "Talking about that worldly foolishness on TV. You know I don't pay that mess any attention." She did not want the Reverend to know that she secretly watched afternoon soap operas, just like Emma and all the other women in the congregation. Usually she gossiped to beat the band about this rich heifer and that handsome hunk whenever she found a fellow TV-gazer. Buck-toothed hypocrite, Maggie thought. She knew the truth: Henrietta, herself a widow now on ten years, was sweet on the widower minister, who in turn, alas, had his eye on Maggie.

"Now, Miss Henrietta, we was talking about it t'other day. Don't you think he's apt to marry her soon?" Emma's tone was insistent.

"*I don't know,* Emma." Visibly agitated, Henrietta donned her glasses and looked into the fields. "I wonder who that is anyhow?"

Annoyed by Henrietta's rebuff, Emma stood and began to collect the few remaining dishes. Her purple-and-yellow floral print dress hugged her ample hips. "It's that ole Morton Henry that Miss Maggie leases that piece of land to." She walked toward the door, into the house. "He ain't no God-fearing man."

"Well, that's plain to see." The Reverend glanced over to Maggie. She shrugged.

They are ignoring Gabriel, Maggie thought. She had invited them to dinner after church services thinking it would be pleasant for Gabriel to meet other people in Tims Creek. But generally they chose not to see him, and when they did it was with ill-concealed scorn or petty curiosity or annoyance. At first the conversation seemed civil enough. But the ice was never truly broken, questions still buzzed around the talk like horse-flies, Maggie could tell. "Where you from?" Henrietta had asked. "What's your line of work?" Barden had asked. While Gabriel sat there with a look on his face somewhere between peace and pain. But Maggie refused to believe she had made a mistake. At this stage of her life she depended on no one for anything, and she was certainly not dependent on the approval of these self-important fools.

She had been steeled by anxiety when she picked Gabriel up at the airport that Friday night. But as she caught sight of him stepping from the jet and greeted him, asking about the weather in Boston; and after she had ushered him to her car and watched him slide in, seeming quite at home; though it still felt awkward, she thought: I'm doing the right thing.

II

"Well, thank you for inviting me, Mrs. Williams. But I don't under-stand... Is something wrong?"

"*Wrong?* No, nothing's wrong, Gabriel. I just thought it'd be good to see you. Sit and talk to you. We didn't have much time at the funeral."

"Gee... I—"

"You don't want to make an old woman sad, now do you?"

"Well, Mrs. Williams, if you put it like that, how can I refuse?"

"Weekend after next then?"

There was a pause in which she heard muted voices in the wire. "Okay."

After she hung up the phone and sat down in her favorite chair in the den, she heaved a momentous sigh. Well, she had done it. At last. The weight of uncertainty would be lifted. She could confront him face to face. She wanted to know about her grandboy, and Gabriel was the only one who could tell her what she wanted to know. It was that simple. Surely, he realized what this invitation meant. She leaned back looking out the big picture window onto the tops of the brilliantly blooming crepe myrtle trees in the yard, listening to the grandfather clock mark the time.

III

Her grandson's funeral had been six months ago, but it seemed much longer. Perhaps the fact that Edward had been gone away from home so long without seeing her, combined with the weeks and days and hours and minutes she had spent trying not to think about him and all the craziness that had surrounded his death, somehow lengthened the time.

At first she chose to ignore it, the strange and bitter sadness that seemed to have overtaken her every waking moment. She went about her daily life as she had done for thirty-odd years, overseeing her stores, her land, her money; buying groceries, paying bills, shopping, shopping; going to church and talking to her few good living friends and the few silly fools she was obliged to suffer. But all day, dusk to dawn, and especially at night, she had what the field-workers called "a monkey on your back," when the sun beats down so hot it makes you delirious; but her monkey chilled and angered her, born not of the sun but of a profound loneliness, an oppressive emptiness, a stabbing guilt. Sometimes she even wished she were a drinking woman.

The depression had come with the death of Edward, though its roots reached farther back, to the time he seemed to have vanished.

There had been so many years of asking other members of the family: Have you heard from him? Have you seen him? So many years of only a Christmas card or birthday card a few days early, or a cryptic, taciturn phone call on Sunday mornings, and then no calls at all. At some point she realized she had no idea where he was or how to get in touch with him. Mysteriously, he would drop a line to his half-sister, Clarissa, or drop a card without a return address. He was gone. Inevitably, she had to ask: Had she done something evil to the boy to drive him away? Had she tried too hard to make sure he became nothing like his father and grandfather? I was as good a mother as a woman can claim to be, she thought: from the cradle on he had all the material things he needed, and he certainly didn't want for attention, for care; and I trained him proper, he was a well-mannered and upright young fellow when he left here for college. Oh, I was proud of that boy, winning a scholarship to Boston University. Tall, handsome like his granddad. He'd make somebody a good…

So she continued picking out culprits: school, the cold North, strange people, strange ideas. But now in her crystalline hindsight she could lay no blame on anyone but Edward. And the more she remembered battles with the mumps and the measles and long division and taunts from his schoolmates, the more she became aware of her true anger. He owes me respect, damn it. The least he can do is keep in touch. Is that so much to ask?

But before she could make up her mind to find him and confront him with her fury, before she could cuss him out good and call him an ungrateful, no-account bastard just like his father, a truck would have the heartless audacity to skid into her grandchild's car one rainy night in Springfield and end his life at twenty-seven, taking that opportunity away from her forever. When they told her of his death she cursed her weakness. Begging God for another chance. But instead He gave her something she had never imagined.

Clarissa was the one to finally tell her. "Grandma," she had said, "Edward's been living with another man all these years."

"So?"

"No, Grandma. Like man and wife."

Maggie had never before been so paralyzed by news. One question answered, only to be replaced by a multitude. Gabriel had come with the body, like an interpreter for the dead. They had been living together in

Boston, where Edward worked in a bookstore. He came, head bowed, rheumy-eyed, exhausted. He gave her no explanation; nor had she asked him for any, for he displayed the truth in his vacant and humble glare and had nothing to offer but the penurious tribute of his trembling hands. Which was more than she wanted.

In her world she had been expected to be tearless, patient, comforting to other members of the family; folk were meant to sit back and say, "Lord, ain't she taking it well. I don't think I could be so calm if my grandboy had've died so young." Magisterially she had done her duty; she had taken it all in stride. But her world began to hopelessly unravel that summer night at the wake in the Raymond Brown Funeral Home, among the many somber-bright flower arrangements, the fluorescent lights, and the gleaming bronze casket, when Gabriel tried to tell her how sorry he was… How dare he? This pathetic, stumbling, poor trashy white boy, to throw his sinful lust for her grandbaby in her face, as if to bury a grandchild weren't bad enough. Now this abomination had to be flaunted.—Sorry, indeed! The nerve! Who the hell did he think he was to parade their shame about?

Her anger was burning so intensely that she knew if she didn't get out she would tear his heart from his chest, his eyes from their sockets, his testicles from their sac. With great haste she took her leave, brushing off the funeral director and her brother's wives and husband's brothers—they all probably thinking her overcome with grief rather than anger—and had Clarissa drive her home. When she got to the house she filled a tub with water as hot as she could stand it and a handful of bath oil beads, and slipped in, praying her hatred would mingle with the mist and evaporate, leaving her at least sane.

Next, sleep. Healing sleep, soothing sleep, sleep to make the world go away, sleep like death. Her mama had told her that sleep was the best medicine God ever made. When things get too rough—go to bed. Her family had been known as the family that retreated to bed. Ruined crop? No money? Get some shut-eye. Maybe it'll be better in the morning. Can't be worse. Maggie didn't give a damn where Gabriel was to sleep that night; someone else would deal with it. She didn't care about all the people who would come to the house after the wake to the Sitting Up, talking, eating, drinking, watching over the still body till sunrise; they could take care of themselves. The people came; but Maggie slept. From deeps under deeps of slumber she sensed her granddaughter stick her head in the door and whisper, asking Maggie if she wanted something to eat. Maggie didn't stir. She slept. And in her sleep she dreamed.

She dreamed she was Job sitting on his dung heap, dressed in sack-cloth and ashes, her body covered with boils, scratching with a stick, sending away Eliphaz and Bildad and Zophar and Elihu, who came to counsel her, and above her the sky boiled and churned and the air roared, and she matched it, railing against God, against her life—*Why? Why? Why did you kill him, you heartless old fiend? Why make me live to see him die? What earthly purpose could you have in such a wicked deed? You are God, but you are not good. Speak to me, damn it. Why? Why? Why?* Hurricanes whipped and thunder ripped through a sky streaked by lightning, and she was lifted up, spinning, spinning, and Edward floated before her in the rushing air and quickly turned around into the comforting arms of Gabriel, winged, who clutched her grandboy to his bosom and soared away, out of the storm. Maggie screamed and the winds grew stronger, and a voice, gentle and sweet, not thunderous as she expected, spoke to her from the whirlwind: *Who is this that darkeneth counsel by words without knowledge? Gird up now thy loins like a man; for I will demand of thee, and answer thou me. Where wast thou when I laid the foundations of the earth? Declare if thou hast understanding...* The voice spoke of the myriad cre-ations of the universe, the stupendous glory of the Earth and its inhabitants. But Maggie was not deterred in the face of the maelstrom, saying: *Answer me, damn you: Why?*, and the winds began to taper off and finally halted, and Maggie was alone, standing on water. A fish, what appeared to be a mackerel, stuck its head through the surface and said: *Kind woman, be not aggrieved and put your anger away. Your arrogance has clouded your good mind. Who asked you to love? Who asked you to hate?* The fish dipped down with a plip and gradually Maggie too began to slip down into the water, down, down, down, sinking, below depths of reason and love, down into the dark unknown of her own mind, down, down, down.

Maggie MacGowan Williams woke the next morning to the harsh chatter of a bluejay chasing a mocking-bird just outside her window, a racket that caused her to open her eyes quickly to blinding sunlight. Squinting, she looked about the room, seeing the chest of drawers that had once belonged to her mother and her mother's mother before that, the chairs, the photographs on the wall, the television, the rug thickly soft, the closet door slightly ajar, the bureau, the mirror atop the bureau, and herself in the mirror, all of it bright in the crisp morning light. She saw herself looking, if not refreshed, calmed, and within her the rage had gone, replaced by a numb humility and a plethora of questions. Questions. Questions. Questions.

Inwardly she had felt beatific that day of the funeral, ashamed at her anger of the day before. She greeted folk gently, softly, with a smile, her tones honey-flavored but solemn, and she reassumed the mantle of one-who-comforts-more-than-needing-comfort.

The immediate family had gathered at Maggie's house—Edward's father, Tom, Jr.; Tom, Jr.'s wife, Lucille; the grandbaby, Paul (Edward's brother); Clarissa. Raymond Brown's long black limousine took them from the front door of Maggie's house to the church, where the yard was crammed with people in their greys and navy blues, dark browns, and deep, deep burgundies. In her new humility she mused: When, oh when will we learn that death is not so somber, not something to mourn so much as celebrate? We should wear fire reds, sun oranges, hello greens, ocean-deep blues, and dazzling, welcome-home whites. She herself wore a bright dress of saffron and a blue scarf. She thought Edward would have liked it.

The family lined up and Gabriel approached her. As he stood before her—raven-haired, pink-skinned, abject, eyes bloodshot—she experienced a bevy of conflicting emotions: disgust, grief, anger, tenderness, fear, weariness, pity. Nevertheless she *had* to be civil, *had* to make a leap of faith and of understanding. Somehow she felt it had been asked of her. And though there were still so many questions, so much to sort out, for now she would mime patience, pretend to be accepting, feign peace. Time would unravel the rest.

She reached out, taking both his hands into her own, and said, the way she would to an old friend: "How have you been?"

IV

"But now, Miss Maggie…"

She sometimes imagined the good Reverend Barden as a toad-frog or an impotent bull. His rantings and ravings bored her, and his clumsy advances repelled her; and when he tried to impress her with his holiness and his goodness, well…

"…that man should know better than to be plowing on a Sunday. Sunday! Why, the Lord said…"

"Reverend, I know what the Lord said. And I'm sure Morton Henry knows what the Lord said. But I am not the Lord, Reverend, and if Morton Henry wants to plow the west field on Sunday afternoon, well, it's his soul, not mine."

"But, Maggie. Miss Maggie. It's—"

"Well,"—Henrietta Fuchee sat perched to interject her five cents into the debate—"but, Maggie. It's your land! Now, Reverend, doesn't it say somewhere in Exodus that a man, or a woman in this case, a woman is responsible for the deeds or misdeeds of someone in his or her employ, especially on her property?"

"But he's not an emplo—"

"Well,"—Barden scratched his head—"I think I know what you're talking about, Henrietta. It may be in Deuteronomy...or Leviticus...part of the Mosaic Law, which..."

Maggie cast a quick glance at Gabriel. He seemed to be interested in and entertained by this contest of moral superiority. There was certainly something about his face...but she could not stare. He looked so *normal*...

"Well, I don't think you should stand for it, Maggie."

"Henrietta? What do you...? Look, if you want him to stop, *you* go tell him what the Lord said. I—"

The Right Reverend Hezekiah Barden stood, hiking his pants up to his belly. "Well, *I* will. A man's soul is a valuable thing. And I can't risk your own soul being tainted by the actions of one of your sharecroppers."

"My soul? Sharecropper—he's not a sharecropper. He leases that land. I—wait!... Hezekiah!... This doesn't..."

But Barden had stepped off the patio onto the lawn and was headed toward the field, marching forth like old Nathan on his way to confront King David.

"Wait, Reverend." Henrietta hopped up, slinging her black pocketbook over her left shoulder. "Well, Maggie?" She peered at Maggie defiantly, as if to ask: *Where do you stand?*

"Now, Henrietta, I—"

Henrietta pivoted, her moral righteousness jagged and sharp as a shard of glass. "Somebody has to stand up for right!" She tromped off after Barden.

Giggling, Emma picked up the empty glasses. "I don't think ole Morton Henry gone be too happy to be preached at this afternoon."

Maggie looked from Emma to Gabriel in bewilderment, at once annoyed and amused. All three began to laugh out loud. As Emma got to the door she turned to Maggie. "Hon, you better go see that they don't get into no fistfight, don't you think? You know that Reverend don't know when to be quiet." She looked to Gabriel and nodded knowingly. "You better go with her, son," and was gone into the house; her molasses-thick laughter sweetening the air.

Reluctantly Maggie stood, looking at the two figures—Henrietta had caught up with Barden—a tiny cloud of dust rising from their feet. "Come on, Gabe. Looks like we have to go referee."

Gabriel walked beside her, a broad smile on his face. Maggie thought of her grandson being attracted to this tall white man. She tried to see them together and couldn't. At that moment she understood that she was being called on to realign her thinking about men and women, and men and men, and even women and women. Together…the way Adam and Eve were meant to be together.

V

Initially she found it difficult to ask the questions she wanted to ask. Almost impossible.

They got along well on Saturday. She took him out to dinner; they went shopping. All the while she tried with all her might to convince herself that she felt comfortable with this white man, with this homosexual, with this man who had slept with her grandboy. Yet he managed to impress her with his easygoing manner and openness and humor.

"Mrs. W." He had given her a *nickname,* of all things. No one had given her a nickname since… "Mrs. W., you sure you don't want to try on some swimsuits?"

She laughed at his kind-hearted jokes, seeing, oddly enough, something about him very like Edward; but then that thought would make her sad and confused.

Finally that night over coffee at the kitchen table she began to ask what they had both gingerly avoided.

"Why didn't he just tell me?"

"He was afraid, Mrs. W. It's just that simple."

"Of what?"

"That you might disown him. That you might stop...well, you know, loving him, I guess."

"Does your family know?"

"Yes."

"How do they take it?"

"My mom's fine. She's great. Really. She and Edward got along swell. My dad. Well, he'll be okay for a while, but every now and again we'll have these talks, you know, about cures and stuff and sometimes it just gets heated. I guess it'll just take a little more time with him."

"But don't you *want* to be normal?"

"Mrs. W., I *am*. Normal."

"I see."

They went to bed at one-thirty that morning. As Maggie buttoned up her nightgown, Gabriel's answers whizzed about her brain; but they brought along more damnable questions and Maggie went to bed feeling betrayal and disbelief and revulsion and anger.

In church that next morning with Gabriel, she began to doubt the wisdom of having asked him to come. As he sat beside her in the pew, as the Reverend Barden sermonized on Jezebel and Ahab, as the congregation unsuccessfully tried to disguise their curiosity—("What is that white boy doing here with Maggie Williams? Who is he? Where he come from?")—she wanted Gabriel to go ahead and tell her what to think: *We're perverts* or *You're wrong-headed, your church has poisoned your mind against your own grandson; if he had come out to you, you would have rejected him. Wouldn't you?* Would she have?

Barden's sermon droned on and on that morning; the choir sang; after the service people politely and gently shook Gabriel and Maggie's hands and then stood off to the side, whispering, clearly perplexed.

On the drive back home, as if out of the blue, she asked him: "Is it hard?"

"Ma'am?"

"Being who you are? What you are?"

He looked over at her, and she could not meet his gaze with the same intensity that had gone into her question. "Being gay?"

"Yes."

"Well, I have no choice."

"So I understand. But is it hard?"

"Edward and I used to get into arguments about that, Mrs. W." His tone altered a bit. He spoke more softly, gently, the way a widow speaks of her dead husband. Or, indeed, the way a widower speaks of his dead husband. "He used to say it was harder being black in this country than gay. Gays can always pass for straight; but blacks can't always pass for white. And most can never pass."

"And what do you think now?"

"Mrs. W., I think *life* is hard, you know?"

"Yes. I know."

VI

Death had first introduced itself to Maggie when she was a child. Her grandfather and grandmother both died before she was five; her father died when she was nine; her mother when she was twenty-five; over the years all her brothers except one. Her husband ten years ago. Her first memories of death: watching the women wash a cold body: the look of brown skin darkening, hardening: the corpse laid out on a cooling board, wrapped in a winding-cloth, before interment: fear of ghosts, bodyless souls: troubled sleep. So much had changed in seventy years; now there were embalming, funeral homes, morticians, insurance policies, bronze caskets, a bureaucratic wall between deceased and bereaved. Among the many things she regretted about Edward's death was not being able to touch his body. It made his death less real. But so much about the world seemed unreal to her these dark, dismal, and gloomy days. Now the flat earth was said to be round and bumblebees were not supposed to fly.

What was supposed to be and what truly was. Maggie learned these things from magazines and television and books; she loved to read. From her first week in that small schoolhouse with Miss Clara Oxendine, she had wanted to be a teacher. School: the scratchy chalkboard, the dusty-smelling textbooks, labyrinthine grammar and spelling and arithmetic, geography, reading out loud, giving confidence to the boy who would never learn to read well, correcting addition and subtraction problems, the taste and the scent of the schoolroom, the heat of the potbellied stove in January. She liked that small world; for her it was large. Yet how could she pay for enough education to become a teacher? Her mother would smile, encouragingly, when young Maggie would ask her, not looking up from her sewing, and merely say: "We'll find a way."

However, when she was fourteen she met a man named Thomas Williams, he sixteen going on thirty-nine. Infatuation replaced her dreams and murmured to her in languages she had never heard before, whispered to her another tale: *You will be a merchant's wife.*

Thomas Williams would come a-courting on Sunday evenings for two years, come driving his father's red Ford truck, stepping out with his biscuit-shined shoes, his one good Sunday suit, his hat cocked at an impertinent angle, and a smile that would make cold butter drip. But his true power lay in his tongue. He would spin yarns and tell tales that would make the oldest storyteller slap his knee and declare: "Hot damn! Can't that boy lie!" He could talk a possum out of a tree. He spoke to Maggie about his dream of opening his own store, a dry-goods store, and then maybe two or three or four. An audacious dream for a seventeen-year-old black boy, son of a farmer in 1936—and he promised, oh, how he promised, to keep Maggie by his side through it all.

Thinking back, on the other side of time and dreams, where fantasies and wishing had been realized, where she sat rich and alone, Maggie wondered what Thomas Williams could possibly have seen in that plain brown girl. Himself the son of a farmer with his own land, ten sons and two daughters, all married and doing well. There she was, poorer than a skinned rabbit, and not that pretty. Was he looking for a woman who would not flinch at hard work?

Somehow, borrowing from his father, from his brothers, working two, three jobs at the shipyards, in the fields, with Maggie taking in sewing and laundry, cleaning houses, saving, saving, saving, they opened their store; and were married. Days, weeks, years of days, weeks of days, weeks of inventory and cleaning and waiting on people and watching over the dry-goods store, which became a hardware store in the sixties while the one store became two. They were prosperous; they were respected; they owned property. At seventy she now wanted for nothing. Long gone was the dream of a schoolhouse and little children who skinned their knees and the teaching of the ABCs. Some days she imagined she had two lives and she preferred the original dream to the flesh-and-blood reality.

Now, at least, she no longer had to fight bitterly with her pompous, self-satisfied, driven, blaspheming husband, who worked seven days a week, sixteen hours a day, money-grubbing and mean though—out-wardly—flamboyantly generous; a man who lost interest in her bed after her first and only son, Thomas, Jr., arrived broken in heart, spirit, and brain upon delivery; a son whose only true achievement in life was to illegitimately produce Edward by some equally brainless waif of a girl, now long vanished; a son who practically thrust the few-week-old infant into Maggie's arms, then flew off to a life of waste, sloth, petty crime, and finally a menial job in one of her stores and an ignoble marriage to a woman who could not conceal her greedy wish for Maggie to die.

Her life now was life that no longer had bite or spit or fire. She no longer worked. She no longer had to worry about Thomas's philander-ing and what pretty young thing he was messing with now. She no longer had the little boy whom Providence seemed to have sent her to maintain her sanity, to moor her to the Earth, and to give her vast energies focus.

In a world not real, is there truly guilt in willing reality to cohere through the life of another? Is that such a great sin? Maggie had turned to the boy—young, brown, handsome—to hold on to the world itself. She now saw that clearly. How did it happen? The mental slipping and sliding that allowed her to meld and mess and confuse her life with his, his rights with her wants, his life with her wish? He would not be like his father or his grandfather; he would rise up, go to school, be strong, be honest, upright. He would be; she would be…a feat of legerdemain; a sorcery of vicariousness in which his victory was her victory. He was her champion. Her hope.

Now he was gone. And now she had to come to terms with this news of his being "gay," as the world called what she had been taught was an unholy abomination. Slowly it all came together in her mind's eye: Edward.

He should have known better. I should have known better. I must learn better.

VII

They stood there At the end of the row, all of them waiting for the trac-tor to arrive and for the Reverend Hezekiah Barden to save the soul of Morton Henry.

Morton saw them standing there from his mount atop the green John Deere as it bounced across the broken soil. Maggie could make out the expression on his face: confusion. Three blacks and a white man out in the fields to see him. Did his house burn down? His wife die? The President declare war on Russia?

A big, red-haired, red-faced man, his face had so many freckles he appeared splotched. He had a big chew of tobacco in his left jaw and he spat out the brown juice as he came up the edge of the row and put the clutch in neutral.

"How you all today? Miss Maggie?"

"Hey, Morton."

Barden started right up, thumbs in his suspenders, and reared back on his heels. "Now I spect you're a God-fearing man?"

"Beg pardon?"

"I even spect you go to church from time to time?"

"Church? Miss Maggie, I—"

The Reverend held up his hand. "And I warrant you that your preacher—where *do* you go to church, son?"

"I go to—wait a minute. What's going on here? Miss Maggie—"

Henrietta piped up. "It's Sunday! You ain't supposed to be working and plowing fields on a Sunday!"

Morton Henry looked over to Maggie, who stood there in the bright sun, then to Gabriel, as if to beg him to speak, make some sense of this curious event. He scratched his head. "You mean to tell me you all come out here to tell me I ain't suppose to plow this here field?"

"Not on Sunday you ain't. It's the Lord's Day."

"'The Lord's Day'?" Morton Henry was visibly amused. He tongued at the wad of tobacco in his jaw. "The Lord's Day." He chuckled out loud.

"Now it ain't no laughing matter, young man." The Reverend's voice took on a dark tone.

Morton seemed to be trying to figure out who Gabriel was. He spat. "Well, I tell you, Reverend. If the Lord wants to come plow these fields I'd be happy to let him."

"You..." Henrietta stomped her foot, causing dust to rise. "You can't talk about the Lord like that. You're using His name in vain."

"I'll talk about Him any way I please to." Morton Henry's face became redder by the minute. "I got two jobs, five head of children, and a sick wife, and the Lord don't seem too worried about that. I spect I ain't gone worry too much about plowing this here field on His day none neither."

"Young man, you can't—"

Morton Henry looked to Maggie. "Now, Miss Maggie, this is your land, and if you don't want me to plow it, I'll give you back your lease and you can pay me my money and find somebody else to tend this here field!"

Everybody looked at Maggie. How does this look, she couldn't help thinking, a black woman defending a white man against a black minister? Why the *hell* am I here having to do this? she fumed. Childish, hypocritical idiots and fools. Time is just slipping, slipping away and all they have to do is fuss and bother about other folk's business while their own houses are burning down. God save their souls. She wanted to yell this, to cuss them out and stomp away and leave them to their ignorance. But in the end, what good would it do?

She took a deep breath. "Morton Henry. You do what you got to do. Just like the rest of us."

Morton Henry bowed his head to Maggie, "Ma'am," turned to the others with a gloating grin, "Scuse me," put his gear in first, and turned down the next row.

"Well—"

Barden began to speak but Maggie just turned, not listening, not wanting to hear, thinking: When, Lord, oh when will we learn? Will we ever? *Respect,* she thought. Oh how complicated.

They followed Maggie, heading back to the house, Gabriel beside her, tall and silent, the afternoon sunrays romping in his black hair. How curious the world had become that she would be asking a white man to exonerate her in the eyes of her own grandson; how strange that at seventy, when she had all the laws and rules down pat, she would have to begin again, to learn. But all this stuff and bother would have to come later, for now she felt so, so tired, what with the weekend's activities weighing on her three-score-and-ten-year-old bones and joints; and she wished it were sunset, and she alone on her patio, contemplating the roundness and flatness of the earth, and slipping softly and safely into sleep.

JACQUELINE WOODSON

■ ■ ■

[1963–]

BORN IN COLUMBUS, OHIO, CHILDREN'S BOOK WRITER AND young adult novelist Jacqueline Woodson divided her childhood between her grandmother and older siblings in North Carolina and her mother, living in Brooklyn. The earliest recognition of her literary gifts came in fifth grade, when she won a contest for a tribute poem to Martin Luther King, Jr. Her first "lesbian-related" writings, however, were love letters to other teenaged girls. Eventually, Woodson came out as a lesbian in a creative writing class at New York's Adelphi University, from which she graduated with a degree in English literature in 1985.

Woodson's first job after college was working for a children's book company, where she was encouraged by a coworker to write her first book, *Last Summer with Maizon* (1990). Later, this story about best friends Margaret and Maizon developed into the trilogy that includes *Maizon at Blue Hill* (1992) and *Between Madison and Palmetto* (1993). Her other popular works include *I Hadn't Meant to Tell You This* (1994), named a Coretta Scott King Honor Book in Fiction, and her Lambda Award–winning novel for adults, *Autobiography of a Family Photo* (1995). Woodson has been a fellow at the MacDowell Colony and at the Fine Arts Work Center in Provincetown, Massachusetts, as well as a recipient of the *Kenyon Review* Award for Literary Excellence in Fiction.

Noted for effectively incorporating controversial subject matter such as racism, substance abuse, and AIDS into her work, Woodson is also one of the first writers of color to explicitly address homosexual themes in young adult fiction. Her eighth novel and Scholastic Books'

first gay publication, *From the Notebooks of Melanin Sun* (1995), explores
lesbianism from the point of view of a thirteen-year-old African
American named Melanin, whose mother has recently begun dating a
white woman.

from **From the Notebooks of Melanin Sun**

[1995]

I was sitting at my desk going through my frog stamps when the phone rang a few hours later. "Can I speak to Melanin Sun?" a girl's voice said.

"This is Mel."

"Well, this is Angie."

"What's up, Angie?" I said, then immediately regretted it. It sounded rehearsed because it was. I had dreamed this moment a million times and now here it was. And *she* was calling *me*. Maybe that made me lame, though, 'cause I should have been the man about it.

Angie laughed nervously.

Breathe, Mel. Start all over. "So what's up?"

"Nothing," Angie said, "I was just calling to say hey."

We were silent for a few moments. I couldn't think of a single thing to say. Stupid.

"Oh, well," Angie said. "I just wanted to say hello. It's hard to talk to you in person since you're always with your friends."

"Sometimes I'm not."

"Like when?"

I thought for a moment. "When I'm in the house."

I looked out the kitchen window. It was cloudy again. Would Angie run screaming from here if she knew about Mama? Would she ever speak to me again? What was the use of even talking to her, I wondered, if the minute she found out, she wouldn't even pick up the phone to dial my number?

"What are you doing?" Angie asked.

"Nothing." *Breathe, Mel. Breathe.* "Collecting stamps and stuff…of endangered species. I'm holding one of a Corroboree." *Stupid, stupid me.*

"S'cuse me?"

"Corroboree, bufo bufo, golden toad…"

"You sound like a crazy person."

I smiled, embarrassed. She had a nice voice. "Frogs. I know you probably don't think of them as animals…"

"They're amphibians."

"They're vanishing," I said.

"Oh." The line grew silent again. I wondered if Angie was thinking I was crazy. I didn't care. If she didn't like the way I thought about things, she didn't have to call anymore. The heck with her. The heck with everyone.

"I like all the insects and animals and amphibians that are almost extinct or already extinct," I said, kind of giving up on everything.

"Oh," Angie said again. This time it was a different "oh," like maybe she understood a little better. "Save the world stuff."

I swallowed. *What would you say, Angie? Tell me what you'd say if you knew.* "Not saving it," I said, twisting the phone cord around my thumb. "I don't think anybody can do that 'cause it's already over the edge."

"Yeah," Angie said. "Isn't that messed up?"

We talked for a while longer but it was hard to think of anything except Angie finding out about Mama.

"We should hang out sometimes," Angie said.

"Yeah," I said. "I was gonna call you. Ask you if you wanted to hang out."

"Yeah?" Angie said. "That'd be cool."

After we hung up, I went back into my room and raised the window. It was gray out now, and quiet. Sitting down on the window ledge, I looked up at the cloudy sky. *The amphibians are vanishing*, I kept thinking. Angie. Angie. Angie. I felt like throwing up. I wanted to kiss her. What would it feel like? What would I feel like? Would we fall in love? Maybe. Maybe it could happen.

"Are you ever going to let me read anything in those notebooks?" Mama had asked. And I should have said, *No!* Maybe, *Hell, no!* I should have said, *These are the only things I have that are mine, all mine. The only things I have that won't mess my life up by being gay. The only things that won't stop calling me if they find out.*

Angie. Angie. Angie. I didn't want to hope too much. She was going to find out some way sooner or later. But she had called me. And she hadn't laughed when I told her about the amphibians. Maybe, I couldn't help thinking. Maybe.

I picked up the phone and dialed. She answered after the first ring.

"Angie," I said. "Maybe we could hang out now."

It was raining again and cold, so the park was empty. Angie pulled her jacket closed, over those breasts, hiding those breasts. I remembered something stupid Mama had said—*It's okay to be nice to women*—so I wiped the bench dry with my jacket before we sat down. Angie moved closer to me. So close, our shoulders were touching. Then I was shivering. Not from the cold but from something—shivering from the inside out. We didn't say anything for a long time. Watching the rain. Watching the empty park. Trying hard not to look at each other.

"I always thought you were cool, Mel," Angie said.

"Yeah," I said, kind of glancing at her but mostly looking straight ahead. Sitting on my hands and looking straight ahead. "I thought that about you." I tried to sound calm, but the words came out shaky, like they were barely on the tip of something in the back of my throat. I know it sounds like a lie, but I leaned over and kissed her then, quick so that I wouldn't be thinking about it. So fast my teeth bumped her lips. *Stupid, stupid me.*

Angie laughed. She closed her eyes when she laughed and I had never seen anybody laugh like that. It made me smile, from someplace deep that I had forgotten about.

"You never kissed anybody before?"

"I kissed lots of people," I said, sitting up straighter, looking off.

"No you haven't," Angie said. When I glanced at her again she was looking at me, straight on. She knew I was lying.

"I been kissing girls since I was ten," I said.

"Lie number two," Angie said, laughing.

I swallowed. *No, Angie. Lie number three. There's another one. Bigger and worse.*

We didn't say anything for a long time, looking off, watching the drizzle, slick against grayblack ground. Rain dripped from the hoops. I thought of the hollow bounce of a basketball and the sound repeated itself in my head—over and over. And the silence filled us up.

"I don't have a lot of friends," Angie said quietly, after a long time had passed. "You mad at me for teasing you?"

I shook my head. "It's nothing." I felt lame making her think I was mad.

"Sometimes I don't know the right things to say," Angie said. She wiped her chin with the back of her hand. "I talk to myself a lot. You don't have to worry about saying the wrong things to yourself." She smiled a little bit, the corners of her mouth turning up, but nothing else about her face changed. I wanted to hold her hand. I wanted to know what it would feel like to have her fingers against my palm. "I'm kind of to myself mostly," she said. "It's better that way."

I nodded, taking my hands from beneath my legs and staring at them. I can palm a basketball, almost. Ralphy says it's about control and muscle. Maybe I had weak hands.

If I was a real liar I would say I took Angie's hand then, that I leaned over and kissed her again. But it didn't happen that way. She kissed *me*. Maybe that was okay because only for a little while did I think about Mama and Kristin kissing and then, after that, it was Angie, all Angie. Beautiful, beautiful Angie.

We kissed for a long time. When we stopped, we just sat there, a little bit embarrassed. It was like all of the words went out of us. Maybe we didn't need any right then.

The rain had started coming down harder, but it didn't seem as though Angie was in any hurry to get out of it. Something about her sitting there, like nothing mattered, like it wasn't even raining, made me want to tell her everything. But I just shivered and continued looking straight ahead.

"I don't have a lot going on," I said. "I, you know, collect my stamps and watch some TV and write…"

"Poetry?"

I shook my head.

"I write some poetry sometimes," she said softly. "Stuff about life and my family." When I looked at her, she was smiling. Looking at me and smiling.

"What's your family like?" Maybe she had a dyke mother, too. Maybe this was the perfect ending.

"Mother, father, sister, sister, brother, brother, brother," Angie was saying. I felt myself closing up, switching off—like a light with a dimmer switch. She would run screaming if she knew. Screaming, screaming, back to her big, big family. Back to her normal life.

Toward the middle of August, it got cold suddenly, and me and Sean and Ralphy ended up walking the neighborhood with heavy dungaree jackets hanging like capes from our heads. Ralph said seasons changing depressed the hell out of him. Sean was quiet, too quiet, and Ralph and I kept nudging him with our elbows trying to get him to say something.

We finally gave up and the three of us fell silent for about four blocks. When we passed Angie, I smiled at her.

"Hey," I said.

"Hey yourself," Angie said back, falling in step with us.

I hadn't called her since that day in the park. Maybe she thought I didn't like her.

"Rasta woman," Ralph said.

Angie rolled her eyes at Ralph. "Stupid. *You're* the one with locks."

"Who you calling stupid?" Ralph raised one eyebrow.

"I'm calling you stupid," Angie said over her shoulder.

"Leave her alone, Ralph," I said.

Ralph was frowning. "She's trying to be cute in front of you. I'll show her who's stupid."

"Yeah," I said. "Whatever."

Angie and I walked bumping shoulders. Ralph and Sean gave us glances, but didn't say anything. Sean was glaring. Maybe he was jealous.

I took my jacket off my head and put it on. It was too big. Everything we owned was too big. *"You planning on doing a lot of growing?"* Mama asked last time she took me shopping.

"It's the style," I told her but she just pulled her lips to the side of her face and paid for everything.

Now I pulled the pants up a bit and stole a look at Angie. I could tell she was still mad from Ralphy messing with her.

"Don't listen to him," I said softly.

"Oh, I'm not even hearing it," Angie said.

We walked along silently for a while, Ralphy and Sean a few paces behind us.

"I guess we should double-date sometimes, huh?" Ralphy said. I knew this was his way of apologizing, so I winked at him. Angie smiled and said she guessed it would be fun.

"Yeah," Sean said. "Why don't you take her out on a double date with your mama and that dyke she's seeing."

I turned. *Please, God. Please let me be imagining this.*

"Don't look at me like I'm crazy," he said. "Everybody knows."

"Knows what?" Ralph was asking but I didn't wait to hear Sean's answer before I swung hard and landed a punch across his jaw. Something snapped and Sean seemed to move toward me in slow motion. I caught him around the neck, feeling my fist connect with his nose. Someone was trying to pull us apart and in the distance I could hear Angie telling me to stop. Sean's knee landed hard in my stomach and I felt myself falling backwards.

"Stop it," Ralph was saying. Someone was pulling Sean off of me. I kicked into the air and connected.

Pancho, the guy who owned the store we were standing in front of, was holding Sean's arms, but Sean was struggling against him.

"Your mother's a dyke," Sean yelled. *Angie,* I kept thinking, looking around for her. She was standing in front of the store, where a small group had gathered. She looked confused and angry. Now she knew. Now everyone in the whole stupid world knew.

"Stop talking junk," Ralph said.

I swallowed, breathing hard to keep from crying.

"No fighting here," Pancho was saying. "You want to fight, go back where you live."

"Don't worry, Pancho," Ralph said. "They won't be throwing down anymore." He looked around at the crowd. "Did someone die?" he asked sarcastically, and reluctantly, the group began to scatter. "Man. This is one nosey hood."

Pancho disappeared back inside his store and Ralph loosened his grip on me but didn't let go.

"I've seen her with that white lady," Sean said. "I saw them sitting in her car last night. Your mama touching her like they were in love or something." He spit. Someone else said something, but I couldn't hear anything anymore.

I was backing away, then I was turning and running fast and hard as hell away from there. Away from everyone. *I hated her. I hated her.*

BIL WRIGHT

■ ■ ■

[1963–]

BORN IN THE BRONX, BIL WRIGHT HAS A LONG HISTORY OF community service. While earning his MFA in Playwrighting from Brooklyn College, he worked at The Door, a youth drop-in center, and also taught English at New York's Housing Works, a social service agency for people with HIV. Following graduation, Wright was appointed director of a performing arts program at the Martin Luther King Center for Social Change. His plays, including a stage adaptation of Audre Lorde's *Zami: A New Spelling of My Name,* have been produced at Yale University, Orchestra Hall in Detroit, Dixon Place, Nuyorican Cafe, and the Samuel Beckett Theater in New York. Additionally, Wright's drama has been published in the United States and Germany, and appears in the anthology *Tough Acts to Follow.* His short stories and poetry are also featured in *Men on Men 3, The Road Before Us: 100 Black Gay Poets,* and *Shade: An Anthology of Fiction by Gay Men of African Descent.* The recipient of several awards, including the 1995 Millay Fellowship, Wright teaches in New York.

His debut novel, *Sunday You Learn How to Box* (2000), depicts the coming of age of Louis, an awkward African American thirteen-year-old living amid the violence of the Stratfield Housing Projects in 1968. When his upwardly mobile mother and her abusive second husband, Ben, decide that their bookish son needs to be toughened up to withstand the taunts from local bullies, Ben begins giving Louis boxing lessons. In this passage, a Christmas gift instigates further humiliation for the young protagonist, who is unable to ride his new bicycle regardless of Ben's attempt to teach him. With this round of humiliation, however, comes an unexpected encounter with Ray Anthony Robinson, the enigmatic and sexually alluring neighborhood "hoodlum," whom Louis eventually looks to as means for escape from his anguished existence.

from Sunday You Learn How to Box

[2000]

When I first saw Jackie Wilson on Saturday Hit Parade, I was in seventh grade. Mom heard him singing from the kitchen and asked me, "Who's singing like that, Louis?"

"A new guy named Jackie Wilson," I called back. "He's black." Before he'd come on, I'd been dancing around with Lorelle in my arms, but I put her down now, unable to do anything but stare at the television screen. Jackie Wilson was the prettiest black man I'd ever seen, with high, jutting cheekbones and skin that looked like powdered satin. He was also one of the few black men I'd seen on *Hit Parade*. There were groups sometimes where nobody particularly stood out, but not that many solo acts. No one like this.

"Nothing new about Jackie Wilson. He's just new to you. This must be his comeback," she said. "Some woman shot him up good a few years ago. He almost died. I'm surprised he can talk, much less sing."

Somebody shot him?! Now I had to get down on my knees, closer to the screen. I turned the volume up. Jackie Wilson sang higher than any man I'd ever heard and wore a suit with pants so tight you could see his calf muscles. He'd take off his tie, then his jacket, singing the whole time, and you could see how much he was sweating. Shirt soaked through, his chest and stomach smooth and dark under his white dress shirt. He jerked his head from side to side until his long processed hair fell over his forehead. He looked dangerous.

The song was a warning to somebody they better stop messing around, Jackie's heart was breaking and he didn't know how much longer he'd be able to take the pain. He was holding the microphone as if this was the person he was singing to, with his big, ringed fingers wrapped around their face and neck. He wanted to kiss them, but they'd hurt him so much, he might have to hurt them back. "You'd bettah stop, baby, messin', messin' round," he moaned, his voice swooping from a trembling soprano to a hoarse, rusty shout. He fell to his knees cradling the microphone one moment, looking like he was strangling it the next.

Love. And danger. On his knees, sweating and screaming with his hair hanging. "You bet-tah stop, baby, messin', messin' round." I wanted him to scream about me like that.

When *Hit Parade* was over, Mom started upstairs. "Bring Lorelle, Louis," she instructed. When I looked into their bedroom, she was leaning into her mirror, trying to even out the black hills she'd drawn for eyebrows. "Come in here. I want to talk to you about Christmas."

I went in and sat on the side of the bed where Ben slept. Leaning over onto his pillow, I imagined his face under my elbow.

"Do you realize you have to be the only thirteen-year-old in the world who can't ride a damn bicycle?"

This wasn't the first time she'd asked me if I realized everyone around me could ride a bike. What I wanted to know was, why did it matter so much to her?

"There isn't a child out there who can't ride a bike unless they're blind or crippled. Every year I ask you if you want one and you say no. This year I made up my mind I'm going to get you one and you'll learn to ride it."

Other kids in the projects had bikes, but no one had one that was new. Sure, the older guys rode new bikes, but they were stolen and everybody knew because they bragged about it to anybody who'd listen. A new bike would probably get me killed.

Christmas morning, I knew I was looking at trouble. The first thing I thought when I saw it was that it looked like a brand-new red lipstick with tires. If there was anywhere in the world I could've gotten away with a bike like this, it wasn't the Stratfield Projects.

Right after dinner she told me, "You can take the bike out now. Remember, they say the only way to learn how to ride is to stay on it."

"What about the ice? I shouldn't take it out on the ice, should I?"

"There's not that much ice out there. I'll bet if any other kid in the projects got one, they'd be out there, ice or no ice. Learn now. It'll be spring before you know it."

I walked the bike around and around the courtyard, trying to get up the courage to jump the pedal closest to me with one foot and throw my other leg over the bar to the other side. If I could just get on it, pushing the pedals to keep it going couldn't be that hard. When I did push off on my side, I couldn't get my leg up and over to the other side fast enough before the bike fell over onto the ice. I jumped up, looking down to the other end for Mom, just in case. I tried a few more times. Each time, the bike crashed to the ground. Finally, I looked up and there she was, coming toward me in her coat and bedroom slippers.

"What's going on out here? Can you ride it yet?"

"No, ma'am. Not yet," I told her.

"Well, I want to see you ride it today. I asked Ben to come out here to help you."

"No. Please. I don't need him." A lesson from Ben was the last thing I wanted. I could feel eyes on me from all over the projects. It was only a matter of time before I'd be surrounded.

"What's the matter with you? Maybe if you gave him a chance every once in a while, the two of you could be friends."

I felt trapped in a world like those glass snow scenes with the miniature houses and all the water sloshing from side to side. I would have given anything to be able to disappear through a crack in the ice, leaving the bike to whoever wanted it.

Mom went inside and in moments Ben came out in a jacket, galoshes, and one of those hats with the bib and flaps. It wasn't that cold, but I guessed he thought he'd be out there for a while.

"Your mother seems to think you need help out here."

"Yes, sir."

"Well, this is usually something kids teach themselves. If it was something you wanted to do, I'm sure you'd find a way to learn it. You being as smart as you are." He held the back of the seat and nodded for me to start.

I ran, pushed down hard on the pedal closest to me with my outside leg, and threw my leg up and over to the other side. Ben continued to hold on to the seat, running behind me. I pumped as hard and as fast as I could, especially after he let go. For a moment I thought there'd been a miracle. I seemed to be suspended, held up by invisible strings as the bike sped forward. When I got to the corner, I panicked. I turned the handlebars sharply, feeling the bike quiver beneath me. I'd lost control. I crashed, noisily.

In these few minutes, as I expected, several boys had gathered in the courtyard. At first, they stood in the distance snickering. Ben said nothing as we repeated the sequence. Pedal, pedal, fall. Pedal, pedal, crash. Each time, the snickers got louder. Each time, I glanced at Ben, hoping he'd decide on some way to end the whole thing.

Finally, as I scrambled to get up from what I'd decided was the absolutely last fall I'd let any one of them witness, they surrounded Ben and me yelling, "Why don't ya let me ride? C'mon, let me ride it!"

Ben started to grin at them. "Hold on," he said. "Hold on, guys." I stared at him, waiting to see how he was going to get rid of them.

He stood in front of them, like he was going to try to reason with them. "Who here knows how to ride?" he asked.

They all began yelling, "I do!" "I *been* knowin' how to ride!" "Please, please let me ride it, please!"

If this was a plan to distract them, I thought, Ben was wrong. They'd never give up now.

"Come on," he invited the closest, whose name I didn't even know. "Just a short one, though."

I stood watching as they took turns, fighting over who would go next.

No one spoke to me, not Ben, not any of them. I was shaking with anger, but I couldn't look at him. Mom had to be watching. She had to know what she'd started.

When the last boy had taken his ride around the courtyard, Ben turned to me and asked, "Well, did you learn something by watching at least?"

"Yes, sir," I said evenly, looking past him toward the apartment. "You want to try again?"

"No, sir." I took the handlebars and slowly walked the bike home. I knew Ben was following me. I could hear the boys calling out to him to let them have another chance.

Mom opened the door for me. I left the bike on the stoop, went in and started upstairs. Silently, Mom held the door for Ben. She closed it behind him. "Damn you, Ben," she said, "Damn you."

The next morning I took the bike outside and down to the other end of the projects where it would be harder for Mom to see me from the window, or even the stoop. The day before had been humiliating, but it had shown me something after all. I'd watched boys of all different sizes and shapes ride my bike, some of whom I knew were as old as I was and couldn't read or count. I understood the secret had to be in practice, not in intelligence. Now, I was determined.

When I got tired of falling, I decided to hide out behind the bushes awhile to rest. Even though there weren't any leaves on them, they were too dense for anyone to see me. When I pushed the bike through to the other side, Ray Anthony Robinson was standing behind the bushes, peeing and smoking a cigarette.

Ray Anthony lived across the courtyard with his mother in the 4B apartment building next to where we'd lived in 4A before we moved to the bungalows. Nobody was really sure how old Ray Anthony was, but Miss Helen, Mom's hairdresser, said she thought he had to be seventeen at least. He didn't go to high school and by law, you had to go until you were sixteen. Miss Helen said nobody she knew could remember a time when Ray Anthony had ever gone to school, but she was sure he must have. She whispered to my mother that Ray Anthony was "an out-and-out hoodlum." Miss Helen was always calling somebody's child a hoodlum, but I could tell from the way she said it that to be an "out-and-out hoodlum" was more serious than an ordinary run-of-the-mill hoodlum. So I stared at Ray Anthony after that from my window wondering what kind of crimes he might be on his way to commit.

When I pushed through the bushes to Ray Anthony Robinson standing there peeing and smoking, it felt like I'd pushed through to the other side of the world. He turned in my direction and aimed right through the spokes of my front tire. My eyes followed the arc back to where it came from, Ray Anthony Robinson's dick. It was long, wide and the color of these cookies Miss Odessa used to give me for dessert when I spent the night. Almond Macaroons. Most likely, Ray Anthony was the color of Almond Macaroons all over, but I'd never thought about it until I saw his dick. The way he looked at me, with his cigarette hanging from his lips and his waist pushed forward at me, you'd have thought it was the most natural thing in the world for us to be there, him peeing and me watching.

When he stopped peeing, he didn't put his dick back in his pants. He spat the cigarette in my direction, but he wasn't trying to hit me with it. He started peeing again, aiming at his cigarette until the smoke stopped spiraling up from it. I tried not to look impressed.

"Who gave you the girl's bike for Christmas?"

"It's not a girl's." It was hard to sound as forceful as I wanted, watching him slowly tuck himself back into his pants.

"You gonna let me ride it?"

He'd zipped his pants and I could look him in the face. I'd never been this close to Ray Anthony before, and he'd certainly never said anything to me. It was the first time I realized one of his two front teeth was chipped, just a little on the inside corner. He also had a big dent in his chin.

"No," I said. If I'd thought about it, I might have been scared to say no to him. But it seemed like he didn't expect me to say yes, he'd already figured out I'd say no, that wasn't the point of him asking. He walked closer to me and reached for the handlebars. That's when I saw his hair had a rusty, orange glow to it. I didn't like orange or red much. But Ray Anthony Robinson's hair was unlike any other reds or oranges I'd seen before.

"Leggo," he told me.

I smelled the cigarette on his breath, kept staring at the chipped tooth. I was filling in the space to see what he'd look like if he got it fixed.

"I can't let you ride it. My mom will see."

"I'll go the other way. Leggo."

I'd already let go. Ray Anthony pushed my bike through the bushes. I stood in the opening and watched him throw his leg over it easily without having to get a running start. He was wearing shoes with pointy toes and buckles on the sides. Pushing off, he huddled over the bars like the kids did when they raced each other. Except Ray Anthony wasn't racing anybody. He was just riding my bike wherever he'd decided to take it. I watched his butt lifted in the air and the muscles in his legs as he pumped the pedals. All I could do was wait behind the bushes and hope he wouldn't ride it in front of my house where Mom could see him, and that he'd bring it back. Soon.

I started to feel the cold for the first time that morning. But I couldn't move, playing the whole thing with Ray Anthony backwards and forwards in my mind. His cigarette was lying a few feet away. That and his footprints in the snow with the long, pointy toes were my evidence that he'd really been there.

But evidence wouldn't matter anyway. He hadn't beat me up, knocked me down and ridden over me on my own bike. I was sure he'd seen me coming, sure that he'd waited till I could watch him, smoking and making bridges of piss in the air. But hoodlum or not, he'd told me only once, without sounding any more dangerous than my own mother, to let go of those handlebars. And I had. Without a fight, without even thinking about fighting him.

It might have been a half hour, it might have been longer before Ray Anthony brought my bike back, but by now, the time didn't matter. Whatever happened had happened already, before he left. It's the difference between when something begins and something continues. You can't compare the two.

When he pushed the bike back through the bushes, there was sweat running down from his thick bush of rust colored hair and he had a perfectly folded handkerchief he kept patting his forehead with.

"You want me to ride you now? C'mon. Get behind me."

He was crazy. If I could get the bike away from him, the only thing I wanted to do was run home with it and tell my mother any lie I could think of to keep from coming outside again. The bike had attracted people I never would have spoken to or had anything to do with. If I couldn't lose it or give it away, I had to think of some excuse not to bring it out again anytime soon.

By the time I got home, Miss Odessa had already called Mom and told her she'd seen me behind the bushes with Ray Anthony Robinson. Told her she saw Ray Anthony ride away from the bushes on a red bicycle which by now the whole projects knew was mine. Mom asked me, "Well, what's your story, Louis?" but she was already in a mood to beat some behind.

"You gonna let everybody in the projects ride it but you? I didn't spend months cleaning behind white men for that."

"He made me." I was looking at her, but I was picturing Ray Anthony Robinson with his chipped tooth, his rusty hair.

Mom started with her fists. "No, today was your fault. You can't blame today on anybody else." Then she grabbed the broom. She turned it upside down and used the stick part on me as my sister watched, looking troubled, but helpless.

The following Saturday morning Mom excused me from cleaning the apartment. "Take the bike outside and see how long you can hold on to it."

I wasn't out there five minutes before three kids started running toward me from the south end. I looked back at the window of our apartment. The curtains were pulled almost together. Mom was there, in the almost space.

The three kids formed a V at the front of the bike. Bubba Graves was on one side, this guy called Rat on the other, and some boy I'd never seen before who smelled bad, in the front. We all just looked at each other, like we were waiting for some kind of signal. The one who smelled bad walked in closer, straddling the front tire. He grabbed the handlebars and jerked the front of the bike so hard I was thrown to the side, but I held on and kept my balance so I didn't fall. The other two inched in closer to me.

"Better get the hell outta here." It was what I'd rehearsed to say to anybody about anything, the next time I got picked on.

"Who you cursin', faggot? You cursin' me?" The Smell leaned in over the handlebars so that we were eye to eye. I held my breath.

Rat said, "Yeah, he cursed you. I heard him curse you."

The Smell heaved the front of the bike toward Rat while Bubba Graves pushed it from the other side. Rat jumped out of the way as the bike fell over onto the snow with me halfway underneath it. I was still holding on to the handlebars. The three of them kicked the bike as I scrambled to get from under it. One, I couldn't see who, straddled me from behind with his legs around my neck and started kicking into my ribs with his heels. My ears started to ring. I squeezed my eyes shut, but the ringing only got louder.

"Get the hell off him! You hear me, you little bastard! Get off him now!" My mother's voice cut through.

Instead, he kicked me harder and faster. Each time Mom screamed, it got worse. If she doesn't stop, I thought, he'll kick a hole in my side.

But he stopped suddenly, and someone grabbed me under my arms and pulled me up from behind. I whirled around to try to free myself. It wasn't Bubba or Rat or The Smell who'd lifted me. It was Ray Anthony Robinson. He was in his undershirt. The first thing I saw was how much hair he had under his arm and how it was reddish colored too. Then, I saw my mother standing behind him.

I was dizzy, spitting snow, my head dropped toward the ground again. There was a bloody silhouette in the snow in the shape of a small rabbit.

"Why you gotta jump in for him?" The Smell shouted at Ray Anthony. "The faggot cursed me. Don't nobody curse me. I'm gonna kick his butt good."

"If you gonna kick somebody's butt, kick mine." I looked up to see Ray Anthony step toward him slowly with his legs spread wide, his thick arms swinging free. He was taller than any of us. He looked different to me now, like he was prepared to do whatever he had to win. It wasn't the same as when he'd been behind the bushes. I realized for the first time that he probably hadn't even thought about hurting me that day. He'd just taken what he wanted, because he knew he could. I was ashamed to think he'd probably seen me get pushed around before. Why was he helping me now?

"Why you wanna front for a faggot, man? Let him fight for himself."

My body tensed with a new fear. Would The Smell convince Ray Anthony to leave me alone with them again? Please God, don't let Ray Anthony back down. I knew Mom would probably try to help me, but that would make it worse. They wouldn't fight her, but I'd get beat up again later on because she'd already called them some pretty rough names.

"Come on, you so bad." Ray Anthony stepped in closer to the kid. "Come on and kick my butt."

The Smell did step in closer to Ray Anthony, but my bike was between them. The Smell jumped on the bike so hard, he dented the back fender.

"You good-for-nothing little pig!" my mother shouted and grabbed a fallen tree branch near where she was standing. But The Smell was running backwards yelling, "You wait, faggot. You wait till your big red nigger ain't around."

Bubba and Rat backed off slowly, not even in the same direction as The Smell. The fear hadn't left me, though. I knew as far as Mom was concerned, there was still Ray Anthony to deal with. Saving me from getting my ribs kicked in didn't erase the fact that he'd taken a turn on my bike himself, the bike she said she'd cleaned behind white men to buy me.

"Well, looks like everybody in the projects is gonna ride that damn thing, or kill you trying."

She was talking to me, but glaring at Ray Anthony. He walked past her slowly, back towards his building. I stared at his arms hanging at his sides, wondering if he was cold with only an undershirt on. Maybe arms that looked like Ray Anthony's didn't get cold.

Mom was asking me, "You gonna pick up that bike or just leave it there so they can come back and get it?"

I stooped to pick it up, but I kept my eyes on Ray Anthony to see if he'd turn around before he went inside.

DARIECK SCOTT

■ ■ ■

[1964–]

BORN IN FORT KNOX, KENTUCKY, TO A CAREER MILITARY FATHER, Darieck Scott lived with his family in small towns and army installations throughout Georgia, North Carolina, and Kansas. Many of the most powerfully formative and vivid experiences of his youth took place in Germany, where his family resided for six years. The seminomadic existence of an army child kindled in him an intense longing for community.

Scott attended Stanford University, where he won several writing prizes, though he received his undergraduate degree in human biology. Subsequently he worked as an assistant to R. W. Apple at the *New York Times'* Washington bureau during the year that the Iran-contra scandal came to light. After his brief stint in journalism he attended Yale Law School to pursue his dream of becoming a civil rights lawyer. However, various developments moved Scott in a different direction, including his coming out as gay, the rise of AIDS activism in nearby New York City, the academic and cultural excitement generated by the commercial as well as critical success of black women's fiction, and the upsurge in black gay political and artistic activity, all of which inspired him to seek an MA degree in Afro-American Studies and to begin writing his first novel. He earned JD and MA degrees from Yale University, and then went on to get a PhD in Modern Thought and Literature at Stanford. Scott's writing has appeared in *Callaloo* and the anthologies *Shade, Giant Steps, Ancestral House, Flesh and the Word 4,* and *Gay Travels.* He is assistant professor of English at the University of Texas at Austin, where he teaches African American literature and creative writing, and is also a postdoctoral fellow in the English Department at UCLA.

His novel, *Traitor to the Race* (1995), explores homophobia in the black community and racism among white gays. In the following excerpt, Kenneth, an unemployed African American actor, is forced to come to terms with his identity as a black gay men when his cousin is murdered by gay-bashers. He meets his friend Cyrus to discuss this death, as well as Kenneth's increasingly insecure relationship with his white lover, Evan.

from **Traitor to the Race**

"Fwoinne," Cyrus purrs, red-brown eyebrows arched over cat-eye sunglasses.

I follow his gaze. "Serious fwoin," I agree when I see him.

"Ummnh." Cyrus shakes his head, almost imperceptibly, just enough for me to see. "Positively strapping." He savors the consonants in that way of his that surprises the muscles of my face by the breadth of the smile it cajoles. My laugh is already beginning. "And look at his friend."

His friend saunters by in a thin-strapped, deeply-plunging tank top, and the muscles of his back show, exquisitely sculpted in the sunshine. "Oh my," I intone.

"It almost makes me want to move back to Manhattan," Cyrus says reverently, leaning back in his chair. He lifts a crouton from his salad to his mouth. There is such a style about him even as he does this small thing—overblown, perhaps, just a tad too consciously flamboyant (*too* if we take an Anglo-Saxon norm of "restraint" in all things as our guide—I remind myself of the injustice of this), but dead on. Always. "Some of these b-boys who come around here are the Bomb."

Now I laugh. The Bomb. Precisely. I haven't heard that one before.

"So, my sweet—" (This is what he calls me. He may flatter any number of his friends with the same endearment, but I am always made happy by it, confirmed by it, gathered by it into a grateful communion. I met Cyrus one night through a woman friend I was in a play with, and over hurried drinks at a cafe I came breathlessly to the decision that he was both charming and dangerous, delightful but intimidating, much too sure of himself for me to want to know too well. But weeks later he did a reading of his poetry at a Gay and Lesbian Performance Night and dazzled me with his warm, open assumption of community. I didn't quite buy it, of course—brotherhood, I thought; where's mine? But he made me desperate to believe. I have been chasing his friendship ever since.)

But let me step out of the way, let him speak.

"—there's a new performance piece we're putting on at the theater," he is saying. "It's more of a one-act play than anything else, and I thought you might want to audition."

Suddenly I feel the possibility of a depression flying at me. But let me step out of the way. "What's it called? What's it about?"

Cyrus waves a fork—swallowed clean, of course—at my face; it is the imperial director in him. "Don't play this, Kenneth. Don't start retreating to that oh-it's-a-*black*-thang remove you run to everytime I ask you to audition for one of my shows. No, I'm serious! It is time to *wake up,* little boy." He pounces quickly, as always. Of course I admire his technique. "That's right: *lit-tle boy.* Kenneth, I'll tell you this like I've told you before. You need to stop pouting. You need to start making use of the contacts you have. You can't keep pulling yourself back and stopping before you begin. You have *talent.* You have to *use* it."

"I'm not good at black dialect. I'm just not."

Cyrus rolls his eyes hugely. "Kenneth, that was one audition and one play, and one director. And she was right: traditional black folk's English is not your strength. You sound—a little forced, a little… shaky. There are, however, a good number of plays out there with middle-class, bougie Aframericans in them that you can play, and play well." Having been hunched, his broad, slim shoulders (they give him such carriage, those; were he a woman, he would have been a model in Paris, smooth-swinging boyish hips, pursed lips and all) fall down and he relaxes, a smirk on his lips. This is how he plays with me.

"Phallicist's honor, Kenneth." He places two fingers in a V on either side of his nose, like Agnes Moorehead in *Bewitched.* We share a devotion to Agnes's memory, Cyrus and I. "I really think you could play a number of parts in this piece very, very well. I even told the director you might be a good choice for the lead."

I meet this with silence because I am terrified. Principally terrified of disappointing Cyrus. He is waiting impassively for my reply, golden-skinned face set in quiet judgment. "Can I see a script?" I ask at last.

"They can make a copy for you at the *GMOC Journal* office—the Lesbian/Gay Community Center, third floor." But of course he knows I know this. He has seen me lurking there a number of times.

Now a new silence looms. This is not typical of our conversations, and he must know this. I sip my tea while he watches me. It is a contest of wills now.

Cyrus breaks first. "Uh," he says. This degree of inarticulation is also not typical. "I, uh, heard about your cousin."

The roll I am lifting to my mouth I set back in the basket. "What? Who told you?"

"Daria. She didn't say much," he adds quickly. "I'm really sorry, Kenneth. And I have to say, I feel it, too, a part of it, even though I didn't know him. I remember you mentioned him once." He sighs, shakes his head, looks across the street. "So many perils are out there for our people in this city, Kenneth. If it's not run-of-the-mill cracker bigots, it's homophobic cracker bigots, and if it's not homophobic cracker bigots, it's Jamaican homophobe bigots or Puerto Rican bigots or run-of-the-mill black folks homophobic bigots. Then if it's not men who think beating you to death is a sport that helps them prove something precious to themselves, it's sistas who think that because your penis is black it belongs to them in holy wedlock, or who, if they can't get your penis, know you must be using it to steal their men. Then the police, the government...I mean, you know all this. I just want you to know that it pains me, too. It really does. And not just for you but for myself."

He shakes his head again, more vigorously. I don't think I've ever seen him quite this way, his passion expressed like this. His glasses obscure his eyes like clouds before the sun. "I'm sorry," he says, and touches my hand. "I just keep talking. Do you—want to talk about it?"

I had envisioned, practiced this conversation earlier. But I am not as smooth, as nonchalant as I had hoped to be when I say, "I think I saw him."

I have not said this aloud before. My throat is constricted. "He was walking around, I think, near Different Light bookstore, before it happened. I had just left there, I was walking on one of those little streets behind the bookstore, and I heard someone call my name, and I looked back. I think it was him."

"You didn't speak?" There is no judgment in the question.

"No." There is more to say. "No. No."

"I *hope* you're not thinking you're to blame for his being killed because you didn't *speak* to the man. Cause, child, if every relative I wasn't speaking to at any given time dropped dead, I'd be an orphan by now."

I fake a small smile. I've thought of this, of course. Yet it gives me hope to hear it from his lips.

He smiles back. "The universe is not that bleak, Kenneth. It's not *that* cruel."

This time there is nothing more to say.

But Cyrus will not permit any more silences. "So how's Mr. Marcialis? Being a good boy, I hope?" This with a mock Caribbean lilt in his voice. I marvel at his cleverness—not the accent, but the connection he's discerned, the link that, in a few words, he has uncovered.

"Yes. Mostly," I answer. My turkey sandwich tastes like paper. The sigh comes; he has already—the sorcerer—dragged it out of me. "It's very hard, Cyrus. Very hard sometimes to…"

The fingertips of his hand reach out to rest upon the veins that stand out on the back of my exposed arm. "To love a white boy?" And there is about him a smug but sympathetic certainty, as if his other hand were slowly stroking a sinister goatee at the end of his chin.

"Yes, it's hard." I exhale. "But harder—I don't know; is it harder? just as hard—not to. It's what we're taught, you know, to love them. Even in hate. Hate's just another way to love someone. It's just safer because you don't really need to know them."

He stares at me. One of his brutish fingers circles my thumb in a loving vise. The sensation is of the vampire drawing the bared and willing neck tenderly to his lips, or of the Godfather, pulling an errant Family member's frightened face to his own for the last kiss.

"Kenneth. You are completely, absolutely wrong." This as if he were blowing in my ear.

And now his finger leaves mine, his breath (scented, faintly, with the cinnamon-orange iced tea he has been drinking) leaves my face, his torso recedes from the top of the small white table.

"Your problem, my sweet, is not with white boys or even white men." His fork is raised high for a brief second, tines to the sky. "It's with The Folks." The fork descends and a crouton flies. "Aframerican male Folk to be specific. So it's hard loving white men, is it? Not really, little boy. You don't love white *men;* you happen—as much as anything can just happen, I suppose—to be in love with one white *man.* And you might have loved one in the past, may love another in the future. Of course you're attracted to them, but not every one every day, or even most of the time. I know you, Kenneth. Your desires—like everybody else's, one way or another, and don't let them fool you, baby, because it's true—but your desires are not such that you run around with your tongue hanging out and following after every pale swimmer with a chlorine bleached-out blond crewcut and eyes that look green in bad light.

"Don't laugh! I've seen it happen, and it's funny, but it's not pretty. That's not where you are. Your problem is that you've set yourself up so that the only men you can love are white men—and I'll include Latinos, Asians, native Americans, and Semitic Folk in there, too, because any-one that ain't Folks is white in your little love em or leave em, no middle ground no complications moral world.

"Don't argue! I only read for the benefit of the person being read, so just keep your little ass still in that chair and listen. It's black men or any other kind of man for you, right? Either or. You never felt comfortable, never liked or felt liked by all those beautiful, sexy, het-erosexual Aframerican men who ran around, beloved by all, talkin bout playin ball and gettin pussy and my woman this and your woman that. Right? You hated them. Admit it. *Hate*. That's how you felt, because they were supposed to belong to you, make you belong, right? And they didn't. And *don't*—mostly. So you don't love them, sometimes still hate em. And you think because of that that maybe you don't really love The Folks at all and feel terribly guilty when you read some writer talking about how much he or she loves Our People. Right?

"But this is the thing, Kenneth: You do love The Folks. You love Aframerican women, right? How many times do we sit here and sing their individual praises? Hm? And you never knew a black gay man— that was *out*—before you came to New York. Right? You've convinced yourself that you hate you and hate The Folks, too, but like my grand-mother down South used to say, It don't make no kinda sense, baby. And it don't. You *love* you. Somewhere that's true; otherwise you wouldn't be here, alive and healthy, today. Too many of us don't know how to love ourselves and don't make it, even out of safe bougie Aframerica. You love you. And you love *us,* The Folks. There are plenty of us out here, out there, that aren't those boys you hated and still hate now. Women, Aframerican gay men. And I would be willing to say, even a good num-ber of those boys that you hate and fear so much. See? All that love is right there, waiting for you."

I see this finger—looks huge—like a gun barrel pointed at my chest.

"And Kenneth—in whatever way, however much, even if it doesn't seem in hindsight like it was enough—you loved your cousin. You did. And you have to really know that, believe it. It almost has to show up in your dreams for it to be real."

And now he leans back. The smug sympathetic sinister goatee stroking expression returns. "I'd snap," he says blandly, "but I'm too tired." He really does have a beauty about him.

We are silent.

I'm a stubborn man, I'll admit, and being read does not sit well with me. With confessed vengefulness, then, I can only say that it seems to me that I shall never be able to bring myself to obey one word of his advice, not one whit of it. *It has to show up in your dreams,* he said. That is what plays in my head now, as he asks, "How're the Games?"

He is teasing, but I cannot answer. "Fine," is all I say. And then: "How's your thing?"

"Oh—!" Another fork flourish. "Good. The fucking is delicious. Makes me so thankful I'm a phallicist." My laugh is beginning again; the smile is already there.

"The problem, of course, is that he's a *man*—as unoriginal a thing as *that,* and men have unfortunately all been taught, whatever their race"—he shoots me a look; his lover is black—"that they have something to *say* about things. Which is ridiculous, because most men haven't anything at all to say about most things, unless it's offensive or forgettable. Or *stupid.* Women are better life partners, ultimately. They're taught they have nothing to say, and consequently they have *everything* fascinating and insightful to say, because they kept quiet or pretended to keep quiet and they learned something, and didn't burble out their entire brainload before age ten. *But—!*" He smiles, as pleased with himself as I am. "Men do have penises."

And we both laugh.

Later, I am watching him recede from me as I stand at the corner, his slim shoulders carrying him, his step bouncing him gently away, like a little buoy bobbing slowly up and down in a sea of bodies and chatter.

Why do I find it so easy to love Cyrus?

THOMAS GLAVE

■ ■ ■

[1965–]

BORN TO EXPATRIATE JAMAICAN PARENTS IN THE BRONX, Thomas Glave was raised in both New York City and Kingston, Jamaica. In 1988 he returned as a Fulbright Scholar to Jamaica, where he studied the island's historiography and Jamaican-Caribbean intellectual and literary traditions. During his time in Jamaica, he helped found the Jamaican Forum of Lesbians, All-Sexuals, and Gays (J-FLAG). He is a 1993 honors graduate of Bowdoin College as well as a graduate of Brown University.

Glave's first short story collection, *Whose Song? and Other Stories* (2000), was published to critical acclaim, including the *Village Voice*'s selection of him as one of the most promising new fiction authors of the year. His writing has appeared in *Callaloo* and *The Kenyon Review*, as well as in the anthologies *Children of the Night: The Best Short Stories by Black Writers, Men on Men 6: Best New Gay Fiction*, and *Soulfires: Young Black Men on Love and Violence*. In 1997 Glave became the second gay African American author, after James Baldwin, to win the O. Henry Award for Fiction.

The title story of his collection, "Whose Song?," depicts in disturbing detail the rape of a teenaged African American lesbian by three young black men, all of whom are struggling with their own sexuality.

Whose Song?

[2000]

Yes, now they're waiting to rape her, but how can they know? The girl with strum-vales, entire forests, behind her eyes. Who has already known the touch of moondewed kisses, nightwing sighs, on her teenage skin. Cassandra. Lightskinned, lean. Lovelier to them for the light. How can they know? The darkskinned ones aren't even hardly what they want. They have been taught, have learned well and well. Them black bitches, that's some skank shit, they sing. Give you VD on the woody, make your shit fall off. How can they know? Have been taught. Cassandra, fifteen, in the light. On her way to the forests. In the light. Hasn't known a man yet. Hasn't wanted to. How can they know? She prefers Tanya's lips, the skin-touch of silk. Tanya, girlfriend, sixteen and fine, dark glider, schoolmatelover, large-nippled, -thighed. Tanya. Who makes her come and come again when the mamas are away, when houses settle back into silent time and wrens swoopflutter their wings down into the nightbird's song. Tanya and Cassandra. Kissing. Holding. Climbing and gliding. What the grown girls do, they think, belly-kissing but shy. Holding. She makes me feel my skin, burrowing in. Which one of them thinks that? Which one flies? Who can tell? Climbing and gliding. Coming. Wet. Coming. Laughing. Smelling. Girlsex, she-love, and the nightbird's song. Thrilling and trilling. Smooth bellies, giving face, brushing on and on. Cassandra. Tanya swooping down, brown girls, dusky flesh. How can they know? The boys have been watching them, have begun to know things about them watchers know or guess. The boys, touching themselves in nightly rage, watching them. Wanting more of Cassandra because she doesn't want them. Wanting to set the forests on fire, cockbrush those glens. How can they know? They are there and they are there and they are watching. Now.

Sing this tale, then, of a Sound Hill rape. Sing it, low and mournful, soft, beneath the kneeling trees on either side of the rusty bridge out by Eastchester Creek; where the sun hangs low over the sound and water meets the sky; where the departed walk along Shore Road and the joggers run; where morning rabbits leap away from the pounding jogger's step. Sing it far and wide, this sorrow song woven into the cresting nightbird's blue. Sing it, in that far-off place far up away from it all,

where the black people live and think they've at last found peace; where
there are homes, small homes and large, with modest yards, fruit
hedges, taxus, juniper trees; where the silver hoses, coiled, sag and lean;
where the withered arms hanging out of second-story windows are the
arms of that lingering ghost or aging lonely busybody everybody knows.
In that northerly corner of the city where no elevated IRT train yet
comes; where the infrequent buses to Orchard Beach and Pelham Bay
sigh out spent lives and empty nights when they run; where the sound
pulls watersmell through troubled dreams and midnight pains, the
sleeping loneliness and silence of a distant place. Sound Hill, beneath
your leaning trees and waterwash, who do you grieve for now? Sound
Hill girl of the trees and the girlflesh where are you now? Will those
waters of the sound flow beside you now? Caress you with light-kisses
and bless you now? The City Island currents and the birds rush by you
now? O sing it. Sing it for that yellow girl, dark girl, brown girl homely
or fine, everygirl displaced, neither free nor named. Sing it for that girl
swinging her axe through the relentless days, suckling a child or selling
her ass in the cheap hotels down by the highway truckers' stop for
chump change. Sing it for this girl, swishing her skirt and T-shirt, an
almost-free thing, instinctual, throwing her head back to the breeze.
Her face lifted to the sky. Now, Jesus. Walk here, Lamb. In thy presence
there shall be light and light. Grace. Cadence. A witness or a cry. Come,
now. All together. And.

How could we know? Three boys in a car, we heard, but couldn't be
neighbors of ours. Had to be from some other part of the world, we
thought; the projects or the Valley. Not from here. In this place every
face knows every eye, we thought, what's up here in the heart always is
clear. But they were not kind nor good, neither kin nor known. If they
were anything at all besides unseen, they were maimed. Three boys,
three boys. In a car. Long legs, lean hands. In a car. Bitter mouths, tight
asses, and the fear of fear. Boys or men and hard. In their car. Who did
not like it. Did not like the way those forest eyes gazed out at those
darker desert ones, at the eyes of that other who had known what it was
to be dark and loathed. Yo, darkskinned bitch. So it had been said. Yo,
skillet ass. Don't be cutting your eyes at me, bitch, I'll fuck your black ass
up. It had been said. Ugly black bitch. You need some dick. Them eyes
gone get you killed, rolling them at me like that. It had been said. Had
to be, *had* to be from over by Edenwald, we thought. Rowdy, raunchy, no

kind of class. Nasty homies on the prowl, not from this 'hood. How could we know? Three boys, fretful, frightened, angry. In a row. The burning rope had come to them long ago in willed and willful dreams, scored mean circles and scars into their once-gorgeous throats. The eyes that had once looked up in wonder from their mother's arms had been beaten, hammered into rings, dark pain-pools that belied their depth. Deeper. Where they lived, named and unnamed. How could they know? Know that those butterflies and orchids of the other world, that ice-green velvet of the other world, the precious stones that got up and wept before the unfeeling sky and the bears that slept away entire centuries with memories of that oncewarm sweet milk on their lips, were not for them? So beaten, so denied, as they were and as they believed, their own hands had grown to claws over the years; savaged their own skin. Needles? Maybe, we thought. In the reviling at large, who could tell? Pipes, bottles? Vials? So we thought. Of course. Who could know, and who who knew would tell? Who who knew would sing through the veil the words of that song, about the someone-or-thing that had torn out their insides and left them there, far from the velvet and the butterflies and the orchid-time? The knower's voice, if voice it was, only whispered down bitter rains when they howled, and left us only the curve of their skulls beneath the scarred flesh on those nights, bony white, when the moon smiled.

And she, so she: alone that day. Fresh and wet still from Tanya's arms, pajama invitations and TV nights, after-dark giggles and touches, kisses, while belowstairs the mama slept through world news, terrorist bombings, cleansings ethnic and unclean. Alone that day, the day after, yellow girl, walking out by the golden grayswishing Sound, higher up along the Shore Road way and higher, higher up where no one ever walks alone, higher still by where the dead bodies every year turn up (four Puerto Rican girl-things cut up, garbage-bagged, found there last year: bloated hands, swollen knees, and the broken parts); O higher still, Cassandra, where the fat joggers run, higher still past the horse stables and the smell of hay, higher yet getting on to where the whitefolks live and the sundowns die. Higher. Seeking watersmell and sheen for those forests in her eyes; seeking that summer sundown heat on her skin; seeking something away from 'hood cat calls and yo, bitch, let me in. Would you think she doesn't already know what peacefulness means, contains? She's already learned of the dangers of the too-high skirt, the things some of them say they'd like to put between her knees. The blouse that reveals, the pants that show too much hip. Ropes hers and theirs. Now seeking only a place where she can walk away, across the water if need be, away from the beer cans hurled from cars, the What's up, bitch yells and the burning circle-scars. Cassandra, Cassandra. Are you a bitch out here? The sun wexing goldsplash across her now says no. The water stretching out to Long Island summerheat on the other side says no, and the birds wheeling overhead, *okay, okay,* they cry, call down the skytone, concurring: the word is no. Peace and freedom, seasmell and free. A dark girl's scent riding on her thighs. Cassandra. Tanya. Sing it.

But they watching. The three. Singing. Listen: a bitch ain't nothing but a ho, sing those three. Have been taught. (But by whom?) Taught and taut. Taught low and harsh, that rhythm. Fierce melody. Melodylessness in mixture, lovelessness in joy. Drunk on flame, and who the fuck that bitch think she is anyway? they say—for they had seen her before, spoken to her and her kind; courted her favor, her attentions, in that car. Can't talk to nobody, bitch, you think you all a that? Can't speak to nobody, bitch, you think your pussy talks and shit? How could they know then?—of her forests, smoldering? Know and feel?—how in that growing silent heat those inner trees had uprooted, hurled stark branches at the outer sky? The firestorm and after-rain remained unseen. Only the lashes fluttered, and the inner earth grew hard. With those ropes choking so many of them in dreams, aware of the circles burnt into their skins, how could they know? How could they not know?

Robbie. Dee. Bernard. Three and three. Young and old. Too old for those jeans sliding down their asses. Too young for the rope and the circle's clutch. Too old to love so much their own wet dreams splashed out onto she they summoned out of that uncentered roiling world. She, summoned, to walk forth before their fire as the bitch or cunt. So they thought, would think and sing: still too young for the nursing of that keening need, the unconscious conscious wish to obliterate through vicious dreams who they were and are, have been, and are not. Blackmenbrothers, lovers, sons of strugglers. Sharecroppers, cocksuckers, black bucks and whores. Have been and are, might still be, and are not. A song. To do away with what they have and have not; what they can be, they think, are told by that outer chorus they can be—black boys, pretty boys, big dicks, tight asses, pretty boys, black scum, or funky homie trash—and cannot. Their hearts replaced by gnashing teeth, dirt;

the underscraping grinch, an always-howl. Robbie Dee Bernard. Who have names and eyelids, fears, homiehomes. Watching now. Looking out for a replacement for those shredded skins. Cause that bitch think she all a that, they sing. Word, got that lightskin, good hair, think she fly. Got them titties that need some dick up in between. The flavor. Not like them darkskinned bitches, they sing. (But do the words have joy?) Got to cut this bitch down to size, the chorus goes. A tune. Phat pussy. Word, G! Said hey-ho! Said a-hey-ho! Word, my brother. My nigger. Sing it.

So driving. Looking. Watching. Seeing. Their words a blue song, the undercolor of the nightbird's wing. Is it a song you have heard before? Heard it sung sweet and clear to someone you hate before? Listen: –Oh shit, yo, there she go. Right up there. Straight on. Swinging her ass like a high-yellow ho. Said hey-ho! Turn up the volume on my man J Live J. Drive up, yo. Spook the bitch. Gonna get some serious pussy outa this shit. –Driving, slowing, slowing down. Feeling the circles, feeling their own necks. Burning skins, cockheads fullstretched and hard. Will she have a chance, dreaming of girlkisses, against that hard? In the sun. Here. And.

Pulling up. –So, Miss Lightskin, they sing, what you doing out here? Walking by yourself, you ain't scared? Ain't scared somebody gonna try to get some of your skin? Them titties looking kinda fly, girl. Come on, now. Get in.

Was it then that she felt the smoldering in those glens about to break? The sun gleaming down silver whiteheat on her back? *And O how she had only longed to walk the walk.* To continue on and on and on and through to those copses where, at the feet of that very old and most wise woman-tree of all, she might gaze into those stiller waters of minnow-fishes, minnow-girls, and there yes! quell quell quell quell quell the flames. As one of them then broke through her glens, to shout that she wasn't nothing anyway but a yellow bitch with a whole lotta attitude and a skanky cunt. As (oh yes, it was true, rivers and fire, snake daggers and black bitches, she had had enough) she flung back words on what exactly he should do with his mother's cunt, cause your mother, nigger, is the only motherfucking bitch out here. And then? Who could say or know? The 5-0 were nowhere in sight; all passing cars had passed; only the wheeling birds and that drifting sun above were witnesses to what they could not prevent. Cassandra, Cassandra. –Get in the car, bitch. –Fuck no, I won't. Leave me alone. Leave me—trying to say Fuck off, y'all leave me the fuck alone, but whose hand was that, then, grabbing for her breast? Whose hand is that, on her ass, pressing now, right now, up into her flesh? –Stop it, y'all. Get the fuck off before screaming and crying. Cursing, running. Sneakered feet on asphalt, pursuit, and the laughter loud. An easy catch. –We got you now, bitch. –Who can hear? The sun can only stare, and the sky is gone.

Driving, driving, driving on. Where can they take her? Where will they? They all want some, want to be fair. Fair is fair: three dicks, one cunt. That is their song. Driving on. Pelham Bay Park? they think. But naw, too many people, niggers and Ricans with a whole buncha kids and shit. (The sun going down. Driving on.) How about under the bridge, by Eastchester Creek? That's it, G! Holding her, holding, but can't somebody slap the bitch to make her shut up? Quit crying, bitch. Goddamn. A crying-ass bitch in a little funky-ass car. Now weeping more. Driving on. –Gonna call the police, she says, crying more; choking in that way they like, for then (oh, yes, they know) in that way from smooth head to hairy base will she choke on them. They laugh. –What fucking 5-0 you gonna call, bitch? You lucky we ain't take your yellow ass over to the projects. Fuck your shit in the elevator, throw your ass off the roof. These bitches, they laugh. Just shut up and sit back. Sit back, sit back. –Driving on.

Now the one they call Robbie is talking to her. –Open it, he says. Robbie, O Robbie. Eager and edgy, large-eyed and fine. Robbie, who has a name, unspoken hopes; private dreams. How can they know? Will he be dead within a year like so many others? A mirrored image in a mirror that shows them nothing? A wicked knife's slide from a brother's hand to his hidden chewed-up heart? Shattered glass, regret. Feeling now only the circle around his neck that keeps all in thrall. For now he must be a man for them. Must show the steel. Robbie don't be fronting, he prays they think, Robbie will be hard. Will they like you better, Robbie, then, if you be hard? Will the big boys finally love you, take you in, Robbie, if you be hard? Deep and low…he knows. Knows the clear tint of that pain. Alone and lonely…unknown, trying to be hard. Not like it was back then when *then when he said you was pretty*. Remember? All up in his arms…one of your boys, Darrel J. in his arms. Where nobody couldn't see. Didn't have to be hard. Rubbing up, rubbing. Kissing up on you. Licking. Talking shit about lovelove and all a that. *But naw man* he said the first time (Darrell J., summertime, 10 P.M., off the court, hotwet, crew gone home, had an extra 40, sweaty chest neck face, big hands, shoulders, smile, was fine), *just chillin whyn't you come on hang out?*—so said Darrell J. with the hands and the yo yo yo yo going on and on with them eyes and mouth tongue up in his skin my man—: kissing up on Robbie the second time, pretty Robbie, the third time and the fourth and the we did and he kissing licking holding y'all two and O Robbie Robbie Robbie. A homie's song. Feeling then. Underneath him, pretty. In his arms. *Where nobody couldn't see didn't have to be hard kissing up on him shy shy and* himinyou youinhim Robbie, Robbie. Where has the memory gone? Back then, straddling hips, homiekisses and the nightbird's song. But can't go back there, can you? To feel and feel. Gots to be hard. Can't ever touch him again, undress him, kiss his thing...feel it pressing against the teeth and the slow-hipped song. Black skin on skin and

—but he was *holding onto me and sliding, sliding way up inside sucking coming inside me in me in hot naw didn't need no jimmy aw shit now hold on holding him and I was I was Robbie Robbie Robbie Darrell J. together we was and I we I we came we hotwet on his belly my side sliding over him under him holding and we came we* but naw, man, can't even be *doing* that motherfucking punk shit out here. You crazy? You bugging? Niggers be getting smoked dusty for that shit. Y'all ain't never seen *me* do that. Gots to be hard. –So open it, bitch, he says. Lemme get my fingers on up in there. Awright, awright. Damn, man, he says, nobody don't got a jimmy? This bitch stinks, man, he says, know I'ma probably get some VD shit on my hands and shit. They laugh. –He a man, all right. Robbie! Ain't no faggot, yo. Not like we *heard*. They laugh. –Just put a sock on it, the one they call Dee says. Chillchill, yo. Everybody gonna get their chance.

And the sun. Going down, going down. Light ending now, fire and ice, blue time watersheen and the darkened plunge. Sink, golden sun. Rest your bronze head in the Sound and the sea beyond. The birds, going down, going down. Movement of trees, light swathed in leaves. Going down, going down. And.

Hard to see now, but that's okay, they say. This bitch got enough for everybody here under the bridge. No one's around now, only rusty cars and rats. Who cares if they shove that filthy rag into her mouth and tie it there? It's full of turpentine and shit, but the night doesn't care. The same night that once covered them in swamps from fiery light. Will someone come in white robes to save a lightskinned bitch this time?

Hot. Dark. On the backseat. Burning bright. Burning. On the backseat. Fire and rage. –Naw, man, Robbie, not so hard, man. You gone wear the shit out fore I get my chance. –Who said that? Which one in the dark? O but can't tell, for all are hidden now, and all are hard. The motherfucking *rig*orous shit, one of them says. Shut up, bitch. Was that you, Bernard? Did you miss your daddy when he went off with the one your mama called a dirty nigger whore, Bernard? Was that where you first learned everything there was to learn, and nothing? –There, Bernard? When he punched you in the face and left you behind, little boy Bernard? You cried. Without. A song unheard. A song like the shadowrain—wasn't it? The shadowrain that's always there so deep, deep down inside your eyes, Bernard. Cold rain inside. Tears and tears. Then fists and kicks on a black shitboy's head. Little punk-looking nigger dumped in a foster home, age ten, named Bernard. Fuckhead faggot ass, the boys there said. The ones who stuck it up in you. Again and again. The second and the third... –don't hurt me, don't!—screamed that one they called the faggot ass pussy bitch. You, Bernard. How could they know? Know that the little bitch punk scrunched up under the bed had seen the whole night and afterward and after alone? Bernard? *Hurts, mama. Daddy*—. Rain. Little faggot ass punk. Break his fucking face, yo. Kick his faggot ass down the stairs. Then he gone suck my dick. Suck it, bitch, fore we put this motherfucking hammer up your ass. The one you trusted most of all in that place, in all those places...everywhere? Bernard? The one who said he'd have your back no matter what. Little man, my man, he said. Smiling down. His teeth so white and wide. Smiling down. Smiling when he got you by the throat, sat on your chest and made you swallow it. Swallow it, bitch, he sang. Smiling down. Choking, choked. Deep inside the throat. Where has the memory gone? Something broken, then a hand. A reaching-out howl within the rain. A nightbird's rage. A punk, used up. Leave the nigger there, yo, they said. Til the next time. And the next. On the floor. Under the bed. Under. Bleeding under. You, Bernard.

The words to every song on earth are buried deep somewhere. Songs that must be sung, that must never be sung. That must be released from deep within the chest yet pulled back and held. Plaintive and low, they rail; buried forever beneath the passing flesh, alone and cold, they scream. The singer must clutch them to the heart, where they are sanctified, nurtured, healed. Songs which finally must be released yet recalled, in that place where no one except the singer ever comes, in one hand caressing the keys of life wounded, ravaged, in the other those of the precious skin and life revealed. The three of them and Cassandra know the words. Lying beneath them now and blind, she knows the words. Tasting turpentine and fire, she knows the words. –Hell no, yo, that bitch ain't dead. –A voice. –Fucked up, yo. The rag's in her mouth, how we gone get some mouth action now? –Aw, man, fuck that shit. –Who says that? –My turn. My turn. –They know the words.

Now comes Dee. Can't even really see her, has to navigate. Wiggles his ass a little, farts softly to let off stress. –Damn, Dee, nasty mother-fucker! they laugh. But he is busy, on to something. Sniffs and sniffs. At the bitch's asshole. At her cunt. –Cause yeah, yo, he says, y'all know what's up with this shit. They be saying this bitch done got into some bulldagger shit. Likes to suck pussy, bulldagger shit. –Word? –The phat-test bitch around, yo, he says. Bulldagger shit.

Dee. DeeDee. Someone's boy. Has a place that's home. Eastchester, or Mount V. Has a heart that hates his skin and a mind half gone. Is ugly now, got cut up, but smoked the nigger who did it. Can't sleep at night, wanders seas; really wants to die. The lonely bottle might do it if the whiffs up don't. The empty hand might do it if the desire can't. What has been loved and not loved, what seeks still a place. The same hand, pushed by the once-winsome heart, that before painted angels, animals, miraculous creatures. Blank walls leaped into life, lightspeed and light. When (so it seemed) the whole world was light. But was discouraged, led into tunnels, and then of course was cut. The eyes went dim. Miraculous creatures. Where have the visions gone? Look, now, at that circle around his neck. Will he live? Two young ones and a dark girl waiting back there for him, frightened—will he live? Crushed angels drowned in St. Ides— will he live? When he sells the (yes, that) next week to the undercover 5-0 and is set up, will he live? When they shoot him in the back and laugh at the stain that comforts them, will he live?

But now he's happy, has found it!—the hole. The soft little hole, so tight, down there, as he reaches up to squeeze her breasts. Her eyes are closed but she knows the words. *That bitch ain't dead.* How can they know? When there is time there's time, and the time is now. Time to bang the bulldagger out of her, he sings. Listen to his song. –I'ma give you a baby, bitch. –(She knows the words.) –Got that lightskin, think you all that, right, bitch? Word, I want me some lightskin on my dick, yo. When I get done this heifer ain't gone be *half* a ho. You know know? Gonna get mines, til you know who you dis and who you don't. Til you know we the ones in *control,* sing it! Got the flavor. –Dim-eyed, banging out his rage. Now, a man. Banging out his fear like the others, ain't even hardly no faggot ass. Def jam and slam, bang bang shebam. On and on as he shoots high, shoots far…laughter, but then a sense of falling, careening…sudden fear. It doesn't matter. The song goes on.

Night. Hell, no, broods the dim, that bitch ain't dead. Hasn't uttered half a sound since they began; hasn't opened her eyes to let the night look in again; hasn't breathed to the soft beating of the nightbird's wing. The turpentine rag in place. Cassandra, Cassandra. The rag, in place. Cassandra. Is she feeling something now? Cassandra. Will they do anything more to her now? Cassandra, will they leave you there? Focusing on flies, not meeting each other's eyes, will they leave you there? Running back from the burning forests behind their own eyes, the crackling and the shame? Will they leave you there? –Push that bitch out on the ground, the one they call Dee says. Over there, by them cars and shit. –Rusty cars, a dumping ground. So, Cassandra. Yes. They'll leave you there.

Were they afraid? Happy? Who can tell? Three dark boys, three men, driving away in a battered car. Three boy-men, unseen, flesh, minds, heart. Flame. In their car. O my God, three rapists, the pretty lady in her Volvo thinks, locking her doors at the traffic light. In their car. Blood on the backseat, cum stains, even hair. Who can tell? It's time to get open now. Time to numb the fear. –Get out the whiff, yo. –40s and a blunt. –That bitch got what she deserved. –Those words, whiffs up, retreat, *she deserved it, deserved it*—and they are gone. Mirrored images in shattered glass, desire and longing, chill throbbing, and they are gone. The circles cleaving their necks. Flesh, blood and flame. A whiff and a 40. –We fucked that bitch good, G. –Night. Nightnight. Hush dark silence. Fade. They are gone.

Cassandra. What nightbirds are searching and diving for you now? What plundered forests are waiting for you now? The girltrees are waiting for you, and so is she. Tanya. The girl-trees. Mama. How can they know? Their eyes are waiting, searching, and will soon be gray. The rats are waiting. They are gray. Cassandra, Cassandra. When the red lights come flashing on you, will they know? Fifteen, ripped open. Will they know? Lightskinned bitch nigger ho, went that song. Will they know? Girl-trees in a burning forest…they will know. And the night….

Where is she, they're wondering, why hasn't she come home?

They can't know what the rats and the car-carcasses know.

Cassandra? they are calling. Why don't you answer when night-voices call you home?

Night....

Listen now to the many night voices calling, calling soft, *Cassandra. Come.* Carrying. Up. *Cassandra. Come. Out* and *up.* What remains is what remains. *Out* and *up.* They will carry her. A feeling of hands and light. Then the red lights will come. *Up* and *up.* But will she see? Will she hear? Will she know?

The girl-trees are screaming. That is their song.

It will not appear on tomorrow's morning news.

But then—come now, ask yourself—whose song, finally, shall this be? Of four dark girls, or four hundred, on their way to lasting fire in Sunday school? Of a broken-backed woman, legs bent? Her tune? Of a pair of hands, stitching for—(but they'll never grow). Of four brothers rapping, chugging?—a slapbeat in the chorus? Doing time? Something they should know?

A song of grieving ships, bodies, torch-lit roads?

(*—But then now O yes remember, remember well that time, face place or thing: how those ten thousand million billion other ashes eyelids arms uncountable dark ceaseless burnt and even faces once fluttered, fluttered for—in someone's dream unending, dream of no escape, beneath a blackblueblack sea: fluttered, flutter still and descend, now faces ashes eyelids dark reflection and skin forever flame descend, descend over laughing crowds.*)

A song of red earth roads. Women crying and men. Red hands, gray mouths, and the circle's clutch. A song, a song. Of sorrowing suns. Of destruction, self-destruction, when eyes lay low. A song —

But whose song is it? Is it yours? Or mine?

Hers?

Or theirs...—?

—But a song. A heedless, feckless tune. Here, where the nighttime knows. And, well

Yes, well—

—So, Cassandra. Now, Cassandra.

Sing it.

JAMES EARL HARDY

■ ■ ■

[1966–]

BORN AND RAISED IN THE BEDFORD-STUYVESANT SECTION OF Brooklyn, James Earl Hardy has been credited with launching the Afrocentric gay hip-hop romance genre that began with the publication of his groundbreaking debut novel *B-Boy Blues* (1994). He has worn many hats as a journalist in his twenty-plus year career writing feature articles, book and music reviews, and essays for publications such as *Essence*, the *Washington Post, Entertainment Weekly, VIBE, OUT, The Advocate, The Source*, and The Blackstripe online.

An honors graduate of Columbia University in 1993, Hardy won many prizes for his work, including a Columbia Scholastic Press Association Writing Citation, two Educational Press Association Writing Awards, grants from the E. Y. Harbug Arts Foundation and the American Association of Sunday and Feature Editors, and scholarships from the Paul Rapoport Memorial Foundation and both the national and New York chapters of the Association of Black Journalists.

But after complaining for years about not seeing depictions of African American Same Gender Loving (SGL) men in literature that reminded him of men he knew, he took what he believed would be a brief detour into the world of fiction and wrote *B-Boy Blues* (1994), in which Mitchell Crawford, a journalist, and Raheim Rivers, a bike messenger homeboy from Harlem, fall in love. Praised as the first Afrocentric, gay, hip-hop love story, the novel became an immediate bestseller. Four other titles in the *B-Boy Blues* series have followed: *2nd Time Around* (1996), *If Only for One Nite* (1997), and *The Day Eazy-E Died* (2001). In addition to documenting and celebrating contemporary black SGL life, the series has prompted overdue discussions about racism in the white gay community and homophobia in the heterosexual African American community. And because of its cultural impact, *B-Boy Blues* has become required reading in many multicultural and queer college studies programs around the country.

In this selection from *B-Boy Blues,* Mitchell explains what a b-boy is—and why he's irresistibly drawn to them.

A nd why was he what the doctor ordered? Well, besides being a vision of lust, he's a B-boy—or banjee/banji/banjie boy, or block boy, or homeboy, or homie, or, as MC Lyte tags 'em, "ruffneck." For those who don't know who these fellas are—and, if you don't, just where have you been living, on another planet?—I'll gladly school you on the subject. This is something I love to discuss.

They are the boyz who stand on street corners, doin' their own vogue—striking that "cool pose" against a pole, a storefront, up against or on a car, leanin', loungin', and loiterin' with their boyz, just holding court like a king with a "40" to quench the thirst, tryin' to rap to the females, and daring anyone to stake their territory, to invade their domain.

They are the boyz you see every morning, afternoon, early eve, and late nite on the news, heads down and covered—but nothing can hide the handcuffs.

They are the boyz who stand like a tree—body erect, but somewhat arched, slanted to one side, their arms stretched and reaching like branches. Their eyes are icy cold; they look through you, sizing you up and cutting you down. Their smile is a wicked, wavering one. At one moment, it seems both inviting and harmless; at another, cunning yet calculating.

They are the boyz who dress to thrill. Their heads—clean, close-cropped, or in a funky fade—are wrapped in bandanas, scarves, stocking caps, or sports caps, which are usually worn front, tilted downward, loose, or backwards on the head for full effect. They style and profile in their baggy jeans or pants falling somewhere between their waists and knees, barely holding onto their behinds, their undergear puffed up over their waists. They kick the pavement in sidewalk-stompin' boots and low- and high-top, high-priced sneakers, oftentimes worn loose, unlaced, or open, with their trousers tucked inside.

They are the boyz who move to a rhythm all their own—the swagger in their step, the hulking strut that jerks their bodies to and fro, front to back, side to side, as if they are about to fall. Their arms sway to their own beat. Their hands are right at home in their pockets.

They are the boyz who, whether they are in motion or standing, are always clutching their crotches. In fact, it seems like their hands are surgically attached to their dicks, as if they are holding it in place and fear it will fall off (or are they reaching for something that isn't really there?).

They are the boyz who walk like they are marching off to war—a war that many of them are, unfortunately, fighting against each other and themselves.

They are the epitome of cool.

They are the epitome.

They are *cool.*

They are the boyz who are filling our prisons, where many pump iron to pump up their bodies, when they should be in school pumpin' knowledge into their brains.

They are the boyz who are loud and boisterous; they speak to be heard, not so much to be understood. They are cantankerous and obnoxious; they know everything, and don't even try to tell them they are wrong. They are cocky and egocentric; the world doesn't revolve around them, because they *are* the world. They are self-centered and self-absorbed; they are all true men, 101 percent, and it's all about them.

They are the boyz who are walking stereotypes, walking statistics for commentators, forecasters, academicians, and politicians to discuss and dissect, to berate and blast, to write about and write off.

They are the boyz whose main challenge in life is to gain or sustain props (that's respect). So, don't even think about looking at them the wrong way or looking at them, period, when they don't want to be looked at, for it is over for you. They'll cap you, take you out, snuff you, to prove who is runnin' this motha-fucka.

They are the boyz who just don't give a fuck.

They are the boyz who are the true hip-hopsters, the gangstas, the menaces 2 and of society, the troublemakers, the troubleseekers, the hoods, the hoodlums, the hood-rocks, the MacDaddys, the Daddy-Macs, the rugged hard-rocks...

You get the picture.

We've all seen 'em and one thing is certain—they scare the shit out of a lot of folks, especially The Man and his Woman. They are White America's hellmare—those Big, Black Brutes, those Common Criminals, those Violent Vagrants who have made the streets unsafe, taken the value out of "family values"—since, the logic goes, so many of them make babies but don't care for them—and just, in general, brought down the quality of life. When they are coming down the street, a path is not only cleared for them, it is *cleaned*. And they love it…

"Dat's right, step outa da way, you betta move ta da otha side of da fuckin' street, you white bitch, you ain't impo'tant, I don' want yo' fuckin' purse or yo' pussy…

"Mr. Mutha-Fuckin' Wall Street, I don' need yo' wallet or gold money clip, it ain't about you, it's about me, you cracka jack motha-fucka…"

Here are "men" who throw their masculinity around for the entire world to not only see but swallow (pun intended). Of course, it is a rather grotesquely exaggerated take on manhood. But, when you are on your way to growing into a man (at least in years) and nobody has told you how to be one and almost all the "men" you see around you walk, talk, dress, and act like this, how else do you prove that you are a man but by joining them? Yes, you too have to be one bad motha-fucka, the one they'll fear the most. It's a man thang, nothin' but a man thang, and only the roughest, the toughest survive.

Banjeeness has become a boyz2men rite-of-life for many preteen/teenage/postteen males in the so-called inner city. And, the vibe these fellas give off is an overtly "straight" one. But B-boys do come in all ages (uh-huh, forty-year-olds nursin' a "40"), persuasions (the girlz are down, too), mutations (white boys like the down-with-the-homies-phony and Great-White-Aryan-Muscle-Boy-Hope Marky Mark), and orientations. For many Black heterosexuals, though, there is no such thing as a homosexual, so most would faint if you were to even suggest that a B-boy could be gay. The general rule is that, even if there are homosexuals in our community, there *should*n't be, and those willing to acknowledge that we do exist feel comfortable with us only as flaming faggots (a la Blaine and Antoine of TV's *In Living Color*). Given our history in AmeriKKKa, it has been a struggle defining what manhood means in a society that does not afford us the right to be men.

So, the worst thing for any Black man to be is a cocksucker or someone who takes it up the ass. *We* "want to be women" because we can't handle the harsh reality of being a Black man in America or dealing with a "strong sister," as if sleeping with other men is going to change one's sex or sexual orientation. God forbid if *we* bend over for a Caucasian—that is the ultimate symbol of subjugation, a throwback to slavery, and proof to some that homosexuality is something "the white man forced upon us." In fact, the nation's prisons, which many consider the white man's modern-day slave system, are responsible for helping to perpetuate this "pathology." *We* are worse than females who may be bitches or ho's, for at least they are good for something—pimpin' and puttin' out.

And *we* are a "threat" to the Black family—even though all of us come from Black families, and head or have our own, whether they be blood- or bond-related.

Because homosexuality is still a no-no, an unmentionable topic in most households and churches, too many of us spend our lives in the closet. And, one of the best ways to do that is to adopt the B-boy stance. And B-boys, with the indirect support of the community, fool themselves into thinking that, because they are so hard, because no one knows and probably won't be able to figure them out, they can't be homosexual. They just like to suck dick or have their dick sucked by another man is all; they just like to fuck other men. Hey, they can get an erection with a woman, maybe even have a baby (now *there's* a badge of masculine honor), so they must be straight. They are real men, unlike us, the faggots they fuck. But, as Teddy Pendergrass once vocalized: "You Can't Hide from Yourself."

Gene calls B-boys many things (most of them too vulgar for even me to repeat), but three of his labels are priceless. There's "homiesexuals," "homoboyz," and his fave, "perpetrades": guys who "look" straight, "act" straight, may even think they're straight, but ain't. Since so many B-boys are trapped in this syndrome, Gene doesn't see how anybody could find them appealing. He admits their aura screams sex— lusty, animalistic, ravenous sex—and they do know what to do between them sheets (he has tasted a few himself). But an orgasm can last but so long. And, for people like me, who are looking forward to being "married" someday, they ain't exactly husband material. How can you build something with someone who lives for the moment, who can't or won't grow up? As Gene once remarked: "I want a man, not a boy!"

Still, I find them irresistible.

It took some time for me to notice they could be, though. Like most people, I was intimidated, put off by them. That in-yo'-face, gruff-and-grandiose air would always make me think, "Who the hell do these guys think they are, walking around like they own everything and can run anyone?" I guess because I have always been a softie, a sensitive, sensuous guy who cries at the drop of a hat, I was also somewhat jealous of this quality. But I soon came to find it sexy. It was certainly a smug kind of confidence, but it grew on me. That head-nigga-in-charge atimatude made me wish they would take charge of me!

The next "characteristic" that caught my eye was what Gene calls their "tail waggin'." As mentioned before, B-boys wear their pants hanging off their asses. Most of them have juicy behinds to begin with, so when they bebop down the street, it just jingles and jangles—and *that* is a sight to see. I am convinced that most B-boys, whatever their orientation, really enjoy the attention that their asses attract; I mean, why advertise like that if you don't want it to be seen and salivated over? When you think about it, this is very homoerotic. Homosexuals are often accused of "flaunting" their sexuality (a tired charge, since straight folks bombard us every day with images that glorify their sexuality), but B-boys, who are supposedly a heterosexual lot, seem to do it more, especially in this area. Needless to say, my head began turning a lot to gawk. Of course, this was something I had to do very carefully. Even if the one I was lusting over was gay, they might have kicked my ass for looking at them that way, anyway. I managed to do it well, though, and went from being just an ordinary homosexual to a butt man. It was then that I began daydreaming about having a B-boy.

But the curiosity boiled to the point of deep-seated desire by the spring and summer of 1991. It was the year of new jack cinema: boyz from the ghettos, dealin' and doin' drugs, carousin' and killin' up a storm, getting any and all the pussy they wanted. After seeing one of these flicks, I'd find myself starring in my own version at night, complete with opening and closing credits, soundtrack, narration, and special effects:

In *New Jack Booty,* I was a simple, naive schoolteacher who lectured his students on saying no to drugs, while I was cautioned by my own peers about saying no to a fine crack kingpin. Does my conscience prevail over my carnal instincts? In a word, *No.*

In *Hangin' Out, Over, and Under the Homeboyz,* I am picked up in a bar by one homie, agree to go to his house to have some fun, and we are joined by two of his buddies. They pass me around like a "40," taking turns sipping and gulping me down. And believe me, this one always made me wake up in a hot sweat.

In *Lovin' Large,* this hulky, bulky thug kidnaps me, the "bitch" of a rival, and demands that my hubby, a big-time drug lord, come up with

$1 million in a day or he'll kill me (doesn't sound at all pleasant, does it?). Well, while we're waiting for hubby to decide whether I'm worth saving, I'm doing some serious sleeping with the enemy. I love it so much, I don't want to leave him and he feels the same way. Twenty-four hours later, he tells my now ex-boyfriend that he can keep the mill, cuz he's got something money can't buy, and we blaze off into the sunset in his Jeep.

But the one that gave me some seriously sticky nights was *Boyz under My Hood*. Talk about a romance: My car breaks down on a highway and this tall, dark, handsome B-boy with a bald head (shades of Raheim?) stops to help. He checks under the hood of my car, and then asks if he can check under mine! Of course, I let him, and his monkey wrench turns me out! This dream was too real. When I'd wake up in the morning, I could still taste him, smell him, and feel him in bed with me. While this made me smile the entire day, it also made me mad as hell. I wanted it, for real.

So, after all of this, I couldn't take the hunger anymore. I had to find myself a B-boy to satisfy it or I'd bust. And, when I met Raheim, the fantasy in full-bodied flesh had finally come along. All I could think was that he could definitely be Mr. Boyz under My Hood. He would be The One.

But, of course, I had said this before.

Brian Keith Jackson

■ ■ ■

[1967–]

RAISED IN MONROE, LOUISIANA, BRIAN KEITH JACKSON GREW
up listening to the Deep South stories of his great-grandmother. After
moving to New York City, he published his first novel, the critically
acclaimed *The View from Here* (1997), winner of the First Fiction Award
from the Black Caucus of the American Library Association. Jackson is
also the recipient of fellowships from Art Matters, the Jerome Foundation,
and the Millay Colony of the Arts.

His second novel, *Walking Through Mirrors* (1998), takes place in the
author's home state, where Jeremy Bishop, a young, apparently gay
African American photographer, has returned from New York for his
father's funeral. Known as Patience by his grandmother, Mama B.,
Jeremy tells his story through flashbacks of his boyhood.

from **Walking Through Mirrors**

[1998]

I had often wondered what my mother looked like. I knew she must have been beautiful, for that's what a fantasy demands. It was Mama B who told me that there were no pictures because some people just didn't care for them. But every black family I knew seemed to dote on photographs, so her explanation made little sense to me. She said that the Indians believe that every time someone takes a picture of you, a piece of your spirit is stolen. From this I was led—or rather chose—to believe that my mother was an Indian, maybe even one of the descendants of those who founded Elsewhere.

Just that belief was all it took for me to pass up hide-and-seek and make cowboys and Indians my favorite game. But this meant recruiting others. Having been around mostly adults and believing myself one, I had little tolerance for children my age, but many children are older than they appear—in actions if not intellect.

The Baker boys lived just down the street. Their family had won a plot of land in a lawsuit. It had three houses on it, along with certain areas that resembled a car graveyard. About ten cars populated their yard; not a single one provided mobility. Some were supported on cinder blocks; other were on the ground, weeds substituting for tires. Some had the hood wide open, but others had no hood at all, their rusted wounds becoming a home for yellow jackets, lizards, and the like.

The Bakers were known to produce at the rate of rabbits. No one could say exactly how many people lived on that plot of land. I knew just the three who were somewhere near my age and the mothers who always flirted with me in that way that only older women can.

I'd walk down the street to their place and the Baker boys would be out and about. Pookie was the youngest. He was always the first to be found in a game of hide-and-seek, but he could never seem to figure out that his soiled scent was the giveaway. Chester was the middle child and mean as all get-out. He was two heads above us all and would spit so much you were surprised that there was any more liquid available in his body. Tyrone was the eldest, so I liked him the most. But he rarely had time to hang out with us, as he was on his way to manhood.

Summers garnered notable additions to the clan, as Miss Irene's grandchildren always came from Detroit, carrying the mystique of coming from that unknown place up North. Miss Irene's grand-daughter Shandra and I had been boyfriend and girlfriend ever since we had heard the words. My job was to say mean things to her, then she would do the same to me, and later we'd meet and kiss. Her little sister Precious—"to name a chile Precious is just askin' for a heap o' trouble"—was a crier. I never knew her to do anything but cry or say, "Ooo, I'ma tellit." I believed their brother James to be the coolest thing since "sliced bread," as I had heard the older folks say. I never understood that saying, for I didn't realize that bread came any other way. But I was honored to have James as a friend, if only for the summers.

Miss Irene was probably the most popular adult in the neighbor-hood, for she was the huckabuck lady. A small huckabuck came in a Peanuts Dixie cup for a dime and the larger ones came in a Styrofoam cup for fifteen cents. Because Shandra was my girlfriend, I always got mine free during her visits. Or almost for free. She would steal them for me. Though Miss Irene counted her inventory closely during her grandchildren's stay, she counted only what she made, never the ones that we made while she was out to replace those we'd already consumed.

Huckabucks were either red or purple. If you timed it just perfectly, the Kool-Aid would be frozen just enough that the top was a syrupy treat that you could lap up with your tongue. I always preferred the larger ones because they required less skill to eat. The small ones often entailed the consumer's having to push them up from the bottom of the cup. Many times, the frozen treat, with a mind of its own, would shoot out of the cup to the ground. This episode was always the truest test of friendship, for a friend would understand that after you've washed it off, a dropped huckabuck was good as new.

The larger huckabucks were easier. As you worked your way down the cup, you bit the Styrofoam then spit it out to the ground. Though it hadn't snowed in Elsewhere in a "dog's year," Miss Irene's yard was the closet thing to looking as though it had, but it was a rake, not a shovel, that cleared the ground.

The notion of cowboys and Indians didn't sit well with the others. Evidently, kids in Detroit had stopped playing the game years ago in favor of cops and robbers, leaving James to say, "You all are so backwards down here."

"That shit's for punks," spat out Chester, allying himself with James. I took that statement to be some sort of Bakerism that I didn't quite understand, but I was wise enough not to acknowledge my ignorance.

Punk.

"Fine by me. We can play whatever y'all want to. Cops and robbers is perfectly fine with me. It was just a suggestion."

"Why you talk so country, like white folks? You actin' all proper," said Chester, throwing this out at me like a dart that missed the board all together but stuck to the wall, begging for a reprimand.

I had never before heard anyone comment on how I spoke. All I could muster was "That's just the way I talk." It was Pookie who saved me, for at that moment, he started to pee on himself. "At least I don't pee on myself" rolled out of my mouth with the same bitterness of a plum prematurely picked. That seemed to silence Chester.

Shandra then informed me that girls couldn't play cowboys and Indians. I didn't want to tell her that they could because my mother was an Indian, maybe like Pocahontas. I wanted to explain to Shandra, but I kept mum, as always, on the subject of my mother.

Clark soon appeared. He was their cousin and lived with Miss Irene year 'round. I once asked her why his school bus was smaller than the others; it was then that I gathered he was "special." But summers had him home just like the rest of us. Of everyone, I liked Clark best. He seemed most like me. He was bigger than all of us, and I heard it said that he was twenty. Though twenty seemed old at the time, he made twenty not seem old at all.

He did have the eyes of an old soul—like mine—and when I looked into them, I saw something that would never exist in the eyes of the others. I saw innocence, and wherever that is found, you're certain to find longing. He loved hugging, but hugs were shunned by this tribe. I let Clark hug me once. He wanted so much to embrace everyone that he was unaware of his manly strength compared to that of my eight-year-old body. He was like a child roughly stroking a cat, unable to realize that love is gentle.

Clark would often be tormented to the point of tears. It was as though James resented Clark's presence because it was a visible reminder that he had an imperfect relative. I don't think Clark rightly understood what was being said, but he could feel the words that were as numbing as the ice from the huckabuck, now sucked clear of color and flavor.

It was the last day of summer—well, not really, but it was the day before Miss Irene's grandchildren were returning to Detroit, where James said they were going to have dinner that very next night with Aretha Franklin.

The day remains vivid in my mind; the cold moves on, yet the cough lingers.

It was the boys. Tyrone. Chester. Pookie. Clark. Me.

We were sitting on Miss Irene's back steps, the August heat presenting itself in a blur before us.

"Did you fuck her?" asked James.

"Fuck, yeah. Tore that shit up. Man, yo' sister know how to do it good, too," said Tyrone. "I guess Jeremy warmed it up for me, 'cuz we was all over that mattress."

Everyone exchanged soul shakes. Even I joined in, wanting to be party to the story. Palm cupped. Slide to knuckles. Patted twice with the knuckles of the other hand. Fingers then pinched and swung up to the mouth to indicate smoking reefer, then a slide over the head and back down to a thumbs-up.

James had shown us this shake on his first day. Every summer, another move or two were added. We had attempted, in his absence, to make our own additions, but they never held a candle to what James brought from Detroit.

Miss Irene's backyard was always our private place. Behind her house was a huge field that had grown wild with neglect. A barbed-wire fence separated it from her vacant yard. On numerous occasions, we had played hide-and-seek in that field, but not this summer. Hide-and-seek was replaced with the mattress in the overgrown lot, a place for sex, not child's play.

I'd been shown the mattress, but the thought of ever being on it never interested me. I had never "done it" with Shandra. But if she had not brought that fact to light with Tyrone, I certainly wasn't going to broach the matter. Maybe that was what she wanted and why she broke up with me to be with him. I knew what it was. I'd seen Aunt Jess doing it one time.

Some man was on top of her, jiggling around. She was making these *uh, uh, uh* sounds and so was he, but it didn't seem like they meant disdain, as is usually the case when those sounds are strung together. No, they were continuous, drawn out, the final *uh* always the longest, deflating to nothing.

On the day of my first sexual sighting, I had hidden in the closet in Aunt Jess's room—not with the idea of spying, for I had always hidden in certain places in the house to just get away from it all. Hide-and-seek for one. I peeked out of the crack between the closet-door panels, feeling a bit sweaty up against the plastic-covered dry-cleaned Sunday clothes that surrounded me.

When she entered the room with the man, I dared not present myself. I was trapped there. They undressed, and he climbed on top of her but didn't cover himself with the blankets. I didn't quite understand why she would want this man on top of her like that. The look on her face was as though what he was doing was painful, but he kept right at it. I wanted to jump out and protect her, but when he asked if she liked it, she said that she did. When she opened her eyes, I had to wonder.

With that long last *uh,* he rolled off of her onto his back. She stroked his chest a few times, but just a few, because he popped up from the bed. "I gotta get goin'," he said, motioning for his boxers on the floor.

"You wanna wash up?"

"Nah, I'll do it later. I gotta get goin'. I'll call ya later."

Aunt Jess stayed in bed and watched through the window as he went out the front door. I sat back in the closet, not wanting to see any more. I thought she would stay in bed forever. It wasn't until I heard the bathwater running that I crept out of the place I'd intended for solace, soaked with sweat, feeling I should wash up, but for a different reason.

Still, I couldn't imagine Tyrone and Shandra doing that. The thought of it made me dislike her even more and hate him for his lack of discretion. It seemed peculiar to me that James didn't mind that his sister had done this. It was as though he was proud, not of her, but of Tyrone. "Hey, if you can get them drawers, get 'em," he said to Tyrone. They all laughed, even Clark, but I couldn't imagine that he had ever done it. I doubt he even knew why this was funny.

"Yeah, Jeremy, you missin' out now, man. But I 'preciate you handin' her over to me," said Tyrone, hand cupped over his crotch. I couldn't help but wonder if indeed I had really missed something. "Bitch wouldn't suck my dick, though."

"Ah, man, she wouldn't suck yo' dick?" said James, her own brother. "Nothin' beat gettin' yo' dick sucked."

They all concurred, as though sex and its many acts were as common to them as biting off the Styrofoam that kept the huckabuck from making cherrylike stains on cotton garments.

I too nodded my head, yet not in agreement. I put my hands in my pockets, pushing down as far as they would go, grabbing for anything to distract me, but all I found was lint.

"Don't go puttin' yo' hands in yo' pockets. It's too late to be gettin' hard now. You could still be pokin' that, but you were too busy ackin' like a l'il ol' punk, so I had to step up to the plate. Batter up!" he said, laughing before adding, "Hank Aaron ain't got shit on me."

Punk.

Tyrone had a responsive crowd now, and they followed his lead, hooing and hawing, even Clark. I took my hands out of my pockets posthaste and though I wanted to say something in rebuttal, like "Fuck you" or "Yo' mamma" or one of the many puerile insults that I'd heard thrown around, I knew that coming out of my mouth, they wouldn't carry the same vituperative heft.

"You wanna see somethin'?" asked James. Our excitement was piqued for a moment, for the way he posed it was as though he was going to show us the most amazing feat in the world. If he was going to be supping with the queen of soul, then anything was possible—and it had to be if it was going to top Tyrone's grandstanding.

The yeahs of everyone followed—everyone except Clark, for he rarely answered. The only sound I'd ever heard him make that wasn't laughter was like a yelp that came from deep down. I thought of it as a baby crying in the night, frustrated because no one could understand what the problem was.

"Come on." James shot off the step. He went down to where the middle line of the barbed wire had been cut out of the fence. Tyrone placed his foot on the bottom line, then pulled up the top one as we all stepped through, free of puncture. We walked through the field, me looking down rather than ahead, certain that a ground rattler or some other creature of the grass was ready to defend its home. Later on, I knew I would have preferred that.

We got to the mattress. I wondered how many others had been on it, whose stains covered the striped fabric, and did they too just roll over and wash up later.

James looked around to see if anyone else was in view, as though what he was about to show us was going to be mind shattering. When he saw that the site was secure, his hand found its way to his zipper and he slid it down. With the thumb of the other hand, he pushed down his underwear and kept the zipper's metal teeth pried open. He took his other hand off the zipper and pulled out his dick. There it was, without a thought, privacy relinquished. He began to wiggle it up and down, and in no time, it began to inflate like an inner tube in a bicycle tire until it looked as though it would pop.

"Watch this," said James, as he sat Clark on the mattress. He stepped up onto the mattress, a hand on Clark's shoulder so he could maintain his balance on the worn springs. Clark just sat there, watching us all. James put his dick near Clark's face, and as though they had done it hundreds of times before, Clark took James into his mouth, just like a child sucking on his thumb.

None of us made a sound. I had unknowingly stopped breathing. Clark's eyes just wandered from corner to corner, not at all out of embarrassment or to see if anyone was approaching. They just wandered because that's what they always did. When he looked at me with those old eyes, I wanted to see a tear fall, but none was to be seen. I wanted to do something to stop James, but I couldn't move, couldn't speak. The air was thick and lost, as if a belt squeezed to the last hole was around my neck, making my heart pound frantically. James put his hands on the sides of Clark's head and began moving back and forth. I was not to escape to the comfort of a rocking chair.

"James!" It was Miss Irene. All heads turned at lightning speed. We expected her to be standing over us, but she was calling from the front of the house. James looked up and tried to pull himself away from Clark, but Clark wouldn't let go so easily. James punched him on the side of the face and finally, like a baby burping, Clark released his suction. He looked up at James. The punch was more devastating to him than the deed I had just witnessed; yes, at last, the tears came.

"James!" screamed Miss Irene again.

"I'm comin'."

"Hurry up, then. Ya momma's on the phone."

James zipped his pants and began running back through the field, with the Baker boys closely in tow. Clark tried to find some spring from the mattress to get up, but he was so big that leverage weighed against him.

There we were, together. I walked over to him, trying to help him up, and he reached for my zipper. "No! Clark—no! Don't do that!" My scream shook every strand of overgrown vegetation in the field, and Clark again began to cry. I sat down on the mattress, forgetting its filth. I stroked his back, telling him it was all right, the way Mama B or Aunt Jess had done to me every time I cried. He began to rock back and forth as I always did, and after a while, he stopped crying. I stood, and it took all my strength to help him from the mattress. We began to walk through that field. He grabbed my hand and I let him hold it, and I didn't care about snakes or anything else. We just kept walking.

True to form, I never considered speaking of what I had seen. Though they were all too old to play cowboys and Indians, they still used the word tattletale as if it was Mr. Webster's finest. I didn't want to be likened to Precious. I didn't know what the word punk meant, but I knew that if it meant that I wasn't like James, then I didn't at all mind being called that word.

The next day, Miss Irene sent her grandchildren on their way. Because my life had been filled with things not said and frequent good-byes, I had become accustomed to it. But never had I been so happy to see someone leave as I was when James left for Detroit, where they played cops and robbers, not cowboys and Indians.

A few weeks later, I came in from school and Mama B was in the kitchen, but she wasn't making cornbread for me. She was frying fish. I always considered fish to be our Friday meal, but it wasn't Friday.

"We're having fish today?" I asked, brushing against her side. But she remained distant. No hug hello or questions about my day.

"No, Patience, this ain't for us. I'm makin' it for Miss Irene."

"Is she sick?"

"No, she got a bit of bad news today. I'm just takin' somethin' over to ease the burden."

I knew Mama B wasn't telling me the whole story. She always tried to protect, as was her nature. The truth always came from Aunt Jess. I knew the only two reasons someone took someone else food was when they were ill or someone had died. Since Miss Irene wasn't sick…

I ventured out of the house in search of answers, not at all caring that I would miss Flipper's adventures that day. I went to the rental house to talk to Miss Claire; if death was involved, I knew she would be privy to the information.

As it unfolded, James had been associated with a gang back in Detroit. "He was killed dead, just like his no-'count daddy," said Miss Claire. "I don't know how his mamma kept him outta trouble this long. Now, she could send them down here to Irene, Lawd bless her soul, for the summers, tryin' to get him away from that foolishness, but who was watchin' him the other nine months? I truly feel for Irene."

It was different for me to think that someone thirteen years old, the age of manhood in certain cultures, two years older than me, could be shot. I supposed Detroit was different and we were backward down here. But if this was backward, it was what I wanted.

I can't say I was disappointed by the news about James, for though I couldn't envision him on the ground with bullets in his body and bloodstained clothes, I could remember Clark's eyes.

When Mama B returned from delivering the food, she was out of sorts. She sat in her rocker as if even its frame couldn't support her, an oak turned into a willow.

"Are you alright, Mama B?"

"Yes, Patience."

I could tell by her posture that she didn't want to speak any more about it, so I let it and her rest. I went and sat on the back steps and I looked out into the day. Later that evening, I found Mama B in better spirits.

"Mama B?"

"Yes."

"What's a punk?"

She stopped her brush midway through the length of her hair. She brought it down to her lap and pulled off the excess from its teeth. She balled the hair between her fingers then placed it in the ash-tray and struck a big wooden match, setting the oiled hair ablaze. A sizzle and the smell of burn filled the air for an instant. When the hair had shriveled before me to nothing, she blew out the match. Holding it up she said, "This is a punk, Patience. It's a piece of wood—just a piece of wood."

MARCI BLACKMAN

■ ■ ■

[1969–]

NOVELIST MARCI BLACKMAN, AN OHIO NATIVE, BEGAN HER literary career by reading the novels of Toni Morrison and writing poetry, to which she attributes the lyrical quality of her work. However, it was during an epiphanic moment while bicycling near Florence, Italy, that she committed herself to writing a novel. The work in progress was shaped through readings given with Sister Spit's Ramblin' Road Show, a lesbian performance group Blackman helped found, and was later published by Manic D Press as *Po Man's Child* (1999). She is also coeditor of *Beyond Definition: New Writing from Gay and Lesbian San Francisco* (1996), and her fiction has appeared in the anthologies *Signs of Life, Fetish,* and *Brown Sugar.*

Winner of both the American Library Association's 2000 Gay, Lesbian, Bisexual, Transgendered Book Award and the Firecracker Alternative Book Award for Best New Fiction, *Po Man's Child* was inspired by a news story about teenaged sex workers in Brazil who cut themselves to feel. In this opening chapter, an S/M sex scene between Po and her girlfriend, Mary, slips out of hand, seriously injuring Po. She places herself in a psychiatric hospital for observation, and the novel unfolds in flashbacks to the young woman's past as she recuperates during a seventy-two-hour rest.

Aunt Florida is angry and it's not a good sign. Yesterday the picture of her that adorns my mantel—the one with the cigar in her mouth, and the nickel-sized tar black eyes that glare at you no matter where you stand in the room—tipped over three times. Today all the books on my bookshelf conspired to fall at the exact same moment. And now three mocking liquid shadows dance violently upon my wall even though the candles that cast them burn calm.

"When the Po ladies start turnin their faces down on ya," my mother always warned, "you know they are not happy." It is four A.M. Mary lies flat on her back, knees bent, hands clasped behind her head, breasts off to each side. I'm propped up beside her, leaning on one elbow, my finger circling the labia stencil tattooed across her navel.

"Tell me a story," she whispers in a sultry voice, stopping the motion of my hand with her own.

"Not tonight," I answer, refusing to bite. "Not in the mood."

"Oh," she says coyly, still holding my hand, "but it's not a request." She pinches the skin on the soft side of my forearm, then uses it for leverage as she sits up. It doesn't hurt when she pinches me. It never does in the beginning. We've been through this before. "Tell me the one about your family," she demands.

I let my head fall and rest on her shoulder. "You're not tired of that one yet?" I ask, yawning so she knows that I am. "How many versions have you heard now? Three? Four?"

"So," she answers, still pinching my skin, "tell it to me again." Then letting her mouth slide into the crooked grin reserved for these occasions, junctions in time when she knows she'll have her way, she pinches even harder.

My forearm is starting to burn and it's kind of annoying. I don't want to do this tonight. Something about Aunt Florida's picture lying face down doesn't feel right. "I said I'm not in the mood," I answer again, sternly. "Besides, I'm all out of fresh ideas."

At this last comment, she sits up, tosses her head back and laughs. Her stringy black hair wafts in the breeze stirred up by Aunt Florida. Flanked by the in-your-face arrogance of dancing shadows from the candles, she narrows her pale green eyes and says, "Then try telling the truth this time."

"The what?"

"The truth," she laughs again. "How's that for a fresh idea? Novel concept, isn't it?" The laugh halts abruptly. "When's the last time you told me the truth, Po?"

I sit up on my knees to face her. "Oh, I get it. This is supposed to be some kind of dare."

"No, Po, no dare," she says, coldly. "Just a simple question. Can you remember?"

"You're serious, aren't you?"

She just stares at me.

"You don't think I can do it?" I ask, acting insulted.

Still she says nothing.

"Okay," I smile, responding to the challenge. "The truth? You got it. Starting from where?"

"From the day your parents first met."

On Mary's order, I scoot to the edge of the bed, lay my forearm face up on the nightstand and start talking. "My parents—Gregory Taylor and Lillian Louise Childs—met and fell in love in 1958. Lillian's last name was Smith then, and at the time she met my father, she had no intention of changing it..."

It's an act, a game we play. Mary picks a spot on my body, any spot; tests how hard she can pinch or bite it, how deep she can cut it, or how long she can burn it. While I recount—without flinching—a story that's never happened.

It must be the fifth or sixth time we've played this game. Mary got the idea from a book one of her fag friends loaned her called *Intellectual S/M*. At first the idea was just intriguing. Kind of like one of those endurance tests the Fitness Council makes you take in junior high school. I was curious to see how long my imagination would hold out. How long I could keep the story going. It wasn't something I expected to like. But being forced to focus so intently on something outside the realm of current pain seems to make the endorphins kick in sooner. Before I know it, for a while anyway, the numbness is nowhere to be found.

This time, whether she calls it that or not, there's a dare involved. She wants the truth, a truth she knows I've never been able to share. And

I'm not sure I can now. For as soon as I flinch or falter in the text, the game is over and Mary wins. Otherwise, it continues until Mary believes I've had enough. But I rarely flinch or falter. The real reason Mary stops is because she's had enough. She only tops me because she knows I want her to. She'd much rather have it the other way around. She's never truly understood the numbness that stalks me. Truth is, the levels of pain I endure frighten her. And the thought that I might enjoy the pain is something she doesn't want to think about.

Before the game starts, we agree on a safe word. A word, a non sequitur—usually a color—that I can yell if things get out of hand. Tonight the word is "red," the color of blood, and the spot she has chosen is my arm. It's not coincidence. The small portion of truth I have already revealed is that when I was fifteen going on sixteen, I developed this thing about my arms and cars. A fear that someday someone would forget I was there, halfway in or out, and close one of my arms in the door, roll it up in the window. And though I still can't remember what triggered this fear, the lost moment in time when the bullet ran screeching from the chamber, the overwhelming desire to protect my arms surfaced sometime after the night my parents and I became snow angels.

Everything was spinning. I remember feeling like a flush-faced porcelain doll at holiday time—all hot and bothered and numb—soldered to the plastic floor of one of those miniature snowglobe nativity scenes just after someone has shaken it. Even though I wanted to, I couldn't move. Instead I stood terrified that all the jostling around would cause the bottoms of my feet to rip and tear.

I heard my mother's voice first—wild, out of control. "Goddamn it, Gregory! God-fucking-damn it! I'm not gonna let you do this! I am not going to let you do this!"

His voice soothed, "Lillian, Lil…Lil, baby…"

But my father was calm. Even in the midst of my mother's rabid cries, "What about the kids?" she sobbed, tired and out of breath. "How can you do this to them? How can you do this to me?"

I run from the house, no coat. No one notices the bottoms of my bare feet burned numb in the cold. There in the front yard they're making angels in the snow, my mother on his back, begging.

They are making angels, yelling and screaming and rolling around in the snow. On hot white coals I run from the house, lay my back flat as a board on a flawless patch of snow. Icicle tongues of water drip frigid saliva down the back of my neck, my head crushes its remembrance. Snow white snow. I glue my arms to my ribs, my legs pinch my clit in between, and slowly I breathe. Slowly I begin to move. Ever so slowly I push my legs and my arms out and up until the frozen tips of my fingers touch but do not feel. Then down, arms and legs spread wide; I can touch the sky, I can reach the moon.

"Look! I'm an angel! I'm an angel, Daddy! I can fly."

Ignoring me, my father stands, throws my mother off his back like a fond memory grown indifferent. I remember the hinges on the door of the Falcon squeaking as he pulled it open.

The rules are simple. Once the spot is chosen, it is set; she can never again veer from it. She can, however, add additional means of torture if my tale reeks of bullshit's pungent smell, lacking clarity and attention to detail.

"They were at a party," I go on, still smiling.

"What kind of party?" Mary interrupts, as she walks to the bureau. "Details!" she sings. "Were they with friends or did they go alone? Was it winter and snowing, or did it take place outside, warmed by the hot and muggy stale breath of summer?" She reaches for the cane and cackles loud and hearty, then dramatically raises the thin bamboo stick high in the air before swatting it down on my arm.

"It was a college party," I answer. Matching Mary's playful mood, I pretend to wince from the sting. "A Div party, short for Division. Every year during the six-week winter break between semesters the seniors would throw a big party for themselves. And no, it wasn't snowing. It was cold as a mofo, as my father's friend MacArthur was fond of saying, but not cold enough for snow.

"My mother wasn't supposed to be there. She was a sophomore, just twenty years old. And because it was rumored that other things besides liquor would be on hand, lower-classmen weren't allowed to attend. But my mother's girlfriend, Mavis, insisted on sneaking her in. 'You got to go to the Div party, girl' Mavis told her. 'Everybody who's anybody makes an appearance at the Div party.'"

While I talk, I watch as Mary rummages in the bureau, the bureau that used to belong to Grandma Margret, my grandmother on my father's side. Before her, it had been Great-grandma Cora's. And before Cora, it had been given to my great-great-grandmother Ida. A gift from Bo Jones, the man who owned half the state. And just to prove the power such wealth afforded, in view of his wife and his children, Mr. Bo took to strolling around town, parading my great-great-grandmother on his arm, daring anyone to say word one about it. Now the bureau had been given to me with instructions to give it to my daughter. If, as with Grandma Margret, I happen to be blessed with only boys, I'm to pass it on to one of my granddaughters.

The brown leather satchel Mary takes from the top drawer is worn, frayed at the bottom, its drawstrings calling for the comfort of retirement. I speak slowly, make certain my words are measured and audible, focusing all my energy on enunciation. But my eyes never leave her hands, whose fingers—long, white, slender, and sheathed in a pair of rubber latex gloves—are beginning to turn me on.

"My father played vibes and sang in the band," I go on, staring at the gloved hands. "Jazz. The Gregory Childs Quartet. They were the hot new sensation on campus. And after graduating, all but my father—for reasons that will become clear later—would make the pilgrimage to New York to become the pioneers of a new young scene.

"The campus was small, the number of black students on it even smaller. So it wasn't surprising that Lillian and Greg socialized in the same circles even though my father was three years older and a senior. In fact, whether it was passing each other on their way in or out of BSA headquarters or being embroiled in the same five-person debate about a new breed of poets who called themselves Beatniks, Greg and Lillian ran into each other often. But neither ever stopped to take notice until the night my mother's girlfriend snuck her into the Div party.

"At least that's how my father put it. My mother claimed that my father was making passes at her from the beginning, but she didn't trust him. He was shady, she said. And every time she saw him, every time he winked or smiled at her, he was arm in arm with a different girl.

"Shady vibe or no, there was no escaping the attraction, and on the night of the Div party, the night my father made the senior class swoon from his rendition of *This Little Girl o' Mine,* something magical happened. In just a little over a year, while my mother was dropping out of school pregnant with my sister Onya, my father was running around town, handing out cigars, proclaiming that from now on, Gregory Taylor Childs was a certified one-woman man."

From the satchel Mary removes a brand new disposable scalpel, a bottle of iodine, and a package of extra-long cotton swabs, then splays them out across the nightstand. After dipping one of the cotton swabs into the iodine, she begins to paint burnt orange stripes back and forth across the smoothness of my arm. Taking a deep breath I try to relax but as soon as she unwraps the scalpel from its sterilized disposable package every muscle tightens in anticipation. Its blade is rounded, half-moon shaped. As the white gloves close around its plastic green shaft, it sparkles.

She says she wants the truth this time. But not the whole truth, I'll bet. Only the part that makes a good story. She can't comprehend the real truth. My truth. Even I don't fully understand what's running through my head as I speak. Thoughts like, what does it feel like when the wounds are carved with a dulled and rusted edge? When the hands are not gloved but cold and callused and calculating, caked with the dirt of two solid months in the field? To have them cleaned with salt after? She doesn't want to hear about the curse, about Uncle George. We've been over it before. She can't tag along on this quest I'm on, she says. If she does then she'll be there with me. It's a trip she's just not ready to take. So I go on. On with the story, feeding her the mouthful of truth she's ready to swallow, the morsel with which I'm willing to part.

"They were married at once, in secret. My mother wanted to wait just a little while so she could tell her people in Cleveland: my great-grandma Shirley and my aunt Florida. Grandma Janie, my mother's mother, died in a fire when my mother was a little girl; her father was never in the picture. Shirley and Florida would want her to be married proper, she said. In a church, at least, if she couldn't wear the white dress. But my father insisted, saying that he didn't want to take a chance on his first child being born outside his name. So they said their vows before a justice of the peace and told no one, except my father's younger brother Ray who was needed as a witness, until Onya started showing.

"Although they weren't exactly thrilled about the veil of secrecy (believing that any man who forces his wife to keep her marriage hidden from her family has to be suspect), Aunt Florida and Great-grandma Shirley welcomed my father into the family with open arms. Grandma Margret, on the other hand, was ecstatic. Her prayers had finally been answered. Destiny had smiled on her and she was going to be a grand-mother. And though there was some question about which came first (the marriage or the baby), as the day of delivery drew near, she took out her knitting needles and fashioned two pairs of booties—one pink and one blue—for her eldest son's firstborn."

Scalpel in one hand, bracing my arm with the other, Mary's eyes catch mine to see if I'm ready. One word from me and the game stops. Did Uncle George have a safe word? What was running through his head as the whip came down? Stories? Songs of freedom? Anticipation of the end? Did the overseer ever check to see if he was ready? Holding fast to the cadence of my words, I close my eyes.

"The labor was both difficult and long. From the time my mother's water broke, twenty-three hours would pass with all kinds of false starts and interruptions before Onya poked her head from my mother's womb and let out a fierce cry—the first of many protests at having been born at all. But all through the process, between wondering if she had what it took to be a good mother and leveling threats against my father's life, my mother was making plans. Plans to return to school. She would have to wait till the baby was weaned, of course, until Onya was old enough to have a sitter, but as soon as my mother got her strength back, she was going to finish the education she started.

"Unfortunately for Mama, those plans would have to wait. On the day Grandma Margret had looked forward to, the day she was finally allowed to sit unsupervised with her granddaughter, my mother walked into the admissions building to sign up for classes and fainted. Right there in line, after standing there less than half an hour, her mouth went dry, her knees buckled, her body went limp and she fainted. When she came to, one of the admissions ladies was kneeling over her, extending a cup filled with water, asking, 'How long have you been expecting, sweetheart?' Nine months later, my mother gave birth to my brother Bobby."

The first cut sinks deep, creating a hollow that burns. It is long, much longer than anticipated, from the crease in my elbow stopping just short of my wrist. My chest caves and heaves from the pain, like chattel when informed of the existence of free air.

"Where's your blood, baby?" Mary whispers to herself, this time not wanting to interrupt. And though the pearl white dermis is pretty, seemingly innocent lying next to the darker outer layer of brown, Mary is right; initially there is no blood. Eventually, though, little red dots do matriculate into the hollow's walls, and the latex fingers waste no time spreading the incision wide to release the flow.

All this effort, all this busyness, trying to draw a line, a foothold in the sand, to hold back an enemy I've never been able to see. Aunt Florida called it a curse. The curse of Uncle George. Is it futile, Uncle George? That the conclusion you came to?

Deeper even than the first, the second cut immediately makes the river flow, trickling in forks down the sides of my wrist onto the top of the table.

"Mmmm," Mary sings, green eyes glowing in the first morning light, "there it is." My body starts to tingle. A light swell rises in my head.

But did you get off on it, Uncle George? Did you feel your knees weaken? Your nipples harden? Your body go to shakin? No longer from the beautiful face of pain alone, but from the sheer pleasure of its cheek rubbing against your bones? Did you? Ever? Get off?

"Once again, my mother started making plans. This time, she thought, after Bobby was weaned. This time it would happen. But once again, she was foiled. Just fifteen months after Bobby took his first glimpse of the world, while the nation was still recovering from the death of President Kennedy, my mother discovered another heartbeat thumping away in her womb. A beat that, if allowed to mature, would drum out any remaining hope of returning to school. So she panicked and spoke to my father about the possibility of aborting. Completing her education was her ticket to independence. Without it, she was a cripple who would have to rely on my father for the rest of her life. And what if he died suddenly? Who would take care of her then? But my father was emphatic. Wasn't no way in the world any seed of his was gonna remain unborn.

"Grandma Margret scolded her. Told her she ought to be thankful. And when my mother confided it was too big a burden to bear, that it seemed like she'd been pregnant since the day they were married, Grandma Margret called her an ingrate. 'You lucky the Lord blessed you with children at all' she said. 'Coulda turned out barren, like Mrs. Felder over in Hamilton. Better learn to look on your burdens as blessins, child. You know it's not everybody the Lord chooses to burden.'"

The third cut is sexy. Water flushes my eyes as the tenuous blade glides without interruption, parting my skin. My head is full. I'm certain it will detach itself and fly away. All my juices—begging to come down—splash violently, ready to boil over.

"Turned out I was a bigger burden than anyone expected." The truth drives on. "After they brought me home from the hospital, the two-bedroom house my parents were renting became cramped. It never was meant to hold more than four, and even that was pushing it. So even though they couldn't afford it, they were forced to find something bigger.

"That's when things started to fall apart. My father wanted to buy. Why should they keep paying all that money to the man, he said, and never have anything to show for it? But they didn't have any money saved, my mother argued. And it would be awhile, at best, before she could look for work. What bank in its right mind would give a loan to a family of five with one measly income and no down payment? Even if it did, the new mortgage would be double the rent they paid now. Rent they barely managed to meet as it was. But again my father insisted. He would give up music if he had to. Get a second job. He refused to argue about it any further. If he had to work three jobs, he said, Gregory Taylor Childs' children were going to grow up on their own land. Six months after I was born, we loaded down a U-Haul with all of our belongings and moved across town into my father's dream house."

I do not see the hunting knife when Mary unsheathes it from its distressed leather casing. Not until it is raised high, poised to rain down, do I catch its gleam refracted in the nervous light of the candles. And not until I see its point spiraling downward do I first consider calling out the safe word. But I'm not quite ready to give in, and as usual, I go on.

"The moment we moved into the house, it seemed my parents started arguing and never stopped. And before long, while my mother stayed home to care for the kids, my father took to gambling and drinking and staying out late. Not only did rumors in town have it that he was no longer a one-woman man, but it was whispered that when he was drunk, Gregory Taylor Childs would fuck anything that moved. Even his brother's wife, that is, if his brother had a wife to be fucked."

The blade stops an inch above my forearm and hovers. I do not move. Slowly it ascends again. This is it. The place in the game I sometimes falter, either by stumbling over the text or by calling out the word. Only it's not a game this time. It's the truth. And as Aunt Florida used to say, the truth has a way of forcing its way out even when you try your damnedest to stop it.

"Eventually, Uncle Ray—my father's brother—did get married, to a white woman named Jessica. And shortly thereafter, as if to fulfill the prophesy of the rumor mill, she and my father started fooling around.

The mill couldn't spit out the news fast enough. He's fucking his brother's wife, it said, he's fucking his brother's wife. And the poor brother and his own wife don't even know. What's that they say? The spouse is always the last to know? But Uncle Ray did know. Deep down, my mother did also. They just pretended not to notice."

This time I watch as the jagged blade rises. Again, it comes barreling down, stopping inches from my arm.

"But they couldn't play make-believe forever. And it wasn't long before the truth started to show itself in ways nobody could understand. Out of nowhere, it seemed, Uncle Ray took up trying to kill himself. And my mother just gave up. Like she figured if she couldn't beat the truth, she might as well let it have its way."

The third time, the mesmerizing blade seems to hang, balance awhile at its peak before it starts down. And once in motion it's as though something or someone is trying to resist it. As though if I squinted long enough I could see its tip embedded in the palm of Aunt Florida's blistered, wrinkled, and tired old hand pushing upward to slow its decline.

"Sooner or later, one them was bound to break. Turned out it was Uncle Ray. And when he did, all hell broke loose. When he finally decided to tell my father he knew, he did it with a vengeance. Instead of just trying to take his own life, he tried to take his daughter's as well."

I brace myself for the inevitable. I know the knife is coming down. The truth is on a roll and there's nothing that can stop it. But on the fourth and final turn, instead of raising the knife slowly as she'd done before, Mary unexpectedly stands as though a pair of giant invisible hands has just lifted her to her feet. Then, knife in hand, resting unreliable in her palm, she starts waltzing around the room as if with a partner. But she's not enjoying it. Although her moves appear to be choreographed expertly, with every step she's trying to break free.

"The kidnapping of his daughter was the domino that started the effect. Everything happened so fast, days and events seemed to whiz by in a blur. And by the time they got tired and finished, stood still long enough for us to sort things out, Uncle Ray was in the hospital, nursing a bullet wound to his head, and my parents were bankrupt."

But just as her breasts and the extra skin around her thighs begin to fall into the rhythm of it, just as her hand slips down into that position ready to take over the imaginary partner's lead, her feet throwing in the tricky variances and nuances worthy of the most expert ballroom dancers, almost as abruptly as she started, blade raised high, Mary lunges over to the bed and drives it down…

It wasn't as bad as I thought it would be. That's what I was thinking when I finally heard the phone. I expected it to hurt more, like one of those pains that makes you pray for a quick death. At first, after the blade plunged into my arm, I couldn't think or hear much of anything. Just those words resonating in my head: it wasn't as bad as I thought it would be. The words and a constant ringing. I've since remembered pulling the blade from my arm and getting up from the bed to answer the phone, thinking it had to be stopped. The ringing. It had to be answered.

I remember taking note of the candles as I passed by the mantle. Someone or something had blown them out. Every last one blown right out. Aunt Florida's picture was face down.

I still don't remember how the t-shirt got wrapped around my arm, only that it was still there, sagging and dripping with blood, as we waited in the emergency room. I also don't remember picking up the phone, the actual lifting of the receiver. Just that at some point it was in my hand and the ringing had finally stopped.

"Po, it's Bobby," my brother kept saying on the other end. "Po, it's Bobby," like he didn't think I could hear him or something.

"Oh, hey Bobby, what's up? Uh…listen…it's kind of a bad time, you know? Can I call you back?"

"Po, I'm at the hospital."

"The…? Yeah? What a coincidence. It's kind of a bad time, though…"

"Po!"

"Yeah?"

"I'm at the hospital. Dad had a heart attack. He died on arrival… Po? Did you hear me? I said, Dad had a heart attack. He's dead."

"Yeah, I… Shit! It's just that it's a really bad time right now, Bobby."

"Po!?"

"I heard you, Bobby. But listen, I can't do this right now. I'll call you later, okay? But right now, I gotta go."

NOTES

The Harlem Renaissance 1900–1950

1. David Levering Lewis, *W. E. B. DuBois: Biography of a Race, 1868–1919* (Holt, 1993) xvi.

2. Nathan Huggins, ed., *W. E. B. DuBois: Writings* (Library of America, 1984) 842.

3. David Levering Lewis, ed., *The Portable Harlem Renaissance Reader* (Penguin, 1994) 92, 95.

4. Jonathan Birnbaum and Clarence Taylor, eds., *Civil Rights Since 1787: A Reader on the Black Struggle* (New York UP, 2000) 178.

5. Birnbaum and Taylor 223–24.

6. Kwame Anthony Appiah and Henry Louis Gates, Jr., eds., *Africana: The Encyclopedia of the African and African American Experience* (Basic/Civitas, 1999) 1391.

7. Birnbaum and Taylor 260.

8. Carolyn Wedin, *Inheritors of the Spirit: Mary White Ovington and the Founding of the NAACP* (Wiley, 1998) 107.

9. Wedin 181.

10. Wedin 183.

11. Appiah and Gates 1427.

12. Appiah and Gates 1170.

13. W. E. B. DuBois, *The Autobiography of W. E. B. DuBois* (International, 1968) 282.

14. David Levering Lewis, *W. E. B. DuBois: The Fight for Equality and the American Century, 1919–1963* (Holt, 2000) 379.

15. Lewis, *W. E. B. DuBois* 205.

16. DuBois 282.

17. Steven Watson, *The Harlem Renaissance: Hub of African American Culture, 1920–1930* (Pantheon, 1995) 90.

18. Joseph Beam, *In the Life: A Black Gay Anthology* (Alyson, 1986) 214.

19. Watson 88.

20. John Loughery, *The Other Side of Silence: Men's Lives and Gay Identities: A Twentieth Century History* (Holt, 1998) 50.

21. Beam 214.

22. Steve Hogan and Lee Hudson, *Completely Queer: The Gay and Lesbian Encyclopedia* (Holt, 1998) 164.

23. Gerald Early, ed., *My Soul's High Song: The Collected Writings of Countee Cullen, Voice of the Harlem Renaissance* (Anchor, 1991) 97, 109.

24. Early 169.

25. Watson 78.

26. Alain Locke, ed., *The New Negro: Voices of the Harlem Renaissance* (Boni, 1925) xxv.

27. Watson 25.

28. Watson 58.

29. Watson 24.

30. Arnold Rampersad, ed., *The Collected Poems of Langston Hughes* (Vintage, 1994) 23.

31. Rampersad 122.

32. Rampersad 406, 396.

33. Edward Lueders, *Carl Van Vechten* (Twayne, 1965) 104.

34. Emily Bernard, ed., *Remember Me to Harlem: The Letters of Langston Hughes and Carl Van Vechten, 1925–1964* (Knopf, 2001) 6.

35. Bernard xxi.

36. Bernard xxii.

37. Zora Neale Hurston, *Their Eyes Were Watching God* (Harper, 1937) 25.

38. Barbara Smith, *The Truth That Never Hurts: Writings on Race, Gender, and Freedom* (Rutgers UP, 1998) 33.

39. Smith, *The Truth That Never Hurts* 33.

40. Barbara Smith, *Home Girls: A Black Feminist Anthology* (Kitchen Table, 1983) 73, 77.

41. Smith, *Home Girls* 75.

42. Smith, *Home Girls* 73.

43. Akasha (Gloria) Hull, ed., *Give Us Each Day: The Diary of Alice Dunbar-Nelson* (Norton, 1984) 16.

44. Hull 250.

45. Hull 432.

46. Hull 23.

47. Lillian Faderman, *Odd Girls and Twilight Lovers: A History of Lesbian Life in Twentieth Century America* (Columbia UP, 1991) 322.

48. David Levering Lewis, *When Harlem Was in Vogue* (Knopf, 1981) 166.

49. Lewis, *When Harlem Was in Vogue* 227.

50. Watson 144.

51. Faderman 76.

52. Faderman 76.

53. Gladys Bentley, "I Am a Woman Again," *Ebony* 7 (Aug. 1952) 93–94.

54. Bentley 94.

55. Bentley 98.

56. George Chauncey, *Gay New York: Gender, Urban Culture, and the Making of the Gay Male World 1890–1940* (Basic, 1994) 331.

57. Philip S. Foner, ed., *Paul Robeson Speaks* (Citadel, 1978) 132–33.

58. Mark Naison, *Communists in Harlem During the Depression* (Grove, 1983) 210–11.

59. Martin Duberman, *Paul Robeson: A Biography* (New Press, 1989) 394.

60. Eric Brandt, ed., *Dangerous Liaisons: Blacks, Gays, and the Struggle for Equality* (New Press, 1999) 183.

61. Neil Miller, *Out of the Past: Gay and Lesbian History from 1869 to the Present* (Vintage, 1995) 235.

62. Faderman 120.

63. Darlene Clark Hine and Kathleen Thompson, *A Shining Thread of Hope: The History of Black Women in America* (Broadway, 1998) 264.

64. Faderman 119.

65. Jonathan Katz, *Gay American History: Lesbians and Gay Men in the U.S.A.* (Crowell, 1976) 140.

66. Neil Miller, *Out of the Past: Gay and Lesbian History from 1869 to the Present* (Vintage, 1995) 259.

67. Miller 259.

68. Miller 260.

69. Katz 614.

70. Katz 615.

71. Katz 585–86.

72. Katz 591.

73. Mark Blasius and Shane Phelan, eds., *We Are Everywhere: A Historical Sourcebook of Gay and Lesbian Politics* (Routledge, 1997) 235.

The Protest Era 1950–1980

1. James Baldwin, speaking in the film *The Price of the Ticket, 1989.*

2. Jonathan Birnbaum and Clarence Taylor, eds., *Civil Rights Since 1787: A Reader on the Black Struggle* (New York UP, 2000) 351–52.

3. Richard Delgado and Jean Stefancic, eds., *Critical Race Theory: The Cutting Edge* (New York UP, 2000) 110.

4. Bayard Rustin, "Montgomery, Alabama," in *The War Resister,* 1957.

5. David J. Garrow, *Bearing the Cross: Martin Luther King, Jr. and the Southern Christian Leadership Conference* (Morrow, 1986) 16.

6. Garrow 16.

7. Joan Grant, *Ella Baker: Freedom Bound* (Wiley, 1998) 123.

8. Beverly Guy-Sheftall, ed., *Words of Fire: An Anthology of African American Feminist Thought* (New Press, 1995) 14.

9. Hazel V. Carby, *Race Men* (Harvard UP, 1998).

10. Grant 230.

11. *Jet* magazine, March 1949.

12. Rustin, "Montgomery, Alabama."

13. Jervis Anderson, *Bayard Rustin: Troubles I've Seen* (Harper, 1997) 231.

14. Bayard Rustin interview in *Washington Blade*, 13 Jan. 1984.

15. Anderson 231.

16. John A. Salmond, *My Mind Set on Freedom: A History of the Civil Rights Movement, 1954–1968* (Dee, 1997) 101.

17. Mary King, *Freedom Song: A Personal Story of the 1960s Civil Rights Movement* (Morrow, 1987) 568–69.

18. Clayborne Carson, *In Struggle: SNCC and the Black Awakening of the 1960s* (Harvard UP, 1981) 148.

19. Paula Giddings, *When and Where I Enter: The Impact of Black Women on Race and Sex in America* (Morrow, 1984) 302.

20. David Hilliard interview for *Black Like Us*, Oakland, Calif., 10 June 2001.

21. Eldridge Cleaver, *Soul on Ice* (McGraw-Hill, 1968) 14, 100.

22. Huey P. Newton, "The Women's and Gay Liberation Movement," in *To Die for the People: Selected Writings and Speeches* (Random, 1972) 152.

23. Susan Brownmiller, *In Our Time: Memoir of a Revolution* (Dial, 1999) 7.

24. Karla Jay, *Tales of the Lavender Menace: A Memoir of Liberation* (Basic, 1999) 145.

25. Neil Miller, *Out of the Past: Gay and Lesbian History, from 1869 to the Present* (Vintage, 1995) 375–76.

26. Jay 131.

27. Miriam Schneir, ed., *Feminism in Our Time: The Essential Writings, World War II to the Present* (Vintage, 1994) 163.

28. Schneir 161.

29. Kate Millett, *Sexual Politics* (Doubleday, 1970) 32.

30. Adrienne Rich, *Blood, Bread, and Poetry: Selected Prose 1979–1985* (Norton, 1986) 49.

31. Rich 51.

32. Toni Morrison, "What the Black Woman Thinks," in Barbara A. Crow, ed., *Radical Feminism: A Documentary Reader* (New York UP, 2000) 454.

33. Schneir 173–74.

34. Barbara Smith, *The Truth That Never Hurts: Writings on Race, Gender, and Freedom* (Rutgers UP, 1998) 272.

35. Smith 275.

36. Toni Cade Bambara, ed., *The Black Woman: An Anthology* (Signet, 1970) 7.

37. Bambara 37.

38. bell hooks, *Feminist Theory from Margin to Center* (South End, 1984) 2.

39. Smith 5.

40. Smith 20.

41. Mark Blasius and Shane Phelan, eds., *We Are Everywhere: A Historical Sourcebook of Gay and Lesbian Politics* (Routledge, 1997) 283.

42. Miller 339.

43. Ernestine Eckstein with Barbara Gittings and Kay Tobin, "An Interview with Ernestine," *The Ladder,* June 1966, 5–6.

44. Eckstein 11.

45. Audre Lorde, *Zami: A New Spelling of My Name* (Crossing, 1982) 180.

46. Lorde, *Zami* 181.

47. Dudley Clendinen and Adam Nagourney, eds., *Out for Good: The Struggle to Build a Gay Rights Movement in America* (Simon, 1999) 32.

48. David Deitcher, ed., *The Question of Equality: Lesbian and Gay Politics in America Since Stonewall* (Scribner, 1995) 78.

49. Miller 388.

50. Barbara A. Crow, ed., *Radical Feminism: A Documentary Reader* (New York UP, 2000) 327.

51. Steve Hogan and Lee Hudson, *Completely Queer: The Gay and Lesbian Encyclopedia* (Holt, 1998) 18.

52. Mark Thompson, ed., *The Long Road to Freedom: The Advocate History of the Gay and Lesbian Movement* (St. Martin's Press, 1994) 196.

53. Miller 402.

54. Deitcher 52.

55. Lillian Faderman, *Odd Girls and Twilight Lovers: A History of Life in Twentieth-Century America* (Columbia UP, 1991) 147.

56. Sharon Malinowski, ed., *Gay and Lesbian Literature* (St. James, 1994) 1: xvii.

57. Barbara Smith, ed., *Home Girls: A Black Feminist Anthology* (Kitchen Table, 1983) 83.

58. Smith, *Home Girls* 86.

59. Jonathan Katz, *Gay American History: Lesbians and Gay Men in the U.S.A.* (Crowell, 1976) 639–40.

60. Guy-Sheftall 139.

61. Guy-Sheftall 128.

62. Audre Lorde, *The Black Unicorn: Poems* (Norton, 1978) 82.

63. Lorde, *The Black Unicorn* 28.

64. Mari Evans, ed., *Black Women Writers (1950–1980): A Critical Evaluation* (Doubleday, 1984) 264.

65. Anita Cornwell, *Black Lesbian in White America* (Naiad, 1983) 1.

66. Cornwell 19.

67. Cornwell 18.

68. Pat Parker, *Movement in Black* (Crossing Press, 1983) 11.

69. Parker 99, 77.

70. Parker 17.

71. John D'Emilio, *Sexual Politics, Sexual Communities: The Making of a Homosexual Minority in the United States 1940–1970* (U of Chicago P, 1983) 35.

72. Blasius 280.

73. Blasius 235.

74. Hogan and Hudson 65.

75. James V. Hatch, *Sorrow Is the Only Faithful One: A Life of Owen Dodson* (U of Illinois P, 1993) 179.

76. D'Emilio 181.

77. Samuel R. Delany, *Silent Interviews: On Language, Race, Sex, Science Fiction, and Some Comics* (Wesleyan UP, 1994) 73.

78. Hogan and Hudson 471.

79. Claude J. Summers, ed., *The Gay and Lesbian Literary Heritage: A Reader's Companion to the Writers and Their Works, from Antiquity to the Present* (Holt, 1995) 44.

80. Joseph Beam, ed., *In the Life: A Black Gay Anthology* (Alyson, 1986) 13.

Coming Out Black, Like Us 1980–2000

1. Audre Lorde, "Learning from the 60s," in *Sister Outsider: Essays and Speeches* (Crossing, 1984) 135.

2. Larry Kramer, "1,112 and Counting," in *Reports from the Holocaust: The Making of an AIDS Activist* (St. Martin's, 1989) 33.

3. Cathy Cohen, *The Boundaries of Blackness: AIDS and the Breakdown of Black Politics* (U of Chicago P, 1999) 260.

4. Nathan Hare and Julia Hare, *The Endangered Black Family: Coping with Unisexualization and the Coming Extinction of the Black Race* (Black Think Tank, 1984) 65.

5. Essex Hemphill, "If Freud Had Been a Neurotic Colored Woman: Reading Dr. Frances Cress Wesling," in *Ceremonies: Poetry and Prose* (Dutton, 1992) 61.

6. Devon Carbado, ed., *Black Men on Race, Gender, and Sexuality* (New York UP, 1999) 306.

7. *The Million Man March: Day of Atonement, Reconciliation and Responsibility and Day of Absence—Mission Statement 2* (1995).

8. Dennis Holmes, "An Opportunity to Empower Gay Blacks," *St. Louis Post-Dispatch*, 13 Oct. 1995, 19c.

9. Carbado, 293.

10. Carbado 294.

11. *Romer v. Evans*, 517 U.S. 620, 635 (1996).

12. Wilma Mankiller et al., eds., *The Reader's Companion to U.S. Women's History* (Houghton, 1998) 640.

13. *Frontiers* magazine, Oct. 1989.

14. June Jordan, "On Bisexuality and Cultural Pluralism," in *Affirmative Acts: Political Essays* (Doubleday, 1998) 137.

15. "Rants and Raves" in *The Advocate*, 15 Feb. 2000, 10.

16. Catherine E. McKinley and L. Joyce DeLaney, eds., *Afrekete: An Anthology of Black Lesbian Writing* (Doubleday, 1995) xv.

17. Kathleen E. Morris, *Speaking in Whispers: African American Lesbian Erotica* (Third Side, 1996) 10.

18. Lisa Duggan and Nan D. Hunter, *Sex Wars: Sexual Dissent and Political Culture* (Routledge, 1995) 4.

19. Author's website.

20. Marci Blackman, *Po Man's Child* (Manic D, 1999) 11.

21. Edmund White, "Out of the Closet, on to the Bookshelves," in David Bergman, ed., *The Burning Library: Essays* (Knopf, 1994) 277.

22. Marvin K. White, *Last Rights* (Alyson, 1999) 136.

23. Michael J. Smith, "The Double Life of a Gay Dodger," in Michael J. Smith, ed., *Black Men/White Men: A Gay Anthology* (Gay Sunshine, 1983) 130.

24. Smith 132.

25. Smith 133.

26. Melvin Dixon, *Vanishing Rooms* (Dutton, 1991) 104.

27. James Earl Hardy, *B-Boy Blues* (Alyson, 1994) 201.

28. Marlon Riggs, interview with Bettina Gray, "The Creative Mind," PBS, 1991.

29. E. Lynn Harris, *Invisible Life* (Anchor, 1994) 212.

30. E. Lynn Harris in *The Advocate,* 13 June 1997.

31. Charles Michael Smith, ed., *Fighting Words: Personal Essays by Black Gay Men* (Avon, 1999) 152.

PERMISSIONS

Owen Dodson, excerpt from *Boy at the Window.* © 1951 by Farrar, Straus & Giroux. Reprinted by permission of Farrar, Straus & Giroux, Inc. Owen Dodson photograph reprinted by permission of James V. Hatch.

Alice Dunbar-Nelson photograph reprinted by permission of Alice Dunbar Papers, University of Delaware Library, Newark, Delaware.

Larry Duplechan, excerpt from *Captain Swing.* © 1993 by Alyson Books. Reprinted by permission of the author.

Thomas Glave, *Whose Song?* © 2000 by City Lights Publishers. Reprinted by permission of City Lights Books. Thomas Glave photograph reprinted by permission of Thomas Glave. Thomas Glave photograph by Becket Logan.

Jewelle Gomez, excerpt from *The Gilda Stories.* © 1991 by Firebrand Books. Reprinted by permission of Firebrand Books. Jewelle Gomez photograph reprinted by permission of Tee Corinne.

Rosa Guy, excerpt from *Ruby.* © 1976 by Dell Publishing. Reprinted by permission of Ellen Levine Literary Agency, Inc.

James Earl Hardy, excerpt from *B-Boy Blues.* © 1994 by Alyson Books. Reprinted by permission of Alyson Publications, Inc.

E. Lynn Harris, excerpt from *Invisible Life.* © 1991 by Random House, Inc. Reprinted by permission of Doubleday, a division of Random House, Inc. E. Lynn Harris photograph reprinted by permission of E. Lynn Harris. Photograph by Matthew Jordan Smith.

Langston Hughes, "Blessed Assurance." © 1963 by Farrar, Straus & Giroux. Reprinted by permission of Farrar, Straus & Giroux, Inc. Langston Hughes photograph reprinted by permission of Harold Ober Associates Incorporated.

Brian Keith Jackson, excerpt from *Walking Through Mirrors.* © 1998 by Pocket Books. Reprinted by permission of Simon & Schuster, Inc.

Randall Kenan, *Let the Dead Bury Their Dead.* © 1992 by Little, Brown and Co. (U.K.). Reprinted by permission of Little, Brown and Co. (U.K.).

Helen Elaine Lee, excerpt from *The Serpent's Gift.* © 1994 by Atheneum. Reprinted by permission of Scribner, a division of Simon & Schuster, Inc.

Audre Lorde, excerpt from *Zami.* © 1982 by The Crossing Press, Inc. Reprinted by permission of The Crossing Press, Inc. Audre Lorde photograph reprinted by permission of Tee Corinne.

Richard Bruce Nugent, "Smoke, Lillies, and Jade" reprinted by permission of Thomas H. Wirth.

Canaan Parker, excerpt from *The Color of Trees.* © 1992 by Alyson Books. Reprinted by permission of the author.

Darieck Scott, excerpt from *Traitor to the Race.* © 1995 by Dutton. Reprinted by permission of the author.

April Sinclair, excerpt from *Coffee Will Make You Black.* © 1994 by Hyperion. Reprinted by permission of Hyperion.

Wallace Thurman photograph reprinted by permission of the Beinecke Rare Book and Manuscript Library, Yale University.

Alice Walker, "This Is How It Happened." © 2000 by Random House, Inc. Reprinted by permission of Random House, Inc.

Jacqueline Woodson, excerpt from *From the Notebooks of Melanin Sun.* © 1995 by Sheedy Literary Agency. Reprinted by permission of Sheedy Literary Agency. Jacqueline Woodson photograph reprinted by permission of Jacqueline Woodson.

Bil Wright, excerpt from *Sunday You Learn How to Box.* © 2000 by Simon & Schuster, Inc. Reprinted by permission of Scribner, a division of Simon & Schuster, Inc.

Shay Youngblood, excerpt from *Soul Kiss.* © 1997 by Shay Youngblood. Reprinted by permission of Putnam Berkley, a division of Penguin Putnam Inc.

This page constitutes an extension of the copyright page.

BIBLIOGRAPHY

The following are titles we felt would be of interest to readers of *Black Like Us*. These include books by and about African American lesbian, gay, and bisexual authors, as well as books that contribute to an understanding of African American lesbian, gay, and bisexual life. Where collections include the writings of authors featured in *Black Like Us*, the author's name is noted at the end of the entry. Some books listed may also include the work of other African American lesbian, gay, and bisexual authors who are not featured in *Black Like Us;* those names will be found in each of those books' table of contents rather than in this bibliography.

The bibliography is organized according to year of publication, with titles grouped into three sections, corresponding to the three eras covered in this volume: The Harlem Renaissance 1900–1950; The Protest Era 1950–1980; Coming Out Black, Like Us 1980–2000; and is further gathered into genres: anthologies, drama, fiction, nonfiction, and poetry.

1900–1950: THE HARLEM RENAISSANCE

ANTHOLOGIES

Multiauthor Collections

Beam, Joseph, ed., *In the Life: A Black Gay Anthology* (Alyson, 1986); includes Richard Bruce Nugent.

Bontemps, Arna, ed., *American Negro Poetry* (Hill, 1963); includes Countee Cullen and Angelina Weld Grimké.

————, ed., *The Harlem Renaissance Remembered* (Dutton, 1972).

Boyd, Herb, and Robert Allen, eds., *Brotherman: The Odyssey of Black Men in America* (Ballantine, 1995); includes Countee Cullen and Wallace Thurman.

Cullen, Countee, ed., *Caroling Dusk: An Anthology of Verse by Negro Poets* (Harper, 1927); includes Alice Dunbar-Nelson, Angelina Weld Grimké, Langston Hughes, and Richard Bruce Nugent.

DeCosta-Willis, Miriam, Roseann Bell, and Reginald Martin, eds., *Erotique Noire/ Black Erotica* (Anchor, 1992); includes Richard Bruce Nugent.

Dunbar-Nelson, Alice, ed., *Masterpieces of Negro Eloquence* (Douglass, 1914).

————, ed., *The Dunbar Speaker and Entertainer* (Nichols, 1920).

Guy-Sheftall, Beverly, ed., *Words of Fire: An Anthology of African American Feminist Thought* (New Press, 1995); includes Alice Dunbar-Nelson.

Hatch, James V., and Ted Shine, eds., *Black Theater U.S.A.: Forty-five Plays by Black Americans, 1847–1974* (Free Press, 1974); includes Alice Dunbar-Nelson and Angelina Weld Grimké.

Hughes, Langston, and Arna Bontemps, eds., *The Poetry of the Negro* (Doubleday, 1949); includes Countee Cullen, Alice Dunbar-Nelson, Angelina Weld Grimké, and Langston Hughes.

Hughes, Langston, *The Best Short Stories by Negro Writers* (Little, 1967); includes Langston Hughes.

Johnson, Charles S., ed., *Ebony and Topaz: A Collection* (National Urban League, 1927); includes Countee Cullen, Alice Dunbar-Nelson, Angelina Weld Grimké, and Langston Hughes.

Kerlin, Robert T., ed., *Negro Poets and Their Poems* (Associated, 1923); includes Alice Dunbar-Nelson and Angelina Weld Grimké.

Lewis, David Levering, ed., *The Portable Harlem Renaissance Reader* (Penguin, 1994); includes Countee Cullen, Angelina Weld Grimké, Langston Hughes, Richard Bruce Nugent, and Wallace Thurman.

Locke, Alain, ed., *The New Negro: An Interpretation* (Boni, 1925); includes Countee Cullen, Angelina Weld Grimké, Langston Hughes, and Richard Bruce Nugent.

Roses, Lorraine Elena, and Ruth Elizabeth Randolph, eds., *Harlem's Glory: Black Women Writing, 1900–1950* (Harvard UP, 1996); includes Alice Dunbar-Nelson.

Ruff, Shawn Stewart, ed., *Go the Way Your Blood Beats: An Anthology of Lesbian and Gay Fiction by African American Writers* (Holt, 1996); includes Alice Dunbar-Nelson, Richard Bruce Nugent, and Wallace Thurman.

Smith, Michael J., ed., *Black Men/White Men: A Gay Anthology* (Gay Sunshine, 1983); includes Langston Hughes and Richard Bruce Nugent.

Thurman, Wallace, ed., *Fire!! A Quarterly Devoted to Young Negro Artists* (self-published, 1926); includes Countee Cullen, Langston Hughes, Richard Bruce Nugent, and Wallace Thurman.

Single Author Collections

Berry, Faith, ed., *The Uncollected Social Protest Writings of Langston Hughes* (Lawrence Hill, 1973).

Cooper, Wayne F., ed., *The Dialectic Poetry of Claude McKay* (Books for Libraries, 1972).

———, ed., *The Passion of Claude McKay: Selected Poetry and Prose* (Shocken, 1972).

Cullen, Countee, *My Lives and How I Lost Them* (Harper, 1942).

———, *On These I Stand: An Anthology of the Best Poems of Countee Cullen* (Harper, 1947).

Dewey, John, ed., *The Selected Poems of Claude McKay* (Bookman, 1953).

Dunbar-Nelson, Alice, *Violets and Other Tales* (Monthly Review, 1895).

———, *The Goodness of St. Rocque and Other Stories* (Dodd, 1899).

Early, Gerald, ed., *My Soul's High Song: The Collected Writings of Countee Cullen, Voice of the Harlem Renaissance* (Doubleday, 1991).

Harper, Akiba Sullivan, *Langston Hughes: Short Stories* (Hill, 1996).

Herron, Carolivia, ed., *Selected Works of Angelina Weld Grimké* (Oxford UP, 1991).

Hopkins, Lee Bennett, ed., *Don't You Turn Back* (Knopf, 1969).

Hughes, Langston, *Simple Speaks His Mind* (Knopf, 1934).

———, *The Ways of White Folks* (Knopf, 1934).

———, *Laughing to Keep from Crying* (Holt, 1952).

———, *Simple Takes a Wife* (Simon, 1953).

———, *Simple Stakes a Claim* (Rinehart, 1957).

———, *The Langston Hughes Reader: The Selected Writings of Langston Hughes* (Braziller, 1958).

———, *Selected Poems of Langston Hughes* (Knopf, 1959).

———, *The Best of Simple* (Hill, 1961).

———, *Five Plays by Langston Hughes* (Indiana UP, 1963).

———, *Something Common and Other Stories* (Hill, 1963).

———, *Simple's Uncle Sam* (Hill, 1965).

Hull, Gloria T., ed., *The Works of Alice Dunbar-Nelson* (Oxford UP, 1988).

McKay, Claude, *Gingertown* (Harper, 1932).

———, *Trial by Lynching* (U of Mysore, 1977).

———, *My Green Hills of Jamaica* (Heinemann, 1979).

———, *The Negroes in America* (Kennikat, 1979).

Rampersad, Arnold, ed., *The Collected Poems of Langston Hughes* (Vintage, 1994).

Walker, Alice, ed., *I Love Myself When I Am Laughing...And Then Again When I Am Looking Mean and Impressive: A Zora Neale Hurston Reader* (Feminist, 1979).

DRAMA

Cullen, Countee, *One Way to Heaven,* 1932.

Cullen, Countee, and Arna Bontemps, *St. Louis Woman,* 1946.

Cullen, Countee, and Larry Hamilton, *Heaven's My Home,* 1935.

Dunbar-Nelson, Alice, *Mine Eyes Have Seen,* 1918.

Grimké, Angelina Weld, *Rachel: A Play in Three Acts,* 1920.

Hughes, Langston, and Zora Neale Hurston, *Mule Bone,* 1930.

Hughes, Langston, *Mulatto,* 1935.

———, *Emperor of Haiti,* 1936.

———, *Little Ham,* 1936.

Hughes, Langston, and Arna Bontemps, *When the Jack Hollers,* 1936.

Hughes, Langston, *Joy to My Soul*, 1937.

————, *Soul Gone Home*, 1937.

————, *Don't You Want to Be Free?*, 1938.

————, *The E-Fuehrer Jones*, 1938.

————, *Front Porch*, 1938.

————, *Limitations of Life*, 1938.

————, *Little Eva's End*, 1938.

————, libretto, *The Organizer*, music by James P. Johnson, 1939.

————, *The Sun Do Move*, 1942.

————, *For This We Fight*, 1943.

————, lyrics, *Street Scene*, book by Elmer Rice, music by Kurt Weil, 1947.

————, libretto, *Troubled Island*, music by Grant Still, 1949.

————, libretto, *The Barrier*, music by Jan Meyerowitz, 1950.

————, lyrics, *Just Around the Corner*, 1951.

————, libretto, *The Glory Round His Head*, 1953.

————, libretto, *Esther*, music by Jan Meyerowitz, 1957.

————, *Simply Heavenly*, 1957.

————, libretto, *The Ballad of the Brown King*, music by Margaret Bonds, 1960.

————, *Black Nativity*, 1961.

————, *Gospel Glow*, 1962.

————, libretto, *Let Us Remember Him*, music by David Amram, 1963.

————, *Tambourines to Glory*, 1963.

————, *Jericho-Jim Crow*, 1964.

————, *The Prodigal Son*, 1965.

Nugent, Richard Bruce, *Sahdji, an African Ballet*, late 1920s.

Nugent, Richard Bruce, and Rose McClendon, *Taxi Fare*, 1931.

Thurman, Wallace, *Savage Rhythm*, 1931.

————, *Singing the Blues*, 1932.

————, screenplay, *Tomorrow's Children*, 1934.

————, screenplay, *High School Girl*, 1935.

Thurman, Wallace, and William Jourdan Rapp, *Harlem: A Melodrama of Negro Life in Harlem*, 1929.

————, *Jeremiah the Magnificent*, 1930.

FICTION

Novels

Cullen, Countee, *One Way to Heaven* (Harper, 1932).

Hughes, Langston, *Not Without Laughter* (Knopf, 1930).

Hurston, Zora Neale, *Their Eyes Were Watching God* (Lippincott, 1937).

Larsen, Nella, *Quicksand* (Knopf, 1928).

———, *Passing* (Knopf, 1929).

McKay, Claude, *Home to Harlem* (Harper, 1928).

———, *Banjo: A Story Without a Plot* (Harper, 1929).

———, *Banana Bottom* (Harper, 1933).

Thurman, Wallace, *The Blacker the Berry: A Novel of Negro Life* (Macaulay, 1929).

———, *Infants of the Spring* (Macaulay, 1932).

Thurman, Wallace, and Abraham L. Furman, *The Interne* (Macaulay, 1932).

Young Adult Novels and Children's Books

Cullen, Countee, *The Lost Zoo (A Rhyme for the Young but Not Too Young)* (Harper, 1940).

Hughes, Langston, and Arna Bontemps, *Popo and Fifina: Children of Haiti* (Macmillan, 1932).

Hughes, Langston, *The First Book of Negroes* (Watts, 1952).

———, *Famous American Negroes* (Watts, 1954).

———, *The First Book of Rhythms* (Watts, 1954).

———, *Famous Negro Music Makers* (Dodd, 1955).

———, *The First Book of Jazz* (Watts, 1955).

———, *The First Book of the West Indies* (Watts, 1956).

———, *Famous Negroes in American History* (Dodd, 1958).

———, *The First Book of Africa* (Watts, 1960).

NONFICTION

Autobiography, Biography, Letters, and Memoir

Alexander, Eleanor, *Lyrics and Sunshine: The Tragic Courtship and Marriage of Paul Laurence Dunbar and Alice Ruth Moore* (NY UP, 2001).

Bernard, Emily, ed., *Remember Me to Harlem: The Letters of Langston Hughes and Carl Van Vechten, 1925–1964* (Knopf, 2001).

Cooper, Wayne F., *Claude McKay: Rebel Sojourner in the Harlem Renaissance* (Louisiana State UP, 1987).

Davis, Angela Y., *Blues Legacies and Black Feminism: Gertrude "Ma" Rainey, Bessie Smith, and Billie Holiday* (Pantheon, 1998).

Duberman, Martin, *Paul Robeson: A Biography* (Knopf, 1988).

Ferguson, Blanche E., *Countee Cullen and the New Negro Renaissance* (Dodd, 1966).

Hughes, Langston, *The Big Sea: An Autobiography* (Knopf, 1940).

———, *I Wonder As I Wander: An Autobiographical Journey* (Rinehart, 1956).

Hull, Gloria T., ed., *Give Us Each Day: The Diary of Alice Dunbar-Nelson* (Norton, 1984).

Hurston, Zora Neale, *Dust Tracks on the Road* (Lippincott, 1942).

Kellner, Bruce, ed., *Letters of Carl Van Vechten* (Yale UP, 1987).

Leeming, David Adams, *Amazing Grace: A Life of Beauford Delaney* (Oxford UP, 1998).

McKay, Claude, *A Long Way from Home: An Autobiography* (Harper, 1937).

Nichols, Charles H., ed., *Arna Bontemps–Langston Hughes Letters: 1925–1967* (Dodd, 1980).

Rampersad, Arnold, *The Life of Langston Hughes, Vol. 1, 1902–1941: I, Too, Sing America* (Oxford UP, 1986).

———, *The Life of Langston Hughes, Vol. 2, 1941–1967: I Dream a World* (Oxford UP, 1988).

Roses, Lorraine Elena, and Ruth Elizabeth Randolph, *Harlem Renaissance and Beyond: Literary Biographies of 100 Black Women Writers, 1900–1945* (Harvard UP, 1990).

Shucard, Alan R., *Countee Cullen* (Twayne, 1984).

History and Reference

Birnbaum, Jonathan, and Clarence Taylor, eds., *Civil Rights Since 1787: A Reader on the Black Struggle* (New York UP, 2000).

Black, Allida M., ed., *Modern American Queer History* (Temple UP, 2001).

Blasius, Mark, and Shane Phelan, eds., *We Are Everywhere: A Historical Sourcebook of Gay and Lesbian Politics* (Routledge, 1997).

Chauncey, George, *Gay New York: Gender, Urban Culture, and the Marketing of the Gay Male World 1890–1940* (Basic, 1994).

Clendinen, Dudley, and Adam Nagourney, *Out for Good: The Struggle to Build a Gay Rights Movement in America* (Simon, 1999).

Dickinson, Donald C., *A Bio-Bibliography of Langston Hughes, 1902–1967* (Shoestring, 1967).

Duberman, Martin, Martha Vicinus, and George Chauncey, Jr., eds., *Hidden from History: Reclaiming the Gay and Lesbian Past* (New American Library, 1989).

Faderman, Lillian, *Odd Girls and Twilight Lovers: A History of Lesbian Life in Twentieth-Century America* (Columbia UP, 1991).

Fouts, John, and Maura Tantillo, eds., *American Sexual Politics: Sex, Gender, and Race Since the Civil War* (U of Chicago P, 1993).

Harley, Sharon, and Rosalyn Terborg-Penn, eds., *The Afro-American Woman: Struggles and Images* (National Univ., 1978).

Harrison, Daphne Dural, *Black Pearls: Blues Queens of the 1920s* (Rutgers UP, 1988).

Hawkeswood, William G., *One of the Children: Gay Black Men in Harlem* (U of California P, 1996).

Hine, Darlene Clark, Rosalyn Terborg-Penne, and Elsa B. Brown, eds., *Black Women in America: An Historical Encyclopedia* (Carlson, 1993).

Huggins, Nathan, *Harlem Renaissance* (Oxford UP, 1971).

Hughes, Langston, *The Negro Looks at Soviet Central Asia* (Cooperative Pub. Society of Foreign Workers in the USSR, 1934).

———, *The Sweet Flypaper of Life*, with photographs by Roy DeCarava (Simon, 1955).

Hughes, Langston, with Milton Melzer, *A Pictorial History of the Negro in America* (Crown, 1956).

Hughes, Langston, *Fight for Freedom: The Story of the NAACP* (Berkeley, 1962).

Hughes, Langston, with Milton Melzer, *Black Magic: A Pictorial History of the Negro in American Entertainment* (Prentice, 1967).

Hughes, Langston, *Black Misery* (Knopf, 1969).

Hull, Gloria T., Patricia Bell Scott, and Barbara Smith, eds., *All the Women Are White, All the Blacks Are Men but Some of Us Are Brave: Black Women's Studies* (Feminist, 1982).

Hull, Gloria T., *Color, Sex, and Poetry: Three Women Writers of the Harlem Renaissance* (Indiana UP, 1987).

Katz, Jonathan, ed., *Gay American History: Lesbians and Gay Men in the U.S.A.* (Harper, 1976).

Lerna, Gerda, ed., *Black Women in White America: A Documentary History* (Random, 1972).

Lewis, David Levering, *When Harlem Was in Vogue* (Knopf, 1981).

Locke, Alain, *When Peoples Meet: A Study in Race and Culture Contacts* (Progressive Education Assoc., 1942).

Loughery, John, *The Other Side of Silence: Men's Lives and Gay Identities: A Twentieth Century History* (Holt, 1998).

Mankiller, Wilma, Gwendolyn Mink, Marysa Navarro, Barbara Smith, and Gloria Steinem, eds., *The Reader's Companion to U.S. Women's History* (Houghton, 1998).

McKay, Claude, *Harlem: Negro Metropolis* (Dutton, 1940).

Miller, Neil, *Out of the Past: Gay and Lesbian History from 1869 to the Present* (Vintage, 1995).

Perry, Margaret, *A Bio-Bibliography of Countee P. Cullen, 1903–1946* (Greenwood, 1971).

———, *The Harlem Renaissance: An Annotated Bibliography and Commentary* (Garland, 1982).

Roberts, J. R., ed., *Black Lesbians: An Annotated Bibliography* (Naiad, 1981).

Shockley, Ann Allen, *Afro-American Women Writers, 1746–1933: An Anthology and Critical Guide* (Hall, 1988).

Somerville, Siobhan B., *Queering the Color Line: Race and the Invention of Homosexuality in American Culture* (Duke UP, 2000).

Summers, Claude J., ed., *The Gay and Lesbian Literary Heritage: A Reader's Companion to the Writers and Their Works, from Antiquity to the Present* (Holt, 1995).

Thurman, Wallace, *Negro Life in New York's Harlem* (Haldeman-Julius, 1928).

Van Notten, Eleanor, *Wallace Thurman's Harlem Renaissance* (Rodopi, 1994).

Watson, Steve, *The Harlem Renaissance: Hub of African-American Culture, 1920–1930* (Pantheon, 1995).

POETRY

Cullen, Countee, *Color* (Harper, 1925).

———, *The Ballad of the Brown Girl* (Harper, 1927).

———, *Copper Sun* (Harper, 1927).

———, *The Black Christ and Other Poems* (Harper, 1929).

———, *The Medea and Some Poems* (Harper, 1935).

Hughes, Langston, *Weary Blues* (Knopf, 1926).

———, *Fine Clothes to the Jew* (Knopf, 1927).

———, *Dear Lovely Death* (Troutbeck, 1931).

———, *The Negro Mother and Other Dramatic Recitations* (Golden Stair, 1931).

———, *The Dream Keeper and Other Poems* (Knopf, 1932).

———, *Scottsboro Limited* (Golden Stair, 1932).

Hughes, Langston, with Robert Glenn, *Shakespeare in Harlem* (Knopf, 1942).

Hughes, Langston, *Freedom's Plow* (Musette, 1943).

———, *Jim Crow's Last Stand* (Negro Pub. Society of America, 1943).

———, *Lament for Dark Peoples and Other Poems* (Holland, 1944).

———, *Fields of Wonder* (Knopf, 1947).

———, *One-Way Ticket* (Knopf, 1949).

———, *Montage of a Dream Deferred* (Holt, 1951).

———, *Ask Your Mama: Twelve Moods for Jazz* (Knopf, 1961).

———, *The Panther and the Lash: Poems of Our Times* (Knopf, 1967).

McKay, Claude, *Constab Ballads* (Watts, 1912).

———, *Songs of Jamaica* (Gardner, 1912).

———, *Spring in New Hampshire* (Richards, 1920).

———, *Harlem Shadows: The Poems of Claude McKay* (Harcourt, 1922).

1950–1980: THE PROTEST ERA

ANTHOLOGIES

Multiauthor Collections

Anzaldua, Gloria, and Cherrie Moraga, eds., *This Bridge Called My Back: Writings by Radical Women of Color* (Persephone, 1981); includes Audre Lorde and Cheryl Clarke.

Bambara, Toni Cade, ed., *The Black Woman* (Mentor, 1970); includes Audre Lorde and Alice Walker.

Beam, Joseph, ed., *In the Life: A Black Gay Anthology* (Alyson, 1986); includes Samuel R. Delany.

Boyd, Herb, and Robert Allen, eds., *Brotherman: The Odyssey of Black Men in America* (Ballantine, 1995); includes James Baldwin.

Brandt, Eric, ed., *Dangerous Liaisons: Blacks, Gays, and the Struggle for Equality* (New Press, 1999); includes Cheryl Clarke, Samuel R. Delany, and Audre Lorde.

Crow, Barbara, ed., *Radical Feminism: A Documentary Reader* (New York UP, 2000).

Davis, Angela Y., Bettina Aptheker, and other members of the National United Committee to Free Angela Davis and All Political Prisoners, eds., *If They Come in the Morning: Voices of Resistance* (Third, 1971).

Davis, Arthur P., and Saunders Redding, eds., *Cavalcade: Negro American Writing from 1760 to the Present* (Houghton, 1971); includes James Baldwin and Owen Dodson.

DeCarnin, Camilla, ed., *Worlds Apart: An Anthology of Lesbian and Gay Science Fiction and Fantasy* (AlyCat, 1994); includes Samuel R. Delany.

DeCosta-Willis, Miriam, Roseann Bell, and Reginald Martin, eds., *Erotique Noire/ Black Erotica* (Anchor, 1992); includes Audre Lorde and Alice Walker.

Gallo, Donald R., ed., *Sixteen: Short Stories by Outstanding Writers for Young Adults* (Delacorte, 1984); includes Rosa Guy.

Gates, Henry Lewis, ed., *Bearing Witness: Selections from 150 Years of African American Autobiography* (Pantheon, 1991); includes Samuel R. Delany and Audre Lorde.

Guy-Sheftall, Beverly, ed., *Words of Fire: An Anthology of African American Feminist Thought* (New Press, 1995); includes Cheryl Clarke, Audre Lorde, and Alice Walker.

Hamalian, Leo, and James V. Hatch, eds., *The Roots of African American Drama* (Wayne State UP, 1990); includes Owen Dodson.

Hatch, James V., and Ted Shine, eds., *Black Theater USA* (Free Press, 1974); includes Owen Dodson.

Hughes, Langston, and Arna Bontemps, eds., *The Book of Negro Folklore* (Dodd, 1958); includes Owen Dodson.

Hughes, Langston, ed., *Negro Poets U.S.A.* (Indiana UP, 1964); includes Audre Lorde.

———, *The Best Short Stories by Negro Writers* (Little, 1967); includes James Baldwin, Owen Dodson, and Alice Walker.

Hull, Gloria T., Patricia Bell Scott, and Barbara Smith, eds., *All the Women Are White, All the Blacks Are Men, but Some of Us Are Brave: Black Women's Studies* (Feminist, 1982); includes Alice Walker.

Jordan, June, ed., *Soulscript: Afro-American Poetry* (Doubleday, 1970).

Lassell, Michael, and Elena Georgious, eds., *The World in Us: Lesbian and Gay Poetry of the Next Wave* (St. Martin's, 2000); includes Cheryl Clarke.

Major, Clarence, ed., *The New Black Poetry* (International, 1969); includes Audre Lorde.

———, ed., *Calling the Wind: 20th Century African American Short Stories* (Harper, 1992); includes James Baldwin, Michelle Cliff, Rosa Guy, and Alice Walker.

Mayfield, Julian, ed., *Ten Times Black* (Bantam, 1972); includes Rosa Guy.

McKinley, Catherine E., and L. Joyce DeLaney, eds., *Afrekete: An Anthology of Black Lesbian Writing* (Anchor, 1995); includes Michelle Cliff and Audre Lorde.

McMillan, Terry, ed., *Breaking Ice: An Anthology of Contemporary African American Fiction* (Penguin, 1990); includes Samuel R. Delany and Alice Walker.

Moore, Lisa C., ed., *Does Your Mama Know: An Anthology of Black Lesbian Coming Out Stories* (RedBone, 1997); includes Cheryl Clarke.

Morrow, Bruce, and Charles H. Rowell, eds., *Shade: An Anthology of Fiction by Gay Men of African Descent* (Avon, 1996); includes Samuel R. Delany.

Muse, Daphne, ed., *Prejudice: Stories About Hate, Ignorance, Revelation and Transformation* (Hyperion, 1995); includes Julie Blackwomon.

Naylor, Gloria, ed., *Children of the Night: The Best Short Stories by Black Writers, 1967 to the Present* (Little, 1995); includes James Baldwin and Alice Walker.

Nestle, Joan, ed., *The Persistent Desire: A Butch–Femme Reader Edited by Joan Nestle* (Alyson, 1992); includes Cheryl Clarke and Audre Lorde.

Paris Review, ed., *Best Short Stories of the Paris Review* (Dutton, 1959); includes Owen Dodson.

Poole, Rosey, ed., *Beyond the Blues: New Poems by American Negroes* (Lympne, 1963); includes Audre Lorde.

Rowell, Charles H., ed., *Ancestral House: The Black Short Story in the Americas and Europe* (Westview, 1995); includes Michelle Cliff, Samuel R. Delany, and Alice Walker.

Ruff, Shawn Stewart, ed., *Go the Way Your Blood Beats: An Anthology of Lesbian and Gay Fiction by African American Writers* (Holt, 1996); includes James Baldwin, Samuel R. Delany, Audre Lorde, and Alice Walker.

Schneir, Miriam, ed., *Feminism in Our Time: The Essential Writings, World War II to the Present* (Vintage, 1994).

Sherman, Charlotte Watson, ed., *Sisterfire: Black Womanist Fiction and Poetry* (Harper, 1994); includes Alice Walker.

Silvera, Makeda, ed., *Piece of My Heart: A Lesbian of Colour Anthology* (Sister Vision, 1992); includes Cheryl Clarke.

Smith, Barbara, ed., *Home Girls: A Black Feminist Anthology* (Persephone, 1981); includes Julie Blackwomon, Cheryl Clarke, Michelle Cliff, Audre Lorde, and Alice Walker.

Stadler, Quandra Prettyman, ed., *Out of Our Lives: A Selection of Contemporary Black Fiction* (Howard UP, 1995); includes Alice Walker.

Thomas, Sheree, ed., *Dark Matter: A Century of Speculative Fiction from the African Diaspora* (Warner, 2001); includes Samuel R. Delany.

Turner, Darwin T., ed., *Black Drama in America: An Anthology* (Fawcett, 1971); includes Owen Dodson.

Zahava, Irened, ed., *Lavender Mansions: Forty Contemporary Lesbian and Gay Short Stories* (Westview, 1994); includes Audre Lorde.

Single Author Collections

Arobateau, Red Jordan, *Lesbian Cum Stories with Feeling and Meaning* (Red Jordan Press, 1991).

———, *Suzie-Q: A Collection of Stories* (Red Jordan Press, 1991).

———, *Doing It for the Mistress: Gay, Lesbian, Bisexual, Transsexual Fuck Stories* (Red Jordan Press, 1999).

Baldwin, James, *Notes of a Native Son* (Beacon, 1955).

———, *Nobody Knows My Name: More Notes of a Native Son* (Dial, 1961).

———, *The Fire Next Time* (Dial, 1963).

———, *No Name in the Street* (Dial, 1974).

———, *The Devil Finds Work* (Dial, 1976).

———, *The Evidence of Things Not Seen* (Holt, 1985).

———, *The Price of the Ticket: Collected Nonfiction 1948–1985* (St. Martin's, 1985).

Blackwomon, Julie, and Nona Caspers, *Voyages Out 2: Lesbian Short Fiction* (Seal, 1990).

Cliff, Michelle, *Claiming an Identity They Taught Me to Despise* (Persephone, 1980).

———, *The Land of Look Behind* (Firebrand, 1985).

———, *Bodies of Water* (Dutton, 1990).

———, *The Store of a Million Items: Stories* (Houghton, 1998).

Cornwell, Anita, *Black Lesbian in White America* (Naiad, 1983).

Delany, Samuel R., *Driftglass: Ten Tales of Speculative Fiction* (NAL, 1971).

———, *The Jewel-Hinged Jaw: Notes on the Language of Science Fiction* (Dragon, 1977).

———, *Distant Stars* (Bantam, 1981).

———, *Starboard Wine: More Notes on the Language of Science Fiction* (Dragon, 1984).

———, *The Straits of Messina* (Serconia, 1989).

———, *Silent Interviews: On Language, Race, Sex, Science Fiction, and Some Comics* (Wesleyan UP, 1994).

———, *Atlantis: Three Tales* (Wesleyan UP, 1995).

———, *Longer Views: Extended Essays* (Wesleyan UP, 1995).

———, *Shorter Views: Queer Thoughts and the Politics of the Paraliterary* (Wesleyan UP, 1999).

Duberman, Martin, *Left Out: The Politics of Exclusion/Essays/1964–1999* (Basic, 1999).

Guy, Rosa, *Children of Longing* (Holt, 1971).

Hansberry, Lorraine, *To Be Young, Gifted and Black: Lorraine Hansberry in Her Own Words,* adapted by Robert Nemiroff (Signet, 1969).

———, *The Collected Last Plays: Les Blancs, The Drinking Gourd, What Use Are Flowers?,* ed. by Robert Nemiroff (Vintage, 1983).

———, *A Raisin in the Sun and The Sign in Sidney Brustein's Window* (Vintage, 1995).

Jordan, June, *Civil Wars* (Beacon, 1981).

———, *On Call: Political Essays* (South End, 1985).

———, *Technical Difficulties: African American Notes on the State of the Union* (Pantheon, 1992).

———, *Affirmative Acts: Political Essays* (Doubleday, 1998).

Lorde, Audre, *Sister Outsider: Essays and Speeches* (Crossing, 1984).

———, *A Burst of Light: Essays* (Firebrand, 1988).

———, *The Collected Poems of Audre Lorde* (Norton, 1997).

Maddy, Yulisa Amadu, *Obasai and Other Plays* (Heinemann, 1971).

Morrison, Toni, ed., *Baldwin: Collected Essays* (Library of America, 1998).

Nestle, Joan, *A Restricted Country* (Firebrand, 1987).

———, *A Fragile Union: New and Selected Writings* (Cleis, 1998).

Rich, Adrienne, *Blood, Bread, and Poetry: Selected Prose 1979–1985* (Norton, 1986).

Rustin, Bayard, *Down the Line: The Collected Writings of Bayard Rustin* (Quadrangle, 1971).

Shockley, Ann Allen, *The Black and White of It* (Naiad, 1980).

Smith, Barbara, *The Truth That Never Hurts: Writings on Race, Gender, and Freedom* (Rutgers UP, 1998).

Standley, Fred L., and Louis H. Pratt, eds., *Conversations with James Baldwin* (U of Mississippi P, 1989).

Walker, Alice, *In Love and In Trouble: Stories of Black Women* (Harcourt, 1973).

———, ed., *I Love Myself When I Am Laughing...And Then Again When I Am Looking Mean and Impressive: A Zora Neale Hurston Reader* (Feminist, 1979).

———, *You Can't Keep a Good Woman Down* (Harcourt, 1981).

———, *In Search of Our Mothers' Gardens: Womanist Prose* (Harcourt, 1983).

———, *Living by the Word: Selected Writings, 1973–1987* (Harcourt, 1988).

———, *Her Blue Body Everything We Know: Earthling Poems, 1965–1990* (Harvest, 1993).

———, *The Way Forward Is with a Broken Heart* (Random, 2000).

DRAMA

Baldwin, James, *Blues for Mr. Charlie* (Dial, 1964).

———, *The Amen Corner* (Dial, 1968).

———, *One Day, When I Was Lost: A Scenario Based on "The Autobiography of Malcolm X"* (Dial, 1972).

Dodson, Owen, *Deep in Your Heart*, 1935.

———, *Including Laughter*, 1936.

———, *Divine Comedy*, 1938.

———, *Amistad*, 1939.

———, *Garden of Time*, 1939.

———, *Gargoyles in Florida*, 1941.

———, *Robert Smalls*, 1942.

———, *Booker T. Washington*, 1943.

———, *Don't Give Up the Ship*, 1943.

———, *Dorrie Miller*, 1943.

———, *Everybody Join Hands*, 1943.

———, *Freedom the Banner*, 1943.

———, *John P. Jones*, 1943.

———, *Lord Nelson*, 1943.

———, *Old Ironsides*, 1943.

———, *Tropical Fable*, 1943.

———, *New World A-Coming*, 1944.

———, *Hot Spots*, 1945.

———, *Bayou Legend*, 1948.

———, *Constellation of Women*, 1950.

———, *Christmas Miracle*, 1958.

———, *The Confession Stone*, 1964.

———, *Til Victory Is Won*, 1965.

———, *The Dream Awake*, 1970.

———, *Owen's Song*, 1974.

———, *Soul of Soul*, 1978.

———, *Life in the Streets*, 1982.

Guy, Rosa, *Venetian Blind*, 1954.

Hansberry, Lorraine, *A Raisin in the Sun*, 1959.

———, *The Sign in Sidney Brustein's Window* , 1965.

———, *A Raisin in the Sun: The Unfilmed Original Screenplay* (Signet, 1995).

Jordan, June, *In the Spirit of Sojourner Truth*, 1979.

———, *For the Arrow That Flies by Day*, 1981.

———, *Bang Bang Uber Alles*, 1985.

———, *I Was Looking at the Ceiling and Then I Saw the Sky: Earthquake/Romance* (Simon, 1995).

Walker, Alice, screenplay, *The Color Purple*, 1985.

FICTION

Novels

Arobateau, Red Jordan, *Bars Across Heaven* (Red Jordan Press, 1975).

———, *Ho Stroll* (Red Jordan Press, 1975).

———, *Jailhouse Stud* (Red Jordan Press, 1977).

———, *Dirty Pictures: A Lesbian Novel* (Red Jordan Press, 1991).

———, *Lay, Lady, Lay: A Lesbian Novel* (Red Jordan Press, 1991).

———, *Street Fighter: A Lesbian Novel* (Red Jordan Press, 1992).

———, *Leader of the Pack: A Lesbian Biker Novel* (Red Jordan Press, 1993).

———, *Lucy and Mickey: A Trilogy* (Red Jordan Press, 1993).

———, *Satan's Best: A Lesbian Biker Novel* (Red Jordan Press, 1993).

———, *The Black Biker: A Lesbian Novel* (Red Jordan Press, 1994).

———, *The Big Change: A Transsexual Novel* (Red Jordan Press, 2001).

———, *Tranny Biker* (Red Jordan Press, 2001).

Baldwin, James, *Go Tell It on the Mountain* (Knopf, 1953).

———, *Giovanni's Room* (Dial, 1956).

———, *Another Country* (Dial, 1962).

———, *Tell Me How Long the Train's Been Gone* (Dial, 1968).

———, *If Beale Street Could Talk* (Dial, 1974).

———, *Just Above My Head* (Dial, 1979).

Baxt, George, *A Queer Kind of Love: A Pharaoh Love Mystery* (Simon, 1966).

Cliff, Michelle, *Abeng: A Novel* (Crossing, 1984).

———, *No Telephone to Heaven* (Random, 1987).

———, *Free Enterprise* (Dutton, 1993).

Delany, Samuel R., *The Jewels of Aptor* (Ace, 1962).

———, *The Ballad of Beta-2* (Ace, 1965).

———, *Babel-17* (Ace, 1966).

———, *Empire Star* (Ace, 1966).

———, *The Einstein Intersection* (Ace, 1967).

———, *Nova* (Ace, 1968).

———, *The Fall of the Towers* (Ace, 1970).

———, *The Tides of Lust* (Lancer, 1973); also published as *Equinox.*

———, *Dhalgren* (Bantam, 1975).

———, *Triton* (Bantam, 1976).

———, *Tales of Nevèryon* (Bantam, 1979).

———, *Nevèryon* (Bantam, 1983).

———, *Stars in My Pocket Like Grains of Sand* (Bantam, 1984).

———, *Flight from Nevèryon* (Bantam, 1985).

———, *The Bridge of Lost Desire* (Arbor, 1987).

———, *They Fly at Ciron* (Incunabul, 1993).

———, *The Mad Man* (Kasak, 1994).

———, *Hogg* (Black Ice, 1995).

———, *Bread and Wine: An Erotic Tale of New York City* (Masquerade, 1999).

Dodson, Owen, *Boy at the Window* (Farrar, 1951).

———, *Come Home Early Child* (Popular Library, 1977).

Ellison, Ralph, *Invisible Man* (Random, 1952).

Himes, Chester, *Cast the First Stone* (McGraw, 1952).

Jones, Gayl, *Corregidora* (Random, 1975).

Lorde, Audre, *Zami: A New Spelling of My Name* (Crossing, 1982).

Maddy, Yulisa Amadu, *No Past, No Present, No Future* (Heinemann, 1973).

Morrison, Toni, *Sula* (Knopf, 1973).

Shockley, Ann Allen, *Loving Her* (Avon, 1974).

———, *Say Jesus and Come to Me* (Avon, 1982).

Slim, Iceberg, *Mama Black Widow* (Holloway, 1970).

Walker, Alice, *The Third Life of Grace Copeland* (Harcourt, 1970).

———, *Meridian* (Harcourt, 1976).

———, *The Color Purple* (Harcourt, 1982).

———, *The Temple of My Familiar* (Harcourt, 1989).

———, *Possessing the Secret of Joy* (Harcourt, 1992).

———, *By the Light of My Father's Smile* (Random, 1998).

Young Adult Novels and Children's Books

Baldwin, James, *Little Man, Little Man: A Story of Childhood* (Dial, 1977).

DeVeaux, Alexis, *Na-ni* (Harper, 1973).

———, *Spirits in the Street* (Doubleday, 1973).

Guy, Rosa, *Bird at My Window* (Lippincott, 1966).

———, *The Friends* (Holt, 1974).

———, *Ruby: A Novel* (Viking, 1976).

———, *Edith Jackson* (Viking, 1978).

———, *The Disappearance* (Delacorte, 1979).

———, *Mirror of Her Own* (Delacorte, 1981).

———, *A Measure of Time* (Holt, 1983).

———, *My Love, My Love: or, The Pleasant Girl* (Holt, 1985).

———, *Paris, Pee Wee and Big Dog* (Delacorte, 1985).

———, *And I Heard a Bird Sing* (Delacorte, 1986).

———, *The Ups and Downs of Carl Davis III* (Delacorte, 1989).

Jordan, June, *Who Look At Me?* (Crowell, 1969).

———, *His Own Where* (Crowell, 1971).

———, *Fannie Lou Hamer* (Harper, 1972).

———, *New Life: New Room* (Harper, 1975).

McKissick, Pat, and Frederick L. McKissick, *Young, Black, and Determined: A Biography of Lorraine Hansberry* (Holiday, 1998).

Walker, Alice, *Langston Hughes: American Poet* (Crowell, 1974).

———, *To Hell with Dying* (Harcourt, 1988).

———, *Finding the Green Stone* (Harcourt, 1991).

NONFICTION

Autobiography, Biography, Letters, and Memoir

Ailey, Alvin, and Peter Bailey, *Revelations: The Autobiography of Alvin Ailey* (Birch Lane Press, 1995).

Anderson, Jervis, *Bayard Rustin: Troubles I've Seen* (Harper, 1997).

Angelou, Maya, *I Know Why the Caged Bird Sings* (Random, 1970).

Brown, Elaine, *A Taste of Power: A Black Woman's Story* (Pantheon, 1992).

Brownmiller, Susan, *In Our Time: Memoir of a Revolution* (Dial, 1999).

Chisholm, Shirley, *The Good Fight* (Harper, 1973).

Davis, Angela Y., *Angela Davis: An Autobiography* (Random, 1974).

———, *Blues Legacies and Black Feminism: Gertrude "Ma" Rainey, Bessie Smith, and Billie Holiday* (Pantheon, 1998).

Delany, Samuel R., *Heavenly Breakfast: An Essay on the Winter of Love* (Bantam, 1979).

———, *The Motion of Light in Water: Sex and Science Fiction in the East Village, 1957–1965* (Arbor, 1988).

———, *1984: Selected Letters* (Voyant, 2000).

DeVeaux, Alexis, *Audre Lorde* (Random, 1997).

Grant, Joanne, *Ella Baker: Freedom Bound* (Wiley, 1998).

Hadju, David, *Lush Life: A Biography of Billy Strayhorn* (Farrar, 1996).

Hatch, James V., *Sorrow Is the Only Faithful One: The Life of Owen Dodson* (U of Illinois P, 1995).

Heath, Gordon, *Deep Are the Roots: Memoirs of a Black Expatriate* (U of Massachusetts P, 1992).

Jay, Karla, *Tales of the Lavender Menace: A Memoir of Liberation* (Basic, 1999).

Jordan, June, *Soldier: A Poet's Childhood* (Basic, 2000).

Leeming, David, *James Baldwin: A Biography* (Knopf, 1994).

Levine, Daniel, *Bayard Rustin and the Civil Rights Movement* (Rutgers UP, 2000).

Lorde, Audre, *The Cancer Journals* (Spinsters Ink, 1980).

Robinson, Jo Ann Gibson, *The Montgomery Bus Boycott and the Women Who Started It: The Memoir of Jo Ann Gibson Robinson* (Tennessee UP, 1987).

Walker, Alice, *The Same River Twice: Honoring the Difficult: A Meditation on Life, Spirit, Art and the Making of the Film, The Color Purple, Ten Years Later* (Scribner, 1996).

————, *Anything We Loved Can Be Saved: A Writer's Activism* (Random, 1997).

History and Reference

Baldwin, James, *Nothing Personal,* with photographs by Richard Avedon (Atheneum, 1964).

Baldwin, James, and Margaret Mead, *A Rap on Race* (Lippincott, 1971).

Baldwin, James, and Nikki Giovanni, *A Dialogue* (Lippincott, 1973).

Banks, Erma D., and Keith Byerman, *Alice Walker: An Annotated Bibliography* (Garland, 1989).

Baxandall, Rosalyn, and Linda Gordon, eds., *Dear Sister: Dispatches from the Women's Liberation Movement* (Basic, 2000).

Black, Allida M., ed., *Modern American Queer History* (Temple UP, 2001).

Blasius, Mark, and Shane Phelan, eds., *We Are Everywhere: A Historical Sourcebook of Gay and Lesbian Politics* (Routledge, 1997).

Carson, Clayborne, *In Struggle: SNCC and the Black Awakening of the 1960s* (Harvard UP, 1981).

Clendinen, Dudley, and Adam Nagourney, *Out for Good: The Struggle to Build a Gay Rights Movement in America* (Simon, 1999).

Crenshaw, Kimberlé, Neil Gotanda, Gary Pellar, and Kendall Thomas, eds., *Critical Race Theory: The Key Writings That Formed the Movement* (New Press, 1995).

Dandridge, Rita B., *Ann Allen Shockley: An Annotated Primary and Secondary Bibliography* (Greenwood, 1987).

Davis, Angela Y., *Women, Race, and Class* (Random, 1981).

————, *Women, Culture, and Politics* (Random, 1989).

Delany, Samuel R., *Times Square Red, Times Square Blue* (New York UP, 1999).

D'Emilio, John, *Sexual Politics, Sexual Communities: The Making of a Homosexual Community in the United States, 1940–1970* (U of Chicago P, 1983).

Duberman, Martin, Martha Vicinus, and George Chauncey, Jr., *Hidden from History: Reclaiming the Gay and Lesbian Past* (New American Library, 1989).

Duberman, Martin, *Stonewall* (Dutton, 1993).

Evans, Mari, ed., *Black Women Writers (1950–1980): A Critical Evaluation* (Doubleday, 1984); includes Audre Lorde and Alice Walker.

Faderman, Lillian, *Odd Girls and Twilight Lovers: A History of Lesbian Life in Twentieth-Century America* (Columbia UP, 1991).

Fouts, John, and Maura Tantillo, eds., *American Sexual Politics: Sex, Gender, and Race Since the Civil War* (U of Chicago P, 1993).

Garrow, David, *Bearing the Cross: Martin Luther King, Jr. and the Southern Christian Leadership Conference* (Morrow, 1986).

Gates, Henry Louis, and Anthony Appiah, eds., *Alice Walker: Critical Perspectives* (Amistad, 1993).

Giddings, Paula, *When and Where I Enter: The Impact of Black Women on Race and Sex in America* (Morrow, 1984).

Hansberry, Lorraine, *The Movement: Documentary of a Struggle for Equality* (Simon, 1964).

Hernton, Calvin, *Sex and Racism in America* (Grove, 1965).

Hine, Darlene Clark, Rosalyn Terborg-Penne, and Elsa B. Brown, eds., *Black Women in America: An Historical Encyclopedia* (Carlson, 1993).

Hine, Darlene Clark, and Kathleen Thompson, *A Shining Thread of Hope: The History of Black Women in America* (Broadway, 1998).

Hull, Gloria T., *Color, Sex, and Poetry: Three Women Writers of the Harlem Renaissance* (Indiana UP, 1987).

Hull, Akasha Gloria, *Soul Talk: The New Spirituality of African American Women* (Inner Traditions, 2001); includes Alice Walker.

Katz, Jonathan, ed., *Gay American History: Lesbians and Gay Men in the U.S.A.* (Harper, 1976).

Lerna, Gerda, ed., *Black Women in White America: A Documentary History* (Random, 1972).

Lorde, Audre, *Uses of the Erotic: The Erotic as Power* (Crossing, 1978).

———, *I Am Your Sister: Black Women Organizing Across Sexualities* (Kitchen Table: Women of Color, 1985).

———, *Need: A Chorale for Black Woman Voices* (Kitchen Table: Women of Color, 1991).

Loughery, John, *The Other Side of Silence: Men's Lives and Gay Identities: A Twentieth Century History* (Holt, 1998).

Mankiller, Wilma, Gwendolyn Mink, Marysa Navarro, Barbara Smith, and Gloria Steinem, eds., *The Reader's Companion to U.S. Women's History* (Houghton, 1998).

McBride, Dwight A., ed., *James Baldwin Now* (New York UP, 1999).

Miller, Neil, *Out of the Past: Gay and Lesbian History from 1869 to the Present* (Vintage, 1995).

Millet, Kate, *Sexual Politics* (Doubleday, 1970).

Nelson, Emmanuel S., ed., *Critical Essays: Gay and Lesbian Writers of Color* (Harrington, 1994).

Olson, Lynne, *Freedom's Daughter: The Unsung Heroines of the Civil Rights Movement from 1830 to 1970* (Scribner, 2001).

Peplow, Michael W., and Robert S. Bravard, eds., *Samuel R. Delany: A Primary and Secondary Bibliography, 1962–1979* (Hall, 1980).

Pollack, Sandra, and Denise D. Knight, *Contemporary Lesbian Writers in the United States: A Bio-bibliographical Critical Sourcebook* (Greenwood, 1993).

Roberts, J. R., *Black Lesbians: An Annotated Bibliography* (Naiad, 1981).

Robnett, Belinda, *How Long? How Long?: African American Women in the Struggle for Civil Rights* (Oxford UP, 1997).

Rosen, Ruth, *The World Split Open: How the Modern Women's Movement Changed America* (Viking, 2000).

Rustin, Bayard, *Strategies for Freedom: The Changing Patterns of Black Protest* (Columbia UP, 1976).

Smith, Barbara, Elly Bulkin, and Minnie Bruce Pratt, *Yours in Struggle: Three Feminist Perspectives on Anti-Semitism and Racism* (Long Haul, 1984).

Summers, Claude J., ed., *The Gay and Lesbian Literary Heritage: A Reader's Companion to the Writers and Their Works, from Antiquity to the Present* (Holt, 1995).

Teal, Donn, *The Gay Militants* (Stein, 1971).

Vaid, Urvashi, *Virtual Equality: The Mainstreaming of Gay and Lesbian Liberation* (Anchor, 1995).

Walker, Alice, with Pratibha Parmar, *Warrior Marks: Female Genital Mutilation and the Sexual Binding of Women* (Harcourt, 1993).

———, *Banned* (Aunt Lute, 1996).

———, *Sent by Earth: A Message from the Grandmother Spirit After the Bombing of the World Trade Center and the Pentagon* (Seven Stories, 2001).

Wallace, Michelle, *Black Macho and the Myth of the Superwoman* (Dial, 1979).

Woods, Gregory, *A History of Gay Literature: The Male Tradition* (Yale UP, 1998).

POETRY

Arobateau, Red Jordan, *The Collected Poems of Red Jordan Arobateau* (Red Jordan Press, 1996).

Baldwin, James, *Jimmy's Blues: Selected Poems* (St. Martin's, 1985).

———, *Gypsies and Other Poems* (Gehenna/Eremite, 1989).

Bogus, SDiane, *I'm Off to See the Goddamn Wizard, Alright!* (Woman in the Moon, 1971).

———, *Woman in the Moon* (Soap Box, 1977).

———, *Her Poems: An Annaversaric Chronology* (Woman in the Moon, 1979).

———, *Sapphire's Sampler* (Woman in the Moon, 1982).

———, *Dyke Hands and Sutras: Erotic Lyric* (Woman in the Moon, 1988).

——, *The Chant of the Women of the Magdalene and the Magdalene Poems* (Woman in the Moon, 1990).

——, *For the Love of Men: Shikata Gai Nai* (Woman in the Moon, 1991).

Byrd, Stephanie, *25 Years of Malcontent* (Good Gay Poets, 1976).

Carpenter, Pandoura, *Deal with It!* (She Wolf, 1979).

Clarke, Cheryl, *Narratives: Poems in the Tradition of Black Women* (Kitchen Table: Women of Color, 1983).

——, *Living as a Lesbian* (Firebrand, 1986).

——, *Humid Pitch: Narrative Poetry* (Firebrand, 1989).

——, *Experimental Love* (Firebrand, 1993).

Dodson, Owen, *Powerful Long Ladder* (Farrar, 1946).

——, *The Confession Stone* (Breman, 1970).

Dodson, Owen, with Camille Billops and James Van Der Zee, *The Harlem Book of the Dead* (Morgan, 1978).

Gibbs, Joan, *Between a Rock and a Hard Place* (Third, 1979).

Gomillion, E. Sharon, *Forty Acres and a Mule* (Diana, 1973).

Hopkins, Lea, *I'm Not Crazy, Just Different* (self-published, 1977).

——, *Womyn I Have Known You* (self-published, 1978).

Hull, Gloria T., *Healing Heart: Poems 1973–1988* (Kitchen Table, 1989).

Jemima Writer's Collective, eds., *Jemima from the Heart* (Jemima, 1977).

Jordan, June, *Some Changes* (Dutton, 1971).

——, *New Days: Poems of Exile and Return* (Emerson Hall, 1973).

——, *Things That I Do in the Dark: Selected Poems* (Random, 1977).

——, *Naming Our Destiny: New and Selected Poems* (Thunder's Mouth, 1989).

——, *Kissing God Goodbye: Poems 1991–1997* (Doubleday, 1997).

Lorde, Audre, *The First Cities* (Poets, 1968).

——, *Cables to Rage* (Broadside, 1970).

——, *From a Land Where Other People Live* (Broadside, 1973).

——, *The New York Head Shop and Museum* (Broadside, 1974).

——, *Between Our Selves* (Eidolon, 1976).

——, *Coal* (Norton, 1976).

——, *The Black Unicorn* (Norton, 1978).

——, *Chosen Poems: Old and New* (Norton, 1982).

——, *Our Dead Behind Us* (Norton, 1986).

——, *Undersong: Chosen Poems Old and New* (Norton, 1992).

——, *The Marvelous Arithmetic of Distance: Poems, 1987–1992* (Norton, 1993).

Parker, Pat, *Child of Myself* (Women's Press Collective, 1972).

——, *Pit Stop: Words* (Women's Press Collective, 1974).

——, *Movement in Black: Collected Poetry of Pat Parker, 1961–1978* (Diana, 1978).

——, *Womanslaughter* (Diana, 1978).

——, *Jonestown and Other Madness* (Firebrand, 1985).

Walker, Alice, *Once: Poems* (Harcourt, 1968).

——, *Five Poems* (Broadside, 1972).

——, *Revolutionary Petunias and Other Poems* (Harcourt, 1973).

——, *Goodnight, I'll See You in the Morning* (Dial, 1979).

——, *Horses Make a Landscape Look More Beautiful* (Harcourt, 1984).

1980–2000: COMING OUT BLACK, LIKE US

ANTHOLOGIES

Multiauthor Collections

Anzaldua, Gloria, and Cherrie Moraga, eds., *This Bridge Called My Back: Writings by Radical Women of Color* (Persephone, 1981).

Austin, Doris Jean, ed., *Streetlights: Illuminating Tales of the Urban Black Experience* (Penguin, 1996); includes Steven Corbin.

Bauer, Marion Dane, ed., *Am I Blue?: Coming Out from the Silences* (Harper, 1994); includes Jacqueline Woodson.

Beam, Joseph, ed., *In the Life: A Black Gay Anthology* (Alyson, 1986); includes Melvin Dixon.

Belton, Don, ed., *Speak My Name: Black Men on Masculinity and the American Dream* (Beacon, 1995); includes Randall Kenan.

Blackman, Marci, and Trebor Healey, eds., *Beyond Definition: New Writing from Gay and Lesbian San Francisco* (Manic D, 1994).

Bledsoe, Lucy Jane, ed., *Lesbian Travels: A Literary Companion* (Whereabouts, 1998); includes Donna Allegra.

Blount, Marcellus, and George P. Cunningham, eds., *Representing Black Men* (Routledge, 1996).

Boyd, Herb, and Robert Allen, eds., *Brotherman: The Odyssey of Black Men in American* (Ballantine, 1995); includes Melvin Dixon, E. Lynn Harris, and Randall Kenan.

Brandt, Eric, ed., *Dangerous Liaisons: Blacks, Gays, and the Struggle for Equality* (New Press, 1999); includes Jewelle Gomez and Darieck Scott.

Carbado, Devon W., ed., *Black Men on Race, Gender, and Sexuality* (New York UP, 1999).

Conlon, Faith, Rachel DaSilva, and Barbara Wilson, eds., *The Things That Divide Us* (Seal, 1985); includes Becky Birtha.

Constantine-Simms, Delroy, ed., *The Greatest Taboo: Homosexuality in Black Communities* (Alyson, 2000).

Cruikshank, Margaret, ed., *Lesbian Studies: Present and Future* (Feminist, 1982); includes Becky Birtha.

Datcher, Michael, ed., *My Brother's Keeper: Black Men's Poetry Anthology* (Datcher, 1992).

DeCarnin, Camilla, ed., *Worlds Apart: An Anthology of Lesbian and Gay Science Fiction and Fantasy* (AlyCat, 1994); includes Jewelle Gomez.

DeCosta-Willis, Miriam, Roseann Bell, and Reginald Martin, eds., *Erotique Noire/ Black Erotica* (Anchor, 1992); includes Jewelle Gomez.

Dent, Gina, ed., *Black Popular Culture* (Bay, 1992).

Douglas, Debbi, Courtnay McFarlane, Makeda Silvera, and Douglas Stewart, eds., *Má-ka: Diasporic Juks: Contemporary Writing by Queers of African Descent* (Sister Vision, 1997); includes Cheryl Clarke.

Drucker, Peter, ed., *Different Rainbows* (Gay Men's, 2000).

Elam, Harry J., and Robert Alexander, eds., *Colored Contradictions: An Anthology of Contemporary African-American Plays* (Plume, 1996); includes Shay Youngblood.

Featherstone, Elena, ed., *Skin Deep: Women Writing on Color, Culture, and Identity* (Crossing, 1994).

Fehret, Genevieve, and Robert G. O'Meally, eds., *History and Memory in African American Culture* (Oxford UP, 1994); includes Melvin Dixon.

Gambone, Philip, ed., *Something Inside: Conversations with Gay Fiction Writers* (U of Wisconsin P, 1999); includes Randall Kenan.

Gates, Beatrix, ed., *The Wild Good: Lesbian Photographs and Writings on Love* (Doubleday, 1996); includes Alexis DeVeaux.

Gates, Henry Lewis, ed., *Reading Black/Reading Feminist: A Critical Anthology* (Meridian, 1990); includes Jewelle Gomez.

Got to Be Real: Four Original Love Stories (New American Library, 2000); includes E. Lynn Harris.

Guy-Sheftall, Beverly, ed., *Words of Fire: An Anthology of African American Feminist Thought* (New Press, 1995).

Harper, Michael S., and Anthony Walton, *Every Shut Eye Ain't Asleep: An Anthology of Poetry by African Americans Since 1945* (Little, 1994); includes Melvin Dixon.

Hemphill, Essex, ed., *Brother to Brother: Collected Writings by Black Gay Men* (Alyson, 1991); includes Melvin Dixon.

Hull, Gloria T., Patricia Bell Scott, and Barbara Smith, eds., *All the Women Are White, All the Blacks Are Men but Some of Us Are Brave: Black Women's Studies* (Feminist, 1982).

Hunter, Michael, ed., *Sojourner: Black Gay Voices in the Age of AIDS* (Other Countries, 1993); includes Melvin Dixon, Thomas Glave, and Bil Wright.

Lee, C. Allison, and Makeda Silvera, eds., *Pearls of Passion: A Treasury of Lesbian Erotica* (Sister Vision, 1995).

Lowenthal, Michael, ed., *Flesh and the Word 4: Gay Erotic Confessionals* (Plume, 1997); includes Canaan Parker and Darieck Scott.

Major, Clarence, ed., *Calling the Wind: 20th Century African American Short Stories* (Harper, 1992); includes Larry Duplechan.

Mason-Johnson, Valerie, and Ann Khambatta, eds., *Lesbians Talk: Making Black Waves* (Scarlet, 1994).

Mason-Johnson, Valerie, ed., *Talking Black: Lesbians of African and Asian Descent Speak Out* (Cassell, 1995).

Mass, Larry, ed., *We Must Love One Another or Die: The Life and Loves of Larry Kramer* (St. Martin's, 1997); includes Canaan Parker.

Mazer, Norman F., ed., *Just a Writer's Thing: A Collection of Prose and Poetry from the National Book Foundation 1995 Writing Camp* (National Book Fdtn., 1996); includes Jacqueline Woodson.

McKinley, Catherine E., and L. Joyce DeLaney, eds., *Afrekete: An Anthology of Black Lesbian Writing* (Anchor, 1995); includes Alexis DeVeaux, Jewelle Gomez, Helen Elaine Lee, and Jacqueline Woodson.

McMillan, Terry, ed., *Breaking Ice: An Anthology of Contemporary African American Fiction* (Penguin, 1990); includes Becky Birtha, Steven Corbin, and Melvin Dixon.

Mercer, Kobena, ed., *Welcome to the Jungle: New Positions in Black Cultural Studies* (Routledge, 1994).

Moore, Lisa C., ed., *Does Your Mama Know?: An Anthology of Black Lesbian Coming Out Stories* (RedBone, 1997); includes Alexis DeVeaux, Jewelle Gomez, and Shay Youngblood.

Morrow, Bruce, and Charles H. Rowell, eds., *Shade: An Anthology of Fiction by Gay Men of African Descent* (Avon, 1996); includes Melvin Dixon, Larry Duplechan, James Earl Hardy, Brian Keith Jackson, Randall Kenan, Darieck Scott, and Bil Wright.

Muñoz, José Esteban, ed., *Disidentifications: Queers of Color and the Performance of Politics* (U of Minnesota P, 1999).

Murphy, Timothy F., and Suzanne Poirier, eds., *Writing AIDS: Gay Literature, Language, and Analysis* (Columbia UP, 1993).

Naylor, Gloria, ed., *Children of the Night: The Best Short Stories by Black Women Writers, 1967 to the Present* (Little, 1995); includes Thomas Glave, Jewelle Gomez, Randall Kenan, Helen Elaine Lee, and Shay Youngblood.

Nelson, Emmanuel S., ed., *Critical Essays: Gay and Lesbian Writers of Color* (Harrington, 1994).

Nestle, Joan, and Naomi Holoch, eds., *Women on Women: An Anthology of Lesbian Short Fiction* (Plume, 1990); includes Becky Birtha, Jewelle Gomez, and Jacqueline Woodson.

Nestle, Joan, ed., *The Persistent Desire: A Butch-Femme Reader* (Alyson, 1992); includes Donna Allegra and Jewelle Gomez.

Other Countries Collective, eds., *Other Countries: Black Gay Voices* (Other Countries, 1988).

Patton, Cindy, and Benigno Sanchez-Eppler, eds., *Queer Diasporas* (Duke UP, 2000).

Pilcher, Darryl, ed., *Certain Voices: Short Stories About Gay Men* (Alyson, 1991); includes Larry Duplechan.

Preston, John, ed., *Hometowns: Gay Men Write About Where They Belong* (Alyson, 1991); includes Larry Duplechan.

———, ed., *A Member of the Family: Gay Men Write About Their Families* (Dutton, 1992); includes Larry Duplechan.

Ratner, Rochelle, ed., *Bearing Life: Women's Writings on Childlessness* (Feminist Press at CUNY, 2000); includes Becky Birtha.

Reimonenq, Alden, ed., *Milking Black Bull: 11 Black Gay Poets* (Vega, 1995); includes Thomas Glave.

Rizzo, Cindy, ed., *All the Way Home: Parenting and Children in the Lesbian and Gay Community: A Collection of Short Fiction* (New Victoria, 1995); includes Donna Allegra.

Robotham, Rosemarie, ed., *The Bluelight Corner: Black Women Writing on Passion, Sex and Romantic Love* (Three Rivers, 1999); includes Helen Elaine Lee.

Rowell, Charles H., ed., *Ancestral House: The Black Short Story in the Americas and Europe* (Westview, 1995); includes Helen Elaine Lee.

Ruff, Shawn Stewart, ed., *Go the Way Your Blood Beats: An Anthology of Lesbian and Gay Fiction by African American Writers* (Holt, 1996); includes Becky Birtha, E. Lynn Harris, Randall Kenan, and Jacqueline Woodson.

Saint, Assotto, ed., *The Road Before Us: 100 Black Gay Poets* (Galiens, 1991); includes Melvin Dixon, Thomas Glave, and Bil Wright.

———, ed., *Here to Dare: 10 Gay Black Poets* (Galiens, 1992).

Sherman, Charlotte Watson, ed., *Sisterfire: Black Womanist Fiction and Poetry* (Harper, 1994); includes Jewelle Gomez.

Silvera, Makeda, ed., *Piece of My Heart: A Lesbian of Colour Anthology* (Sister Vision, 1992); includes Jewelle Gomez.

Smith, Barbara, ed., *Home Girls: A Black Feminist Anthology* (Kitchen Table, 1983); includes Donna Allegra, Becky Birtha, Alexis DeVeaux, and Jewelle Gomez.

Smith, Charles Michael, ed., *Fighting Words: Personal Essays by Black Gay Men* (Avon, 1999).

Smith, Michael J., ed., *Black Men/White Men: A Gay Anthology* (Gay Sunshine, 1983); includes Larry Duplechan.

Springer, Kimberly, ed., *Still Lifting, Still Climbing: African American Women's Contemporary Activism* (New York UP, 1999).

Stadler, Quandra Prettyman, ed., *Out of Our Lives: A Selection of Contemporary Black Fiction* (Howard UP, 1995).

Stambolian, George, ed., *Men on Men 2: Best New Gay Fiction* (New American Library, 1988); includes Melvin Dixon.

——, ed., *Men on Men 3: Best New Gay Fiction* (Plume, 1990); includes Bil Wright.

Taormino, Tristan, ed., *Best Lesbian Erotica 1997,* selected by Jewelle Gomez (Cleis, 1997).

Taylor, Carol, ed., *Brown Sugar: A Collection of Erotic Black Fiction* (Plume, 2001); includes Marci Blackman.

Thomas, Sheree, ed., *Dark Matter: A Century of Speculative Fiction from the African Diaspora* (Warner, 2001); includes Jewelle Gomez.

Vega Studios, *In Our Own Image: The Art of Black Male Photography* (Vega, 1993).

Walker, Rebecca, ed., *To Be Real: Telling the Truth and Changing the Face of Feminism* (Anchor, 1995).

Washington, Mary Helen, ed., *Midnight Birds: Stories by Contemporary Black Women Writers* (Anchor, 1986); includes Alexis DeVeaux.

——, ed., *Memory of Kin: Stories of Family by Black Writers* (Doubleday, 1991); includes Alexis DeVeaux.

White, Edmund, ed., *Loss within Loss: Artists in the Age of AIDS* (U of Wisconsin P, 2001); includes Randall Kenan.

White, Evelyn C., ed., *The Black Women's Health Book* (Seal, 1994).

Whitmore, Suzanne, ed., *Crossing the Color Line: Readings in Black and White* (U of South Carolina P, 2000); includes Randall Kenan.

Wideman, Daniel J., and Rothan B. Preston, eds., *Soulfires: Young Black Men on Love and Violence* (Penguin, 1996).

Wilkerson, Margaret B., *9 Plays by Black Women* (Penguin, 1986); includes Alexis DeVeaux.

Wing, Adrien Katherine, ed., *Critical Race Feminism: A Reader* (New York UP, 1997).

Woodson, Jacqueline, ed., *A Way Out of No Way: Writings about Growing Up Black in America* (Ballantine, 1997); includes Randall Kenan.

Yan, John, ed., *Fetish: An Anthology of Fetish Fiction* (Four Walls, 1998); includes Marci Blackman.

Young, Kevin, ed., *Giant Steps: The New Generation of African American Writers* (Harper, 2000); includes Randall Kenan and Darieck Scott.

Zahava, Irene, ed., *Hear the Silence: Stories by Women of Myth, Magic, and Renewal* (Crossing, 1986); includes Becky Birtha.

————, ed., *Lavender Mansions: Forty Contemporary Lesbian and Gay Short Stories* (Westview, 1994); includes Donna Allegra, Jewelle Gomez, and Shay Youngblood.

Single Author Collections

Allegra, Donna, *Witness to the League of Blond Hip Hop Dancers: A Novella and Short Stories* (Alyson, 2000).

Barnett, LaShonda, *Callaloo and Other Lesbian Love Tales* (New Victoria, 1999).

Belasco, *Brothers of New Essex: Afro-Erotic Adventures* (Cleis, 2000).

Birtha, Becky, *For Nights Like This One: Stories* (Frog in the Well, 1983).

————, *Lovers' Choice: Stories* (Seal, 1987).

Boykin, Keith, *Respecting the Soul: Daily Reflections for Black Lesbians and Gays* (Avon, 1999).

Brand, Dionne, *Sans Souci and Other Stories* (Firebrand, 1989).

Cornwell, Anita, *Black Lesbian in White America* (Naiad, 1983).

Dixon, Melvin, trans., *The Collected Poems of Léopold Sédor Senghor* (UP of Virginia, 1991).

————, *The Collected Poetry* (UP of Virginia, 1991).

Glave, Thomas, *Whose Song? and Other Stories* (City Lights, 2000).

Gomez, Jewelle, *Forty-three Septembers: Essays* (Firebrand, 1993).

————, *Don't Explain: Short Fiction* (Firebrand, 1998).

Hardy, James Earl, *Back 2 Back: An Anthology Featuring the Bestsellers B-Boy Blues and 2nd Time Around* (Alyson, 1994).

Hemphill, Essex, *Ceremonies: Prose and Poetry* (Plume, 1992).

Kenan, Randall, *Let the Dead Bury the Dead* (Harper, 1992).

Kinard, Rupert, *B. B. and the Diva* (Alyson, 1992).

Mann, G. B., *Low-Hanging Fruit* (Grape Vine, 1996).

Morris, Kathleen E., *Speaking in Whispers: African American Lesbian Erotica* (Third Side, 1996).

Reid-Pharr, Robert F., *Black Gay Man: Essays* (New York UP, 2001).

Saint, Assotto, *Spells of a Voodoo Doll: The Poems, Fiction, Essays, and Plays of Assotto Saint* (Kasak, 1996).

Schulman, Sarah, *My American History: Lesbian and Gay Life During the Reagan/Bush Years* (Routledge, 1994).

Sedgwick, Eve Kosofsky, ed., *Gary in Your Pocket: Stories and Notebooks of Gary Fisher* (Duke UP, 1996).

Silvera, Makeda, *Remembering G. and Other Stories* (Sister Vision, 1991).

————, *Her Head: A Village and Other Stories* (Press Gang, 1994).

Smith, Barbara, *The Truth That Never Hurts: Writings on Race, Gender, and Freedom* (Rutgers UP, 1998).

Vega, *Men of Color: An Essay on the Black Male Couple in Prose, Illustrations, and Photographs* (Vega, 1989).

Youngblood, Shay, *The Big Mama Stories* (Firebrand, 1989).

DRAMA

DeVeaux, Alexis, *Circles*, 1973.

——, *A Little Play and Whip Cream*, 1973.

——, *Tapestry*, 1976.

——, *The Fox Street War*, 1979.

——, *A Season to Unravel*, 1979.

——, *No*, 1981.

——, *Elbow Rooms*, 1987.

Wolfe, George C., Susan Birkenhead, and John Lahr, eds., *Jelly's Last Jam* (Theatre Communication Group, 1993).

Wolfe, George C., *The Colored Museum* (Grove, 1998).

Youngblood, Shay, *Shakin' the Mess Outta Misery* (Dramatic Pub., 1994).

——, *Talking Bones* (Dramatic Pub., 1994).

——, *Amazing Grace*, stage adaptation of the novel by Mary Hoffman (Dramatic Pub., 1998).

FICTION

Novels

Baker, Nikki, *In the Game: A Virginia Kelly Mystery* (Naiad, 1991).

Blackman, Marci, *Po Man's Child* (Manic D, 1999).

Blair, Alaric Wendell, *The End of Innocence: A Journey into the Life* (Writers Club, 2001).

Boyd, Randy, *Uprising* (West Beach, 1998).

——, *Bridge Across the Ocean* (West Beach, 2000).

Braithewaite, Lawrence Ytzhak, *Wigger* (Arsenal Pulp, 1995).

——, *Ratz Are Nice (PSP)* (Alyson, 2000).

Brand, Dionne, *In Another Place Not Here* (Grove, 1997).

——, *At the Full Change of the Moon* (Grove, 2000).

Bridgforth, Sharon, *The Bull Jean Stories* (RedBone, 1998).

Brown, Laurinda D., *Fire and Brimstone* (Creative Enterprises, 2001).

Butler, Octavia, *Imago* (Warner, 1989).

Caminha, Adolfo, *Bom-Crioulo: The Black Man and the Cabin Boy* (Gay Sunshine, 1982).

Carter, Dwayne, *The Best Man* (Ishai, 1999).

Clay, Stanley Bennett, *In Search of Pretty Young Black Men* (SBC, 2001).

Corbin, Steven, *No Easy Place to Be* (Simon, 1989).

———, *Fragments That Remain* (Alyson, 1993).

———, *A Hundred Days from Now* (Alyson, 1994).

DeVeaux, Alexis, *The Woolu Hat* (Random, 1995).

Dixon, Angelo, *DL Brothaz: Double Life* (Dixon Books, 2001).

Dixon, Melvin, *Trouble the Water* (U of Colorado P, 1988).

———, *Vanishing Rooms* (Dutton, 1991).

Duplechan, Larry, *Eight Days a Week* (Alyson, 1985).

———, *Blackbird* (Alyson, 1986).

———, *Tangled Up in Blue* (Alyson, 1990).

———, *Captain Swing* (Alyson, 1993).

Gomez, Jewelle, *The Gilda Stories* (Firebrand, 1991).

Gordon, John R., *Black Butterflies* (Gay Men's, 1993).

———, *Skin Deep* (Gay Men's, 1997).

Hardy, James Earl, *B-Boy Blues: A Seriously Sexy, Fiercely Funny, Black-on-Black Love Story* (Alyson, 1994).

———, *2nd Time Around* (Alyson, 1996).

———, *If Only for One Night* (Alyson, 1997).

———, *The Day Eazy-E Died* (Alyson, 2001).

Harris, E. Lynn, *Invisible Life* (Consortium, 1991).

———, *Just as I Am* (Doubleday, 1994).

———, *And This Too Shall Pass* (Doubleday, 1996).

———, *If This World Were Mine* (Doubleday, 1997).

———, *Abide with Me* (Doubleday, 1999).

———, *Not a Day Goes By* (Doubleday, 2000).

———, *Any Way the Wind Blows* (Doubleday, 2001).

Jackson, Brian Keith, *The View from Here* (Pocket, 1997).

———, *Walking Through Mirrors* (Pocket, 1998).

Kay, Jackie, *Trumpet* (Random, 1999).

Keene, John, *Annotations* (New Directions, 1995).

Kenan, Randall, *A Visitation of Spirits* (Grove, 1989).

Lee, Helen Elaine, *The Serpent's Gift* (Simon, 1994).

———, *Watermarked* (Simon, 1999).

Mickelbury, Penny, *Keeping Secrets: A Gianna Maglione Mystery* (Naiad, 1994).

———, *One Must Wait: A Carol Gibson Mystery* (Simon, 1998).

Muhanji, Cherry, *Her: A Novel* (Aunt Lute, 1990).

Naylor, Gloria, *The Women of Brewster Place* (Viking, 1983).

———, *Linden Hills* (Penguin, 1986).

———, *Bailey's Cafe* (Harcourt, 1992).

Parker, Canaan, *The Color of Trees* (Alyson, 1992).

———, *Sky Daddy* (Alyson, 1997).

Powell, Patricia, *The Pagoda* (Knopf, 1998).

Randall, Alice, *The Wind Done Gone: A Novel* (Houghton, 2001).

Rollins, Ricc, *Like Breathing* (Ishai Creative Group, 1998).

Rose, Odessa, *Water in a Broken Glass* (Caille Nous, 2000).

Sapphire, *Push* (Knopf, 1996).

Scott, Darieck, *Traitor to the Race* (Dutton, 1995).

Scruggs, Michangelo, *Blood Thicker Than Water* (Footprint Media, 2001).

Sinclair, April, *Coffee Will Make You Black* (Hyperion, 1994).

———, *Ain't Gonna Be the Same Fool Twice* (Hyperion, 1996).

———, *I Left My Back Door Open* (Hyperion, 1999).

Teamer, Blaine, *Shady* (iUniverse, 2000).

Thompson, H. Nigel, *Spirits in the Dark* (Heinemann, 1994).

Watson, K. Rhydell, *From Mardi Gras wit' Love* (Sheken, 1997).

Williams, John A., *Clifford's Blues* (Coffee House, 1999).

Woodson, Jacqueline, *Autobiography of a Family Photo* (Dutton, 1994).

Wright, Bil, *Sunday You Learn How to Box* (Scribner, 2000).

Youngblood, Shay, *Soul Kiss* (Riverhead, 1997).

———, *Black Girl in Paris* (Riverhead, 2000).

Young Adult Novels and Children's Books

DeVeaux, Alexis, *Na-ni* (Harper, 1973).

———, *Spirits in the Street* (Doubleday, 1973).

———, *Don't Explain: A Song of Billie Holiday* (Harper, 1980).

———, *Adventures of the Dread Sisters* (self-published, 1982).

———, *An Enchanted Hair Tale* (Harper, 1987).

Woodson, Jacqueline, *Last Summer with Maizon* (Delacorte, 1990).

———, *Martin Luther King Jr. and His Birthday* (Silver, 1990).

———, *The Dear One* (Delacorte, 1991).

———, *Maizon at Blue Hill* (Delacorte, 1992).

———, *Between Madison and Palmetto* (Delacorte, 1993).

———, *The Book Chase* (Bantam, 1994).

———, *I Hadn't Meant to Tell You This* (Delacorte, 1994).

———, *From the Notebooks of Melanin Sun* (Scholastic, 1995).

———, *The House You Pass on the Way* (Delacorte, 1997).

———, *We Had a Picnic This Past Sunday* (Hyperion, 1997).

———, *Lena* (Dell, 1999).

———, *If You Come Softly* (Puffin, 2000).

———, *Miracle's Boys* (Thorndike, 2000).

———, *Sweet, Sweet Memory* (Putnam, 2000).

———, *The Other Side* (Putnam, 2001).

———, *Our Gracie Aunt* (Hyperion, 2001).

NONFICTION

Autobiography, Biography, Letters, and Memoir

Als, Hilton, *The Women* (Farrar, 1996).

Burke, Glenn, Erik Sherman, and Michael Sherman, *Out at Home: The Glenn Burke Story* (Excel, 1995).

DeVeaux, Alexis, *Audre Lorde* (Random, 1997).

Hardy, James Earl, *Boys II Men* (Chelsea, 1996).

———, *Spike Lee* (Chelsea, 1996).

Jones, Bill T., *Last Night on Earth* (Pantheon, 1995).

Julien, Isaac, and Colin MacCabe, *Diary of a Young Soul Rebel* (British Film Institute, 1991).

Kincaid, Jamaica, *My Brother* (Farrar, 1997).

Lady Chablis and Theodore Bouloukis, *Hiding My Candy: The Autobiography of the Grand Empress of Savannah* (Simon, 1996).

RuPaul, *Lettin' It All Hang Out: An Autobiography* (Hyperion, 1995).

Walker, Rebecca, *Black, White and Jewish: Autobiography of a Shifting Self* (Riverhead, 2000).

Ward, Roger T., *Anger Is What I Do Best: The Journal of a Black Gay Man in America* (Ward, 2000).

History and Reference

Black, Allida M., ed., *Modern American Queer History* (Temple UP, 2001).

Boykin, Keith, *One More River to Cross: Black and Gay in America* (Doubleday, 1996).

Castle, Terry, *The Apparitional Lesbian: Female Homosexuality and Modern Culture* (Columbia UP, 1993).

Clendinen, Dudley, and Adam Nagourney, *Out for Good: The Struggle to Build a Gay Rights Movement in America* (Simon, 1999).

Cohen, Cathy J., *The Boundaries of Blackness: AIDS and the Breakdown of Black Politics* (U of Chicago P, 1999).

Collins, Patricia Hill, *Black Feminist Thought: Knowledge, Consciousness, and the Politics of Empowerment* (Unwin, 1990).

Comstock, Gary David, *A Whosoever Church: Welcoming Lesbians and Gay Men into African American Congregations* (Knox, 2001).

Dixon, Melvin, *Ride Out the Wilderness: Geography and Identity in Afro-American Literature* (U of Illinois P, 1987).

Faderman, Lillian, *Odd Girls and Twilight Lovers: A History of Lesbian Life in Twentieth-Century America* (Columbia UP, 1991).

Gomes, Peter, *The Good Book: Reading the Bible with Mind and Heart* (Avon, 1996).

Grahn, Judy, *Another Mother Tongue: Gay Words, Gay Worlds* (Beacon, 1984).

Hine, Darlene Clark, Rosalyn Terborg-Penne, and Elsa B. Brown, eds., *Black Women in America: An Historical Encyclopedia* (Carlson, 1993).

Hine, Darlene Clark, and Kathleen Thompson, *A Shining Thread of Hope: The History of Black Women in America* (Broadway, 1998).

hooks, bell, *Ain't I a Woman: Black Women and Feminism* (South End, 1981).

———, *Feminist Theory: From Margin to Center* (South End, 1984).

———, *Black Looks: Race and Representation* (South End, 1992).

Hull, Akasha Gloria, *Soul Talk: The New Spirituality of African American Women* (Inner Traditions, 2001); includes Alexis DeVeaux.

James, Joy, *Shadow Boxing: Representations of Black Feminist Politics* (St. Martin's, 1999).

Kenan, Randall, *Walking on Water: Black Lives at the Turn of the Twenty-first Century* (Random, 1999).

Loughery, John, *The Other Side of Silence: Men's Lives and Gay Identities: A Twentieth Century History* (Holt, 1998).

Mankiller, Wilma, Gwendolyn Mink, Marysa Navarro, Barbara Smith, and Gloria Steinem, eds., *The Reader's Companion to U.S. Women's History* (Houghton, 1998).

Miller, Neil, *Out of the Past: Gay and Lesbian History from 1869 to the Present* (Vintage, 1995).

Murray, Steven O., and Will Roscoe, eds., *Boy-Wives and Female Husbands: Studies of African Homosexualities* (St. Martin's, 2001).

Pettiway, Leon E., *Honey, Honey, Miss Thang: Being Black, Gay and On the Streets* (Temple UP, 1996).

Pollack, Sandra, and Denise D. Knight, *Contemporary Lesbian Writers in the United States: A Bio-bibliographical Critical Sourcebook* (Greenwood, 1993).

Shilts, Randy, *And the Band Played On: Politics, People, and the AIDS Epidemic* (St. Martin's, 1987).

Smith, Valerie, *Not Just Race, Not Just Gender: Black Feminist Readings* (Routledge, 1998).

Summers, Claude J., ed., *The Gay and Lesbian Literary Heritage: A Reader's Companion to the Writers and Their Works, from Antiquity to the Present* (Holt, 1995).

Vaid, Urvashi, *Virtual Equality: The Mainstreaming of Gay and Lesbian Liberation* (Anchor, 1995).

White, E. Francis, *Dark Continent of Our Bodies: Black Feminism and the Politics of Respectability* (Temple UP, 2001).

POETRY

Birtha, Becky, *The Forbidden Poems* (Seal, 1991).

Brand, Dionne, *No Language Is Neutral* (McClelland, 1990).

Cassell, Cyrus, *The Mud Actor* (Holt, 1982).

———, *Soul Make a Path through Shouting* (Copper Canyon, 1995).

———, *Beautiful Signor* (Copper Canyon, 1997).

Clinton, Michelle T., *Good Sense and the Faithless Plays* (U of New Mexico P, 1994).

Cook, Carl, *Postscripts* (Vega, 1995).

Davenport, Doris, *it's like this* (self-published, 1980).

———, *eat thunder and drink rain* (self-published, 1983).

———, *Voodoo Chile* (Soque Street, 1991).

DeVeaux, Alexis, *Blue Heat: Poems and Drawings* (Diva, 1985).

Dixon, Melvin, *Climbing Montmartre* (Broadside, 1974).

———, *Change of Territory* (UP of Virginia, 1983).

———, *Love's Instrument* (Tia Chucha, 1995).

Gomez, Jewelle, *The Lipstick Papers* (self-published, 1980).

———, *Flamingoes and Bears* (Grace, 1986).

———, *Oral Tradition: Selected Poems Old and New* (Firebrand, 1995).

Hamer, Forrest, *Call and Response* (Alice James, 1995).

———, *Middle Ear* (Heyday, 2000).

Hemphill, Essex, *Conditions* (self-published, 1985).

———, *Earth Life* (self-published, 1985).

James, G. Winston, *Lyric: Poems along a Broken Road* (Grape Vine, 1999).

Jones, Cy K., *Sweep* (Bloody Someday, 1996).

Phillips, Carl, *In the Blood* (Northeastern UP, 1992).

———, *Cortege* (Graywolf, 1995).

———, *From the Devotions* (Graywolf, 1997).

———, *Pastoral* (Graywolf, 2000).

Rushin, Kate, *The Black Back-ups* (Firebrand, 1993).

Saint, Assotto, *Stations* (Galiens, 1989).

———, *Wishing for Wings* (Galiens, 1995).

Sapphire, *Meditations on the Rainbow* (Crystal Bananas, 1987).

———, *American Dreams* (Vintage 1996).

———, *Black Wings and Blind Angels* (Knopf, 1999).

Shepherd, Reginald, *Some Are Drowning* (U of Pittsburgh P, 1993).

———, *Angel Interrupted* (U of Pittsburgh P, 1996).

———, *Wrong* (U of Pittsburgh P, 1999).

Sneed, Pamela, *Imagine Being More Afraid of Freedom than Slavery* (Holt, 1998).

Taylor, Cheryl Boyce, *Night When Moon Follows* (Long Shot, 2000).

———, *Raw Air* (Fly by Night, 2000).

Thompson, Jerry, *What Happens!* (Cosmo, 1994).

Vega Studios, *A Warm December* (Vega, 1992).

White, Marvin, *Last Rights* (Alyson, 1999).

About the Editors

DEVON CARBADO is Professor of Law and African American Studies at the University of California–Los Angeles. He teaches and writes in the areas of constitutional criminal procedure, critical race/feminist theory, gay and lesbian studies, and criminal adjudication. His scholarship appears in law reviews at, among other institutions, Harvard, UCLA, Cornell, and Michigan. He was recently elected Professor of the Year and is the editor of *Black Men on Race, Gender, and Sexuality: A Critical Reader* (New York UP, 1999).

DWIGHT A. MCBRIDE is Chair of the Department of African-American Studies and an Associate Professor of English and African-American Studies at Northwestern University. His published essays are in the areas of race theory and black cultural studies. He is the author of *Impossible Witnesses: Truth, Abolitionism, and Slave Testimony* (New York UP, 2001), a book-length study of abolitionist discourse and the problem of witnessing slavery in Britain and the United States. He is the editor of *James Baldwin Now* (New York UP, 1999). He also coedited a special issue of the journal *Callaloo* entitled "Plum Nelly: New Essays in Black Queer Studies" (winter 2000).

DONALD WEISE is a coeditor of *The Huey P. Newton Reader* (Seven Stories, 2002) with Black Panther Party leader David Hilliard. He is also editor of Gore Vidal's book of essays *Gore Vidal: Sexually Speaking— Collected Sex Writings* (Cleis, 1999). His collection of writings by the black gay civil rights pioneer Bayard Rustin, entitled *Time on Two Crosses*, is being coedited with Devon Carbado for Cleis Press.

Index